C. S. FORESTER

Captain Hornblower RN

Comprising

Hornblower and the 'Atropos'
The Happy Return
A Ship of the Line

CLAREMONT BOOKS
LONDON

PENGUIN BOOKS

Published by the Penguin Group
Penguin Books Ltd, 27 Wrights Lane, London W8 5TZ, England
Penguin Books USA Inc., 375 Hudson Street, New York, New York 10014, USA
Penguin Books Australia Ltd, Ringwood, Victoria, Australia
Penguin Books Canada Ltd, 10 Alcorn Avenue, Toronto, Ontario, Canada M4V 3B2
Penguin Books (NZ) Ltd, 182-190 Wairau Road, Auckland 10, New Zealand

Penguin Books Ltd, Registered Offices: Harmondsworth, Middlesex, England

This edition first published in Great Britain by Michael Joseph Ltd, 1965
Published in Penguin Books, 1987
This edition published by Claremont Books,
an imprint of Godfrey Cave Associates Limited,
42 Bloomsbury Street, London WC1B 3QJ,
under licence from Penguin Books Ltd, 1995

ISBN 1 85471 475 9

Hornblower and the "Atropos"

CLAREMONT BOOKS

CAPTAIN HORNBLOWER RN

C. S. Forester was born in Cairo in 1899, where his father was stationed as a government official. He studied medicine at Guy's Hospital and, after leaving Guy's without a degree, he turned to writing as a career. His first success was *Payment Deferred*, a novel written at the age of twenty-four and later dramatized and filmed with Charles Laughton in the leading role. In 1932 Forester was offered a Hollywood contract, and from then until 1939 he spent thirteen weeks of every year in America. On the outbreak of war he entered the Ministry of Information and later he sailed with the Royal Navy to collect the material for *The Ship*. He made a voyage to the Bering Sea to gather material for a similar book on the United States Navy, and it was during this trip that he was stricken with arteriosclerosis, a disease which left him crippled. However, he continued to write and in the *Hornblower* novels created the most renowned sailor in contemporary fiction. He died in 1966.

I

Having climbed up through the locks, the canal boat was now winding over the pleasant Cotswold country. Hornblower was bubbling with good spirits, on his way to take up a new command, seeing new sights, travelling in an entirely new way, at a moment when the entirely unpredictable English weather had decided to stage a clear sunny day in the middle of December. This was a delightful way of travelling, despite the cold.

"Your pardon for a moment, ma'am," said Hornblower.

Maria, with the sleeping little Horatio in her arms, gave a sigh at her husband's restlessness and shifted her knees to allow him passage, and he rose under the restricted height of the first-class cabin and stepped out through the forward door into the open bow of the passage-boat. Here he could stand on his sea chest and look round him. It was a queer craft, fully seventy feet long and, judging by eye as he looked aft, he would think hardly five feet in beam—the same proportions as had the crazy dugout canoes he had seen in use in the West Indies. Her draught must be less than a foot; that was clear as she tore along behind the cantering horses at a speed that must certainly be all of eight knots—nine miles an hour he told himself, hurriedly, for that was the way they measured speeds here inland.

The passage-boat was making her way from Gloucester to London along the Thames and Severn Canal; going far more smoothly than the stage coach, it was very nearly as fast and decidedly cheaper, at a penny a mile, even in the first class. He and Maria, with the child, were the only first-class passengers, and the boatman, when Hornblower had paid the fares, had cocked an eye at Maria's condition and had said that by rights they ought to pay two children's fares instead of one. Maria had snorted with disdain at such vulgarity, while the onlookers chuckled.

Standing on his sea chest, Hornblower could look over the canal banks, at the grey stone boundary walls and the grey stone farms. The rhythmic sound of the hoofs of the cantering tow horses accentuated the smoothness of the travel; the boat itself made hardly a sound as it slid along over the surface of the water—Hornblower noticed that the boatmen had the trick of lifting the bows, by a sudden acceleration, on to the crest of the bow wave raised by her passage, and retaining them there. This reduced turbulence in the canal to a minimum; it was only when he looked aft that he could see, far back, the reeds at the banks bowing and straightening again long after they had gone by. It was this trick that made the fantastic speed possible. The cantering horses maintained their nine miles an hour, being changed every half hour. There were two tow lines, attached to timber heads at bow and stern; one boatman rode as postillion on the rear horse, controlling the lead horse with shouts and the cracking of his whip. In the stern sat the other boatman, surly and with one hand missing and replaced by a hook; with the other he held the tiller and steered the boat round the curves with a skill that Hornblower admired.

A sudden ringing of the horses' hoofs on stone warned Hornblower just in time. The horses were dashing, without any slackening of pace, under a low bridge, where the tow-path, cramped between the water and the arch, gave them barely room to pass. The mounted boatman buried his face in his horse's mane to pass under; Hornblower had just time to leap down from his sea chest and seat himself as the bridge hurried over him. Hornblower heard the helmsman's loud laugh at his momentary discomfiture.

"You learn to move fast in a canal boat, Captain," the steersman called to him from his place by the tiller. "Two dozen for the last man off the yard! None o' that here on Cotswold, Captain, but a broken head for *you* if you don't look lively."

"Don't let that fellow be so rude to you, Horatio," said Maria from the cabin. "Can't you stop him?"

"Not so easy, dear," replied Hornblower. "It's he who's captain of this craft, and I'm only a passenger."

"Well, if you can't stop him, come in here where he can't be rude to you."

"Yes, my dear, in a minute."

Hornblower chose to risk the jeers of the boatman rather than miss looking round him; this was the best opportunity he had had of watching the working of the canals which in the last thirty years had changed the economic face of England. And not far ahead was Sapperton Tunnel, the engineering marvel of the age, the greatest achievement of the new science. He certainly wanted to see that. Let the steersman laugh his head off if he wanted to. He must be an old sailor, discharged as disabled by the loss of his hand. It must be a wonderful experience for him to have a naval captain under his command.

The grey stone tower of a lock-house showed ahead, with the minute figure of the lock-keeper opening the gates. A yell from the postillion-boatman checked the speed of the horses; the boat glided on, its speed diminishing greatly as the bows slid off the bow wave. As the boat entered the lock the one-handed steersman leaped ashore with a line which he flipped dexterously round a bollard; a smart tug or two took most of the way off the boat, and the boatman, running forward, secured the line to another bollard.

"Heave us that line, Captain," he cried, and Hornblower obediently threw up the bow line for him to secure forward. The law of the sea applied equally in inland waters—the ship first and personal dignity a long way second.

Already the lock-keeper was closing the gates behind them and the lock-keeper's wife was opening the paddles of the upper gate, the water swirling in. The lower gates closed with a crash with the mounting pressure, and the boat rose with the gurgling water. The horses were changed in a twinkling; the postillion scrambled into his saddle, and proceeded to tilt a black bottle against his lips during the remaining few seconds while the lock filled. The steersman was casting off the lines—Hornblower took the bow-line from him—and the lock-keeper's wife was thrusting at one upper gate while the lock-keeper, running up from the lower gate, thrust at the other. The postillion yelled and cracked his whip, the boat sprang forward while the helmsman leaped to his place astern, and they were off again with not a second wasted. Assuredly this canal traffic was a miracle of modernity, and it was gratifying to be on board the very fastest of the canal boats, the *Queen Charlotte*, that took priority over all other traffic. On her bow she carried a glittering scythe-blade as the proud symbol of her superior importance. It would sever the towline of any approaching boat which did not drop her line quickly enough to let her through. The two score of farmers' wives and wenches who sat aft in the second class with their chickens and ducks and eggs and butter were all of them travelling as much as twenty miles to market, in the confident expectation of returning the same day. Quite astonishing.

Here, as they climbed to the summit level, lock succeeded lock at frequent intervals, and at each the postillion held his black bottle to his lips, and his yells to his horses became more raucous and his whip-cracking more continuous. Hornblower obediently handed the bow-line at each lock, despite Maria's urgings to the contrary.

"My dear," said Hornblower, "we save time if I do."

"But it isn't right," said Maria. "He knows you're a captain in the Navy."

"He knows it too well," said Hornblower with a lopsided smile. "And after all I have a command to take up."

"As if it couldn't wait," snorted Maria.

It was hard to make Maria understand that to a captain his command was all in all, that he wished to lose not an hour, not a minute, in his journey to assume command of his sloop of war in London River; he was yearning to see what *Atropos* was like, with the mingled hope and apprehension that might be expected of an Oriental bridegroom affianced to a veiled bride—that was not a simile that it would be wise to mention to Maria, though.

Now they were gliding down the summit level of the canal; the cutting was growing deeper and deeper, so that the echo of the sound of the horses' hoofs came ringing from the rocky banks. Round the shallow curve must surely be Sapperton Tunnel.

"Hold hard, Charlie!" suddenly yelled the steersman. A moment later he sprang to the after towline and tried to cast it off from the timber head, and there was wild confusion. Shouts and yells on the towpath, horses whinnying, hoofs clattering. Hornblower caught a glimpse of the lead horse leaping frantically up the steep slope of the cutting—just ahead of them was the castellated but gloomy mouth of the tunnel and there was no other way for the horse to turn. The *Queen Charlotte* lurched hideously against the bank to the accompaniment of screams from the second-class cabin; for a moment Hornblower was sure she would capsize. She righted herself and came to a stop as the towlines slackened; the frantic struggles of the second horse, entangled in two towlines, ended as it kicked itself free. The steersman had scrambled on to the towpath and had dropped the after line over a bollard.

"A pretty kettle o' fish," he said.

Another man had shown up, running down the bank from the top whence spare horses looked down at them, whinnying. He held the heads of the *Queen Charlotte's* horses, and near his feet lay Charlie, the boatman-postillion, his face a mask of blood.

"Get ye back in there!" bellowed the steersman to the women who were all scrambling out of the second-class cabin. "All's well. Get ye back! Once let them loose on the country"—he added to Hornblower—"and they'd be harder to catch than their own chickens."

"What is it, Horatio?" asked Maria, standing at the door of the first-class cabin with the baby in her arms.

"Nothing to alarm yourself about, my dear," said Hornblower. "Compose yourself. This is no time for agitation."

He turned and looked at the one-handed steersman, who bent down to examine Charlie; taking a hold of the breast of his coat with his steel hook he hauled up, but Charlie's head only hung back helplessly, the blood running over his cheeks.

"Not much use out of Charlie," said the steersman, letting him drop with a thump. As Hornblower stooped to look he could catch the reek of gin three feet from the bleeding mouth. Half stunned and half drunk—more than half of both for that matter.

"We've the tunnel to leg through," said the steersman. "Who's up at the Tunnel House?"

"Ne'er a soul," replied the man with the horses. "The trade all went through in the early morning."

The steersman whistled.

"You'll have to come wi' us," he said.

"Not I," said the horseholder. "I've sixteen horses—eighteen with these two. I can't leave 'em."

The steersman swore a couple of astonishing oaths—astonishing even to Hornblower, who had heard many in his time.

"What d'you mean by 'legging' through the tunnel?" Hornblower asked.

The steersman pointed with his hook at the black, forbidding tunnel mouth in the castellated entrance.

"No towpath through the tunnel, o' course, Captain," he said. "So we leaves our horses here an' we legs through. We puts a pair o' 'wings' on the bows—sort o' catheads, in a way. Charlie lies on one an' I lies on the other, wi' our heads inboard an' our feet agin the tunnel wall. Then we sort o' walks, and we gets the boat along that way, and we picks up another pair o' horses at the south end."

"I see," said Hornblower.

"I'll souse this sot wi' a couple o' buckets o' water," said the steersman. "Mebbe it'll bring him round."

"Maybe," said Hornblower.

But buckets of water made no difference to the unconscious Charlie, who was clearly concussed. The slow blood flowed again after his battered face had been washed clean. The steersman produced another couple of oaths.

"The other trade'll be coming up arter you," said the horseholder. " 'Nother couple o' hours, mebbe."

All he received in reply was a further series of oaths.

"We have to have daylight to run the Thames staunches," said the steersman. "Two hours? We'll only just get there by daylight if we go now."

He looked round him, at the silent canal cut and tunnel mouth, at the chattering women in the boat and the few doddering old gaffers along with them.

"Twelve hours late, we'll be," he concluded, morosely.

A day late in taking up his command, thought Hornblower.

"Damn it," he said, "I'll help you leg through."

"Good on ye, sir," said the steersman, significantly dropping the equalitarian "captain" for the "sir" he had carefully eschewed so far. "D'ye think you can?"

"Likely enough," said Hornblower.

"Let's fit those wings," said the steersman, with sudden decision.

They were small platforms, projecting out from either bow.

"Horatio," asked Maria, "whatever are you doing?"

That was just what Maria *would* ask. Hornblower was tempted to make use of the rejoinder he had heard used once in the *Renown*, to the effect that he was getting milk from a male ostrich, but he checked himself.

"Just helping the boatman, dear," he said patiently.

"You don't think enough of your position," said Maria.

Hornblower was by now a sufficiently experienced married man to realize the advantages of allowing his wife to say what she liked as long as he could continue to do as he liked. With the wings fitted he and the steersman on board, and the horseholder on the bank, took their places along the side of the *Queen Charlotte*. A strong united shove sent the boat gliding into the cut, heading for the tunnel.

"Keep 'er goin', sir," said the steersman, scrambling forward to the port side wing. It was obvious that it would be far easier to maintain gentle way on the boat than to progress in fits and starts of alternate stopping and moving. Hornblower hurried to the starboard side wing and laid himself down on it as the bows of the boat crept into the dark tunnel. Lying on his right side, with his head inboard, he felt his feet come into contact with the brick lining of the tunnel. He pressed with his feet, and then by a simple backwards walking motion he urged the boat along.

"Hold hard, sir," said the steersman—his head was just beside Hornblower's—"there's two miles an' more to go."

A tunnel two miles long, driven through the solid rock of the Cotswolds! No wonder it was the marvel of the age. The Romans with all their aqueducts had achieved nothing to compare with this. Farther and farther into the tunnel they went, into darkness that increased in intensity, until it was frightfully, astonishingly dark, with the eye recording nothing at all, strain as it might. At their entrance into the tunnel the women had chattered and laughed, and had shouted to hear the echoes in the tunnel.

"Silly lot o' hens," muttered the steersman.

Now they fell silent, oppressed by the darkness, all except Maria.

"I trust you remember you have your good clothes on, Horatio," she said.

"Yes, dear," said Hornblower, happy in the knowledge that she could not possibly see him.

It was not a very dignified thing he was doing, and not at all comfortable. After a few minutes he was acutely aware of the hardness of the platform on which he was lying; nor was it long before his legs began to protest against the effort demanded of them. He tried to shift his position a little, to bring other muscles into play and other areas of himself into contact with the platform, but he learned fast enough that it had to be done with tact and timing, so as not to disturb the smooth rhythm of the propulsion of the boat—the steersman beside him grunted a brief protest as Hornblower missed a thrust with his right leg and the boat baulked a little.

"Keep 'er goin', sir," he repeated.

So they went on through the darkness, in the strangest sort of mesmeric nightmare, suspended in utter blackness, utterly silent, for their speed was not sufficient to raise a ripple round the *Queen Charlotte*'s bows. Hornblower went on thrusting with his feet, urging his aching legs into further efforts; he could tell by the sensations conveyed through the soles of his shoes that the tunnel was no longer brick-lined—his feet pressed against naked rock, rough and irregular as the tunnellers' picks and gunpowder had left it. That made his present employment more difficult.

He became aware of a slight noise in the distance—a low muttering sound, at first so feeble that when he first took note of it he realized that he had been hearing it already for some time. It gradually increased in volume as the boat crept along, until it was a loud roaring; he had no idea what it could be, but as the steersman beside him seemed unconcerned he decided not to ask about it.

"Easy a minute, sir," said the steersman, and Hornblower, wondering, rested his aching legs, while the steersman, still recumbent, fumbled and tugged beside him. Next moment he had dragged a tarpaulin completely over both of them, except for their feet protruding from under the edges. It was no darker under the tarpaulin than outside it, but it was considerably stuffier.

"Carry on, sir," said the steersman, and Hornblower recommenced pushing with his feet against the wall, the roaring he had heard before somewhat muffled by the tarpaulin. A trickle of water volleyed loudly on the tarpaulin, and then another, and he suddenly understood what the roaring was.

"Here it comes," said the steersman under the tarpaulin.

An underground spring here broke through the roof of the tunnel and tumbled roaring into the canal. The water fell down on them in deafening cataracts. It thundered upon the roofs of the cabins, quite drowning the cries of the women within. The weight of its impact pressed the tarpaulin upon him. Then the torrent eased, fell away to trickles, and then they were past it.

"Only one more o' those," said the steersman in the stuffy darkness beside him. "It's better arter a dry summer."

"Are you wet, Horatio?" asked Maria's voice.

"No, dear," said Hornblower, the simple negative having the desired cushioning effect and smothering further expostulation.

Actually his feet were wet, but after eleven years at sea that was not a new experience; he was much more concerned with the weariness of his legs. It seemed an age before the next trickling of water and the steersman's "Here it comes" heralded the next deluge. They crawled on beyond it, and the steersman, with a grunt of relief, dragged the tarpaulin from off them. And with its removal Hornblower, twisting his neck, suddenly saw something far ahead. His eyes were by now accustomed to the darkness, and in that massive darkness, incredibly far away, there was something to be seen, a minute something, the size apparently of a grain of sand. It was the farther mouth of the tunnel. He worked away with his legs with renewed vitality. The tunnel opening grew in size, from a grain of sand to a pea; it assumed the crescentic shape to be expected of it; it grew larger still, and with its growth the light increased in the tunnel by infinitesimal gradations, until Hornblower could see the dark surface of the water, the irregularities of the tunnel roof. Now the tunnel was brick-lined again, and progress was easier—and seemed easier still.

"Easy all," said the steersman with a final thrust.

It seemed unbelievable to Hornblower that he did not have to work his legs any more, that he was emerging into daylight, that no more underground springs would cascade upon him as he lay, suffocating under a tarpaulin. The boat slowly slid out of the tunnel's mouth, and despite its slow progress, and despite the fact that outside the sun shone with only wintry brilliance, he was quite blinded for a while. The chatter of the passengers rose into a roar almost comparable with the sound of the underground spring upon the tarpaulin. Hornblower sat up and blinked round him. There was a horseholder on the towpath with a pair of horses; he caught the line the steersman tossed to him and between them they drew the boat to the bank. Many of the passengers were leaving at this point, and they began to swarm out at once with their packages and their chickens. Others were waiting to board.

"Horatio," said Maria, coming out of the first-class cabin; little Horatio was awake now and was whimpering a little.

"Yes, my dear?"

Hornblower was conscious of Maria's eyes taking in the disorder of his clothes. He knew that Maria would scold him, brush him down, treat him with the same maternal possessiveness as she treated his son, and he knew that at the moment he did not want to be possessed.

"One moment, dear, if you will pardon me," he said, and stepped nimbly out on to the towpath, joining himself to the conversation of the steersman and the horseholder.

"Ne'er a man here," said the latter. "An' you won't find one before Oxford, that I'll warrant you."

In reply the steersman said much the same things as he had said to the other horseholder.

"That's how it is, an' all," said the horseholder philosophically, "you'll have to wait for the trade."

"No spare men here?" asked Hornblower.

"None, sir," said the steersman, and then, after a moment's hesitation, "I suppose, sir, you wouldn't care to drive a pair o' horses?"

"Not I," answered Hornblower hastily—he was taken sufficiently by surprise by the question to make no attempt to disguise his dismay at the thought of driving two horses in the manner of the injured Charlie; then he saw how to recover his dignity and keep himself safe from Maria's ministrations, and he added: "But I'll take the tiller."

"O' course you could, sir," answered the steersman. "Not the first time you've handled a tiller. Not by a long chalk. An' I'll drive the nags, me an' my jury fist an' all."

He glanced down at the steel hook that replaced his missing hand.

"Very well," said Hornblower.

"I'm grateful to you, sir, that I am," said the steersman, and to emphasize his sincerity he swore a couple more oaths. "I've a contract on this here v'yage—that's two chests o' tea for'rard there, first o' the China crop for Lunnon delivery. You'll save me pounds, sir, an' my good name as well. Grateful I am, by—"

He emphasized his sincerity again.

"That's all right," said Hornblower. "The sooner we start the sooner we arrive. What's your name?"

"Jenkins, sir." Tom Jenkins, the steersman—now to be the postillion—tugged at his forelock, "main topman in the old *Superb*, Cap'n Keates, sir."

"Very well, Jenkins. Let's start."

The horseholder tended to the business of attaching the horses' towlines, and while Jenkins cast off the bow-line, Hornblower cast off the stern one and stood by with a single turn round the bollard; Jenkins climbed nimbly into the saddle and draped the reins about his hook.

"But, Horatio," said Maria, "whatever are you thinking about?"

"About arriving in London, my dear," said Hornblower, and at that moment the whip cracked and the towlines tightened.

Hornblower had to spring for the stern sheets, line in hand, and he had to grab for the tiller. Maybe Maria was still expostulating, but if she were, Hornblower was already far too busy to hear anything she said. It was impressive how quickly the *Queen Charlotte* picked up speed as the horses, suddenly breaking into a trot, pulled her bows up on to her bow wave. From a trot they changed to a canter, and the speed seemed fantastic—far faster, to Hornblower's heated imagination, now that he was at the helm instead of being a mere irresponsible passenger. The banks were flying by; fortunately in this deep cut of the summit level the channel was straight at first, for the steering was not perfectly simple. The two towlines, one at the bow and one at the stern, held the boat parallel to the bank with the smallest use of the rudder—an economic employment of force that appealed to Hornblower's mathematical mind, but which made the feel of the boat a little unnatural as he tentatively tried the tiller.

He looked forward at the approaching bend with some apprehension, and as they neared it he darted his eyes from bank to bank to make sure he was holding in mid-channel. And round the bend, almost upon them, was a bridge—another of these infernal canal bridges, built for economy, with the towpath bulging out under the arch, so that it was hard to sight for the centre of the greatly narrowed channel. Maria was certainly saying something to him, and little Horatio was undoubtedly yelling like a fury, but this was no moment to spare them either a glance or a thought. He steadied the boat round the bend. The hoofs of the lead horse were already ringing on the cobbles under the bridge. God! He was over too far. He tugged the tiller across. Too far the other way! He pushed the tiller back, straightening the boat on her course even as her bows entered the narrows. She turned, very nearly fast enough—her starboard quarter, just where he stood, hit with a solid thump against the elbow of the brick-faced canal side, but she had a thick rope rubbing strake there—presumably to meet situations of this sort—which cushioned the shock; it was not violent enough to throw the passengers off their benches in the cabin, although it nearly threw Hornblower, crouching low under the arch, on to his face. No time to think, not even though little Horatio had apparently been bumped by the shock and was now screaming even more wildly in the bows; the canal was curving back again and he had to guide the *Queen Charlotte* round the bend.

Crack-crack-crack-crack—that was Jenkins with his whip—was not the speed already great enough for him? Round the bend, coming towards them, there was another canal boat, creeping peacefully along towed by a single horse. Hornblower realized that Jenkins' four whip cracks were a signal, demanding a clear passage. He hoped most sincerely and fervently that one would be granted, as the canal boat hastened down upon the barge.

The bargee at the tow horse's head brought the beast to a standstill, edging him over into the hedge beside the towpath; the bargee's wife put her tiller over and the barge swerved majestically, with her residual way, towards the reeds that lined the opposite bank; so between horse and barge the tow-rope sank to the ground on the towpath, and into the water in a deep bight. Over the tow-rope cantered Jenkins' horses, and Hornblower headed the passage boat for the narrow space between the barge and the towpath. He could guess that the water beside the path was shallow; it was necessary to steer the passage boat to shave the barge as closely as possible, and in any case the bargee's wife, accustomed to encountering skilled steersmen, had only left him the minimum of room. Hornblower was in a fair way towards panic as the passage boat dashed forward.

Starboard—meet her. Port—meet her. He was giving these orders to himself, as he might to his coxswain; like a streak of lightning through the dark confusion of his mind flashed the thought that although he might give the orders he could not trust his clumsy limbs to execute them with the precision of a skilled helmsman. Into the gap now; the stern was still swinging and at the last moment he got the tiller over to check her. The barge seemed to flash by; out of the tail of his eye he was dimly aware of the bargee's wife's greeting, changing to surprise as she noted that the *Queen Charlotte* was being steered by a man quite unknown to her. Faintly to his ear came the sound of what she said, but he could distinguish no word—he had no attention to spare for compliments.

They were through, in that flash, and he could breathe again, he could smile, he could grin; all was well in a marvellous world, steering a passage boat at nine miles an hour along the Thames and Severn Canal. But that was another yell from Jenkins: he was checking his horses, and there was the grey tower of a lock-house ahead. The gates were open, the lock-keeper standing by them. Hornblower steered for them, greatly helped by the Queen Charlotte's abrupt reduction in speed as her bow wave passed ahead of her. Hornblower grabbed for the stern rope, leaped for the bank, and miraculously kept his footing. The bollard was ten feet ahead; he ran forward and dropped a loop over it and took the strain. The ideal method was to take nearly all the way off the boat, let her creep into the lock, and stop her fully at the next bollard, but it was too much to hope that he could at his first attempt execute all this exactly. He let the line slip through his hands, watching the boat's progress, and then took too sudden a pull at it. Line and bollard creaked; the *Queen Charlotte* swung her bows across the lock to bump them against the farther side, and she lay there half in and half out, helpless, so that the lock-keeper's wife had to run along from the farther gates, lean over, shove the bows clear while seizing the bowline, and, with the line over her sturdy shoulder, haul the boat the final dozen yards into the lock—a clear waste of a couple of minutes. Nor was this all, for as they had now passed the summit level, this was a downward lock, and Hornblower had not readied his mind for this transition. He was taken by surprise when the *Queen Charlotte* subsided abruptly, with the opening of the gate paddles, along with the emptying water, and he had only just time to slack away the stern-line, or else the boat might have been left hanging on it.

"Ee, man, you know little about boats," said the lock-keeper's wife, and Hornblower's ears burned with embarrassment. He thought of the examination he had passed in navigation and seamanship; he thought of how often he had tacked a monstrous ship of the line in heavy weather. That experience was not of much use to him here in inland Gloucestershire—or perhaps it was Oxfordshire by now—and in any case the lock was empty, the gates opening, the towlines tightening, and he had to leap down six feet or more in a hurry into the already moving stern, remembering to take the stern-line down with him. He managed it, clumsily as ever, and he heard the lock-keeper's wife's hearty laugh as he glided on below her; and she said something more, too, but he could pay no attention to it, as he had to grab for the tiller and steer the hurrying boat out under the bridge. And when he had first paid for their passages he had pictured to himself the leisurely life of the canal boatman!

And, heavens and earth! Here was Maria beside him having made her way aft through the second-class cabin.

"How can you let these people be so insolent to you, dear?" she was asking. "Why don't you tell them who you are?"

"My dear—" began Hornblower, and then stopped.

If Maria could not see the incongruity of a naval captain mishandling a canal boat it was hopeless to argue. Besides, he had no attention to spare for her, not with those cantering horses whisking the *Queen Charlotte* along like this.

"And this all seems very unnecessary, dear," went on Maria. "Why should you demean yourself like this? Is there all this need for haste?"

Hornblower took the boat round a bend—he congratulated himself that he was getting the feel of the tiller now.

"Why don't you answer me?" went on Maria. "And I have our dinner waiting for us, and little Horatio—"

She was like the voice of conscience—for that matter that was exactly what she was.

"Maria," snapped Hornblower. "Get for'rard! Get for'rard, I say. Go back to the cabin."

"But, my dear—"

"Get for'rard!"

Hornblower roared this out—here was another barge approaching and he could spare no time for the niceties of married life.

"You are very heartless," said Maria, "and in my condition, too."

Heartless, maybe, but certainly preoccupied. Hornblower pulled the tiller over, and Maria put her handkerchief to her eyes and flounced—as much of a flounce as was possible to her as she was—back into the second-class cabin again. The *Queen Charlotte* shot neatly down the gap between the barge and the towpath, and Hornblower could actually spare enough attention to acknowledge with a wave of his hand the greeting of the bargee's wife. He had time, too, now, for a prick of conscience about his treatment of Maria, but only a momentary one. He still had to steer the boat.

II

There was still plenty of daylight when they came out into the Thames valley and Hornblower, looking down to starboard, could see the infant river—not such an infant at its winter level—running below. Every turn and every lock brought the canal nearer to the stream, and at last they reached Inglesham, with Lechlade church steeple in view ahead, and the junction with the river. At Inglesham lock Jenkins left his horses and came back to speak to Hornblower.

"There's three staunches on the river next that we have to run, sir," he said.

Hornblower had no idea what a staunch was, and he very much wanted to know before he had to "run" them, but at the same time he did not want to admit ignorance. Jenkins may have been tactful enough to sense his difficulty; at least he gave an explanation.

"They're dams across the river, sir," he told Hornblower. "At this time o' year, with plenty of water, some o' the paddles are kept out for good, at the towpath end o' the staunch. There's a fall o' five or six feet."

"Five or six feet?" repeated Hornblower, startled.

"Yes, sir. 'Bout that much. But it isn't a real fall, if you know what I mean, sir. Steep, but no more."

"And we have to run down it?"

"Yes, sir. It's easy enough, sir—at the top, leastways."

"And at the bottom?"

"There's an eddy there, sir, like as you'd expect. But if you hold her straight, sir, the nags'll take you through."

"I'll hold her straight," said Hornblower.

"O' course you will, sir."

"But what the devil do they have these staunches on the river for?"

"They keeps back the water for the mills—an' the navigation, sir."

"But why don't they have locks?"

Jenkins spread his hand and his hook in a gesture of ignorance.

"Dunno, sir. There's locks from Oxford down. These 'ere staunches are a plague. Takes six horses to get the old *Queen Charlotte* up 'em, sometimes."

Hornblower's thinking about the subject had not yet progressed as far as thinking about how the staunches were passed up-river; and he was a little annoyed with himself at not having raised the point. But he managed to nod sagely at the information.

"I daresay," he said. "Well, it doesn't concern us this voyage."

"No, sir," said Jenkins. He pointed down the canal. "The first 'un is half a mile below Lechlade Bridge, there. It's well over on the port side. You can't miss it, sir."

Hornblower hoped he was right about that. He took his place in the stern and seized the tiller with a bold attempt to conceal his misgivings, and he waved to the lock-keeper as the boat moved rapidly out of the lock—he was adept enough by now to be able to spare attention for that even with a gate to negotiate. They shot out on to the surface of the young river; there was plenty of current running in their direction —Hornblower noted the eddy at the point—but the speed of the horses gave them plenty of steerage-way.

Lechlade Bridge just ahead of them—the staunch was half a mile beyond, Jenkins said. Although the air was distinctly cold now Hornblower was conscious that his palms, as they rested on the tiller, were distinctly damp. To him now it appeared a wildly reckless thing to do, to attempt to shoot the staunch inexperienced as he was. He would prefer—infinitely prefer—not to try. But he had to steer through the arch of the bridge—the horses splashed fetlock deep there—and then it was too late to do anything about his change of mind. There was the line of the staunch across the stream, the gap in it plainly visible on the port side. Beyond the staunch the surface of the river was not visible because of the drop, but above the gap the water headed down in a steep, sleek slope, higher at the sides than in the middle; the fragments which floated on the surface were all hurrying towards it, like people in a public hall all pressing towards a single exit. Hornblower steered for the centre of the gap, choking a little with excitement; he could feel the altered trim of the boat as her bows sank and her stern rose on the slope. Now they were flying down, down. Below, the smooth slope narrowed down to a point, beyond which and on each side was the turbulent water of the eddy. He still had steerage way enough to steer down the point; as he felt the boat answer the helm he was momentarily tempted to follow up the mathematical line of thought presented by that situation, but he had neither time nor really the inclination. The bows hit the turbulent water with a jar and a splash; the boat lurched in the eddy, but next moment the towlines plucked them forward again. Two seconds' careful steering and they were through the eddy and they were gliding over a smooth surface once more, foam-streaked but smooth, and Hornblower was laughing out loud. It had been simple, but so exhilarating that it did not occur to him to condemn himself for his earlier misgivings. Jenkins looked back, turning in his saddle, and waved his whip, and Hornblower waved back.

"Horatio, you *must* come and have your dinner," said Maria. "And you have left me alone all day."

"Not long before we reach Oxford now, dear," said Hornblower—he was just able to conceal the fact that he had temporarily, until then, forgotten the existence of his wife and child.

"Horatio—"

"In a little while, dear," said Hornblower.

The winter evening was closing round them, the light mellowing while it faded over ploughland and meadow, over the pollard willows knee-deep in the stream, over the farmhouses and cottages. It was all very lovely; Hornblower had the feeling that he did not want this moment ever to end. This was happiness, as his earlier feelings of well-being changed to something more peaceful, just as the surface of the river had changed below the eddy. Soon he would be back in another life again, plunged once more into a world of cruelty and war—the world he had left behind in the tide-water of the Severn and would meet again in the tide-water of the Thames. It was symbolic that it should be here in the centre of England, at the midpoint of his journey, that he should reach this momentary summit of happiness. The cattle in the fields, the rooks in the trees—were they part of this happiness? Possibly, but not certainly. The happiness came from within him, and depended on even more transitory factors than those. Hornblower breathed the evening air as though it were divine poetry, and then he noticed Jenkins waving to him from his saddle and pointing with his whip, and the moment was over, lost for ever.

That was the next staunch at which Jenkins was pointing. Hornblower steered boldly for it, without a moment of nervousness; he steadied the boat on her course above it, felt the heave and sudden acceleration as she topped the slope, and grinned with delight as she shot down it, hit the eddy below, and emerged as before after a brief period of indecision. Onward, down the river, through the gathering night. Bridges; another staunch—Hornblower was glad it was the last; there had been much point to what Jenkins had said about needing daylight in which to run them—villages, churches. Now it was quite dark, and he was cold and weary. The next time Maria came aft to him he could address her sympathetically, and even share her indignation that Oxford was so far away. Jenkins had lighted candle-lanterns; one hung on the collar of the lead horse and the other from the cantle of the saddle of the horse he rode. Hornblower, in the stern sheets of the *Queen Charlotte*, saw the specks of light dancing on the towpath—they gave him an indication of the turns the river was making, and just enabled him to steer a safe course, although twice his heart was in his mouth as the side of the boat brushed against the reeds at the river bank. It was quite dark when Hornblower felt the boat slow up suddenly with the easing of the towlines, and in response to Jenkins' quiet hail he steered the boat towards a lantern-lit landing-stage; ready hands took the lines and moored the boat, and the passengers began to swarm out.

"Captain—sir?" said Jenkins.

That was not the way he had used the word "captain" at their first acquaintance. Then it had been with an equalitarian gibe; now he was using the formula and the intonation that would be used by any member of a ship's company addressing his captain.

"Yes?" said Hornblower.

"This is Oxford, sir, and the relief is here."

In the wavering lantern light Hornblower could see the two men indicated.

"So now I can have my dinner?" he asked, with gentle irony.

"That you can, sir, an' it's sorry I am that you have had to wait for it. Sir, I'm your debtor. Sir—"

"Oh, that's all right, Jenkins," said Hornblower testily. "I had my own reasons for wishing to get to London."

"Thank'ee sir, and—"

"How far to London now?"

"A hundred miles to Brentford, sir, by the river. You'll be there at the first light. How'll the tide be then, Jem?"

"Just at the flood," said the member of the relief crew holding the whip. "You can take water there, sir, an' be at Whitehall Steps in an hour."

"Thank you," said Hornblower. "I'll say good-bye to you, then, Jenkins."

"Good-bye, sir and thank'ee agen for a true gennelman."

Maria was standing by the bows of the boat, and even in the dim light Hornblower thought he could detect reproach in her attitude. But it was not immediately apparent in her words.

"I've found you a hot supper, Horatio," was what she said.

"By Jingo!" said Hornblower.

Standing on the quay were a few boys and young women come to sell food to the river travellers. The one who caught Hornblower's eye was a sturdy lad with a keg, clearly containing beer, on a barrow, and Hornblower realized that he was consumed with thirst even more acutely than with hunger.

"That's what I want," he said. "Give me a quart."

"On'y pints, sir," said the boy.

"Two pints then, you lubber."

He emptied the first wooden piggin without an effort, without even taking breath, and started on the second, before he remembered his manners. He had honestly been so consumed with thirst that he had forgotten them completely.

"How about you, dear?" he asked Maria.

"I think I'd like half a pint," said Maria—Hornblower could have guessed at her reply beforehand; Maria would think it was a sign of a lady to drink beer only by the half pint.

"On'y pints, sir," said the boy again.

"Well, give the lady a pint and I'll finish it," said Hornblower, his second piggin two-thirds empty.

"All aboard!" called the new steersman. "All aboard!"

"That'll be a shilling, sir," said the boy.

"Fourpence a pint for this beer!" marvelled Maria.

"Cheap at the price," said Hornblower. "Here, boy."

Out of sheer lightness of heart he gave the boy a florin, and the boy spun it in the air delightedly before putting it in his pocket. Hornblower took the piggin from Maria's hand and drained it and tossed it to the boy.

"All aboard!"

Hornblower stepped down into the boat and elaborately handed Maria down too. He was taken a little aback to find that the *Queen Charlotte* had acquired some more first-class passengers either here or farther back along their route. There were two or three men and a half dozen women sitting in the cabin lit by the light of a lamp; little Horatio was asleep in one corner. Maria was fluttered; she wanted to speak about domestic subjects, but was self-conscious about it in the presence of strangers. She whispered what she had to say, while her hands now and then gesticulated towards the stony-faced strangers to indicate how much more she would have said if there were no fellow passengers.

"That was two shillings you gave the boy, dear," she said. "Why did you do it?"

"Just lunacy, my dear, lunacy," said Hornblower, speaking light-heartedly but not so far from the truth.

Maria sighed as she looked at this unpredictable husband of hers who could throw away a shilling, and talk about lunacy in the hearing of strangers without dropping his voice.

"And here's the supper I bought," said Maria, "while you were talking to the men. I hope it's still hot. You've not had a bite all day, and by now the bread and meat I brought for dinner will be stale."

"I'll eat whatever there is, and more," said Hornblower, with more than a quart of beer inside his otherwise empty stomach.

Maria indicated the two wooden platters awaiting them on the bench beside little Horatio.

"I got out our spoons and forks," explained Maria. "We leave the platters on board here."

"Excellent," said Hornblower.

There were two sausages on each platter, embedded in masses of pease pudding, still steaming. Hornblower sat down with his platter on his lap and began to eat. Those were beef sausages, naturally, if they were not mutton or possibly goat or horse, and they apparently were made from the purest gristle. The skins were as tough as their contents. Hornblower stole a sideways glance at Maria, eating with apparent contentment. He had hurt her feelings several times today and he could not bear to do it again; otherwise he would have pitched those sausages over the side into the river where possibly the fish could deal with them. But as it was he made a valiant effort to eat them. By the time he had started the second he decided it was beyond him. He made his handkerchief ready in his left hand.

"We'll be at the first lock any moment," he said to Maria, with a gesture of his right hand calling her attention to the dark window. Maria tried to peer out, and Hornblower flipped the second sausage into his handkerchief and stuffed it into his side pocket. He caught the eye of the elderly man sitting nearly opposite him across the narrow cabin. This individual had been sitting muffled up in great coat and scarf, his hat pressed down low on his forehead, grouchily keeping watch from under his eyebrows at every movement the Hornblowers had made. Hornblower gave him an elaborate wink in reply to the astonishment which replaced the grouchy old gentleman's bad-tempered curiosity. It was not a conspiratorial wink, nor did Hornblower attempt the hopeless task of trying to pretend that he stuffed hot greasy sausages into his pocket every day of his life; the wink simply dared the old gentleman to comment on or even think about the remarkable act. He applied himself to finishing off the pease pudding.

"You eat so fast, dear," said Maria. "It cannot be good for your stomach."

She herself was struggling desperately with her own sausages.

"I'm hungry enough to eat a horse," said Hornblower. "Now I'll start on our dinner, stale or not."

"I am delighted," said Maria. "Let me—"

"No, dear. Sit still. I'll look after myself."

Hornblower took the food parcel and opened it.

"Quite excellent," he said, with his mouth full of bread and meat.

At every moment he was making amends to Maria for his cavalier treatment of her during the day. The larger the meals he ate, the more appetite he evinced, the better Maria was pleased. A little gesture like helping himself to his own dinner gratified her absurdly. He could give her so much happiness; he could hurt her so easily.

"I regret having seen so little of you during the day, dear," he said. "It was my loss. But if I had not helped with the working of the boat we should still be at Sapperton Tunnel."

"Yes, dear," said Maria.

"I would have liked to point out the scenery to you as we passed it," went on Hornblower, battling with the self-contempt that his hypocrisy was arousing. "I trust you enjoyed it even so?"

"Not nearly as much as if you had been with me, dear," said Maria, but gratified beyond all measure. She darted glances at the other women in the cabin to detect the envy they must feel on account of her having such a wonderful husband.

"The boy was good?" asked Hornblower. "He ate his pap?"

"Every bit of it," answered Maria proudly, looking down at the sleeping child. "He was inclined to whimper at times, but now he is sleeping happily."

"If it had been two years from now that we made this journey," said Hornblower, "how interested he would have been! He would have helped with the lines, and I could have taught him to hold the tiller."

Now he was not being hypocritical at all.

"He showed a lively interest even now," said Maria.

"And what about his little sister?" asked Hornblower. "Did she behave well?"

"Horatio!" said Maria, a little scandalized.

"I hope not badly, dear," said Hornblower, smiling away her embarrassment.

"No, excellently," admitted Maria.

They were gliding into a lock; Hornblower heard the rattle of the paddles being let down behind them.

"You made very little progress with your sausages, dear," he said. "Let me dispose of them while you tackle some of this bread and meat, which is really delicious."

"But, dear—"

"I insist."

He took Maria's platter and his own, and stepped out into the bows of the boat in the darkness. It was the work of a moment to give the platters a quick rinse overside; the work of another moment to drop overside the sausage from his pocket, and he returned with the dripping platters to a Maria both scandalized and delighted at the condescension of her husband in thus doing menial work.

"Too dark to enjoy any scenery," he said—already the boat was moving out of the lock—"Maria, my dear, when you have completed your supper I will endeavour to make you as comfortable as is possible for the night."

He bent over the sleeping child while Maria repacked the remains of the supper.

"Now, my dear."

"Horatio, really you should not. Horatio, please, I beg of you—"

"No need for a hat at this time of night. Let's have it off. Now there's plenty of room for you on the bench. Put your feet up here. No need for shoes either. Not a word, now. Now a pillow for your head. The bag will make a good foundation. Comfortable like that? Now, the coat over you to keep you warm. There, now sleep well, my dear."

Maria was carried away by his masterful attentions so that she could not protest. She had lain still for a full two minutes before she opened her eyes again to ask what he was doing for his own comfort.

"I shall be supremely comfortable, my dear. I'm an old campaigner. Now close those eyes again, and sleep in peace, my dear."

Hornblower was by no means supremely comfortable, although he had often spent worse nights, in open boats, for instance. With Maria and the child lying on the thinly-cushioned bench he had necessarily to sit upright, as the other passengers were doing. What with the lamp and the breathing of all those people in the cramped little cabin the air was stuffy; his legs were cramped, the small of his back ached, and the part on which he sat protested against bearing his weight unrelieved. But it was only one night to live through, after all. He crammed his hands into his pockets and settled himself again, while the boat went on down the river through the darkness, stopping at intervals at the locks, bumping gently against the walls, gliding forward again. He knew nothing, naturally, of the river between Oxford and London, so he could not guess where they were at any time. But they were heading downstream and towards his new command.

Lucky he was to have a command, he told himself. Not a frigate, but a sloop so big—twenty-two guns—as to justify having a captain and not a commander. It was the best that could be hoped for, for the man who a month ago was the six hundred and first captain out of the six hundred and two on the list. Apparently Caldecott, the previous captain of the *Atropos*, had broken down in health while fitting her out at Deptford, which accounted for his unexpected summons thither to replace him. And the orders had no sooner reached him than the news of Nelson's victory at Trafalgar had arrived in England. Since that time no one had had a thought save for Nelson and Trafalgar. The country was wild with delight at the destruction of Villeneuve's fleet, and in the depths of sorrow at Nelson's death. Nelson—Trafalgar—Nelson—Trafalgar—no column in a newspaper, no momentary gossip with a stranger, but contained those names. The country had been lavish with its rewards. A state funeral was promised for Nelson; for the Navy there were peerages and knighthoods and promotions. With the re-creation of the rank of Admiral of the Red twenty new admirals had been promoted from the top of the captains' list; two captains had fallen at Trafalgar, and two more had died; so that Hornblower was now the five hundred and seventy-seventh captain in seniority. But at the same time promotion had been lavish among the commanders and lieutenants. There were forty-one new captains on the list—there was something gratifying in in the thought that now he was senior to forty-two captains. But it meant that now there were six hundred and nineteen captains seeking employment, and even in the vast Royal Navy there were not enough vacancies for all those. A hundred at least—more likely a hundred and fifty—would be on half-pay awaiting employment. That was as it should be, one might think. That proportion not only made allowance for sickness and old age among the captains, but also made it unnecessary to employ those who had been proved to be inefficient.

Unless the inefficient had friends in high places; then it would be the friendless and the unfortunate who languished on half-pay. Hornblower knew himself to be friendless, and even though he had just been congratulating himself on his good fortune he always thought himself ultimately doomed to misfortune. He was on his way to take over a ship that someone else had fitted out, with officers and men he knew nothing of; those facts were sufficient basis on which his gloomy pessimism could build itself.

Maria sighed and turned herself on the bench; Hornblower crept down to her to rearrange the heavy coat over her body.

III

At Brentford, in the early light of the winter's morning, it was cold and damp and gloomy. Little Horatio whimpered ceaselessly; Maria was uncomfortable and weary, as she stood beside Hornblower while her trunk and Hornblower's two sea chests were being hoisted out of the boat.

"Is it far to Deptford, my dear?" she asked.

"Far enough," said Hornblower; between Brentford and Deptford lay the whole extent of London and much more besides, while the river on which they were to travel wound sinuously in wide curves, backwards and forwards. And they had arrived late, and the tide would barely serve.

The wherrymen were soliciting for his custom.

"Boat, sir? Sculls, sir? Oars, sir?"

"Oars," said Hornblower.

It cost twice as much for a wherry rowed by two oarsmen as for one rowed by a single man with sculls, but with the ebbing tide it was worth it. Hornblower helped Maria and the baby down into the stern-sheets and looked on while the baggage was handed down.

"Right, Bill. Give way," said stroke-oar, and the wherry shot away from the slip out on to the grey river.

"Ooh," said Maria, a little afraid.

The oars ground in the rowlocks, the boat danced on the choppy water.

"They say the old King's fair mazed, sir, at Lord Nelson's death," said stroke, with a jerk of his hand towards Kew, across the river. "That's where he lives, sir. In the Palace there."

"Yes," said Hornblower; in no mood to discuss the King or Lord Nelson or anyone else.

The wind was brisk and westerly; had it been easterly the river would have been far more choppy, and their progress would be delayed, so there was something at least to be said in favour of this grey world.

"Easy, 'Arry," said bow, and the wherry began to round the bend.

"Hush, baby. Don't you like the nasty boat?" said Maria to little Horatio, who was making it plain that Maria had guessed at the truth of the matter.

"Nipper's cold, likely," volunteered stroke.

"I think he is," agreed Maria.

The boatman and Maria fell into conversation, to Hornblower's relief; he could immerse himself in his thoughts then, in his hopes and his apprehensions—the latter predominating—about his ship that awaited him down river. It would only be an hour or two before he would go on board. Ship, officers and crew were all unknown to him.

"The Dook lives there, ma'am," said the boatman, through little Horatio's yells, "an' you can see the Bishop's Palace through the trees."

This was Maria's first visit to London; it was convenient that they should have a loquacious boatman.

"See the pretty houses," said Maria, dancing the baby in her arms. "Look at the pretty boats."

The houses were getting thicker and thicker; they shot bridge after bridge, and the boat traffic on the river was growing dense, and suddenly Hornblower became aware they were at London's edge.

"Westminster, ma'am," said the boatman. "I used to ply on the ferry here until they built the bridge. A ha'penny toll took the bread out of the mouths of many an honest boatman then."

"I should think so, indeed," said Maria, sympathetically. By now she had forgotten the dignity of her position as a captain's wife.

"White'all Steps, ma'am, and that 'ere's the Strand."

Hornblower had taken boat to Whitehall Steps often, during those bitter days of half-pay when he was soliciting employment from the Admiralty.

"St Paul's, ma'am."

Now they were really within the City of London. Hornblower could smell the smoke of the coal fires.

"Easy, 'Arry," said bow again, looking back over his shoulder. Boats, lighters, and barges covered the surface of the river, and there was London Bridge ahead of them.

"Give way, 'ard," said bow, and the two oarsmen pulled desperately through a gap in the traffic above the bridge. Through the narrow arches the tide ran fast; the river was piled up above the constriction of the bridge. They shot down through the narrow opening.

"Goodness!" said Maria.

And here was the greatest port in the world; ships at anchor, ships discharging cargo, with only the narrowest channel down the centre. North country collier brigs, Ramsgate trawlers, coasters, grain ships, with the grey tower looking down on them.

"The Pool's always a rare sight, ma'am," said stroke. "Even wi' the war an' all."

All this busy shipping was the best proof that Bonaparte across the water was losing his war against England. England could never be conquered while the Navy dominated the sea, strangling the continental powers while allowing free passage to British commerce.

Below the Pool lay a ship of war, idly at anchor, topmasts sent down, hands at work on stages overside painting. At her bows was a crude figurehead of a draped female painted in red and white; in her clumsily carved hands she carried a large pair of gilded shears, and it was those which told Hornblower what the ship was, before he could count the eleven gunports aside, before they passed under her stern and he could read her name, *Atropos*. He choked down his excitement as he stared at her, taking note of her trim and her lines, of the petty officer of the anchor watch—of everything that in that piercing moment he could possibly observe.

"*Atropos, twenty-two*," said stroke-oar, noting Hornblower's interest.

"My husband is captain of her," said Maria proudly.

"Indeed, sir?" answered stroke, with a new respect that must have been gratifying to Maria.

Already the boat was swinging round; there was Deptford Creek and Deptford Hard.

"Easy!" said bow. "Give way again. Easy!"

The boat rasped against the shore, and the journey from Gloucester was over. No, not over, decided Hornblower preparing to disembark. There was now all the tedious business before them of getting a lodging, taking their baggage there, and settling Maria in before he could get to his ship. Life was a succession of pills that had to be swallowed. He paid the boatman under Maria's watchful eye; fortunately a riverside lounger came to solicit custom, and produced a barrow on which he piled the luggage. Hornblower took Maria's arm and helped her up the slippery Hard as she carried the baby.

"Glad I'll be," said Maria, "to take these shoes off. And the sooner little Horatio is changed the better. There, there, darling."

Only the briefest walk, luckily, took them to the "George". A plump landlády received them, running a sympathetic eye over Maria's condition. She took them up to a room while a maid under her vigorous urgings sped to get hot water and towels.

"There, my poppet," said the landlandy to little Horatio.

"Ooh," said Maria, sitting down on the bed and already beginning to take off her shoes.

Hornblower was standing by the door waiting for his sea chests to be brought up.

"When are you expecting, ma'am?" asked the landlady.

It seemed not a moment before she and Maria were discussing midwives and the rising cost of living—the latter subject introduced by Maria's determination to chaffer over the price of the room. The potman and the riverside lounger carried the baggage up and put it down on the floor of the room, interrupting the discussion. Hornblower took out his keys and knelt eagerly at his chest.

"Horatio, dear," said Maria, "we're speaking to you."

"Eh—what?" asked Hornblower absently over his shoulder.

"Something hot, sir, while breakfast is preparing?" asked the landlady. "Rum punch? A dish o' tea?"

"Not for me, thank you," said Hornblower.

He had his chest open by now and was unpacking it feverishly.

"Cannot that wait until we've had breakfast, dear?" asked Maria. "Then I could do it for you."

"I fear not, ma'am," said Hornblower, still on his knees.

"Your best shirts! You're crumpling them," protested Maria.

Hornblower was dragging out his uniform coat from beneath them. He laid the coat on the other chest and searched for his epaulette.

"You're going to your ship!" exclaimed Maria.

"Of course, my dear," said Hornblower.

The landlady was out of the room and conversation could run more freely.

"But you must have your breakfast first," expostulated Maria.

Hornblower made himself see reason.

"Five minutes for breakfast, then, after I've shaved," he said.

He laid out his coat on the bed, with a frown at its creases, and he unlatched the japanned box which held his cocked hat. He threw off the coat he was wearing and undid, feverishly, his neckcloth and stock. Little Horatio decided at that moment to protest again against a heartless world, and Hornblower unrolled his housewife and took out his razor and addressed himself to shaving while Maria attended to the baby.

"I'll take Horatio down for his bread and milk, dear," said Maria.

"Yes, dear," said Hornblower through the lather.

The mirror caught Maria's reflection, and he forced himself back into the world again. She was standing pathetically looking at him, and he put down his razor, and took up the towel and wiped the lather from his mouth.

"Not a kiss since yesterday!" he said. "Maria, darling, don't you think you've been neglecting me?"

She came to his outheld arms; her eyes were wet, but the gentleness of his voice and the lightness of his tone brought a smile to her lips despite her tears.

"I thought I was the neglected one," she whispered.

She kissed him eagerly, possessively, her hands at his shoulders, holding him to her swollen body.

"I have been thinking about my duty," he said to her, "to the exclusion of the other things I should have thought about. Can you forgive me, dearest?"

"Forgive!" the smile and the tears were both more evident as she spoke. "Don't say that, darling. Do what you will—I'm yours. I'm yours."

Hornblower felt a wave of real tenderness rise within him as he kissed her again; the happiness, the whole life, of a human creature depended on his patience and his tact. His wiping off of the lather had not been very effective; there were smears of it on Maria's face.

"Sweetness," he said, "that makes you my very dearest possession."

And while he kissed her he thought of *Atropos* riding to her anchor out there in the river, and despised himself as a hypocritical unfaithful lover. But his concealment of his impatience brought its reward, for when little Horatio began to wail again it was Maria who drew back first.

"The poor lamb!" she said, and quitted Hornblower's arms to go and attend to him. She looked up at her husband from where she bent over the child, and smiled at him. "I must see that both of these men of mine are fed."

There was something Hornblower had to say, but it called for tact, and he fumbled in his mind before he found the right way to say it.

"Dearest," he said. "I do not mind if the whole world knows I have just kissed you, but I fear lest you would be ashamed."

"Goodness!" said Maria, grasping his meaning and hurrying to the mirror to wipe off the smears of lather. Then she snatched up the baby. "I'll see that your breakfast is ready when you come down."

She smiled at him with so much happiness in her face, and she blew him a kiss before she left the room. Hornblower turned again to renew the lather and prepare himself for going on board. His mind was full of his ship, his wife, his child, and the child to be. The fleeting happiness of yesterday was forgotten; perhaps, not being aware that he was unhappy now, he could be deemed happy today as well, but he was not a man with a gift for happiness.

With breakfast finished at last he took boat again at the Hard to go the short distance to his ship; as he sat in the stern-sheets he settled his cocked hat with its gold loop and button, and he let his cloak hang loose to reveal the epaulette on his right shoulder that marked him as a captain of less than three years' seniority. He momentarily tapped his pocket to make sure that his orders were in it, and then sat upright in the boat with all the dignity he could muster. He could imagine what was happening in *Atropos*—the master's mate of the watch catching sight of the cocked hat and the epaulette, the messenger scurrying to tell the first lieutenant, the call for sideboys and bosun's mates, the wave of nervousness and curiosity that would pass over the ship at the news that the new captain was about to come on board. The thought of it made him smile despite his own nervousness and curiosity.

"Boat ahoy!" came the hail from the ship.

The boatman gave an inquiring glance at Hornblower, received a nod in return, and turned to hail back with a pair of lungs of leather.

"*Atropos*!"

That was positive assurance to the ship that this was her captain approaching.

"Lay her alongside," said Hornblower.

Atropos sat low in the water, flush-decked; the mizzen chains were within easy reach of Hornblower where he stood. The boatman coughed decorously.

"Did you remember my fare, sir?" he asked, and Hornblower had to find coppers to pay him.

Then he went up the ship's side, refusing, as far as his self-control would allow, to let the incident fluster him. He tried to conceal his excitement as he reached the deck amid the twittering of the pipes, with his hand to his hatbrim in salute, but he was not capable of seeing with clarity the faces that awaited him there.

"John Jones, First Lieutenant," said a voice. "Welcome aboard, sir."

Then there were other names, other faces as vague as the names. Hornblower checked himself from swallowing in his excitement for fear lest it should be noticed. He went to some pains to speak in a tone of exactly the right pitch.

"Call the ship's company, Mr Jones, if you please."

"All hands! All hands!"

The cry went through the ship while the pipes twittered and squealed again. There was a rush of feet, a bustling and a subdued murmur. Now there was a sea of faces before him in the waist, but he was still too excited to observe them in detail.

"Ship's company assembled, sir."

Hornblower touched his hat in reply—he had to assume that Jones had touched his hat to him, for he was not aware of it—and took out his orders and began to read.

"Orders from the Commissioners for executing the office of Lord High Admiral of Great Britain and Ireland, addressed to Captain Horatio Hornblower of His Majesty's Navy.

"You are hereby required—"

He read them through to the end, folded them, and returned them to his pocket. Now he was legally captain of the *Atropos*, holding a position of which only a court martial—or an Act of Parliament—or the loss of the ship—could deprive him. And from this moment his half-pay ceased and he would begin to draw the pay of a captain of a sixth-rate. Was it significant that it was from this moment the mists began to clear from before his eyes? Jones was a lantern-jawed man, his close-shaven beard showing blue through his tan. Hornblower met his eyes.

"Dismiss the ship's company, Mr. Jones."

"Aye aye, sir."

This might have been the moment for a speech, Hornblower knew. It was even customary to make one. But he had prepared nothing to say; and he told himself it was better to say nothing. He had it in mind that he would give a first impression of someone cold and hard and efficient and unsentimental. He turned to the waiting group of lieutenants; now he could distinguish their features, recognize that they were distinct individuals, these men whom he would have to trust and use for years in the future; but their names had escaped him completely. He had really heard nothing of them in those excited seconds after arriving on the quarterdeck.

"Thank you, gentlemen," he said to them. "We shall know each other better soon, I do not doubt."

There was a touching of hats and a general turning away of them all except Jones.

"There's an Admiralty letter waiting for you, sir," said the latter.

An Admiralty letter! Orders! The key to the future, which would reveal what was to be their fate—the words which might despatch him and the *Atropos* to China or Greenland or Brazil. Hornblower felt his excitement surge up again—it had hardly subsided in any case. Once more he checked himself from swallowing.

"Thank you, Mr. Jones. I'll read it as soon as I have leisure."

"Would you care to come below, sir?"

"Thank you."

The captain's quarters in the *Atropos* were as minute as Hornblower had expected; the smallest possible day-cabin and night-cabin. They were so small that they were not bulkheaded off from one another; a curtain was supposed to be hung between them, but there was no curtain.

There was nothing at all—no cot, no desk, no chair, nothing. Apparently Caldecott had made a clean sweep of all his belongings when he left the ship. There was nothing surprising about that, but it was inconvenient. The cabin was dark and stuffy, but as the ship was newly out of dry dock she had not yet acquired all the manifold smells which would impregnate her later.

"Where are these orders?" demanded Hornblower, brusque with his suppressed excitement.

"In my desk, sir. I'll fetch 'em at once."

It could not be too quickly for Hornblower, who stood under the little skylight awaiting Jones' return. He took the sealed package into his hand and stood holding it for a moment. This was an instant transition. The journey of the last twenty-four hours had been a longer period, but of the same kind—an interval between one kind of activity and another. The next few seconds would eventually transform the *Atropos* from an idle ship in the Thames to an active ship at sea, lookouts at the mastheads, guns ready for action, peril and adventure and death only just over the horizon if not alongside. Hornblower broke the seal—the foul anchor of the Admiralty, the most inappropriate emblem conceivable for a nation that ruled the sea. Looking up, he met Jones' eyes, as the first lieutenant waited anxiously to hear what their fate was to be. Hornblower knew that he should have sent Jones away before breaking the seal, but it was too late now. Hornblower read the opening lines—he could have announced beforehand what would be the first six words, or even the first twelve.

> You are hereby requested and required, immediately upon receipt of these orders—

This was the moment; Hornblower savoured it for one half of one second.

> —to wait upon Henry Pallender, Esq., Blue Mantle Pursuivant at Arms, at the College of Heralds—

"God bless my soul," said Hornblower.

"What is it, sir?" asked Jones.

"I don't know yet," answered Hornblower.

> —there to consult with him upon the arrangements to be made for the funeral Procession by water of the late Vice-Admiral Lord Viscount Nelson—

"So that's it," said Hornblower.

"It's *what*, sir?" asked Jones, but Hornblower could not spare the time at present to enlighten him.

—You will take upon yourself, by the authority of these orders, the command of all officers, seamen, and Royal Marines to be engaged in the Procession aforesaid, likewise of all vessels, boats and barges belonging to the Cities of London and Westminster and to the City Companies. You will issue all the orders necessary for the Procession to be conducted in a seaman-like manner. You will, by your consultations with Henry Pallender, Esq., aforesaid, ascertain the requirements of Ceremonial and Precedence, but you are hereby charged, upon your peril, to pay strict attention to conditions of Tide and Weather so that not only may Ceremonial be observed, but also that no Danger or Damage may be incurred by the boats, barges, and vessels aforesaid, nor by their Crews and Passengers.

"Please, sir. *Please*, sir," said Jones.

His thoughts came back into the little cabin.

"These are orders for me personally," he said. "Oh—very well, you can read them if you wish to."

Jones read them with moving lips and finally looked up at Hornblower with a bewildered expression.

"So the ship stays here, sir?" he asked.

"She certainly does. She is from this moment the flagship of the funeral procession," said Hornblower. "I shall need a boat and boat's crew at once. Oh yes, pen and paper to send a message to my wife."

"Aye aye, sir."

"See there's a good petty officer in the boat. She'll be waiting a good deal ashore."

"Aye aye, sir. We're having men run every day."

Of course desertion could be a very serious problem in a ship anchored here in the river, within swimming distance of shore and innumerable boats plying about, with the whole City of London close at hand into which a deserter might disappear. And there could be the question of liquor being surreptitiously sold on board from shore boats. And Hornblower had been on board for a full ten minutes and he was no wiser about the things he most wanted to know—about how *Atropos* was manned and officered, what she lacked, what was her material condition—than he had been yesterday. But all the problems with which he was so anxious to deal must for the moment be shelved, to be dealt with at intervals when this new strange duty permitted. The mere question of the furnishing of his cabin might demand more attention than he could spare at present. Hornblower knew from the newspaper he had read yesterday that Nelson's body was at the Nore, awaiting a fair wind before being brought up to Greenwich. Time was pressing, and there were orders in hundreds to be written, he did not doubt.

And so the moment of transition was over. If he had been allowed a thousand guesses as to what his orders would contain, he would never have thought of this particular duty. He could laugh about it if it were not so serious. He could laugh in any case, and he did. After a moment's glance of surprise Mr. Jones decided that he should laugh too, and did so, obsequiously.

IV

"Black breeches?" asked Hornblower, startled.

"Of course. Black breeches and stockings, and mourning bands," said Mr. Pallender solemnly.

He was an aged man, and although the top of his head was bald he wore the remainder of his white hair long, clubbed at the nape of his neck in a thick short queue tied with black ribbon. He had pale blue eyes, rheumy with age, and a thin pointed nose which in the chill of the room bore a small drop at its reddish tip—perhaps always bore one. Hornblower made a note on the sheet of paper before him regarding the black breeches and stockings and mourning bands. He also made a mental note that he would have to obtain these things for himself as well, and he wondered where the money was coming from to do it.

"It would be best," went on Mr. Pallender, "if the procession were to pass through the City at midday. Then the populace will have plenty of time to assemble, and the apprentices can do a morning's work."

"I can't promise that," said Hornblower. "It depends on the tide."

"The tide, Captain Hornblower? You must realize that this is a ceremonial in which the Court—His Majesty himself—is deeply interested."

"But it has to depend on the tide all the same," said Hornblower. "And even on the winds too."

"Indeed? His Majesty will be most provoked if his ideas are scouted."

"I see," said Hornblower.

He thought of remarking that although His Majesty ruled the waves he had no more control over the tides than had his illustrious predecessor King Canute, but he thought better of it. Mr. Pallender was not the type to appreciate jokes about the limitations of the royal power. Instead Hornblower decided to imitate Mr. Pallender's solemnity.

"Since the actual day of the ceremonial hasn't yet been decided upon," he said, "it might be possible to choose such a day as the tide serves best."

"I suppose so," conceded Mr. Pallender.

Hornblower made a note of the necessity of immediately consulting the tide-tables.

"The Lord Mayor," said Mr. Pallender, "will not be present in person, but his representative will."

"I understand."

There would be some small relief in not being responsible for the person of the Lord Mayor, but not much, seeing that the eight most senior admirals in the Navy were going to be present, and were going to be his responsibility.

"Are you sure you won't try a little of this brandy?" asked Mr. Pallender, giving the decanter a little push.

"No, thank you."

Hornblower had no desire at all to drink brandy at this time of day; but now he knew what gave Mr. Pallender's nose that reddish tip. Mr. Pallender sipped appreciatively before going on.

"Now as regards the minute guns—"

Along the processional route apparently there were fifteen points at which minute guns were to be fired, and his Majesty would be listening to see that they were properly timed. Hornblower covered more paper with notes. There would be thirty-eight boats and barges in the procession, to be assembled in the tricky tideway at Greenwich, marshalled in order, brought up to Whitehall Steps, and dispersed again after delivering over the body to a naval guard of honour assembled there which would escort it to the Admiralty to lie there for the night before the final procession to St. Paul's.

"Can you tell me, sir," asked Hornblower, "what kind of vessel these ceremonial barges are?"

He regretted the question as soon as he asked it; Mr. Pallender showed surprise that any man should not be familiar with ceremonial barges, but as for knowing how handy they were in choppy water, or even how many oars aside they rowed, that was of course more than could be expected of Mr. Pallender. Hornblower realized that the sooner he took one over, and rowed it over the course of the procession in the appropriate tidal conditions, timing every stage, the better. He went on adding to his pages of notes while Mr. Pallender went on with what to him was most important—the order of precedence of the boats; how the whole College of Heralds would be present, including Norroy King of Arms and himself, Blue Mantle Pursuivant; the Royal Dukes and the Admirals; the formalities to be observed at the embarkation and the landing; the Chief Mourner and the train-bearer, the pall-bearers and the Family of the Deceased.

"Thank you, sir," said Hornblower at last, gathering up his notes. "I will begin these preparations at once."

"Greatly obliged, I'm sure, sir," said Mr. Pallender, as Hornblower took his leave.

This was an operation as elaborate as Abercrombie's landing on the Egyptian coast—and in the Mediterranean there were no tides to complicate arrangements. Thirty-eight boats with their crews and oarsmen; guards of honour; mourners and officials; there would be a thousand officers and men at least under Hornblower's command. And Hornblower's heart sank a little when he was able to take one of the barges from the hands of the workmen who were attaching the insignia to it in Deptford Yard, and conduct his own trials with it. It was a vast clumsy vessel, not much smaller and no more manageable than a cargo lighter. Forward in the open bows she pulled twelve oars; from midships aft she was covered with a vast canopy of solid construction, exposing an enormous area to the wind. The barge allotted to the conveyance of the Body (Mr. Pallender had made that capital letter quite obvious in their discussion) was being so covered with plumes that she would catch the wind like a frigate's mainsail. There must be lusty oarsmen detailed to the task of rowing that barge along—and it would be best to have as nearly as complete a relief available as possible, hidden away under the canopy. But as she would head the procession, with the other boats taking station upon her, he must be careful not to overdo that. He must time everything exactly—up with the flood tide, arriving at Whitehall Steps precisely at slack water so that the complicated manoeuvres there could be carried out with the minimum of risk, and then back with the ebb, dispersing barges and crews along the route as convenient.

"My dear," said Maria to him, in their bedroom at the "George" "I fear I have little of your attention at present."

"Your pardon, dear?" said Hornblower, looking round from the table at which he was writing. He was deep in plans for issuing a solid breakfast to a thousand men who would have small chance of eating again all day.

"I was telling you that I spoke to the midwife today. She seems a worthy woman. She will hold herself free from tomorrow. As she lives only in the next street there is no need for her to take up residence here until the time comes, which is fortunate—you know how little money we have, Horatio."

"Yes, dear," said Hornblower. "Have those black breeches of mine been delivered yet?"

It was a perfectly natural step from Maria's approaching confinement to Hornblower's black breeches, *via* the question of money, but Maria resented her husband's apparent heartlessness.

"Do you care more for your breeches than for your child?" she asked, "—or for me?"

"Dearest," answered Hornblower. He had to put down his pen and rise from his chair to comfort her. "I have much on my mind. I can't tell you how much I regret it at this moment."

This was the very devil. The eyes not only of London but of all England would be on that procession. He would never be forgiven if there was any blunder. But he had to take Maria's hands in his and reassure her.

"You, my dear," he said, smiling into her eyes, "are my all in all. There is nothing in my world as important as you are."

"I wish I could be sure," said Maria.

He kissed the hands he held.

"What can I say to make you sure?" he asked. "That I love you?"

"That would be pleasant enough," said Maria.

"I love you, dear," he said, but he had not had now a smile from her as yet, and he went on, "I love you more dearly even than my new black breeches."

"Oh!" said Maria.

He had to labour the point to make sure that she understood he was both joking and tender.

"More dearly than a thousand pair of black breeches," he said. "Could any man say more?"

She was smiling now, and she took her hands from his and laid them on his shoulders.

"Is that a compliment for me to treasure always?" she asked.

"It will always be true, my dear," he said.

"You are the kindest of husbands," she said, and the break in her voice showed that she meant it.

"With the sweetest of wives," he answered. "And now may I go on with my work?"

"Of course, darling. Of course. I fear I am selfish. But—but—darling, I love you so. I love you so!"

"There, there," said Hornblower patting her shoulder. Perhaps he felt as strongly over this business as Maria did, but he had much else to feel strongly about. And if he mismanaged these ceremonial arrangements the child to come might go on short commons with him on half-pay for life. And Nelson's body was at this very moment lying in state at Greenwich, and the day after tomorrow was the date fixed for the procession, with the tide beginning to flood at eleven, and there was still much to be done. He was glad to get back to the writing of his orders. He was glad to go back on board *Atropos* and plunge into business there.

"Mr. Jones, I'd be glad if you'd call the midshipmen and master's mates. I need half a dozen who can write a fair round hand."

The cabin of the *Atropos* took on the appearance of a schoolroom, with the midshipmen sitting on mess stools at improvised tables, with inkwells and pens, copying out Hornblower's drafts of the orders, and

Hornblower going from one to another, like a squirrel in a cage, answering questions.

"Please, sir, I can't read this word."

"Please, sir, do I start a new paragraph here?"

It was one way of finding out something of the junior officers, of distinguishing them as individuals out of what had been so far a formless mass of officers; there were the ones who appealed for help at every turn, and the ones who could make deductions from the context; there were the stupid ones who wrote orders that made nonsense.

"Damn it, man," said Hornblower. "Would anyone out of Bedlam say a thing like that—far less write it?"

"That's what it looked like, sir," said the midshipman stubbornly.

"God help us all," said Hornblower in despair.

But that was the man who wrote a very clear hand; Hornblower put him on to the task of writing the beginnings of each letter.

H.M.S. *Atropos* at Deptford
Jan 6th 1806
Sir

By virtue of the powers entrusted to me by the Lords Commissioners of the Admiralty—

Other men could carry on from there, with a saving of time. The ninety different written orders with their duplicates were written at last, and distributed by midnight; crews and petty officers had been found from various sources for every boat that was to take part in the procession, rations allotted to them, their place in the line clearly stated—"You will take the seventeenth position, immediately after the barge of the Commander-in-Chief at the Nore and immediately preceding that of the Worshipful Company of Fishmongers."

The final arrangements were made with Mr. Pallender at two in the morning of the day of the procession, and Hornblower, yawning, could think of nothing else to be done. Yes, there was a final change to be made.

"Mr. Horrocks, you will come with me with the Body in the first barge. Mr. Smiley, you'll command the second with the Chief Mourner."

Horrocks was the stupidest of the midshipmen and Smiley the brightest—it had been natural to reserve the latter for himself, but now he realized how stupid Horrocks was, and how necessary it was to keep him under his own eye.

"Aye aye, sir."

Hornblower fancied Smiley looked pleased at thus escaping from the direct supervision of his captain, and he pricked that bubble.

"You'll have nine admirals and four captains as passengers, Smiley," he said. "Including Admiral of the Fleet Sir Peter Parker and Lord St Vincent."

Smiley did not look nearly as pleased at that.

"Mr. Jones, have the longboat with the hands at Greenwich Pier at six o'clock, if you please."

"Aye aye, sir."

"And call away the gig for me now."

"Aye aye, sir."

"I'll be at the "George" until five. Send any messages there."

"Aye aye, sir."

He still had a personal life; Maria was very near her time now.

On the deck there was a brisk westerly wind harping in the rigging, gusty, Hornblower noted. The barges would call for careful handling unless it dropped considerably. He stepped down into the gig.

"Make for Deptford Hard," he ordered the coxswain, and clasped his coat close tightly round him, for the cabin of the *Atropos* had been hot with lamps and candles and many people. He walked up the Hard and knocked at the door of the "George"; from the window at the side there was a faint light showing and the window of their room above was illuminated. The door opened to reveal the landlady."

"Oh, it's you, sir. I thought it was the midwife. I've just sent Davie for her. Your good lady—"

"Let me by," said Hornblower.

Maria was walking about the bedroom in her dressing-gown; two candles illuminated the room, and the shadows of the bed-tester and the other furniture moved in sinister fashion as Hornblower opened the door.

"Darling!" said Maria.

Hornblower came towards her, his hands held out.

"I hope all is well with you, dear," he said.

"I think so. I—I hope so. It has only just begun," said Maria.

They kissed.

"Darling," said Maria. "How good of you to come here. I—I was hoping I should see you again before—before—my time came."

"Not good of me," said Hornblower. "I came because I wanted to come. I wanted to see you."

"But you are so busy. Today is the day of the procession, is it not?"

"Yes," said Hornblower.

"And our child will be born today. A little girl, dear? Or another little boy?"

"We'll know soon," said Hornblower. He knew which Maria wanted. "Whichever it is we'll love her—or him."

"That we shall," said Maria.

The last syllable was jerked out of her more forcibly than necessary, and Maria's face took on an expression of preoccupation.

"How is it, dearest?" asked Hornblower, concerned.

"Only a pain," said Maria, smiling—forcing a smile, as Hornblower well knew. "They are not coming close together yet."

"I wish I could help," said Hornblower, in the manner of uncounted millions of fathers.

"You have helped by coming to me, my darling," said Maria.

A bustle outside the door and a knock heralded the entrance of the midwife and the landlady.

"Well, well," said the midwife. "So it has began, has it?"

Hornblower looked her over carefully. She was not neat—no one could be expected to be in those conditions—but she was at least sober, and her gap-toothed smile was kindly.

"I'll have a look at you, ma'am," said the midwife, and then, with a sidelong glance, "Gentlemen will retire."

Maria looked at him. She was trying so hard to appear unconcerned.

"I'll see you again, dear," said Hornblower, trying equally hard.

Outside the bedroom the landlady was cordial in her offers of hospitality.

"How about a go of brandy, sir? Or a glass o' rum, hot?"

"No, thank you," said Hornblower.

"The young gennelman's sleeping in with one o' the maids now," explained the landlady. "He didn't cry, no, not a sound, when we carried him in. A fine little fellow he is, sir."

"Yes," said Hornblower. He could smile at the thought of his little son.

"You'd better come into the coffee-room, sir," said the landlady. "There's still what's left of the fire there."

"Thank you," said Hornblower, with a glance at his watch. God, how time was passing!

"Your good lady will be all right," said the landlady maternally. "It'll be a boy, as sure as fate. I can tell by the way she was carrying."

"Perhaps you'll be right," said Hornblower, and he looked at his watch again. He really must start preparations for the day.

"Now see here, please," he said, and then he paused, as he made his mind clear itself of its preoccupation with Maria, and of its deadly fatigue. He began to list the things he needed from the bedroom upstairs, ticking them off on his fingers as he told them to the landlady. The black breeches and stockings, the epaulette and the best cocked hat, the sword and the mourning band.

"I'll get 'em, sir. You can dress in here—no one won't disturb you, not at this time o' night."

She came back later with her arms full of the things Hornblower had asked for.

"A marvel that I should forget this was the day of the Funeral, sir," she said. "No one hasn't talked o' nothing else along the river not for the last week. There's your things, sir."

She looked closely at Hornblower in the candlelight.

"You'd better shave, sir," she went on. "You can use my husband's razor if yours is in the ship."

One mention of maternity, it seemed, turned all women into mothers.

"Very well," said Hornblower.

Later he was dressed and looking at his watch again.

"I must leave now," he said. "Will you find out if I can see my wife?"

"I'll tell you now you can't, sir," said the landlady. "Not if you can hear what I can hear."

Much of what Hornblower felt must have shown in his expression, for the landlady went on—

"It'll all be over in a hower, sir: whyn't you wait a bit?"

"Wait?" repeated Hornblower, looking at his watch again. "No, I can't do that. I'll have to go."

The landlady lighted the candle of his lantern at that on the coffee-room mantel.

"Lord a mercy," she said. "You look just the picture. But it's cold out."

She fastened the button of his coat close at his neck.

"Can't have you catching cold. There! Don't you worry, now."

Good advice, thought Hornblower, walking down the slope towards the river again, but as difficult to act upon as most good advice. He saw the light of the gig at the water's edge, and a sudden movement of shadowy figures there. The gig's crew must have appointed one of its members to keep watch for his lantern, while the others snatched what sleep they could in the exceedingly uncomfortable spaces of the gig. But however uncomfortable they were, they were better off than he was. He felt he could sleep on the bobstay of the *Atropos* if only he had the chance. He got into the gig.

"Down river," he ordered the coxswain.

At Greenwich Pier it was still dark, no sign as yet of the late January dawn. And the wind was blowing steadily from the west, downstream. It would probably freshen as the day went on. A loud challenge halted him as he walked down the pier.

"Friend," said Hornblower, opening his cloak for his lantern to show his uniform.

"Advance and give the countersign!"

"The Immortal Memory," said Hornblower—he had chosen that countersign himself; one detail out of a thousand details of the day before.

"Pass, friend. All's well," said the sentry.

He was a private in the Blackheath Militia; during the time the Body had been lying in state at Greenwich there had had to be guards posted at all points to prevent the public from straying into areas where they were not wanted. The Hospital was lighted up; there was already bustle and excitement there.

"The Governor's dressing now, sir," said a wooden-legged lieutenant. "We're expecting the quality at eight."

"Yes," said Hornblower. "I know."

It was he who had drawn up the time-table; the national, naval, and civic dignitaries were to come by road from London, to accompany the Body back by water. And here was the Body, in its coffin, the trestles on which it lay concealed by flags and trophies and heraldic insignia. And here came the Governor, limping with his rheumatism, his bald head shining in the lamplight.

"Morning, Hornblower."

"Good morning, sir."

"Everything settled?"

"Yes, sir. But the wind's blowing very fresh from the west. It'll hold back the flood."

"I feared as much."

"It will delay the boats, too, of course, sir."

"Of course."

"In that case, sir, I'd be obliged if you would do all you can to see that the Mourners leave on time. There'll be little to spare, sir."

"I'll do my best, Hornblower. But you can't hurry an Admiral of the Fleet. You can't hurry Lord St Vincent. You can't hurry a Lord Mayor—not even his representative."

"It will be difficult, I know, sir."

"I'll do my best, Hornblower. But they have to have their bite of breakfast."

The Governor gestured towards the next room where, under the supervision of the wooden-legged lieutenant, seamen with black scarves round their necks were laying out a meal. There were cold pies, there were hams, there were cold roasts of beef being assembled on the buffet; silver was being set out on the dazzling white cloth. At the smaller buffet a trusted petty officer was setting out decanters and bottles.

"A bite and a glass of something?" asked the Governor.

Hornblower looked as always at his watch.

"Thank you, sir. I've three minutes to spare."

It was gratifying to have a meal when he expected to have none; it was gratifying to gulp down slices of ham which otherwise would have gone down the throat of an Admiral of the Fleet. He washed the ham down with a glass of water, to the ill-concealed amazement of the petty officer at the wine buffet.

"Thank you, sir," he said to the Governor. "I must take my leave now."

"Good-bye, Hornblower. Good luck."

At the pier now it was almost dawn—light enough to satisfy the Mohammedan definition of being able to distinguish a black thread from a white. And the river was alive now with boats. From upstream the wind carried down the sound of the splash of oars and sharp naval commands. Here was the *Atropos*' longboat, with Smiley and Horrocks in the stern; here were the boats from the guardship and the receiving ship; measured tread on the pier heralded the arrival of another contingent of seamen. The day was beginning in earnest.

Really in earnest. The thirty-eight boats had to be manned and arranged in their correct order, stretching a mile down-stream. There were the fools who had mislaid their orders, and the fools who could not understand theirs. Hornblower dashed up and down the line in the gig, that watch of his continually in and out of his pocket. To complicate matters, the grog sellers, anticipating a good day's business, were already out and rowing along the line, and they obviously had effected some surreptitious sales. There were red faces and foolish grins to be seen. The ebb was still running strongly, with the wind behind it. Horrocks, in the state barge that was to carry the Body, completely misjudged his distances as he tried to come alongside. The clumsy great boat, swept round by the wind and borne by the tide, hit the pier on her starboard quarter with a resounding crash. Hornblower on the pier opened his mouth to swear, and then shut it again. If he were to swear at every mishap he would be voiceless soon. It was enough to dart a glance at the unhappy Horrocks. The big raw-boned lout wilted under it; and then turned to rave at the oarsmen.

These ceremonial barges were heartbreaking boats to manage, admittedly. Their twelve oars hardly sufficed to control their more than forty feet of length, and the windage of the huge cabin aft was enormous. Hornblower left Horrocks struggling to get into his station, and stepped down into his gig again. They flew downstream; they toiled up. Everything seemed to be in order. Hornblower, looking over the side from the pier when he landed again, thought he could detect a slacking of the ebb. Late, but good enough. High and clear from the Hospital came the notes of a trumpet. Tone-deaf as he was, the notes meant nothing to him. But the sound itself was sufficient. The militia were forming up along the road from the Hospital to the pier, and here came the dignitaries in solemn procession, walking two by two, the least important leading. The boats came to the pier to receive them, in inverted order of numbers—how hard that had been for Hornblower to impress upon the petty officers commanding—and dropped back again downstream to wait, reversing their order. Even now there was a boat or two out of correct order, but this was not a moment for trifles. The dignitaries on the pier were hustled into even inappropriate boats without a chance of protesting. More and more important were the dignitaries advancing on to the pier—here were the Heralds and Pursuivants, Mr. Pallender among them. And here at last was the Chief Mourner, Admiral of the Fleet Sir Peter Parker, with Blackwood bearing his train, and eight other admirals with—as the drill-book stated—melancholy aspects; perhaps their aspects would be melancholy even without the drill-book. Hornblower saw them down into their boat, all of them. The tide had turned, and already the flow was apparent. Minutes would be precious now.

The shattering boom of a gun from not far away made Hornblower start, and he hoped nobody would notice it. That was the first of the minute guns, that would boom on from now until the Body reached its next temporary resting-place at the Admiralty. For Hornblower it was the signal that the Body had started from the Hospital. He handed Sir Peter Parker into the barge. A loud order from the militia colonel, and the troops reversed their arms and rested on them. Hornblower had seen them doing that drill every available minute during the last two days. He reversed his own sword with as much military precision as he could manage—a couple of days ago Maria, coming into the bedroom at the "George", had caught him practising the drill, and had laughed immoderately. The mourners' barge had shoved off, and Horrocks was gingerly bringing his up to the pier. Hornblower watched from under his eyebrows, but now that the wind was against the tide it was not such a difficult operation. The band approached; all tunes were dreary to Hornblower, but he gathered that the one they were playing was drearier than most. They wheeled to the right at the base of the pier, and the seamen drawing the gun-carriage, stepping short, with bowed heads, came into view behind them. Hornblower thought of the long line of boats struggling to keep position all down the reach, and wished they would step out, although he knew such a wish was nonsense. The monotonous booming of the minute gun marked the passage of valuable time. Up to the pier's end came the carriage. It was a tricky business to transfer the coffin from the gun-carriage to the top of the state barge; Hornblower caught some of the words whispered, savagely, by the petty officer supervising the operation, and tried not to smile at their incongruity. But the coffin was put safely in place, and quickly lashed into position, and while the wreaths and flags were being arranged to conceal the lashings Hornblower advanced to the barge. He had to make himself step short, with his back bowed and the melancholy aspect on his face, his reversed sword under his right arm, and he strove to maintain the attitude while making the wide stride from the pier on to the stern of the barge behind the canopy.

"Shove off!" he ordered, out of the side of his mouth. The minute guns bellowed a farewell to them as the barge left the pier, the oar-blades dragging through the water before she gathered way. Horrocks beside him put the tiller over, and they headed out for midstream. Before they straightened on their course Hornblower, his head still bowed, was able to steal a sideways glance downstream at the waiting procession. All seemed to be well; the boats were bunched in places, crowded in others, with the effort of maintaining station in difficult weather conditions, but once everyone was under way it would be easier.

"Slow at first," he growled to Horrocks, and Horrocks translated the order to the rowers; it was necessary to give the boats time to take up station.

Hornblower wanted to look at his watch. Moreover, he realized that he would have to keep his eye continually on his watch, and he certainly could not be pulling it out of his pocket every minute. The foot of the coffin was there by his face. With a quick movement he hauled out both watch and chain, and hung them on the end handle, the watch dangling conveniently before his nose. All was well; they were four minutes late, but they still had a full eleven minutes in reserve.

"Lengthen the stroke," he growled to Horrocks.

Now they were rounding the bend. The shipping here was crowded with spectators, so was the shore, even as far from London as this. The *Atropos* had her yards manned by the remnant of her crew, as Hornblower had ordered. He could see that out of the tail of his eye; and as they approached the clear sharp bang of her aftermost nine-pounder took up the tale of minute guns from the one at Greenwich. All well, still. Of all the ungrateful duties a naval officer ever had to perform, this one must be the worst. However perfect the performance, would he receive any credit? Of course not. Nobody—not even the Admiralty—would stop and think how much thought and labour were necessary to arrange the greatest water procession London had ever seen, on one of the trickiest possible tideways. And if anything went wrong there were hundreds of thousands of pairs of eyes ready to observe it, and hundreds of thousands of pairs of lips ready to open in condemnation.

"Sir! Sir!"

The curtains at the after end of the cabin had parted; an anxious seaman's face was peering out, from where the reserve rowers lay concealed; so anxious was the speaker that he put out his hand to twitch at Hornblower's black breeches to call attention to himself.

"What is it?"

"Sir! We've sprung a leak!"

My God! The news chimed in with his thoughts with perfectly devilish accuracy of timing.

"How bad?"

"Dunno, sir. But it's up over the floorboards. That's 'ow we know. Must be making pretty fast, sir."

That must have been when Horrocks allowed the barge to crash against the pier. A plank started. Up over the floorboards already? They would never get to Whitehall Steps in time, then. God, if they were to sink here in the middle of the river! Never, never, *never*, would England forgive the man who allowed Nelson's coffin to sink, unceremoniously, in Thames mud beside the Isle of Dogs. Get in to shore and effect repairs? With the whole procession behind them—God, what confusion there would be! And without any doubt at all they would miss the tide, and disappoint the waiting thousands, to say nothing of His Majesty. And tomorrow was the final ceremony, when the Body would be carried from the Admiralty to St. Paul's—dukes, peers, the royal family, thousands of troops, hundreds of thousands of people were to take part in or to watch the ceremonies. To sink would be disaster. To stop would be disaster. No; he could get into shore and effect repairs, causing today's ceremony to be abandoned. But then they could get the Body up to the Admiralty tonight, enabling tomorrow's funeral to be carried out. It would ruin him professionally, but it was the safest half-measure. No, no, no! To hell with half-measures.

"Mr. Horrocks!"

"Sir!"

"I'll take the tiller. Get down in there. Wait, you fool, and listen to me. Get those floorboards up and deal with that leak. Keep bailing—use hats or anything else. Find that leak and stop it if you can—use one of the men's shirts. Wait. Don't let all the world see you bailing. Pitch the water out here, past my legs. Understand?"

"Er—yes, sir."

"Give me the tiller, then. Get below. And if you fail I'll have the hide off you, if it's the last thing I do on earth. Get below."

Horrocks dived down through the curtains, while Hornblower took the tiller and shifted his position so as to see forward past the coffin. He had to let his sword drop, and of course had had to abandon his melancholy aspect, but that was no hardship. The westerly wind was blowing half a gale now, right in their teeth; against the tide it was raising a decided chop on the water—spray was flying from the bows and now and then the oar-blades raised fountains. Perhaps it was a fitting homecoming for the dead hero whose corpse lay just before him. As they came to the bend a fresher gust set them sagging off to leeward, the wind acting powerfully on all the top hamper in the stern.

"Put your backs into it!" shouted Hornblower to the rowers, throwing much of his dignity to the wind, although he was the leading figure in the procession.

The rowers clenched their teeth, snarling with the effort as they tugged at the oars, dragging the obstinate barge by main force forward. Here the wind, acting directly against the tide, was raising some quite respectable rollers, and the barge plunged over them, bows up, bows down, stagger, and heave, like a fishing smack in a gale at sea, lurching and plunging; it was hard to stand upright in her, harder to hold her on her course. And surely—surely—Hornblower was conscious of the water on board cascading forward and back as she plunged. With the ponderous coffin stowed so high up he was nervous about the stability of the absurd craft. Inch by inch they struggled round the bend, and once round it the massed shipping on the north side gave them a lee.

"Haven't you got those floorboards up, Mr. Horrocks?" said Hornblower, trying to hurl the words down into the cabin without stooping in the sight of the crowds.

He heard a splintering crash at that moment, and Horrocks' face emerged between the curtains.

"They were all nailed down tight here," he said. "I had to prise 'em up. We're down by the stern an' we'd have to bail from here, anyways."

What with the coffin and the auxiliary rowers they would, of course, be down by the stern.

"How much water?"

"Nigh on a foot, I should say, sir."

"Bail like hell!"

Horrocks' nose had hardly been withdrawn from between the curtains when a hatful of water shot out past Hornblower's legs, and was followed by another and another and another. A good deal of it soused Hornblower's new black breeches. He cursed but he could not complain. That was Bermondsey on the Surrey shore; Hornblower glanced at his watch dangling from the coffin. They were dropping very slightly behind time, thanks to this wind. Not dangerously, though. They were not nearly in as much danger of missing the tide as they were of sinking in mid-river. Hornblower shifted position miserably in his soaking breeches and glanced back. The procession was keeping station well enough; he could see about half of it, for the centre of it was just now fighting round the bend he had already negotiated. Ahead lay another bend, this time to starboard. They would have a head-wind there again.

So indeed they had. Once more they plunged and staggered over the rollers. There was one moment when the barge put her bows down and shipped a mass of water over them—as much must have come in as Horrocks had been able by now to bail out. Hornblower cursed again, forgetting all about the melancholy aspect he should maintain. He could hear and feel the water rolling about in her as she plunged. But the hatfuls of water were still flying out from between the curtains, past—and on to—Hornblower's legs. Hornblower did not worry now about the effect on the crowd of the sight of the funeral barge bailing out; any seamen among the crowd, seeing that rough water, would appreciate the necessity for it without making allowance for a leak. They fought their way round the bend; for a few desperate moments it seemed as if they were making no progress at all, with the oar-blades dragging through the water. But the gust was succeeded by a momentary lull and they went on again.

"Can't you plug that leak, Mr. Horrocks?"

" 'Tain't easy, sir," said Horrocks, putting his nose out again. "There's a whole plank stove in. The tree-nails at the ends are on'y just holding, sir. If I plug too hard—"

"Oh, very well. Get on with the bailing again."

Make for the shore? Over there, beside the Tower? That would be a convenient place. No, damn it. Never. Bail, bail, bail. Steer a course that gave them the utmost advantage from the flood and from the lee afforded by the shipping—that calculation was a tricky one, something to occupy his mind. If he could spare a moment to look round he could see the thousands of spectators massed along the shores. If he could spare a moment—God, he had forgotten all about Maria! He had left her in labour. Perhaps—most likely—the chiid was born by now. Perhaps—perhaps—no, that did not bear thinking about.

London Bridge, with its narrow arches and the wicked swirls and eddies beyond. He knew by the trials he had made two days ago that the oars were too wide for the arches. Careful timing was necessary; fortunately the bridge itself broke most of the force of the wind. He brought the tiller over and steadied the barge as best he could on a course direct for the arch's centre.

"Now, pull!" he bellowed to the oarsmen; the barge swept forward, carried by the tide and the renewed efforts of the oarsmen. "In oars!"

Fortunately they did it smartly. They shot into the arch, and there the wind was waiting for them, shrieking through the gap, but their way took them forward. Hornblower measured their progress with his eye. The bows lurched and began to swing in the eddy beyond, but they were just clear enough even though he himself was still under the arch.

"Pull!" he yelled—under the bridge he had no fear of being seen behaving without dignity.

Out came the oars. They groaned in their rowlocks. The eddy was turning her—the oars were dragging her forward—now the rudder could bite again. Through—with the eddies left behind.

The water was still cascading out through the curtains, still soaking his dripping breeches, but despite the rate at which they were bailing he did not like the feel of the barge at all. She was sluggish, lazy. The leak must be gaining on them, and they were nearing the danger point.

"Keep pulling!" he shouted to the rowers; glancing back he saw the second barge, with the Chief Mourners, emerging from the bridge. Round the bend to sight the churches in the Strand—never did shipwrecked mariner sight a sail with more pleasure.

"Water's nearly up to the thwarts, sir," said Horrocks.

"Bail, damn you!"

Somerset House, and one more bend, a shallow one, to Whitehall Steps. Hornblower knew what orders he had given for the procession —orders drawn up in consultation with Mr. Pallender. Here the funeral barge was to draw towards the Surrey bank, allowing the next six barges in turn to come alongside the Steps and disembark their passengers. When the passengers had formed up in proper order, and not until then, the funeral barge was to come alongside for the coffin to be disembarked with proper ceremony. But not with water up to the thwarts—not with the barge sinking under his feet. He turned and looked back to where Smiley was standing in the stern-sheets of the second barge. His head was bowed as the instructions stated, but fortunately the coxswain at the tiller noticed, and nudged Smiley to call his attention. Hornblower put up his hand with a gesture to stop; he accentuated the signal by gesturing as though pushing back. He had to repeat the signal before Smiley understood and nodded in reply. Hornblower ported his helm and the barge came sluggishly round, creeping across the river. Round farther; no; with that wind, and with the flood slacking off, it would be better to come alongside bows upstream. Hornblower steadied the tiller, judging his distances, and the barge crept towards the Steps.

"Easy all!"

Thank God, they were alongside. There was a Herald at Arms, tabard and all, standing there with the naval officer in command of the escort.

"Sir!" protested the Herald, as vehemently as his melancholy aspect allowed, "You're out of your order—you—"

"Shut your mouth!" growled Hornblower, and then, to the naval officer, "Get this coffin ashore, quick!"

They got it ashore as quickly as dignity would permit; Hornblower, standing beside them, head bowed, a sword reversed again, heaved a genuine sigh of relief as he saw, from under his lowered brows, the barge rise perceptibly in the water when freed from the ponderous weight of the coffin. Still with his head bowed he snapped his orders.

"Mr. Horrocks! Take the barge over to the jetty there. Quick. Get a tarpaulin, put it overside and plug that leak. Get her bailed out. Give way, now."

The barge drew away from the Steps; Hornblower could see that Horrocks had not exaggerated when he said the water was up to the thwarts. Smiley, intelligently, was now bringing the Mourners' barge up to the Steps, and Hornblower, remembering to step short, moved out of the way. One by one they landed, Sir Peter Parker with Blackwood bearing his train, Cornwallis, St Vincent. St Vincent, labouring on his gouty feet, his shoulders hunched as well as his head bent, could hardly wait to growl his complaints, out of the corner of his mouth as he went up the Steps.

"What the devil, Hornblower?" he demanded. "Don't you read your own orders?"

Hornblower took a few steps—stepping slow and short—alongside him.

"We sprung a leak, sir—I mean, my lord," he said, out of the corner of his mouth in turn. "We were nigh on sinking. No time to spare."

"Ha!" said St Vincent. "Oh, very well then. Make a report to that effect."

"Thank you, my lord," said Hornblower.

He halted again, head bowed, sword reversed, and allowed the other mourners to flow on past him. This was extemporized ceremonial, but it worked. Hornblower tried to stand like a statue, although no statue he had ever seen was clothed in breeches streaming with wet. He had to repress a start when he remembered again about Maria. He wished he knew. And then he had more difficulty in repressing another start. His watch! That was still dangling on the coffin, now being put into the waiting hearse. Oh well, he could do nothing about that at the moment. And nothing about Maria. He went on standing in his icy breeches.

V

The sentry at the Admiralty was worried but adamant. "Pardon, sir, but them's my orders. No one to pass, not even a Admiral, sir."

"Where's the petty officer of the guard?" demanded Hornblower.

The petty officer was a little more inclined to listen to reason.

"It's our orders, sir," he said, however. "I daren't, sir. You understand, sir."

No naval petty officer gladly said "no" to a Post Captain, even one of less than three years' seniority.

Hornblower recognized a cocked-hatted lieutenant passing in the background.

"Bracegirdle!" he hailed.

Bracegirdle had been a midshipman along with him in the old *Indefatigable*, and had shared more than one wild adventure with him.

Now he was wearing a lieutenant's uniform with the aigullettes of a staff appointment.

"How are you, sir?" he asked, coming forward.

They shook hands and looked each other over, as men will, meeting after years of war. Hornblower told about his watch, and asked permission to be allowed in to get it. Bracegirdle whistled sympathetically.

"That's bad," he said. "If it was anyone but old Jervie I'd risk it. But that's his own personal order. I've no desire to beg my bread in the gutter for the rest of my days."

Jervie was Admiral Lord St Vincent, recently become First Lord of the Admiralty again, and once Sir John Jervis whose disciplinary principles were talked of with bated breath throughout the Navy.

"You're his flag-lieutenant?" asked Hornblower.

"That's what I am," said Bracegirdle. "There are easier appointments. I'd exchange for the command of a powder hulk in Hell. But I only have to wait for that. By the time I've gone through my period of servitude with Jervie that'll be the only command they'll offer me."

"Then I can say good-bye to my watch," said Hornblower.

"Without even a farewell kiss," said Bracegirdle. "But in after years when you visit the crypt of St. Paul's you will be able to look at the hero's tomb with the satisfaction of knowing that your watch is in there along with him."

"Your humour is frequently misplaced, Mr. Bracegirdle," replied Hornblower, quite exasperated, "and you seem to have forgotten that the difference in rank between us should invite a more respectful attitude on the part of a junior officer."

Hornblower was tired and irritated; even as he said the words he was annoyed with himself for saying them. He was fond of Bracegirdle, and there was still the bond of perils shared with him, and the memory of lighthearted banter in the days when they were both midshipmen. It was not good manners, so to speak, to make use of his superior rank (which only good fortune had brought him) to wound Bracegirdle's feelings—as undoubtedly he had, and merely to soothe his own. Bracegirdle brought himself stiffly to attention.

"I beg your pardon, sir," he said. "I allowed my tongue to run away with me. I hope you will overlook the offence, sir."

The two officers eyed each other for a moment before Bracegirdle unbent again.

"I haven't said yet how sorry I am about your watch, sir," he said. "I'm genuinely sorry on your account. Really sorry, sir."

Hornblower was about to make a pacific reply, when another figure appeared behind Bracegirdle, huge and ungainly, still in gold-laced full dress, and peering from under vast white eyebrows at the two officers. It was St Vincent; Hornblower touched his hat and the gesture informed Bracegirdle that his superior was behind him.

"What's the young man so sorry about, Hornblower?" asked St Vincent.

Hornblower explained as briefly as he could, with hardly a stumble this time over saying "my Lord".

"I'm glad to see Mr. Bracegirdle was carrying out my orders," said St Vincent. "We'd have the Admiralty chock a block with sightseers in a moment otherwise. But you have my personal permission, Captain Hornblower, to pass the sentries."

"Thank you, my lord. I am most grateful."

St Vincent was about to hobble on his way when he checked himself and looked more acutely than ever at Hornblower.

"Have you been presented to His Majesty yet, young Hornblower?"

"No sir—my lord."

"You should be. Every officer should show his respect to his king. I'll take you myself."

Hornblower thought about his wife, about the new baby, about his ship at Deptford, about his wet uniform which would have to be pressed into incredible smartness before he could show it at court. He thought about the rich, and the great, and the powerful, who frequented courts, and knew he would be out of place there and would be unhappy every minute he was compelled to appear there. It might be possible to make an excuse. But—but it would be a new adventure. The distasteful aspects about which he had been thinking were really so many challenges, which he felt spurred to meet.

"Thank you, my lord," he said, searching in his mind for the words appropriate to the subject, "I should be most honoured, most deeply obliged."

"Settled, then. Today's Monday, isn't it? Levee's on Wednesday. I'll take you in my coach. Be here at nine."

"Aye aye, sir—my lord."

"Pass Captain Hornblower through, Mr. Bracegirdle," said St Vincent, and hobbled on his way.

Bracegirdle led Hornblower through to where the coffin stood on its trestles, and there, sure enough, the watch still hung on the end handle. Hornblower unhooked it with relief and followed Bracegirdle out again. There he stood and offered his hand to Bracegirdle in farewell; as they clasped hands Bracegirdle's expression was one of hesitant inquiry.

"Two bells in the forenoon watch the day after tomorrow, then, sir," he said; there was the faintest accent on the "forenoon".

"Yes, I'll see you then," said Hornblower.

His other responsibilities were crowding in upon him, and he turned and hurried back to Whitehall Steps. But as he walked, with his mind busily engaged in planning his activities for the next two days, that slight stress came back into his mind. Bracegirdle had relieved him of one small extra worry—by tomorrow at the latest he would have been in painful doubt as to whether his appointment with St Vincent had been for the morning or the evening.

At the Steps the ebb was already running full; there were broad strips of mud visible on either side of the river. Over at the Lambeth jetty the funeral barge could be seen with Horrocks and his men completing their task of getting a tarpaulin over the bottom of the boat. The other boats which had taken part in the procession were clustered here, there, and everywhere, and it was with pleasure that Hornblower saw his own gig clinging to the steps below him. He climbed down into it, picked up his speaking trumpet, and plunged into the business of dispersing the craft in accordance with the scheme he had laid down in his previous orders. The wind was blowing as briskly as ever, but now that the tide had turned the water was more smooth, and the only new difficulty he encountered was the great number of small craft that now were pulling about the river, bearing sightseers to a closer inspection of the ceremonial vessels.

Aldermen and City Companies, Heralds at Arms and Admirals, had all landed and gone home to their respective dinners, and the January darkness had hardly closed in before Hornblower dismissed the last of his charges at Greenwich and, getting back into his gig, was able with relief to give the order to pull for Deptford Hard. He climbed wearily up to the "George", cold and hungry and fatigued. That busy day seemed to stretch back in his memory for a week at least—except that he had left Maria in labour only that morning.

He came walking into the "George", and the first face that he caught sight of was the landlord's—a shadowy figure with whom he was scarcely acquainted, in this house where the landlady assumed all the responsibility.

"How's my wife?" demanded Hornblower.

The landlord blinked.

"I don't rightly know, sir," he said, and Hornblower turned away from him impatiently and ran up the stairs. He hesitated at the bedroom door, with his hand on the handle; his heart was beating fast. Then he heard a murmur of voices within and opened the door. There was Maria in bed, lying back on the pillows, and the midwife moving about by the window. The light of a candle faintly illuminated Maria's face.

"Horry!" said Maria; the glad surprise in her voice accounted for her use of the diminutive.

Hornblower took her hand.

"All well, dearest?" he asked.

"Yes," said Maria.

She held up her lips to be kissed, but even before the kiss was completed she was turning her eyes towards the wicker basket which stood on a small table beside the bed.

"It's a little girl, darling," she said. "Our little girl."

"And a fine little babby too," added the midwife.

Hornblower walked round the bed and peered into the basket. The blanket there concealed a diminutive figure—Hornblower, grown accustomed to playing with little Horatio, had forgotten how tiny a thing was a new-born baby—and a minute red face, a sort of caricature of humanity, was visible on the little pillow. He gazed down upon it; the little lips opened and emitted a squall, faint and high-pitched, so that little Horatio's remembered cries were lusty bellows by comparison.

"She's beautiful," said Hornblower, gallantly, while the squalling continued and two minute clenched fists appeared above the edge of the blanket.

"Our little Maria," said Maria, "I'm sure her hair is going to curl."

"Now, now," said the midwife, not in reproof of this extravagant prophecy but because Maria was trying to lift herself in bed to gaze at the child.

"She has only to grow up like her mother," said Hornblower, "to be the best daughter I could wish for."

Maria rewarded him with a smile as she sank back on the pillow again.

"Little Horatio's downstairs," she said. "He has seen his sister."

"And what did he think of her?"

"He cried when she did," said Maria.

"I had better see how he is," suggested Hornblower.

"Please do," said Maria, but she extended her hand to him again, and Hornblower bent and kissed it.

The room was very warm with a fire burning briskly in the grate, and it smelt of sickness, oppressive to Hornblower's lungs after the keen January air that had filled them all day.

"I am happy beyond all measure to see you so well, dear," said Hornblower, taking his leave.

Downstairs as he stood hesitating in the hall the landlady popped her head out from the kitchen.

"The young gennelman's in here, sir," she said, "if you don't mind stepping in."

Little Horatio was sitting up in a high-chair. His face lit up with a smile as he caught sight of his father—the most flattering experience Hornblower had ever known—and he bounced up and down in his chair and waved the crust he held in his fist.

"There! See him smile 'cause his daddy's come home!" said the landlady; then she hesitated before she put forward a suggestion which she knew to verge on the extravagant. "His bedtime's coming soon, sir. Would you care to play with him until then, sir?"

"Yes," said Hornblower.

"There, baby!" said the landlady. "Daddy's going to play with you. Oops-a-daisy, then. The bar parlour's empty now, sir. This way, sir. Emily, bring a candle for the captain."

Little Horatio was in two minds, once he found himself on the parlour floor, as to which of two methods of progression was most satisfactory to a man almost a year old. On hands and knees he could make prodigious speed, and in any direction he chose. But on the other hand he could pull himself upright by clinging to the leg of a chair, and the radiant expression on his face when he did so was proof of the satisfaction this afforded him. Then, having let go of the chair, provided he had already been successful in the monstrous effort necessary to turn away from it, he could manage to take a step towards his father; he was then compelled to stop and sway perilously on widely separated feet before taking another step, and it was rarely that he could accomplish a step before sitting down on the floor with something of a bump. And was it possible that the monosyllable he said so frequently—"Da" it sounded like—was an attempt to say "Daddy"?

This was happiness again, fleeting, transient, to have his little son tottering towards him with a beaming smile.

"Come to Daddy," said Hornblower, hands outstretched.

Then the smile would turn to a mischievous grin, and down on his hands and knees went young Horatio, galloping like lightning across the room, and gurgling with delirious joy when his father came running after him to seize him and swing him into the air. Simple and delightful pleasure; and then as Hornblower held the kicking gurgling baby up at arm's length he had a fleeting recollection of the moment when he himself had hung suspended in the mizzen rigging on that occasion when the *Indefatigable's* mizzen mast fell when he was in command of the top. This child would know peril and danger—and fear; in later years. He would not let the thought cloud his happiness. He lowered the baby down and then held him at arm's length again—a most successful performance, judging by the gurgles it elicited.

The landlady came in, knocking at the door.

"That's a big man," she said, and Hornblower forced himself not to feel self-conscious at being caught enjoying the company of his own child.

"Dunno what come over me, sir," went on the landlady. "I clear forgot to ask if you wanted supper."

"Supper?" said Hornblower. The last time he had eaten was in the Painted Hall at Greenwich.

"Ham an' eggs?" asked the landlady. "A bite o' cold beef?"

"Both, if you please," said Hornblower.

"Three shakes of a duck's tail an' you'll have 'em," said the landlady. "You keep that young feller busy while I get it."

"I ought to go back to Mrs. Hornblower."

"She'll do for another ten minutes without you," said the landlady, briskly.

The smell of bacon and eggs when they came was heavenly. Hornblower could sit down with appetite while Emily bore little Horatio off to bed. And after bacon and eggs, cold beef and pickled onions, and a flagon of beer—another simple pleasure, that of eating his fill and more, the knowledge that he was eating too much serving as a sauce to him who kept himself almost invariably within bounds and who looked upon over-indulgence usually with suspicion and contempt. With his duty carried out successfully today he had for once no care for the morrow, not even when the day after tomorrow would see him engaged in the rather frightening experience of attending the King's levee. And Maria had come safely through her ordeal, and he had a little daughter who would be as adorable as his little son. Then he sneezed three times running.

VI

"Whitehall Steps," said Hornblower, stepping down into his gig at Deptford Hard.

It was convenient having his gig for use here; it was faster than a wherryman's boat and it cost him nothing.

"Give way!" said the coxswain.

Of course it was raining. The westerly wind still blew and bore with it today flurries of heavy rain, which hissed down on the surface of the river, roared on the tarpaulins of the wretched boat's crew, and rattled loudly on the sou'wester which Hornblower wore on his head while he sheltered his cocked hat under his boat cloak. He sniffed lamentably. He had the worst cold he had ever experienced, and he needed to use his handkerchief. But that meant bringing a hand out from under his cloak, and he would not do that—with the boat cloak spread round him like a tent as he sat in the stern-sheets, and with the sou'wester on top, he could hope to keep himself reasonably dry as far as Whitehall if he did not disturb the arrangement. He preferred to sniff.

Up the river, through the rain; under London Bridge, round the bends he had come to know so well during the last few days. He cowered in misery under his boat cloak, shuddering. He was sure he had never felt so ill in his life before. He ought to be in bed, with hot bricks at his feet and hot rum-and-water at his side, but on the day when the First Lord was going to take him to the Court of St. James's he could not possibly plead illness, not even though the shivers ran up and down his spine and his legs felt too weak to carry him.

The Steps were slippery where the tide had receded from them; in his weak state he could hardly keep his footing as he climbed them. At the top, with the rain still beating down, he put his appearance to rights as well as he could. He rolled up the sou'wester and put it in the pocket of his cloak, put on his cocked hat, and hurried, bending forward into the driving rain, the hundred and fifty yards to the Admiralty. Even in the short time that took him his stockings were splashed and wet, and the brim of his cocked hat was filled with water. He was glad to stand before the fire in the Captain's Room while he waited until Bracegirdle came in with the announcement that His Lordship was ready for him.

"Morning, Hornblower," said St Vincent, standing under the portico.

"Good morning, my lord."

"No use waiting for a smooth," growled St Vincent, looking up at the rain and eyeing the distance between him and his coach. "Come on."

He hobbled manfully forward. Hornblower and Bracegirdle advanced with him. They had no cloaks on—Hornblower had left his at the Admiralty—and had to wait in the rain while St Vincent walked to the coach and with infinite slowness hauled himself into it. Hornblower followed him and Bracegirdle squeezed in after him, perching on the turn-down seat in front. The coach rumbled forward over the cobbles, with a vibration from the iron-rimmed wheels that found an echo in the shudders that were still playing up and down Hornblower's spine.

"All nonsense, of course, having to use a coach to St. James's from the Admiralty," growled St Vincent. "I used to walk a full three miles on my quarterdeck in the old *Orion*."

Hornblower sniffed again, miserably. He could not even congratulate himself on the fact that as he felt so ill he knew almost no qualms about his new experience which was awaiting him, because, stupefied by his cold, he was unable even to indulge in his habitual self-analysis.

"I read your report last night, Hornblower," went on St Vincent. "Satisfactory."

"Thank you, my lord." He braced himself into appearing intelligent. "And did the funeral at St. Paul's go off well yesterday?"

"Well enough."

The coach rumbled down the Mall.

"Here we are," said St Vincent. "You'll come back with me, I suppose, Hornblower? I don't intend to stay long. Nine in the morning and I haven't done a third of my day's work yet."

"Thank you, my lord. I'll take station on you, then."

The coach door opened, and Bracegirdle nimbly stepped out to help his chief down the steps. Hornblower followed; now his heart was beating faster. There were red uniforms, blue and gold uniforms, blue and silver uniforms, in evidence everywhere; many of the men were in powder. One powdered wig—the dark eyes below it were in startling contrast—detached itself and approached St Vincent. The uniform was black and silver; the polished facets of the silver-hilted sword caught and reflected the light at a myriad points.

"Good morning, my lord."

"Morning, Catterick. Here's my protégé, Captain Horatio Hornblower."

Catterick's keen dark eyes took in every detail of Hornblower's appearance in one sweeping glance, coat, breeches, stockings, sword, but his expression did not change. One might gather he was used to the appearance of shabby naval officers at levees.

"His Lordship is presenting you, I understand, Captain. You accompany him into the Presence Chamber."

Hornblower nodded; he was wondering how much was implied by that word "protégé". His hat was in his hand, and he made haste to cram it under his arm as the others did.

"Follow me, then," said St Vincent.

Up the stairs; uniformed men on guard on the landings; another black and silver uniform at the head of the stairs; a further brief exchange of sentences; powdered footmen massed about the doorway; announcements made in a superb speaking voice, restrained but penetrating.

"Admiral the Right Honourable Earl St Vincent. Captain Horatio Hornblower. Lieutenant Anthony Bracegirdle."

The Presence Chamber was a mass of colour. Every possible uniform was represented there. The scarlet of the infantry; light cavalry in all the colours of the rainbow, be-frogged and be-furred, cloaks swinging, sabres trailing; heavy cavalry in jack boots up to the thigh; foreign uniforms of white and green; St Vincent carried his vast bulk through them all, like a battleship among yachts. And there was the King, seated in a throne-like chair with a lofty back; it was an odd surprise to see him, in his little tie-wig, looking so exactly like his pictures. Behind him stood a semi-circle of men wearing ribbons and stars, blue ribbons, red ribbons, green ribbons, over the left shoulder and over the right; Knights of the Garter, of the Bath, of St. Patrick, these must be, the great men of the land. St Vincent was bending himself in clumsy obeisance to the King.

"Glad to see you, my lord, glad to see you," said the latter. "Haven't had a moment since Monday. Glad all went well."

"Thank you, sir. May I present the officer responsible for the naval ceremonial?"

"You may."

The King turned his eyes on Hornblower; light blue eyes, prominent, but kindly.

"Captain Horatio Hornblower," said St Vincent, and Hornblower did his best to bow, as his French émigré dancing teacher had tried to teach him ten years before, left foot forward, hand over his heart. He did not know how far down to bend; he did not know how long to stay there when he had bent. But he came up again at last, with something of the sensation of breaking the surface of the water after a deep dive.

"What ship, sir? What ship?" asked the King.

"*Atropos, twenty-two,* Your Majesty."

Sleepless during the previous night Hornblower had imagined that question might be put to him, and so the answer came fast enough.

"Where is she now?"

"Deptford, Your Majesty."

"But you go to sea soon?"

"I—I—" Hornblower could not answer that question, but St Vincent spoke up for him.

"Very shortly, sir," he said.

"I see," said the King. "I see."

He put up his hand and stroked his forehead with a gesture of infinite weariness before recalling himself to the business in hand.

"My great-nephew," he said, "Prince Ernst—did I speak to you about him, my lord?"

"You did, sir," answered St Vincent.

"Do you think Captain Hornblower would be a suitable officer for the duty?"

"Why yes, sir. Quite suitable."

"Less than three years' seniority," mused the King, his eyes resting on Hornblower's epaulette. "But still. Harmond!"

"Your Majesty."

A glittering figure with ribbon and star came gliding forward from the semi-circle.

"Present Captain Hornblower to His Serene Highness."

"Yes, Your Majesty."

There was a smile in the pale blue eyes.

"Thank you, Captain," said the King. "Do your duty as you have done it, and your conscience will always be clear."

"Yes, Your Majesty," said Hornblower.

St Vincent was bowing again; Hornblower bowed. He was aware of the fact that he must not turn his back upon the King—that was almost the sum of his knowledge of court ceremonial—and he found it not so difficult to withdraw. Already there was a line formed of people waiting their turn to reach the royal presence, and he sidled away from them in St Vincent's wake.

"This way, if you please," said Harmond, directing their course to the farther side of the room. "Wait a moment."

"His Majesty's service makes strange bedfellows sometimes," said St Vincent as they waited. "I hardly expected you would be saddled with this, Hornblower."

"I—I have not yet understood," said Hornblower.

"Oh, the Prince is—"

"This way, if you please," said Harmond, appearing again.

He led them towards a diminutive figure who awaited them with composure. A young man—no, only a boy—wearing an outlandish uniform of gold and green, a short gold-hilted sword at his side, orders on his breast, and two more hanging from his neck. Behind them towered a burly figure in a more moderate version of the same uniform, swarthy, with fat pendulous cheeks. The boy himself was handsome, with fair hair falling in ringlets about his ears, frank blue eyes and a nose slightly turned upwards. The burly figure stepped forward, intercepting the approach of the group to the boy. Harmond and he exchanged glances.

"Presentations should be made to me first," said the burly figure; he spoke thickly, in what Hornblower guessed to be a German accent.

"And why, sir?" asked Harmond.

"By the fundamental law of Seitz-Bunau only the High Chamberlain can make presentations to His Serene Highness."

"Yes?"

"And I, sir, am the High Chamberlain. As you know."

"Very well, sir," said Harmond with resignation. "Then may I have the honour to present—Admiral the Right Honourable Earl St Vincent; Captain Horatio Hornblower; Lieutenant Anthony Bracegirdle."

Hornblower was about to bow, but out of the tail of his eye he caught sight of St Vincent still holding himself ponderously erect, and he restrained himself.

"To whom have I the honour of being presented?" asked St Vincent, coldly. It appeared as if St Vincent entertained some prejudice against Germans.

"Doctor Eisenbeiss," said Harmond.

"His Excellency the Baron von Eisenbeiss, High Chamberlain and Secretary of State to His Serene Highness the Prince of Seitz-Bunau," said the burly man, in further explanation. "It is with much pleasure that I make your acquaintance."

He stood meeting St Vincent's eyes for a moment, and then he bowed;

St Vincent bowed only after Eisenbeiss had begun to bow; Hornblower and Bracegirdle followed his example. All four of them straightened up at the same moment.

"And now," said Eisenbeiss, "I have the honour to present—"

He turned to the Prince and continued his speech in German, apparently repeating his first words and then mentioning the names in turn. The little Prince gave a half bow at each name, but as St Vincent bowed low—nearly as low as he had bowed to the King—Hornblower did likewise. Then the Prince spoke in German to Eisenbeiss.

"His Serene Highness says," translated the latter, "that he is delighted to make the acquaintance of officers of His Majesty's Navy, because it is His Highness's will that he should make war against the French tyrant in their company."

"Tell His Serene Highness," said St Vincent, "that we are all delighted, too."

The translation was made, and the Prince produced a smile for each of them. Then there was an uncomfortable moment as they looked at each other. Finally Eisenbeiss said something again to the Prince, received a reply, and then turned to the group.

"His Serene Highness," he announced, "says that he will not detain you longer."

"Hm'ph," said St Vincent, but he bent himself once more in the middle, as did the others, and then they withdrew themselves, backwards and sideways, from out of His Serene Highness's presence.

"Damned upstart whippersnapper," mumbled St Vincent to himself, and then added, "At any rate, our duty's done. We can leave. Follow me over to that door."

Down below loud bawling by a footman in the courtyard brought up the Earl's coach again, and they climbed in, Hornblower utterly dazed by reason of his cold, the excitement he had been through, and his puzzlement about the incident in which he had taken part.

"Well, that's your midshipman, Hornblower," said St Vincent. His voice was so like the rumbling of the iron tyres over the cobbles that Hornblower was not sure that he had heard aright—especially as what St Vincent had said was so strange.

"I beg your pardon, my lord?"

"I have no doubt you heard me. I said that's your midshipman—the Prince of Seitz-Bunau."

"But who is he, my lord?"

"One of those German princes. Boney chased him out of his principality last year, on his way to Austerlitz. Country's brimful of German princes chased out by Boney. The point is that this one's the King's great-nephew, as you heard."

"And he's to be one of my midshipmen?"

"That is so. He's young enough to learn sense, not like most of 'em. Most of 'em go in the army. On the staff, God help the staff. But now the navy's fashionable—first time since the Dutch Wars. We've been winning battles, and God knows the soldiers haven't. So all the ne'er do well young lords join the Navy nowadays instead of the Light Dragoons. It was His Majesty's own idea that this young fellow should do the same."

"I understand, my lord."

"It won't do him any harm. *Atropos* won't be any palace, of course."

"That's what I was thinking, my lord. The midshipmen's berth in *Atropos*—"

"You'll have to put him there, all the same. Not much room in a flush-decked sloop. If it were a ship of the line he might berth by himself, but if it's to be *Atropos* he'll have to take what comes. And it won't be caviar and venison, either. I'll send you orders on the subject, of course."

"Aye aye, my lord."

The coach was grinding to a stop at the Admiralty; someone opened the door, and St Vincent began to heave himself out of his seat. Hornblower followed him in under the portico.

"I'll bid you good-bye, then, Hornblower," said St Vincent, offering his hand.

"Good-bye, my lord."

St Vincent stood looking at him from under his eyebrows.

"The Navy has two duties, Hornblower," he said. "We all know what one is—to fight the French and give Boney what for."

"Yes, my lord?"

"The other we don't think about so much. We have to see that when we go we leave behind us a Navy which is as good as the one in which we served. You've less than three years' seniority now, Hornblower, but you'll find you'll grow older. It'll seem you've hardly had time to look round before you'll have forty-three years' seniority, like me. It goes fast enough, I assure you. Perhaps then you'll be taking another young officer to present him at the Palace."

"Er—yes, my lord."

"Choose carefully, Hornblower, if it ever becomes your duty. One can make mistakes. But let them be honest mistakes."

"Yes, my Lord."

"That's all."

The old man turned away without another word, leaving Hornblower with Bracegirdle under the portico.

"Jervie's in a melting mood," said Bracegirdle.

"So it seems."

"I think he wanted to say he had his eye on you, sir."

"But he had an anchor out to windward all the same," said Hornblower, thinking of what St Vincent had said about the chance of one making mistakes.

"Jervie never forgives, sir," said Bracegirdle, seriously.

"Well—"

Twelve years of service in the Navy had gone far to make Hornblower, on occasions, fatalist enough to be able to shrug off that sort of peril—at least until it was past.

"I'll take my boat cloak, if you please," he said, "and I'll say good-bye, and thank you."

"A glass of something? A cup of tea? A mouthful to eat, sir?"

"No, thank you, I'd better shove off."

Maria was waiting for him at Deptford, longing to hear about his visit to Court and his presentation to the King. Maria had been wildly excited when Hornblower had told her what he was going to do. The thought that he was going to meet face to face the Lord's anointed was almost too much for her—the midwife had come forward with a warning that all this excitement might bring on a fever. And he had not merely been presented to the King, but the King had actually spoken to him, had discussed his professional career with him. Besides, he was to have a real Prince as a midshipman on board his ship—a dispossessed prince, admittedly, but to counter-balance that was the fact that the prince was a great-nephew of the King, related by blood to the Royal Family. That would delight Maria as much as his presentation at Court.

She would want to know all about it, who was there (Hornblower found himself wishing he had been able to identify a single one of the figures who had stood behind the throne) and what everyone was wearing—that would be easier, as there had been no women present, of course, at the levee, and practically everyone had been in uniform. He would have to be careful in his account, as it was possible to hurt Maria's feelings. Hornblower himself fought for his country; it might be better said that he fought for the ideals of liberty and decency against the unprincipled tyrant who ruled across the Channel; the hackneyed phrase "for King and Country" hardly expressed his feelings at all. If he was ready to lay down his life for his King that really had no reference to the kindly pop-eyed old gentleman with whom he had been speaking this morning; it meant that he was ready to die for the system of liberty and order that the old gentleman represented. But to Maria the King was representative of something other than liberty and order; he had received the blessing of the Church; he was somebody to be spoken about with awe. To turn one's back on the King was to Hornblower a breach of good manners, something damaging, in some degree, to the conventions which held the country together in the face of its imminent peril; but to

Maria it would be something very close to sacrilege. He would have to be careful not to speak too lightly of the old gentleman.

And yet (the gig was carrying him through the Pool now, under the walls of the Tower) Hornblower had to admit it to himself that Maria's views about his service in the Navy were not on as lofty a plane as his own. To Maria it was a gentlemanly trade; it gave her a certain social status to which she otherwise would not have attained, and it put food into the mouth of her precious child—children, now that little Maria was born. But self-sacrifice for a cause; the incurring of danger beyond the dictates of duty; honour; glory; these were conceptions that Maria cared little about. She was in fact rather inclined to turn up her nose at them as purely masculine notions, part of an elaborate game or ritual devised by men to make them feel superior to and different from women whose self-respect and sublime certainty of superiority needed no such puerile bolstering.

It was a surprise to Hornblower to find that the gig was now passing the *Atropos* as she lay at the edge of the stream. He should have been all eyes to see that all was well with her and that the officer of the watch had been on the alert to detect the gig as she came down the river; as it was Hornblower merely had time to acknowledge the salute of Lieutenant Jones as the gig left the ship behind. There was Deptford Dock, and beside it the enormous activities of the Victualling Yard. From a sailing barge lying beside the jetty a gang of men were at work driving a herd of pigs up into the yard, destined for slaughter and salting down to feed the Navy.

"Eyes in the boat, there!" growled the coxswain.

One of the gig's crew had made a *sotto voice* joke about those pigs, evidently. It was hard to believe, even with this evidence before their eyes, that the unrecognizable, wooden hard chunks of matter that were issued from the brine barrels to the men at sea, really came from decent respectable animals like those there. Hornblower's sympathies were with his men. The coxswain was putting his tiller over to bring the gig up to Deptford Hard. Hornblower disembarked, to walk up to the "George", to where his family was awaiting him. He would sit by Maria's bed and tell her about the pageantry of the Court of St. James's. He would hold his little daughter in his arms; he would play with his little son. It might well be for the very last time; at any moment his orders would come, and he would take *Atropos* to sea. Battle, storm, shipwreck, disease—what were the chances that he would never come back again? And if ever he did the squalling baby he was leaving behind would be a trim little miss playing with her dolls; little Horatio would be at least starting with slate and pencil writing his letters and figures; he might be beginning to decline mensa and learning the Greek alphabet. And he himself? He hoped he would be able to say he had done his duty; he hoped that those weaknesses of which he was so conscious would not prevent him from achieving something of which his children might be proud.

VII

So it was to be the Mediterranean. Hornblower sat in his canvas chair in his cabin in *Atropos*, re-reading the orders which had come for him.

Sir—

I am commanded by the Lords Commissioners of the Admiralty—

He was to prepare himself with the utmost diligence ready to proceed to Gibraltar, and there he was to call for orders which the Vice-Admiral Commanding in the Mediterranean might send to him there. In the event that no such orders should be forthcoming, he was to ascertain where the Vice-Admiral was likely to be found, and to proceed with the same diligence to put himself under the Vice-Admiral's orders.

That must be Cuthbert Collingwood—Lord Collingwood now that he had received his peerage after Trafalgar. The fleet that had won the battle there—or such ships of it as were still seaworthy—had been sent into the Mediterranean after the battle, he knew. The destruction of the French and Spanish fleets outside Cadiz had definitely established British command of the Atlantic, so now the Navy was carrying its ponderous weight into the Mediterranean to head off there any moves that Bonaparte might make now that Austerlitz had given him command of Continental Europe. Austerlitz—Trafalgar. The French army—and the Royal Navy. The one might be balanced against the other. There was no corner of Europe whither French troops might not march—as long as there was land for them to march on; there was no corner of the sea where British ships might not bring their influence to bear—as long as there was water in which they could float. In the landlocked Mediterranean with its peninsulas and islands sea power could best confront land power. The bloody and seemingly endless conflict between tyranny and liberty would be fought out there. He would play his part in it. The Secretary to the Lords Commissioners signed himself "your obedient humble servant", but before he did so he went on to say that Their Lordships rested assured that *Atropos* was ready for immediate departure, so that on receipt of final orders and of the last minute despatches which would be entrusted to her she would be able to leave at once. Hornblower and his ship, in other words, were being put on notice of instant readiness

Hornblower felt a slight feeling of apprehension, a sensation of goose-flesh at the back of his neck. He did not believe that his ship was prepared in all respects to leave at a moment's notice.

Hornblower lifted up his voice in a call to the sentry outside his door. "Pass the word for Mr. Jones."

He heard the cry repeated in 'tween decks like an echo, as he sat on with the orders in his hands. It was only a few moments before Mr. Jones came in hastily, and it was only when he arrived that Hornblower realized that he had not prepared himself to give the necessary orders and make the necessary inquiries. As a result Hornblower found himself compelled to look Jones over without speaking. His mind was sorting out his thoughts without reacting at all to the reports his eyes were making to it, but Hornblower's steady stare discomposed the unfortunate Jones, who put his hand up nervously to his face. Hornblower saw a dab of dry lather in front of Jones's right ear, and as the lieutenant's gesture recalled him to himself he noticed something more; one lantern cheek was smooth and well shaved, while the other bristled with a fair growth of black beard.

"Pardon, sir," said Jones, "but your call caught me half shaved, and I judged it best to come at once."

"Very well, Mr. Jones," said Hornblower; he was not sorry that Jones had something to explain away while he himself was not ready with the definite orders that a good officer should be able to issue.

Under that embarrassing stare Jones had to speak again.

"Did you want me, sir?"

"Yes," said Hornblower. "We are under orders for the Mediterranean."

"Indeed, sir?" Mr. Jones's remarks did not make any great contribution to the progress of the conversation.

"I want your report on how soon we can be ready for sea."

"Oh, sir—"

Jones put his hand up to his face again; perhaps it was as long as it was because of his habit of pulling at his chin.

"Are stores and water complete?"

"Well, sir, you see—"

"You mean they are not?"

"N—no, sir. Not altogether."

Hornblower was about to ask for an explanation, but changed his approach at the last second.

"I won't ask why at present. How short are we?"

"Well, sir—" The wretched Jones entered into a hurried statement. They were twenty tons of water short. Bread, spirits, meat—

"You mean that with the Victualling Yard only across the river you have not kept the ship complete with stores?"

"Well, sir—" Jones tried to explain that he had not thought it necessary to draw supplies from day to day. "There was plenty of other work for the hands, sir, fitting out."

"Watch bills? Station bills?"

These were the lists that allocated the hands to their duties and quarters in the ship.

"We're twenty topmen short, sir," said Jones pitifully.

"All the more reason to make the most of what we have."

"Yes, sir, of course, sir." Jones sought desperately in his mind for excuses for himself. "Some of our beef, sir—it—it isn't fit to eat."

"Worse than usual?"

"Yes, sir. Must be some of an old batch. Real bad, some of it."

"In which tier?"

"I'll ask the purser, sir."

"You mean you don't know?"

"No, sir—yes, sir."

Hornblower fell into deep thought again, but as once more he did not take his eyes from Jones's face that did not help the delinquent first lieutenant to recover his equanimity. Actually Hornblower was condemning himself. During the few days he had held command of the *Atropos* he had been hard at work on the details of Nelson's funeral, and then he had been preoccupied with his own family affairs, but all that was no excuse. The captain of a ship should be aware at every moment of the state of his command. He was savagely angry with himself. He hardly knew his officers' names; he could not even estimate what sort of fight *Atropos* could put up—and yet he would not have to go very far down the river to find his ship likely to be in action.

"What about the gunner's stores?" he asked. "Powder? Shot? Wads? Cartridges?"

"I'll send for the gunner, sir, shall I?" asked Jones. He was desperate at all this revelation of his own inadequacies.

"I'll see 'em all in a minute," said Hornblower. "Purser, gunner, bos'n, cooper, master's mate."

These were the subordinate heads of department responsible through the first lieutenant to the captain for the proper functioning of the ship.

"Aye aye, sir."

"What the devil's that noise?" asked Hornblower pettishly. For some minutes now there had been some sort of altercation on the quarterdeck over their heads. Strange voices were making themselves heard through the skylight.

"Shall I find out, sir?" asked Jones eagerly, hoping for some distraction. But as he spoke there was a knock at the cabin door.

"This'll tell us," said Hornblower. "Come in!"

Midshipman Horrocks opened the door.

"Mr. Still's respects, sir, an' there are some gentlemen come on board with an Admiralty letter for you, sir."

"Ask them to come here."

It could only be trouble of one sort or another, Hornblower decided, as he waited. One more distraction at a moment when he was about to be desperately busy. Horrocks ushered in two figures, one large and one diminutive, wearing glittering uniforms of green and gold—Hornblower had last seen them only yesterday at the Court of St. James's, the German princeling and his bear-leader. Hornblower rose to his feet, and Eisenbeiss stepped forward with an elaborate bow, to which Hornblower replied with a curt nod.

"Well, sir?"

Eisenbeiss ceremoniously handed over a letter; a glance showed Hornblower that it was addressed to him. He opened it carefully and read it.

> You are hereby requested and required to receive into your ship His Serene Highness Ernst Prince of Seitz-Bunau, who has been rated as midshipman in His Majesty's Navy. You will employ your diligence in instructing His Serene Highness in his new profession as well as in continuing his education in readiness for the day which under Providence may not be far distant, when His Serene Highness will again assume the government of his hereditary dominions. You will also receive into your ship His Excellency the Baron Otto von Eisenbeiss, Chamberlain and First Secretary of State to His Serene Highness. His Excellency was until recently practising as a surgeon, and he has received from the Navy Office a warrant as such in His Majesty's Navy. You will make use of His Excellency's services, therefore, as Surgeon in your ship while, as far as naval discipline and the Articles of War allow, he continues to act as Chamberlain to His Serene Highness.

"I see," he said. He looked at the odd pair in their resplendent uniforms. "Welcome aboard, Your Highness."

The prince nodded and smiled, clearly without understanding.

Hornblower sat down again, and Eisenbeiss began to speak at once, his thick German accent stressing his grievances.

"I must protest, sir," he said.

"Well?" said Hornblower, in a tone that might well have conveyed a warning.

"His Serene Highness is not being treated with proper respect. When we reached your ship I sent my footman on board to announce us so that His Highness could be received with royal honours. They were absolutely refused, sir. The man on the deck there—I presume he is an officer—said he had no instructions. It was only when I showed him that letter, sir, that he allowed us to come on board at all."

"Quite right. He had no instructions."

"I trust you will make amends, then. And may I remind you that you are sitting in the presence of royalty?"

"You call me 'sir'," snapped Hornblower. "And you will address me as my subordinate should."

Eisenbeiss jerked himself upright in his indignation, so that his head came with a shattering crash against the deck-beam above; this checked his flow of words and enabled Hornblower to continue.

"As officers in the King's service you should have worn the King's uniform. You have your dunnage with you?"

Eisenbeiss was still too stunned to answer, even if he understood the word, and Horrocks spoke for him.

"Please, sir, it's in the boat alongside. Chests and chests of it."

"Thank you, Mr. Horrocks. Now, doctor, I understand you have the necessary professional qualifications to act as surgeon in this ship. That is so?"

Eisenbeiss still strove to retain his dignity.

"As Secretary of State I am addressed as 'Your Excellency'," he said.

"But as surgeon in this ship you are addressed as 'doctor'. And that is the last time I shall overlook the omission of the word 'sir'. Now. Your qualifications?"

"I am a surgeon—sir."

The last word came out with a jerk as Hornblower's eyebrows rose.

"You have been in practice recently?"

"Until a few months ago—sir. I was surgeon to the Court of Seitz-Bunau. But now I am—"

"Now you are surgeon in H.M.S. *Atropos*, and we can leave off the farce of your being Secretary of State."

"Sir—"

"Silence, if you please, doctor. Mr. Horrocks!"

"Sir!"

"My compliments to Mr. Still. I'll have these two gentlemen's baggage swayed up. They are to make immediate selection of their necessities to the extent of one sea chest each. You will be able to help them in their choice. The remainder is to leave the ship within ten minutes by the boat in which it came. Is that quite clear, Mr. Horrocks?"

"Aye aye, sir. If you please, sir, there's a couple of footmen with the baggage."

"Footmen?"

"Yes, sir, in uniforms like these," Horrocks indicated the green and gold of the Germans.

"That's two more hands, then. Read 'em in and send 'em for'rard."

The Navy could always use more men, and a couple of fat, well-fed footmen would make useful hands in time to come.

"But sir—" said Eisenbeiss.

"Speak when you're spoken to, doctor. Now Mr. Horrocks, you will take the prince and settle him into the midshipmen's berth. I'll introduce you. Mr. Midshipman Horrocks—er, Mr. Midshipman Prince."

Horrocks automatically offered his hand, and the prince as automatically took it, displaying no immediate change at the contamination of a human touch. He smiled shyly, without understanding.

"And my compliments to the master's mate, too, Mr. Horrocks. Ask him to be good enough to show the doctor where he berths for'rard."

"Aye aye, sir."

"Now, doctor, in half an hour I wish to see you both in the King's uniform. You can take up your duties then. There will be a court of inquiry opened at that time, consisting of the first lieutenant, the purser, and yourself, to decide whether certain hogsheads of beef are fit for human consumption. You will be secretary of that court and I want your written report by noon. Go with Mr. Horrocks now."

Eisenbeiss hesitated a moment under Hornblower's sharp glance before he turned to leave the cabin, but at the curtain his indignation overcame him again.

"I shall write to the Prime Minister, sir," he said. "He shall hear about this treatment of His Majesty's Allies."

"Yes, doctor. If you contravene the Mutiny Act you'll swing at the yardarm. Now, Mr. Jones, with regard to these station and quarter bills."

As Hornblower turned to Jones to re-enter into the business of getting *Atropos* ready for sea he was conscious of feeling some contempt for himself. He could browbeat a silly German doctor effectively enough; he could flatter himself that he had dealt adequately with what might have been a difficult though petty situation. But that was nothing to be proud of, when he had to realize that with regard to his real duties he had been found wanting. He had wasted precious hours. During the last two days he had twice played with his little son; he had sat by his wife's bedside and held his little daughter in his arms, when really he should have been on board here looking after his ship. It was no excuse that it was Jones's duty to have attended to the matters under consideration; it had been Hornblower's duty to see that Jones had attended to them. A naval officer should not have a wife or children—this present situation was the proof of that trite saying. Hornblower found himself setting his mouth hard as he came to that conclusion. There were still eight hours of daylight left today. He began an orderly planning of those eight hours. There were the matters that would call for his own personal activity like appealing to the superintendent of the dockyard; there were the matters he could safely leave to his subordinates. There was work that could be done on one side of the ship, leaving the other side clear; there was work that would demand the services of skilled seamen, and work that landsmen could do. There were some jobs that could not be started until other jobs were finished. If he was not careful some of his officers would have to be in two places at once, there would be confusion, delay, ridiculous disorder. But with good planning it could be done.

Purser and gunner, boatswain and cooper, each in turn was summoned to the after cabin. To each was allotted his tasks; to each was grudgingly conceded a proportion of the men that each demanded. Soon the pipes were shrilling through the ship.

"Launch's crew away!"

Soon the launch was pulling across the river, full of the empty barrels the cooper and his mates had made ready, to begin ferrying over the twenty tons of water necessary to complete the ship's requirements. A dozen men went scurrying up the shrouds and out along the yards under the urging of the boatswain; yardarm tackles and stay tackles had to be readied for the day's work.

"Mr. Jones! I am leaving the ship now. Have that report on the beef ready for me by the time I return from the dockyard."

Hornblower became aware of two figures on the quarterdeck trying to attract his attention. They were the prince and the doctor. He ran his eye over their uniforms, the white collar patches of the midshipman and the plain coat of the surgeon.

"They'll do," he said, "your duties are awaiting you, doctor. Mr. Horrocks! Keep Mr. Prince under your lee for today. Call away my gig."

The captain superintendent of the dockyard listened to Hornblower's request with the indifference acquired during years of listening to requests from urgent officers.

"I've the men ready to send for the shot, sir. Port side's clear for the powder hulk to come alongside—slack water in half an hour, sir. I can send men to man her too if necessary. It's only four tons that I need. Half an hour with the hulk."

"You say you're ready now?"

"Yes, sir."

The captain superintendent looked across at the *Atropos* lying in the stream.

"Very well. I hope what you say is quite correct, captain, for your sake. You can start warping the hulk alongside—I warn you I want her back at her moorings in an hour."

"Thank you, sir."

Back in the *Atropos* the cry went round the ship.

"Hands to the capstan! Waisters! Sailmakers! Loblolly boys!"

The inmost recesses of the ship were cleared of men to man the capstan bars—any pairs of arms, any stout backs, would serve for that purpose. A drum went roaring along the deck.

"All lights out!"

The cook and his mates dumped the galley fire overside and went reluctantly to man the yardarm and stay tackles. The powder hulk came creeping alongside. She had stout sheers and wide hatchways, efficient equipment for the rapid transfer of explosives. Four tons of powder, eighty kegs of one hundredweight each, came climbing out of the hulk's holds to be swayed down the hatchways of the *Atropos*, while down below the gunner and his mates and a sweating working party toiled in near darkness—barefooted to avoid all chance of friction or sparks—to range the kegs about the magazines. Some day *Atropos* might be fighting for her life, and her life would depend on the proper arrangement of those kegs down below so that the demands of the guns on deck might be met.

The members of the court of inquiry, fresh from their investigation of the defective beef barrels, made their appearance on deck again.

"Mr. Jones, show the doctor how to make his report in due form." Then to the purser, "Mr. Carslake, I want to be able to sign your indents as soon as that report is ready."

One final look round the deck, and Hornblower could dive below, take pen and ink and paper, and devote himself single-mindedly to composing a suitable covering letter to the Victualling Yard (worded with the right urgency and tactfully coaxing the authorities there into agreement without annoying them by too certain assumption of acquiescence) beginning: "Sir, I have the honour to enclose—" and concluding: "—in the best interests of His Majesty's service, Your Obedient Servant—"

Then he could come on deck again to see how the work was progressing and fume for a space before Jones and Carslake appeared with the documents they had been preparing. Amid the confusion and din he had to clear his head again to read them with care before signing them with a bold "H. Hornblower, Captain".

"Mr. Carslake, you can take my gig over to the Victualling Yard. Mr. Jones, I expect the Yard will need hands to man their lighter. See to that, if you please."

A moment to spare now to observe the hands at work, to settle his cocked hat square on his head, to clasp his hands behind him, to walk slowly forward, doing his best to look quite cool and imperturbable, as if all this wild activity were the most natural thing in the world.

"Avast heaving there on that stay-tackle. Belay!"

The powder keg hung suspended just over the deck. Hornblower forced himself to speak coldly, without excitement. A stave of the keg had started a trifle. There was a minute trail of powder grains on the deck; more were dribbling very slowly out.

"Sway that keg back into the hulk. You, bos'n's mate, get a wet mop and swill that powder off the deck."

An accident could have fired that powder easily. The flash would pass in either direction; four tons of powder in *Atropos*, forty, perhaps in the hulk—what would have happened to the massed shipping in the Pool in that event? The men were eyeing him; this would be a suitable moment to encourage them with their work.

"Greenwich Hospital is over there, men," said Hornblower, pointing down river to the graceful outlines of Wren's building. "Some of us will wind up there in the end, I expect, but we don't want to be blown straight there today."

A feeble enough joke, perhaps, but it raised a grin or two all the same.

"Carry on."

Hornblower continued his stroll forward, the imperturbable captain who was nevertheless human enough to crack a joke. It was the same sort of acting that he used towards Maria when she seemed likely to be in a difficult mood.

Here was the lighter with the shot, coming along the starboard side. Hornblower looked down into it. Nine-pounder balls for the four long guns, two forward and two aft; twelve-pounder balls for the eighteen carronades that constituted the ship's main armament. The twenty tons of iron made a pathetically small mass lying in the bottom of the lighter, when regarded with the eye of a man who had served in a ship of the line; the old *Renown* would have discharged that weight of shot in a couple of hours' fighting. But this dead weight was a very considerable proportion of the load *Atropos* had to carry. Half of it would be distributed fairly evenly along the ship in the shot-garlands; where he decided to stow the other ten tons would make all the difference to *Atropos*, could add a knot to her speed or reduce it by a knot, could make her stiff in a breeze or crank, handy or awkward under sail. He could not reach a decision about that until the rest of the stores were on board and he had had an opportunity of observing her trim. Hornblower ran a keen eye over the nets in which the shot were to be swayed up at the starboard fore-yardarm, and went back through his mind in search of the data stored away there regarding the breaking strain of Manila line —this, he could tell, had been several years in service.

"Sixteen rounds to the load," he called down into the lighter, "no more."

"Aye aye, sir."

It was typical of Hornblower's mind that it should spend a moment or two thinking about the effect that would be produced if one of those nets was to give way; the shot would pour down into the lighter again; falling from the height of the yardarm they could go clear through the bottom of the lighter; with all that deadweight on board, the lighter would sink like a stone, there on the edge of the fairway, to be an intolerable nuisance to London's shipping until divers had painfully cleared the sunken wreck of the shot, and camels had lifted the wreck clear of the channel. The vast shipping of the Port of London could be seriously impeded as a result of a momentary inattention regarding the condition of a cargo net.

Jones was hastening across the deck to touch his hat to him.

"The last of the powder's just coming aboard, sir."

"Thank you. Mr. Jones. Have the hulk warped back to her moorings. Mr. Owen can send the powder boys here to put the shot in the garlands as they come on board."

"Aye aye, sir."

And the gig was coming back across the river with Carslake sitting in the stern.

"Well, Mr. Carslake, how did the Victualling Yard receive those indents?"

"They've accepted them, sir. They'll have the stores on the quayside tomorrow.

"Tomorrow? Didn't you listen to my orders, Mr. Carslake? I don't want to have to put a black mark against your name. Mr. Jones! I'm going over to the Victualling Yard. Come back with me, Mr. Carslake."

The Victualling Yard was a department of the Navy Office, not of the Admiralty. The officials there had to be approached differently from those of the dockyard. One might almost think the two organizations were rivals, instead of working to a common patriotic end against a deadly enemy.

"I can bring my own men to do the work," said Hornblower. "You needn't use your own gangs at all."

"M'm," said the victualling superintendent.

"I'll move everything to the quayside myself, besides lightering it over."

"M'm," said the victualling superintendent again, a trifle more receptively.

"I would be most deeply obliged to you," went on Hornblower. "You need only instruct one of your clerks to point out the stores to the officer in command of my working party. Everything else will be attended to. I beg of you, sir."

It was highly gratifying to a Navy Office official to have a captain, metaphorically, on his knees to him, in this fashion. Equally gratifying was the thought that the Navy would do all the work, with a great saving of time-tallies to the Victualling Yard. Hornblower could see the satisfaction in the fellow's fat face. He wanted to wipe it off with his fist, but he kept himself humble. It did him no harm, and by this means he was bending the fellow to his will as surely as if he was using threats.

"There's the matter of those stores you have condemned," said the superintendent.

"My court of inquiry was in due form," said Hornblower.

"Yes," said the superintendent thoughtfully.

"Of course I can return you the hogsheads," suggested Hornblower. "I was intending to do so, as soon as I had emptied the beef over into the tide."

"No, please do not go to that trouble. Return me the full hogsheads."

The working of the minds of these government Jacks-in-office was beyond normal understanding. Hornblower could not believe—although it was just possible—that the superintendent had any personal financial interest in the matter of those condemned stores. But the fact that the condemnation had taken place presumably was a blot on his record, or on the record of the yard. If the hogsheads were returned to them no mention of the condemnation need be made officially, and presumably they could be palmed off again on some other ship—some ship that might go to sea without the opportunity of sampling the stuff first. Sailors fighting for their country might starve as long as the Victualling Yard's records were unsmirched.

"I'll return the full hogsheads gladly, sir," said Hornblower. "I'll send them over to you in the lighter that brings the other stores over."

"That might do very well," said the superintendent.

"I am delighted, and, as I said, intensely obliged to you, sir. I'll have my launch over here with a working party in ten minutes."

Hornblower bowed with all the unction he could command; this was not the moment to spoil the ship for a ha'porth of tar. He bowed himself out before the discussion could be reopened. But the superintendent's last words were:

"Remember to return those hogsheads, captain."

The powder hulk had been warped back to her moorings; the other ordnance stores that were being taken on board seemed trifling in appearance, bundles of wads, and bales of empty serge cartridges, a couple of sheaves of flexible rammers, spare gun trucks, reels of slow-match—the multifarious accessories necessary to keep twenty-two guns in action. Hornblower sent off Midshipman Smiley with the working party promised to the Victualling Yard.

"Now I'll have those condemned hogsheads got up on deck, Mr. Carslake. I must keep my promise to return them."

"Aye aye, sir," said Carslake.

Carslake was a bull-headed, youngish man with expressionless pale-blue eyes. Those eyes were even more expressionless than usual. He had been a witness of the interview between Hornblower and the superintendent, and he did not allow his feelings to show. He could not guess whether as a purser he thoroughly approved of saving the stores to be fobbed off on another ship or whether as a sailor certain to endure privations at sea he despised Hornblower's weakness in agreeing to the superintendent's demands.

"I'll mark 'em before I return 'em," said Hornblower.

He had thought of paint when he had been so accommodating towards the superintendent, but was not quite happy in his mind about it, for turpentine would remove paint fast enough. A better idea occurred to him, marvellously, at that very moment.

"Have the cook relight the fire in the galley," he ordered. "I'll have —I'll have a couple of iron musket ramrods heated in the fire. Get them from the armourer, if you please."

"Aye aye, sir. If you please, sir, it's long past the hands' dinner-time."

"When I've time for my own dinner the hands can have theirs," said Hornblower.

He was glad that the deck was crowded so that those words of his could be overheard, for he had had the question of the men's dinner-time in his mind for some time although he was quite resolved not to waste a moment over it.

The first of the condemned hogsheads came creaking and swaying up from the hold and was lowered to the deck. Hornblower looked round him; there was Horrocks with the young prince, quite bewildered with all the continuous bustle, trailing after him.

"You'll do, Mr. Horrocks. Come here," said Hornblower. He took the chalk from beside the slate at the binnacle; and wrote with it, in large letters diagonally round the hogshead, the word "CONDEMNED". "There are two irons heating in the galley fire. You and Mr. Prince can spend your time branding these hogsheads. Trace out those letters on every one. Understand?"

"Er—yes, sir."

"Good and deep, so there is no chance of planing it off. Look sharp about it."

"Aye aye, sir."

The next lighter for the Dockyard was alongside now, at the port side recently vacated by the powder hulk. It was full of boatswain's stores, cordage, canvas, paint; and a weary party of men were at work swaying the bundles up. There seemed no end to this business of getting *Atropos* fully equipped for sea. Hornblower himself felt as leg-weary as a foundered horse, and he stiffened himself up to conceal his fatigue. But as he looked across the river he could see the Victualling Yard's lighter already emerging from the Creek. Smiley had his men at work on the sweeps, straining to row the ponderous thing across the ebbing tide.

From the quarterdeck he could see the lighter was crammed with the hogsheads and kegs and biscuit bags. Soon *Atropos* would be full-gorged. And the acrid smell of the red-hot irons burning into the brine-soaked staves of the condemned hogsheads came to his nostrils. No ship would ever accept those stores. It was a queer duty for a Serene Highness to be employed upon. How had those orders read? "You will employ your diligence in instructing His Serene Highness in his new profession." Well, perhaps it was not a bad introduction to the methods of fighting men and civilian employees.

Later—ever so much later, it seemed—Mr. Jones came up and touched his hat.

"The last of the stores are on board, sir," he said. "Mr. Smiley's just returning the Victualling Yard's lighter."

"Thank you, Mr. Jones. Call away my gig, please."

Hornblower stepped down into the boat conscious of many weary eyes on him. The winter afternoon was dissolving in a cold and gloomy drizzle as a small rain was beginning to fall. Hornblower had himself rowed round his ship at a convenient distance to observe her trim. He looked at her from ahead, from broadside on, from astern. In his mind's eye he was visualizing her underwater lines. He looked up at the spread of her lower yards; the wind would be pressing against the canvas there, and he worked out the balance of the forces involved, wind against lateral resistance, rudder versus headsails. He had to consider seaworthiness and handiness as well as speed. He climbed back on deck to where Jones was awaiting him.

"I want her more down by the head," he announced. "I'll have those beef casks at the for'rard end of the tier, and the shot for'rard of the magazine. Get the hands to work, if you please."

Once more the pipes shrilled through the ship as the hands began to move the stores ranged upon the deck. It was with anxiety that Hornblower's return was awaited from his next pull round the ship.

"She'll do for the present," said Hornblower.

It was not a casual decision, no stage-effect. The moment *Atropos* should clear the land she would be in danger, she might find herself in instant action. She was only a little ship; even a well found privateer might give her a hard battle. To overtake in pursuit; to escape in flight; to handle quickly when manoeuvring for position in action; to claw off to windward should she be caught on a lee shore; she must be capable of all this, and she must be capable of it today, for tomorrow, even tomorrow, might be too late. The lives of his crew, his own life, his professional reputation, could hang on that decision.

"You can strike everything below now, Mr. Jones."

Slowly the littered decks began to clear, while the rain grew heavier and the night began to close in round the little ship. The tiers of great casks, down against the skin of the ship, were squeezed and wedged into position; the contents of the hold had to be jammed into a solid mass, for once at sea *Atropos* would roll and pitch, and nothing must budge, nothing must shift, lest the fabric of the ship be damaged or even perhaps the ship might be rolled completely over by the movement of an avalanche of her cargo. The Navy still thought of Sir Edward Berry as the officer who, when captain of Nelson's own *Vanguard,* allowed the masts of his ship to be rolled clear out of her in a moderate gale of wind off Sardinia.

Hornblower stood aft by the taffrail while the rain streamed down on him. He had not gone below; this might be part of the penance he was inflicting on himself for not having sufficiently supervised the management of his ship.

"The decks are cleared, sir," said Jones, looming up in the wet darkness before him.

"Very well, Mr. Jones. When everything is swabbed down the men can have their dinners."

The little cabin down below was cold and dark and cheerless. Two canvas chairs and a trestle-table stood in the day cabin; in the night cabin there was nothing at all. The oil lamp shone gloomily over the bare planks of the deck under his feet. Hornblower could call for his gig again; it would whisk him fast enough half a mile downstream to Deptford Hard, and there at the "George" were his wife and his children. There would be a roaring fire of sea coal, a spluttering beef steak with cabbage, a feather bed with the sheets made almost too hot to bear by the application of a warming pan. His chilled body and aching legs yearned inexpressibly for that care and warmth. But in his present mood he would have none of them. Instead he dined, shivering, off ship's fare hastily laid out for him on the trestle-table. He had a hammock slung for himself in the night cabin, and he climbed into it and wrapped himself in clammy blankets. He had not lain in a hammock since he was a midshipman, and his spine had grown unused to the necessary curvature. He was too numb, both mentally and physically, to feel any glow of conscious virtue.

VIII

Fog in the Downs, cold, dense, and impenetrable over the surface of the sea. There was no breath of air to set it stirring; overside the surface of the sea, just visible when Hornblower looked down at it from the deck, was black and glassy. Only close against the side could be detected the faintest of ripples, showing how the tide was coursing beside the ship as she lay anchored in the Downs. Condensing on the rigging overhead the fog dripped in melancholy fashion on to the deck about him, an occasional drop landing with a dull impact on his cocked hat; the heavy frieze pea-jacket that he wore looked as if it were frosted with the moisture that hung upon it. Yet it was not freezing weather, although Hornblower felt chilled through and through inside his layers of clothing as he turned back from his gloomy contemplation of the sea.

"Now, Mr. Jones," he said, "we'll start again. We'll have topmasts and yards struck—all top hamper down and stowed away. Order 'out pipes', if you please."

"Aye aye, sir," said Jones.

The hands had already spent half the morning at sail drill; Hornblower was taking advantage of the fogbound calm to exercise his ship's company. With so many landsmen on board, with officers unfamiliar with their divisions, this fog actually could be used to advantage; the ship could be made more of a working, fighting unit during this interval of grace before proceeding down Channel. Hornblower put his cold hand inside his coat and brought out his watch; as if the gesture had called forth the sound five bells rang out sharply from beside the binnacle, and from the thick fog surrounding them came the sound of other bells—there were many ships anchored in the Downs all about them, so many that it was some minutes before the last sound died away; the sand-glasses on board the ships were by no means in agreement.

While the bells were still sounding Hornblower took note of the position of the minute hand of his watch and nodded to Jones. Instantly came a roar of orders; the men, already called to attention after their brief stand-easy came pouring aft with their petty officers urging them on. Watch in hand, Hornblower stood back by the taffrail. From where he stood only the lower part of the main rigging was visible; the foremast was completely hidden in fog. The hands went hurrying up the ratlines, Hornblower watching keenly to see what proportion of them were vague about their stations and duties. He could have wished that he could see all that was going on—but then if there had been no fog there would have been no sail drill, and *Atropos* would have been making the best of her way down Channel. Here was the Prince, hurried along by Horrocks with a hand at his shoulder.

"Come on," said Horrocks, leaping at the ratlines.

The Prince sprang up beside him. Hornblower could see the bewildered expression on the boy's face. He had small enough idea of what he was doing. He would learn, no doubt—he was learning much even from the fact that the blood-royal, the King's nephew, could be shoved about by the plebeian hand of a midshipman.

Hornblower got out of the way as the mizzen topsail came swaying down. A yelping master's mate came running up with a small pack of waisters at his heels; they fell upon the ponderous roll and dragged it to the side. The mizzen mast hands were working faster than the main-mast, apparently—the main topsail was not lowered yet. Jones, his head drawn back so that his Adam's apple protruded apparently by inches, was bellowing the next orders to the masthead. A shout from above answered him. Down the ratlines came a flood of men again.

"Let go! Haul! Lower away!"

The mizzen topsail yard turned in a solemn arc and made its slow descent down the mast. There was an exasperating delay while the main-stay tackle was applied—organization at this point was exceedingly poor—but at last the yard was down and lying along the booms beside its fellows. The complicated and difficult business of striking the topmasts followed.

"An hour and a quarter, Mr. Jones. More nearly an hour and twenty minutes. Far too long. Half an hour—half an hour with five minutes' grace; that's the longest you should ever take."

"Yes, sir," said Jones. There was nothing else he could say.

As Hornblower was eyeing him before giving his next orders a faint dull thud came to his ears, sounding flatly through the fog. A musket shot? A pistol shot? That was certainly what it sounded like, but with the fog changing the quality of all the sounds he could not be sure. Even if it were a shot, fired in one of the numerous invisible ships round about, there might be endless innocent explanations of it; and it might not be a shot. A hatch cover dropped on a deck—a grating being pushed into place—it could be anything.

The hands were grouped about the deck, looming vaguely in the fog, awaiting further orders. Hornblower guessed that they were sweating despite the cold. This was the way to get that London beer out of them, but he did not want to drive them too hard.

"Five minutes stand-easy," said Hornblower. "And, Mr. Jones, you had better station a good petty officer at that mainstay tackle."

"Aye aye, sir."

Hornblower turned away to give Jones an opportunity to arrange his reorganization. He set himself to walk the deck to bring some life back into his cold body; his watch was still in his hand through sheer forget-fulness to replace it in his pocket. He ended his walk at the ship's side, glancing over into the black water. Now what was that floating down beside the ship? Something long and black; when Hornblower first caught sight of it it had bumped one end against the ship's side under the main chains, and as he watched it swung solemnly round, drawn by the tide, and came down towards him. It was an oar. Curiosity overcame him. In a crowded anchorage like this there was nothing very surprising about a floating oar, but still—

"Here, quartermaster," said Hornblower. "Get down into the mizzen chains with a line to catch that oar."

It was only an oar; Hornblower looked it over as the quartermaster held it for his inspection. The leather button was fairly well worn—it was by no means a new oar. On the other hand, judging by the fact that the leather was not entirely soaked through, it had not long been in the water, minutes rather than days, obviously. There was the number "27" burned into the loom, and it was that which caused Hornblower to look more sharply. The "7" bore a crossbar. No Englishman ever wrote a "7" with a crossbar. But everyone on the Continent did; there were Danes and Swedes and Norwegians, Russians and Prussians, at sea, either neutrals in the war or allies of England. Yet a Frenchman or a Dutchman, one of England's enemies, would also write a "7" in that way.

And there had certainly been something that sounded like a shot. A floating oar and a musket shot made a combination that would be hard to explain. Now if they had been connected in causation—! Hornblower still had his watch in his hand. That shot—if it was a shot—had made itself heard just before he gave the order for stand-easy, seven or eight minutes ago. The tide was running at a good two knots. If the shot had caused the oar to be dropped into the water it must have been fired a quarter of a mile or so—two cables' length—upstream. The quartermaster still holding the oar was looking at him curiously, and Jones was waiting, with the men poised for action, for his next orders. Hornblower was tempted to pay no more attention to the incident.

But he was a King's officer, and it was his duty to make inquiry into the unexplainable at sea. He hesitated in inward debate; the fog was horribly thick. If he sent a boat to investigate it would probably lose itself; Hornblower had had much experience of making his way by boat in a fog-ridden anchorage. Then he could go himself. Hornblower felt a qualm at the thought of blundering about trying to find his way in the fog—he could make a fool of himself so easily in the eyes of his crew. Yet on the other hand that was not likely to be as exasperating as fuming on board waiting for a dilatory boat to return.

"Mr. Jones," he said, "call away my gig."

"Aye aye, sir," said Jones, the astonishment in his voice hardly concealed at all.

Hornblower walked to the binnacle and took a careful reading of how the ship's head lay. It was the most careful reading he could possibly take, not because his comfort or his safety but because his personal dignity depended on getting that reading right. North by East half East. As the ship lay riding to her anchor bows to the tide he could be sure that the oar had come down from that direction.

"I want a good boat compass in the gig, Mr. Jones, if you please."

"Aye aye, sir."

Hornblower hesitated before the last final order, which would commit him to a public admission that he thought there was a chance of something serious awaiting him in the fog. But not to give the order would be to strain at a gnat and swallow a camel. If that had really been a musket shot that he had heard there was a possibility of action; there was a likelihood that at least a show of force would be necessary.

"Pistols and cutlasses for the gig's crew, Mr. Jones, if you please."

"Aye aye, sir," said Jones, as if nothing could astonish him again.

Hornblower turned back as he was about to step down into the boat.

"I shall start timing you from this moment, Mr. Jones. Try to get those tops'l yards across in half an hour from now—I'll be back before then."

"Aye aye, sir."

The ship broke into a roar of activity as Hornblower took his place in the stern-sheets of the gig.

"I'll take the tiller," he said to the coxswain. "Give way."

He steered the gig along the *Atropos* from stern to bow. He took one last look up at her bows, at her bowsprit and bobstay, and then the fog swallowed them up. The gig was instantly in a world of its own, constricted about by the walls of mist. The sounds of activity on board the ship died rapidly away.

"Pull steady!" growled Hornblower to the man at the oars. That little boat compass would be swinging about chasing its tail in ten seconds if he allowed the gig to keep anything except an exactly straight course. North by East half East.

"Seventeen," said Hornblower to himself. "Eighteen. Nineteen."

He was counting the strokes of the oars; it was a rough way of estimating the progress made. At seven feet to the stroke less than two hundred strokes meant a quarter of a mile. But there was the speed of the tide to be allowed for. It would be nearer five hundred strokes—all very vague, but every possible precaution must be taken on a foolish expedition like this.

"Seventy-four, seventy-five," said Hornblower, his eyes glued to the compass.

Even with the brisk tide running the surface of the sea was a glassy flat calm; the oar-blades, lifting from the water at the completion of each stroke, left whirlpools circling on the surface.

"Two hundred," said Hornblower, suppressing a momentary fear that he had miscounted and that it was really three hundred.

The oars groaned on monotonously in the rowlocks.

"Keep your eyes ahead," said Hornblower to the coxswain. "Tell me the moment you see anything. Two sixty-four."

It seemed only yesterday that he had sat in the stern-sheets of the jolly boat of the *Indefatigable*, rowing up the estuary of the Gironde to cut out the *Papillon*. But that was more than ten years ago. Three hundred. Three hundred and fifty.

"Sir," said the coxswain, tersely.

Hornblower looked forward. Ahead, a trifle on the port bow, there was the slightest thickening in the fog, the slightest looming of something solid there.

"Easy all!" said Hornblower, and the boat continued to glide over the surface; he put the tiller over slightly so as to approach whatever it was more directly. But the boat's way died away before they were near enough to distinguish any details, and at Hornblower's command the men began to row again. Distantly came a low hail out of the fog, apparently called forth by the renewal of the sound of the oars.

"Boat ahoy!"

At least the hail was in English. By now there was visible the vague outlines of a large brig; from the heaviness of her spars and fast lines she looked like one of the West India packets.

"What brig's that?" hailed Hornblower in reply.

"*Amelia Jane* of London, thirty-seven days out from Barbados."

That was a direct confirmation of Hornblower's first impression. But that voice? It did not sound quite English, somehow. There were foreign captains in the British merchant service, plenty of them, but hardly likely to be in command of a West India packet.

"Easy," said Hornblower to the rowers, the gig glided silently on over the water. He could see no sign of anything wrong.

"Keep your distance," said the voice from the brig.

There was nothing suspicious about the words. Any ship at anchor hardly more than twenty miles from the coast of France was fully entitled to be wary of strangers approaching in a fog. But that word sounded more like "deestance" all the same. Hornblower put his helm over to pass under the brig's stern. Several heads were now apparent at the brig's side; they moved round the stern in time with the gig. There was the brig's name, sure enough. *Amelia Jane*, London. Then Hornblower caught sight of something else; it was a large boat lying under the brig's port quarter from the main chains. There might be a hundred possible explanations of that, but it was a suspicious circumstance.

"Brig ahoy!" he hailed, "I'm coming aboard."

"Keep off!" said the voice in reply.

Some of the heads at the brig's side developed shoulders, and three or four muskets were pointed at the gig.

"I am a King's officer," said Hornblower.

He stood up in the stern-sheets and unbuttoned his pea-jacket so that his uniform was visible. The central figure at the brig's side, the man who had been speaking, looked for a long moment and then spread his hands in a gesture of despair.

"Yes," he said.

Hornblower went up the brig's side as briskly as his chilled limbs would permit. As he stood on the deck he felt a trifle self-conscious of being unarmed, for facing him were more than a dozen men, hostility in their bearing, and some of them with muskets in their hands. But the gig's crew had followed him on the deck and closed up behind him, handling their cutlasses and pistols.

"Cap'n, sir!" It was the voice from overside of one of the two men left down in the gig. "Please, sir, there's a dead man in the boat here."

Hornblower turned away to look over. A dead man certainly lay there, doubled up in the bottom of the boat. That accounted for the floating oar, then. And for the shot, of course. The man had been killed by a bullet from the brig at the moment the boat was laid alongside; the brig had been taken by boarding. Hornblower looked back towards the group on the deck.

"Frenchmen?" he asked.

"Yes, sir."

The fellow was a man of sense. He had not attempted a hopeless resistance when his coup had been discovered. Although he had fifteen men at his back and there were only eight altogether in the gig he had realized that the presence of a King's ship in the immediate vicinity made his final capture a certainty.

"Where's the crew?" asked Hornblower.

The Frenchman pointed forward, and at a gesture from Hornblower one of his men ran to release the brig's crew from their confinement in the forecastle, half a dozen coloured hands and a couple of officers.

"Much obliged to you, mister," said the captain, coming forward.

"I'm Captain Hornblower of His Majesty's ship *Atropos*," said Hornblower.

"I beg your pardon, Captain." He was an elderly man, his white hair and blue eyes in marked contrast with his mahogany tan. "You've saved my ship."

"Yes," said Hornblower, "you had better disarm those men."

"Gladly, sir. See to it, Jack."

The other officer, presumably the mate, walked aft to take muskets and swords from the unresisting Frenchmen.

"They came out of the fog and laid me alongside before I was aware, almost, sir," went on the captain. "A King's ship took my four best hands when we was off the Start, or I'd have made a better account of them. I only got one crack at them as it was."

"It was that crack that brought me here," said Hornblower shortly. "Where did they come from?"

"Now that's just what I was asking myself," said the captain. "Not from France in that boat, they couldn't have come."

They turned their gaze inquiringly upon the dejected group of Frenchmen. It was a question of considerable importance. The Frenchmen must have come from a ship, and that ship must be anchored somewhere amid the crowded vessels in the Downs. And at that rate she must be disguised as a British vessel or a neutral, coming in with the others before the wind dropped and the fog closed down. There had been plenty of similar incidents during the war. It was an easy way to snap up a prize. But it meant that somewhere close at hand there was a wolf in sheep's clothing, a disguised French privateer, probably crammed with men—she might have made more than one prize. In the bustle and confusion that would ensue when a breeze should get up, with everyone anxious to up anchor and away, she could count on being able to make her escape along with her prizes.

"When the fog closed down," said the captain, "the nearest vessel to us was a Ramsgate trawler. She anchored at the same time as we did. I doubt if it could be her."

It was a matter of so much importance that Hornblower could not keep still. He turned and paced the deck for a space, his mind working rapidly. Yet his mind was not completely made up when he turned back and gave his first order in execution of the vague plan. He did not know if he would have the resolution to go through with it.

"Leadbitter," he said to the coxswain.

"Sir!"

"Tie those men's hands behind them."

"Sir?"

"You heard what I said."

To bind prisoners was almost a violation of the laws of war. When Leadbitter approached to carry out his orders the Frenchmen showed evident resentment. A buzz of voices arose.

'You can't do this, sir," said their spokesman. "We have—"

"Shut your mouth," snapped Hornblower.

Even having to give that order put him in a bad temper, and his bad temper was made worse by his doubts about himself. Now that the Frenchmen were disarmed they could offer no resistance in face of the drawn pistols of the British sailors. With loud protests they had to submit, as Leadbitter went from man to man tying their wrists behind their backs. Hornblower was hating himself for the part he had to play, even while his calculating mind told him that he had a fair chance of success. He had to pose as a bloodthirsty man, delighting in the taking of human life, without mercy in his soul, gratified by the sight of the death struggles of a fellow-human. Such men did exist, he knew. There were gloomy tyrants in the King's service. In the past ten years of war at sea there had been some outrages, a few, on both sides. These Frenchmen did not know him for what he really was, nor did the West India crew. Nor for that matter his own men. Their acquaintance had been so short that they had no reason to believe him not to have homicidal tendencies, so that their behaviour would not weaken the impression he wished to convey. He turned to one of his men.

"Run aloft," he said. "Reeve a whip through the block at the main yardarm."

That portended a hanging. The man looked at him with a momentary unbelief, but the scowl on Hornblower's face sent him scurrying up the ratlines. Then Hornblower strode to where the wretched Frenchmen were standing bound; their glance shifted from the man at the yardarm to Hornblower's grim face, and their anxious chattering died away.

"You are pirates," said Hornblower, speaking slowly and distinctly. "I am going to hang you."

In case the English-speaking Frenchman's vocabulary did not include the word "hang" he pointed significantly to the man at the yardarm. They could all understand that. They remained silent for a second or two, and then several of them began to speak at once in torrential French which Hornblower could not well follow, and then the leader, having pulled himself together, began his protest in English.

"We are not pirates," he said.

"I think you are," said Hornblower.

"We are privateersmen," said the Frenchman.

"Pirates," said Hornblower.

The talk among the Frenchmen rose to a fresh height; Hornblower's French was good enough for him to make out that the leader was translating his curt words to his companions, and they were urging him to explain more fully their position.

"I assure you, sir," said the wretched man, striving to be eloquent in a strange language, "we are privateersmen and not pirates."

Hornblower regarded him with a stony countenance, and without answering turned away to give further orders.

"Leadbitter," he said, "I'll have a hangman's noose on the end of that line."

Then he turned back to the Frenchmen.

"Who do you say you are then?" he asked. He tried to utter the words as indifferently as he could.

"We are from the privateer *Vengeance* of Dunkirk, sir. I am Jacques Lebon, prizemaster."

Privateers usually went to sea with several extra officers, who could be put into prizes to navigate them back to a French port without impairing the fighting efficiency of the privateer, which could continue her cruise. These officers were usually selected for their ability to speak English and for the knowledge of English seagoing ways, and they bore the title of "prizemaster". Hornblower turned back to observe the noose now dangling significantly from the yardarm, and then addressed the prizemaster.

"You have no papers," he said.

He forced his lips into a sneer as he spoke; to the wretched men studying every line in his face his expression appeared quite unnatural, as indeed it was. And Hornblower was gambling a little when he said what he did. If the prizemaster had been able to produce any papers the whole line of attack would have to be altered; but it was not much of a gamble. Hornblower was certain when he spoke that if Lebon had had papers in his pocket he would have already mentioned them, asking someone to dive into his pocket for them. That would be the first reaction of any Frenchman whose identity had been put in question.

"No," said Lebon, crestfallen. It was hardly likely that he would have, when engaged on an ordinary operation of war.

"Then you hang," said Hornblower. "All of you. One by one."

The laugh he forced himself to produce sounded positively inhuman, horrible. Anyone hearing it would be justified in thinking that he was inspired by the anticipated pleasure of watching the death struggles of a dozen men. The white-haired captain of the *Amelia Jane* could not bear the prospect, and came forward to enter into the discussion.

"Sir," he said. "What are you going to do?"

"I am going to attend to my own business, sir," said Hornblower, striving to throw into his voice all the harshness he had ever heard employed by all the insolent officers he had met during his service. "May I ask you to be kind enough to do the same?"

"But you can't be meaning to hang the poor devils," went on the captain.

"But that is what I do mean."

"But not in my ship, sir—not now—not without trial."

"In your ship, sir, which you allowed to be captured. And now. Pirates taken red-handed can be hanged instantly, as you know, sir. And that is what I shall do."

It was a stroke of good fortune that the captain should have entered into the discussion. His appearance of sick dismay and the tone of his protests were convincingly genuine—they would never have been so if he had been admitted previously to a planned scheme. Hornblower's attitude towards him was brutal, but it was for the good of the cause.

"Sir," persisted the captain, "I'm sure they're only privateersmen—"

"Please refrain from interfering with a King's officer in the execution of his duty. You two men, there, come here."

The two of the crew of the gig that he indicated approached obediently. Probably they had seen hangings before, along with every kind of brutality in a brutal service. But the imminent certainty of taking personal part in a hanging obviously impressed them. There was some reluctance visible in their expressions, but the hard discipline of the service would make certain they would obey the orders of this one man, unarmed and outnumbered.

Hornblower looked along the line of faces. Momentarily he felt a horrid sickness in his stomach as it occurred to him to wonder how he would be feeling if he really was selecting a victim.

"I'll have that one first," he said, pointing.

The bull-throated swarthy man whom he indicated paled and shuddered; backing away he tried to shelter himself among his fellows. They were all speaking at once, jerking their arms frantically against the bonds that secured their wrists behind them.

"Sir!" said Lebon. "Please—I beg of you—I implore—"

Hornblower condescended to spare him a glance, and Lebon went on in a wild struggle against the difficulties of language and the handicap of not being free to gesticulate.

"We are privateersmen. We fight for the Empire, for France." Now he was on his knees, his face lifted. As he could not use his hands he was actually nuzzling with his mouth against the skirts of Hornblower's pea-jacket. "We surrendered. We did not fight. We caused no death."

"Take this man away from me," said Hornblower, withdrawing out of reach.

But Lebon on his knees followed him over the deck, nuzzling and pleading.

"Captain," said the English captain, interceding once again. "Can't you at least wait and land 'em for trial? If they're pirates it'll be proved quick enough."

"I want to see 'em dangling," said Hornblower, searching feverishly in his mind for the most impressive thing he could say.

The two English seamen, taking advantage of the volume of protest, had paused in the execution of their orders. Hornblower looked up at the noose, dangling dimly but horribly in the fog.

"I don't believe for one single moment," went on Hornblower, "that these men are what they say they are. Just a band of thieves, pirates. Leadbitter, put four men on that line. I'll give the word when they are to walk away with it."

"Sir," said Lebon, "I assure you, word of honour, we are from the privateer *Vengeance*."

"Bah!" replied Hornblower. "Where is she?"

"Over there," said Lebon. He could not point with his hands; he pointed with his chin, over the port bow of the anchored *Amelia Jane*. It was not a very definite indication, but it was a considerable help, even that much.

"Did you see any vessel over there before the fog closed down, captain?" demanded Hornblower, turning to the English captain.

"Only the Ramsgate trawler," he said, reluctantly.

"That is our ship!" said Lebon. "That is the *Vengeance*! She was a Dunkirk trawler—we—we made her look like that."

So that was it. A Dunkirk trawler. Her fish-holds could be crammed full of men. A slight alteration of gear, an "R" painted on her mainsail, a suitable name painted on her stern and then she could wander about the narrow seas without question, snapping up prizes almost at will.

"Where did you say she lay?" demanded Hornblower.

"There—oh!"

Lebon checked himself as he realized how much information he was giving away.

"I can hazard a good guess as to how she bears from us," interposed the English captain, "I saw—oh!"

He broke off exactly as Lebon had done, but from surprise. He was staring at Hornblower. It was like the denouement scene in some silly farce. The lost heir was at last revealed. The idea of now accepting the admiration of his unwitting fellow players, of modestly admitting that he was not the monster of ferocity he had pretended to be, irritated Hornblower beyond all bearing. All his instincts and good taste rose against the trite and the obvious. Now that he had acquired the information he had sought he could please himself as long as he acted instantly on that information. The scowl he wished to retain rested the more easily on his features with this revulsion of feeling.

"I'd be sorry to miss a hanging," he said, half to himself, and he allowed his eye to wander again from the dangling noose to the shrinking group of Frenchmen who were still ignorant of what had just happened. "If that thick neck were stretched a little—"

He broke off and took a brief turn up and down the deck, eyed by every man who stood on it.

"Very well," he said, halting. "It's against my better judgment, but I'll wait before I hang these men. What was the approximate bearing of that trawler when she anchored, captain?"

"It was at slack water," began the captain, making his calculations. "We were just beginning to swing. I should say—"

The captain was obviously a man of sober judgment and keen observation. Hornblower listened to what he had to say.

"Very well," said Hornblower when he had finished. "Leadbitter, I'll leave you on board with two men. Keep an eye on these prisoners and see they don't retake the brig. I'm returning to the ship now. Wait here for further orders."

He went down into his gig; the captain accompanying him to the ship's side was clearly and gratifyingly puzzled. It was almost beyond his belief that Hornblower could be the demoniac monster that he had appeared to be, and if he were it was strange good fortune that his ferocity should have obtained, by pure chance, the information that the prisoners had just given him. Yet on the other hand it was almost beyond his belief that if Hornblower had employed a clever ruse to gain the information he should refuse to enjoy the plaudits of his audience and not to bask in their surprise and admiration. Either notion was puzzling. That was well. Let him be puzzled. Let them all be puzzled—although it seemed as if the sobered hands pulling at the oars of the gig were not at all puzzled. Unheeding of all that had been at stake they were clearly convinced that their captain had shown himself in his true colours, and was a man who would sooner see a man's death agonies than eat his dinner. Let 'em think so. It would do no harm. Hornblower could spare them no thought in any case, with all his attention glued upon the compass card. It would be ludicrous—it would be horribly comic—if after all this he were to miss *Atropos* on his way back to her, if he were to blunder about in the fog for hours looking for his own ship. The reciprocal of North by East half East was South by West half West, and he kept the gig rigidly on that course. With what still remained of the ebb tide behind them it would only be a few seconds before they ought to sight *Atropos*. It was a very great comfort when they did.

Mr. Jones received Hornblower at the ship's side. A glance had told him that the gig's crew was two men and a coxswain short. It was hard to think of any explanation of that, and Mr. Jones was bursting with curiosity. He could not help but wonder what his captain had been doing, out there in the fog. His curiosity even overcame his apprehension at the sight of the scowl which Hornblower still wore—now that he was back in his ship Hornblower was beginning to feel much more strongly the qualms that should have influenced him regarding what Their Lordships might think of his absence from his ship. He ignored Jones's questions.

"You got those tops'l yards across, I see, Mr. Jones."

"Yes, sir. I sent the hands to dinner when you didn't come back, sir. I thought—"

"They'll have five minutes to finish their dinners. No longer. Mr. Jones, if you were in command of two boats sent to capture a hostile vessel at anchor in this fog, how would you set about it? What orders would you give?"

"Well, sir, I'd—I'd—"

Mr. Jones was not a man of quickness of thought or rapid adaptability to a new situation. He hummed and he hawed. But there were very few officers in the Navy who had not been on at least one cutting-out and boarding operation. He knew well enough what he should do, and it slowly became apparent.

"Very well, Mr. Jones. You will now hoist out the long boat and the launch. You will man them and see that the boats' crews are fully armed. You will proceed North by East half East—fix that in your mind, Mr. Jones, North by East half East—from this ship for a quarter of a mile. There you find a West India brig the *Amelia Jane*. She has just been recaptured from a French prize crew, and my coxswain is on board with two men. From her you will take a new departure. There's a French privateer, the *Vengeance*. She's a Dunkirk trawler disguised as a Ramsgate trawler. She is probably heavily manned—at least fifty of a crew left—and she is anchored approximately three cables' lengths approximately north-west of the *Amelia Jane*. You will capture her, by surprise if possible. Mr. Still will be in command of the second boat. I will listen while you give him his instructions. That will save repetition. Mr. Still!"

The despatch that Hornblower wrote that evening and entrusted to the *Amelia Jane* for delivery to the Admiralty was couched in the usual Navy phraseology.

Sir

I have the honour to report to you for the information of Their Lordships that this day while anchored in dense fog in the Downs I became aware that it seemed likely that some disturbance was taking place near at hand. On investigating I had the good fortune to recapture the brig *Amelia Jane*, homeward bound from Barbados, which was in possession of a French prize crew. From information gained from the prisoners I was able to send my first lieutenant, Mr. Jones, with the boats of H.M. ship under my command, to attack the French private ship of war *Vengeance* of Dunkirk. She was handsomely carried by Mr. Jones and his officers and men including Mr. Still, second lieutenant, Messrs. Horrocks and Smiley, and His Serene Highness the Prince of Seitz-Bunau, midshipmen, after a brief action in which our loss was two men slightly wounded while the French Captain, Monsieur Ducos, met with a severe wound while trying to rally his crew. The *Vengeance* proved to be a French trawler masquerading as an English fishing boat. Including the prize crew she carried a crew of seventy-one officers and men, and she was armed with one four-pounder carronade concealed under her net.

I have the honour to remain,

Your obed't servant,

H. Hornblower, Captain.

Before sealing it Hornblower read through this report with a lopsided smile on his face. He wondered if anyone would ever read between the lines of that bald narrative, how much anyone would guess, how much anyone would deduce. The fog, the cold, the wet; the revolting scene on the deck of the *Amelia Jane*; the interplay of emotion; could anyone ever guess at all the truth? And there was no doubt that his gig's crew was already spreading round the ship horrible reports about his lust for blood. There was some kind of sardonic satisfaction to be derived from that, too. A knock at the door. Could he never be undisturbed?

"Come in," he called.

It was Jones. His glance took in the quill in Hornblower's fingers, and the inkwell and papers on the table before him.

"Your pardon, sir," he said. "I hope I don't come too late."

"What is it?" asked Hornblower; he had little sympathy for Jones and his undetermined manners.

"If you are going to send a report to the Admiralty, sir—and I suppose you are, sir—"

"Yes, of course I am."

"I don't know if you're going to mention my name, sir—I don't want to ask if you are, sir—I don't want to presume—"

If Jones was soliciting a special mention of himself in the Admiralty letter he would get none at all.

"What is it you're saying to me, Mr. Jones?"

"It's only that my name's a common one, sir. John Jones, sir. There are twelve John Jones's in the lieutenants' list, sir. I didn't know if you knew, sir, but I am John Jones the Ninth. That's how I'm known at the Admiralty, sir. If you didn't say that, perhaps—"

"Very well, Mr. Jones. I understand. You can rely on me to see that justice is done."

"Thank you, sir."

With Jones out of the way Hornblower sighed a little, looked at his report, and drew a fresh sheet towards him. There was no chance of inserting "the Ninth" legibly after the mention of Jones's name. The only thing to do was to take a fresh sheet and write it all over again. An odd occupation for a bloodthirsty tyrant.

IX

Hornblower watched with a keen eye his crew at work as they took in sail while *Atropos* came gliding into Gibraltar Bay. He could call them well-drilled now. The long beat down the Channel, the battles with the Biscay gales, had made a correlated team of them. There was no confusion and only the minimum number of orders. The men came hurrying off the yards; he saw two figures swing themselves on to the main backstays and come sliding down all the way from the masthead, disdaining to use the shrouds and ratlines. They reached the deck simultaneously and stood grinning at each other for a moment—clearly they had been engaged in a race. One was Smiley, the midshipman of the maintop. The other—His Serene Highness the Prince of Seitz-Bunau. That boy had improved beyond all expectation. If ever he should sit on his throne again in his princely German capital he would have strange memories to recall.

But this was not the time for a captain to let his attention wander.

"Let go, Mr. Jones!" he hailed, and the anchor fell, dragging the grumbling hawser out through the hawsehole; Hornblower watched while *Atropos* took up on her cable and then rode to her anchor. She was in her assigned berth; Hornblower looked up at the towering Rock and over at the Spanish shore. Nothing seemed to have changed since the last time—so many years ago—that he had come sailing into Gibraltar Bay. The sun was shining down on him, and it was good to feel this Mediterranean sun again, even though there was little warmth in it during this bleak winter weather.

"Call away my gig, if you please, Mr. Jones."

Hornblower ran below to gird on his sword and to take the better of his two cocked hats out of its tin case so as to make himself as presentable as possible when he went ashore to pay his official calls. There was a very decided thrill in the thought that soon he would be reading the orders that would carry him forward into the next phase of his adventures—adventures possibly; more probably the mere dreariness of beating about on eternal blockade duty outside a French port.

Yet in Collingwood's orders to him, when he came to read them, there was a paragraph which left him wondering what his fate was to be.

> You will take into your ship Mr. William McCullum, of the Honourable East India Company's Service, together with his native assistants, and you will give them passage when, in obedience to the first paragraph of these orders, you come to join me.

Mr. McCullum was awaiting him in the Governor's anteroom. He was a burly, heavy-set man in his early thirties, blue-eyed and with a thick mat of black hair.

"Captain Horatio Hornblower?" there was a roll to the "r's" which betrayed the county of his origin.

"Mr. McCullum?"

"Of the Company's Service."

The two men eyed each other.

"You are to take passage in my ship?"

"Aye."

The fellow carried himself with an air of vast independence. Yet judging by the scantiness of the silver lace on his uniform, and by the fact that he wore no sword, he was not of a very lofty position in the Company's hierarchy.

"Who are these native assistants of yours?"

"Three Sinhalese divers."

"Sinhalese?"

Hornblower said the word with caution. He had never heard it before, at least pronounced in that way. He suspected that it meant something to do with Ceylon, but he was not going to make a display of his ignorance.

"Pearl divers from Ceylon," said McCullum.

So he had guessed right. But he could not imagine for one moment why Collingwood, at grips with the French in the Mediterranean, should need Ceylonese pearl divers.

"And what is your official position, Mr. McCullum?"

"I am wreck-master and salvage director of the Coromandel Coast."

That went far to explain the man's ostentatious lack of deference. He was one of those experts whose skill made them too valuable to be trifled with. He might have drifted out to India as a cabin boy or apprentice; presumably he had been treated like a menial while young, but he had learned a trade so well as now to be indispensable and in a position to repay the slights he had endured earlier. The more the gold lace he was addressing the brusquer was likely to be his manner.

"Very well, Mr. McCullum. I shall be sailing immediately and I shall be glad if you will come on board with your assistants at the earliest possible moment. Within an hour. Do you have any equipment with you to be shipped?"

"Very little besides my chests and the divers' bundles. They are ready, along with the food for them."

"Food?"

"The poor bodies"—McCullum narrowed the vowel sound until the word sounded like "puir"—"are benighted heathen, followers of Buddha. They wellnigh died on the voyage here, never having known what it was to have a full belly before. A scrap of vegetable, a drop of oil, a bit of fish for a relish. That's what they're used to living on."

Oil? Vegetables? Ships of war could hardly be expected to supply such things.

"I've a puncheon of Spanish olive oil for them," explained McCullum. "They've taken kindly to it, although it's far removed from their buffalo butter. Lentils and onions and carrots. Give them salt beef and they'll die, and that would be poor business after shipping them all round the Cape of Good Hope."

The statement was made with apparent callousness, but Hornblower suspected that the manner concealed some consideration for his unfortunate subordinates so far from their homes. He began to like McCullum a little better.

"I'll give orders for them to be well looked after," he said.

"Thank you." That was the first shade of politeness that had crept into McCullum's speech. "The poor devils have been perishing of cold here on the Rock. That makes them homesick, like, and a long way they are from home, too."

"Why have they been sent here in any case?" asked Hornblower. That question had been striving for utterance for some time; he had not asked it because it would have given McCullum too good an opportunity to snub him.

"Because they can dive in sixteen and a half fathoms," said McCullum, staring straight at him.

It was not quite a snub; Hornblower was aware that he owed the modification to his promise that they would be well treated. He would not risk another question despite his consuming curiosity. He was completely puzzled as to why the Mediterranean Fleet should need divers who could go down through a hundred feet of water. He contented himself with ending the interview with an offer to send a boat for McCullum and his men.

The Ceylonese when they made their appearance on the deck of the *Atropos* were of an appearance to excite pity. They held their white cotton clothes close about them against the cold; the keen air that blew down from the snow-clad Spanish mountains set them shivering. They were thin, frail-looking men, and they looked about them with no curiosity, but with only a dull resignation in their dark eyes. They were of a deep brown colour, so as to excite the interest of the hands who gathered to stare. They spared no glances for the white men, but conversed briefly with each other in high piping musical voices.

"Give them the warmest corner of the 'tween decks, Mr. Jones," said Hornblower. "See that they are comfortable. Consult with Mr. McCullum regarding anything they may need. Allow me to present Mr. McCullum—Mr. Jones. I would be greatly obliged if you will extend to Mr. McCullum the hospitality of the wardroom."

Hornblower had to phrase it that way. The wardroom theoretically was a voluntary association of officers, who could make their own choice as to what members they might admit. But it would be a bold set of officers who decided to exclude a wardroom guest recommended by their captain, as Jones and Hornblower both knew.

"You must provide a cot for Mr. McCullum, too, Mr. Jones, if you please. You can decide for yourself where you will put it."

It was comforting to be able to say that. Hornblower knew perfectly well—and so did Jones, as his slightly dismayed expression revealed—that in a twenty-two gun sloop there was not a square foot of deck space to spare. Everyone was already overcrowded, and McCullum's presence would add seriously to the overcrowding. But it was Jones who would have to find a way round the difficulty.

"Aye aye, sir," said Jones; the interval that elapsed before he said it was the best indication of the involved train of thought he had been following out.

"Excellent," said Hornblower. "You can attend to it after we're under way. No more time to waste, Mr. Jones."

Minutes were always valuable. The wind might always shift, or drop. An hour wasted now might mean the loss of a week. Hornblower was in a fever to get his ship clear of the Gut and into the wider waters of the Mediterranean, where he would have sea room in which to beat against a head wind should a Levanter come blowing out of the East. Before his mind's eye he had a picture of the Western Mediterranean; the north-westerly blowing at present could carry him quickly along the southern coast of Spain, past the dangerous shoal of Alboran, until at Cape de Gata the Spanish coast trended away boldly to the northward. Once there he would be less restricted; until Cape de Gata was left behind he could not be happy. There was also—Hornblower could not deny it—his own personal desire to be up and doing, to find out what was awaiting him in the future, to put himself at least in the possible path of adventure. It was fortunate that his duty and his inclination should coincide in this way; one of the few small bits of good fortune, he told himself with amused grimness, that he had experienced since he had made his original choice of the career of a naval officer.

But at least he had come into Gibraltar Bay after dawn and he was leaving before nightfall. He could not be accused of wasting any time. They had rounded the Rock; Hornblower looked into the binnacle and up at the commission pendant blowing out from the masthead.

"Full and bye," he ordered.

"Full and bye, sir," echoed the quartermaster at the wheel.

A keen gust of wind came blowing down out of the Sierra de Ronda, laying the *Atropos* over as the trimmed yards braced the sails to catch it. Over she lay; a short steep wave came after them, the remnants of an Atlantic roller that had survived its passage through the Gut. *Atropos* lifted her stern to it, heaving jerkily in this unnatural opposition of wind and wave. Spray burst under her counter, and spray burst round her bows as she plunged. She plunged again in the choppy sea. She was only a little ship, the smallest three-masted vessel in the service, the smallest that could merit a captain to command her. The lofty frigates, the massive seventy-fours, could condescend to her. Hornblower looked round him at the wintry Mediterranean, at the fresh clouds obscuring the sinking sun. The waves could toss his ship about, the winds could heel her over, but standing there, braced on the quarter-deck, he was master of them. Exultation surged within him as his ship hurried forward into the unknown.

The exultation even remained when he quitted the deck and descended into the cabin. Here the prospect was cheerless in the extreme. He had mortified his flesh after he had come on board his ship at Deptford. His conscience had nagged at him for the scanty hours he had wasted with his wife and children; and he had never left his ship again for a moment after he had reported her ready for sea. No farewell to Maria lying in childbed, no last parting from little Horatio and little Maria. And no purchase of cabin equipment. The furniture about him was what the ship's carpenter had made for him, canvas chairs, a rough-and-ready table, a cot whose frame was strung with cordage to support a coarse canvas mattress stuffed with straw. A canvas pillow, straw-filled, to support his head; coarse Navy blankets to cover his skinny body. There was no carpet on the deck under his feet; the light came from a swinging and odorous ship's lantern. A shelf with a hole in it supported a tin wash-basin; on the bulkhead above it hung the scrap of polished steel mirror from Hornblower's meagre canvas dressing-roll. The most substantial articles present were the two sea chests in the corners; apart from them a monk's cell could hardly have been more bare.

But there was no self-pity in Hornblower's mind as he crouched under the low deck beams unhooking his stock preparatory to going to bed. He expected little from this world, and he could lead an inner life of the mind that could render him oblivious to discomfort. And he had saved a good deal of money by not furnishing his cabin, money which would pay the midwife's fee, the long bill at the "George", and the fare for the carrier's cart which would convey Maria and the children to lodge with her mother at Southsea. He was thinking about them—they must be well on their way now—as he drew the clammy blankets over himself and rested his cheek on the rough pillow. Then he had to forget Maria and the children as he reminded himself that as the *Atropos*' junction with the fleet was so imminent he must exercise the midshipmen and the signal ratings in signalling. He must devote a good many hours to that, and there would not be much time to spare, for the creaking of the timbers, the heave of the ship, told him that the wind was holding steady.

The wind continued to hold fair. It was at noon on the sixth day that the lookout hailed the deck.

"Sail ho! Dead to loo'ard."

"Bear down on her, Mr. Jones, if you please. Mr. Smiley! Take a glass and see what you make of her."

This was the second of the rendezvous which Collingwood had

named in his orders. Yesterday's had been barren, off Cape Carbomara. Not a sail had been sighted since leaving Gibraltar. Collingwood's frigates had swept the sea clear of French and Spanish shipping, and the British Levant convoy was not due for another month. And no one could guess what was going on in Italy at this moment.

"Captain, sir! She's a frigate. One of ours."

"Very well. Signal midshipman! Be ready with the private signal and our number."

Thank Heaven for all the signalling exercise he had been giving during the last few days.

"Captain, sir! I can see mastheads beyond her. Looks like a fleet."

"Very well, Mr. Jones, I'll have the gunner make ready to salute the flag, if you please."

"Aye aye, sir."

There was the Mediterranean Fleet, a score of ships of the line, moving slowly in two columns over the blue sea under a blue sky.

"Frigate's *Maenad*, 28, sir."

"Very well."

Reaching out like the tentacles of a sea monster, the scouting frigates lay far ahead of the main body of the fleet, four of them, with a fifth far to windward whence most likely would appear ships hostile or friendly. The air was clear; Hornblower on the quarter-deck with his glass to his eye could see the double column of topsails of ships of the line, close hauled, every ship exactly the same distance astern of her predecessor. He could see the vice-admiral's flag at the foremast of the leader of the weather line.

"Mr. Carslake! Have the mail-bags ready for sending off."

"Aye aye, sir."

His own packet of despatches for Collingwood was handy in his cabin.

"Signal midshipman! Can't you see the flagship's making a signal?"

"Yes, sir, but the flags are blowing straight away from us. I can't make them out."

"What do you think the repeating frigate's for? Use your eyes."

"General signal, sir. Number 41. That is 'tack', sir."

"Very well."

As *Atropos* had not yet officially joined the Mediterranean squadron a general signal could not apply to her. Down came the signal from the flagship's yardarm; that was the executive moment. Round came the flagship's yards; round came the yards of the scouting frigates, and of the leader of the lee column. One by one, at precise intervals, the succeeding ships in the columns came round in order; Hornblower could see the momentary backing and filling of the mizzen-topsails which maintained the ships so exactly spaced. It was significant that the drill was being carried out under all plain sail, and not merely under the "fighting sails". There was something thrilling in the sight of this perfection of drill; but at the same time something a little disturbing. Hornblower found himself wondering, with a qualm of doubt, if he would be able to maintain *Atropos* so exactly in station now that the time had come to join the fleet.

The manoeuvre was completed now; on its new tack the fleet was steadily plunging forward over the blue sea. There was more bunting fluttering at the flagship's yardarm.

"General signal, sir. 'Hands to dinner.' "

"Very well."

Hornblower felt a bubbling of excitement within him as he stood and watched. The next signal would surely be for him.

"Our number, sir! Flag to *Atropos*. Take station to windward of me at two cables' lengths."

"Very well. Acknowledge."

There were eyes turned upon him everywhere on deck. This was the moment of trial. He had to come down past the screening frigates, cross ahead of what was now the weather column, and come to the wind at the right moment and at the right distance. And the whole fleet would be watching the little ship. First he had to estimate how far the flagship would progress towards his starboard hand while he was running down to her. But there was nothing for it but to try; there was some faint comfort in being an officer in a fighting service where an order was something that must be obeyed.

"Quartermaster! Port a little. Meet her. Steady as you go! Keep her at that! Mr. Jones!"

"Aye aye, sir."

No need for an order to Jones. He was more anxious—at least more apparently anxious—than Hornblower was. He had the hands at the braces trimming the yards already. Hornblower looked up at yards and commission pendant to assure himself that the bracing was exact. They had left the *Maenad* behind already; here they were passing *Amphion*, one of the central frigates in the screen. Hornblower could see her lying over as she thrashed to windward, the spray flying from her bows. He turned back to look at the flagship, nearly hull up, at least two of her three rows of checkered gunports visible.

"Port a little! Steady!"

He resented having to give that additional order; he wished he could have headed straight for his station with no alteration of course. The leading ship—she wore a rear admiral's flag—of the weather column was now nearly on his port beam. Four cables' length was the distance between the two columns, but as his station was to windward of the flagship, nearly on her starboard beam, he would be by no means between the two ships, nor equidistant from them. He juggled in his mind with the scalene triangle that could be drawn connecting *Atropos* with the two flagships.

"Mr. Jones! Clue up the mizzen tops'l." Now *Atropos* would have a reserve of speed that he could call for if necessary. He was glad that he had subjected his crew to ceaseless sail drill ever since leaving Deptford. "Stand by the mizzen tops'l sheets."

The reduction in the after-sail would make *Atropos* a little slower in coming to the wind; he must bear it in mind. They were fast approaching their station. His eye darted from one column of ships to the other; he could see all the starboard sides of one and all the port sides of the other. It might be useful to take sextant angles, but he would rather trust his eye in a trigonometrical problem as uncomplicated as this. His judgment told him this must be the moment. The bows were pointing at the flagship's jib-boom.

"Port your helm," he ordered. Perhaps he was wrong. Perhaps the little ship's response would be delayed. Perhaps— He had to keep his voice steady. "Bring her to the wind."

The wheel spun over. There was a nervous second or two. Then he felt the heel of the ship alter under his feet; and he saw the flagship come round on *Atropos*' port beam, and he knew *Atropos* was turning.

"Steady!"

The yards were braced up; strong arms were hauling on the tacks. A moment or two while *Atropos* regained the small amount of way she had lost through her turn; but even making allowance for that he could see that the flagship was slowly head-reaching on her.

"Mr. Jones! Sheet home the mizzen tops'l."

With the mizzen topsail drawing full they would head-reach in turn upon the flagship.

"Keep the hands at the braces there!"

Occasionally spilling the wind from the mizzen topsail would enable *Atropos* to keep her speed equal to the flagship's. Hornblower felt the wind on his neck; he looked up at the pendant and at the flagship. He was exactly to windward of her, and there was two cables' lengths between them.

"Mr. Jones! You may begin the salute."

Fifteen guns for a vice-admiral, a minute and a quarter to fire them. That might be long enough for him to regain his composure, and for his heart to resume its normal rate of beating. Now they were part of the Mediterranean Fleet, the tiniest, most insignificant part of it. Hornblower looked down the massive lines of ships ploughing along behind them, three-deckers, two-deckers, ships of a hundred guns and ships of seventy-four, the ships which had fought at Trafalgar, the roar of whose cannons had dashed from Bonaparte's lips the heady cup of world domination. On the invisibly distant Mediterranean shores that encompassed them armies might march, kings might be set up and kings might be pulled down; but it was these ships which in the end would decide the destiny of the world, as long as the men who sailed them retained their skill, as long as they remained ready to endure danger and hardship, as long as the government at home remained resolute and unafraid.

"Our number, sir! Flag to *Atropos*. 'Welcome.' "

"Reply to Flag. 'Respectful greetings.' "

Eager hands worked vigorously on the signal halliards.

"Signal '*Atropos* to Flag. Have aboard dispatches and letters for fleet'."

"Flagship acknowledges, sir."

"Flagship's signalling again," announced Still; from a point of vantage on the weather side he could see through his glass enough of the flagship's quarter-deck, despite the fact that she was heeling away from him, to make out that signal ratings were bending fresh flags on the halliards. The dark lumps soared up to the flagship's yardarm and broke into gaily-coloured bunting.

"General signal. 'Heave to on the starboard tack.' "

"Acknowledge, Mr. Jones! Clue up the courses."

Hornblower watched the hands at the clue-garnets and buntlines, the hands at the tacks and sheets.

"Signal's down, sir."

Hornblower had already seen the first movement of descent.

"Back the mizzen tops'l. Let her come up."

Atropos rode easily, just meeting the waves with her bow, as the sharp struggle with the wind changed to yielding acquiescence, like a girl's resistance giving way in her lover's arms. But this was no time for that sort of sentimental simile—here was another long signal from the flagship.

"General signal. 'Send to'—our number, sir—'for letters.' "

"Mr. Carslake! Have those mail-bags on deck at once. You'll have a boat from every ship in the fleet alongside."

It was at least a month—it might well be two—since any letters had reached the Fleet from England. Not a newspaper, not a word. Possibly some of the ships present had not yet seen the accounts in the press of the victory they had won at Trafalgar four months before. *Atropos* had brought a respite from the dreadful isolation in which a fleet at sea habitually lived. Boats would be hastening as fast as sail or oar could drive them to collect the pitifully lean mail-bags.

Another signal.

"Our number, sir. 'Flag to *Atropos*. Come and report.' "

"Call away my gig."

He was wearing the shabbier of his two coats. There was just time, when he ran below to get the packets of dispatches, to change his coat, to pass a comb through his hair, and twitch his neckcloth into position. He was back on deck just as his gig touched the water. Lusty work at the oars carried him round to the flagship. A chair dangled at her side, now almost lipped as a wave rose at it, now high above the water as the wave passed on. He had to watch carefully for his chance; as it was there was an uncomfortable moment when he hung by his arms as the gig went away from under him. But he managed to seat himself, and he felt the chair soar swiftly upwards as the hands above hauled on the tackle. The pipes shrilled as his head reached the level of the main-deck and the chair was swung in. He stepped aboard with his hand to the brim of his hat.

The deck was as white as paper, as white as the gloves and the shirts of the sideboys. Gold leaf gleamed in the sun, the most elaborate Turks' heads adorned the ropework. The King's own yacht could not be smarter than the quarter-deck of the *Ocean*—that was what could be done in the flagship of a victorious admiral. It was as well to remember that Collingwood's previous flagship, the *Royal Sovereign*, had been pounded into a mastless hulk, with four hundred dead and wounded on board her, at Trafalgar. The lieutenant of the watch, his telescope quite dazzling with polished brass and pipe-clayed twine, wore spotless and unwrinkled white trousers; the buttons on his well-fitting coat winked in the sunshine. It occurred to Hornblower that to be always as smart as that, in a ship additionally crowded by the presence of an admiral and his staff, could be by no means easy. Service in a flagship might be the quick way to promotion, but there were many crumpled petals in the bed of roses. The flag captain, Rotherham—Hornblower knew his name; it had appeared in a hundred newspaper accounts of Trafalgar—and the flag lieutenant were equally smart as they made him welcome.

"His Lordship is awaiting you below, sir," said the flag lieutenant. "Will you come this way?"

Collingwood shook hands with him in the great cabin below. He was a large man, stoop-shouldered, with a pleasant smile. He eagerly took the packets Hornblower offered him, glancing at the superscriptions. One he kept in his hands, the others he gave to his secretary. He remembered his manners as he was about to break the seal.

"Please sit down, captain. Harkness, a glass of Madeira for Captain Hornblower. Or there is some Marsala that I can recommend, sir. Please forgive me for a moment. You will understand when I tell you these are letters from my wife."

It was an upholstered chair in which Hornblower sat; under his feet was a thick carpet; there were a couple of pictures in gilt frames on the bulkheads; silver lamps hung by silver chains from the deck-beams. Looking round him while Collingwood eagerly skimmed through his letters, Hornblower thought of all this being hurriedly bundled away when the *Ocean* cleared for action. But what held his attention most was two long boxes against the great stern windows. They were filled with earth and were planted with flowers—hyacinths and daffodils, blooming and lovely. The scent of the hyacinths reached Hornblower's nostrils where he sat. There was something fantastically charming about them here at sea.

"I've been successful with my bulbs this year," said Collingwood, putting his letters in his pocket and following Hornblower's glance. He walked over and tilted up a daffodil bloom with sensitive fingers, looking down into its open face. "They are beautiful, aren't they? Soon the daffodils will be flowering in England—some time, perhaps, I'll see them again. Meanwhile these help to keep me contented. It is three years since I last set foot on land."

Commanders-in-Chief might win peerages and pensions, but their children, too, grew up without knowing their fathers. And Collingwood had walked shot-torn decks in a hundred fights; but Hornblower, looking at the wistful smile, thought of other things than battles—thirty thousand turbulent seamen to be kept disciplined and efficient, court-martial findings to be confirmed, the eternal problems of provisions and water, convoys and blockade.

"You will give me the pleasure of your company at dinner, Captain?" asked Collingwood.

"I should be honoured, my lord."

It was gratifying to bring that phrase out pat like that, with hardly more than the least feeling of embarrassment.

"That is excellent. You will be able to tell me all the gossip of home. I fear there will be no other opportunity for some time, as *Atropos* will not be staying with the Fleet."

"Indeed, my lord?"

This was a moment of high excitement, when the future was about to be revealed to him. But of course the excitement must not be allowed to appear; only the guarded interest of a self-contained captain ready for anything.

"I fear so—not that you young captains with your saucy little ships want to stay tied to a fleet's apron strings."

Collingwood was smiling again, but there was something in the words that started a new train of thought in Hornblower's mind. Of course, Collingwood had watched the advent of the newest recruit to his fleet with a keen eye. Hornblower suddenly realized that if *Atropos* had been clumsy in taking up station, or dilatory in answering signals, his reception here might not have been so pleasant. He might be standing at attention at this moment submitting with a tight-shut mouth to a dressing-down exemplary in its drastic quality. The thought caused a little prickling of gooseflesh at the back of his neck. It reduced his reply to a not very coherent mumble.

"You have this man McCullum and his natives on board?" asked Collingwood.

"Yes, my lord."

Only a little self-restraint was necessary to refrain from asking what the mission would be; Collingwood would tell him.

"You are not acquainted with the Levant?"

"No, my lord."

So it was to be the Levant, among the Turks and the Greeks and the Syrians.

"You soon will be, captain. After taking my dispatches to Malta you will convey Mr. McCullum to Marmorice Bay and assist him in his operations there."

Marmorice Bay? That was on the coast of Asia Minor. The fleet and transports which had attacked Egypt some years ago had rendezvoused there. It was a far cry from Deptford.

"Aye aye, my lord," said Hornblower.

"I understand you have no sailing master in *Atropos*."

"No, my lord. Two master's mates."

"In Malta you will have a sailing master assigned to you. George Turner; he is familiar with Turkish waters and he was with the fleet in Marmorice. He took the bearings when *Speedwell* sank."

Speedwell? Hornblower raked back in his memory. She was the transport which had capsized and sunk at her anchors in a sudden gale of wind in Marmorice Bay.

"Yes, my lord."

"She had on board the military chest of the expeditionary force. I don't expect you knew that."

"No, indeed, my lord."

"A very considerable sum in gold and silver coin for the pay and subsistence of the troops—a quarter of a million sterling. She sank in water far deeper than any diver in the service could reach. But as no one knew what our gallant allies the Turks might contrive by way of salvage with infinite leisure it was decided to keep the loss a secret. And for once a secret remained a secret."

"Yes, my lord."

Certainly it was not common knowledge that a quarter of a million in coin lay at the bottom of Marmorice Bay.

"So the Government had to send to India for divers who could reach those depths."

"I see, my lord."

"Now it will be your duty to go to Marmorice Bay and with the assistance of McCullum and Turner to recover that treasure."

"Aye aye, my lord."

No imagination could ever compass the possible range of duties of a naval officer. But it was satisfactory that the words he had just uttered were the only ones a naval officer could say in such circumstances.

"You will have to be careful in your dealings with our friend the Turk. He will be curious about your presence in Marmorice, and when he ascertains the object of your visit he may raise objections. You will have to conduct yourself according to the circumstances of the moment."

"Aye aye, my lord."

"You will not find all this in your orders, captain. But you must understand that the Cabinet has no wish for complications with the Turks. Yet at the same time a quarter of a million sterling in cash would be a Godsend to the Government today—or any day. The money is badly needed, but no offence should be offered to the Turks."

It was necessary to steer clear of Scylla and yet not fall into Charybdis, said Hornblower to himself.

"I think I understand, my lord."

"Fortunately it is an unfrequented coast. The Turks maintain very small forces, either military or naval, in the locality. That does not mean that you should attempt to carry off matters with a high hand."

Not in *Atropos* with eleven popguns a side, thought Hornblower, and then he mentally withdrew the sneer. He understood what Collingwood meant.

"No, my lord."

"Very well then, captain, thank you."

The secretary at Collingwood's elbow had a pile of opened despatches in hand, and was clearly waiting for a break in the conversation to give him an opportunity to intervene, and the flag lieutenant was hovering in the background. Both of them moved in at once.

"Dinner will be in half an hour, my lord," said the flag lieutenant.

"These are the urgent letters, my lord," said the secretary.

Hornblower rose to his feet in some embarrassment.

"Perhaps, captain, you would enjoy a turn on the quarterdeck, eh?" asked Collingwood. "Flags here would keep you company, I'm sure."

When a vice-admiral made suggestions to a captain and a flag lieutenant he did not have to wait long before they were acted upon. But out on the quarterdeck, pacing up and down making polite conversation, Hornblower could have wished that Collingwood had not been so thoughtful as to provide him with company. He had a great deal to think about.

X

Malta; Ricasoli Point on the one hand and Fort St. Elmo returning the salute on the other, and the Grand Harbour opening up between them; Valetta with its palaces on the promontory; gaily painted small craft everywhere; a fresh north-easterly wind blowing. That wind—the Gregale, the sailing directions called it—did not allow Hornblower any leisure at present for sightseeing. In confined waters a sailing ship before the wind always seemed pig-headedly determined to maintain her speed however much her canvas was reduced, even under bare poles. It called for accurate timing to round-to at the right moment, to take her way off her, to clue up, and drop anchor at the right moment.

Nor would there be any leisure for Hornblower, it appeared, during the few hours that he would be here. He could combine his official calls with his personal delivery of the despatches entrusted to him, which would save a good deal of time, but that saving was immediately eaten up—as the fat kine of Pharaoh's dream were eaten up by the lean kine—by the demands on his attention, and, just as the lean kine were no fatter after their meal, so he was just as busy even when his planning had saved that much time. It would be quarter-day, or as near to it as made no matter, by the time letters from Malta would reach England, so that now he could draw against his pay. Not to any great extent, of course—there were Maria and the children to be considered—but enough to provide himself with a few luxuries in this island where bread was dear and luxuries cheap. Oranges and olives and fresh vegetables—the bum-boats were already awaiting permission to come alongside.

McCullum, with his salvage operations in mind, was anxious for an indent to be made for supplies he considered necessary. He wanted a mile of half-inch line and a quarter mile of slow match—a fantastic demand, to Hornblower's mind, but McCullum knew more about his business than he did, presumably—and five hundred feet of leather "fuse-hose", which was something Hornblower had hardly heard of. Hornblower signed the indent wondering vaguely whether the Navy Office would surcharge him with it, and turned away to face the inevitable fact that every officer in the ship wished to go ashore and was presenting irrefutable reasons to Jones in favour of his so doing. If *Atropos* had been on fire they could not be more passionately anxious to be out of her.

And here was another complication; a note from His Excellency the

Governor. Would Captain Hornblower and one of his officers dine at the Palace this afternoon? It would be impossible to refuse, so no time need be wasted on debate regarding that point—His Excellency was just as anxious as any ordinary mortal to hear the gossip from England and to see a new face—while there was equally no debate regarding which officer he should take with him. His Excellency would never forgive him if he heard who had been on board *Atropos* and he had not been afforded the opportunity of seating royalty at his table.

"Pass the word for Mr. Prince," said Hornblower, "and the doctor."

It would be necessary to have the doctor to interpret to the Prince exactly what was going to happen; the boy had learned a good deal of English during his month on board, but the vocabulary of the gunroom was hardly inclusive enough to permit of discussions of vice-regal etiquette. The Prince came in a little breathless, still twitching his uniform into some kind of order; Eisenbeiss was breathing hard too—he had to come the whole length of the ship and through a narrow hatchway.

"Please explain to His Serene Highness," said Hornblower, "that he is coming ashore with me to dine with the Governor."

Eisenbeiss spoke in German, and the boy gave his mechanical little bow. The use of German evoked the manners of royalty from under the new veneer of a British midshipman.

"His Serene Highness is to wear his court dress?" asked Eisenbeiss.

"No," said Hornblower, "his uniform. And if ever I see him again with his shoes as badly brushed as those are I'll take the cane to him."

"Sir—" said Eisenbeiss, but words failed him. The thought of the cane being applied to his Prince struck him dumb; fortunately, perhaps.

"So that I am to wear this uniform too, sir?" asked Eisenbeiss.

"I fear you have not been invited, doctor," said Hornblower.

"But I am First Chamberlain to His Serene Highness, sir," exploded Eisenbeiss. "This will be a visit of ceremony, and it is a fundamental law of Seitz-Bunau that I make all presentations."

Hornblower kept his temper.

"And I represent His Britannic Majesty," he said.

"Surely His Britannic Majesty cannot wish that his ally should not be treated with the honours due to his royal position? As Secretary of State it is my duty to make an official protest."

"Yes," said Hornblower. He put out his hand and bent the Prince's head forward. "You might be better employed seeing that His Serene Highness washes behind his ears."

"Sir! Sir!" said Eisenbeiss.

"Be ready and properly dressed in half an hour, if you please, Mr. Prince."

Dinner at the Palace ran the dreary course it might be expected to take. It was fortunate that, on being received by the Governor's aide-de-camp, Hornblower was able to shuffle on to his shoulders the burden of the difficult decision regarding the presentations—Hornblower could not guess whether His Serene Highness should be presented to His Excellency or vice versa, and he was a little amused to note Her Excellency's hurried asides when she heard the quality of her second guest; the seating arrangements for dinner needed hasty revision. So Hornblower found himself between two dull women, one of them with red hands and the other with a chronic sniff. He struggled to make polite conversation, and he was careful with his wine-glass, contriving merely to sip when the others drank deep.

The Governor drank to His Serene Highness the Prince of Seitz-Bunau, and the Prince, with the most perfect aplomb, drank to His Majesty the King of Great Britain; presumably those were the first words of English he had ever learned, long before he had learned to shout "Vast heaving" or "Come on, you no-sailors, you". When the ladies had withdrawn Hornblower listened to His Excellency's comments about Bonaparte's threatening invasion of Southern Italy, and about the chances of preserving Sicily from his clutches; and a decent interval after returning to the drawing-room he caught the Prince's eye. The Prince smiled back at him and rose to his feet. It was odd to watch him receiving the bows of the men and the curtseys of the ladies with the assurance of ingrained habit. Tomorrow the boy would be in the gunroom mess again—Hornblower wondered whether he was able yet to stand up for his rights there and make sure he received no more than his fair share of gristle when the meat was served.

The gig whisked them across the Grand Harbour from the Governor's steps to the ship's side, and Hornblower came on to the quarter-deck with the bos'n's mates' pipes to welcome him. He was conscious even before he had taken his hand from his hat brim that there was something wrong. He looked round him at the ship illuminated by the wild sunset the Gregale had brought with it. There was no trouble with the hands, judging by their attitudes as they stood crowded forward. The three Ceylonese divers were there in their accustomed isolation by the knight-heads. But the officers grouped aft wore an apprehensive look; Hornblower's eyes moved from face to face, from Jones to Still, the two lieutenants, to Carslake, the purser, and to Silver, the master's mate of the watch. It was Jones as senior officer who came forward to report.

"If you please, sir—"

"What is it, Mr. Jones?"

"If you please, sir, there has been a duel."

No one could ever guess what would be the next burden to be laid on a captain's shoulders. It might be an outbreak of plague, or the discovery of dry rot in the ship's timbers. And Jones's manner implied not merely that there had been a duel, but that someone had been hurt in it.

"Who fought?" demanded Hornblower.

"The doctor and Mr. McCullum, sir."

Well, somewhere they could pick up another doctor, and if the worst came to the worst they could manage without one at all.

"What happened?"

"Mr. McCullum was shot through the lungs, sir."

God! That was something entirely different, something of vital importance. A bullet through the lungs meant death almost for certain, and what was he to do with McCullum dead? McCullum had been sent for all the way from India. It would take a year and a half to get someone out from there to replace him. No ordinary men with salvage experience would do—it had to be someone who knew how to use the Ceylonese divers. Hornblower wondered with sick despair whether a man had ever been so plagued as he was. He had to swallow before he could speak again.

"Where is he now?"

"Mr. McCullum, sir? He's in the hands of the garrison surgeon in the hospital ashore."

"He's still alive?"

Jones spread despairing hands.

"Yes, sir. He was alive half an hour ago."

"Where's the doctor?"

"Down below in his berth, sir."

"I'll see him. No, wait. I'll send for him when I want him."

He wanted to think; he needed time and leisure to decide what was to be done. It was his instinct to walk the deck; that was how he could work off the high internal pressure of his emotions. It was only incidentally that the rhythmic exercise brought his thoughts into orderly sequence. And this little deck was crowded with idle officers—his cabin down below was of course quite useless. That was the moment when Jones came forward with something else to bother him.

"Mr. Turner's come aboard, sir."

Mr. Turner? Turner? That was the sailing master with experience of Turkish waters whom Collingwood had detailed specially to service in *Atropos*. He came from behind Jones as the words were said, a wizened old man with a letter in his hand, presumably the orders which had brought him on board.

"Welcome aboard, Mr. Turner," said Hornblower, forcing himself into cordiality while wondering whether he would ever make use of Turner's services.

"Your servant, sir," said Turner with old-fashioned politeness.

"Mr. Jones, see that Mr. Turner's comfortable."

"Aye aye, sir."

That was the only reply Jones could make, however hard of execution the order might be. But clearly Jones meditated some supplementary remark; it could be that he was going to suggest putting Turner into McCullum's quarters. Hornblower could not bear the thought of having to listen to anything of the sort while he had yet to reach a decision. It was the final irritation that roused him to the pitch of acting with the arbitrariness of a captain of the old school.

"Get below, all of you," he snapped. "I want this deck clear."

They looked at him as if they had not heard him aright, and he knew they had.

"Get below, if you please," he said, and the "if you please" did nothing to soften the harshness of his request. "Master's mate of the watch, see that this deck is kept clear, and keep out of my way yourself."

They went below—this was an order from the captain who (according to the reports of his gig's crew) had barely been diverted from hanging a dozen French prisoners for no other reason than a desire to see their death struggles. So he had the quarter-deck to himself, on which to stride up and down, from taffrail to mizzen mast and back again, in the fast-fading twilight. He walked rapidly, turning with a jerk at each end, irritation and worry goading him on.

He had to reach a decision. The obvious thing to do was to report to Collingwood and await further orders. But how long would it be before any vessel left Malta with letters for Collingwood, and how long would it be before another returned? A month altogether, probably. No captain worth his salt would keep *Atropos* lying idle in Grand Harbour for a month. He could guess what Collingwood would think of a man who evaded responsibility like that. He could take *Atropos* and seek out Collingwood himself, but the same objections applied. And how would he appear in Collingwood's eyes if he were to arrive off Toulon or Leghorn or wherever the chances of war might have summoned Collingwood, at the moment when he was supposed to be two thousand miles away? No. No. It would never do. At least he had reduced two apparent possibilities to impossibilities.

Then he must proceed with his orders as if nothing had happened to McCullum. That meant he must undertake the salvage operations himself, and he knew nothing about the subject. A wave of fury passed over him as his mind dwelt on the inconvenience and loss occasioned by the duel. The idiotic Eisenbeiss and the bad-tempered McCullum. They had no business incommoding England in her struggle with Bonaparte merely to satisfy their own ridiculous passions. He himself had borne with Eisenbeiss's elephantine nonsense. Why could not McCullum have done the same? And in any event why could not McCullum have held his pistol straighter and killed the ridiculous doctor instead of getting killed himself? But that sort of rhetorical question did not get him any further with his own urgent problems; he must not think along those lines. Moreover, with a grinding feeling of guilt another consideration crept in. He should have been aware of bad blood between the people in his ship. He remembered the lighthearted way in which he had put on Jones's shoulders the responsibility for accommodating McCullum in his crowded little ship. In the wardroom the doctor and McCullum had probably got on each other's nerves; there could be no doubt about that—and presumably ashore, over wine in some tavern, the enmity had flared up and brought about the duel. He should have known about the possibility and nipped it in the bud. Hornblower scourged himself spiritually for his remissness. He experienced bitter self-contempt at that moment. Perhaps he was unfit to be captain of one of His Majesty's ships.

The thought brought about an even greater internal upheaval. He could not bear it. He must prove to himself that there was no truth in it, or he must break himself in the attempt. He must carry through that salvage operation by his own efforts if necessary. He must. He *must*.

So that was the decision. He had only to reach it for the emotion to die down within him, to leave him thinking feverishly but clearly. He must of course do everything possible to ensure success, omit nothing that could help. McCullum had indented for "leather fuse-hose"; that was some indication of how the salvage problem was to be approached. And McCullum was not yet dead, as far as he knew. He might—no, it was hardly possible. No one ever survived a bullet through the lungs. And yet—

"Mr. Nash!"

"Sir!" said the master's mate of the watch, coming at the run.

"My gig. I'm going over to the hospital."

There was still just a little light in the sky, but overside the water was black as ink, reflecting in long, irregular lines the lights that showed in Valetta. The oars ground rhythmically in the rowlocks. Hornblower restrained himself from urging the men to pull harder. They could never have rowed fast enough to satisfy the pressing need for instant action that seethed inside him.

The garrison officers were still at mess, sitting over their wine, and the mess sergeant, at Hornblower's request, went in and fetched out the surgeon. He was a youngish man, and fortunately still sober. He stood with the candle-light on his face and listened attentively to Hornblower's questions.

"The bullet hit him in the right armpit," said the surgeon. "One would expect that, as he would be standing with his shoulder turned to his opponent and his arm raised. The actual wound was on the posterior margin of the armpit, towards the back, in other words, and on the level of the fifth rib."

The heart was on the level of the fifth rib, as Hornblower knew, and the expression had an ominous sound.

"I suppose the bullet did not go right through?" he asked.

"No," replied the surgeon. "It is very rare for a pistol bullet, if it touches bone, to go through the body, even at twelve paces. The powder charge is only one drachm. Naturally the bullet is still there, presumably within the chest cavity."

"So he is unlikely to live?"

"Very unlikely, sir. It is a surprise he has lived so long. The haemoptysis—the spitting of blood, you understand, sir—has been extremely slight. Most chest wounds die of internal bleeding within an hour or two, but in this case the lung can hardly have been touched. There is considerable contusion under the right scapula—that is the shoulder blade—indicating that the bullet terminated its course there."

"Close to the heart?"

"Close to the heart, sir. But it can have touched none of the great vessels there, most surprisingly, or he would have been dead within a few seconds."

"Then why do you think he will not live?"

The doctor shook his head.

"Once an opening has been made in the chest cavity, sir, there is little chance, and with the bullet still inside the chance is negligible. It will certainly have carried fragments of clothing in with it. We may expect internal mortification, in general gathering of malignant humours, and eventual death within a few days."

"You could not probe for the bullet?"

"Within the chest wall? My dear sir!"

"What action have you taken, then?"

"I have bound up the wound of entry to put an end to the bleeding there. I have strapped up the chest to ensure that the jagged ends of the broken ribs do no more damage to the lungs. I took two ounces of blood from the left basilar vein, and I administered an opiate."

"An opiate? So he is not conscious now?"

"Certainly not."

Hornblower felt hardly wiser than he had done when Jones first told him the news.

"You say he may live a few days? How many?"

"I know nothing about the patient's constitution, sir. But he is a powerful man in the prime of life. It might be as much as a week. It might even be more. But on the other hand if events take a bad turn he might be dead tomorrow."

"But if it is several days? Will he retain his senses during that time?"

"Likely enough. When he ceases to, it is a sign of the approaching end. Then we can expect fever, restlessness, delirium, and death."

Several days of consciousness were possible, therefore. And the faintest, remotest chance that McCullum would live after all.

"Supposing I took him to sea with me? Would that help? Or hinder?"

"You would have to ensure his immobility on account of the fractured ribs. But at sea he might even live longer. There are the usual Mediterranean agues in this island. And in addition there is an endemic low fever. My hospital is full of such cases."

Now this was a piece of information that really helped in coming to a decision.

"Thank you, doctor," said Hornblower, and he took his decision. Then it was only a matter of minutes to make the arrangements with the surgeon and to take his leave. The gig took him back through the darkness, over the black water, to where *Atropos*' riding light showed faintly.

"Pass the word for the doctor to come to my cabin at once," was Hornblower's reply to the salute of the officer of the watch.

Eisenbeiss came slowly in. There was something of apprehension and something of bravado in his manner. He was prepared to defend himself against the storm he was certain was about to descend on him. What he did not expect was the reception he actually experienced. He approached the table behind which Hornblower was seated and stood sullen, meeting Hornblower's eyes with the guilty defiance of a man who has just taken another human's life.

"Mr. McCullum," began Hornblower, and the doctor's thick lips showed a trace of a sneer, "is being sent on board here tonight. He is still alive."

"On board here?" repeated the doctor, surprised into a change of attitude.

"You address me as 'sir'. Yes, I am having him sent over from the hospital. My orders to you are to make every preparation for his reception."

The doctor's response was unintelligible German, but there could be no doubt it was an ejaculation of astonishment.

"Your answer to me is 'aye aye, sir'," snapped Hornblower, his pent-up emotion and strain almost making him tremble as he sat at the table. He could not prevent his fist from clenching, but he just managed to refrain from allowing it to pound the table. The intensity of his feelings must have had their effect telepathically.

"Aye aye, sir," said the doctor grudgingly.

"Mr. McCullum's life is extremely valuable, doctor. Much more valuable than yours."

The doctor could only mumble in reply to that.

"It is your duty to keep him alive."

Hornblower's fist unclenched now, and he could make his points slowly, one by one, accentuating each with the slow tap of the tip of a lean forefinger on the table.

"You are to do all you can for him. If there is anything special that you require for the purpose you are to inform me and I shall endeavour to obtain it for you. His life is to be saved, or if not, it is to be prolonged as far as possible. I would recommend you to establish a hospital for him abaft No. 6 carronade on the starboard side, where the motion of the ship will be least felt, and where it will be possible to rig a shelter for him from the weather. You will apply to Mr. Jones for that. The ship's pigs can be taken for'rard where they will not discommode him."

Hornblower's pause and glance called forth an "aye aye, sir" from the doctor's lips like a cork from out of a bottle, so that Hornblower could proceed.

"We sail at dawn tomorrow," he went on. "Mr. McCullum is to live until we reach our destination, and until long after, long enough for him to execute the duty which has brought him from India. That is quite clear to you?"

"Yes, sir," answered the doctor, although his puzzled expression proved that there was something about the orders which he could not explain to himself.

"You had better keep him alive," continued Hornblower. "You had certainly better. If he dies I can try you for murder under the ordinary laws of England. Don't look at me like that. I am speaking the truth. The common law knows nothing about duels. I can hang you, doctor."

The doctor was a shade paler, and his big hands tried to express what his paralyzed tongue would not.

"But simply hanging you would be too good for you, doctor," said Hornblower. "I can do more than that, and I shall. You have a fat, fleshy back. The cat would sink deeply into it. You've seen men flogged—you saw two flogged last week. You heard them scream. You will scream at the gratings too, doctor. That I promise you."

"No!" said the doctor—"you can't—"

"You address me as 'sir', and you do not contradict me. You heard my promise? I shall carry it out. I can, and I shall."

In a ship detached far from superior authority there was nothing a captain might not do, and the doctor knew it. And with Hornblower's grim face before him and those remorseless eyes staring into his the doctor could not doubt the possibility. Hornblower was trying to keep his expression set hard, and to pay no attention to the internal calculations that persisted in maintaining themselves inside him. There might be terrible trouble if the Admiralty ever heard he had flogged a warranted doctor, but then the Admiralty might never hear of an incident in the distant Levant. And there was the other doubt—with McCullum once dead, so that nothing could bring him to life, Hornblower could not really believe he would torture a human being to no practical purpose. But as long as Eisenbeiss did not guess that, it did not matter.

"That is all quite clear to you now, doctor?"

"Yes, sir."

"Then my order is that you start making your arrangements now."

It was a really great surprise to Hornblower when Eisenbeiss still hesitated. He was about to speak more sharply still, cutting into the feverish gestures of the big hands, when Eisenbeiss spoke again.

"Do you forget something, sir?"

"What do you think I have forgotten?" asked Hornblower, playing for time instead of flatly refusing to listen to any arguments—proof enough that he was a little shaken by Eisenbeiss's persistence.

"Mr. McCullum and I—we are enemies," said Eisenbeiss.

It was true that Hornblower had forgotten that. He was so engrossed with his chessboard manipulation of human pieces that he had overlooked a vital factor. But he must not admit it.

"And what of that?" he asked coldly, hoping his discomfiture was not too apparent.

"I shot him," said Eisenbeiss. There was a vivid gesture by the big right hand that had held the pistol, which enabled Hornblower to visualize the whole duel. "What will he say if I attend him?"

"Whose was the challenge?" asked Hornblower, still playing for time.

"He challenged me," said Eisenbeiss. "He said—he said I was no Baron, and I said he was no gentleman. 'I will kill you for that,' he said, and so we fought."

Eisenbeiss had certainly said the thing that would best rouse McCullum's fury.

"You are convinced you are a Baron?" asked Hornblower—curiosity urged him to ask the question as well as the need for time to reassemble his thoughts. The Baron drew himself up as far as the deck-beams over his head allowed.

"I know I am, sir. My patent of nobility is signed by His Serene Highness himself."

"When did he do that?"

"As soon as—as soon as we were alone. Only His Serene Highness and I managed to cross the frontier when Bonaparte's men entered Seitz-Bunau. The others all took service with the tyrant. It was not fit that His Serene Highness should be attended only by a bourgeois. Only a noble could attend him to bed or serve his food. He had to have a High Chamberlain to regulate his ceremonial, and a Secretary of State to manage his foreign affairs. So His Serene Highness ennobled me—that is why I bear the title of Baron—and gave me the high offices of State.

"On your advice?"

"I was the only adviser he had left."

This was very interesting and much as Hornblower had imagined it, but it was not the point. Hornblower was more ready now to face the real issue.

"In the duel," he asked, "you exchanged shots?"

"His bullet went past my ear," answered Eisenbeiss.

"Then honour is satisfied on both sides," said Hornblower, more to himself than to the doctor.

Technically that was perfectly correct. An exchange of shots, and still more the shedding of blood, ended any affair of honour. The principals could meet again socially as if there had been no trouble between them. But to meet in the relative positions of doctor and patient might be something different. He would have to deal with that difficulty when it arose.

"You are quite right to remind me about this, doctor," he said, with the last appearance of judicial calm that he could summon up. "I shall bear it in mind."

Eisenbeiss looked at him a little blankly, and Hornblower put on his hard face again.

"But it makes no difference at all to my promise to you. Rest assured of that," he continued. "My orders still stand. They—still—stand."

It was several seconds before the reluctant answer came.

"Aye aye, sir."

"On your way out would you please be good enough to pass the word for Mr. Turner, the new sailing master?"

"Aye aye, sir."

That showed the subtle difference between an order and a request—but both of them had to be obeyed.

"Now, Mr. Turner," said Hornblower when Turner arrived in the cabin, "our destination is Marmorice Bay, and we sail at dawn tomorrow. I want to know about the winds we can expect at this time of year. I want to lose no time at all in arriving there. Every hour—I may say every minute is of importance."

Time was of importance, to make the most of a dying man's last hours.

XI

These were the blue waters where history had been made, where the future of civilization had been decided, more than once and more than twice. Here Greek had fought against Persian, Athenian against Spartan, Crusader against Saracen, Hospitaller against Turk. The penteconters of Byzantium had furrowed the seas here, and the caracks of Pisa. Great cities had luxuriated in untold wealth. Only just over the horizon on the port beam was Rhodes, where a comparatively minor city had erected one of the seven wonders of the world, so that two thousand years later the adjective colossal was part of the vocabulary of people whose ancestors wore skins and painted themselves with woad at the time when the Rhodians were debating the nature of the Infinite. Now conditions were reversed. Here came *Atropos*, guided by sextant and compass, driven by the wind harnessed to her well-planned sails, armed with her long guns and carronades—a triumph of modern invention, in short —emerging from the wealthiest corner of the world into one where misgovernment and disease, anarchy and war, had left deserts where there had been fertile fields, villages where there had been cities, and hovels where there had been palaces. But there was no time to philosophize in this profound fashion. The sands in the hour-glass beside the binnacle were running low, and the moment was approaching when course should be altered.

"Mr. Turner!"

"Sir!"

"We'll alter course when the watch is called."

"Aye aye, sir."

"Doctor!"

"Sir!"

"Stand by for a change of course."

"Aye aye, sir."

McCullum's invalid bed was disposed athwart ships between Nos. 6 and 7 carronades on the starboard side; a simple tackle attached to the bedhead enabled the level of the bed to be adjusted with the change of course, so that the patient lay as horizontal as might be, whichever way the ship might be heeling. It was the doctor's responsibility to attend to that.

The watch was being called.

"Very good, Mr. Turner."

"Headsail sheets! Hands to the braces!"

Turner was an efficient seaman, despite his age. Hornblower could be sure of that by now. He stood by and watched him lay the ship close to the wind. Still came and touched his hat to Turner to take over the watch.

"We ought to raise the Seven Capes on this tack, sir," said Turner, coming over to Hornblower.

"I fancy so," said Hornblower.

The passage from Malta had been comfortingly rapid. They had lain becalmed for a single night to the south of Crete, but with the morning the wind had got up again from a westerly quarter. There had not been a single breath of Levanter—the equinox was still too far off for that, apparently—and every day had seen at least a hundred miles made good. And McCullum was still alive.

Hornblower walked forward to where he lay. Eisenbeiss was bending over him, his fingers on his pulse, and with the cessation of the bustle of going about the three Ceylonese divers had returned, to squat round the foot of the bed, their eyes on their master. To have those three pairs of melancholy eyes gazing at him would, Hornblower thought, have a most depressing effect, but apparently McCullum had no objection.

"All well, Mr. McCullum?" asked Hornblower.

"Not—quite as well as I would like."

It was distressing to see how slowly and painfully the head turned on the pillow. The heavy beard that had sprouted over his face could not conceal the fact that McCullum was more hollow-cheeked, more feverish-eyed, than yesterday. The decline had been very marked; the day they sailed McCullum had appeared hardly more than slightly wounded, and the second day he had seemed better still—he had protested against being kept in bed, but that night he had taken a turn for the worse and had sunk steadily ever since, just as the garrison surgeon and Eisenbeiss had gloomily predicted.

Of course those had not been his only protests. McCullum had been as angry as his muddled condition would allow when he emerged from his narcotic to find he was under the treatment of the man who had shot him. He had struggled against his weakness and his bandages. It had called for Hornblower's personal intervention—fortunately *Atropos* was clear of the harbour mouth when McCullum regained consciousness—to calm him down. "It's a blackguard trick to pursue an affair of honour after an exchange of shots," Hornblower had said, and "It's the Doctor who's attending to you, not the Baron," and then the clinching argument "Don't be a fool, man. There's no other surgeon within fifty miles. Do you want to die?" So McCullum had yielded, and had submitted his tortured body to Eisenbeiss's ministrations, perhaps deriving some comfort from the ignoble things the doctor had to do for him.

And now all that spirit had gone. McCullum was a very sick man. He closed his eyes as Eisenbeiss laid his hand on his forehead. The pale lips muttered, and Hornblower, stooping, could only hear disjointed phrases. There was something about "fuses under water". McCullum was thinking, then, of the salvage operation ahead. Hornblower looked up and met Eisenbeiss's eyes. There was deep concern in them, and there was the least perceptible shake of the head. Eisenbeiss thought McCullum was going to die.

"It hurts—it hurts," said McCullum, moaning a little.

He moved restlessly, and Eisenbeiss's large powerful hands eased him into a more comfortable position on his left side. Hornblower noticed that Eisenbeiss laid one hand, as if inquiringly, over McCullum's right shoulder-blade, and then lower down, towards the short ribs, and McCullum moaned again. There was no change in the gravity of Eisenbeiss's expression.

This was horrible. It was horrible to see this magnificently constructed creature dying. And it was equally horrible that Hornblower was aware that his deep sympathy was allayed with concern for himself. He could not imagine how he would carry through the salvage operation with McCullum dead, or even with McCullum as helpless as he was at present. He would return empty-handed, to face Collingwood's wrath and contempt. What was the use of all his endeavours? Hornblower suddenly boiled with exasperation at the duelling convention which had claimed the life of a valuable man and at the same time had imperilled his own professional reputation. Within himself he was a whirlpool of emotions conflicting with each other.

"Land! Land ho! Land on the starboard bow!"

The cry came ringing down from the fore topmast head. No one could hear it without at least a little excitement. McCullum opened his eyes and turned his head again, but Eisenbeiss, stooping over him, endeavoured to soothe him. Hornblower's place was aft, and he turned away from the bed and walked back, trying to restrain himself from appearing too eager. Turner was already there, brought up from his watch below at the cry, and by the lee bulwark the other officers were rapidly assembling in a group.

"A good landfall, sir," said Turner.

"An hour earlier than I was led to expect," answered Hornblower.

"The current sets northerly here with steady winds from the West, sir," said Turner. "We'll raise Atairo in Rhodes to port soon, and then we'll have a cross-bearing."

"Yes," replied Hornblower. He was aware of his shortness of manner, but only dimly aware of its cause; he was uneasy with a sailing master on board who knew more about local conditions than he did, although that sailing master had been assigned to him to save him from uneasiness.

Atropos was shouldering her way valiantly through the short but steep seas that came hurrying forward to assail her port bow. Her motion was easy; she was carrying exactly the right amount of sail for that wind. Turner put a telescope in his pocket and walked forward to ascend the main shrouds, while Hornblower stood on the weather side with the wind blowing against his sunburned cheeks. Turner came aft again, his smile denoting self-satisfaction.

"That's the Seven Capes, sir," he said. "Two points on the starboard bow."

"There's a northerly set here, you say?" asked Hornblower.

"Yes, sir."

Hornblower walked over and looked at the compass, and up at the trim of the sails. The northerly set would help, and the wind was coming from the southward of west, but there was no sense in going unnecessarily far to leeward.

"Mr. Still! You can come closer to the wind than this. Brace her up."

He did not want to have to beat his way in at the last, and he was making allowance for the danger of the current setting in on Cape Kum.

Now here was the doctor, touching his hat to demand attention.

"What is it, doctor?" asked Hornblower.

The hands were hauling on the maintack.

"May I speak to you, sir?"

That was exactly what he was doing, and at a moment by no means opportune. But of course what he wanted was a chance to speak to him in privacy, and not on this bustling deck.

"It's about the patient, sir," supplemented Eisenbeiss. "I think it is very important."

"Oh, very well," said Hornblower, restraining himself from using bad language. He led the way down into the cabin, and seated himself to face the doctor. "Well? What do you have to say?"

Eisenbeiss was nervous, that was plain.

"I have formed a theory, sir."

He failed, as ever, with the "th" sound, and the word was so unusual and his pronunciation of it was so odd that Hornblower had to think for a moment before he could guess what it was Eisenbeiss had said.

"And what is this theory?"

"It is about the position of the bullet, sir," answered Eisenbeiss; he, too, took a moment to digest what was the English pronunciation of the word.

"The garrison surgeon at Malta told me it was in the chest cavity. Do you know any more than that?"

That expression "chest cavity" was an odd one, but the garrison surgeon had used it. It implied an empty space, and was an obvious misnomer. Lungs and heart and the great blood-vessels must fill that cavity full.

"I believe it may not be in there at all, sir," said Eisenbeiss, clearly taking a plunge.

"Indeed?" This might be exceedingly important news if it were true. "Then why is he so ill?"

Now that Eisenbeiss had committed himself he became voluble again. Explanations poured out of him, accompanied by jerky gestures. But the explanations were hard to follow. In this highly technical matter Eisenbeiss had been thinking in his native language even more than usual, and now he was having to translate into technical terms unfamiliar to him and still more unfamilar to Hornblower, who grasped despairingly at one contorted sentence.

"You think that the bullet, after breaking those ribs, may have bounced off again?" he asked. At the last moment he substituted the word "bounce" for "ricochet" in the hope of retaining clarity.

"Yes, sir. Bullets often do that."

"And where do you say you think it went then?"

Eisenbeiss tried to stretch his left hand far under his right armpit; his body was too bulky to permit it to go far enough to make his demonstration quite complete.

"Under the scapula, sir—the—the shoulder-blade."

"Land ho! Land on the port bow?"

Hornblower heard the cry come down through the skylight from above. That must be Rhodes they had sighted. Here they were heading into Rhodes Channel, and he was down below talking about ribs and scapulas. And yet the one was as important as the other.

"I can't stay down here much longer, doctor. Tell me why you think this is the case?"

Eisenbeiss fell into explanation again. He talked about the patient's fever, and about his comparative wellbeing the morning after he had been wounded, and about the small amount of blood he had spat up. He was in the full flood of his talk when a knock at the door interrupted him.

"Come in," said Hornblower.

It was His Serene Highness the Prince of Seitz-Bunau, with a speech that he had obviously prepared carefully on his way down.

"Mr. Still's respects, sir," he said. "Land in sight on the port bow."

"Very well, Mr. Prince. Thank you."

It was a pity there was not time to compliment the boy on his rapid acquirement of English. Hornblower turned back to Eisenbeiss.

"So I think the bullet went round the back, sir. The skin is—is tough, sir, and the ribs are—are elastic."

"Yes?" Hornblower had heard of bullets going round the body before this.

"And the patient has much muscle. Much."

"And you think the bullet has lodged in the muscles of the back?"

"Yes. Deep against the ribs. Under the lower point of the scapula, sir."

"And the fever? The illness?"

They could be accounted for, according to Eisenbeiss's torrential explanation, by the presence of the foreign body deep inside the tissues, especially if, as was probable, it had carried fragments of clothing in along with it. It all seemed plausible enough.

"And you are trying to say that if the bullet is there and not inside the chest you might be able to extract it?"

"Yes, sir."

Eisenbeiss showed by his manner that he knew that those words had finally committed him.

"You think that you can do that? It means using the knife?"

As soon as Hornblower finished asking the second question he was aware that it was impolitic to ask two questions at once of a man who had enough trouble answering one. Eisenbeiss had to think a long time over the phrasing of his answers.

"It means using the knife," he said at length. "It means a difficult operation. I do not know if I can do it."

"But you hope you can?"

"I hope so."

"And do you think you will be successful?"

"I do not think. I hope."

"And if you are not successful?"

"He will die."

"But you think he will die in any case if you do not attempt the operation?"

That was the point. Eisenbeiss twice opened his mouth and shut it again before he answered.

"Yes."

Down through the skylight, as Hornblower sat studying Eisenbeiss's expression, came a new cry, faintly borne from the weather main-chains.

"No bottom! No bottom with this line!"

Turner and Still had very properly decided to take a cast of the lead; they were still out of soundings, as was to be expected. Hornblower brought his mind back from the situation of the ship to the decision regarding McCullum. The latter might have some claim to be consulted on the matter, but the claim was specious. His life was his country's.

A seaman was not consulted first when he was carried into the ordeal of battle.

"So that is your opinion, doctor. If you operate and fail you will only have shortened the patient's life by a few hours?"

"A few hours. A few days."

A few days might suffice for the salvage operation; but with McCullum as sick as he was he would be no use during those few days. On the other hand there was no knowing at present whether or not he might possibly recover after those few days, without being operated on.

"What are the difficulties of the operation?" asked Hornblower.

"There are several layers of muscle there," explained Eisenbeiss. "Infraspinatus. Subscapularis, many of them. In each case the—the threads run in a different direction. That makes it difficult to work quickly and yet without doing great damage. And there is the big artery, the subscapular. The patient is weak already and unable to withstand much shock."

"Have you everything you need for this operation if you carry it out?"

Eisenbeiss hunched his thick shoulders.

"The two attendants—loblolly boys, you call them, sir—are experienced. They have both served in ships in action. I have my instruments. But I should like—"

Eisenbeiss clearly wanted something he believed to be difficult to grant.

"What?"

"I should like the ship to be still. At anchor. And a good light."

That turned the scale of the decision.

"Before nightfall," said Hornblower, "this ship will be at anchor in a landlocked harbour. You can make your preparations for the operation."

"Yes, sir." Again a pause before Eisenbeiss asked an important question. "And your promise, sir?"

Hornblower did not have to think very long about the question as to whether Eisenbeiss would work more efficiently or not if he were faced with the certainty of flogging and hanging if he failed. The man would do all he could out of sheer professional pride. And the thought that his life was at stake might possibly make him nervous.

"I'll take my promise back," said Hornblower. "You'll suffer no harm, whatever happens."

"Thank you, sir."

"No bottom!" called the leadsman in the chains.

"Very well, then. You have until this evening to make what preparations you can."

"Yes, sir. Thank you, sir."

With Eisenbeiss out of the cabin Hornblower sat for hardly a moment retracing the grounds of his decision. His ship was entering Rhodes Channel and he must be on deck.

"Wind's come southerly a point, sir," said Still, touching his hat.

The first thing, of course, that Hornblower had noticed as he came up the companion was that *Atropos* was still braced up as close to the wind as she would lie. Still and Turner had acted correctly without troubling him about it.

"Very well, Mr. Still."

Hornblower put his glass to his eye and swept the horizon. A bold, wildly rugged coast on the one hand; on the other a low sandy shore. He bent to study the chart.

"Cape Angistro to starboard, sir," said Turner at his side. "Cape Kum abaft the port beam."

"Thank you."

Everything was as it should be. Hornblower straightened up and turned his glass upon the Turkish coast. It was steep, with bold cliffs, behind which rose a chain of steeply undulating hills.

"They're only green at this time of year, sir," explained Turner. "The rest of the year they're brown."

"Yes."

Hornblower had read all he could about the Eastern Mediterranean, and he knew something of the climatic conditions.

"Not many people live there now, sir," went on Turner. "Farmers, a few. Shepherds. Little fishing villages in some of the coves. A little coasting trade in caiques from Rhodes—not so much of that now, sir. There's piracy in all these waters, on account of the feuds between the Greeks and the Turks. There's a bit of trade in honey an' timber, but precious little."

"Yes."

It was fortunate the wind had backed southerly, even by so little. It eased one of the myriad complications in his complicated life.

"Ruins a-plenty along that coast, though, sir," droned on Turner. "Cities—temples—you'd be surprised."

Ancient Greek civilization had flourished here. Over there had stood Artemisia and a score of other Greek cities, pulsating with life and beauty.

"Yes," said Hornblower.

"The villages mostly stand where the old cities were," persisted Turner. "Ruins all round 'em. Half the cottages are built of marble from the temples."

"Yes."

In other circumstances Hornblower could have been deeply interested, but as it was Turner was merely distraction. There was not merely the immediate business in hand of taking *Atropos* up into Marmorice harbour; there was the business of how to deal with the Turkish authorities; of how to set about the problems of salvage; there was the question—the urgent, anxious question—as to whether McCullum would live. There was the routine of the ship; when Hornblower looked round him he could see the hands and the officers clustered along the ship's sides gazing out eagerly at the shores. There were Greeks dwelling among the Mohammedans of the mainland—that would be important when it came to a question of keeping liquor from the men. And he would like to fill his water barrels; and there was the matter of obtaining fresh vegetables.

Here was Still with a routine question. Hornblower nodded in agreement.

"Up spirits!"

The cry went through the little ship, and when they heard it the men had no ears for any siren song from the shore. This was the great moment of the day for most of them, when they would pour their tiny issue of rum-and-water down their eager throats. To deprive a man of his ration was like barring a saint from Paradise. The speculations that went on among the men, their dealings with their rum rations, the exchanging, the buying, the selling, made the South Sea Bubble seem small by comparison. But Hornblower decided he need not vaunt himself above the herd, he need not look down with condescension at the men as if they were Circe's hogs swilling at a trough; it was perfectly true that this was the great moment of their day, but it was because they had no other moment at all, for months and for years, confined within the wooden walls of their little ship, often seeing not a shilling of money in all that time, not a fresh face, not a single human problem on which to exercise their wits. Perhaps it was better to be a captain and have too many problems.

The hands went to dinner. Cape Kum went by on the one hand and the Turkish coast on the other, the breeze freshening with the bright sunny day, and Turner droning on as the landmarks went by.

"Cape Marmorice, sir," reported Turner.

The coast dipped here, revealing mountains more lofty close behind. Now was the time to take in sail, ready to enter. It was the time when decisive action had to be taken, too; when *Atropos* changed from a peaceful ship, cruising placidly along outside territorial waters, to a stormy petrel, whose entrance into a foreign harbour might send despatches hastening from embassies, and might cause cabinets to assemble at opposite ends of Europe. Hornblower tried to give his orders as if he had no care for the importance of the moment.

"All hands! All hands shorten sail! All hands!"

The watch below came running to their posts. The officers, at the call of all hands, went to their stations, the one or two who had been dozing down below coming hastily on deck. Courses and top gallants were got in.

"Mr. Jones!" said Hornblower harshly.

"Sir!"

"Ease that sheet and take the strain off the tack! Where did you learn your seamanship?"

"Aye aye, sir," answered Jones rather pathetically, but he ran up both clues smartly together.

The reprimand was deserved, but Hornblower wondered if he would have administered it in just that way if he had not been anxious to show that the responsibilities he was carrying could not distract him from any detail of the management of the ship. Then he decided bitterly that it was unnecessary in any event; not one of those hurrying figures on deck gave a single thought to the responsibilities of his captain, or of what international crisis this shortening of sail might be the preliminary.

"Red Cliff Point, sir," said Turner. "Passage Island. Cape Sari over there. The east passage is better, sir—there's a rock in the middle of the west passage."

"Yes," said Hornblower. There was not much detail in the chart, but that much was clear. "We'll take the east passage. Quartermaster! Port your helm. Steady! Steady as you go!"

With the wind on her quarter *Atropos* headed for the entrance like a stag, even with her sail reduced to topsails and headsails. The entrance became better defined as she approached; two bold points running to meet each other with a lofty island in between. It was obvious why Red Cliff Point was so named; elsewhere there was a dark, straggling growth of pine trees on capes and island, while on the summits could just be seen the rectangular outlines of small forts.

"They don't keep those manned, sir," said Turner. "Gone to rack and ruin like everything else."

"You say the east passage is absolutely clear?"

"Yes, sir."

"Very well."

Atropos headed in, with Hornblower giving his orders to the wheel. There was no flag flying on shore, and until one could be seen there was no question of firing a salute. From point to island the entrance extended a scant half mile, possibly less; now they could see through it, to the wide waters of Marmorice Bay, with high mountains surrounding it on nearly every side, except to the northward.

"There's the town, sir," said Turner. "Not much of a place."

A white tower—a minaret—caught the afternoon sun.

"You can see the red mound behind the town now, sir."

"Where did the *Speedwell* go down?" asked Hornblower.

"Over to port, there, sir. Right in line between the red mound and the fort on Passage Island. The fort on Ada bore sou'-sou' east half south."

"Take the bearing now," ordered Hornblower.

They were through the entrance now. The water was smooth, not smooth enough to reflect the blue sky. Turner was calling the bearing of the fort on Capa Ada. With his own eye Hornblower could judge the other cross-bearing. There was no harm in anchoring close to the projected scene of operations; that would attract less attention than to anchor in one place first and to move to another anchorage later. Jones took in fore and main topsails and headsails smartly enough. *Atropos* glided quietly on.

"Hard a-starboard," said Hornblower to the quartermaster. Round came *Atropos*, the mizzen topsail helping the turn as Jones clued it up. The ship's way died away almost imperceptibly, the tiny waves lapping against her bows.

"Let go!"

The hawser rumbled out. *Atropos* swung to her anchor, in Turkish waters. The crossing of the three-mile limit, even the entrance through the Pass, had been actions that might be argued about, disavowed. But that anchor, its flukes solidly buried in the firm sand, was something of which a diplomatic note could take definite notice.

"Pass the word for the doctor," said Hornblower.

There were many things to do; it was his duty to make contact with the Turkish authorities if they did not make contact with him. But first of all, without wasting a moment, it was necessary to make arrangements for the operation on McCullum. The man's life hung in the balance, and far more than his life.

XII

Hornblower sat waiting in his cabin. "A few minutes" had been Eisenbeiss's estimate of the time necessary for the operation. It was necessary, Hornblower knew, to work as quickly as possible, so as to minimize the shock to the patient.

"In the old *Hannibal*, sir," said the sickberth attendant whom Hornblower had questioned regarding his experience, "we took off eleven legs in half an hour. That was at Algeciras, sir."

But amputations were relatively simple. A full half of all amputation cases survived—Nelson himself had lost an arm, amputated on a dark night in a moderate storm at sea, and he had lived until a musket bullet killed him at Trafalgar. This was not an amputation. It was something which would be worse than useless if Eisenbeiss's diagnosis was incorrect and which could easily fail in any case.

The ship was very still and quiet. Hornblower knew that all his crew were taking a morbid interest in the fate of the "poor gentleman". They were sentimental about McCullum, lying at death's door as a result of a bullet wound he need never have received; the fact that he was going to be cut about with a knife had an unholy attraction for them; the fact that in a few minutes he might be dead, might have gone through those mysterious doors they all feared to go through invested his personality with some special quality in their eyes. Sentries had to be posted to keep out all the sentimental, the inquisitive, and the morbid-minded among the crew, and now Hornblower could tell by the silence that his men were waiting in shuddering silence for the climax, hoping perhaps to hear a scream or a groan, waiting as they would wait to see a condemned criminal turned off the hangman's cart. He could hear the heavy ticking of his watch as he waited.

Now there were distant sounds, but sounds in the little wooden ship were susceptible to so many possible interpretations that he would not at first allow himself to think that they might arise as a result of the ending of the operation. But then there were steps and voices outside his cabin door, the sentry speaking and then Eisenbeiss, and then came a knock.

"Come in," said Hornblower, trying to keep his voice indifferent; the first sight of Eisenbeiss as he entered was enough to tell Hornblower that all was as well as could be hoped. There was an obvious lightheartedness about the doctor's elephantine movements.

"I found the bullet," said Eisenbeiss. "It was where I thought—at the inferior angle of the scapula."

"Did you get it out?" asked Hornblower; the fact that he did not correct Eisenbeiss for omitting the "sir" was proof—if anyone had been present to notice it—that he was not as calm as he appeared.

"Yes," said Eisenbeiss.

He laid something on the table in front of Hornblower, with a gesture positively dramatic. It was the bullet, mis-shapen, flattened to an irregular disc, with a raw scratch on one surface.

"That is where my scalpel cut into it," said Eisenbeiss proudly. "I went straight to the right place."

Hornblower picked the thing up gingerly to examine it.

"You see," said Eisenbeiss, "it was as I said. The bullet struck the ribs, breaking them, and then glanced off, passing back between the bone and the muscle."

"Yes, I see," said Hornblower.

"And there are these as well," went on Eisenbeiss, laying something else in front of Hornblower with the same sort of conscious pride as a conjuror at a fair bringing the rabbit out of the hat.

"Is this the wad?" asked Hornblower, puzzled, and making no attempt to pick up the horrid little object.

"No," said Eisenbeiss, "that is how my forceps brought it out. But see—"

Eisenbeiss's large fingers plucked the object into successive layers.

"I have looked at these through my lens. That is a piece of a blue coat. That is a piece of silk lining. That is a piece of linen shirt. And those are threads of a knitted undershirt."

Eisenbeiss beamed with triumph.

"The bullet carried these in with it?" asked Hornblower.

"Exactly. Of course. Between the bullet and the bone these portions were cut off, as they might be between the blades of scissors, and the bullet carried them on with it. I found them all. No wonder the wound was suppurating."

"You address me as 'sir'," said Hornblower, realizing, now that the tension had eased, that Eisenbeiss had been omitting the honorific. "The operation was otherwise successful as well?"

"Yes—sir," said Eisenbeiss. "The removal of these foreign bodies and the draining of the wound brought immediate relief to the patient."

"He did not suffer too much?"

"Not too much. The men who were ready to hold him still had hardly anything to do. He submitted with good spirit, as he promised you he would. It was well that he lay still. I feared further injury to the lung from the broken ribs if he struggled."

"You address me as 'sir'," said Hornblower. "That is the last time, doctor, that I shall overlook the omission."

"Yes—sir."

"And the patient is going on well?"

"I left him as well as I could hope—sir. I must return to him soon, of course."

"Do you think he will live?"

Some of the triumph evaporated from Eisenbeiss's expression as he concentrated on phrasing his reply.

"He is more likely to live now, sir," he said. "But with wounds—one cannot be sure."

There was always the likelihood, the unpredictable likelihood, of a wound taking a turn for the worse, festering and killing.

"You cannot say more than that?"

"No, sir. The wound must remain open to drain. When applying the sutures I inserted a bristle—"

"Very well," said Hornblower, suddenly squeamish. "I understand. You had better return to him now. You have my thanks, doctor, for what you have done."

Even with Eisenbeiss gone there was no chance of quietly reviewing the situation. A knock on the door heralded the appearance of Midshipman Smiley.

"Mr. Jones' compliments, sir, and there are boats heading for us from the shore."

"Thank you. I'll come up. And if Mr. Turner's not on deck tell him I want to see him there."

Some of the gaily-painted boats in the distance were under oars, but the nearest one was under a lateen sail, lying very close to the wind. As Hornblower watched her she took in her sail, went about, and reset it on the other tack. The lateen rig had its disadvantages. On the new tack the boat would fetch up alongside *Atropos* easily enough.

"Now listen to me, Mr. Turner," said Hornblower, reaching the decision he had had at the back of his mind—overlain until now by a host of other considerations—for the last two days. "When you speak to them you are to tell them that we are looking for a French squadron."

"Beg pardon, sir?"

"We are looking for a French squadron. Two sail—that will do. A ship of the line and frigate, escaped from Corfu three weeks back. The first thing you ask is whether they have touched here."

"Aye aye, sir."

Turner was not very clear on the point yet.

"Admiral—Admiral Harvey has sent us in for news. He's cruising off Crete looking for them with four sail of the line. Four will do. Enough force to make them respect us."

"I see, sir."

"You're quite sure you do?"

"Yes, sir."

It was irksome being dependent on Turner to interpret for him. With Spanish authorities, or French, Hornblower could have conducted his own negotiations, but not with Turks.

"Remember, that's the first thing you ask, the very first. Have two French ships touched here? Then you can go on to get permission to fill the water casks. We'll buy fresh vegetables, too, and a couple of bullocks, if we can."

"Yes, sir."

"Keep it in your mind all the time that we're scouting for Admiral Harvey. Don't forget it for a moment, and then everything will be all right."

"Aye aye, sir."

The lateen boat was nearing them fast, making surprising speed with the small evening wind; there was a respectable bubble of foam under her bow. She came running close alongside and hove-to, the lateen sail flapping until they brailed up the upper portion.

"Turks, sir, not Greeks," said Turner.

Hornblower could have guessed that without Turner's help; the boat's crew was dressed in dirty white gowns; they wore on their heads round red hats wreathed in dirty white turbans. The grey-bearded man who stood up in the stern wore a red sash about his waist, from which hung a curved sword. He hailed *Atropos* in a thin high voice. Turner hailed back; the jargon he spoke was the lingua franca of the Levant, and Hornblower tried to guess at what was being said. Italian, French, English, Arabic, Greek, all contributed to the language, he knew. It was a little strange to hear the words "Horatio Hornblower" come clearly through the incomprehensible remainder.

"Who is this fellow?" he asked.

"The Mudir, sir. The local Jack-in-office. Harbour master—preventive officer. He is asking about our bill of health, sir."

"Don't forget to ask about the French ships," said Hornblower.

"Aye aye, sir."

The shouted conversation went on; Hornblower caught the word "fregata" more than once. The grey-beard in the boat extended his hands in a negative gesture and went on to supplement it with a further sentence.

"He says there have been no French ships in here for years, sir," said Turner.

"Ask him if he has heard about any along the coast or in the islands?"

The grey-beard clearly disclaimed all knowledge.

"Tell him," said Hornblower, "I'll give him five pieces of gold for news of the French."

There was something infectious in the atmosphere, in this Oriental talk—that was the only explanation Hornblower could think of for his using the outlandish expression "pieces of gold". There was no reason why he should not have said "guineas" to Turner. The grey-beard shook his head again; Hornblower, looking keenly at him fancied that the offer impressed him nevertheless. He asked another question and Turner answered.

"I've told him about the British squadron in the offing, sir," he reported.

"Good."

There was no harm in having the Turks believe he had a powerful force to back him up. Now the grey-beard was gesturing with the fingers of one hand outstretched as he answered some question of Turner's.

"He says he wants five piastres a hogshead for us to fill our water casks, sir," said Turner. "That's a shilling each."

"Tell him—tell him I'll give him half."

The conversation continued; the western sky was beginning to redden with the sunset as the sun sank lower. At last the grey-beard waved in farewell, and the boat turned away and unfurled her sail to the dying wind.

"They've gone back to spread their mats for the evening prayer, sir," said Turner. "I've promised him ten guineas for everything. That gives us the right to land at the jetty over there, to fill our water casks, and to buy in the market that he'll open in the morning. He'll take his share of what we pay there, you can be sure, sir."

"Very well, Mr. Turner. Mr. Jones!"

"Sir!"

"With the first light in the morning I'm going to start sweeping for the wreck. I'll have the sweep prepared now."

"Er—aye aye, sir."

"A hundred fathoms of one-inch line, if you please, Mr. Jones. Two nine-pounder shot. Have a net made for each, and attach them ten fathoms apart at equal distances from the ends of the line. Is that clear?"

"Not—not quite, sir."

Because he was honest about it Hornblower refrained from remarking on his slowness of comprehension.

"Take a hundred fathoms of line and attach one shot forty-five fathoms from one end and another forty-five fathoms from the other end. Is that clear now?"

"Yes, sir."

"You can get the launch and long boat into the water now, ready for the morning. They'll carry the sweep between them, dragging the bottom for the wreck. Tell off the boats' crews for duty. I want to start work at first dawn, as I said. And we'll need grapnels and buoys to mark what we find. Nothing conspicuous—planks will do, with seventeen fathoms of line to each. You understand all that?"

"Yes, sir."

"Carry on, then, Mr. Turner, report in my cabin in fifteen minutes' time, if you please. Messenger! My compliments to the doctor, and I'd like to see him in my cabin immediately."

Hornblower felt like a juggler at a fair, keeping half a dozen balls in the air at once. He wanted to hear from the doctor how McCullum was progressing after the operation; he wanted to discuss with Turner the question of what local authorities might be likely to be present in Marmorice to interfere with his work there; he wanted to make all preparations for the next morning; he wanted to be ready with his own plans for raising the treasure if McCullum was unable to give advice; and night orders for the care of the ship in this harbour of doubtful neutrality had to be written; it was only late in the evening that he remembered something else—something of which he was reminded only by a suddenly noticed feeling of emptiness inside him. He had eaten nothing since breakfast. He ate biscuit and cold meat, crunching the flinty fragments hurriedly at his cabin table before hurrying on deck again into the darkness.

It was a chilly night, and the young moon had already set. No breath of air now ruffled the black surface of the water of the bay, smooth enough to bear faint reflections of the stars. Black and impenetrable was the water, beneath which lay a quarter of a million pounds sterling. It was as impenetrable as his future, he decided, leaning on the bulwark. An intelligent man, he decided, would go to bed and sleep, having done all that his forethought and ingenuity could devise, and an intelligent man would worry no further for the moment. But he had to be very firm with himself to drive himself to bed and allow his utter weariness of body and mind to sweep him away into unconsciousness.

It was still dark when he was called, dark and cold, but he ordered coffee for himself and sipped it as he dressed. Last night when he had given the time for his being called he had allowed for a leisurely dressing before daylight, but he felt tense and anxious as he got out of bed, much as he had felt on other occasions when he had been roused in the night to take part in a cutting-out expedition or a dawn landing, and he had to restrain himself from putting on his clothes in haphazard fashion and hurrying on deck. He forced himself to shave, although that was an operation which had mostly to be carried out by touch because the hanging lamp gave almost no illumination to the mirror. The shirt he pulled on felt clammy against his ribs; he was struggling with his trousers when a knock at the door brought in Eisenbeiss, reporting in obedience to overnight orders.

"The patient is sleeping well, sir," he announced.

"Is his condition good?"

"I thought I should not disturb him, sir. He was sleeping quietly, so I could not tell if he had fever nor could I examine the wound. I can wake him if you wish, sir—"

"No, don't do that, of course. I suppose it's a good symptom that he's sleeping in any case?"

"A very good one, sir."

"Then leave him alone, doctor. Report to me if there is any change."

"Aye aye, sir."

Hornblower buttoned his trousers and thrust his feet into his shoes. His eagerness to be on deck overcame his self-restraint to the extent that he was still buttoning his coat as he went up the companion. On deck as well the atmosphere seemed to be charged with that feeling of impending attack at dawn. There were the dimly-seen figures of the officers, silhouetted against the sky. To the east there was the faintest illumination, a little light reaching half-way up to the zenith, so faint as almost to be unnoticed, and its colour, in its turn, was so faint a shade of pink as hardly to be called that.

"Morning," said Hornblower in response to the touched hats of his subordinates.

In the waist he could hear orders being quietly given—just like manning the boats for a cutting-out expedition.

"Longboat's crew starboard side," said Smiley's voice.

"Launch's crew port side." That was the Prince's voice. He was acquiring a better accent than Eisenbeiss's.

"There's some surface mist, sir," reported Jones. "But it's very patchy."

"So I see," replied Hornblower.

"Last night we were lying two cables' lengths from the wreck as near as makes no matter, sir," said Turner. "We've swung during the night, with the wind dropping, but little enough."

"Tell me when it's light enough for you to get your bearings."

"Aye aye, sir."

In that short time the eastern sky had changed. One might almost have said it had darkened, but perhaps that was because with the tiny increase in the general illumination the contrast was not so marked.

"You took a third bearing at the time when *Speedwell* went down, Mr. Turner?"

"Yes, sir. It was—"

"No matter."

Turner could be relied upon to manage a simple piece of business of that sort.

"I don't expect the wreck has moved an inch, sir," said Turner. "There's no tide here. No scour. The two rivers that run into the Bay don't set up any current you can measure."

"And the bottom's firm sand?"

"Firm sand, sir."

That was something to be thankful for. In mud the wreck might have sunk beyond discovery.

"How the devil did *Speedwell* come to capsize?" asked Hornblower.

"Sheer bad luck, sir. She was an old ship and she'd been at sea a long time. The weeds and the barnacles were thick along her waterline—she wasn't coppered high enough, sir. So they were heeling her, cleaning her port side, with the guns run out to starboard and all the weights they could shift over to starboard too. It was a still day, baking hot. Then, before you could say Jack Robinson, there came a gust out of the mountains. It caught her square on the port beam and laid her over before she could pay off. The gun ports were open and the water came up over the sills. That laid her over still more—at least, that's what the court of inquiry found, sir—and with her hatchways open the water rose over the coamings and down she went."

"Did she right herself as she sank?"

"No, sir. I looked over at her when I heard the shout, and I saw her keel. Bottom upwards she went. Her top-masts were snapped clean off. They came up soon enough, main and fore top-masts still anchored to the wreck by a shroud or two. That was a help when it came to taking the bearings."

"I see," said Hornblower.

Dawn was coming up fast. It actually seemed—an optical illusion, of course—as if great arms of colour were climbing up the sky from the eastern horizon at a pace perceptible to the eye.

"It's light enough now, sir," said Turner.

"Thank you. Mr. Jones! You can carry on."

Hornblower watched them go, Turner leading the way in the gig with his instruments and compass, Still following behind in the launch with Smiley in the longboat attached to the launch by the sweep. Hornblower became acutely aware that despite the cup of coffee he had drunk he wanted his breakfast. It seemed almost against his will that he lingered. This dead still calm at dawn was the ideal time for an operation of this sort; it enabled the gig to take up and maintain a position with the least possible effort. The ripples caused by the boat's passage, slow though it was, spread far over the glassy surface of the Bay before dying out at last. He saw the gig stop, and clearly over the water came the sound of Turner's voice as he spoke through his speaking trumpet to the other boats. They jockeyed round into position awkwardly, like two beetles tied together with a thread, and then they paid out the sweep between them, manoeuvred awkwardly again for a moment as they laid themselves exactly upon the correct bearing, and then the oars began to swing rhythmically, slowly, like the pendulum of Fate, as the boats began to sweep the area ahead of them. Hornblower's heart beat faster despite himself, and he swallowed with excitement. Around him the ship was beginning her normal life. Amid the peculiar patter of bare feet on wooden planking—a sound unlike any other on earth—the watch below were bringing their hammocks to stow in the nettings. Swabs and holystones, buckets and pump; the hands not at work in the boats began the eternal daily routine of washing down the decks. Not for the first time on the voyage Hornblower found himself experiencing a momentary envy of the seamen at their work. Their problems were of the simplest, their doubts were minute. To holystone a portion of planking to the whiteness demanded by a petty officer, to swab it off, to swab it dry, working in amicable companionship with friends of long standing, dabbling their naked feet in the gush of clear water—that was all they had to do, as they had done for an infinity of mornings in the past and would do for an infinity of mornings in the future. He would be glad to exchange with them his loneliness, his responsibility, the complexity of his problems; so he felt for a moment before he laughed at himself, knowing perfectly well he would be horrified if some freak of Fate forced such an exchange on him. He turned away, changing the subject of his thoughts; a generous slice of fat pork, fried to a pale brown—there had been a leg in soak for him for the past two days, and the outside cut would be not too salty now. It would smell delicious —he could almost smell it at this very moment. Holy Jerusalem, unless it was still spluttering on his plate when it was put before him despite the journey from galley to cabin he'd make someone wish he had never been born. And he would have biscuit crumbs fried with it, and he would top it off with black treacle smeared on a biscuit, thick. That was a breakfast worth thinking about.

XIII

Hornblower stood with his purse in his hand, having taken it from his sea chest where it had lain in the inner compartment. He knew exactly how many guineas there were in it, and he was trying not to wish there were more. If he were a wealthy captain he would be generous towards his ship's company, and to the wardroom and gunroom. But as it was— He shook his head. He did not want to appear miserly or mean, but he certainly did not want to be foolish. He walked along to the wardroom door and paused there; Still caught his eye.

"Please come in, sir."

The other officers rose from their chairs; there was nowhere for them to sit unless they sat round the table in the tiny wardroom.

"I was hoping," said Hornblower to Carslake the purser, "that you would be kind enough to make some purchases for me."

"Of course, sir. Honoured, I'm sure," said Carslake. He could say nothing else, in any case.

"A few chickens—half a dozen, say, and some eggs."

"Yes, sir."

"Is it the intention of the wardroom to buy fresh meat for itself?"

"Well, sir—"

That had been the subject under discussion at his entrance.

"At this time of year there might be lambs to sell. I could have one—two young ones, if they're cheap. But an ox—what am I to do with a whole ox?"

Everyone in the wardroom had been up against this problem at some time or other.

"If the wardroom decides to buy an ox I would be glad to pay a quarter of the price," said Hornblower, and the wardroom cheered up perceptibly.

A captain who bought a share in an animal would always get the best cuts—that was in the course of nature. And they had all known captains who would pay no more than their share. But with five wardroom officers Hornblower's offer was generous.

"Thank you very much, sir," said Carslake. "I think I can sell a couple of joints to the gunroom."

"On advantageous terms, I trust?" said Hornblower, with a grin. He could remember well enough as a midshipman occasions when wardroom and gunroom had gone shares in an animal.

"I expect so, sir," said Carslake and then, changing the subject, "Mr. Turner says that it'll be goat here, mainly. Do you care for goat, sir?"

"Young kid, stewed with turnips and carrots!" said Jones. "You can do worse than that, sir."

Jones's lantern-jawed face was alight with appetite. These grown men, continuously fed on preserved food, were like children at a gingerbread stall at a fair with the thought of fresh meat.

"Do what you can," said Hornblower. "I'll eat kid or lamb, or I'll share in an ox, as you find the market provides. You know what you're buying for the crew?"

"Yes, sir," said Carslake.

The penny-pinching clerks of a penurious government at home would scrutinize those expenditures in time. Nothing very generous could be bought for the hands.

"I don't know what vegetables we'll find, sir, at this time of year," went on Carslake, "winter cabbage, I suppose."

"Nothing wrong with winter cabbage," interposed Jones.

"Carrots and turnips out of winter store," said Carslake. "They'll be pretty stringy, sir."

"Better than nothing," said Hornblower. "There won't be enough in the market for all we need, nor will there be until the word goes round the countryside. So much the better. Then we'll have an excuse to linger. You're going to interpret, Mr. Turner?"

"Yes, sir."

"Keep your eyes open. And your ears."

"Aye aye, sir."

"Mr. Jones, you will attend to the water casks, if you please."

"Aye aye, sir."

That was the transition between the social visit and the official issuing of orders.

"Carry on."

Hornblower went to the bedside where McCullum lay. Sailcloth pillows supported him in a position half on his side. It was a comfort to see how comparatively well he looked. The fever and its accompanying distortion of thought had left him.

"Glad to see you looking so well, Mr. McCullum," said Hornblower.

"Well enough," answered McCullum.

He croaked a little, but his speech was almost normal.

"A full night's sleep," said Eisenbeiss, hovering on the far side of the bed. He had already made his report to Hornblower—the wound showed every sign of healing, the sutures had not at least as yet caused undue inflammation, and the draining where the bristle kept the wound in the back open had been apparently satisfactory.

"And we've started a full morning's work," said Hornblower. "You have heard that we have located the wreck?"

"No. I had not heard that."

"It's located and buoyed," said Hornblower.

"Are you sure it is the wreck?" croaked McCullum. "I've known some queer mistakes made."

"It is exactly where the bearings were taken when she sank," said Hornblower. "It is the right size as far as the sweep can show. And no other obstructions were found by the sweep, either. The bottom here is firm sand, as I expect you know."

"It sounds plausible," said McCullum grudgingly. "I could have wished I'd had the direction of the sweeping, nevertheless."

"You must trust me, Mr. McCullum," said Hornblower patiently.

" 'Tis little that I know about you and your capabilities," answered McCullum.

Hornblower, swallowing his irritation at that remark, wondered how McCullum had managed to live so long without previously being shot in a duel. But McCullum was the irreplaceable expert, and even if he were not a sick man it would be both foolish and undignified to quarrel with him.

"I presume the next thing to do is to send your divers down to report on the condition of the wreck," he said, trying to be both firm and polite.

"Undoubtedly that will be the first thing I do as soon as I am allowed out of this bed," said McCullum.

Hornblower thought of all that Eisenbeiss had told him about McCullum's wound, about gangrene and suppuration and general blood-poisoning, and he knew there was a fair chance that McCullum would never rise from his bed.

"Mr. McCullum," he said, "this is an urgent matter. Once the Turks get wind of what we want to do, and can assemble sufficient force to stop us, we will never be allowed to conduct salvage operations here. It is of the first importance that we get to work as quickly as we can. I was hoping that you would instruct your divers in their duties so that they could start now, immediately."

"So that is what you were thinking, is it?" said McCullum.

It took some minutes of patient argument to wear McCullum down, and the grudging agreement that McCullum gave was tempered by an immediate pointing out of the difficulties.

"That water's mortal cold," said McCullum.

"I'm afraid so," answered Hornblower, "But we have always expected that."

"The Eastern Mediterranean in March is nothing like the Bay of Bengal in summer. My men won't stand it for long."

It was a great advance that McCullum should admit that they might stand it at all.

"If they work for short intervals—?" suggested Hornblower.

"Aye. Seventeen fathoms beside the wreck?"

"Seventeen fathoms all round it," said Hornblower.

"They can't work for long at that depth in any case. Five dives a day will be all. Then they bleed at the nose and ears. They'll need lines and weights—nine-pounder shot will serve."

"I'll have them got ready," said Hornblower.

Hornblower stood by while McCullum addressed his divers. He could guess at the point of some of the speeches. One of the divers was raising objections; it was clear, when he clasped his arms about his chest and shuddered dramatically with a rolling of his pathetic dark eyes, what he was saying. All three of them talked at once for a space in their twittering language. A sterner note came into McCullum's voice when he replied, and he indicated Hornblower with a gesture, directing all eyes to him for a moment. All three clung to each other and shrank away from him like frightened children. McCullum went on speaking, energetically—Eisenbeiss leaned over him and restrained the left hand that gesticulated; the right was strapped into immobility against McCullum's chest.

"Do not move," said Eisenbeiss. "We shall have an inflammation."

McCullum had winced more than once after an incautious movement, and his appearance of well-being changed quickly to one of fatigue.

"They'll start now," he said at length, his head back on his pillow. "You can take 'em. Looney, here—that's what I call him—will be in charge. I've told 'em there are no sharks. Generally when one of 'em's down at the bottom the other two pray against sharks—they're all three of 'em shark doctors. A good thing they've seen men flogged on board here. I promised 'em you'd give 'em a taste of the cat if there was any nonsense."

Hornblower had seen very plainly what the reactions of these twittering, bird-like creatures had been to that horror.

"Take 'em away," said McCullum, lying back on his pillow.

With longboat and launch over at the far side of the Bay for stores and water only the gig and the tiny jolly boat were available. The gig was uncomfortably crowded but it served, with four hands at the oars, Hornblower and Leadbitter in the stern—Hornblower felt he could not possibly endure not taking part in this first essay—and the Ceylonese crowded into the bows. Hornblower had formed a shrewd notion about the extent of McCullum's ability to speak the divers' language. He had no doubt that McCullum made no attempt to speak it accurately or with any attempt at inflection. He made his points, Hornblower guessed, with a few nouns and verbs and some energetic gestures. McCullum's command of the Ceylonese tongue could not compare with Hornblower's Spanish, nor even with his French. Hornblower felt a sense of grievance about that, as he sat with his hand on the tiller and steered the gig over the dancing water—already the flat calm of dawn had given way to a moderate breeze that ruffled the surface.

They reached the first of the buoys—a plank wallowing among the wavelets at the end of its line—and Hornblower stood to identify the others. A stroke or two of the oars carried the gig into the centre of the area, and Hornblower looked down the boat to where the divers huddled together.

"Looney," he said.

Now that he had been paying special attention to them he could distinguish each of the three divers from the others. Until that time they might as well have been triplets as far as his ability went to tell them apart.

"Looney," said Hornblower again.

Looney rose to his feet and dropped the grapnel over the side. It went down fast, taking out the coiled-down line rapidly over the gunwale. Slowly Looney took off his clothes until he stood naked. He sat himself on the gunwale and swung his legs over. As his feet felt the cold of the water he cried out, and the other two joined with him in cries of alarm or commiseration.

"Shall I give 'im a shove, sir?" asked the hand at the bow oar.

"No," said Hornblower.

Looney was sitting systematically inflating and deflating his chest, inhaling as deeply as he could, forcing air into his lungs. Hornblower could see how widely the ribs moved at each breath. One of the other two Ceylonese put a cannon-ball into Looney's hands, and he clasped it to his naked chest. Then he let himself slip from the gunwale and disappeared below the surface, leaving the gig rocking violently.

Hornblower took out his watch; it had no second hand—watches with second hands were far too expensive for him to afford—but he could measure the time roughly. He watched the tip of the minute hand creep from one mark to the next, from there to the next, and into the third minute. He was concentrating so deeply on the task that he did not hear Looney break water; his attention was called by a word from Leadbitter. Looney's head was visible twenty yards astern, his long thick switch of black hair, tied with a string, beside his ear.

"Back water!" said Hornblower promptly. "Pay out that line, there!"

The second order was understood clearly enough by the Ceylonese, or at least they knew their business, for as a vigorous stroke or two sent the gig down to Looney one of them attended to the line over the bows. Looney put his hands up to the gunwale and the other two pulled him on board. They talked volubly, but Looney at first sat still on the thwart, his head down by his thighs. Then he lifted his head, the water streaming from his wet hair. Clearly he talked about the cold—that sharp breeze must have been icy upon his wet skin—for the others towelled him and assisted him to cover himself with his clothes.

Hornblower wondered how he would set them to work again, but there was no need for him to interfere. As soon as Looney had his white garments about his shoulders he stood up in the bows of the gig and looked about him, considering. Then he pointed to a spot in the water a few yards away, looking round at Hornblower.

"Give way!" said Hornblower.

One of the Ceylonese hauled in on the grapnel and let it go again when the boat reached the spot indicated. Now it was his turn to strip, to inflate and deflate his chest, and to take a cannonball into his hands and drop over the side. Cannonballs cost money, thought Hornblower, and a time might come when he would need them to fire at the enemy. It would be better in the future to play in a supply of small rocks gathered on the shore. The diver came up to the surface and scrambled on board, to be received by his companions just as Looney had been. There was some kind of discussion among the divers, which was ended by the third one going down in the same place, apparently to settle the point in dispute. What he discovered led on his return to Looney requesting by signs a further shifting of the gig, and then Looney took off his clothes again to go down.

The divers were working industriously and, as far as Hornblower could see, intelligently. Later on Looney and one of his mates made a simultaneous descent, and it was on this occasion that Hornblower noticed that Looney's legs and feet, when he climbed in, were scratched and bleeding. For a moment Hornblower thought of sharks and similar underwater perils, but he revised his opinion at once. Looney must have been scrambling about on the wreck itself. There were decaying timbers down there, deep in the bright water, overgrown with barnacles and razor-edged sea shells. Hornblower felt confirmed in his opinion when Looney desired to buoy this particular spot. They anchored a plank there by a grapnel, and then dived more than once again in the neighbourhood.

Now the divers were exhausted, lying doubled up and huddled together beside the bow thwart.

"Very well, Looney," said Hornblower, and he pointed back to the ship.

Looney gave him a weary nod.

"Up anchor," ordered Hornblower, and the gig pulled back towards *Atropos*.

A mile away were visible the lug sails of longboat and launch also on their return journey, coming down with the freshening wind abeam. It seemed to Hornblower as if things could never happen to him one at a time; he had hardly set foot on the deck of the *Atropos* before they were running alongside, and as the Ceylonese made their weary way forward to report to McCullum here were Carslake and Turner demanding his attention.

"The water casks are refilled, sir," said Carslake. "I used the little stream that comes in half a mile from the town. I thought that would be better than those in the town."

"Quite right, Mr. Carslake," said Hornblower. On account of what he had seen in North Africa, Hornblower agreed with Carslake that a water supply that had not passed through a Turkish town would be preferable.

"What stores did you get?"

"Very little, sir, today, I'm afraid."

"There was only the local market, sir," supplemented Turner. "The Mudir has only sent out word today. The goods will be coming in for sale tomorrow."

"The Mudir?" asked Hornblower. That was the word Turner had used before.

"The head man, sir, the local governor. The old man with the sword who came out to us in the boat yesterday."

"And he is the Mudir?"

"Yes, sir. The Mudir is under the Kaimakam, and the Kaimakam is under the Vali, and the Vali is under the Grand Vizier, and he's under the Sultan, or at least that's how it's supposed to be—all of 'em try to be independent when they get the chance."

"I understand that," said Hornblower.

No one who had given any study at all to the military and naval history of the last few years in the Eastern Mediterranean could be ignorant of the anarchy and distintegration prevailing in the Turkish Empire. What Hornblower wanted to hear about was the effect these were producing locally and today. He turned back to Carslake to listen patiently first to his account of what had been bought and what would be available later.

"I bought all the eggs there were, sir. Two and a half dozen," said Carslake in the course of his report.

"Good," said Hornblower, but without any fervour, and that was clear proof that his mind was not on what Carslake was saying. Normally the thought of eggs, boiled, scrambled, or poached, would have excited him. The untoward events at Malta had prevented his buying any there for himself. He had not even laid in a store of pickled eggs at Deptford.

Carslake droned himself to a stop.

"Thank you, Mr. Carslake," said Hornblower. "Mr. Turner, come below and I'll hear what you have to say."

Turner had apparently kept his eyes and ears open, as Hornblower had ordered him to.

"The Mudir has no force here at all worth mentioning, sir," said Turner, his wizened old face animated and lively. "I doubt if he could raise twenty-five armed men all told. He came down with two guards as old as himself."

"You spoke with him?"

"Yes, sir. I gave him—Mr. Carslake and I gave him—ten guineas to open the market for us. Another ten guineas tomorrow, is what we've promised him."

No harm in keeping local authority on his side as long as possible, thought Hornblower.

"And was he friendly?" he asked.

"We-ell, sir. I wouldn't say that, not exactly, sir. Maybe it was because he wanted our money. I wouldn't call him friendly, sir."

He would be reserved and cautious, Hornblower decided, not anxious to commit himself without instructions from superior authority, and yet not averse to pocketing twenty pieces of gold—pickings for an average year, Hornblower guessed—when the opportunity presented itself.

"The Vali's carried off the local army, sir," went on Turner. "That was plain enough from the way the Mudir talked. But I don't know why, sir. Maybe there's trouble with the Greeks again. There's always trouble in the Archipelago."

Rebellion was endemic among the Greek subjects of Turkey. Fire and sword, massacre and desolation, piracy and revolt, swept islands and mainland periodically. And nowadays with French influence penetrating from the Seven Islands, and Russia taking a suspiciously humanitarian interest in the welfare of Turkey's Orthodox subjects, there were fresh sources of trouble and unrest.

"One point's clear, anyway," said Hornblower, "and that is that the Vali's not here at present."

"That's so, sir."

It would take time for a message to reach the Vali, or even the Vali's subordinate, the—the Kaimakam, decided Hornblower, fishing the strange title out of his memory with an effort. The political situation was involved beyond any simple disentanglement. Turkey had been Britain's enthusiastic ally recently, when Bonaparte had conquered Egypt and invaded Syria and threatened Constantinople. But Russia and Turkey were chronic enemies—they had fought half a dozen wars in the last half century—and now Russia and England were allies, and Russia and France were enemies, even though since Austerlitz there was no way in which they could attack each other. There could be no doubt in the world that the French ambassador in Constantinople was doing his best to incite Turkey to a fresh war with Russia; no doubt at all that Russia since the days of Catherine the Great was casting covetous eyes on Constantinople and the Dardanelles.

The Greek unrest was an established fact. So was the ambition of the local Turkish governors. The tottering Turkish government would seize any opportunity to play off one possible enemy against the other, and would view with the deepest suspicion—there was even the religious factor to be borne in mind—any British activity amid Turkish possessions. With England and France locked in a death struggle the Turks could hardly be blamed if they suspected England of buying Russia's continued alliance with a promise of a slice of Turkish territory; luckily France, with a far worse record, was liable to be similarly suspected. When the Sultan heard—if ever he did hear—of the presence of a British ship of war in Marmorice Bay, he would wonder what intrigues were brewing with the Vali, and if Sultan or Vali heard that a quarter of a million in gold and silver lay at the bottom of Marmorice Bay it could be taken for granted that none would be salvaged unless the lion's share went into Turkish hands.

There was just no conclusion to be reached after all this debate, except for the one he had reached a week ago, and that was to effect as prompt a recovery of the treasure as possible and to leave the diplomats to argue over a *fait accompli*. He walked forward to hear from McCullum's lips how much had been learned regarding this possibility.

McCullum had just finished hearing what the divers had reported to him. They were squatting round his cot, with all the attention of their big eyes concentrated on his face, and with all their clothes draped about them until they looked something like beehives.

"She is there," said McCullum. Apparently he had been quite prepared to find that some gross blunder or other had been committed, either in plotting the original bearings or in the recent sweeping operations.

"I'm glad to hear it," replied Hornblower, as politely as he could make himself endure these temperamental liberties of an expert and an invalid.

"She's greatly overgrown, except for her copper, but she shows no sign of breaking up at all."

A wooden ship, fastened together with wooden pegs, and untouched by storm or current, might well lie for ever on a sandy bed without disintegration.

"Did she right herself?" asked Hornblower.

"No. She's nearly bottom up. My men could tell bow from stern."

"That's fortunate," said Hornblower.

"Yes." McCullum referred to some pages of written notes that he held in his free hand. "The money was in the lower lazarette, aft, abaft the mizzen mast and immediately below the main deck. A ton and a half of coined gold in iron chests and nearly four tons of coined silver in bags."

"Ye-es," said Hornblower, trying to look as if that exactly agreed with his own calculations.

"The lazarette was given an additional lining of oak to strengthen it before the treasure was put on board," went on McCullum. "I expect the money's still there."

"You mean—?" asked Hornblower, quite at a loss.

"I mean it will not have fallen through the deck on to the sea bottom," said McCullum, condescending to explain to this ignorant amateur.

"Of course," said Hornblower, hastily.

"*Speedwell's* main cargo was half the battering train of the army," went on McCullum. "Ten long eighteen pounders. Bronze guns. And the shot for them. Iron shot."

"That's why she went down the way she did," said Hornblower brightly. As he spoke he realized as well the implications of the words "bronze" and "iron" which McCullum had accented. Bronze would endure under water longer than iron.

"Yes," said McCullum. "As soon as she heeled, guns and shot and all would shift. I'll wager on that, from what I know of first mates in these days. With the war, any jumped-up apprentice is a first mate."

"I've seen it myself," said Hornblower, sorrowfully.

"But that's neither here nor there," went on McCullum. "Looney here says she is still, most of her, above the sand. He could get in under the break of the poop, just."

From McCullum's significant glance when he made this announcement Hornblower could guess that it was of great importance, but it was hard to see just why this should be.

"Yes?" said Hornblower, tentatively.

"Do you think they can break in through the ship's side with crowbars?" asked McCullum testily. "Five minutes' work on the bottom a day each for three men! We'd be here a year."

Hornblower suddenly remembered the "leather fuse-hoses" for which McCullum had indented at Malta. He made a hasty guess, despite the fantastic nature of what he had to say.

"You're going to blow up the wreck?" he said.

"Of course. A powder charge in that angle should open the ship at exactly the right place."

"Naturally," said Hornblower. He was dimly aware that it was possible to explode charges under water, but his knowledge of the technical methods to be employed was dimmer still.

"We'll try the fuse-hoses first," announced McCullum. "But I've little hope of them at that depth. The joints can't resist the pressure."

"I suppose not," said Hornblower.

"I expect it'll mean a flying fuse in the end," said McCullum. "These fellows here are always afraid of 'em. But I'll do it."

The bulky figure of Eisenbeiss loomed up beside the cot. He put one hand on McCullum's forehead and the other on his wrist.

"Take your hands off me!" snarled McCullum. "I'm busy."

"You must not do too much," said Eisenbeiss. "Excitement increases the morbid humours."

"Morbid humours be damned!" exclaimed McCullum. "And you be damned, too."

"Don't be a fool, man," said Hornblower, his patience exhausted. "He saved your life yesterday. Don't you remember how sick you were? 'It hurts. It hurts.' That's what you were saying."

Hornblower found his voice piping in imitation of McCullum's yesterday, and he turned his face feebly from side to side like McCullum's on the pillow. He was aware that it was an effective bit of mimicry, and even McCullum was a trifle abashed by it.

"Sick I may have been," he said, "but I'm well enough now."

Hornblower looked across at Eisenbeiss.

"Let Mr. McCullum have five more minutes," he said. "Now, Mr. McCullum, you were talking about leather fuse-hoses. Will you please explain how they are used?"

XIV

Hornblower came forward to where the gunner and his mates were squatting on the deck at work upon the fuse-hose in accordance with McCullum's instructions.

"You are making a thorough job of those seams, I hope, Mr. Clout," he said.

"Aye aye, sir," said Clout.

They had an old sail spread out to sit on, for the purpose of saving the spotless deck from the warm pitch in the iron pot beside them.

"Five seconds to the foot, this quick match burns, sir. You said one foot of slow match, sir?"

"I did."

Hornblower bent to look at the work. The leather hose was in irregular lengths, from three to five feet; it was typical of the cross-grained ways of nature that animals could not provide longer pieces of leather than that. One of the gunner's mates was at work with a slender wooden bodkin, dragging the end of a vast length of quick match through a section of hose. When the bodkin emerged he proceeded to slip the hose along the quick match until it joined the preceding section.

"Easy with that, now," said Clout. "We don't want a break in that match."

The other gunner's mate set to work with needle and palm to sew and double sew the new length to its neighbour. The joint completed, Clout proceeded to apply warm pitch liberally over the joint and down the seam of the new section. Eventually there would be a hundred and twenty feet of hose joined and pitched and with quick match threaded all the way through it.

"I've picked a couple of sound kegs, sir," said Clout. "Fifty-pound kegs, they are. I have bags of dry sand to fill 'em up."

"Very well," said Hornblower.

Thirty pounds of powder was what McCullum wanted for his explosve charge, no more and no less.

"I don't want to shatter the wreck to pieces," McCullum had said. "I only want to split her open."

That was a part of McCullum's special knowledge; Hornblower could not possibly have guessed how much powder, at a depth of a hundred feet, would achieve this result. In a long nine-pounder, he knew, three pounds of powder would throw the shot a mile and a half, random shooting, but this was something entirely different, and in the incompressible medium of water, too. With a fifty-pound keg and only thirty pounds of powder it was necessary to have some indifferent substance like sand to fill the keg full.

"Send me word the moment you are ready," said Hornblower, and turned back aft again.

Here was Turner, newly come from the shore, hovering about to attract his attention.

"Well, Mr. Turner?"

Turner kept his distance, his manner indicating that he had something very private to say. He spoke in a low voice when Hornblower walked over to him.

"Please, sir, it's the Mudir. He wants to visit you. I can't make him out, but there's something he wants."

"What did you tell him?"

"I said—I'm sorry, sir, but I didn't know what else to do—I said you'd be delighted. There's something fishy, I think. He said he'd come at once."

"He did, did he?"

Things were bound to be fishy in these troubled waters, thought Hornblower, with a simultaneous disapproval of the style of that sentiment.

"Midshipman of the watch!"

"Sir!"

"What do you see over towards the town?"

Smiley trained his glass across the Bay.

"Boat putting out, sir. She's the same lateen we saw before."

"Any flag?"

"Yes, sir. Red. Turkish colours, it looks like."

"Very well. Mr. Jones, we're going to have an official visitor. You may pipe the side for him."

"Aye aye, sir."

"Now, Mr. Turner, you don't know what the Mudir wants?"

"No, sir. He wanted to see you, urgently, it seems like. 'Il capitano' was all he'd say when we landed—the market was supposed to be ready for us, but it wasn't. What he wanted was to see the Captain, and so I said you'd see him."

"He gave no hint?"

"No, sir. He wouldn't say. But he was agitated, I could see."

"Well, we'll know soon enough," said Hornblower.

The Mudir mounted to the deck with a certain dignity, despite the difficulties the awkward ascent presented to his old legs. He looked keenly about him as he came on board; whether or not he understood the compliment that was being paid him by the bosn's mates and the sideboys could not be determined. There was a keen hawk-like face above the white beard, and a pair of lively dark eyes took in the scene about him without revealing whether it was a familiar one or not. Hornblower touched his hat and the Mudir replied with a graceful gesture of his hand to his face.

"Ask him if he will come below," said Hornblower. "I'll lead the way"

Down in the cabin Hornblower offered a chair, with a bow, and the Mudir seated himself. Hornblower sat opposite him with Turner at his side. The Mudir spoke and Turner translated.

"He hopes God has given you the gift of health, sir," said Turner.

"Make the correct reply," said Hornblower.

As he spoke he met the glance of the sharp brown eyes and smiled politely.

"Now he's asking you if you have had a prosperous voyage, sir," reported Turner.

"Say whatever you think fit," answered Hornblower.

The conversation proceeded from one formal politeness to another. This was the way of the Levant, Hornblower knew. It could be neither dignified nor tactful to announce one's business in one's opening sentences.

"Should we offer him a drink?" asked Hornblower.

"Well, sir, it's usual over business to offer coffee."

"Then don't you think we'd better?"

"You see, sir, it's the coffee—it'll be different from what he calls coffee."

"We can hardly help that. Give the order, if you please."

The conversation continued, still without reaching any point. It was interesting to note how an intelligent and mobile face like the Mudir's could give no hint at all of any emotion behind it. But the coffee brought about a change. The sharp eyes took in the thick mugs, the battered pewter coffee pot, while the face remained impassive, and while the Mudir was going through the ceremony of polite refusal and then grateful acceptance; but the tasting of the coffee effected a transformation. Willy nilly, the Mudir could not prevent an expression of surprise, even though he instantly brought his features under control again. He proceeded to sweeten his coffee to a syrup with sugar, and he did not touch the cup, but raised it to his lips by means of the saucer.

"There ought to be little cakes and sweetmeats, too, sir," said Turner. "But we couldn't offer him blackstrap and biscuit."

"I suppose not," said Hornblower.

The Mudir sipped cautiously at his coffee again, and resumed his speech.

"He says you have a very fine ship, sir," said Turner. "I think he is coming to the point soon."

"Thank him and tell him what a wonderful village he has, if you think that's the right thing," said Hornblower.

The Mudir sat back in his chair—it was plain that he was not accustomed to chairs—studying first Hornblower's face and then Turner's. Then he spoke again; his voice was well modulated, well controlled.

"He's asking if *Atropos* is going to stay long, sir," said Turner.

It was the question Hornblower was expecting.

"Say that I have not completed my stores yet," he said.

He was quite sure that the preliminary operations of salvage, sweeping for the wreck, buoying it, and sending down the divers, had escaped observation, or at least would be quite unintelligible from the shore. He did not take his eyes from the Mudir's face as Turner translated and the Mudir replied.

"He says he presumes you will be leaving as soon as you've done that," said Turner.

"Tell him it's likely."

"He says this would be a good place to wait for information about French ships, sir. The fishing boats often come in with news."

"Tell him I have my orders."

The suspicion began to form in Hornblower's mind that the Mudir did not want *Atropos* to leave. Perhaps he wanted to keep him here until an ambush could be laid, until the guns at the fort could be manned, until the Vali returned with the local army. This was a good way to carry on a diplomatic conversation. He could watch the Mudir all the time, while any unguarded statement of Turner's could be disavowed on the grounds of poor translation if no other way.

"We can keep an eye on the Rhodes Channel from here, sir, he says," went on Turner. "It's the most likely course for any Frenchy. It looks as if he wants to get his twenty guineas, sir."

"Maybe so," said Hornblower, trying to convey by his tone that he saw no need for Turner to contribute to the conversation. "Say that my orders give me very little discretion."

With the conversation taking this turn it was obvious that the best tactics would be to display a reluctance that might with great difficulty be overcome. Hornblower hoped that Turner's command of lingua franca was equal to this demand upon it.

The Mudir replied with more animation than he had previously shown; it was as if he were about to show his hand.

"He wants us to stay here, sir," said Turner. "If we do there'll be much better supplies coming in from the country."

That was not his real reason, obviously.

"No," said Hornblower. "If we can't get the supplies we'll go without them."

Hornblower was having to be careful about the expression on his face; he had to say these things to Turner as if he really meant them—the Mudir was not letting anything escape his notice.

"Now he's coming out in the open, sir," said Turner. "He's asking us to stay."

"Then ask him why he wants us to."

This time the Mudir spoke for a long time.

"So that's it, sir," reported Turner. "Now we know. There are pirates about."

"Tell me exactly what he said, if you please, Mr. Turner."

"There are pirates along the coast, sir," explained Turner, accepting the rebuke. "A fellow called Michael—Michael the—the Slayer of Turks, sir. I've heard of him. He raids these coasts. A Greek, of course. He was at Fettech two days back. That's just along the coast, sir."

"And the Mudir's afraid this'll be the next place he raids?"

"Yes, sir. I'll ask him so as to make sure, sir," added Turner, when Hornblower glanced at him.

The Mudir was quite eloquent now that he had taken the plunge. Turner had to listen for a long time before he could resume his translation.

"Michael burns the houses, sir, and takes the women and cattle. He's the sworn enemy of the Mohammedans. That's where the Vali is with the local army, sir. He went to head off Michael, but he guessed wrong. He went to Adalia, and that's a week's march away, sir."

"I see."

With *Atropos* lying in Marmorice Bay a pirate would never venture in, and the Mudir and his people were safe as long as she stayed there. The purpose of the Mudir's visit was plain; he wanted to persuade Hornblower to stay until this Michael was at a safe distance again. It was a remarkable piece of good fortune; it was, thought Hornblower, ample compensation for the freak of fate which had left McCullum wounded in a duel. In the same way that in a long enough session the whist player found that the luck evened itself out, so it was with war. Good luck followed bad—and for Hornblower that was an astonishing admission, although he was ready enough to admit that bad luck followed good. But he must on no account show any pleasure.

"It's a stroke of luck for us, sir," said Turner.

"Please keep your conclusions to yourself, Mr. Turner," said Hornblower bitingly.

The tone of his voice and Turner's crestfallen expression puzzled the Mudir, who had not ceased to watch them closely. But he waited patiently for the unbelievers to make the next move.

"No," said Hornblower decisively, "tell him I can't do it."

At Hornblower's shake of the head the Mudir actually showed a little dismay even before Turner translated. He stroked his white beard and spoke again, choosing his words carefully.

"He's offering to bribe us, sir," said Turner. "Five lambs or kids for every day we stay here."

"That's better," said Hornblower. "Tell him I'd rather have money."

It was the Mudir's turn to shake his head when he heard what Turner had to say. He looked, to Hornblower's searching eye, like a man quite sincere.

"He says there isn't any money, sir. The Vali took all there was when he was here last."

"He has our twenty guineas, anyway. Tell him I want them back, and six lambs a day—no kids—and I'll stay."

That was how it was decided in the end. With Turner escorting the Mudir back in the launch Hornblower went forward to inspect the gunner's work. It was nearly completed. A hundred odd feet of hose, carefully coiled, lay on the deck, and one end disappeared into a powder keg covered over with canvas which the gunner was smearing thickly with pitch. Hornblower stooped to examine what must be the weakest point, where the canvas cover of the keg was sewn round the hose.

"That's as good as I can make it, sir," said the gunner. "But it's a mighty long length of hose."

At a hundred feet below water the pressures were enormous. A minute, indetectable pinprick anywhere in the fabric and water would be forced in.

"We can try it," said Hornblower. "The sooner the better."

That was how it always was—"the sooner the better" might be found written on a naval officer's heart like Queen Mary's Calais. Man the gig, see that all necessary equipment was packed into it, herd the divers into the bows after their last-minute instructions from McCullum, and start off without a minute wasted. Drink coffee with a Turkish Mudir at one hour, and dabble in underwater explosives the next. If variety was the spice of life, thought Hornblower, his present existence must be an Oriental curry.

"Easy!" he ordered, and the gig drifted slowly up to the moored plank which marked the accessible point of the wreck underneath.

Looney knew his business. The canvas-covered powder keg lay beside him; it was bound with line, and Looney took another short length of line, secured one end to the keg, passed the line round the mooring line of the buoy, and secured the other end to the keg again. He checked to see that the free end of the fuse-hose was properly fastened to the empty keg that was to buoy it up, and then gave a piping order to one of his colleagues, who stood up to take off his clothes. Looney laid hold of the powder keg, but it was too heavy for his spindly arms.

"Help him, you two," said Hornblower to the two seamen nearest. "See that the line's clear and see that the hose is clear, too."

Under Looney's direction the powder keg was lifted up and lowered over the side.

"Let go! Handsomely! Handsomely!" ordered Hornblower.

It was a tense moment—one more tense moment—to watch the powder keg sink below the choppy surface. By the line attached to it the seamen lowered it slowly down, the fuse-hose uncoiling after it as the keg sank. The loop of line which Looney had passed round the mooring line of the buoy made certain that the keg would sink to the right place.

"Bottom, sir," said a seaman, as the lowering line went slack in his hands. Several feet of hose remained in the boat.

The diver was sitting on the opposite gunwale; he carried a sheath knife on a string round his naked waist, and he took in his hands the cannon ball that Looney gave him. Then he lowered himself over and vanished under the surface. They waited until he came up; they waited while the next diver went down and came up again, they waited while Looney took his turn too. Dive succeeded dive; apparently it was not too easy an operation to move the powder keg to exactly the right place under the break of the *Speedwell's* poop. But presumably, down below the surface, the thing was achieved in the end. Looney came up from what seemed to be an extra long dive; he had to be helped over the gunwale and he lay gasping in the bows for some time recovering. Then at last he sat up and made to Hornblower the unmistakable gesture of handling flint and steel.

"Strike a light," said Hornblower to Leadbitter. In all his life he had never properly acquired the knack of it.

Leadbitter opened the tinder box, and struck, and struck again. It did not take Leadbitter more than six times before he succeeded. He bent and blew the spark on the tinder into life, took the piece of slow match and caught the fire on it, blew that into life too, and looked to Hornblower for further orders.

"I'll do it," said Hornblower.

Leadbitter handed him the glowing match, and Hornblower sat with it in his hand for a second while he checked once more to see that all was ready. He was tingling with excitement.

"Stand by with the cask!" he said. "Leadbitter, have the stopper ready."

There were four or five inches of quick match hanging out of the fuse-hose; Hornblower dabbed the glowing match upon it. A second's hesitation and it took fire. Hornblower watched the spark run along the quick match and vanish down into the hose.

"Stopper it!" said Hornblower, and Leadbitter forced the wooden stopper into the end of the hose, grinding down upon the brittle ashes of the match.

At five seconds to the foot the fire was now, he hoped, travelling down the hose, down, down, far below the level of the sea. At the far end, next to the powder keg, there was a foot of slow match. That burned at five minutes to the foot; they had plenty of time—no need for feverish haste, however great the urge to hurry.

"Over with it!" said Hornblower, and Leadbitter picked up the empty cask and lowered it gently into the water. It floated there, holding up above the surface the stoppered end of the fuse-hose.

"Oars!" said Hornblower. "Give way!"

The gig swung away from the floating keg. The spark was still travelling along the quick match, Hornblower presumed; it would be some seconds yet before it even reached the slow match down there by the wreck of the *Speedwell*. He remembered to take the time by his watch.

"Take her back to the ship," he ordered Leadbitter; he looked back to where the empty cask bobbed on the surface.

McCullum had said, "I advise you to keep clear of the explosion." Apparently the explosion of a barrel of powder, even far down under the water, created a turmoil on the surface that would endanger the gig. Beside the ship they would be a quarter of a mile away; that should be safe enough. When the bowman hooked on to the main chains of the *Atropos*, Hornblower looked at his watch again. It was exactly five minutes since he had seen the spark passing into the end of the fuse-hose. The explosion could be expected at any time from now.

Naturally the side of the ship was lined with every idler who could find a place there. The preparation of the charge and the fuse had excited gossip throughout the ship.

Hornblower changed his mind about awaiting the explosion in the gig and mounted to the deck.

"Mr. Jones!" he bellowed. "Is this a raree-show? Keep the hands at work, if you please."

"Aye aye, sir."

He very much wanted to see the explosion himself, but he feared to display curiosity inconsonant with his dignity. And there was the chance —a likely chance, according to McCullum—that there would be no explosion at all. A glance at his watch showed him that it was by now overdue. With an appearance of the utmost indifference he strolled forward to McCullum's bedside, where McCullum was listening to the reports of his divers.

"Nothing as yet?" said McCullum.

"Nothing."

"I never trust a fuse-hose beyond five fathoms," said McCullum, "even when I handle it myself."

Hornblower kept back an irritated answer, and gazed out towards the scene of his recent activities. In the choppy water he could just perceive at intervals the dark spot which was the keg that floated the end of the fuse-hose. He glanced at his watch again.

"Long overdue," he said.

"Water's in that hose. You'll have to use a flying-fuse after all."

"The sooner the better," said Hornblower. "How do I set about it?"

He was glad for the sake of his precious dignity that he had not waited in sight of the men.

XV

This time so many men were wanted for the operation that Hornblower was using the launch instead of the gig. As usual the three Ceylonese divers were huddled in the bows, but next to them in the bottom of the boat stood an iron pot of melted pitch, and beside it squatted a sail-maker's mate, and Mr. Clout, the gunner, sat amidships with the powder keg between his legs. The canvas covering to the keg was incompletely sewn, gaping wide at the upper end. They dropped the grapnel and the launch rode on the little waves beside the little keg that floated with the end of the useless fuse-hose, a monument to the previous failure.

"Carry on, Mr. Clout," said Hornblower.

This was something more than exciting. This was dangerous. The divers stripped themselves for their work, and sat up to begin their exercises of inflating and deflating their lungs. There would not be any time to spare later. Clout took the tinderbox and proceeded to strike a spark upon the tinder, crouching low to shelter it from the small breeze which blew over the surface of the Bay. He caught fire upon the slow match, brought it to a glow, and looked over at Hornblower.

"Carry on, I said," said Hornblower.

Clout dabbed the slow match upon the fuse that protruded through a hole in the end of the powder keg. Hornblower could hear the faint irregular hissing of the fuse as Clout waited for it to burn down into the hole. Among them now, in the middle of the boat, fire was creeping towards thirty pounds of gunpowder. If there were a few powder grains out of place, if the fuse were the least faulty, there would come a sudden crashing explosion which would blow them and the boat to fragments. There was not a sound in the boat save the hissing of the fuse. The spark crept down into the hole. The powder keg at this upper end had a double head, the result of the most careful work by the ship's cooper.

In the space between the two heads was coiled the fuse, whose farther end penetrated the inner head to rest amid the powder. Along that coil stapled to the inner head the fire was now moving unseen, creeping round on its way to dive down along its final length through the inner head.

Clout took from his pocket the canvas-covered stopper, and dipped it into the warm pitch.

"Make sure of it, Mr. Clout," said Hornblower.

Clout rammed the stopper into the hole in the outer head. The action cut off the sound of the hissing fuse, but everyone in the boat knew that the fire was still pursuing its inexorable way inside. Clout smeared pitch thickly about the stopper and then moved out of the way.

"Now, my hearty," he said to the sailmaker's mate.

This last needed no urging. Needle and palm in hand, he took Clout's place and sewed up the canvas cover over the top of the keg.

"Keep those stitches small," said Hornblower; the sailmaker's mate, crouching over instant death, was not unnaturally nervous. So was Hornblower, but the irritation caused by the previous failure made him anxious that the work should be well done.

The sailmaker's mate finished the last stich, oversewed it, and, whipping out his sheath knife, cut the twine. There could be hardly anything more harmless in appearance than that canvas-covered keg. It looked a stupid, a brainless object, standing there in the boat. Clout was already daubing pitch over the newly-sewn end; the sides and the other end had been thickly pitched before the keg was put into the launch.

"Now the line," said Hornblower.

As on the previous occasion a loop of line attached to the keg was passed round the mooring line of the buoy and secured to the keg again.

"Hoist it, you two. Lower away. Handsomely."

The keg sank below the surface, dangling on the lowering line as the men let it down hand over hand. There was a sudden relief from tension in the boat, marked by a sudden babble of talk.

"Silence!" said Hornblower.

Even though the thing was invisible now, sinking down to the bottom of the Bay, it was still deadly—the men did not understand that. One of the divers was already sitting on the gunwale, a cannon-ball in his hands—that was a ridiculous moment for Hornblower to remember that he had not carried out his earlier resolution to get in a store of rocks for that purpose—and his chest expanding and contracting. Hornblower would have liked to tell him to make certain to place the powder keg to the best advantage, but that was impossible owing to the difficulties of language. He had to content himself with a glance, half encouragement and half threat.

"Bottom, sir," announced the seaman at the lowering line.

The diver slipped from the gunwale and vanished under the surface. Down there with the powder charge and the glowing fuse he was in worse peril even than before. "They've seen one of their mates blown to bits using a flying fuse off Cuddalore," McCullum had said. Hornblower wanted nothing like that to happen now. It occurred to him that if it were to happen the launch, with him in it, would be on top of the explosion and turmoil, and he wondered what was the mysterious force that always drove him into voluntarily taking part in dangerous adventures. He thought it must be curiosity, and then he realized that it was a sense of shame as well; and it never occurred to him that a sense of duty had something to do with it too.

The second diver was sitting on the gunwale, cannon-ball in hand and breathing deeply, and the moment the first diver's head broke water he let himself slip down and vanished. "I've put the fear of God into 'em," McCullum had said. "I've told 'em that if the charge explodes without being properly placed they'll all get two dozen. An' I've said we're here to stay. No matter how long we try to get the money up. So you can rely on 'em. They'll do their best."

And they certainly were doing their best. Looney was waiting on the gunwale now, and down he went as soon as the second diver appeared. They wanted to waste no time at all. Not for the first time Hornblower peered overside in the attempt to see down through the water, unsuccessfully again. It was clear, and the loveliest deep green, but there was just sufficient lop and commotion on the surface to make it impossible to see down. Hornblower had to take it for granted that deep down below, in semi-darkness at least, and amid paralysing cold, Looney was dragging the powder charge towards the wreck and shoving it under the break of the poop. That powder keg under water could weigh little enough, thanks to the upthrust that Archimedes discovered, twenty centuries ago.

Looney reappeared, and the first diver instantly went down to replace him. This business was for the divers a gamble with life and death, a losing lottery. If the charge were to explode prematurely it would be chance that would dictate who would happen to be down there with it at that moment. But surely it could not take long to move the charge a few yards along the bottom and into the right place. And down there, he hoped, the fire was creeping along the coils of the fuse, sandwiched tight between the two barrel-heads. The philosophers had decided that fuses were able to burn in the absence of air—unlike candles—because the nitre that permeated the cord supplied the same combustible substance that air supplied. It was a discovery that went close to solving the problem of life—a human being's life went out like a candle's in the absence of air. It might be reasonably expected soon that the discovery might be made as to how to maintain life without air.

Yet another dive. The fire was hurrying along the fuse. Clout had allowed enough for an hour's burning—it must not be too little, obviously, but also it must not be too much, for the longer the keg was exposed to the water pressure the greater the chance of a weak point giving way and water seeping in. But Clout had pointed out that in that confined space between the barrel-heads the heat would not be able to escape; it would grow hotter and hotter in there and the fuse would burn faster—the fire might even jump from one part of the coil to another. The rate of burning, in other words, was unpredictable.

The diver who had just appeared gave a sharp cry, in time to prevent the next one—Looney—from going down. An eager question and answer, and Looney turned to Hornblower with a waving of hands.

"Get that man on board," ordered Hornblower. "Up anchor!"

A few strokes of the oars got the launch under weigh; the Ceylonese in the bows were chattering like sparrows at dawn.

"Back to the ship," ordered Hornblower.

He would go straight on board without looking back once; he would not compromise his dignity by awaiting an explosion which might never come. The tiller was put over and the launch began her steady course towards *Atropos*.

And then it happened, while Hornblower's back was turned to it. A sullen, muffled roar, not very loud, as if a gun had been fired in a distant cave. Hornblower swung round in his seat just in time to see a bulging wave overtake them, heaving up the stern of the launch. The stern sank and bow rose, the launch pitching violently, like a child's toy boat in a tub. The water that surged round them was discoloured and dark. It was only for a few seconds that the violent commotion lasted, and then it passed on, leaving the launch rocking jerkily.

"She's gone up, sir," said Clout, quite unnecessarily.

The hands were chattering as much as the Ceylonese.

"Silence in the boat!" said Hornblower.

He was angry with himself because the unexpected sound had caused him to leap in his seat. He glowered at the men, and they fell into a hushed silence.

"Starboard your helm," growled Hornblower. "Give way!"

The launch swung round and retraced its course towards the scene of the explosion, marked by a dirty patch of water. Half a dozen big bubbles rose to the surface and burst as he watched. Then something else came up, and something else, dead fish floating up to the surface, their white bellies gleaming under the sky. The launch passed one which was not quite dead; it was making feeble efforts, just perceptible, to right itself and descend again.

"Silence!" said Hornblower again—the irrepressible chatter had broken out again. "Easy!"

In silence the launch floated over the scene of the explosion. Dead fish, a stain, and nothing else. Nothing else at all. Hornblower felt a sick feeling of disappointment; there should be fragments from the wreck covering the surface, shattered bits of timber to show that the powder charge had done its work. The fact that there was none was proof that no gap had been blown in the wreck. His mind was racing into the future. Another charge with another flying fuse would have to be used, he supposed, and the most brutal threats would have to be employed towards the divers to make them put it into position. They had escaped the last explosion by not more than thirty seconds, he supposed, and they would be chary of running the risk again.

There was a bit of timber! No, it was the plank which had been used as a marker buoy.

"Haul in on that line," said Hornblower to the man pulling stroke oar. There was only ten feet of line attached to the plank—the line had been broken at that point; so the explosion had effected something, at least. It was ironical that that was all—just a marker buoy torn loose.

"Put on another grapnel and line," ordered Hornblower. They must still be close enough to the spot for the marker to be better than nothing.

Hornblower caught Looney's eye; he seemed willing enough to all appearance. It would save time if an examination of the scant results were made now.

"Looney," said Hornblower, and pointed overside. He had only to point a second time for Looney to nod his agreement and pull off his clothes again. As far as Hornblower could remember Looney had not yet made his daily quota of five dives yet. Looney inflated his chest and slipped in, and the launch lay drifting. The little waves that slapped against her sides had a different quality from usual; they had not even the small amount of system arising from the wind that agitated the surface—they seemed to come from all points at once. Hornblower realized that they were the last dying remnants of turbulence which the explosion had set up.

Up came Looney, his slender bundle of black hair bobbing beside his face. His white teeth showed in what might almost be thought to be a smile, except that of course he was gasping for breath. He struck out towards the launch, saying something to his colleagues as he did so which set them off twittering volubly. Apparently the explosion which had torn the marker buoy loose had not driven it any distance from its position. They hauled Looney on board into the bows. The chattering went on; now Looney was making his way aft over the thwarts and between the men. He was rubbing something in a portion of his clothing as he came—something which he put into Hornblower's hand with a broad grin. Something disc-shaped and heavy, tarnished, encrusted, and yet—and yet—

"God bless my soul," said Hornblower.

It was a shilling; Hornblower could only stare at it, and turn it over in his fingers. Every eye in the boat was directed at it; the men were quick enough to guess even if they could not see it clearly. Someone started to cheer, and the others took it up. Hornblower looked down the boat at the grinning faces. Even Clout was waving his hat and yelling.

"Silence!" shouted Hornblower. "Mr. Clout, you ought to be ashamed of yourself."

But the noise did not stop instantly as before; the men were too excited. But it died away at length, and the men waited. Hornblower had to think now about the next move, completely at a loss—this development had taken him by surprise and he had no idea for the moment what to do next. It would have to be anti-climax, he decided at last. For the recovery of the treasure fresh equipment would be necessary; that was certain. The divers had made nearly as many dives that day as they could. Moreover, McCullum must be informed of the results of the explosion and his decision heard regarding further steps. Hornblower even realized that there was no certainty that subsequent operations would be easy. One shilling did not make a quarter of a million sterling. There might be much further work necessary.

"Oars!" he snapped at the waiting men. The oar-looms clattered into the rowlocks and the men bent forward ready to pull. "Give way!"

The oar-blades bit into the water and the launch slowly gathered way.

"Head for the ship!" he growled at the coxswain.

He sat glowing in the stern-sheets. Anyone seeing his face might well have thought that the launch was returning after a complete failure, but it was merely that he was annoyed with himself at not being quick-witted enough to have had the appropriate orders ready at once when that astonishing shilling was put into his hand. The whole boat's crew had seen him at a loss. His precious dignity was hurt. When he got on board he was inclined to sulk in his cabin, but common sense made him go forward soon to discuss the situation with McCullum.

"There's a cascade of silver," said McCullum, who had been listening to the reports of the divers. "The bags have rotted, and when the treasure room was blown open the silver poured out. I think that's clear enough."

"And the gold?" asked Hornblower.

"Looney can't tell me as yet," said McCullum. "If I had been in the launch I daresay I should have acquired more information."

Hornblower bit back an angry retort. Nothing would please McCullum better than a quarrel, and he had no wish to indulge him.

"At least the explosion served its purpose," he said pacifically.

"Like enough."

"Then why," asked Hornblower—the question had been awaiting the asking for a long time—"if the wreck was blown open why didn't wreckage come to the surface?"

"You don't know?" asked McCullum in reply, clearly gratified at possessing superior knowledge.

"No."

"That's one of the elementary facts of science. Timber submerged at great depths soon becomes waterlogged."

"Indeed?"

"Wood only floats—as I presume you know—by virtue of the air contained in the cavities in its substance. Under pressure that air is squeezed out, and, deprived of this upthrust, the residual material has no tendency to rise."

"I see," said Hornblower. "Thank you, Mr. McCullum."

"I am accustomed by now," said McCullum, "to supplementing the education of King's officers."

"Then I trust," said Hornblower, still keeping his temper, "you will continue with mine. What is the next step to take?"

McCullum pursed his lips.

"If that damned Dutch doctor," he said, "would only have the sense to allow me out of this bed I could attend to it all myself."

"He'll have the stitches out of you soon," said Hornblower. "Meanwhile time is of importance."

It was infuriating that a captain in his own ship should have to endure this sort of insolence. Hornblower thought of the official complaints he could make. He could quarrel with McCullum, abandon the whole attempt, and in his report to Collingwood he would declaim that "owing to the complete lack of co-operation on the part of Mr. William McCullum, of the Honourable East India Company's Service" the expedition had ended in failure. No doubt McCullum would then be rapped on the knuckles officially. But it was better to achieve success, even without receiving any sympathy for the trials he was enduring, than to return with the best of excuses empty-handed. It was just as meritorious to pocket his pride and to coax McCullum into giving clear instructions as it was to head a boarding party on to an enemy's deck. Just as meritorious—although less likely to achieve a paragraph in the Gazette. He forced himself to ask the right questions and to listen to McCullum's grudging explanations of what should next be done.

And it was pleasant, later, when eating his dinner, to be able to congratulate himself on his duty done, orders given, all prepared. Those words of McCullum's, "a cascade of silver," ran in his mind as he sat and ate. It called for little imagination to conjure up a mental picture of the wreck down there in the translucent water, with her strong-room torn open and the silver in a frozen stream pouring out of it. Gray could have written a poem about it; and somewhere in that strong-room there was the gold. Life was good, and he was a fortunate man. He slowly consumed his last mouthful of roast lamb, and addressed himself to his lettuce salad, tender young plants, sweet and delicious, the first fruits of the Turkish spring.

XVI

The Turkish spring was not going to give way to summer without a last struggle, without calling the vanished winter back to her aid. The wind blew wildly and cold from the north-westward; the skies were grey, and the rain lashed down torrentially. It drummed upon the deck, streaming out through the scuppers; it poured in unexpected streams down from points in the rigging; even though it grudgingly gave to the crew the chance to wash their clothes in fresh water it denied them the opportunity of drying them again. *Atropos* swung fitfully to her anchor as the gusts blowing down from the surrounding mountains backed and veered, whipping the surface of the Bay into turbulent white-caps. Wind and rain seemed peculiarly searching. Everyone seemed to be colder and wetter than if the ship were battling a storm in mid-Atlantic, with the deck leaking as she worked in a sea way and the waves crashing down upon it; sulkiness and bad temper made their appearance among the ship's company along with the cold and wet—lack of exercise and lack of occupation combined with the constant drumming of the rain to bring that about.

Walking upon the quarterdeck with the raindrops rattling upon his oilskin seemed to Hornblower to be a cheerless business, the more so until this gale dropped there would be no chance of continuing the salvage operations. Boxes of gold lay over there under that wind-whipped surface; he hated having to wait through these empty hours before knowing if they could be recovered. He hated the thought of having to rouse himself from his inertia and exert himself to re-establish the good spirits of the ship's company, but he knew he must.

"Messenger!" he said, "my compliments to Mr. Smiley and Mr. Horrocks, and I'll see them at once in my cabin."

Half an hour later both watches were assembled on deck by divisions ("Half an hour I'll give you to get it all arranged," Hornblower had said) wearing only their duck trousers in the rain, the cold drops beating on their bare chests and feet. There was plenty of growling at the discomfort, but there was amusement among the topmen because every idler in the ship was there—"I'll have 'em all," Hornblower had said, "waisters and holders, gunner's crew and sailmaker's crew." And there was the excitement always attendant upon a race; and there was the compensation of seeing the three senior watch-keeping officers, Jones and Still and Turner, climbing the ratlines to take their places in the cross-trees to see that the racing was fair. Hornblower stood forward by the knightheads with his speaking trumpet so that the wind would carry his voice plainly along the deck.

"One to get steady!" he shouted. "Two to be ready! Three—and you're *off*!"

It was a relay race, up the rigging of each mast in turn and down again, port watch against starboard; it was the inclusion of the men who rarely, if ever, went aloft that gave spice to the proceedings. Soon divisions down on deck were dancing with excitement as they watched the slow ascent and descent of some lumbering gunner's mate or ship's corporal; until he completed the journey they were not free to dash to the next mast and start again.

"Come on, Fatty!"

The Pegasus-winged topmen to whom the ascent was a trifle leaped up and down on deck with never a thought for the streaming rain as some rival division, set free by the eventual descent of its last man, rushed joyfully along the deck to the next mast while they were forced to stand and witness the cautious movements of the slowest of their own side.

Up went the men and down, round and across. The Prince of Seitz-Bunau came shrieking round the deck, wild with excitement; Horrocks and Smiley, captains of the two sides, were croaking like crows, their voices failing them with the continual shouting as they organized and encouraged. The cook's mate, who was the last man of the port watch, was already close to the mainmast head when Horrocks, who had reserved himself to be the last of the starboard watch, began the ascent on the other side. Everyone in the ship seemed to be shouting and gesticulating. Up ran Horrocks, the shrouds vibrating with the ape-like speed of his passage. The cook's mate reached the cross-trees and started down again.

"Come on, Fatty!"

The cook's mate did not even look to see where to put his feet, and he was coming down two ratlines at a time. Horrocks reached the cross-trees and leaped for the deck stay. Down he came, sliding at a speed that must burn his hands. Cook's mate and midshipman reached the deck together, but Horrocks had farther to run to reach his place with his division than did the cook's mate. There was a final yell as both of them staggered gasping to their places, but the cook's mate was first by a full yard, and every eye was turned towards Hornblower.

"Port watch wins!" he announced. "Starboard watch provides the entertainment tomorrow night!"

The port watch cheered again, but the starboard watch—Hornblower was observing them closely—was not humiliated. He could guess that there were plenty of men among them who were not too displeased at the thought of tomorrow exhibiting their talents to an audience and who were already planning their turns. He put his speaking trumpet to his lips again.

"Attention! Mr. Horrocks! Mr. Smiley! Dismiss your teams."

Aft, beside the wardroom door, as Hornblower was returning to his cabin, there was an unusual figure, walking with slow steps under the supervision of the doctor.

"This is a pleasure, Mr. McCullum," said Hornblower. "It's good to see you out of your bed."

"The incision has entirely healed, sir," said Eisenbeiss, proudly. "Not only are the sutures removed, but I have judged it safe to remove the bristle from the wound, as the drainage was complete."

"Excellent!" said Hornblower. "Then that arm will come out of its sling soon?"

"Within a few days. The broken ribs secm to have knitted well."

"Still a bit stiff round here," said McCullum, feeling his right armpit with his left hand. He was displaying none of his usual ill temper; but a convalescent, making his first attempt to walk, and with his wound under discussion, could feel so much in the centre of the picture as to be well disposed towards humanity.

"Well it might be," said Hornblower. "A pistol bullet at twelve paces is not a welcome visitor. We thought we had lost you. At Malta they thought that bullet was in your lungs."

"It would have been easier," said Eisenbeiss, "if he had not been so muscular. The bullet could not be felt in that mass of muscle."

McCullum fished from his left trouser pocket a small object which he handed to Hornblower.

"D'you see that?" asked McCullum. It was the bullet which Eisenbeiss had extracted, flattened and irregular. Hornblower had seen it before, but this was not the moment to say so. He marvelled over it in suitable terms, much to McCullum's gratification.

"I think," said Hornblower, "that this occasion should be observed with a fitting ceremony. I shall invite the wardroom to dine with me, and I can ask you two gentlemen first of all."

"Honoured, I'm sure," said McCullum, and Eisenbeiss bowed.

"Let us say tomorrow, then. We can dine in comfort before the entertainment which the starboard watch is providing."

He retired to his cabin well pleased with himself. He had exercised his crew; he had given them something to think about; he had found a suitable occasion to entertain his officers socially; his salvage expert had returned from the jaws of death and in a better temper than usual —all this, and the *Speedwell's* treasure lay on the Tom Tiddler's Ground of the sandy bottom of the Bay, with gold and silver only waiting to be picked up. His good opinion of himself even enabled him to endure the tedium of the concert given by the starboard watch that night. There were the sentimental songs which a handsome young foretopman sang; Hornblower found their glutinous sentimentality as wearisome to his soul as the music was to his tone-deaf ear. "The Flowers on Mother's Grave" and "The Empty Cradle"—the young seaman squeezed out every lugubrious drop from their funereal substance, and his audience, with the exception of Hornblower, revelled in it. And an elderly bos'n's mate sang sea songs in a thunderous bass while Hornblower marvelled that a seagoing audience could tolerate the misuse of nautical terms in those songs; if his "good sail" were to "rustle" with a following wind, his officer of the watch would hear from him in good round terms, and there was, of course, the usual landsman's confusion between the sheet and the sail, and Dibdin had never bothered to find out that a "sheer hulk" was still leading a useful existence thanks to its sheers—the term did not imply a complete hulk or anything like it. And of course the song laid stress on the statement that Tom Bowling was dead, like the fore-topman's mythical mother and baby. He had "Gone aloft" and everybody in the ship's company, apparently, felt the better for it.

The hornpipes were more agreeable; Hornblower could admire the lightness and grace of the dancers and could manage to ignore the squeaky sweetness of the flute that accompanied them, played by the same cook's mate whose final effort had won the race for the port watch —his services as accompanist were so necessary, apparently, that they were called for even though the port watch were officially the guests at the concert. To Hornblower the most amusing part of the evening's entertainment, in fact, was the difference in attitude between the two watches, the starboard watch as anxious hosts and the port watch as critical guests. He could congratulate himself again at the end of the evening on a successful piece of work. He had a willing and orderly crew, and a satisfied complement of officers.

And next morning came the real triumph, no less satisfactory in that Hornblower stayed on board the ship and allowed McCullum, his arm still in a sling, to go out with launch and longboat and all the new apparatus that had been constructed for the salvage operations. Hornblower stood at the side of the ship, warmed by the newly returned sunshine, as the boats returned. McCullum pointed with his left hand to a vast heap piled between the centre thwarts of the launch, and turned and pointed to another in the longboat. Silver! The divers must have worked fast down in the depths, shovelling the coins with their hands into the lowered buckets.

The boats came alongside, and a working party prepared to hoist the mass of silver on board. A sudden sharp order by McCullum halted the three Ceylonese divers as they were about to make their way forward to their own particular lair. They looked at him a little sheepishly as he gave a further order in their strange tongue, and he repeated it. Then slowly they began to take off their clothes; Hornblower had seen them stripping themselves so often before in the days—they seemed weeks ago—when the salvage operations had begun. The voluminous cotton garments came off one by one.

"I'll lay a bet," said McCullum, "they've got fifty pounds between them."

One of the garments gave out a mysterious chink as it was laid on the deck, despite the care of the owner.

"Master at arms!" said Hornblower, "search those clothes!"

With a grinning crew looking on the seams and folds of the clothing were emptied of coins, dozens of them.

"They never make a dive," said McCullum, "without trying this on."

Hornblower could only wonder how a naked man climbing from the sea into a boat could possibly manage to convey silver coins into his clothing unobserved, but anything was possible to human ingenuity.

"That would have made them rich for life if they could have taken it back to Jaffra," said McCullum. Reverting to the foreign speech he dismissed the divers, who picked up their clothes again and vanished, while McCullum turned back to Hornblower. "It might be quicker to weigh this than to count it. If we get it all up there'll be four tons altogether."

Silver by the ton! The sailmaker stitched sacks out of new canvas to hold it, and just as in the lost *Speedwell*, the lower lazarette was cleared to store it. And Hornblower found there was a profound truth in the story of Midas, who received the gift of the Golden Touch not so very far from where *Atropos* swung at anchor. Just as Midas lost his happiness at a moment when the world must have deemed him the happiest man on earth, so Hornblower lost his happiness at this moment of success. For as the silver was piled in the lazarette so he came to worry about the coins. He was in no doubt about the ingenuity and persistence and skill of the seamen under his orders; nor was he in doubt about the criminal pasts of many of them, the sweepings of Newgate Gaol. Tales innumerable were told about the remarkable ways in which seamen managed to steal liquor, but the man who stole liquor inevitably revealed himself sooner or later. This was money, English coins, and there was only a frail wooden bulkhead to keep out thieves. So, as in the *Speedwell*, the bulkheads and decks were reinforced by stout timbers nailed across them; the careful and well-planned arrangement of the stores in the hold had to be altered so that the biggest beef casks, the ones that could only be moved by block and tackle, were ranged outside the bulkheads to hinder thieves from breaking through. And even then Hornblower spent wakeful nights visualizing the situation of the lower lazarette and wondering first how he would set about breaking into it and second how he would defeat such an attempt. These feelings intensified each day as the piles of sacks of silver grew larger; and they grew ten times more intense on the triumphant day when McCullum's divers reached the gold.

McCullum knew his work, no doubt about that. One day he told Hornblower of the discovery of one of the chests of gold; the next morning Hornblower watched launch and longboat start off with strong-backs erected in their sterns, and blocks and tackles rigged on them, miles of line coiled in readiness, timbers, buckets, everything that human ingenuity could think of for use in this new task. Hornblower watched through his glass as the boats lay together over the wreck. He saw the divers go down and come up again, time after time. He saw the weighted lines lowered from the tackles; more than once he saw the hands begin to haul in on the falls and then desist while another diver went down, presumably to clear the line. Then at the end he saw the hands haul in again, and stay at work, hauling in, coiling down, until at last, between the two boats, something broke water and a yell of exultation came echoing over to the ship.

It was something quite large which was gingerly swung into the stern of the launch—Hornblower could see the stern of the launch sink and the bows rise as the weight was transferred. His calculations had already told him that a cubic foot of gold weighed half a ton—and gold was at a premium, five guineas in paper or more to the ounce. That was a king's ransom; Hornblower looked at it as the launch came pulling back alongside, a strange object lying in the bottom of the boat, half obscured by weed.

"Those must be wrought iron bars on it," said McCullum, standing beside him while Jones fussily supervised the transfer to the ship, "and best Sussex iron at that. Steel would have rusted to nothing a year ago, but some of those bars are still whole. The weeds growing from the oak must have been a yard long—my boys had to trim 'em off before they got the tackles round."

"Easy there! Easy!" shouted Jones.

"Vast heaving at the yardarm!" shouted the bos'n. "Now, you at the stay tackle, walk away with it!"

The chest dangled over the deck, balancing on its supporting lines.

"Easy! Lower away, yardarm! Easy! Lower away stay tackle! Handsomely!"

The chest sank to the deck; there were little dribbles of water still flowing from inside it. The gold that lay concealed inside it would have built, armed, and equipped the whole *Atropos*, have filled her holds with stores for a year, have provided a month's advance pay for the crew, and still have left a handsome balance.

"Well, that's one of them," said McCullum. "I have a feeling that it won't be so easy to get up the other two. This is the easiest job I've ever done, so far. We've been lucky—inexperienced as you are, you will never know how lucky."

But Hornblower knew how lucky he was. Lucky that McCullum had survived a pistol shot in the ribs; lucky that the Ceylonese divers had survived the journey all round Africa from India to Asia Minor; lucky—incredibly lucky—that the Turks had been so complacent, allowing him to carry out the salvage operation in the Bay without guessing what he was doing and without interfering. It was consideration of this good fortune that reconciled him at last to the worry regarding the guarding of the treasure in the lower lazarette. He was the most fortunate man on earth; fortunate (he told himself) and yet at the same time he owed some of his success to his own merits. He had been clever in his handling of the Mudir. It had been a cunning move to accept a bribe to stay here anchored in the Bay, to appear reluctant to do the very thing he wanted most to do. Collingwood would approve, no doubt. He had recovered the silver; he had recovered one-third of the gold already. He would receive a pat on the back from authority even if McCullum should find it impossible to recover the rest.

XVII

These Mediterranean mornings were beautiful. It was a pleasure to come on deck as the dawn brightened into daylight; usually the night wind had died down, leaving the Bay glassy smooth, reflecting, as the light increased, the intense blue of the sky as the sun climbed up over the mountains of Turkey. There was a refreshing chill in the air—not enough to necessitate wearing a pea-jacket—so that the increasing warmth of the sun brought a sensuous pleasure with it. During a walk on deck with his mind leisurely working out the plans for the day, Hornblower soaked in the beauty and freshness; and right at the back of his mind, flavouring his pleasure as a sauce might give the finishing touch to some perfect dish, was the knowledge that when he went below he could sit down to a plate of fried eggs and a pot of coffee. Beauty all round him, a growing appetite and the immediate prospect of satisfying it—at least they brought the realization that he was a fortunate man.

Today he was not quite as fortunate as usual, because instead of indulging in solitary thought he had to give some attention to McCullum and his problems.

"We'll have one more try along the present lines," said McCullum. "I'll send the boys down again today, and hear what they have to say. But I'm afraid that chest is out of reach at present. I came to suspect that yesterday."

Two days ago the second of the three chests of gold had been recovered, but only after an explosive charge had blown a wide entrance into the wreck.

"Yes," said Hornblower, "that was the substance of your report."

"It's not easy to make 'em go down right in among the wreckage."

"I shouldn't think it was," said Hornblower.

In the dimly-lit depths, under the intolerable weight of a hundred feet of water, to hold one's breath, suffocating, and to make one's way in among the tangled timbers, must be a frightful thing to do.

"The deck sloped away from the gap in the side, and I fancy the last explosion sent that third chest through and down. The whole wreck's on top of it now," said McCullum.

"Then what do you propose to do?"

"It'll be a couple of weeks' work, I expect. I'll use half a dozen charges—with flying fuses, of course—and blow the whole wreck to pieces. But I must inform you officially that the result may still be unsatisfactory."

"You mean you may not recover the gold even then?"

"I may not."

Two thirds of the gold and nearly all the silver lay already in the lower lazarette of the *Atropos*—a good second best, but as unsatisfactory as any other second best.

"I'm sure you'll do the best you can, Mr. McCullum," said Hornblower.

Already the morning breeze was blowing. The first gentle breaths had swung *Atropos* round from where she lay completely inert upon the water. Now she rode to her anchor again, with a fair breeze coursing along her deck. Hornblower felt it about his ears.

And for the last few seconds something had been troubling him. Subconsciously he had become aware of something, while he had addressed that final sentence to McCullum, like a gnat seen out of the corner of his eye. He looked over at the pineclad slopes of Ada peninsula, at the square outline of the fort on the summit. The beauty of the morning seemed suddenly to turn harsh and grey; the feeling of intense well-being was suddenly replaced by sharp apprehension.

"Give me that glass," he snapped at the master's mate of the watch.

There was really no need for the glass; Hornblower's powers of deduction had already reinforced his naked eye, and the telescope merely revealed what he was sure he would see. There was a flag waving over the fort on the peninsula—the red flag of Turkey, where no flag had flown yesterday, nor ever since his arrival in the Bay of Marmorice. There could be only one conclusion. There was a garrison in that fort now; troops must have come back to Marmorice—they must have manned the guns of the fort. He was a fool, a stupid, insensitive idiot, blinded by his own complacency. Now that the revelation had come to him his mind worked feverishly. He had been utterly deceived; the Mudir with his white beard and his innocent anxiety had played upon him the very trick he thought he was playing himself—had lulled him into self-confidence, gaining time for troops to be gathered while he thought he was gaining time to carry out the salvage operation. With bitter self-contempt it dawned upon him that all the work on the wreck must have been carefully noted from the shore. Even the Turks had telescopes—they must have seen all that was done. They must know of the treasure being recovered, and now they had manned the guns guarding the exit, shutting him in.

From where he stood aft he could not see Passage Island—Red Cliff Point lay in line with it. Without a word to the astonished master's mate he ran forward and threw himself into the foremast shrouds. He ran up them, gasping for breath, as fast as any of the competitors in that foolish relay race; back downward, he went up the futtock shrouds, and then up the fore topmast shrouds to the fore topmast head. There was a flag flying above the fort on Passage Island too; the glass revealed a couple of boats drawn up on the beach in the little cove there, showing how during the night, or at first dawn, the garrison had been conveyed there. The guns on Passage Island could cross their fire with those on Ada and sweep the entrance, and could sweep also the tortuous passage between the island and Kaia Rock. The cork was in the bottle. He and the *Atropos* were trapped.

Not by guns alone. The easterly sun, shining behind him, was reflected back from far off in the Rhodes Channel by three geometrical shapes close together on the horizon, two rectangles and a triangle—the sails of a big ship, a Turkish ship, obviously. Equally obvious was the fact that it could not be pure coincidence that the hoisting of the flags on the forts occurred at the same moment that those sails appeared. The flags had been hoisted as soon as the lofty fort on Ada had perceived the sails; the despised Turk was perfectly capable of executing a well-planned coup. In an hour—in less—that ship would be stemming the entrance to the Bay. With the wind blowing straight in he could not hope to escape, even discounting the fact that if he tried to beat out of the entrance the guns on Ada would dismast him. Hornblower was sunk in despair as he clung to his lofty perch, glass in hand; to the despair of a man faced by overwhelming odds was added the frightful self-contempt of a man who found himself out-tricked, out-deceived. The memory of his recent self-congratulation was like the echoing laughter of a crowd of scornful spectators, drowning his thoughts and paralysing his mental processes.

It was a bad moment, up there at the fore topmast head, perhaps the worst moment Hornblower had ever known. Self-control came back slowly, even though hope remained quite absent. Looking again through his glass at the approaching sails Hornblower found that the telescope was trembling with the shaking of his hands, the eyepiece blinding him by vibrating against his eyelashes. He could admit to himself that he was a fool—bitter though such an admission might be—but he could not admit to himself that he was a coward, at least that kind of coward. And yet was anything worth the effort? Did it matter if a grain of dust in a whirlwind retained its dignity? The criminal in the cart on the way to Tyburn strove to retain his self-control, strove not to give way to his pitiful human fears and weaknesses, tried to "die game" for the sake of his own self-respect under the gaze of the heartless crowd, and yet did it profit him when in five minutes he would be dead? There was a horrible moment when Hornblower thought how easy something else would be. He had only to let go his hold, to fall, down, down, to a final crash upon the deck and the end of all this, no need for further effort, the end, oblivion; that would be far easier than to face, trying to appear not to notice, the pity or contempt of his fellow men. He was being tempted to cast himself down, as Christ had been by Satan.

Then he told himself again that he was not that kind of coward. He was calm now; the sweat that had streamed down him lay cold upon his skin. He shut the telescope with a click that sounded clear amid the noise of the wind about his ears. He had no idea what he was going to do, but it was a healing mechanical exercise to set himself to descend the rigging, to lodge first one foot and then the other upon the ratlines, to make sure that despite the weakness he felt he accomplished the descent in safety. And, having set foot on deck, it was further good exercise to try to appear quite unruffled and unperturbed, the grain of dust unchanging in the whirlwind, even though he had a feeling that his cheeks were pale under their sunburn. Habit was a useful thing too; to put back his head and bellow an order could set his mechanism working again, as the stopped clock would start to tick again and would go on ticking after a single shake.

"Mr. McCullum! Belay those arrangements, if you please. Officer of the watch! Pipe all hands. Get the launch hoisted in. Leave the longboat for the present."

A surprised Jones came hurrying on deck at the call of all hands.

"Mr. Jones! Get a hawser passed out through a stern port. I want a spring on the cable."

"A spring, sir? Aye aye, sir."

It was a minute compensation for his own misery to see how a glance called forth the last three words after the astonished utterance of the first three. Men who went to sea, and ten times more so men who went to sea in a fighting ship, must be ready for the execution of the most unexpected orders, at any moment, even the shattering of the routine of a peaceful morning by an order to put a spring on the cable—a hawser passed out through a stern port and made fast to the anchor cable, so that by hauling in on the spring with the capstan the ship could be swung even though she was stationary, and her guns trained to sweep a different arc at will. It happened to be very nearly the only exercise in which Hornblower had not drilled his ship's company so far.

"You're too slow, Mr. Jones! Master-at-arms, take the names of those three men there!"

Midshipman Smiley went off with the hawser end in the longboat; Jones, running forward, bellowed himself hoarse through his speaking trumpet with instructions to Smiley, to the man beside him at the capstan, to the man aft with the hawser. Cable was taken in; cable was paid out.

"Spring's ready, sir."

"Very well, Mr. Jones. Hoist in the longboat and clear for action."

"Er—aye aye, sir. Pipe 'hands to quarters'. Clear for action. Drummer! Beat to quarters."

There was no marine detachment in a little ship like *Atropos*. The ship's boy who had been appointed drummer set his sticks rolling on his drumhead. That warlike sound—there was nothing quite as martial as the rolling of a drum—would drift over the water and would bear a message of defiance to the shore. The longboat came swaying down on the chocks; excited men, with the drum echoing in their ears, braced the lines about her and secured her; already the pump crew were directing a stream of water into her to fill her up—a necessary precaution against her catching fire while providing a convenient reservoir of water to fight other fires. The hands at the tackles broke off and went racing away to their other duties.

"Guns loaded and run out, if you please, Mr. Jones!"

"Aye aye, sir."

Mr. Jones was startled again. In a mere exercise of clearing for action it was usual merely to simulate the loading of the guns; otherwise when the exercise ended there was the difficulty and waste of drawing wads and charges. At the cry the powder boys went scurrying to bring up from below the cartridges that Mr. Clout was laying out in the magazine. Some gun captain gave a yell as he flung his weight on the tackle to run out his gun.

"Silence!"

The men were well enough behaved; despite the excitement of the moment they had worked in silence save for that one yell. Much drill and relentless discipline showed their effects.

"Cleared for action, sir!" reported Jones.

"Rig the boarding netting, if you please."

That was a harassing, irritating exercise. The nettings had to be roused out, laid in position along the ship's sides, and their lower edges made fast in the chains all round. Then lines from the yardarms and bowsprit end had to be rove through the upper edges. Then with steady hauling on the falls of the tackles the nettings rose into position, sloping up and out from the ship's sides from bow to stern, making it impossible for boarders to come in over the ship's side.

"Belay!" ordered Jones as the tricing lines came taut.

"Too taut, Mr. Jones! I told you that before. Slack away on those falls!"

Taut boarding nettings, triced up trimly as far as they would go, might look seamanlike, but were not as effective when their function as obstacles was considered. A loose, sagging netting was far more difficult to climb or to cut. Hornblower watched the netting sag down again into lubberly festoons.

"Belay!"

That was better. These nettings were not intended to pass an admiral's inspection, but to keep out boarders.

"Boarding nettings rigged, sir," reported Jones, after a moment's interval, to call his captain's attention to the fact that the ship's company was awaiting further orders; Hornblower had given the last one himself.

"Thank you, Mr. Jones."

Hornblower spoke a trifle absently; his gaze was not towards Jones, but was directed far away. Automatically Jones followed his glance.

"Good God!" said Jones.

A big ship was rounding Red Cliff Point, entering into the bay. Everyone else saw her at the same moment, and a babble of exclamation arose.

"Silence, there!"

A big ship, gaudily painted in red and yellow, coming in under topsails, a broad pendant at her mainmast head and the flag of the Prophet at her peak. She was a great clumsy craft, old-fashioned in the extreme, carrying two tiers of guns so that her sides were unnaturally high for her length; and her beam was unnaturally wide, and her bowsprit steved higher than present fashions in European navies dictated. But the feature which first caught the eye was the lateen rig on the mizzen mast; it was more than thirty years since the last lateen mizzen in the Royal Navy had been replaced by the square mizzen topsail. When Hornblower had first seen her through his glass the triangular peak of her mizzen beside her two square topsails had revealed her nationality unmistakably to him. She looked like something in an old print; without her flag she could have taken her place in the fighting line in Blake's navy or Van Tromp's without exciting comment. She must be almost the last survivor of the small clumsy ships of the line that had now been replaced by the stately 74; small, clumsy, but all the same with a weight of metal that could lay the tiny *Atropos* into a splintered wreck at one broadside.

"That's a broad pendant, Mr. Jones," said Hornblower. "Salute her."

He spoke out of the side of his mouth, for he had his glass trained on her. Her gun ports were closed; on her lofty forecastle he could see men scurrying like ants making ready to anchor. She was crowded with men; as she took in sail it was strange to see men balanced across the sloping mizzen yard—Hornblower had never expected to see a sight like that in his life, especially as the men wore long loose shirts like gowns which flapped round them as they hung over the yard.

The nine-pounder forward gave its sharp bang—some powder boy must have run fast below to bring up the one-pound saluting charges—and a puff of smoke, followed by a report, showed that the Turkish ship was replying. She had goose-winged her main topsail—another outlandish sight in these circumstances—and was slowly coming into the Bay towards them.

"Mr. Turner! Come here please, to interpret. Mr. Jones, send some hands to the capstan, if you please. Take in on the spring if necessary so that the guns bear."

The Turkish ship glided on.

"Hail her," said Hornblower to Turner.

A shout came back from her.

"She's the *Mejidieh*, sir," reported Turner. "I've seen her before."

"Tell her to keep her distance."

Turner hailed through his speaking trumpet, but the *Mejidieh* still came on.

"Tell her to keep off. Mr. Jones! Take in on the spring. Stand by at the guns, there!"

Closer and closer came the *Mejidieh*, and as she did so the *Atropos* swung round, keeping her guns pointed at her. Hornblower picked up the speaking trumpet.

"Keep off, or I'll fire into you!"

She altered course almost imperceptibly and glided by, close enough for Hornblower to see the faces that lined the side, faces with moustaches and faces with beards; mahogany-coloured faces, almost chocolate-coloured faces. Hornblower watched her go by. She rounded-to, with the goose-winged main topsail close-hauled, held her new course for a few seconds, and then took in her sail, came to the wind and anchored, a quarter of a mile away. The excitement of action ebbed away in Hornblower, and the old depression returned. A buzz of talk went up from the men clustered at the guns—it was quite irrepressible by now, with this remarkable new arrival.

"The lateener's heading this way, sir," reported Horrocks.

From the promptitude with which she appeared she must have been awaiting the *Mejidieh's* arrival. Hornblower saw her pass close under the *Mejidieh's* stern; he could almost hear the words that she exchanged with the ship, and then she came briskly up close alongside the *Atropos*. There in the stern was the white-bearded Mudir, hailing them.

"He wants to come on board, sir," reported Turner.

"Let him come," said Hornblower. "'Unlace that netting just enough for him to get through."

Down in the cabin the Mudir looked just the same as before. His lean face was as impassive as ever; at least he showed no signs of triumph. He could play a winning game like a gentleman; Hornblower, without a single trump card in his hand, was determined to show that he could play a losing game like a gentleman, too.

"Explain to him," he said to Turner, "that I regret there is no coffee to offer him. No fires when the ship's cleared for action."

The Mudir was gracious about the absence of coffee, as he indicated by a gesture. There was a polite interchange of compliments which Turner hardly troubled to translate, before he approached the business in hand.

"He says the Vali is in Marmorice with his army," reported Turner. "He says the forts at the mouth are manned and the guns loaded."

"Tell him I know that."

"He says that ship's the *Mejidieh*, sir, with fifty-six guns and a thousand men."

"Tell him I know that too."

The Mudir stroked his beard before taking the next step.

"He says the Vali was very angry when he heard we'd been taking treasure from the bottom of the Bay."

"Tell him it is British treasure."

"He says it was lying in the Sultan's waters, and all wrecks belong to the Sultan."

In England all wrecks belonged to the King.

"Tell him the Sultan and King George are friends."

The Mudir's reply to that was lengthy.

"No good, sir," said Turner. "He says Turkey's at peace with France now and so is neutral. He said—he said that we have no more rights here than if we were Neapolitans, sir."

There could not be any greater expression of contempt anywhere in the Levant.

"Ask him if he has ever seen a Neapolitan with guns run out and matches burning."

It was a losing game that Hornblower was playing, but he was not going to throw in his cards and yield all the tricks without a struggle, even though he could see no possibility of winning even one. The Mudir stroked his beard again; with his expressionless eyes he looked straight at Hornblower, and straight through him, as he spoke.

"He must have been watching everything through a telescope from shore, sir," commented Turner, "or it may have been those fishing boats. At any rate, he knows about the gold and the silver, and it's my belief, sir, that they've known there was treasure in the wreck for years. That secret wasn't as well kept as they thought it was in London."

"I can draw my own conclusions, Mr. Turner, thank you."

Whatever the Mudir knew or guessed, Hornblower was not going to admit anything.

"Tell him we have been delighted with the pleasure of his company."

The Mudir, when that was translated to him, allowed a flicker of a change of expression to pass over his face. But when he spoke it was with the same flatness of tone.

"He says that if we hand over all we have recovered so far the Vali will allow us to remain here and keep whatever else we find," reported Turner.

Turner displayed some small concern as he translated, but yet in his old man's face the most noticeable expression was one of curiosity; he bore no responsibility, and he could allow himself the luxury—the pleasure—of wondering how his captain was going to receive this demand. Even in that horrid moment Hornblower found himself remembering Rochefoucauld's cynical epigram about the pleasure we derive from the contemplation of our friends' troubles.

"Tell him," said Hornblower, "that my master King George will be angry when he hears that such a thing has been said to me, his servant, and that his friend the Sultan will be angry when he hears what his servant has said."

But the Mudir was unmoved by any suggestion of international complications. It would take a long, long time for a complaint to travel from Marmorice to London and then back to Constantinople. And Hornblower could guess that a very small proportion of a quarter of a million sterling, laid out in the proper quarter, would buy the support of the Vizier for the Vali. The Mudir's face was quite unrelenting—a frightened child might have a nightmare about a face as heartless as that.

"Damn it," said Hornblower, "I won't do it."

There was nothing he wanted more in this world than to break through the iron serenity of the Mudir.

"Tell him," said Hornblower, "I'll drop the gold back into the Bay sooner than hand it over. By God, I will. I'll drop it down to the bottom and they can fish for it themselves, which they can't do. Tell him I swear that, by—by the Koran or the beard of the Prophet, or whatever they swear by."

Turner nodded in surprised approval; that was a move he had not thought of, and he addressed himself eagerly to the task of translation. The Mudir listened with his eternal patience.

"No, it's no good, sir," said Turner, after the Mudir had replied. "You can't frighten him that way. He says—"

Turner was interrupted by a fresh sentence from the Mudir.

"He says that after this ship has been seized the idolaters—that's the Ceylonese divers, sir—will work for him just as they work for us."

Hornblower, desperate, thought wildly of cutting the divers' throats after throwing the treasure overboard; that would be consonant with this Oriental atmosphere, but before he could put the frightful thought into words the Mudir spoke again, and at considerable length.

"He says wouldn't it be better to go back with *some* treasure, sir—whatever more we can recover—than to lose everything? He says—he says—I beg your pardon, sir, but he says that if this ship is seized for breaking the law your name would not be held in respect by King George."

That was phrasing it elegantly. Hornblower could well imagine what their Lordships of the Admiralty would say. Even at the best, even if he fought it out to the last man, London would not look with favour on the man who had precipitated an international crisis and whose behaviour necessitated sending a squadron and an army into the Levant to restore British prestige at a moment when every ship and man was needed to fight Bonaparte. And at worst—Hornblower could picture his little ship suddenly overwhelmed by a thousand boarders, seized, emptied of the treasure, and then dismissed with contemptuous indulgence for him to take back to Malta with a tale possibly of outrage but certainly of failure.

It took every ounce of his moral strength to conceal his despair and dismay—from Turner as well as from the Mudir—and as it was he sat silent for a while, shaken, like a boxer in the ring trying to rally after a blow had slipped through his guard. Like a boxer, he needed time to recover.

"Very well," he said at length, "tell him I must think over all this. Tell him it is too important for me to make up my mind now."

"He says," translated Turner when the Mudir replied, "he says he will come tomorrow morning to receive the treasure."

XVIII

In the old days, long ago, Hornblower as a midshipman had served in the *Indefatigable* on cutting-out expeditions more numerous than he could remember. The frigate would find a coaster anchored under the protection of shore batteries, or would chase one into some small harbour; then at night—or even in broad day—the boats would be manned and sent in. The coaster would take all the precautions she could; she could load her guns, rig her boarding nettings, keep her crew on the alert, row guard round the ship, but to no avail. The boarders would fight their way on board, clear the decks, set sail, and carry off the prize under the nose of the defences. Often and often had Hornblower seen it close, had taken part. He had noted with small enough sympathy the pitiful precautions taken by the victim.

Now the boot was on the other leg; now it was even worse, because *Atropos* lay in the broad Bay of Marmorice without even the protection of shore batteries and with ten thousand enemies around her. Tomorrow, the Mudir had said, he would come for the treasure, but there was no trusting the Turks. That might be one more move to lull the *Atropos* into security. She might be rushed in the night. The *Mejidieh*, over there, could put into her boats more men than *Atropos* could boast altogether, and they could be supplemented with soldiers crammed into fishing boats from the shore. If she were attacked by twenty boats at once, from all sides, by a thousand Moslem fanatics, what could she do to defend herself?

She could rig her boarding nettings—they were already rigged. She could load her guns—they were already loaded, grape on top of round shot, depressed so as to sweep the surface of the Bay at close range round the ship. She could keep anxious watch—Hornblower was going round the ship himself, to see that the lookouts were all awake, the guns' crews dozing no more deeply than the hard decks would allow as they lay at their posts, the remainder of the hands stationed round the bulwarks with pike and cutlass within easy reach.

It was a novel experience to be the mouse instead of the cat, to be on the defensive instead of the offensive, to wait anxiously for the moon to rise instead of hurrying to the attack while darkness endured. It might be counted as another lesson in war, to know how the waiting victim thought and felt—some day in the future Hornblower might put that lesson to use, and, paralleling the thought of the ship he was going to attack, contrive to circumvent the precautions she was taking.

That was one more proof of the levity and inconstancy of his mind, said Hornblower to himself, bitterness and despair returning in overwhelming force. Here he was thinking about the future, about some other command he might hold, when there was no future. No future. Tomorrow would see the end. He did not know for certain yet what he would do; vaguely in his mind he had the plan that at dawn he would empty the ship of her crew—non-swimmers in the boats, swimmers sent to seek refuge in the *Mejidieh*—while he went down below to the magazine, with a loaded pistol, to blow the ship and the treasure, himself with his dead ambitions, his love for his children and his wife, to blow it all to fragments. But would that be better than bargaining? Would it be better than returning not only with *Atropos* intact but with whatever further treasure McCullum could retrieve? It was his duty to save his ship if he could, and he could. Seventy thousand pounds was far less than a quarter of a million, but it would be a godsend to an England at her wits' ends for gold. A Captain in the Navy should have no personal feelings; he had a duty to do.

That might be so, but all the same he was convulsed with anguish. This deep, dark sorrow which was rending him was something beyond his control. He looked across at the dark shape of the *Mejidieh*, and sorrow was joined to an intense hatred, like some ugly pattern of red and black before his mind's eye. The vague shape of the *Mejidieh* was drawing back abaft the *Atropos*' quarter—the soft night wind was backing round, as might be expected at this hour, and swinging the ships at their anchors. Overhead there were stars, here and there obscured by patches of cloud whose presence could just be guessed at, moving very slowly over the zenith. And over there, beyond the *Mejidieh*, the sky was a trifle paler; the moon must be rising above the horizon beyond the mountains. The loveliest night imaginable with the gentle breeze—this gentle breeze! Hornblower glowered round in the darkness as if he feared someone might prematurely guess the thought that was forming in his mind.

"I am going below for a few minutes, Mr. Jones," he said, softly.

"Aye aye, sir."

Turner, of course, had been talking. He had told the wardroom all about the quandary in which their captain found himself. One could hear curiosity in the tone of even those three words of Jones's. Resolution came to lacquer over the pattern of red and black.

Down in the cabin the two candles he sent for lit the whole little space, save for a solid shadow here and there. But the chart that he laid out between them was brightly illuminated. He stooped over it, peering at the tiny figures that marked the soundings. He knew them already, as soon as he came to think about them; there was really no need to refresh his memory. Red Cliff Point, Passage Island, Kaia Rock; Point Sari beyond Kaia Rock—he knew them all. He could weather Kaia Rock with this breeze if it should hold. God, there was need for haste! He blew out the candles and felt his way out of the cabin.

"Mr. Jones! I want two reliable bosn's mates. Quietly, if you please."

That breeze was still blowing, ever so gently, a little more fitful than might be desired, and the moon had not cleared the mountains yet.

"Now, you two, pay attention. Go quietly round the ship and see that every man is awake. Not a sound—you hear me? Topmen are to assemble silently at the foot of the masts. Silently."

"Aye aye, sir," was the whispered reply.

"Carry on. Now, Mr. Jones—"

The gentle patter of bare feet on the deck as the men assembled acted as accompaniment to the whispered orders Hornblower was giving to Jones. Over there was the vast bulk of the *Mejidieh*; two thousand ears which might catch the slightest unusual noise—an axe being laid ready on the deck, for instance, or capstan bars being gently eased into their sockets. The boatswain came aft again to rejoin the little group of officers round Hornblower and to make his report in a whisper that accorded ill with his bulk and power.

"The capstan pawl's thrown out, sir."

"Very good. Yours is the first move. Go back, count a hundred, and take up on the spring. Six turns, and hold it. Understand?"

"Aye aye, sir."

"Then off you go. You others are clear about your duties? Mr. Carslake, with the axe at the cable. I'll attend to the axe at the spring. Mr. Smiley, fore tops'l sheets. Mr. Hunt, main tops'l sheets. Go to your stations."

The little ship lay there quietly. A tiny rim of the moon came up over the mountains, and broadened momentarily, revealing her lying peacefully at anchor. She seemed inert, incapable of action. Silent men had swarmed up the rigging and were waiting for the signal. There was a gentle creaking as the spring to the cable tightened, but there was no clank from the capstan, for the pawl had been thrown out from the ratchet; the men at the capstan bars walked silently round, and when their six turns had been completed they stood, breasts against the bars, feet braced on the deck, holding the ship steady. Under the pull of the spring she lay at an angle to the breeze, so that when sail should be set not a moment would be wasted gathering stern way and paying off. She would be under command at once.

The moon had cleared the mountains; the seconds went slowly by.

Ting-ting went the ship's bell—two bells; the signal.

Feet pattered in unison. Sheaves squealed in blocks, but even as the ear caught that sound topsail yards and forestay had blossomed into sail. Forward and aft came brief sullen thumpings as axe blades cut through cable and spring—with the sudden end of the resistance of the spring the capstan spun round, precipitating the men at the bars to the deck. There were bruises and grazes, but nobody paid attention to the injuries; *Atropos* was under way. In five seconds, without giving any warning at all, she had transformed herself from something stationary and inert to a living thing, gliding through the water towards the entrance to the Bay. She was clear of the peril of the *Mejidieh's* broadside, for the *Mejidieh* had no spring on her cable to swing her round. She would have to weigh her anchor, or cut or slip her cable; she would have to set sail enough to give her steerage way, and then she would have to yaw round before she could fire. With an alert crew, awake and ready for the summons, it would be at least several minutes before she could turn her broadside upon *Atropos*, and then it would be at a range of half a mile or more.

As it was *Atropos* had gathered speed, and was already more than clear before *Mejidieh* gave her first sign of life. The deep booming of a drum came sounding over the water; not the high-pitched rattle of the *Atropos*' side-drum, but the far deeper and slower tone of a bass drum monotonously beaten.

"Mr. Jones!" said Hornblower. "Rig in those boarding nettings, if you please."

The moon was shining brightly, lighting the water ahead of them.

"Starboard a point," said Hornblower to the helmsman.

"Starboard a point," came the automatic reply.

"You're taking the west pass, sir?" asked Turner.

As sailing master and navigator his station in action was on the quarter-deck beside his captain, and the question he asked was strictly within his province.

"I don't think so," said Hornblower.

The booming of the *Mejidieh's* drum was still audible; if the sound reached the batteries the guns' crews there would be on the alert. And when he reached that conclusion there was an orange flash from far astern, as if momentarily a furnace door had been opened and then closed. Seconds later came the heavy report; the *Mejidieh* had fired a gun. There was no sound of the passage of the shot—but if it had even been a blank charge it would serve to warn the batteries.

"I'm going under Sari Point," said Hornblower.

"Sari Point, sir!"

"Yes."

It was surprise and not discipline that limited Turner's protests to that single exclamation. Thirty years of service in the merchant navy had trained Turner's mind so that nothing could induce him to contemplate subjecting his ship voluntarily to navigational hazards; his years of service as sailing master in the Royal Navy had done little to change that mental attitude. It was his duty to keep the ship safe from shoal and storm and let the captain worry about cannon-balls. He would never have thought for a moment of trying to take *Atropos* through the narrow channel between Sari Point and Kaia Rock, not even by daylight, and ten times never by night, and the fact that he had not thought of it left him without words.

Another orange flash showed astern; another report reached their ears.

"Take a night glass and go for'rard," said Hornblower. "Look out for the surf."

"Aye aye, sir."

"Take a speaking trumpet as well. Make sure I hear you."

"Aye aye, sir."

The gunfire from *Mejidieh* would have warned the garrisons of the batteries; there would be plenty of time for the men to rouse themselves to wakefulness at their guns, to get their linstocks well alight, so as to sweep the channels with their salvos. Turkish gunners might not be efficient, but the cross fire at East Pass could hardly miss. The West Pass, between Kaia Rock and Passage Island, would not be so efficiently swept; but on the other hand the range was negligible, and with the double turn that had to be made (*Atropos* would be like a sitting duck) there would be no chance of coming through uninjured. Dismasted, or even only crippled, *Atropos* would fall an easy prey to *Mejidieh* coming down through East Pass at her leisure. And, crippled and out of control, *Atropos* might run aground; and she was only a little ship, her scantlings were frail—a salvo from the huge stone cannon-balls that the Turks favoured, plunging from a height, could tear her to pieces, tear open her bottom and sink her in a minute. He would have to take her under Sari Point; that would double, treble the range from the guns on Passage Island; it would be a surprise move; and very likely the guns there would be trained upon Kaia Rock, to sweep the narrowest passage—their aim would have to be hurriedly changed and for a moment at least he would have the rock itself to shelter him. It was his best chance.

"Starboard a point," he said to the quartermaster. That was the moment, like playing his King as third player to the first trick in hand of whist; it was the best thing to do, taking all chances into consideration, and so, the decision taken, there was no room for second thoughts.

The moderate breeze was holding; that meant not merely that he had *Atropos* under full command, but also that wavelets would be breaking at the foot of Kaia Rock and Sari Point, reflecting back the moonlight visibly to Turner's night glass. He could see Ada Peninsula plainly enough. At this angle it looked as if there was no exit at all from the Bay; *Atropos* seemed to be gliding down, unhurried, as though to immolate herself upon an unbroken coast.

"Mr. Jones, hands to the braces and head sail sheets, if you please."

The gunners on Ada would be able to see the ship plainly enough now, silhouetted against the moon; they would be waiting for her to turn. Passage Island and Sari Point were still blended together. He held on.

"Breakers on the port bow!"

That was Turner hailing from forward.

"Breakers ahead!" A long pause, and then Turner's high, thin voice again, sharpened with anxiety. "Breakers ahead!"

"Mr. Jones, we'll be wearing ship soon."

He could see well enough. He carried the chart before his mental eyes, and could superimpose it upon the shadowy landscape before him.

"Breakers ahead!"

The closer he came the better. That shore was steep-to.

"Now, Mr. Jones. Quartermaster—hard a-starboard."

She was coming round on her heel like a dancer. Too fast!

"Meet her! Steady!"

He must hold on for a moment; and it would be as well, too, for then *Atropos* could regain the way and handiness of which the sharp turn had deprived her.

"Breakers ahead! Breakers on the starboard bow! Breakers to port!"

A chain of long, bright flashes over port quarter; a thunder-roll of reports, echoing again from the hills.

"Hard a-starboard. Brace her up, Mr. Jones. Full and by!"

Coming round now, with Sari Point close alongside; not merely alongside but right ahead with the hollow curve of it.

"Keep your luff!"

"Sir—sir—"

The quartermaster at the wheel was croaking with anxiety; she would be in irons in a moment. The headsails were flapping. From the feel of her she was losing her way, sagging off to leeward; she would be aground before long.

"Port a little."

That would keep her going for a moment. The black bulk of Kaia was plainly visible to port. Sari was ahead and to starboard, and the wind was in their teeth. They were creeping forward to destruction. But there must be—there *must* be—a back lash of wind from Sari Point. It could not be otherwise with that land formation. The headsails flapped again as the quartermaster at the wheel vacillated between going aground and being taken aback.

"Keep her going."

"Sir—!"

It would be close under the land that air would be found if at all. Ah! Hornblower could feel the transition with the acute sensitivity of the seaman; the cessation of wind and then the tiny gentle breath on the other cheek. The headsails flapped again, but in a different mood from before; before Hornblower could speak the quartermaster was turning the wheel in agonized relief. It would only be a second or two that would be granted them, small enough time in which to gather steerage way to get the ship under command again, to gain distance from the cliffs.

"Stand by to go about!"

Steerage way so that the rudder would bite; that was what was wanted now. A flash and a roar from Passage Island—Kaia Rock nearly intercepted the flash; perhaps the shot was intercepted as well. That would be the first gun to be reloaded. The others would undoubtedly follow soon. Another flash, another roar, but no time to think about them, for Hornblower's perceptions told him of the fresh alteration in the feel of the ship. They were passing out into the wind again.

"Headsail sheets!"

One moment more. Now!

"Hard a-starboard!"

He could feel the rudder bite. She was coming round. She would not miss stays. As she emerged into the wind she was on her new tack.

"Breakers right ahead!"

That was Kaia Rock, of course. But they must gather way again.

"Stand by to go about!"

They must hold on until the bowsprit was almost touching. Wait. Now!

"Hard over!"

The wheel spun. She was sluggish. Yes—no—yes. The fore staysail was drawing. She was coming round. The yards turned as the hands came aft with the lee-braces. One moment's hesitation, and then she gathered way on the fresh tack, leaving Kaia close beside them, Sari Point ahead; no chance of weathering it on this tack.

"Stand by to go about!"

Hold on as far as possible; this would be the last tack that would be necessary. A howl close overhead. That was a cannon-ball from Passage Island.

"Stand by! Hard over!"

Round she came, the rocks at the foot of Sari Point clearly visible as she wheeled away from them. A flaw, an eddy in the wind again, but only a second's hesitation as she caught the true breeze. Hold on for safety a moment more, with Kaia close abeam. Now all was safe.

"Mr. Jones! Course South by East."

"Course South by East, sir!"

They were heading into the open sea, with Rhodes to starboard and Turkey left behind, and with a King's ransom in the lazarette. They were leaving behind a prince's ransom, so to speak, but Hornblower could think of that with hardly a twinge.

XIX

His Majesty's sloop of war *Atropos*, admittedly, was the smallest ship in the British Navy. There were brigs of war smaller than she was, and schooners and cutters smaller still, but she was the smallest ship in the technical sense, with three masts and a captain in command, that King George owned, yet Hornblower was well content with her. There were times when he looked at the captains' list, and saw below his name those of the fifty captains junior to him, and when he noted above his name the slowly dwindling number of captains senior to him—as captains died or attained flag rank—and it occurred to him that some day, with good fortune, he might be posted to a frigate or even a ship of the line, yet at the moment he was content.

He had completed a mission and was entering upon another one. He had discharged at Gibraltar two hundred thousand pounds sterling in gold and silver coin, and he had left there the unpleasant Mr. McCullum and his Ceylonese divers. The money was to await shipment to London, where it would constitute some part of the "British gold" that sustained the fainting spirits of England's allies and against which Bonaparte raved so violently in his bulletins; McCullum and his men would wait for an opportunity to travel in the opposite direction, round Africa back to India. And *Atropos* was running before a heavy westerly gale in a third direction, back up the Mediterranean to rejoin Collingwood and the Mediterranean Fleet.

She seemed to be lightheartedly free of her encumbrances as she heaved and pitched on the quartering sea; after six months afloat, with hardly six hours on land, Hornblower's seasickness was no longer apparent and he was lighthearted on that account too, along with his ship. Collingwood had seen fit to approve of his report on his proceedings at Marmorice before sending him on to Gibraltar with the treasure, and had given him, for his return journey, orders that an adventurous young captain would approve of. He was to scour the Mediterranean coast of southern Spain, disorganize the Spanish coasting trade, gather up any information he could by personal observation of the harbours, and then look in at Corsica before rejoining the Fleet off the Italian coast, where it was damming back, at the water's edge, Bonaparte's new flood of conquest. Naples had fallen, but Sicily was held intact; Bonaparte's monstrous power ended when the salt water reached the saddle-girths of his horse. His armies could march where they would, but his ships cowered in port, or only ventured forth on furtive raids, while the little *Atropos*, with her twenty-two tiny guns, had twice sailed the whole length of the Mediterranean, from Gibraltar to Marmorice and back again, without once seeing the tricolor flag.

No wonder Hornblower felt pleased with himself, standing on the plunging deck without a qualm, looking over at the serrated skyline which, in the clear Mediterranean air, indicated the mountains of Spain. He had sailed boldly in within gunshot of the harbours and roadsteads of the coast; he had looked into Malaga and Motril and Almeria; fishing boats and coasters had fled before him like minnows before a pike. He had rounded Cape de Gata and had clawed his way back to the coast again so as to look into Cartegena. Malaga and Almeria had sheltered no ships of war. That was negative information, but even negative information could be of value to Collingwood as he directed the activities of his enormous fleet, covering the ramifications of British commerce over two thousand miles of sea, with his finger on the pulse of a score of international enmities and alliances. Cartagena was the principal Spanish naval base. An examination of it would reveal whether the bankrupt Spanish government had made any effort to reconstitute the fleet shattered at Trafalgar. Perhaps a French ship or two would be sheltering there, on one stage of some adventurous cruise planned by Bonaparte to enable them to strike at British convoys.

Hornblower looked up at the straining rigging, felt the heave and plunge of the ship under his feet. There were two reefs in the topsails already—it was more than half a gale that was blowing. He considered, and then dismissed, the notion of a third reef. *Atropos* could carry that amount of canvas safely enough. Cape Cope lay on the port beam; his glass revealed that a little cluster of coasters had taken refuge in the shallows under its lee, and he looked at them longingly. But there were batteries to protect them, and this wind made any attempt on them quite impracticable—he could not send in boats in the teeth of half a gale. He gave an order to the helmsman and the *Atropos* went hurtling on towards Cartagena. It was exhilarating to stand here by the taffrail with the wind screaming round him and a creamy wake emerging from under the stern beneath his feet. He smiled to watch Mr. Turner's navigation class at work; Turner had the midshipmen and master's mates around him giving them instruction in coastwise navigation. He was trying to ballast their feather-brains with good solid mathematics about the "running fix" and "doubling the angle on the bow" and the "four-point bearing", but it was a difficult task to retain their attention in these stimulating surroundings, with the wind setting the chart fluttering wildly in Turner's hand and even making it hard for the young men to hold their slates steady as it caught their inclined surfaces.

"Mr. Turner," said Hornblower. "Report any case of inattention to me at once and I will deal with it as it deserves."

That steadied the young men to a noticeable extent and made them restrain their animal spirits. Smiley checked himself in the midst of a wink at the young Prince, and the Prince's embryo guffaw was stillborn as a guilty grin. That boy was perfectly human now—it was a far cry from the stuffy German court into which he had been born to the windy deck of the *Atropos*. If ever he were restored to the throne of his fathers he would be free of the thraldom of a sextant, but perhaps he might remember these breezy days with regret. The great-nephew of King George—Hornblower looked at him pretending to study the equilateral triangle scrawled on his slate, and smiled to himself again, remembering Dr. Eisenbeiss's horror at the suggestion that perhaps corporal punishment might come the way of a reigning Prince. It had not so far, but it might.

Four bells sounded, the sand glass was turned, the wheel was relieved, and Turner dismissed his class.

"Mr. Smiley! Mr. Horrocks!"

The released midshipmen turned to their captain.

"I want you at the mastheads now with your glasses."

Sharp young eyes would be best for looking into Cartagena. Hornblower noticed the appeal in the Prince's expression.

"Very well, Mr. Prince. You can go too. Fore topmast head with Mr. Smiley."

It was a frequent punishment to send a young officer up to the discomforts of the masthead, but it was no punishment today, not with an enemy's harbour to be examined, and reports made on the shipping inside. Cartagena was fast coming into sight; the castle and the towers of the churches were visible now beyond the sheltering island of La Escombrera. With this westerly wind it was simple enough to stand right in so that from the masthead a view could be had of the inner harbour.

"Deck, there! Captain, sir—"

Smiley was hailing down from the fore topmast head. Hornblower had to walk forward to hear what he had to say, for the wind was sweeping away his words.

"There's a ship of war in the outer bay, sir! Spanish, she looks like. One of their big frigates. She's got her yards across."

That was likely to be the *Castilla*, one of the survivors of Trafalgar.

"There's seven sail of coasters anchored close in, sir."

They were safe enough from the *Atropos* in these conditions.

"What about the inner harbour?"

"Four—no five ships moored there, sir. And two hulks."

"What d'you make of them?"

"Four of the line, sir, and a frigate. No yards across. Laid up in ordinary, I should say, sir."

In past years the Spanish government had built fine ships, but under the corruption and inefficiency of Godoy they were allowed to rot at their moorings for want of crews and stores. Four of the line and a frigate laid up at Cartagena was what had last been reported there, so there was no change; negative information for Collingwood again, but useful.

"She's setting sail!"

That was the prince's voice, high-pitched and excited, screaming down. A moment later Horrocks and Smiley were supplementing the warning.

"The frigate, sir! She's getting sail on her!"

"I can see her cross, sir!"

Spanish ships of war had the habit of hoisting huge wooden crosses at the mizzen peak when action seemed likely. The frigate must be intending to make a sortie, to chase away this inquisitive visitor. It was high time to beat a retreat. A big Spanish frigate such as the *Castilla* carried forty-four guns, just twice as many as *Atropos*, and with three times their weight of metal. If only over the horizon *Atropos* had a colleague to whom she could lure the *Castilla*! That was something to bear in mind and to suggest to Collingwood in any case; this Spanish captain was enterprising and energetic, and might be rash—he might be smouldering with shame after Trafalgar, and he might be lured out to his destruction.

"She's under way, sir!"

"Fore tops'l set! Main tops'l set, sir!"

No sense in courting danger, even though with this wind *Atropos* had a clear run to safety.

"Keep her away a point," said Hornblower to the helmsman, and *Atropos* turned a little to show a clean pair of heels to the Spaniard.

"She's coming out, sir!" reported Horrocks from the main topmast head. "Reefed tops'ls. Two reefs, I think, sir."

Hornblower trained his glass over the quarter. There it was, the white oblong just showing above the horizon as *Atropos* lifted—the reefed fore topsail of the *Castilla*.

"She's pointing straight at us now, sir," reported Smiley.

In a stern chase like this *Atropos* had nothing to fear, newly coppered as she was and with a pretty turn of speed. The high wind and the rough sea would favour the bigger ship, of course. The *Castilla* might contrive to keep the *Atropos* in sight even though she had no chance of overtaking her. It would be a useful object lesson to officers and men to see *Atropos* making the best use of her potentiality for speed. Hornblower looked up again at sails and rigging. Certainly now there could be no question of taking in a third reef. He must carry all possible sail, just as the *Castilla* was doing.

Mr. Still, as officer of the watch, was touching his hat to Hornblower with a routine question.

"Carry on, Mr. Still."

"Up spirits!"

With a powerful enemy plunging along behind her the life of the *Atropos* went on quite normally; the men had their grog and went to their dinners, the watch changed, the wheel was relieved. Palos Point disappeared over the port quarter as *Atropos* went flying on into the open Mediterranean, and still that white oblong kept its position on the horizon astern. The *Castilla* was doing well for a Spanish frigate.

"Call me the moment there is any change, Mr. Jones," said Hornblower, shutting his glass.

Jones was nervous—he might be imagining himself in a Spanish prison already. It would do him no harm to be left on deck with the responsibility, even though, down in his cabin, Hornblower found himself getting up from his dinner table to peer aft through the scuttle to make sure the *Castilla* was not gaining on them. In fact, Hornblower was not sorry when, with his dinner not yet finished, a knock at the door brought a messenger from the quarter-deck.

"Mr. Jones's respects, sir, and the wind is moderating a little, he thinks, sir."

"I'm coming," said Hornblower, laying down his knife and fork.

In a moderate breeze *Atropos* ought to be able to run *Castilla* topsails-under in an hour or two, and any reduction in the wind was to the advantage of *Atropos* as long as she spread all the canvas she could carry. But it would call for judgement to shake out the reefs at the right time, without imperilling spars on the one hand or losing distance on the other. When Hornblower arrived on deck a glance told him that it was time.

"You are quite right, Mr. Jones," he said—no harm in giving him a pat on the back—"we'll shake out a reef."

The order sped along the deck.

"Hands make sail!"

Hornblower looked aft through his glass; as *Atropos* lifted her stern he could get the *Castilla's* fore topsail right in the centre of the field. The most painstaking thought could not bring a decision as to whether or not it was any nearer. She must be exactly maintaining her distance. Then as the topsail hung dizzily in the lens he saw—he was nearly sure he saw—the oblong broaden into a square. He rested his eye and looked again. No doubt about it. *Castilla* had decided that was the moment to shake out a reef too.

Hornblower looked up at the *Atropos*' main topsail yard. The topmen, bent over the yard at that dizzy height, had completed the untying of the reef points. Now they came running in from the yard. Smiley had the starboard yardarm, and His Serene Highness the Prince of Seitz-Bunau the port. They were having their usual race, flinging themselves on to the backstays and sliding down without a thought for their necks. Hornblower was glad that boy had found his feet—of course he was wild with the excitement of the flight and pursuit; Hornblower was glad that Smiley had adopted that amused paternal attitude towards him.

With the letting out of the reef *Atropos* increased her speed again; Hornblower could feel the renewed thrust of the sail upon the fabric of the ship under his feet; he could feel the more frantic leap of the vessel on the wave crests. He directed a wary glance aloft. This would not be the moment to have anything carry away, not with *Castilla* tearing along in pursuit. Jones was standing by the wheel. The wind was just over the starboard quarter, and the little ship was answering well to her rudder, but it was as important to keep an eye on the helmsman as it was to see that they did not split a topsail. It called for some little resolution to leave Jones in charge again and go below to try to finish his dinner.

When the message came down again that the wind was moderating it was like that uncanny feeling which Hornblower had once or twice experienced of something happening again even though it had not happened before—the circumstances were so exactly similar.

"Mr. Jones's respects, sir, and the wind is moderating a little, he thinks, sir."

Hornblower had to compel himself to vary his reply.

"My compliments to Mr. Jones, and I am coming on deck."

Just as before, he could feel that the ship was not giving her utmost. Just as before, he gave the order for a reef to be shaken out. Just as before, he swung round to train his glass on the *Castilla's* topsail. And just as before he turned back as the men prepared to come in from the yard. But that was the moment when everything took a different course, when the desperate emergency arose that always at sea lies just over the horizon of the future.

Excitement had stimulated the Prince into folly. Hornblower looked up to see the boy standing on the port yardarm, not merely standing but dancing, taking a clumsy step or two to dare Smiley at the starboard yardarm to imitate him, one hand on his hip, the other over his head. Hornblower was going to shout a reprimand; he opened his mouth and inflated his chest, but before he could utter a sound the Prince's foot slipped. Hornblower saw him totter, strive to regain his balance, and then fall, heavily through the air, and turning a complete circle as he fell.

Later on Hornblower, out of curiosity, made a calculation. The Prince fell from a height of a little over seventy feet, and without the resistance of the air and had he not bounced off the shrouds he would have reached the surface of the sea in something over two seconds. But the resistance of the air could have been by no means negligible—it must have got under his jacket and slowed his fall considerably, for the boy was not killed and was in fact only momentarily knocked unconscious by the impact. Probably it took as much as four seconds for the Prince to fall into the sea. Hornblower was led to make the calculation when brooding over the incident later, for he could remember clearly all the thoughts that passed through his mind during those four seconds. Momentary exasperation came first and then anxiety, and then followed a hasty summing up of the situation. If he hove-to to pick up the boy the *Castilla* would have all the time needed to overhaul them. If he went on the boy would drown. And if he went on he would have to report to Collingwood that he had left the King's great-nephew without lifting a finger to help him. He had to choose quickly—quickly. He had no right to risk his ship to save one single life. But—but—if the boy had been killed in battle by a broadside sweeping the deck it would be different. To abandon him was another matter again. On the heels of that conclusion came another thought, the beginnings of another thought, sprouting from a seed that had been sown outside Cartagena. It did not have time to develop in those four seconds; it was as if Hornblower acted the moment the green shoot from the seed showed above ground, to reach its full growth later.

By the time the boy had reached the sea Hornblower had torn the emergency lifebuoy from the taffrail; he flung it over the port quarter as the speed of the ship brought the boy nearly opposite him, and it smacked into the sea close beside him. At the same moment the air which Hornblower had drawn into his lungs to reprimand the Prince was expelled in a salvo of bellowed orders.

"Mizzen braces! Back the mizzen topsail! Quarter boat away!"

Maybe—Hornblower could not be sure later—everyone was shouting at once, but everyone at least responded to orders with the rapidity that was the result of months of drill. *Atropos* flew up into the wind, her way checked instantly. It was Smiley—Heaven only knew how he had made the descent from the starboard main topsail yardarm in that brief space—who got the jolly boat over the side, with four men at the oars, and dashed off to effect the rescue, the tiny boat soaring up and swooping down as the waves passed under her. And even before *Atropos* was hove-to Hornblower was putting the next part of the plan into action.

"Mr. Horrocks! Signal 'Enemy in sight to windward'."

Horrocks stood and gaped, and Hornblower was about to blare out with, "Blast you, do what I tell you," but he restrained himself. Horrocks was not a man of the quickest thought in the world, and he had failed entirely to see any purpose in signalling to a vacant horizon. To swear at him now would simply paralyse him with nervousness and lead to a further delay.

"Mr. Horrocks, kindly send up the signal as quickly as you can. 'Enemy in sight to windward.' Quickly, please."

The signal rating beside Horrocks was luckily quicker witted—he was one of the dozen men of the crew who could read and write, naturally—and was already at the halliards with the flag-locker open, and his example shook Horrocks out of his amazement. The flags went soaring up to the main topmast yardarm, flying out wildly in the wind. Hornblower made a mental note that that rating, even though he was no seaman as yet—lately a City apprentice who had come hurriedly aboard at Deptford to avoid something worse in civilian life—was deserving of promotion.

"Now another signal, Mr. Horrocks. 'Enemy is a frigate distant seven miles bearing west course east.' "

It was the sensible thing to do to send up the very signals he would have hoisted if there really were help in sight—the *Castilla* might be able to read them or might make at least a fair guess at their meaning. If there had been a friendly ship in sight down to leeward (Hornblower remembered the suggestion he had been going to make to Collingwood) he would never have hove-to, of course, but would have gone on tearing down to lure the *Castilla* as near as possible, but the captain of the *Castilla* was not to know that.

"Keep that signal flying. Now send up an affirmative, Mr. Horrocks Very good. Haul it down again. Mr. Jones! Lay the ship on the starboard tack, a good full."

A powerful English ship down there to leeward would certainly order *Atropos* to close on *Castilla* as quickly as possible. He must act as if that were the case. It was only when Jones—almost as helpless with astonishment as Horrocks had been—had plunged into the business of getting *Atropos* under way again that Hornblower had time to use his telescope. He trained it on the distant topsail again; not so distant now. Coming up fast, and Hornblower felt a sick feeling of disappointment and apprehension. And then as he watched he saw the square of the topsail narrow into a vertical oblong, and two other oblongs appear beside it. At the same moment the masthead lookout gave a hail.

"Deck there! The enemy's hauled his wind, sir!"

Of course he would do so—the disappointment and apprehension vanished instantly. A Spanish frigate captain once he had put his bowsprit outside the safety of a defended port would ever be a prey to fear.

Always there would be the probability in his mind that just over the horizon lay a British squadron ready to pounce on him. He would chase a little sloop of war eagerly enough, but as soon as he saw that sloop sending up signals and swinging boldly round on a course that challenged action he would bethink him of the fact that he was already far to leeward of safety; he would imagine hostile ships only just out of sight cracking on all sail to cut him off from his base, and once his mind was made up he would not lose a single additional mile or minute before turning to beat back to safety. For two minutes the Spaniard had been a prey to indecision after *Atropos* hove-to, but the final bold move had made up his mind for him. If he had held on for a short time longer he might have caught sight of the jolly boat pulling over the waves and then would have guessed what *Atropos* was doing, but as it was, time was gained and the Spaniard, close-hauled, was clawing back to safety in flight from a non-existent enemy.

"Masthead! What do you see of the boat?"

"She's still pulling, sir, right in the wind's eye!"

"Do you see anything of Mr. Prince?"

"No, sir, can't say as I do."

Not much chance in that tossing sea of seeing a floating man two miles away, not even from the masthead.

"Mr. Jones, tack the ship."

It would be best to keep *Atropos* as nearly straight down wind from the boat as possible, allowing it an easy run to leeward when its mission was accomplished. *Castilla* would not be able to make anything of the manoeuvre.

"Deck there! The boat's stopped pulling, sir. I think they're picking up Mr. Prince, sir."

Thank God for that. It was only now that Hornblower could realize what a bad ten minutes it had been.

"Deck there! Yes, sir, they're waving a shirt. They're pulling back to us now."

"Heave-to, Mr. Jones, if you please. Doctor Eisenbeiss, have everything ready in case Mr. Prince needs treatment."

The Mediterranean at midsummer was warm enough; most likely the boy had taken no harm. The jolly boat came dancing back over the waves and turned under *Atropos*' stern into the little lee afforded by her quarter as she rode with her starboard bow to the waves. Here came His Serene Highness, wet and bedraggled but not in the least hurt, meeting the concentrated gaze of all on deck with a smile half sheepish and half defiant. Eisenbeiss came forward fussily, talking voluble German, and then turned to Hornblower to explain.

"I have a hot blanket ready for him, sir."

It was at that moment that the dam of Hornblower's even temper burst.

"A hot blanket! I know what'll warm him quicker than that. Bos'n's mate! My compliments to the bos'n, and ask him to be kind enough to lend you his cane for a few minutes. Shut your mouth, doctor, if you know what's good for you. Now, young man—"

Humanitarians had much to say against corporal punishment, but in their arguments, while pointing out the harm it might do to the one punished, they omitted to allow for the satisfaction other people derived from it. And it was some further training for the Blood Royal to display his acquired British imperturbability, to bite off the howl that a well-applied cane tended to draw forth, and to stand straight afterwards with hardly a skip to betray his discomfort, with hardly a rub at the smarting royal posterior, and with the tears blinked manfully back. Satisfaction or not, Hornblower was a little sorry afterwards.

XX

There was everything to be said in favour of keeping *Castilla* under observation for a while at least, and almost nothing to be said against it. The recent flight and pursuit had proved that *Atropos* had the heels of her even under reefed topsails, so that it could be taken for granted that she was safe from her in any lesser wind—and the wind was moderating. The *Castilla* was now a full thirty miles dead to leeward of Cartagena; it would be useful to know—Collingwood would certainly want to know—whether she intended to beat back there again or would fetch some easier Spanish port. Close-hauled she could make Alicante to the north or perhaps Almeria to the south; she was close-hauled on the starboard tack, heading south, at this moment. And there was the possibility to be borne in mind that she did not intend to return to Spain as yet, that her captain might decide to range through the Mediterranean for a while to see what prizes he could snap up. On her present course she could easily stretch over to the Barbary coast and pick up a victualler or two with grain and cattle intended for the Fleet.

Hornblower's orders were that he should rejoin Collingwood in Sicilian waters after looking into Malaga and Cartagena; he was not the bearer of urgent despatches, nor, Heaven knew, was *Atropos* likely to be an important addition to the strength of the Fleet; while on the other hand it was the duty of every English captain, having once made contact with a ship of the enemy in open water, to maintain that contact as long as was possible. *Atropos* could not hope to face *Castilla* in battle, but she could keep her under observation, she might warn merchant shipping of danger, and she might with good fortune meet some big British ship of war—in actual fact, not make-believe—to whom she could indicate the enemy.

"Mr. Jones," said Hornblower. "Lay her on the starboard tack again, if you please. Full and by."

"Aye aye, sir."

Jones, of course, showed some surprise at the reversal of the roles, at the pursued becoming the pursuer, and that was one more proof that he was incapable of strategic thought. But he had to engage himself on carrying out his orders, and *Atropos* steadied on a southerly course, running parallel to *Castilla's*, far to windward; Hornblower trained his glass on the topsails just visible over the horizon. He fixed the shape of them firmly in his memory; a slight alteration in the proportion of length to breadth would indicate any change of course on the part of the *Castilla*.

"Masthead!" he hailed. "Keep your eye on the enemy. Report anything you see."

"Aye aye, sir."

Atropos was like a terrier now, yapping at the heels of a bull in a field—not a very dignified role—and the bull might turn and charge at any moment. Eventually the captain of the *Castilla* would make up his mind that a trick had been played on him, that *Atropos* had been signalling to non-existent friends, and there was no guessing what he might decide to do then, when he grew certain that there was no help following *Atropos* up just beyond the horizon. Meanwhile the wind was still moderating, and *Atropos* could set more canvas. When beating to windward she behaved best under all the sail she could carry, and he might as well keep as close to the enemy as the wind allowed.

"Try setting the mainsail, Mr. Jones, if you please."

"Aye aye, sir."

The main course was a big sail, and the little *Atropos* seemed to take wings under the tremendous pressure of it when it was sheeted home, with the tack hauled forward to the chess-trees by the united strength of half a watch. Now she was thrusting along bravely in the summer evening, lying over to the wind, and shouldering off the hungry waves with her starboard bow in great fountains of spray, through which the setting sun gleamed in fleeting rainbows of fiery beauty, and leaving behind her a seething wake dazzling white against the blue. It was a moment when it was good to be alive, driving hard to windward like this, and with all the potentiality of adventure at hand in the near unknown. War at sea was a dreary business usually, with boredom and discomfort to be endured day and night, watch and watch, but it had moments of high exaltation like this, just as it had its moments of black despair, of fear, of shame.

"You may dismiss the watch below, Mr. Jones."

"Aye aye, sir,"

Hornblower glanced round the deck. Still would have the watch.

"Call me if there's any change, Mr. Still. I want to set more sail if the wind moderates further."

"Aye aye, sir."

A moment of exaltation, come and gone. He had been on his feet nearly all day, since dawn, and his legs were weary, and if he stayed on deck they would grow wearier still. Down below there were the two books he had bought at Gibraltar for a badly needed guinea—Lord Hodge's "Statement of the Present Political Condition of Italy", and Barber's "New Methods of Determining Longitude, with some Remarks on Discrepancies in Recent Charts". He wanted to inform himself on both subjects, and it was better to do so now than to stay up on deck growing more and more weary while the hours passed.

At sunset he emerged again; *Castilla* was still holding the same course, with *Atropos* head-reaching upon her very slightly. He looked at those distant topsails; he read the slate that recorded the day's run, and he waited while the log was hove again. Surely if *Castilla* intended to put back into Cartagena she would have gone about by now. She had made a very long reach to the southward, and any backing of the wind round to the north—a very likely occurrence at this season—would nullify much of her progress so far. If she did not come about by the time darkness set in it would be a strong indication that she had something else in mind. He waited as the sunset faded from the western sky, and until the first stars began to appear overhead; that was when his aching eye, straining through the glass, could see no more of *Castilla*. But at the last sight of her she was still standing to the southward. All the more reason to keep her under observation.

It was the end of the second dogwatch and the hands were being called.

"I'll have the main-course taken in, Mr. Turner," he said.

He wrote his night orders by the faint light of the binnacle; the ship to be kept close-hauled on the starboard tack; he was to be called if the wind shifted more than two points, and in any event he was to be called immediately before moonrise in the middle watch. The gloomy little cabin when he retired into it was like a wild beast's lair with its dark corners where the light of the lamp did not penetrate. He lay down fully clothed, endeavouring to keep his tired mind from continuing to try to solve the problem of what the *Castilla* intended to do. He had shortened sail, as she would probably do. If she did not, he had the heels of her and might overtake her in daylight. If she did anything else, if she tacked or wore, he was doing what was probably best to find her again next day. His eyes closed with fatigue, and did not open again until they came to tell him the middle watch had been called.

The west wind, dying away though it was, had brought a slight overcast with it, enough to obscure the stars and deprive the small moon, almost in its last quarter, of most of its light. *Atropos*, still close-hauled, was now, in the lessening wind, only flitting with the waves that came on to her starboard bow, meeting them elegantly like a stage beauty extending her hand to a stage lover. The dark water all around seemed to fall in with the mood and to murmur pretty conventionalities. There seemed no imminence of blazing death. The minutes passed in warm idleness.

"Deck there!" That was the masthead lookout hailing. "I think I can see something, sir. Right away on the starboard bow."

"Get aloft with the night glass, youngster," said Turner, who had the watch, to the master's mate beside him.

A minute passed, two minutes.

"Yes, sir," came the new voice from the masthead. "It's the loom of a ship. Three miles—four miles—fine on the starboard bow."

The night glasses trained round more forward.

"Maybe," said Turner.

There was a tiny patch of something darker than the surrounding night; Hornblower's night glass could tell him no more than that. He watched it painstakingly. The bearing of it seemed to be altering.

"Steer small!" he growled at the helmsman.

For a moment he wondered if the patch was really there; it might be something his mind suggested to his eye—a whole ship's company could sometimes imagine the same thing if the idea was once put in their heads. No, it was undoubtedly there, and drawing across *Atropos*' bows, more than could be accounted for by any wavering of her course with bad steering. It must be *Castilla*; she must have swung round at midnight and come hurrying down wind in the hope of pouncing on her prey by surprise. If he had not shortened sail she would be right on him. The Spanish lookouts were not up to their work, for she was holding on her course.

"Heave-to, Mr. Turner," he said, and walked across to the port side to keep the *Castilla* under observation as *Atropos* came up into the wind. *Castilla* had already lost most of the advantage of the weather gage, and in a few minutes would lose it all. The slowly-moving clouds overhead were parting; there was a faint gleam of light through a thin patch, further darkness, and then the moon shone through a gap. Yes, that was a ship; that was the *Castilla*, already far down to leeward.

"Deck, there! I can see her plainly now, sir. On the port quarter. Captain, sir! She's wearing round!"

So she was. Her sails gleamed momentarily bright in the moonlight as they swung round. She had failed in her attempt to surprise her enemy, and was making a fresh one.

"Lay her on the port tack, Mr. Turner."

The little *Atropos* could play catch-as-catch-can with any big frigate in this sort of weather. She swung round and headed into the wind, her stern to her pursuer again.

"Masthead! What sail has the enemy set?"

"She's setting her royals, sir. All plain sail to the royals."

"Call all hands, Mr. Turner. Set all plain sail."

There was still enough wind for the addition of courses and royals to lay *Atropos* over and send her flying once more. Hornblower looked back at *Castilla's* topsails and royals, silhouetted now against clear sky below the moon. It did not take very long to determine that now *Atropos* was gaining fast. He was pondering a decision regarding shortening sail when he was saved the trouble. The silhouettes narrowed again abruptly.

"Deck there!" hailed the masthead. "Enemy's hauled her wind, sir."

"Very well! Mr. Turner, wear ship, if you please. Point our bows right at her, and take in the fore course."

The terrier had evaded the bull's charge and was now yapping at its heels again. It was easy to follow the *Castilla* for the rest of the night, keeping a sharp lookout during the periods of darkness lest she should play on them the same trick as *Atropos* had played once. Dawn, rising ahead, revealed the *Castilla's* royals and topsails an inky black before they changed to ivory white against the blue sky. Hornblower could imagine the rage of the Spanish captain at the sight of his pertinacious pursuer, dogging him in this fashion with insolent impunity. Seven miles separated the ships, but as far as the *Castilla's* big eighteen-pounders mattered it might as well be seventy, and moreover the invisible wind, blowing direct from *Atropos* to *Castilla,* was an additional protection, guarding her from her enemy like the mysterious glass shield that turned the hero's sword in one of the Italian epics. *Atropos,* seven miles to windward, was as safe and yet as visible as the Saracen magician.

Hornblower was conscious of weariness again. He had been on his feet since midnight, after less than four hours' rest. He wanted, passionately, to rest his legs; he wanted, hardly less, to close his aching eyes. The hammocks had been brought up, the decks swabbed, and it only remained now to cling to *Castilla's* heels, but when any moment might bring the need for a quick decision he dared not leave the deck—odd that now he was safely to windward the situation was more dynamic than yesterday when he had been to leeward, but it was true. *Castilla* might come to the wind at any unforeseen moment, and moreover the two ships were driving into the blue Mediterranean where any surprise might be over the horizon.

"I'll have a mattress up here," said Hornblower.

They brought one up and laid it aft beside the weather scuppers. He eased his aching joints down on to it, settled his head on his pillow, and closed his eyes. The lift and send of the ship were soporific, and so was the sound of the sea under the *Atropos'* counter. The light played backward and forward over his face as the shadows of sails and rigging followed the movement of the ship. He could sleep—he could sleep, heavily and dreamlessly, while the ships flew on up the Mediterranean, while they called the watch, while they hove the log, even while they trimmed the yards as the wind came a little northerly, moving round ahead of the sun.

It was afternoon when he woke. He shaved with the aid of a mirror stuck in the hammock nettings; he took his bath under the washdeck pump and put on the clean shirt that he sent for; he sat on the deck and ate cold beef and the last of the goodly soft bread taken on board at Gibraltar, somewhat stale now but infinitely better than ship's biscuit; and the fresh butter from the same source, kept cool so far in an earthenware crock was quite delicious. It struck seven bells as he finished his last mouthful.

"Deck there! Enemy's altering course."

He was on his feet in a flash, his plate sliding into the scuppers, the telescope in his hand without conscious volition on his part. No doubt about it. *Castilla* had altered to a more northerly course, with the wind abeam. It was not very surprising for they had run a full two hundred miles from Cartagena; unless the *Castilla* was prepared to go right up the Mediterranean far to leeward of all Spanish bases, it was time for her to head north to fetch Minorca. He would follow her there, the terrier harassing the bull, and he would give a final yap at the bull's heels outside Port Mahon. Besides, the *Castilla's* alteration of course might not portend a mere flight to Minorca. They were right on the track of convoys beating up the Mediterranean from Sicily and Malta.

"Port your helm, Mr. Still, if you please. Maintain a parallel course."

It was only sensible to stay up to windward of *Castilla* as much as possible. The intense feeling of wellbeing of five minutes ago was replaced now by excitement, a slight tingling under the skin. Ten to one the *Castilla's* alteration of course meant nothing at all, but there was the tenth chance. Eight bells; hands mustered for the first dogwatch.

"Deck there! There's a sail ahead of the enemy, sir!"

That was it, then.

"Get aloft with you, Mr. Smiley. You can go too, Mr. Prince."

That would show His Serene Highness that a punishment cleared the record in the Navy, and that he was being trusted not to risk any more monkey tricks. It was a detail that had to be borne in mind despite the flood of excitement following the masthead report. There was no knowing what that sail over there, invisible from the deck, might imply. But there was a chance that it was a British ship of war, fair in *Castilla's* path.

"Two sail! Three sail! Captain, sir, it looks like a convoy, dead to leeward."

A convoy could only be a British convoy, and a convoy meant the presence of a British ship of war ahead there in *Castilla's* path.

"Up helm and bear down on the enemy. Call all hands, Mr. Still, if you please. Clear for action."

During all the long flight and pursuit he had not cleared for action. He had not wanted action with the vastly superior *Castilla*, and had been determined on avoiding it. Now he hoped for it—hoped for it with that tremor of doubt that made him hate himself, all the more so as the repeating of the order brought a cheer from the men, the watch below pouring on deck for duty with expectant grins and schoolboy excitement. Mr. Jones came bustling up on deck buttoning his coat; apparently he had been dozing comfortably through the afternoon watch. To Jones would fall the command of the *Atropos* if any accident should befall him, if a shot should take off his leg or dash him into bloody fragments. Odd that the thought of Jones becoming responsible for handling *Atropos* was as disturbing as the rest of it. But all the same Jones must be brought up to date on the situation and told what should be done. He did it in three sharp sentences.

"I see, sir," said Jones, pulling at his long chin. Hornblower was not so sure that he did see, but there was no more time to spare for Jones.

"Masthead! What of the convoy?"

"One sail has tacked, sir. She's standing towards us."

"What d'you make of her?"

"She looks like a ship of war, sir. I can only see her royals, sir."

"Mr. Horrocks, make the private signal and our number."

A ship standing towards *Castilla* could only be a ship of war, the escorting vessel. Hornblower could only hope she would be one of the larger frigates, able to meet the big *Castilla* on something like equal terms. But he knew most of the frigates Collingwood had—*Sirius, Naiad, Hermione*—thirty-two gun twelve-pounder frigates most of them, hardly a match for *Castilla's* forty-four eighteen-pounders unless well handled, and unless *Castilla* fought badly, and unless he himself had a chance to intervene. He strained his eyesight staring forward through his glass, but the British ship was not yet in sight from the deck, and *Castilla* was still running boldly down before the wind. Clearing for action was nearly completed; they were casting loose the guns.

"Signal, sir!"

Horrocks was ready with the book as the masthead reported the flags.

"Private signal correctly answered, sir. And her number. She's *Nightingale*, sir, 28, Captain Ford, sir."

Almost the smallest of the frigates, with only nine-pounders on her maindeck. Please God Ford would have the sense not to close with *Castilla*. He must out-manoeuvre her, keep her in play, and then when *Atropos* came up there could be some pretty tactics until they could shoot away some of *Castilla's* spars and take her at a disadvantage. Then they could rake her and weaken her before closing in for the kill. The captain of the *Castilla* was showing proof of having grasped the essentials of the situation; caught between two hostile ships so that he could not avoid action if it were forced on him he was plunging down at his best speed to the attack on the one most accessible to him; he was still carrying all sail to bring him most quickly into action before *Atropos* could intervene. He could well hope to batter *Nightingale* into a wreck and then turn on *Atropos*. If he succeeded—oh, if he succeeded! —it would be a terrible problem for *Atropos*, to decide whether or not to accept action.

"Ship cleared for action, sir," reported Jones.

"Very well."

Now his glass picked her up; the distant sail, far beyond *Castilla*. As he looked, as the top gallants appeared below the royals, the royals disappeared. *Nightingale* was shortening down to "fighting sails" ready for action. Hornblower knew a little about Ford. He had the reputation of a good fighting captain. Please God he had discretion as well. Ford was far his senior in the Navy list; there was no possibility of giving him orders to keep clear.

Castilla was still hurtling down upon *Nightingale*.

"Signal, sir. Number 72. 'Engage the enemy more closely!'"

"Acknowledge."

Hornblower was conscious of Jones's and Turner's eyes upon him. There might be an implied rebuke in that signal, a hint that he was not doing his best to get into action. On the other hand it might be a mere signal that action was imminent. *Nightingale's* topsails were over the horizon now; close-hauled, she was doing her best to come to meet *Castilla*. If only Ford would hold off for half an hour—*Atropos* was steadily gaining on *Castilla*. No, he was still hurrying to the encounter before *Atropos* could arrive; he was playing *Castilla's* game for her. Now *Castilla* was clewing up her courses; she was taking in her royals, ready for the clash. The two ships were hastening together; white sails on a blue sea under a blue sky. They were right in line from where Hornblower stood staring at them through his glass; right in line so that it was hard to judge the distance between them. Now they were turning, *Nightingale* paying off before the wind as *Castilla* approached. All the masts seemed blended together. Ford *must* keep clear and try to shoot away a spar.

A sudden billowing of smoke round the ships; the first broadsides were being fired. It looked as if the ships were already close-locked in action—surely it could not be. Not time yet to take in courses and royals; the sooner they got down into action the better. Now, heavily over the blue water, came the sound of those first broadsides, like the rumbling of thunder. The smoke was blowing clear of the fight, drifting away from the ships in a long bank. More smoke billowing up; the guns had been reloaded and were firing away, and still the masts were close together—had Ford been fool enough to lock yardarms? Again the long rumble of the guns. The ships were swinging round in the smoke cloud; he could see the masts above it changing their bearing, but he could not distinguish ship from ship. There was a mast falling, yards, sails and all; it must be *Nightingale's* main topmast, hideous though the thought was. This seemed like a lifetime, waiting to get into action. Cannon smoke and cannon thunder. He did not want to believe the glass was really revealing the truth to him as he looked, the details becoming clearer as he approached. The two ships were locked together, no doubt about it. And that was *Nightingale*, main topmast gone. She was lying at an angle to *Castilla's* side, bows towards her. The wind was still turning the two ships, and it was turning them as if they were one. *Nightingale* must be locked against *Castilla*, bowsprit or possibly anchor hooked into *Castilla's* fore chains. All *Castilla's* guns could bear, practically raking *Nightingale* with every broadside, and *Nightingale's* fire must be almost ineffectual. Could she tear herself loose? There went her foremast, everything, over the side; almost impossible to tear herself loose now.

The men at the guns were yelling at the sight.

"Silence! Mr. Jones, get the courses in."

What was he to do? He ought to cross *Castilla's* bows or stern and rake her, come about and rake her again. Not so easy to fire into *Castilla's* bows without hitting *Nightingale*; not so easy to cross her stern; that would put him to leeward and there would be delay in getting back into action again. And the two ships were still swinging considerably, not only with the wind but with the recoil of their guns. Supposing that as he took *Atropos* to lie a little clear they swung so that *Nightingale* intercepted his fire and he had to work back again to windward to get back into action? That would be shameful, and other captains hearing the story would think he had deliberately stayed out of fire. He could lay his ship alongside *Castilla* on her unoccupied side, but her slender scantlings would bear little of *Castilla's* ponderous broadside; his ship would be a wreck in a few minutes. And yet *Nightingale* was already a wreck. He must bring her instant, immediate relief.

Now they were only a mile from the locked ships and running down fast. Years of experience at sea told him how rapidly those last few minutes passed when ships needed each other.

"Muster the port side guns' crews," he said. "Every man, gun captains and all. Arm them for boarding. Arm every idler in the ship. But leave the hands at the mizzen braces."

"Aye aye, sir."

"Pikes, pistols and cutlasses, lads," said Hornblower to the eager men thronging round the arms chests. "Mr. Smiley, muster your topmen for'rard by No. 1 gun. Starboard side. Stand by for a rush."

Young Smiley was the best fighting man of them all, better than the nervous Jones or the stupid Still or the aged Turner. It was best to give him the command at the other end of the ship. Aft here he would have things under his own eye. And he realized he was still unarmed himself. His sword—the sword he had worn at the court of his King—was a cheap one. He could guess its temper was unreliable; he had never been able to afford a good sword. He stepped to the arms chest and took a cutlass for himself, drawing it and dropping the scabbard discarded on the deck; looping the knot over his wrist he stood with the naked blade in his hand and the sunlight beating down in his face.

Now they were closing on *Castilla*; only a cable's length apart and it looked closer. It called for accurate judgment to come close alongside.

"Starboard a point," he said to the helmsman.

"Starboard a point," came the repetition of the order.

Discipline kept the helmsman entirely attentive to his particular duty, even though *Castilla's* port side gun ports were opening, even though at that close range the gun muzzles were glaring straight at them, and the faces of the gunners could be seen through the ports looking along the guns. Oh God, it was just coming!

"Now, starboard slowly. Bring her gently round."

Like the end of the world that broadside came, ripping and smashing into the ship; there were screams, there were frightful crashes, the sunlight was full of dust particles flung up by the hurtling cannon-balls as the splinters whizzed through the air, and then the ship sidled into the powder smoke jutting forth from the gun muzzles. But he must think about only one thing at this moment.

"Now! Hard a-port. Braces there! Back the mizzen tops'l!"

There was a tiny gap between the sides of the two ships, closing by inches. If she struck violently she might rebound and open the gap again; if her forward way was not checked she might scrape forward and swing. In the loftier sides of the *Castilla* the gun ports were above the level of those of the *Atropos*. The dish-shaped *Atropos* had no "tumble-home" to her sides. Her bulwarks would make contact—he had been counting on that.

"Starboard side! Fire!"

The infernal crash of the broadside; the smoke whirling round, the orange-painted side of *Castilla* torn by the carronade balls; but not a moment to think about it.

"Come on!"

Up over *Castilla's* side in the eddying smoke pierced by sunbeams; up over the side, cutlass in hand, wild with fighting madness. A distorted face looking up at him. Strike, swinging the heavy blade like an axe. Wrench the blade free, and strike again at this new face. Plunge forward. Gold lace here, a lean brown face gashed by a black moustache, a slender blade lunging at him; beat it aside and strike and strike and strike with every ounce of strength, with all the speed possible to him; beat down the feeble guard and strike again without pity. Trip over something and recover again. The terrified eyes of the men at the wheel looking round at him before they ran from his fury. A uniformed soldier with white cross-belts extending his arms in surrender; a pike appearing from nowhere beside him and plunging into the soldier's unprotected breast. The quarterdeck cleared but no time to breathe; shout "Come on" and plunge down on to the maindeck.

Something hit his cutlass blade and sent a numbing shock up his arm—a pistol bullet, most likely. There was a crowd of men massed round the main mast, but before he could reach it a surge of pikes from the side broke it up into fleeing fragments. Now a sudden rally on the part of the enemy, pistols banging, and then suddenly opposition ceased and Hornblower found himself glaring into a pair of wild eyes and realized that it was an English uniform, an English face although unknown to him—a midshipman from *Nightingale*, leading the boarding party which had stormed into the *Castilla* along *Nightingale's* bowsprit.

He could stand there now amid the wreckage and the dead with the madness ebbing out of him, sweat running into his eyes and blinding him; and yet once more he had to clear his mind and brace himself. He had to stop the killing that was still going on, he had to organize the disarming of the prisoners and the herding of them against the ship's side. He had to remember to say a word of thanks to Smiley, covered with blood and smoke, when he met him on the gangway forward. Here was the huge hulk of Eisenbeiss, chest heaving, the bloody cutlass like a toy in his vast hand. The sight roused his wrath.

"What the hell are you doing here, doctor? Get back on board and attend to the wounded. You've no business to neglect them."

A smile for the Prince, and then his attention was demanded by a thin-nosed, long-faced rat of a man.

"Captain Hornblower? My name's Ford."

He was going to shake the proffered hand, but discovered that first he must slip the cutlass lanyard from his wrist and transfer the weapon to his other hand.

"All's well that ends well," said Ford. "You arrived in time, but only just in time, captain."

It was no use trying to point out to a senior the senior's errors. They shook hands there, standing on the gangway of the captured *Castilla*, looking round at the three ships clinging together, battered and shattered. Far down to leeward, drifting over the blue sea, the long trail of powder smoke was slowly dissipating under the blue heaven.

XXI

The church bells of Palermo were ringing, as always, in the drowsy heat of the morning. The sound of them drifted over the water of the bay, the Conca d'Oro, the golden shell which holds the pearl of Palermo in its embrace. Hornblower could hear them as he brought *Atropos* in, echoing round from Monte Pellegrino to Zaffarano, and of all musical noises that was the one that annoyed him most. He looked over at the senior ship, impatient for her to start firing her salute to shatter this maddening sound. If it were not for the church bells this would be almost a happy moment, dramatic enough in all conscience. *Nightingale* under her jury rig, the clear water gushing out of her as the pumps barely kept her afloat, *Atropos* with the raw plugs in the shot holes in her sides, and then *Castilla*, battered and shot torn, too, and with the White Ensign proudly flying over the red and gold of Spain. Surely even the Sicilians must be struck by the drama of this entrance, and for additional pleasure, there were a trio of English ships of war at anchor over there; their crews at least would gape at the proud procession; they at least would be sensitive to all that the appearance of the newcomers implied; they would know of the din and the fury, the agony of the wounded and the distressing ceremony of the burial of the dead.

Palermo looked out idly as the ships came to anchor, and as the boats (even the boats were patched-up fabrics, hurriedly repaired after being shattered by shot) were swung out and began new activities. The wounded had to be carried ashore to hospital, boat-load after boat-load of them, moaning or silent with pain; then the prisoners under guard —there was pathos in those boat-loads of men, too, of a proud nation, going into captivity within four gloomy walls, under all the stigma of defeat. Then there was other ferrying to be done; the forty men that *Atropos* had lent to *Nightingale* had to be replaced by another forty.

The ones that came back were gaunt and hollow-cheeked, bearded and dirty. They fell asleep sitting on the thwarts, and they fell asleep again the moment they climbed on board, falling like dead men between the guns, for they had laboured for eleven days and nights bringing the shattered *Nightingale* in after the victory.

There was so much to do that it was not until evening that Hornblower had leisure to open the two private letters that were awaiting him. The second one was only six weeks old, having made a quick passage out from England and not having waited long for *Atropos* to come in to Palermo, the new base of the Mediterranean Fleet. Maria was well, and so were the children. Little Horatio was running everywhere now, she said, as lively as a cricket, and little Maria was as good as gold, hardly crying at all even though it seemed likely that she was about to cut a tooth, a most remarkable feat at five months old. And Maria was happy enough in the Southsea house with her mother, although she was lonely for her husband, and although her mother tended to spoil the children in a way that Maria feared would not be approved by her very dearest.

Letters from home; letters about little children and domestic squabbles; they were the momentary lifting of a curtain to reveal another world, utterly unlike this world of peril and hardship and intolerable strain. Little Horatio was running everywhere on busy little legs, and little Maria was cutting her first tooth, while here a tyrant's armies had swept through the whole length of Italy and were massed at the Straits of Messina for an opportunity to make another spring and effect another conquest in Sicily, where only a mile of water—and the Navy—opposed their progress. England was fighting for her life against all Europe combined under a single tyrant of frightful energy and cunning.

No, not quite all Europe, for England still had allies—Portugal under an insane queen, Sweden under a mad king, and Sicily, here, under a worthless king. Ferdinand, King of Naples and Sicily—King of the Two Sicilies—bad, cruel, selfish; brother of the King of Spain, who was Bonaparte's closest ally; Ferdinand, a tyrant more bloodthirsty and more tyrannical than Bonaparte himself, faithless and untrustworthy, who had lost one of his two thrones and was only held on the other by British naval might and who yet would betray his allies for a moment's gratification of his senses, and whose gaols were choked with political prisoners and whose gallows creaked under the weight of dead suspects. Good men, and brave men, were suffering and dying in every part of the world while Ferdinand hunted in his Sicilian preserves and his wicked queen lied and intrigued and betrayed, and while Maria wrote simple little letters about the babies.

It was better to think about his duties than to brood over these insoluble anomalies. Here was a note from Lord William Bentinck, the British Minister in Palermo. "The latest advices from the Vice-Admiral Commanding in the Mediterranean are to the effect that he may be expected very shortly in Palermo with his flagship. His Excellency therefore begs to inform Captain Horatio Hornblower that in His Excellency's opinion it would be best if Captain Horatio Hornblower were to begin the necessary repairs to *Atropos* immediately. His Excellency will request His Sicilian Majesty's naval establishment to afford Captain Horatio Hornblower all the facilities he may require."

Lord William might be—undoubtedly was—a man of estimable character and liberal opinions unusual in a son of a Duke, but he knew little enough about the workings of a Sicilian dockyard. In the three days that followed Hornblower succeeded in achieving nothing at all with the help of Sicilian authorities. Turner was voluble to them in lingua franca, and Hornblower laid aside his dignity to plead with them in French with o's and a's added to the words in the hope that in that manner he might convey his meaning in Italian, but even when the requests were intelligible they were not granted. Canvas? Cordage? Sheet lead for shot holes? They might never have heard of them. After those three days Hornblower warped *Atropos* out into the harbour again and set about his repairs with his own resources and with his own men, keeping them labouring under the sun, and deriving some little satisfaction from the fact that Captain Ford's troubles—he had *Nightingale* over at the careenage—were even worse than his own. Ford, with his ship heeled over while he patched her bottom, had to put sentries over the stores he had taken out of her, to prevent the Sicilians from stealing them, even while his men vanished into the alleys of Palermo to pawn their clothing in exchange for the heady Sicilian wine.

It was with relief that Hornblower saw *Ocean* come proudly into Palermo, vice-admiral's flag at the fore; he felt confident that when he made his report that his ship would be ready for sea in all respects in one day's time he would be ordered out to join the Fleet. It could not happen too quickly.

And sure enough the orders came that evening, after he had gone on board to give a verbal account of his doings and to hand in his written reports. Collingwood listened to all he had to say, gave in return a very pleasant word of congratulation, saw him off the ship with his invariable courtesy, and of course kept his promise regarding the orders. Hornblower read them in the privacy of his cabin when the *Ocean's* gig delivered them; they were commendably short. He was "requested and required, the day after tomorrow, the 17th instant", to make the best of his way to the island of Ischia, there to report to Commodore Harris and join the squadron blockading Naples.

So all next day the ship's company of *Atropos* toiled to complete their ship for sea. Hornblower was hardly conscious of the activity going on around *Ocean*—it was what might be expected in the flagship of the Commander-in-Chief in his ally's capital. He regretted the interruption to his men's work when the admiral's barge came pulling by, and still more when the royal barge, with the Sicilian colours and the Bourbon lilies displayed, came pulling by to visit *Ocean*. But that was only to be expected. When the flaming afternoon began to die away into the lovely evening he found time to exercise his men in accordance with the new station and quarter bills—so many had been the casualties that all the organization had to be revised. He stood there in the glowing sunset watching the men coming running down from aloft after setting topsails.

"Signal from the flag, sir," said Smiley, breaking in on his concentrated thought. " 'Flag to *Atropos*. Come on board!' "

"Call my gig," said Hornblower. "Mr. Jones, you will take command."

A desperate rush to change into his better uniform, and then he hurled himself down the ship's side to where his gig awaited him. Collingwood received him in the well-remembered cabin; the silver lamps were alight now, and in the boxes under the great stern windows were strange flowers whose names he did not know. And on Collingwood's face was a strange expression; there was a hint of distress in it, and of sympathy, as well as something of irritation. Hornblower stopped short at the sight of him, with a sudden pounding of the heart. He could hardly remember to make his bow properly. It flashed through his mind that perhaps Ford had reported adversely on his behaviour in the recent action. He might be facing court martial and ruin.

At Collingwood's shoulder stood a large elegant gentleman in full dress, with the ribbon and star of an order.

"My lord," said Collingwood, "this is Captain Horatio Hornblower, I believe you have already had correspondence with His Excellency, Captain. Lord William Bentinck."

Hornblower made his bow again, his feverish mind telling him that at least this could not be anything to do with the action with the *Castilla*—that would not be the Minister's business; on the other hand, in fact, Collingwood would keep strangers out of any scandal in the service.

"How d'ye do, sir?" asked Lord William.

"Very well, thank you, my Lord."

The two Lords went on looking at Hornblower, and Hornblower looked back at them, trying to appear calm during those endless seconds.

"There's bad news for you, Hornblower, I fear," said Collingwood at last, sadly.

Hornblower restrained himself from asking "What is it?" He pulled himself up stiffer than ever, and tried to meet Collingwood's eyes without wavering.

"His Sicilian Majesty," went on Collingwood, "needs a ship."

"Yes, my lord?"

Hornblower was none the wiser.

'When Bonaparte conquered the mainland he laid hands on the Sicilian Navy. Negligence—desertion—you can understand. There is no ship now at the disposal of His Majesty."

"No, my Lord." Hornblower could guess now what was coming.

"While coming out to visit *Ocean* this morning His Majesty happened to notice *Atropos*, with her paint all fresh. You made an excellent business of your refitting, Captain, as I noticed."

"Thank you, my Lord."

"His Majesty does not think it right that, as an island King, he should be without a ship."

"I see, my Lord."

Here Bentinck broke in, speaking harshly.

"The fact of the matter, Hornblower, is that the King has asked for your ship to be transferred to his flag."

"Yes, my Lord."

Nothing mattered now. Nothing was of any value.

"And I have advised His Lordship," went on Bentinck, indicating Collingwood, "that for the highest reasons of state it would be advisable to agree to the transfer."

The imbecile monarch coveting the newly-painted toy. Hornblower could not keep back his protest.

"I find it hard to believe it necessary, my Lord," he said.

For a moment His Excellency looked down in astonishment at the abysmal junior captain who questioned his judgment, but His Excellency kept his temper admirably all the same, and condescended to explain.

"I have six thousand British troops in the island," he said in his harsh voice. "At least, they call them British, but half of 'em are Corsican Rangers and Chasseurs Brittaniques—French deserters in British uniforms. I can hold the Straits against Bonaparte with them, all the same, as long as I have the goodwill of the King. Without it—if the Sicilian army turns against us—we're lost."

"You must have heard about the King, Captain," interposed Collingwood, gently.

"A little, my Lord."

"He'd ruin everything for a whim," said Bentinck. "Now Bonaparte finds he can't cross the Straits he'd be willing to reach an agreement with Ferdinand. He'd promise him his throne here in exchange for an alliance. Ferdinand is capable of agreeing, too. He'd as lief have French troops in occupation as British, and be a satellite—or so he thinks at present—if it would mean paying off a score against us."

"I see, my Lord," said Hornblower.

"When I have more troops I'll talk to him in a different fashion," said Bentinck. "But at present—"

"*Atropos* is the smallest ship I have in the Mediterranean," said Collingwood.

"And I am the most junior captain," said Hornblower. He could not restrain himself from the bitter comment. He even forgot to say "my Lord".

"That is true as well," said Collingwood.

In a disciplined service an officer was only a fool if he complained about treatment received on account of being junior. And it was clear that Collingwood disliked the present situation intensely.

"I understand, my Lord," said Hornblower.

"Lord William has some suggestions to make which may soften the blow," said Collingwood, and Hornblower shifted his glance.

"You can be retained in command of *Atropos*," said Bentinck—what a moment of joy, just one fleeting moment!—"if you transfer to the Sicilian service. His Majesty will appoint you Commodore, and you can hoist a broad pendant. I am sure he will also confer upon you an order of high distinction as well."

"No," said Hornblower. That was the only thing he could possibly say.

"I thought that would be your answer," said Collingwood. "And if a letter from me to the Admiralty carries any weight you can hope, on your return to England, to be appointed to the frigate to which your present seniority entitles you."

"Thank you, my Lord. So I am to return to England?"

He would have a glimpse of Maria and the children then.

"I see no alternative, Captain, I am afraid, as of course you understand. But if Their Lordships see fit to send you back here with your new command, no one would be more delighted than I."

"What sort of a man is your first lieutenant?" demanded Bentinck.

"Well, my Lord—" Hornblower looked from Bentinck to Collingwood. It was hard to make a public condemnation even of the abject Jones. "He is a worthy enough man. The fact that he is John Jones the Ninth in the lieutenants' list may have held him back from promotion."

A wintry twinkle appeared in Bentinck's eye.

"I fancy he would be John Jones the First in the Sicilian Navy List."

"I expect so indeed, my Lord."

"Do you think he would take service as captain under the King of the Two Sicilies?"

"I should be surprised if he did not."

That would be Jones's only chance of ever becoming a captain, and most likely Jones was aware of it, however he might excuse himself for it in his own thoughts.

Collingwood entered the conversation again at this point.

"Joseph Bonaparte over in Naples has just proclaimed himself King of the Two Sicilies as well," he remarked. "That makes four Sicilies."

Now they were all smiling together, and it was a moment before Hornblower's unhappiness returned to him, when he remembered that he had to give up the ship he had brought to perfection and the crew he had trained so carefully, and his Mediterranean station of honour. He turned to Collingwood.

"What are your orders, my Lord?"

"You will receive them in writing, of course. But verbally you are under orders not to move until you are officially informed of the transfer of your ship to the Sicilian flag. I'll distribute your ship's company through the Fleet—I can use them."

No doubt about that; probably every ship under Collingwood's command was undermanned and would welcome a contingent of prime seamen.

"Aye aye, my Lord."

"I'll take the Prince into my flagship here—there's a vacancy."

The Prince had had seven months in a sloop of war; probably he had learned as much in that time as he would learn in seven years in an Admiral's flagship.

"Aye aye, my Lord." Hornblower waited for a moment; it was hard to go on. "And your orders for me personally?"

"The *Aquila*—she's an empty troop transport—sails for Portsmouth immediately without convoy, because she's a fast ship. The monthly convoy is assembling, but it's far from complete as yet. As you know, I am only responsible for their escort as far as Gibraltar, so that if you choose to go in a King's ship you will have to transfer there. *Penelope* will be the escorting vessel, as far as I can tell at present. And when I can spare her—God knows when that will be—I shall send the old *Temeraire* to England direct."

"Yes, my Lord."

"I would be glad if you would choose for yourself, Captain. I'll frame my orders in accordance with your wishes. You can sail in *Aquila*, or *Penelope*, or wait for *Temeraire*, whichever you prefer."

Aquila was sailing for Portsmouth immediately, and she was a fast ship, sailing alone. In a month, even in less with fair winds, he could be setting foot on shore half an hour's walk from where Maria was living with the children. In a month he might be making his request to the Admiralty for further employment. He might be posted to that frigate that Collingwood had mentioned—he did not want to miss any opportunity. The sooner the better, as always. And he would see Maria and the children.

"I would like orders for *Aquila*, if you would be so kind, my Lord."

"I expected you would say that."

So that was the news that Hornblower brought back to his ship. The dreary little cabin which he had never had time to fit out properly seemed sadly homelike when he sat in it again; the sailcloth pillow supported once more a sleepless head, as so often before, when at last he could force himself to go to bed. It was strangely painful to say good-bye to the officers and crew, good characters and bad, even though he felt a little spurt of amusement at sight of Jones, gorgeous in the uniform of a captain in the Sicilian Navy, and another at the sight of the twenty volunteers from the ship's company whom Jones had been permitted to recruit into the Sicilian service. They were the bad characters, of course, laughed at by the others for exchanging the grog and hardtack of old England for the pasta and the daily quart of wine of Sicily. But even to the bad characters it was hard to say good-bye—a sentimental fool, Hornblower called himself.

It was a dreary two days that Hornblower waited for *Aquila* to make ready to sail. Bentinck had advised him to see the Palace chapel, to take a carriage out to Monreale and see the mosaics there, but like a sulky child he would not. The dreamlike city of Palermo turns its back upon the sea, and Hornblower turned his back upon Palermo, until *Aquila* was working her way out round Monte Pellegrino, and then he stood aft, by the taffrail, looking back at *Atropos* lying there, and *Nightingale* at the careenage, and the palaces of Palermo beyond. He was forlorn and lonely, a negligible passenger amid all the bustle of getting under way.

"By your leave, sir," said a seaman, hastening to the peak halliards—a little more, and he would have been elbowed out of the way.

"Good morning, sir," said the captain of the ship, and instantly turned to shout orders to the men at the main topsail halliards; the captain of a hired transport did not want to offer any encouragement to a King's captain to comment on the handling of the ship. King's officers would only grudgingly admit that even admirals came between them and God.

Aquila dipped her colours to the flagship, and *Ocean* returned the compliment, the White Ensign slowly descending and rising again. That was the last memory Hornblower was to have of Palermo and of his voyage in the *Atropos*. *Aquila* braced round her sails and caught the first of the land breeze, heading boldly northward out to sea, and Sicily began to fade into the distance, while Hornblower tried to displace his unaccountable sadness by telling himself that he was on his way to Maria and the children. He tried to stimulate himself into excitement over the thought that a new command awaited him, and new adventures. Collingwood's flag lieutenant had passed on to him the gossip that the Admiralty was still commissioning ships as fast as they could be made ready for sea; there was a frigate, the *Lydia*, making ready, which would be an appropriate command for a captain of his seniority. But it was only slowly that he was able to overcome his sense of loss and frustration, as slowly as the captain of the *Aquila* made him welcome when he was taking his noon sights, as slowly as the days passed while *Aquila* beat her way to the Straits and out into the Atlantic.

Autumn was waiting for them beyond the straits, with the roaring westerly gales of the equinox, gale after gale, when fortunately they had made westing enough to keep them safe from the coast of Portugal while they lay hove-to for long hours in the latitude of Lisbon, in the latitude of Oporto, and then in the Bay of Biscay. It was on the tail of the last of the gales that they drove wildly up the Channel, storm-battered and leaky, with pumps going and topsails treble reefed. And there was England, dimly seen, but well remembered, the vague outline to be gazed at with a catch in the breath. The Start, and at last St. Catharine's, and the hour of uncertainty as to whether they could get into the lee of the Wight or would have to submit to being blown all the way up-channel. A fortunate slant of wind gave them their opportunity, and they attained the more sheltered waters of Spithead, with the unbelievable green of the Isle of Wight on their left hand, and so they attained to Portsmouth, to drop anchor where the quiet and calm made it seem as if all the turmoil outside had been merely imagined.

A shore boat took Hornblower to the Sally Port, and he set foot on English soil again, with a surge of genuine emotion, mounting the steps and looking round him at the familiar buildings of Portsmouth. A shore loafer—an old, bent man—hurried away on twisted legs to fetch his barrow while Hornblower looked round him; when he returned Hornblower had to help him lift his chests on to the barrow.

"Thank'ee, cap'n, thank'ee," said the old man. He used the title automatically, without knowing Hornblower's rank.

No one in England knew as yet—Maria did not know—that Hornblower was in England. For that matter no one in England knew as yet about the last exploit of the *Atropos* and the capture of *Castilla.* Copies of Ford's and Hornblower's reports to Collingwood were on board *Aquila,* in the sealed mailbag in the captain's charge, to be sent on to the Secretary of the Admiralty "for the information of Their Lordships". In a day or two they might be in the Gazette, and they might even be copied to appear in the Naval Chronicle and the daily newspapers. Most of the honour and glory, of course, would go to Ford, but a few crumbs might come Hornblower's way; there was enough chance of that to put Hornblower in a good temper as he walked along with the wooden wheels of the barrow thumping and squeaking over the cobbles behind him.

The sadness and distress he had suffered when he parted from *Atropos* had largely died away by now. He was back in England, walking as fast as the old man's legs would allow towards Maria and the children, free for the moment from all demands upon his patience or his endurance, free to be happy for a while, free to indulge in ambitious dreams of the frigate Their Lordships might give him, free to relax in Maria's happy and indifferent chatter, with little Horatio running round the room, and with little Maria making valiant efforts to crawl at his feet. The thumping of the barrow wheels beat out a pleasant rhythm to accompany his dreams.

Here was the house and the well-remembered door. He could hear the echo within as he let the knocker fall, and he turned to help the old man lift off the chests. He put a shilling into the shaky hand and turned back quickly as he heard the door open. Maria was there with a child in her arms. She stood beside the door looking at him without recognition for a long second, and when at last she spoke it was as if she were dazed.

"Horry!" she said. "Horry!"

There was no smile on her bewildered face.

"I've come home, dearest," said Hornblower.

"I—I thought you were the apothecary," said Maria, speaking slowly, "the—the babies aren't so well."

She offered the child in her arms for his inspection. It must be little Maria, althought he did not know the flushed, feverish face. The closed eyes opened, and then shut again with the pain of the light, and the little head turned away fretfully but wearily, and the mouth opened to emit a low cry.

"Sh—sh," said Maria, folding the child to her breast again, bowing her head over the wailing bundle. Then she looked up at Hornblower again.

"You must come in," she said. "The—the cold. It will strike the fever inward."

The remembered hall; the room at the side where he had asked Maria to marry him; the staircase to the bedroom. Mrs. Mason was there, her grey hair untidy even in the curtained twilight of the room.

"The apothecary?" she asked from where she bent over the bed.

"No, mother. It's Horry come back again."

"Horry? Horatio!"

Mrs. Mason looked up to confirm what her daughter said, and Hornblower came towards the bedside. A tiny little figure lay there, half on its side, one hand outside the bedclothes holding Mrs. Mason's finger.

"He's sick," said Mrs. Mason. "Poor little man. He's so sick."

Hornblower knelt beside the bed and bent over his son. He put out his hand and touched the feverish cheek. He tried to soothe his son's forehead as the head turned on the pillow. That forehead; it felt strange; like small shot felt through velvet. And Hornblower knew what that meant. He knew it well, and he had to admit the certainty to himself before telling the women what it meant. Smallpox.

Before he rose to his feet he had reached another conclusion, too. There was still duty to be done, his duty to his King and Country and to the Service and to Maria. Maria must be comforted. He must always comfort her, as long as life lasted.

The Happy Return

I

It was not long after dawn that Captain Hornblower came up on the quarterdeck of the *Lydia*. Bush, the first lieutenant, was officer of the watch, and touched his hat but did not speak to him; in a voyage which had by now lasted seven months without touching land he had learned something of his captain's likes and dislikes. During this first hour of the day the captain was not to be spoken to, nor his train of thought interrupted.

In accordance with standing orders – hallowed by now with the tradition which is likely to accumulate during a voyage of such incredible length – Brown, the captain's coxswain, had seen to it that the weather side of the quarterdeck had been holystoned and sanded at the first peep of daylight. Bush and the midshipman with him withdrew to the lee side at Hornblower's first appearance, and Hornblower immediately began his daily hour's walk up and down, up and down the twenty-one feet of deck which had been sanded for him. On one hand his walk was limited by the slides of the quarterdeck carronades; on the other by the row of ringbolts in the deck for the attachment of the carronade train tackles; the space of deck on which Captain Hornblower was accustomed to exercise himself for an hour each morning was thus five feet wide and twenty-one feet long.

Up and down, up and down, paced Captain Hornblower. Although he was entirely lost in thought, his subordinates knew by experience that his sailor's instinct was quite alert; subconsciously his mind took note of the shadow of the main rigging across the deck, and of the feel of the breeze on his cheek, so that the slightest inattention on the part of the quartermaster at the wheel called forth a bitter rebuke from the captain – the more bitter in that he had been disturbed in this, the most important hour of his day. In the same way he was aware, without having taken special note, of all the salient facts of the prevailing conditions. On his awakening in his cot he had seen (without willing it) from the tell tale compass in the deck over his head that the course was north east, as it had been for the last three days. At the moment of his arrival on deck he had subconsciously noted that the wind was from the west, and just strong enough to give the ship steerage way, with all sail set to the royals, that the sky was of its perennial blue, and that the sea was almost flat calm, with a long peaceful swell over which the *Lydia* seared and swooped with profound regularity.

The first thing Captain Hornblower was aware of thinking was that the Pacific in the morning, deep blue overside and changing to silver towards the horizon, was like some heraldic blazon of argent and azure – and then he almost smiled to himself because that simile had come up in his mind every morning for the last fortnight. With the thought and the smile his mind was instantly working smoothly and rapidly. He looked down the gangways at the men at work holystoning; down on the maindeck, as he came forward, he could see another party engaged on the same task. They were talking in ordinary tones. Twice he heard a laugh. That was well. Men who could talk and laugh in that fashion were not likely to be plotting mutiny – and Captain Hornblower had that possibility much in mind lately. Seven months at sea had almost consumed the ship's stores. A week ago he had cut the daily ration of water to three pints a day, and three pints a day was hardly sufficient for men living on salt meat and biscuit in ten degrees north latitude, especially as water seven months in cask was half solid with green living things.

A week ago, too, the very last of the lemon juice had been served out, and there would be scurvy to reckon with within a month and no surgeon on board. Hankey the surgeon had died of all the complications of drink and syphilis off the Horn. For a month now tobacco had been doled out in half ounces weekly – Hornblower congratulated himself now on having taken the tobacco under his sole charge. If he had not done so the thoughtless fools would have used up their whole store, and men deprived of tobacco were men who could not be relied upon. He knew that the men were more concerned about the shortage of tobacco than about the shortage of fuel for the galley which caused them each day to be given their salt pork only just brought to the boil in seawater.

The shortage of tobacco, of water and of wood was nothing nearly as important, however, as the imminent shortage of grog. He had not dared to cut that daily issue, and there was only rum for ten more days in the ship. Not the finest crew in the world could be relied on if deprived of their ration of rum. Here they were in the South Sea, with no other King's ship within two thousand miles of them. Somewhere to the westward were islands of romance, with beautiful women, and food to be got without labour. A life of happy idleness was within their reach. Some knave among the crew, better informed than the rest, would give the hint. It would not be attended to at present, but in the future, with no blessed interval of grog at noon, the men would be ready to listen. Ever since the crew of the *Bounty* had mutinied, seduced by the charms of the Pacific, the captain of every ship of His Britannic Majesty whose duty took him there was haunted by this fear.

Hornblower, pacing the deck, looked sharply once more at the crew. Seven months at sea without once touching land had given an admirable opportunity for training the gang of gaolbirds and pressed men into seamen, but it was too long without distraction. The sooner now that he could reach the coast of Nicaragua, the better. A run ashore would distract the men, and there would be water and fresh food and tobacco and spirits to be got. Hornblower's mind began to run back through his recent calculations of the ship's position. He was certain about his latitude, and last night's lunar observations had seemed to confirm the chronometer's indication of the longitude – even though it seemed incredible that chronometers could be relied upon at all after a seven months' voyage. Probably less than one hundred miles ahead, at most three hundred, lay the Pacific coast of Central America. Crystal the master had shaken his head in doubt at Hornblower's positiveness, but Crystal was an old fool, and of no use as a navigator. Anyway, two or three more days would see who was right.

At once Hornblower's mind shifted to the problem of how to spend the next two or three days. The men must be kept busy. There was nothing like long idle days to breed mutiny – Hornblower never feared mutiny during the wild ten weeks of beating round the Horn. In the forenoon watch he would clear for action and practise the men at the guns, five rounds from each. The concussion might kill the wind for a space, but that could not be helped. It would be the last opportunity, perhaps, before the guns would be in action in earnest.

Another calculation came up in Hornblower's mind. Five rounds from the guns would consume over a ton weight of powder and shot. The *Lydia* was riding light already with her stores nearly all consumed. Hornblower called up before his mental eye a picture of the frigate's hold and the positions of the store rooms. It was time that he paid attention to the trim of the ship again. After the men had had their dinner he would put off in the quarter boat and pull round the ship. She would be by the stern a little now, he expected. That could be put right tomorrow by shifting the two No. 1 carronades on the forecastle forward to their original positions. And as the ship would have to shorten sail while he was in the quarter boat he might as well do the job properly and give Bush a free hand in exercising the crew aloft. Bush had a passion for that kind of seamanship, as a first lieutenant quite rightly should. Today the crew might beat their previous record of eleven minutes fifty-one seconds for sending up topmasts, and of twenty-four minutes seven seconds for setting all sail starting with topmast housed. Neither of those times, Hornblower agreed with Bush, was nearly as good as they might be; plenty of ships had set up better figures – at least so their captains had said.

Hornblower became aware that the wind had increased a tiny amount, sufficiently to call forth a faint whispering from the rigging. From the feel of it upon his neck and cheek he deduced it must have shifted aft a point or perhaps two, as well, and even as his mind registered these observations, and began to wonder how soon Bush would take notice of it, he heard the call for the watch. Clay, the midshipman on the quarterdeck, was bellowing like a bull for the afterguard. That boy's voice had broken since they left England; he was learning to use it properly now, instead of alternately squeaking and croaking. Still without taking visual notice of what was going on, Hornblower as he continued pacing the quarterdeck listened to the familiar sequence of sounds as the watch came tumbling aft to the braces. A crack and a yelp told him that Harrison the boatswain had landed with his cane on the stern of some laggardly or unlucky sailor. Harrison was a fine seaman, but with a weakness for using his cane on well-rounded sterns. Any man who filled his trousers out tight was likely to get a welt across the seat of them solely for that reason, especially if he was unluckily engaged as Harrison came by in some occupation which necessitated bending forward.

Hornblower's meditations regarding Harrison's weakness had occupied nearly all the time necessary for the trimming of the sails; as they came to an end Harrison roared 'Belay!' and the watch trooped back to their previous duties. Ting-ting, ting-ting, ting-ting, *ting* went the bell. Seven bells in the morning watch. Hornblower had been walking for well over his covenanted hour, and he was aware of a gratifying trickle of sweat under his shirt. He walked over to where Bush was standing by the wheel.

'Good morning, Mr Bush,' said Captain Hornblower.

'Good morning, sir,' said Bush, exactly as if Captain Hornblower had not been walking up and down within four yards of him for the last hour and a quarter.

Hornblower looked at the slate which bore the rough log of the last twenty-four hours; there was nothing of special note – the hourly casting of the log had given speeds of three knots, four and a half knots, four knots, and so on, while the traverse board showed that the ship had contrived to hold to her north easterly course throughout the day. The captain was aware of a keen scrutiny from his first lieutenant, and he knew that internally the lieutenant seethed with questions. There was only one man on board who knew whither the *Lydia* was bound, and that was the captain. He had sailed with sealed orders, and when he had opened and read them, in accordance with his instructions, in 30° N. 20° W., he had not seen fit to tell even his second in command what they contained. For seven months Lieutenant

Bush had contrived to refrain from asking questions, but the strain was visibly telling on him.

'Ha – h'm,' said Hornblower, clearing his throat non-committally. Without a word he hung up the slate and went down the companion and entered his sleeping-cabin.

It was unlucky for Bush that he should be kept in the dark in this fashion, but Hornblower had refrained from discussing his orders with him not through any fear of Bush's garrulity, but through fear of his own. When he had first sailed as captain five years ago he had allowed his natural talkativeness full play, and his first lieutenant of that time had come to presume upon the licence allowed him until Hornblower had been unable to give an order without having it discussed. Last commission he had tried to limit discussion with his first lieutenant within the ordinary bounds of politeness, and had found that he had been unable to keep himself within those limits – he was always opening his mouth and letting fall one word too many to his subsequent regret. This voyage he had started with the firm resolve (like a drinker who cannot trust himself to drink only in moderation) to say nothing whatever to his officers except what was necessitated by routine, and his resolution had been hardened by the stress which his orders laid upon the need for extreme secrecy. For seven months he had held to it, growing more and more silent every day as the unnatural state of affairs took a firmer grip upon him. In the Atlantic he had sometimes discussed the weather with Mr Bush. Round in the Pacific he only condescended to clear his throat.

His sleeping-cabin was a tiny morsel of space bulkheaded off from his main cabin. Half the room was occupied by an eighteen pounder; the remainder was almost filled by his cot, his desk, and his chest. His steward Polwheal was putting out his razor and lather bowl on a bracket under a strip of mirror on the bulkhead – there was just room for the two of them to stand. Polwheal squeezed himself against the desk to allow his captain to enter; he said nothing, for Polwheal was a man of gratifyingly few words – Hornblower had picked him for that reason, because he had to guard against his besetting sin of garrulity even with servants.

Hornblower stripped off his wet shirt and trousers and shaved standing naked before the mirror. The face he regarded in the glass was neither handsome nor ugly, neither old nor young. There was a pair of melancholy brown eyes, a forehead sufficiently high, a nose sufficiently straight; a good mouth set with all the firmness acquired during twenty years at sea. The tousled curly brown hair was just beginning to recede and leave the forehead a little higher still, which was a source of irritation to Captain Hornblower, because he hated the thought of going bald. Noticing it, he was reminded of his other trouble and glanced down his naked body. He was slender and well muscled; quite a prepossessing figure, in fact, when he drew himself to his full six feet. But down there where his ribs ended there was no denying the presence of a rounded belly, just beginning to protrude beyond the line of his ribs and of his iliac bones. Hornblower hated the thought of growing fat with an intensity rare in his generation; he hated to think of his slender smooth-skinned body being disfigured by an unsightly bulge in the middle, which was the reason why he, a naturally indolent individual who hated routine forced himself to take that regular morning walk on the quarterdeck.

When he had finished shaving he put down razor and brush for Polwheal to wash and put away, and stood while Polwheal hung a ragged serge dressing gown over his shoulders. Polwheal followed him along the deck to the head-pump, removed the dressing gown, and then pumped up seawater from overside while his captain solemnly rotated under the stream. When the bath was finished Polwheal hung the dressing down again over his dripping shoulders and followed him back to the cabin. A clean linen shirt – worn, but neatly mended – and white trousers were laid out on the cot. Hornblower dressed himself, and Polwheal helped him into the worn blue coat with its faded lace, and handed him his hat. All this was without a word being spoken, so well by now had Hornblower trained himself into his self-imposed system of silence. And he who hated routine had by now so fully called in routine to save himself from speech that exactly as he stepped out again on the quarterdeck eight bells rang, just as happened every single morning.

'Hands to punishment, sir?' asked Bush, touching his hat.

Hornblower nodded. The pipes of the boatswain's mates began to twitter.

'All hands to witness punishment,' roared Harrison on the maindeck, and from all parts of the ship men began to pour up and toe their lines in their allotted positions.

Hornblower stood rigid by the quarterdeck rail, setting his face like stone. He was ashamed of the fact that he looked upon punishment as a beastly business, that he hated ordering it and dreaded witnessing it. The two or three thousand floggings he had witnessed in the last twenty years had not succeeded in hardening him – in fact he was much softer now (as he was painfully aware) than as a seventeen year old midshipman. But there had been no avoiding the punishment of this morning's victim. He was a Welshman called Owen who could somehow never refrain from spitting on the decks. Bush, without referring to his captain, had sworn that he would have him flogged for every offence, and Hornblower had necessarily to endorse the decision and back up his officer in the name of discipline, although

Hornblower had the gravest doubts as to whether a man who was fool enough not to be deterred from spitting on the decks by the fear of a flogging would benefit by receiving it.

Happily the business was got over quickly. The boatswain's mates triced Owen, naked to the waist, up to the main rigging, and laid into him as the drum rolled. Owen, unlike the usual run of seamen, howled with pain as the cat of ninetails bit into his shoulders, and danced grotesquely, his bare feet flapping on the deck until at the end of his two dozen he hung from his bound wrists motionless and silent. Someone soused him with water and he was hustled below.

'Hands to breakfast, Mr Bush,' snapped Hornblower; he hoped that the tan of the tropics saved him from looking as white as he felt. Flogging a half witted man was not to his taste as a before breakfast diversion and he was sick with disgust at himself at neither being strong enough to stop it nor ingenious enough to devise a way out of the dilemma Bush's decision had forced him into.

The row of officers on the quarterdeck broke up as each turned away. Gerard, the second lieutenant, took over the deck from Bush. The ship was like a magic tessellated pavement. It presented a geometrical pattern; someone shook it up into confusion, and at once it settled itself into a new and orderly fashion.

Hornblower went below to where Polwheal had his breakfast awaiting him.

'Coffee, sir,' said Polwheal. 'Burgoo.'

Hornblower sat down at table; in the seven months' voyage every luxury had long since been consumed. The coffee was a black extract of burnt bread, and all that could be said in its favour was that it was sweet and hot. The burgoo was a savoury mess of unspeakable appearance compounded of mashed biscuit crumbs and minced salt beef. Hornblower ate absentmindedly. With his left hand he tapped a biscuit on the table so that the weevils would all be induced to have left it by the time he had finished his burgoo.

There were ship-noises all round him as he ate. Every time the *Lydia* rolled and pitched a trifle as she reached the crest of the swell which was lifting her, the woodwork all creaked gently in unison. Overhead came the sound of Gerard's shod feet as he paced the quarterdeck, and sometimes the pattering of horny bare feet as some member of the crew trotted by. From forward came a monotonous steady clanking as the pumps were put to the daily task of pumping out the ship's bilges. But these noises were all transient and interrupted; there was one sound which went on all the time so steadily that the ear grew accustomed to it and only noticed it when the attention was specially directed to it – the sound of the breeze in the innumerable ropes of the rigging. It was just the faintest singing, a harmony of a thousand high-pitched tones and overtones, but it could be heard in every part of the ship, transmitted from the chains through the timbers along with the slow, periodic creaking.

Hornblower finished his burgoo, and was turning his attention to the biscuit he had been rapping on the table. He contemplated it with calm disfavour; it was poor food for a man, and in the absence of butter – the last cask had gone rancid a month back – he would have to wash down the dry mouthfuls with sips of burnt-bread coffee. But before he could take his first bite a wild cry from above caused him to sit still with the biscuit half way to his mouth.

'Land ho!' he heard. 'Deck there! Land two points on the larboard bow, sir.'

That was the lookout in the foretop hailing the deck. Hornblower, as he sat with his biscuit in mid air, heard the rush and bustle on deck; everyone would be wildly excited at the sight of land, the first for three months, on this voyage to an unknown destination. He was excited himself. There was not merely the imminent thrill of discovering whether he had made a good landfall; there was also the thought that perhaps within twenty-four hours he would be in the thick of the dangerous and difficult mission upon which my lords of the Admiralty had despatched him. He was conscious of a more rapid beating of his heart in his breast. He wanted passionately to rush out on deck as his first instincts dictated, but he restrained himself. He wanted still more to appear in the eyes of his officers and crew to be a man of complete self-confidence and imperturbability – and this was only partially to gratify himself. The more respect in which a captain was held, the better for his ship. He forced himself into an attitude of complete composure, crossing his knees and sipping his coffee in entire unconcern as Mr Midshipman Savage knocked at the cabin door and came bouncing in.

'Mr Gerard sent me to tell you land's in sight on the larboard bow, sir,' said Savage, hardly able to stand still in the prevailing infection of excitement. Hornblower made himself take another sip of coffee before he spoke, and he made his words come slowly and calmly.

'Tell Mr Gerard I shall come on deck in a few minutes when I have finished my breakfast,' he said.

'Aye aye, sir.'

Savage bolted out of the cabin; his large clumsy feet clattered on the companion.

'Mr Savage! Mr Savage!' yelled Hornblower. Savage's large moonlike face reappeared in the doorway.

'You forgot to close the door,' said Hornblower, coldly. 'And please don't make so much noise on the companionway.'

'Aye aye, sir,' said the crestfallen Savage.

Hornblower was pleased with himself for that. He pulled at his chin in self congratulation. He sipped again at his coffee, but found himself quite unable to eat his biscuit. He drummed with his fingers on the table in an effort to make the time pass more rapidly.

He heard young Clay bellowing from the masthead, where presumably Gerard had sent him with a glass.

'Looks like a burning mountain, sir. Two burning mountains. Volcanoes, sir.'

Instantly Hornblower began to call up before his mind's eye his memory of the chart which he had so often studied in the privacy of this cabin. There were volcanoes all along this coast; the presence of two of the larboard bow was no sure indication of the ship's position. And yet – and yet – the entrance of the Gulf of Fonseca would undoubtedly be marked by two volcanoes to larboard. It was quite possible that he had made a perfect landfall, after eleven weeks out of sight of land. Hornblower could sit still no longer. He got up from the table, and, remembering just in time to go slowly and with an air of complete unconcern, he walked up on deck.

II

The quarterdeck was thronged with officers, all the four lieutenants, Crystal the master, Simmonds of the marines, Wood the purser, the midshipmen of the watch. The rigging swarmed with petty officers and ratings, and every glass in the ship appeared to be in use. Hornblower realised that a stern coldblooded disciplinarian would take exception to this perfectly natural behaviour, and so he did the same.

'What's all this?' he snapped. 'Has no one in this ship anything to do? Mr Wood, I'll trouble you to send for the cooper and arrange with him for the filling of the water casks. Get the royals and stun'-sails off her, Mr Gerard.'

The ship burst into activity again with the twittering of the pipes and Harrison's bellowing of 'All hands shorten sail' and the orders which Gerard called from the quarterdeck. Under plain sail the *Lydia* rolled smoothly over the quartering swell.

'I think I can see the smoke from the deck, sir, now,' said Gerard, apologetically raising the subject of land again to his captain. He proffered his glass and pointed forward. Low on the horizon, greyish under a wisp of white cloud, Hornblower could see something through the telescope which might be smoke.

'Ha-h'm,' said Hornblower, as he had trained himself to say instead of something more conversational. He went forward and began to climb the weather foremast shrouds. He was nothing of an athlete, and he felt a faint dislike for this task, but it had to be done – and he was uncomfortably aware that every idle eye on board was turned on him. Because of this he was morally compelled, although he was hampered by the telescope, to refrain from going through the lubbers' hole and instead to make the difficult outward climb up the futtock shrouds. Nor could he pause for breath – not when there were midshipmen under his command who in their follow-my-leader games thought nothing of running without a stop from the hold to the main royal truck.

The climb hand over hand up the fore top gallant shrouds tried him severely; breathing heavily, he reached the fore top gallant masthead, and settled himself to point the telescope as steadily as his heaving chest and sudden nervousness would allow. Clay was sitting nonchalantly astride the yardarm fifteen feet away, but Hornblower ignored him. The slight corkscrew roll of the ship was sweeping him in a vast circle, up, forward, sideways, and down; at first he could only fix the distant mountains in snatches, but after a time he was able to keep them under fairly continuous observation. It was a strange landscape which the telescope revealed to him. There were the sharp peaks of several volcanoes; two very tall ones to larboard, a host of smaller ones both to starboard and to port. As he looked he saw a puff of grey steam emerge from one peak – not from the summit, but from a vent in the side – and ascend lazily to join the strip of white cloud which hung over it. Besides these cones there was a long mountain range of which the peaks appeared to be spurs, but the range itself seemed to be made up of a chain of old volcanoes, truncated and weathered down by the passage of centuries; that strip of coast must have been a hell's kitchen when they were all in eruption together. The upper parts of the peaks and of the mountains were a warm grey – grey with a hint of pink – and lower he could see what looked like green cataracts which must be vegetation stretching up along gullies in the mountain sides. Hornblower noted the relative heights and positions of the volcanoes, and from these data he drew a map in his mind and compared it with the section of the chart which he also carried in his mind's eye. There was no doubting their similarity.

'I thought I saw breakers just then, sir,' said Clay. Hornblower's gaze changed direction from the tops of the peaks to their feet.

Here there was a solid belt of green, unbroken save where lesser volcanoes jutted out from it. Hornblower swept his glass along it, along the very edge of the horizon, and then back again. He thought he saw a tiny flash of white, sought for the place again, experienced a moment of doubt, and then saw it again – a speck of white which appeared and disappeared as he watched.

'Quite right. Those are breakers sure enough,' he said, and instantly regretted it. There had been no need to make any reply to Clay at all. By that much his reputation for immobility diminished.

The *Lydia* held her course steadily towards the coast. Looking down, Hornblower could see the curiously foreshortened figures of the men on the forecastle a hundred and forty feet below, and round the bows a hint of a bow wave which told him the ship must be making four knots or very nearly. They would be up with the shore long before nightfall, especially as the breeze would freshen as the day went on. He eased himself out of his cramped position and stared again at the shore. As time went on he could see more breakers stretching on each side of where he had originally seen them. That must be a place where the incoming swell broke straight against a vertical wall of rock and flung its white foam upwards into sight. His belief that he had made a perfect landfall was growing stronger. On each side of the breakers was a stretch of clear water on the horizon, and beyond that again, on each side, was a medium-sized volcano. A wide bay, an island in the middle of the entrance, and two flanking volcanoes. That was exactly how the Gulf of Fonseca appeared in the chart, but Hornblower was painfully aware that no very great error in his navigation would have brought them anything up to two hundred miles from where he thought he was, and he realised that on a coast like this, littered with volcanoes, one section would appear very like another. Even the appearance of a bay and an island might be simulated by some other formation of the coast. Besides, he could not rely on his charts. They had been drawn from those Anson had captured in these very waters sixty years ago, and every one knew about Dago charts – and Dago charts submitted to the revision of useless Admiralty draughtsmen might be completely unreliable.

But as he watched his doubts were gradually set at rest. The bay opening before him was enormous – there could be no other of that size on that coast which could have escaped even Dago cartographers. Hornblower's eyes estimated the width of the entrance at something over ten miles including the islands. Farther up the bay was a big island of a shape typical of the landscape – a steep circular cone rising sheer from the water. He could not see the far end of the bay, not even now when the ship was ten miles nearer than when he first saw the entrance.

'Mr Clay,' he said, not condescending to take his eye from the telescope. 'You can go down now. Give Mr Gerard my compliments and ask him please to send all hands to dinner.'

'Aye aye, sir,' said Clay.

The ship would know now that something unusual was imminent, with dinner advanced by half an hour. In British ships the officers were always careful to see that the men had full bellies before being called upon to exert themselves more than usual.

Hornblower resumed his watch from the mast head. There could be no possible doubt now that the *Lydia* was heading into the Gulf of Fonseca. He had performed a most notable feat of navigation, of which anyone might be justifiably proud, in bringing the ship straight here after eleven weeks without sighting land. But he felt no elation about it. It was Hornblower's nature to find no pleasure in achieving things he could do; his ambition was always yearning after the impossible, to appear a strong silent capable man, unmoved by emotion.

At present there was no sign of life in the gulf, no boats, no smoke. It might be an uninhabited shore that he was approaching, a second Columbus. He could count on at least one hour more without further action being called for. He shut his telescope, descended to the deck, and walked with self conscious slowness aft to the quarterdeck.

Crystal and Gerard were talking animatedly beside the rail. Obviously they had moved out of earshot of the man at the wheel and had sent the midshipman as far away as possible; obviously also, as indicated by the way they looked towards Hornblower as he approached, they were talking about him. And it was only natural that they should be excited, because the *Lydia* was the first British ship of war to penetrate into the Pacific coast of Spanish America since Anson's time. They were in waters furrowed by the famous Acapulco galleon which carried a million sterling in treasure on each of her annual trips, along this coast crept the coasting ships bearing the silver of Potosi to Panama. It seemed as if the fortune of every man on board might be assured if only those unknown orders of the captain permitted it. What the captain intended to do next was of intense importance to them all.

'Send a reliable man with a good glass to the fore t'gallant masthead, Mr Gerard,' was all Hornblower said as he went below.

III

Polwheal was waiting with his dinner in the cabin. Hornblower meditated for a moment upon the desirability of a dinner of fat salt pork at noontide in the tropics. He was not in the least hungry, but the desire to appear a hero in the eyes of his steward overrode his excited lack of appetite. He sat down and ate rapidly for ten minutes, forcing himself to gulp down the distasteful mouthfuls. Polwheal, too, was watching every movement he made with desperate interest. Under his avid gaze he rose and walked through, stooping his head under the low deck, to his sleeping cabin and unlocked his desk.

'Polwheal!' he called.

'Sir!' said Polwheal instantly appearing at the door.

'Get out my best coat and put the new epaulettes on it. Clean white trousers – no, the breeches and the best white silk stockings. The buckled shoes, and see that the buckles shine. And the sword with the gold hilt.'

'Aye aye, sir,' said Polwheal.

Back in the main cabin Hornblower stretched himself on the locker below the stern window and once more unfolded his secret Admiralty orders. He had read them so often that he almost knew them by heart, but it was prudent to make certain that he understood every word of them. They were comprehensive enough, in all conscience. Some Admiralty clerk had given his imagination loose rein in the wording of them. The first ten paragraphs covered the voyage up to the present; firstly the need for acting with the utmost possible secrecy so that no hint could reach Spain of the approach of a British frigate to the Pacific shores of her possessions. 'You are therefore requested and required—' to sight land as little as possible on the voyage, and 'you are hereby entirely prohibited—' from coming within sight of land at all in the Pacific until the moment of his arrival at the mouth of the Gulf of Fonseca. He had obeyed these orders to the letter, although there were few enough captains in the service who could have done and who would have done. He had brought his ship here all the way from England without seeing any land save for a glimpse of Cape Horn, and if he had allowed Crystal to have his way regarding the course to be set a week ago, the ship would have gone sailing into the Gulf of Panama, completely forfeiting all possibility of secrecy.

Hornblower wrenched his mind away from the argument regarding the amount of compass-variation to be allowed for in these waters and forced himself to concentrate on a further study of his orders. 'You are hereby requested and required—' to form an alliance as soon as he reached the Gulf of Fonseca with Don Julian Alvarado, who was a large landowner with estates along the western shore of the bay. Don Julian intended, with the help of the British, to rise in rebellion against the Spanish monarchy. Hornblower was to hand over to him the five hundred muskets and bayonets, the five hundred pouch-belts, and the million rounds of small arm ammunition which were to be provided at Portsmouth, and he was to do everything which his discretion dictated to ensure the success of the rebellion. If he were to think it necessary, he could present to the rebels one or more of the guns of his ship, but the fifty thousand guineas in gold which were entrusted to him as well were only to be disbursed if the rebellion would fail without them, on pain of his being brought to a court-martial. He was to succour the rebels to the utmost of his power, even to the extent of recognising Don Julian Alvarado's sovereignty over any territory that he might conquer, provided that in return Don Julian would enter into commercial treaties with His Britannic Majesty.

This mention of commercial treaties apparently had acted as an inspiration to the Admiralty clerk, for the next ten paragraphs dealt in highflown detail with the pressing necessity for opening Spanish possessions to British commerce. Peruvian balsam and logwood, cochineal and gold, were awaiting exchange for British manufactures. The clerk's quill had fairly dipped with excitement as it penned these details in a fair round hand. Furthermore, there was an arm of the bay of Fonseca, called, it was believed, the Estero Real, which approached closely to the inland lake of Managua, which was thought to communicate with the lake of Nicaragua, which drained to the Caribbean by the river San Juan. Captain Hornblower was requested and required to do his utmost to open up this route across the isthmus to British commerce, and he was to guide Don Julian's efforts in this direction.

It was only after Don Julian's rebellion should be successful and all this accomplished that the orders went on to give Captain Hornblower permission to attack the treasure ships to be found in the Pacific, and moreover no shipping was to be interfered with if doing so should give offence to those inhabitants who might otherwise be favourable to the rebellion. For Captain Hornblower's information it was noted that the Spaniards were believed to maintain in these waters a two-decked ship of fifty guns, by the name the *Natividad,* for the enforcement of the royal authority. Captain Hornblower was therefore requested and required to 'take, sink, burn or destroy' this ship at the first opportunity.

Lastly, Captain Hornblower was ordered to open communications as soon as might be convenient with the Rear Admiral commanding the Leeward Islands station for the purpose of receiving further orders.

Captain Hornblower folded up the crackling paper again and fell into contemplation. Those orders were the usual combination of the barely-possible and the quite Quixotic, which a captain on detached service might expect to receive. Only a landsman would have given those opening orders to sail to the Gulf of Fonseca without sighting other land in the Pacific – only a succession of miracles (Hornblower gave himself no credit for sound judgment and good seamanship) had permitted of their being carried out.

Starting a rebellion in the Spanish American colonies had long been a dream of the British government – a dream which had been a nightmare to the British officers ordered to make it a reality. Admiral Popham and Admiral Stirling, General Beresford and General Whitelocke, had, during the last three years, all lost in honour and reputation in repeated efforts to raise rebellion on the River Plate.

Opening up a channel to British trade across the Isthmus of Darien had long been a similar dream cherished by Admiralty clerks with small scale maps before them and no practical experience. Thirty years ago Nelson himself, as a young captain, had nearly lost his life in command of an expedition up that very river San Juan which Hornblower was ordered to clear from its source.

And to crown it all was the casual mention of the presence of a fifty-gun ship of the enemy. It was typical of Whitehall to send a thirty-six gun frigate so lightly to attack an enemy of nearly double that force. The British navy had been so successful in single ship duels during these wars that by now victory was expected of its ships against any odds. If by any chance the *Natividad* should overwhelm the *Lydia* no excuse would be accepted. Hornblower's career would be wrecked. Even if the inevitable courtmartial did not break him, he would be left to languish on half pay for the rest of his life. Failure to capture the *Natividad,* failure to start a successful rebellion, failure to open the isthmus to trade – any one of these quite probable failures would mean a loss of reputation, of employment, of having to face his wife on his return condemned as a man inferior to his fellows.

Having contemplated all these gloomy possibilities Hornblower thrust them aside with determined optimism. First and foremost he must make contact with this Don Julian Alvarado, which seemed to be a duty involving some little interest and only small difficulty. Later there would be treasure-ships to capture and prize money to be won. He would not allow himself to worry about the rest of the future. He heaved himself off the locker and strode back to his sleeping-cabin.

Ten minutes later he stepped up on the quarterdeck; he noted with sardonic amusement how his officers tried without success to appear not to notice his splendid best coat with the epaulettes, his silk stockings, his shoes with the cut steel buckles, his cocked hat and his gold-hilted sword. Hornblower cast a glance at the fast-nearing shore.

'Beat to quarters, Mr Bush,' he said. 'Clear for action.'

The roll of the drum set the ship into a wild fury as the watch below came tumbling up. Urged on by the cries and blows of the petty officers the crew flung themselves into the business of getting the ship ready for action. The decks were soused with water and strewn with sand; the bulkheads were knocked away; the fire parties took their places at the pumps; the boys ran breathless with cartridges for the guns; down below the purser's steward who had been appointed acting surgeon was dragging together the midshipmen's chests in the cockpit to make an operating table.

'We'll have the guns loaded and run out, if you please, Mr Bush,' said Hornblower.

That was only a sensible precaution to take, seeing that the ship was about to sail before the wind straight into Spanish territory. The guns' crews cast off the frappings of the breeches, tugged desperately at the train tackles to draw the guns inboard, rammed home the powder and the shot, depressed the gun muzzles, strained madly at the gun tackles, and ran the guns out through the opened ports.

'Ship cleared for action. Ten minutes twenty-one seconds, sir,' said Bush as the last rumble died away. For the life of him he still could not tell whether this was an exercise or in earnest, and it gratified Hornblower's vanity to leave him in doubt.

'Very good, Mr Bush. Send a good man with the lead into the main chains, and make ready to anchor.'

The breeze off the sea was strengthening every minute now, and the *Lydia's* speed was steadily increasing. With his glass from the quarterdeck Hornblower could see every detail of the entrance to the bay, and the broad westerly channel between Conchaquita Island and the westerly mainland which the chart assured him afforded twenty fathoms for five miles inland. But there was no trusting these Spanish charts.

'What have you in the chains, there?' called Hornblower.

'No ground with this line, sir.'

'How many fathom have you out? Pass along the deep sea line.'

'Aye aye, sir.'

A dead hush descended on the ship, save for the eternal harping of the rigging and the chatter of the water under the stern.

'No ground, sir, within a hundred fathom.'

The shore must be very steep-to, then, because they were within two miles of land now. But there was no purpose in risking running aground under full sail.

'Get the courses in,' said Hornblower. 'Keep that lead going in the chains, there.'

Under topsails alone the *Lydia* crept in towards land. Soon a cry from the chains announced that bottom had been reached in a hundred fathoms, and the depth diminished steadily at every cast. Hornblower would have been glad to know what was the state of the tide – if he was going aground at all it would be far better to do so on the flow than on the ebb – but there was no possible means of calculating that.

He went halfway up the mizzen rigging to get a better view, everyone else in the ship save for the man in the chains was standing rigid in the blinding heat. They were almost in the entrance channel now. Hornblower sighted some driftwood afloat on the the near side, and training his glass on it, he saw that it was floating in up the bay. The tide was making, then; better and better.

'By the deep nine,' chanted the leadsman.

So much for the Dago chart which indicated ten fathoms.

'And a half eight.'

The channel was shoaling fast. They would have to anchor soon in this case.

'And a half eight.'

Plenty of water still for the present. Hornblower called down to the helmsman, and the *Lydia* swung to starboard round the slight bend.

'And a half eight.'

Well enough still. The *Lydia* steadied on her new course.

'By the mark seven.'

Hornblower's eyes searched the channel in an attempt to determine the line of deepest water.

'By the mark seven.'

An order from Hornblower edged the *Lydia* towards the further side. Bush quietly sent the men to the braces to trim the yards on the new course.

'And a half eight.'

That was better.

'By the deep nine.'

Better still. The *Lydia* was well up the bay now, and Hornblower could see that the tide was still making. They crept on over the glassy water, with the leadsman chanting monotonously, and the steep conical mountain in the middle of the bay drawing nearer.

'Quarter less eight,' called the leadsman.

'Are the anchors clear?' asked Hornblower.

'All clear, sir.'

'By the mark seven.'

No useful object could be served in going in farther.

'Let go the anchor.'

The cable roared through the hawsehole while the watch sprang to furl the topsails, and the *Lydia* swung round to wind and tide while Hornblower descended to the quarterdeck.

Bush blinked at him as at a miracle worker. Seven weeks after sighting the Horn, Hornblower had brought the *Lydia* straight in to her destination; he had arrived in the afternoon with the sea breeze and a flowing tide to bring him in, and if there were danger for them here nightfall would soon bring them the ebb tide and the land breeze to take them out again. How much was fluke and how much was calculation Bush could not guess, but as his opinion of Hornblower's professional merit was far higher than Hornblower himself cherished he was inclined to give him more credit than was really his due.

'Keep the watch at quarters, Mr Bush,' said Hornblower. 'Dismiss the watch below.'

With the ship a mile from any possible danger and cleared for action there was no need to keep every man at his station. The ship broke into a cheerful buzz as the watch below lined the rails to stare out at this land of green jungle and grey rock, but Hornblower was puzzled for a moment, wondering what to do next. The excitement of bringing the ship into an unknown harbour had prohibited his usual careful planning of his next step. His mind was made up for him by a hail from the lookout.

'Deck there! Boat putting out from shore. Two points abaft the starboard beam.'

A double speck of white was creeping out towards them; Hornblower's glass resolved it into an open boat under two tiny lateen sails, and as she drew nearer he could see that she was manned by half a dozen swarthy men wearing wide straw hats. She hove-to fifty yards away, and someone stood up in the stern sheets and shouted across the water with hands cupped round his mouth. It was Spanish that he spoke.

'Is that an English ship?' he asked.

'Yes. Come on board,' replied Hornblower. Two years as a prisoner of Spain had given him the opportunity of learning the language – he had long before decided that it was merely on account of this accomplishment that he had been selected for this special service.

The boat ran alongside and the man who had hailed scrambled lightly up the ladder to the deck. He stopped at the side and looked round him with a certain curiosity at the spotless decks and the rigid order which prevailed on every hand. He wore a sleeveless black waistcoat aflame with gold embroidery; beneath it a dirty white shirt, and on his legs dirty white trousers terminating raggedly just below the knees. His feet were bare, and in a red sash round his waist he carried two pistols and a short heavy sword. He spoke Spanish as his native tongue, but he did not look like a Spaniard; the black hair which hung over his ears was long, lustreless, and lank; there was a tinge of red in his brown complexion and a tinge of yellow in the whites of his eyes. A long thin moustache drooped from his upper lip. His eyes at once picked out the captain, gorgeous in his best coat and cocked hat, and he advanced towards him. It was in anticipation of just such a meeting that Hornblower had donned his best, and he was pleased with his foresight now.

'You are the captain, sir?' asked the visitor.

'Yes. Captain Horatio Hornblower of His Britannic Majesty's frigate *Lydia,* at your service. And whom have I the pleasure of welcoming?'

'Manuel Hernandez, lieutenant general of el Supremo.'

'El Supremo?' asked Hornblower, puzzled. The name was a little difficult to render into English. Perhaps 'The Almighty' might be the nearest translation.

'Yes, of el Supremo. You were expected here four months, six months back.'

Hornblower thought quickly. He dared not disclose the reason of his coming to any unauthorised person, but the fact that this man knew he was expected seemed to indicate that he was a member of Alvarado's conspiracy.

'It is not to el Supremo that I am ordered to address myself,' he temporised. Hernandez made a gesture of impatience.

'Our lord el Supremo was known to men until lately as His Excellency Don Julian Maria de Jesus de Alvarado y Moctezuma,' he said.

'Ah!' said Hornblower. 'It is Don Julian that I want to see.'

Hernandez was clearly annoyed by this casual mention of Don Julian.

'El Supremo,' he said, laying grave accent on the name, 'has sent me to bring you into his presence.'

'And where is he?'

'He is in his house.'

'And which is his house?'

'Surely it is enough, Captain, that you should know that el Supremo requires your attendance.'

'Do you think so? I would have you know, señor, that a captain of one of His Britannic Majesty's ships is not accustomed to being at anyone's beck and call. You can go, if you like, and tell Don Julian so.'

Hornblower's attitude indicated that the interview was at an end. Hernandez went through an internal struggle, but the prospect of returning to face el Supremo without bringing the captain with him was not alluring.

'The house is there,' he said sullenly, at last, pointing across the bay. 'On the side of the mountain. We must go through the town which is hidden behind the point to get there.'

'Then I shall come. Pardon me for a moment, General.'

Hornblower turned to Bush, who was standing by with the half puzzled, half admiring expression on his face so frequently to be seen when a man is listening to a fellow countryman talking fluently in an unknown language.

'Mr Bush,' he said, 'I am going ashore, and I hope I shall return soon. If I do *not,* if I am not back nor have written to you by midnight, you must take steps to ensure the safety of the ship. Here is the key of my desk. You have my orders that at midnight you are to read the government's secret orders to me, and to act on them as you think proper.'

'Aye aye, sir,' said Bush. There was anxiety in his face, and Hornblower realised with a thrill of pleasure that Bush was actually worried about his captain's well being. 'Do you think – is it safe for you on shore alone, sir?'

'I don't know,' said Hornblower, with honest indifference. 'I must go, that is all.'

'We'll bring you off, sir, safe and sound, if there is any hanky-panky.'

'You'll see after the safety of the ship first,' snapped Hornblower, visualising a mental picture of Bush with a valuable landing party blundering about in the fever-haunted jungles of Central America. Then he turned to Hernandez. 'I am at your service, señor.'

IV

The boat ran softly aground on a beach of golden sand round the point, and her swarthy crew sprang out and hauled the boat up so that Hornblower and Hernandez could step ashore dry shod. Hornblower looked keenly about him. The town came down to the edge of the sand; it was a collection of a few hundred houses of palmetto leaves, only a few of them roofed with tiles. Hernandez led the way up towards it.

'Agua, agua,' croaked a voice as they approached. 'Water, for the love of God, water.'

A man was bound upright to a six foot stake beside the path; his hands were free and his arms thrashed about frantically. His eyes were protruding from his head and it seemed as if his tongue were too big for his mouth, like an idiot's. A circle of vultures crouched and fluttered round him.

'Who is that?' asked Hornblower, shocked.

'A man whom el Supremo has ordered to die for want of water,' said Hernandez. 'He is one of the unenlightened.'

'He is being tortured to death?'

'This is his second day. He will die when the noontide sun shines on him tomorrow,' said Hernandez casually. 'They always do.'

'But what is his crime?'

'He is one of the unenlightened, as I said, Captain.'

Hornblower resisted the temptation to ask what constituted enlightenment; from the fact that Alvarado had adopted the name of el Supremo he could fairly well guess. And he was weak enough to allow Hernandez to guide him past the unhappy wretch without a protest – he surmised that no expostulation on his part would override the orders given by el Supremo, and an unavailing protest would only be bad for his prestige. He would postpone action until he was face to face with the leader.

Little miry lanes, filthy and stinking, wound between the palmetto huts. Vultures perched on the roof ridges and squabbled with the mongrel dogs in the lanes. The Indian population were going about their usual avocations without regard for the man dying of thirst within fifty yards of them. They were all brown with a tinge of red, like Hernandez himself; the children ran naked, the women were dressed either in black or in dirty white; the few men to be seen wore only short white trousers to the knees and were naked from the waist up. Half the houses appeared to be shops – open on one side; where were displayed for sale a few handfuls of fruits, or three or four eggs. At one place a black robed woman was bargaining to make a purchase.

Tethered in the little square in the centre of the town some diminutive horses warred with the flies. Hernandez' escort made haste to untether two of them and stood at their heads for them to mount. It was a difficult moment for Hornblower; he was not a good horseman, as he knew, and he was wearing his best silk stockings, and he felt he would not cut a dignified figure on horseback with his cocked hat and his sword. There was no help for it, however. He was so clearly expected to mount and ride that he could not draw back. He got his foot into his stirrup and swung up into the saddle, and was relieved to find that the tiny horse was submissive and quiet. He trotted alongside Hernandez, bumping awkwardly. The sweat ran down his face, and every few seconds he had to reach up hurriedly and adjust his cocked hat. A path wound steeply up the hillside out of the town, only wide enough for one horseman at a time, so that Hernandez, with a courteous gesture, preceded him. The escort clattered along fifty yards behind them.

The narrow path was stifling hot, hemmed by trees and bush on either hand. Insects buzzed round them, biting viciously. Half a mile up the path some lounging sentries came awkwardly to attention, and beyond this point there were other men to be seen – men like the first one Hornblower had encountered, bound to stakes and dying of thirst.

There were dead men, too – mere stinking masses of corruption with a cloud of flies which buzzed more wildly as the horses brushed by them. The stench was horrible; gorged vultures, hideous with their naked necks, flopped along the path ahead of the horses, unable to fly, seeking escape into the forest.

Hornblower was about to say 'More of the unenlightened, General?' when he realised the uselessness of comment. It was better to say nothing than to say anything ineffectual. He rode silently through the stink and the flies, and tried to estimate the mentality of a man who would allow rotting corpses to remain, so to speak, on his doorstep.

The path rose over a shoulder of the mountain, and for a moment Hornblower had a glimpse of the bay below, blue and silver and gold under the evening sun, with the *Lydia* riding to her anchor in the midst of it. Then suddenly the forest at each side changed as if by magic into cultivated land. Orange groves, and trees laden with fruit, bordered the path, and through the trees Hornblower could gain a glimpse of fields bearing crops. The sun, sinking fast to the horizon, illuminated the golden fruit, and then, as they turned a corner, shone full on a vast white building, stretching low and wide on either hand, before them.

'The house of el Supremo,' said Hernandez.

In the patio servants came and took their horses, while Hornblower stiffly dismounted and contemplated the ruin which riding had caused to his best silk stockings. The superior servants who conducted them into the house were dressed in clothes similar in their blend of rags and finery to those Hernandez wore – scarlet and gold above, bare feet and rags below. The most gorgeous of all, whose features seemed to indicate a strong dash of negro blood in his ancestry along with the Indian and the slight trace of European, came up with a worried look on his face.

'El Supremo has been kept waiting,' he said. 'Please come this way as quickly as you can.'

He almost ran before them down a corridor to a door studded with brass. On this he knocked loudly, waited a moment, knocked again, and then threw open the door, bending himself double as he did so. Hornblower, at Hernandez' gesture, strode into the room, Hernandez behind him, and the major-domo closed the door. It was a long room, lime-washed to a glittering white, whose ceiling was supported by thick wooden beams, painted and carved. Towards the farther end, solitary in the bleak bareness of the room, stood a treble dais, and in a canopied chair on the dais sat the man Hornblower had been sent half round the world to see.

He did not seem very impressive or dignified; a small swarthy man, restless and fidgety, with piercing black eyes and lank black hair beginning to turn grey. From his appearance one might have guessed at only a small admixture of Indian blood in his European ancestry, and he was dressed in European fashion, in a red coat laced with gold, a white stock, and white breeches and stockings; there were gold buckles on his shoes. Hernandez cringed before him.

'You have been a long time,' snapped Alvarado. 'Eleven men have been flogged during your absence.'

'Supremo,' sighed Hernandez – his teeth were chattering with fright – 'the captain came instantly on hearing your summons.'

Alvarado turned his piercing eyes upon Hornblower, who bowed stiffly. His mind was playing with the suspicion that the eleven men who had been flogged had suffered, unaccountably, because of the length of time it took to ride a horse from the beach to the house.

'Captain Horatio Hornblower, of His Britannic Majesty's frigate *Lydia,* at your service, sir,' he said.

'You have brought me arms and powder?'

'They are in the ship.'

'That is well. You will make arrangements with General Hernandez here for landing them.'

Hornblower thought of his frigate's almost empty storerooms; and he had three hundred and eighty men to feed. Moreover, as with every ship's captain, he was already feeling irritation at dependence on the shore. He would be restless and uncomfortable until the *Lydia* was fully charged again with food and water and wood and every other necessary, sufficient to take her back round the Horn at least as far as the West Indies or St Helena, if not home.

'I can hand nothing over, sir, until my ship's needs are satisfied,' he said. He heard Hernandez drawing his breath sharply at this sacrilegious temporising in the face of orders from el Supremo. The latter's eyebrows came together; for a moment it seemed likely that he would attempt to impose his imperious will upon the captain, but immediately afterwards his expression cleared as he realised the folly of quarrelling with his new ally.

'Certainly,' he said. 'Please make known to General Hernandez what you require, and he will supply you.'

Hornblower had had dealing with officers of the Spanish services, and knew what they could accomplish in the way of fair promises not carried out, and procrastination and shiftiness and doubledealing. He guessed that Spanish American rebel officers would be proportionately less trustworthy. He decided to make known his wants now, so that there might be a fair chance of seeing a part at least of his demands satisfied in the near future.

'My watercasks must be refilled tomorrow,' he said.

Hernandez nodded.

'There is a spring close to where we landed. If you wish, I will have men to help you.'

'Thank you, but that will not be necessary. My ship's crew will attend to it. Besides water I need—'

Hornblower's mind began to total up all the multifarious wants of a frigate seven months at sea.

'Yes, señor?'

'I shall need two hundred bullocks. Two hundred and fifty if they are thin and small. Five hundred pigs. One hundred quintals of salt. Forty tons of ship's bread, and if biscuit is unobtainable I shall need the equivalent amount of flour, with ovens and fuel provided to bake it. The juice of forty thousand lemons, oranges or limes – I can supply the casks to contain it. Ten tons of sugar. Five tons of tobacco. A ton of coffee. You grow potatoes on this coast, do you not? Then twenty tons of potatoes will suffice.'

Hernandez' face had grown longer and longer during this formidable recital.

'But, captain—' he ventured to protest, but Hornblower cut him short.

'Then for our current needs, while we are in harbour,' he went on 'I shall need five bullocks a day, two dozen chickens, as many eggs as you can provide, and sufficient fresh vegetables for the daily consumption of my ship's company.'

By nature Hornblower was the mildest of men, but in any matter regarding his ship fear of being deemed a failure drove him into unexpected hardness and temerity.

'Two hundred bullocks!' said the wretched Hernandez. 'Five hundred pigs?'

'That is what I said,' replied Hornblower, inexorably. 'Two hundred *fat* bullocks.'

At this point el Supremo intervened.

'See that the captain's wants are satisfied,' he said, with an impatient wave of his hand. 'Start now.'

Hernandez only hesitated for a further tenth of a second, and then retired. The big brass bound door closed silently behind him.

'That is the only way to deal with these people,' said el Supremo, lightly. 'They are no better than beasts. Any kind of refinement is wasted upon them. Doubtless you saw on your way here various criminals suffering punishment?'

'I did.'

'My ancestors on earth,' said el Supremo 'went to much trouble in arranging elaborate punishments. They burned people to death with elaborate ceremonial. They cut out their hearts to the accompaniment of music and dances, or pressed them to death in wrappings of raw hide exposed to the sun. I find all that quite unnecessary. A simple order to have the man tied up to die of thirst is sufficient. The man dies, and there is an end of him.'

'Yes,' said Hornblower.

'They are incapable of absorbing even the simplest of conceptions. There are some who to this very day cannot understand the very obvious principle that the blood of Alvarado and Moctezuma must be divine. They still cling to their absurd Christs and Virgins.'

'Indeed?' said Hornblower.

'One of my earliest lieutenants could not shake himself free from the influence of early education. When I announced my divinity he actually made suggestions that missionaries should be sent out to preach to the tribes so as to convert them, as though I were putting forward a new religion. He could never realise that it was not a matter of opinion but a matter of fact. He was of course one of the first to die of thirst.'

'Of course.'

Hornblower was utterly bewildered by all this. But he clung to the fact that he had to ally himself to this madman. The revictualling of the *Lydia* depended upon his acting in concert with him, if nothing else did – and that was a matter of the most vital primary importance.

'Your King George must have been delighted to hear that I had decided to act in concert with him,' continued el Supremo.

'He charged me with messages to you assuring you of his friendship,' said Hornblower cautiously.

'Of course,' said el Supremo 'he would not venture to push himself forward beyond that point. The blood of the family of Guelph naturally cannot compare with that of Alvarado.'

'Ha – h'm,' said Hornblower. He found that noncommittal noise as useful in conversation with el Supremo as with Lieutenant Bush.

El Supremo's brows approached each other a trifle.

'I suppose you are aware,' he said a little sternly, 'of the history of the family of Alvarado? You know who was the first of that name to reach this country?'

'He was Cortez' lieutenant—' began Hornblower.

'Lieutenant? Nothing of the sort. I am surprised that you should believe such lies. He was the leader of the Conquistadores; it is only by the falsification of history that Cortez is represented as in command. Alvarado conquered Mexico, and from Mexico he descended upon this coast and conquered it all, as far as the Isthmus. He married the daughter of Moctezuma the last of the Emperors; and as a direct descendant from that union I have chosen to select from my family names those of Alvarado and Moctezuma. But in Europe; long before the head of the house came to the Americas, the name of Alvarado can be traced back, beyond the Hapsburgs and the Visigoths, beyond the Romans and the empire of Alexander, to the ultimate sources of time. It is only natural, therefore, that in this present generation the family should have attained to the divine state in my person. I find it satisfactory that you agree with me, Captain – Captain—'

'Hornblower.'

'I thank you. And now I think we had better, Captain Hornblower, discuss the plans for the extension of my Empire.'

'As you please,' said Hornblower. He felt he must at least agree with this madman until the *Lydia* was revictualled, although his already faint hope of heading a successful insurrection in this country was fast becoming fainter.

'The Bourbon who calls himself King of Spain,' said el Supremo, 'maintains in this country an official who calls himself Captain General of Nicaragua. I sent to this gentleman some time ago a message ordering him to announce his fealty to me. This he had not done, and he was even misguided enough to hang my messenger publicly in Managua. Of the insolent men whom he subsequently sent to secure my divine person some were killed on the road and some died while attached to stakes, while a few were fortunate enough to see the light and are now included in my army. The Captain General is now, I hear, at the head of an army of three hundred men in the city of El Salvador. When you have landed the weapons consigned to me I propose to move on this town, which I shall burn, along with the Captain General and the unenlightened among his men. Perhaps, Captain, you will accompany me? A burning town is worth seeing.'

'My ship must be revictualled first,' said Hornblower, sturdily.

'I have given the orders for that,' replied el Supremo with a trace of impatience.

'And further,' continued Hornblower 'it will be my duty first to ascertain the whereabouts of a Spanish ship of war, the *Natividad,* which I believe to be on this station. Before I can engage in any operations on land I must see that she can do no harm to my ship. I must either capture her or know for certain that she is too distant to interfere.'

'Then you had better capture her, captain. I expect, from the information I have received, she will be sailing into the bay here at any moment.'

'Then I must go back to my ship immediately,' said Hornblower, all agitation. The possibility that his frigate might be attacked in his absence by a fifty-gun ship threw him into a seething panic. What would the Lords of the Admiralty say if the *Lydia* were lost while her captain was on shore?

'There is food being brought in. Behold,' said el Supremo.

The door at the end of the hall was flung open as he spoke. A crowd of attendants began to walk slowly in, carrying a large table covered with silver dishes, and bearing four large silver candelabra each supporting five lighted candles.

'Your pardon, but I cannot wait for food. I must not,' said Hornblower.

'As you will,' said el Supremo indifferently. 'Alfonso!'

The negroid major-domo came forward, bowing.

'See that Captain Hornblower goes back to his ship.'

El Supremo had no sooner spoken the words than he relapsed into an attitude of contemplation. The bustle attendant upon the bringing in of the banquet he allowed to pass unheeded. He did not bestow another glance on Hornblower, who stood before him, regretting already his precipitation in deciding to rejoin his ship, anxious to cause no offence by a breach of good manners, worried by the need to revictual the *Lydia,* and acutely conscious that his present attitude of uncertainty before a man who was paying him no attention whatever was quite undignified.

'This way, señor,' said Alfonso, at his elbow, while el Supremo still gazed blankly over his head. Hornblower yielded, and followed the major-domo out to the patio.

Two men and three horses awaited him there, in the half light. Without a word, bewildered by this sudden turn of events, Hornblower set his foot in the linked hands of a half naked slave who knelt at his horse's side and swung himself up into the saddle. The escort clattered before him out through the gates, and he followed them; night was falling fast.

At the corner of the path the wide bay opened before them. A young moon was fast fading down th sky. A shadowy shape in the centre of the silver water showed where the *Lydia* swung to her anchor – she, at least, was something solid and matter-of-fact in this mad world. Eastward a mountain top suddenly glowed red, illuminating the clouds above it, and then died away into darkness. They rode at a sharp trot down the steep path, past the moaning men tied to the stakes, past the stinking corpses, and into the little town. Here there was neither light nor movement; Hornblower had to leave his horse to the task of following the escort round the corners. The sound of the horses' hoofs ceased as they reached the soft sand of the beach; and simultaneously he heard the pitiful moaning of the first man he had seen tied to a stake and saw the faint phosphorescence of the edge of the sea.

He felt his way in the darkness into the waiting boat, and sat on a thwart while to the accompaniment of an explosion of orders the unseen crew pushed off. There was not a breath of wind – the sea breeze had died with the sunset and the land breeze had not yet sprung up. The unseen crew tugged at six oars, and the water sprang into view, the foam faintly visible as each stroke waked the phosphorescence. Slowly they made their way out into the bay to the rhythmical sound of the oars. Far out across the water he could see the faint loom of the *Lydia,* and a minute later he heard the welcome sound of Bush's voice as he hailed.

'Boat ahoy!'

Hornblower made a speaking trumpet of his hands and hailed back '*Lydia!*'

The captain of a King's ship calls himself by the name of that ship when he is on board a small boat.

Hornblower could hear all the expected noises now, could see all the expected sights; the bustle and clatter as boatswain's mate and sideboys ran to the gangway, the measured tramp of the marines, the flickering of lanterns. The boat ran alongside and he sprang to the ladder. It was good to feel solid oak under his feet again. The pipes of the boatswain's mates twittered in chorus; the marines brought their muskets to the present, and Bush was at the gangway to receive him, with all the pomp and ceremony due to a Captain arriving on board.

Hornblower saw, by the lantern light, the relief in Bush's honest face. He glanced round the decks; one watch, wrapped in blankets, was lying on the bare boards of the deck, while the other squatted by the guns ready for action. Bush had very properly maintained all precautions while thus at anchor in a presumably hostile port.

'Very good, Mr Bush,' said Hornblower. Then he became conscious that his white breeches were stained by the dirty saddle, and that his best silk stockings were in threads about his calves. He felt discontented with his appearance; he was ashamed of the fact that he had come back to his ship in this undignified fashion, and without, as far as he knew, having settled anything for the future. He was angry with himself; he feared lest Bush should have a worse opinion of him should he come to know the facts. He felt his cheeks go hot with self-consciousness, and he took refuge, as ever, in uncommunicativeness.

'Ha – h'm,' he rasped. 'Call me if there is anything unusual to justify it.'

With that, and no other word, he turned and went below to his cabin, where canvas screens replaced the torn down bulkheads.

Bush stared at his disappearing form. The volcanoes flicked and glowed round the bay. The crew, excited at their arrival in this strange land and anxious to hear about the future, saw themselves doomed to disappointment, just like the officers, who watched with dropped jaws their captain descending the companion ladder.

For one brief instant Hornblower felt that his dramatic appearance and exit compensated him for his consciousness of failure, but it was only for an instant. Seated on his cot, having sent away Polwheal, he felt his spirits fall again. His weary mind set itself vaguely again to debate the question of whether he would be able to obtain stores on the morrow. He fretted about whether he would be able to raise a rebellion successful enough to satisfy the Admiralty. He fretted about the approaching duel with the *Natividad*.

And throughout these considerations he continually found himself blushing again at the recollection of his abrupt dismissal by el Supremo. He felt that there were few captains in His Britannic Majesty's service who would have submitted so meekly to such cavalier treatment.

'But what the devil could I have *done*?' he asked himself pathetically.

Without turning out his lantern he lay on his cot sweating in the still tropical night while his mind raced back and forth through past and future.

And then the canvas screen flapped. A little breath of wind came stealing along the decks. His sailor's instincts kept him informed of how the *Lydia* was swinging to her anchor. He felt the tiny tremor which ran through the ship as she brought up short to her anchor cable in a new direction. The land breeze had begun at last. The ship was cooler at once. Hornblower wriggled over on to his side, and slept.

V

Those doubts and fears which encompassed Hornblower while he was trying to go to sleep the night before vanished with the day. Hornblower felt a new strength running through his veins when he awoke. His mind was teeming with plans as he drank the coffee which Polwheal brought him at dawn, and for the first time for weeks he dispensed with his morning walk on the quarterdeck. He had decided as he stepped on the deck that at least he could fill the watercasks and restock with fuel, and his first orders sent parties of men hurriedly to the tackles to hoist out the launch and lower the quarter boats. Soon they were off for the shore, charged with the empty casks and manned by crews of excited chattering men; in the bows of each boat sat two marines in their red coats with their muskets loaded and bayonets fixed, and in their ears echoing their final orders from their sergeant, to the effect that if a single sailor succeeded in deserting while on shore every man among them would have his back well scratched with the cat.

An hour later the launch came back under sail, deep laden with her watercasks full, and while the casks were being swayed out of her and lowered into the hold Mr Midshipman Hooker came running up to Hornblower and touched his hat.

'The beef cattle are coming down to the shore, sir,' he said.

Hornblower had to struggle hard to keep his face immobile and to receive the news as if he expected it.

'How many?' he snapped; it seemed a useful question to ask in order to waste time, but the answer was more surprising still.

'Hundreds, sir. There's a Dago in charge with a lot to say, but there's no one ashore who can speak his lingo.'

'Send him out to me when you go ashore again,' said Hornblower.

Hornblower spent the interval granted him in making up his mind. He hailed the lookout at the main royal masthead to ensure that a careful watch was kept to seaward. On the one hand there was the chance that the *Natividad* might come sailing in from the Pacific, in which case the *Lydia,* caught with half her crew ashore, would have no time to clear from the bay and would have to fight in confined waters and with the odds necessarily against her. On the other hand there was the opportunity of filling up completely with stores and regaining entire independence of the shore. From what Hornblower had seen of conditions prevailing there he judged that to postpone regaining that independence would be dangerous in the extreme; at any moment Don Julian Alvarado's rebellion might come to a hurried and bloody ending.

It was Hernandez who came out to him, in the same boat with the two tiny lateen sails in which Hornblower had been ferried across last night. They exchanged salutes on the quarterdeck.

'There are four hundred cattle awaiting your orders, Captain,' said Hernandez. 'My men are driving them down to the beach.'

'Good,' said Hornblower, his mind still not made up.

'I am afraid it will take longer to assemble the pigs,' went on Hernandez. 'My men are sweeping the country for them, but pigs are slow animals to drive.'

'Yes,' said Hornblower.

'With regard to the salt, it will not be easy to collect the hundred quintals you asked for. Until our lord declared his divinity salt was a royal monopoly and scarce in consequence, but I have sent a party to the salt pans at Jiquilisio and hope to find sufficient there.'

'Yes,' said Hornblower. He remembered demanding salt, but he had no distinct recollection of the quantity he had asked for.

'The women are out collecting the lemons, oranges, and limes which you ordered,' continued Hernandez, 'but I am afraid it will be two days before we shall have them all ready.'

'Ha – h'm,' said Hornblower.

'The sugar is ready at el Supremo's mill, however. And with regard to the tobacco, señor, there is a good deal in store. What special kind do you prefer? For some time we have only been rolling cigars for our own consumption, but I can set the women to work again after the fruit has been collected.'

'Ha – h'm,' said Hornblower again, suppressing just in time the cry of delight which nearly escaped him involuntarily at the mention of cigars – it was three months since he had last smoked one. Virginia pigtail twist was what his men used, but that, of course, would be unobtainable on this coast. However, he had often seen British sailors chewing and enjoying the half-cured native leaf.

'Send as many cigars as will be convenient to you,' he said, lightly. 'For the rest, it is of no importance what you send.'

Hernandez bowed.

'Thank you, señor. The coffee, the vegetables, and the eggs will of course be easy to supply. But with regard to the bread—'

'Well?'

Hernandez was obviously nervous about what he was going to say next.

'Your excellency will forgive me, but in this country we have only maize. There is a little wheat grown in the tierra templeda, but it rests still in the hands of the unenlightened. Would maize flour suffice?'

Hernandez' face was working with anxiety as he gazed at Hornblower. It was only then that Hornblower realised that Hernandez was in terror of his life, and that el Supremo's lighthearted endorsement of the requisitions he had made was far more potent than any stamped and sealed order addressed to a Spanish official.

'This is very serious,' said Hornblower sternly. 'My English sailors are unaccustomed to maize flour.'

'I know that,' said Hernandez, his interlocked fingers working galvanically. 'But I assure your excellency that I can only obtain wheat flour for them by fighting for it, and I know that el Supremo would not like me to fight at present. El Supremo will be angry.'

Hornblower remembered the abject fright with which Hernandez had regarded el Supremo the night before. The man was in terror lest he should be denounced as having failed to execute his orders. And then, suddenly, Hornblower remembered something he had unaccountably forgotten to ask for – something more important, if possible, than tobacco or fruit, and certainly far more important than the difference between maize flour and wheat.

'Very well,' he said. 'I will agree to use maize flour. But in consequence of this deficiency there is something else I must ask for.'

'Certainly, Captain. I will supply whatever you ask. You have only to name it.'

'I want drink for my men,' said Hornblower. 'Is there wine to be had here? Ardent spirits?'

'There is a little wine, your excellency. Only a little. The people on this coast drink an ardent spirit with which you are perhaps not acquainted. It is good when of good quality. It is distilled from the waste of the sugar mills, from the treacle, your excellency.'

'Rum, by God!' exclaimed Hornblower.

'Yes, señor, rum. Would that be of any use to your excellency?'

'I shall accept it in lieu of anything better,' said Hornblower sternly.

His heart was leaping with joy. It would appear like a miracle to his officers that he should conjure rum and tobacco from this volcano-riddled coast.

'Thank you, Captain. And shall we begin to slaughter the cattle now?'

That was the question on which Hornblower had been postponing a decision ever since he had heard about the arrival of the cattle on the beach. Hornblower looked up at the lookout at the masthead. He tested the strength of the wind. He gazed out to sea before he took the plunge.

'Very well,' he said at length. 'We will start now.'

The sea breeze was not nearly as strong as yesterday, and the weaker the breeze the less chance there was of the *Natividad* coming in to interrupt the *Lydia's* revictualling. And as events turned out the *Lydia* completed the work undisturbed. For two days the boats plied back and forth between the beach and the ship. They came back piled high with bloody joints of meat; the sand of the shore ran red with the blood of the slaughtered animals, while the half-tame vultures gorged themselves into a coma in the piled offal. On board the ship the purser and his crew toiled like slaves in the roasting heat, cramming the brine barrels with the meat and tugging them into position in the storerooms. The cooper and his mates worked for two days with hardly a break, making and repairing casks. Sacks of flour, ankers of rum, bales of tobacco – the hands at the tackles sweated as they swayed these up from the boats. The *Lydia* was gorging herself full.

So obvious were the good intentions of those on shore that Hornblower was able to give orders that the cargo consigned to this coast should be released, and so the boats which bore the meat and flour to the ship returned laden with cases of muskets and kegs of powder and shot. Hornblower had his gig hoisted out, and was rowed periodically round his ship inspecting her trim, in the anticipation lest at any moment he would have to hoist up his anchor and beat out to sea to fight the *Natividad*.

The work proceeded by night as well as by day; in fifteen years at sea – every one a year of warfare – Hornblower had seen many opportunities lost as a result of some trivial lack of energy, some omission to drive a crew into exerting the last ounce of its strength. He had lost opportunities himself like that, for that matter. He still felt a revulsion of shame at the recollection of how he had missed that privateer off the Azores, for example. For fear of standing condemned again in his own eyes he drove his men until they dropped.

There was no time for enjoyment of the pleasures of land at the moment. The shore party did indeed cook their rations before a huge bonfire, and revel in roast fresh meat after seven months of boiled salt meat, but with the characteristic contrariness of British sailors they turned with revulsion from the delicious fruit which was offered them – bananas and pawpaws, pineapples and guavas, and considered themselves the victims of sharp practice because these were substituted for their regulation ration of boiled dried peas.

And then, on the second evening, as Hornblower walked the quarterdeck enjoying the sea breeze at its freshest, and revelling in the thought that he was free of the land if necessary for another six months, and looking forward with the sheerest joy to his imminent dinner of roast fowl, there came the sound of firing from the beach. A scattering volley at first; a few dropping shots, and then another ragged volley. Hornblower forgot his dinner, his feeling of wellbeing, everything. Trouble on the mainland, of whatever sort, meant that the success of his mission was being imperilled. In hot haste he called for his gig, and he was pulled to the shore by a crew who made the stout oars bend as they flung their weight on the handles in response to the profane urgings of Coxswain Brown.

The scene that greeted his eyes as he rounded the point excited his worst apprehensions. The whole landing party was clubbed together on the beach; the dozen marines were in line on one flank, reloading their muskets; the sailors were bunched beside them armed with whatever weapons had come to their hands. In a wide semicircle round them were the inhabitants, brandishing swords and muskets, and in the no man's land between the two parties lay one or two corpses. At the water's edge, behind the sailors, lay one of the hands with two of his mates bending over him. He was propped up on his elbow and he was vomiting floods of blood.

Hornblower sprang into the shallows; he paid no attention to the wounded sailor, but pushed his way through the mob before him. As he emerged into the open there came a puff of smoke from the half circle up the beach and a bullet sang over his head. He paid no attention to that either.

'Put those muskets down!' he roared at the marines, and he turned towards the gesticulating inhabitants and held up his hand palm forward, in the universal and instinctive gesture of peace. There was no room in his mind for thought of personal danger, so hot was he with anger at the thought that someone was botching his chance of success.

'What's the meaning of this?' he demanded.

Galbraith was in command. He was about to speak, but he was given no opportunity. One of the sailors who had been attending to the dying man came pushing forward, discipline forgotten in the blind whirl of sentimental indignation which Hornblower instantly recognised as characteristic of the lower deck – and which he despised and distrusted.

'They been torturing a pore devil up there, sir,' he said. 'Lashed him to a spar and left him to die of thirst.'

'Silence!' bellowed Hornblower, beside himself with rage not merely at this breach of discipline but at realising the difficulties ahead of him. 'Mr Galbraith!'

Galbraith was slow of speech and of mind.

'I don't know how it started, sir,' he began; although he had been at sea since childhood there was still a trace of Scotch in his accent. 'A party came running back from up there. They had Smith with them, wounded.'

'He's dead now,' put in a voice.

'Silence!' roared Hornblower again.

'I saw they were going to attack us, and so I had the marines fire, sir,' went on Galbraith.

'I'll speak to you later, Mr Galbraith,' snapped Hornblower. 'You, Jenkins. And you, Poole. What were you doing up there?'

'Well, sir, it was like this, sir—,' began Jenkins. He was sheepish and crestfallen now. Hornblower had pricked the bubble of his indignation and he was being publicly convicted of a breach of orders.

'You knew the order that no one was to go beyond the creek?'

'Yessir.'

'Tomorrow morning I'll show you what orders mean, and you, too, Poole. Where's the sergeant of marines?'

'Here, sir.'

'A fine guard you keep, sergeant, to let these men get by. What were your pickets about?'

The sergeant could say nothing; he could only stand rigidly at attention in face of this incontrovertible proof of his being found wanting.

'Mr Simmonds will speak to you in the morning,' went on Hornblower. 'I don't expect you'll keep those stripes on your arm much longer.'

Hornblower glowered round at the landing party. His fierce rebukes had them all cowed and subservient now, and he felt his anger ebbing away as he realised that he had managed this without having to say a word in extenuation of Spanish-American justice. He turned to greet Hernandez, who had come riding up as fast as his little horse would gallop, reining up on his haunches in a shower of sand.

'Did el Supremo give orders for this attack on my men?' asked Hornblower, getting in the first broadside.

'No, Captain,' said Hernandez, and Hornblower rejoiced to see how he winced at the mention of el Supremo's name.

'I think he will not be too pleased with you when I tell him about this,' went on Hornblower.

'Your men tried to release a man condemned to death,' said Hernandez, half sullenly, half apologetically. He was clearly not too sure of his ground, and was nervous about what would be Alvarado's attitude towards this incident. Hornblower kept a rasp in his voice as he went on speaking. None of the Englishmen round him, as far as he knew, could speak Spanish, but he was anxious for his crew to believe (now that discipline was restored) that he was wholeheartedly on their side.

'That does not permit your men to kill mine,' he said.

'They are angry and discontented,' said Hernandez. 'The whole country has been swept to find food for you. The man your men tried to save was condemned for driving his pigs into the bush to keep them from being taken and given to you.'

Hernandez made this last speech reproachfully and with a hint of anger; Hornblower was anxious to be conciliatory if that were possible without exasperating his own men. Hornblower had in mind the plan of leading Hernandez out of earshot of the Englishmen, and then softening his tone, but before he could act upon it his attention was caught by the sight of a horseman galloping down the beach at full speed, waving his wide straw hat. Every eye turned towards this new arrival – a peon of the ordinary Indian type. Breathlessly he announced his news.

'A ship – a ship coming!'

He was so excited that he lapsed into the Indian speech, and Hornblower could not understand his further explanations. Hernandez had to interpret for him.

'This man has been keeping watch on the top of the mountain up there,' he said. 'He says that from there he could see the sails of a ship coming towards the bay.'

He addressed several more questions rapidly, one after the other, to the lookout, and was answered with nods and gesticulations and a torrent of Indian speech.

'He says,' went on Hernandez, 'that he has often seen the *Natividad* before, and he is sure this is the same ship, and she is undoubtedly coming in here.'

'How far off is she?' asked Hornblower and Hernandez translated the answer.

'A long way, seven leagues or more,' he said. 'She is coming from the south eastward – from Panama.'

Hornblower pulled at his chin, deep in thought.

'She'll carry the sea breeze down with her until sunset,' he muttered to himself, and glanced up at the sun. 'That will be another hour. An hour after that she'll get the land breeze. She'll be able to hold her course, close hauled. She could be here in the bay by midnight.'

A stream of plans and ideas was flooding into his mind. Against the possibility of the ship's arrival in the dark must be balanced what he knew of the Spanish habit at sea of snugging down for the night, and of attempting no piece of seamanship at all complicated save under the best possible conditions. He wished he knew more about the Spanish captain.

'Has this ship, the *Natividad*, often come into this bay?' he asked.

'Yes, Captain, often.'

'Is her captain a good seaman?'

'Oh yes, Captain, very good.'

'Ha – h'm,' said Hornblower. A landsman's opinion of the seamanship of a frigate captain might not be worth much, but still it was an indication.

Hornblower tugged at his chin again. He had fought in ten single ship actions. If he took the *Lydia* to sea and engaged the *Natividad* on open water the two ships might well batter each other into wrecks. Rigging and spars and hulls and sails would be shot to pieces. The *Lydia* would have a good many casualties which would be quite irreplaceable here in the Pacific. She would expend her priceless ammunition. On the other hand, if he stayed in the bay and yet the plan he had in mind did not succeed – if the *Natividad* waited off shore until the morning – he would have to beat his way out of the bay against the sea breeze, presenting the Spaniards with every possible advantage as he came out to fight them. The *Natividad's* superiority of force was already such that it was rash to oppose the *Lydia* to her. Could he dare to risk increasing the odds? But the possible gains were so enormous that he made up his mind to run the risk.

VI

Ghostlike in the moonlight, with the first puffs of the land breeze, the *Lydia* glided across the bay. Hornblower had not ventured to hoist sail, lest a gleam of canvas might be visible to the distant ship at sea. The launch and the cutter towed the ship, sounding as they went, into the deep water at the foot of the island at the entrance of the bay – Manguera Island, Hernandez called it when Hornblower had cautiously sketched out his plan to him. For an hour the men laboured at the oars, although Hornblower did his best to aid them, standing by the wheel and making as much use as possible of the lee-way acquired by the ship through the force of the puffs of wind on the *Lydia's* rigging. They reached the new anchorage at last, and the anchor splashed into the water.

'Have that cable buoyed and ready to slip, Mr Bush,' said Hornblower.

'Aye aye, sir.'

'Call the boats alongside. I want the men to rest.'

'Aye aye, sir.'

'Mr Gerard, you have charge of the deck. See that the lookouts keep awake. I want Mr Bush and Mr Galbraith to come below with me.'

'Aye aye, sir.'

The ship was seething quietly with excitement. Everyone on board had guessed the captain's plan, even though the details of its execution, which he was now explaining to his lieutenants, were still unknown. In the two hours which had elapsed since the arrival of the news of the *Natividad's* approach Hornblower's mind had worked busily at the perfection of his plan. Nothing must go wrong. Everything that could possibly contribute to success must be done.

'That is all understood?' he asked finally; he stood stooping under the deck beams in his screened off cabin while his lieutenants fiddled awkwardly with their hats.

'Aye aye, sir.'

'Very good,' said Hornblower, dismissing them.

But within five minutes impatience and anxiety drove him up on deck again.

'Masthead, there? What can you see of the enemy?'

'She's just come up over the island, sir. She's more than hull down. I can only see her torps'ls, sir, below her t'garns.'

'What's her course?'

'She's holding her wind, sir. She ought to make the bay on this tack.

'Ha – h'm,' said Hornblower, and went below again.

It would be four hours at least before the *Natividad* reached the entrance, and before he could take any further action. He found himself pacing, stoopshouldered, up and down the tiny limits of his cabin, and checked himself furiously. The iron-nerved captain of his dreams would not allow himself to work himself into this sort of fever, even though his professional reputation was to be at stake in four hours' time. He must show the ship that he, too, could face uncertainty with indifference.

'Pass the word for Polwheal!' he snapped, coming out through the screen and addressing a group by a maindeck gun; and when Polwheal appeared he went on 'My compliments to Mr Bush, and tell him that if he can spare Mr Galbraith and Mr Clay and Mr Savage from their duties I would be glad if they would sup with me and have a hand of a whist.'

Galbraith was nervous, too. Not merely was he anticipating a battle, but hanging over his head there was still the promised reprimand for his part in the skirmish of the afternoon. His rawboned Scotch figure moved restlessly, and his face was flushed over his high cheek bones. Even the two midshipmen were subdued as well as fidgety.

Hornblower compelled himself to play the part of the courtly host, while every word he uttered was designed to increase his reputation for imperturbability. He apologised for his shortcomings of the supper – the ship being cleared for action involved the extinction of all fires and the consequent necessity for serving cold food. But the sight of the cold roast chickens, the cold roast pork, the golden cakes of maize, the dishes of fruit, roused Mr Midshipman Savage's sixteen year old appetite and caused him to forget his embarrassment.'

'This is better than rats, sir,' he said, rubbing his hands.

'Rats?' asked Hornblower, vaguely. For all his appearance and attention his thoughts were up on deck, and not in the cabin.

'Yes, sir. Until we made this harbour rats had become a favourite dish in the midshipmen's berth.'

'That they had,' echoed Clay. He carved himself substantial slices of cold pork, and plenty of crackling, and added them to the half chicken on his plate. 'I was paying that thief Bailey threepence apiece for prime rats.'

Desperately Hornblower jerked his mind away from the approaching *Natividad* and delved into the past when he had been a half-starved midshipman, homesick and seasick. His seniors then had eaten rats with gusto, and maintained that a biscuit-fed rat was far more delicate a dish than beef two years in cask. He had never been able to stomach them himself, but he would not admit it to these boys.

'Threepence apiece for rats seems a trifle dear,' he said. 'I can't remember paying as much as that when I was a midshipman.'

'Why, sir, did you ever eat them yourself?' asked Savage, amazed.

In reply to this direct question Hornblower could only lie.

'Of course,' he said. 'Midshipmen's berths were much the same twenty years ago as now. I always maintained that a rat who had had the run of the bread-locker all his life made a dish fit for a king, let alone a midshipman.'

'God bless my soul!' gasped Clay, laying down his knife and fork. He had never thought for a moment that this stern and inflexible captain of his had once been a rat-eating midshipman.

The two boys blinked at their captain with admiration. This little human touch had won their hearts completely, as Hornblower had known it would. At the end of the table Galbraith sighed audibly. He had been eating rats himself only three days ago, but he knew full well that to admit it would not increase the boys' respect for him, but would rather diminish it, for he was that sort of officer. Hornblower had to make Galbraith feel at home, too.

'A glass of wine with you, Mr Galbraith,' he said, raising his glass. 'I must apologise because this is not my best Madeira, but I am keeping the last two bottles for when I entertain the Spanish captain as our prisoner tomorrow. To our victories of the future!'

The glasses were drained, and constraint dwindled. Hornblower had spoken of '*our* prisoner' when most captains would have said '*my* prisoner.' And he had said 'our victories.' The strict cold captain, the stern disciplinarian, had for a moment revealed human characteristics and had admitted his inferiors to his fellowship. Any one of the three junior officers would at that moment have laid down his life for his captain – and Hornblower, looking round at their flushed faces, was aware of it. It gratified him at the same moment as it irritated him; but with a battle in the immediate future which might well be an affair of the utmost desperation, he knew that he must have behind him a crew not merely loyal but enthusiastic.

Another midshipman, young Knyvett, came into the cabin.

'Mr Bush's compliments, sir, and the enemy is hull up from the masthead now, sir.'

'Is she holding her course for the bay?'

'Yes, sir. Mr Bush says two hours ought to see her within range.'

'Thank you, Mr Knyvett,' said Hornblower, dismissing him. The reminder that in two hours he would be at grips with a fifty-gun ship set his heart beating faster again. It took a convulsive effort to maintain an unmoved countenance.

'We still have ample time for our rubber, gentlemen,' said Hornblower.

The weekly evening of whist which Captain Hornblower played

with his officers was for these latter – especially the midshipmen – a sore trial. Hornblower himself was a keen good player; his close observation and his acute study of the psychology of his juniors were of great help to him. But to some of his officers, without card sense, and floundering helplessly with no memory for the cards that had been played, Hornblower's card evenings were periods of torment.

Polwheal cleared the table, spread the green tablecloth and brought the cards. When play began Hornblower found it easier to forget about the approaching battle. Whist was enough of a passion with him to claim most of his attention whatever the distraction. It was only during the intervals of play, during the deals and while making the score, that he found his heart beating faster again and felt the blood surging up in his throat. He marked the fall of the cards with close attention, making allowances for Savage's schoolboy tendency to dash out his aces, and for the fact that Galbraith invariably forgot, until it was too late, to signal a short suit. One rubber ended quickly; there was almost dismay on the faces of the other three as Hornblower proffered the cards for cutting for a second one. He kept his face expressionless.

'You really must remember, Clay,' he said 'to lead the king from a sequence of king, queen, knave. The whole art of leading is based upon that principle.'

'Aye aye, sir,' said Clay, rolling his eyes drolly at Savage, but Hornblower looked up sharply and Clay hurriedly composed his expression. Play continued – and to all of them seemed interminable. It came to an end at last, however.

'Rubber,' announced Hornblower, marking up the score. 'I think, gentlemen, that it is almost time that we went on deck.'

There was a general sigh of relief and a scraping of feet on the deck. But at all costs Hornblower felt that he must consolidate his reputation for imperturbability.

'The rubber would not be over,' he said dryly 'if Mr Savage had paid attention to the score. It being nine, Mr Savage and Mr Galbraith had only to win the odd trick to secure the rubber. Hence Mr Savage, at the eighth trick, should have played his ace of hearts instead of risking the finesse. I grant that if the finesse had been successful he would have won two more tricks, but—'

Hornblower droned on, while the other three writhed in their chairs. Yet they glanced at each other with admiration for him in their eyes as he preceded them up the companion ladder.

Up on deck everything was deathly still as the crew lay at their posts. The moon was setting fast, but there was ample light still as soon as the eye grew accustomed to it. Bush touched his hat to the captain.

'The enemy is still heading for the bay, sir,' he said hoarsely.

'Send the crews into the launch and cutter again,' replied Hornblower. He climbed the mizzen rigging to the mizzen top gallant yard. From here he could just see over the island; a mile away, with the setting moon behind her, he could see the white canvas of the *Natividad* as she stood in, close hauled, across the entrance. He struggled with his agitation as he endeavoured to predict her movements. There was small chance of her noticing, against the dark sky, the top gallant masts of the *Lydia;* and it was on the assumption that she would not that all his plans were based. She must go about soon, and her new course would bring her directly to the island. Perhaps she would weather it, but not likely. She would have to go about again to enter the bay, and that would be his opportunity. As he watched, he saw her canvas gleam brighter for a space and then darken again as she came round. She was heading for the middle of the entrance, but her leeway and the beginning of the ebb tide would carry her back to the island. He went down again to the deck.

'Mr Bush,' he said, 'send the hands aloft ready to set sail.'

The ship was filled with gentle noises as bare feet padded over the deck and up the rigging. Hornblower brought the silver whistle out of his pocket. He did not trouble to ask whether everyone was ready for the signal and properly instructed in the part he had to play; Bush and Gerard were efficient officers.

'I am going for'rard, now, Mr Bush,' he said. 'I shall try and get back to the quarterdeck in time, but you know my orders if I do not.'

'Aye aye, sir.'

Hornblower hurried forward along the gangway, past the forecastle carronades with their crews crouching round them, and swung himself over on to the bowsprit. From the sprit sail yard he could see round the corner of the island; the *Natividad* was heading straight for him. He could see the glimmer of phosphorescent foam about her cutwater. He could almost hear the sound of her passage through the water. He swallowed hard, and then all his excitement vanished and he was left deadly cool. He had forgotten about himself, and his mind was making calculations of time and space like a machine. Now he could hear the voice of a man at the lead on board the *Natividad,* although he could distinguish no word. The Spaniard was coming very close. By now he could hear the babble of the Spanish crew, every one busy talking like every Spaniard, and no one looking out sufficiently well to catch sight of the *Lydia's* bare spars. Then he heard orders being shouted from the *Natividad's* deck; she was going about. At the very first sound he put the whistle to his lips and blew, and the whole of the *Lydia* sprang into activity. Sail was loosed from every yard simultaneously. The cable was slipped, the boats were cast off. Hornblower, racing aft again, collided with the hands at the braces as the ship paid off. He picked himself off the deck and ran on, while the *Lydia* gathered way and surged forward. He reached the wheel in time.

'Steady!' he called to the quartermaster. 'Port a little! A little more! Now, hard-a-starboard!'

So quickly had it all happened that the Spaniard had only just gone about and had gathered no way on her new course when the *Lydia* came leaping upon her out of the blackness behind the island and rasped alongside. Months of drill bore their fruit in the English ship. The guns crashed out in a single shattering broadside as the ships touched, sweeping the deck of the *Natividad* with grape. Overhead the topmen ran out along the yards and lashed the ships together. On deck the cheering boarders came rushing to the portside gangway.

On board the Spaniard there was utter surprise. One moment all hands had been engrossed with the work of the ship, and the next, seemingly, an unknown enemy had come crashing alongside; the night had been torn to shreds with the flare of hostile guns; on every hand men had been struck down by the hurtling shot, and now an armed host, yelling like fiends from the pit, came pouring on to the deck. Not the most disciplined and experienced crew could have withstood the shock of that surprise. During the twenty years the *Natividad* had sailed the Pacific coast no enemy had been nearer to her than four thousand miles of sea.

Yet even then there were some stout hearts who attempted resistance. These were officers who drew their swords; on the high quarterdeck there was an armed detachment who had been served out with weapons in consequence of the rumours of rebellion on shore; there were a few men who grasped capstan bars and belaying pins; but the upper deck was swept clear immediately by the wave of boarders with their pikes and cutlasses. A single pistol flashed and exploded. The Spaniards who offered resistance were struck down or chased below; the others were herded together under guard.

And on the lower deck the men sought blindly round for leaders, for means of resistance. They were gathering together in the darkness ready to oppose the enemy above them, and to defend the hatchways, when suddenly a new yelling burst out behind them. Gerard's two boats' crews had reached the *Natividad's* port side, and prising open the lower deck ports, came swarming in, yelling like fiends as their orders bid them do – Hornblower had foreseen that the moral effect of a surprise attack would be intensified, especially against undisciplined Spaniards, if the attackers made as much noise as possible. At this new surprise the resistance of the lower deck broke down completely, and Hornblower's prescience in detaching the two boats' crews to make this diversion was justified.

VII

The Captain of the *Lydia* was taking his usual morning walk on the quarterdeck of his ship. Half a dozen Spanish officers had attempted, on his first appearance, to greet him with formal courtesy, but they had been hustled away by the *Lydia's* crew, indignant that their captain's walk, sacrosanct after so many months, should be disturbed by mere prisoners.

The captain had a good deal to think about, too – so much, in fact, that he could spare no time to rejoice in the knowledge that his frigate last night, in capturing a two-decker without losing a man, had accomplished a feat without precedent in the long annals of British naval history. He wanted instead to think about his next move. With the capture of the *Natividad* he was lord of the South Sea. He knew well enough that the communications by land were so difficult that the whole trade – the whole life, it might he said – of the country depended upon the coastwise traffic; and now not a boat could move without his licence. In fifteen years of warfare he had learned the lessons of sea power. There was at least a chance now that with Alvarado's aid he might set the whole of Central America into such a flame that the Spanish Government would rue the day when they had decided to throw in their lot with Bonaparte.

Hornblower paced up and down the sanded deck. There were other possibilities, too. North westward along the coast lay Acapulco, whither came and whence departed yearly galleons bearing a million sterling in treasure. The capture of a galleon would at a stroke make him a wealthy man – he could buy an estate in England then; could buy a whole village and be a squire, with the country folk touching their hats to him as he drove by in his coach. Maria would like that, although he could not imagine Maria playing the part of a great lady with any grace.

Hornblower tore his mind away from the contemplation of Maria snatched from her Southsea lodgings and settled in a country home. To the east was Panama, with its stored silver from Peru, its pearling fleet, its whitewashed golden altar which had escaped Morgan but would not escape him. A blow there, at the central knot of the transcontinental communications, would be the best strategy perhaps, as well as being potentially profitable. He tried to think about Panama.

Forward Sullivan, the red-haired Irish vagabond, was perched on a carronade slide with his fiddle, and round him a dozen sailors, their horny feet flapping on the deck, were setting to partners. Twenty-five guineas apiece, at least, the men would get as prize money for the capture of *Natividad,* and they were already spending it in imagination. He looked across to where the *Natividad* swung at anchor. Her waist was black with her crew, crammed on her upper deck. On her old-fashioned poop and quarterdeck he could see the red coats and shakoes of his marines, and he could see, too, the carronades pointing down into the waist and the men posted beside them with lighted matches. Gerard, whom he had left on board as prizemaster, had served in a Liverpool slaver in his day and knew well how to keep a ship full of hostile humanity in subjection – although, parted from their officers, Hornblower for one did not anticipate trouble from the crew.

Hornblower knew that he must make up his mind about what to do with the *Natividad,* and more especially with his prisoners. He could not hand them over to the tender mercies of el Supremo; his own crew would hardly permit that. He tried to think about the problem. A long line of pelicans came flying by, more rigid in their formation that the Channel fleet at drill. A frigate bird, superb with its forked tail, came wheeling above them with motionless wings, and having obviously decided that they were not worth plundering, swooped away again towards the island where the cormorants were fishing industriously. The sun was already hot and the water of the bay was as blue as the sky above.

Hornblower cursed sun and pelicans and frigate birds as he tried to concentrate on the problems before him. He paced moodily up and down the deck another half dozen times. Then Midshipman Knyvett barred his way, touching his hat.

'What the devil is it now?' snapped Hornblower.

'Boat coming alongside, sir. Mr – Mr Hernandez on board.'

That was only to be expected.

'Very good,' said Hornblower, and went down the gangway to greet Hernandez as he came up the side. Hernandez wasted no time on felicitations for the late victory. In the service of el Supremo apparently even Spanish-Americans grew abrupt and businesslike.

'El Supremo wishes to see you at once, Captain,' said Hernandez. 'My boat is waiting.'

'Indeed,' said Hornblower. He knew well that dozens of his brother captains in the British service would be infuriated at such a cavalier message. He toyed with the idea of sending back to tell el Supremo to come out to the ship himself if he wanted to interview her captain. But he knew that it would be foolish to imperil his cordial relations with the shore, upon which so much of his success depended, upon a mere question of dignity. The captain of the *Natividad* could afford to overlook the presumption of others.

A compromise suggested itself to him; he could keep Hernandez waiting for an hour or two so as to bolster up his own dignity. But his commonsense rejected the notion. Hornblower hated compromises, and this one would only (like most compromises) irritate one side and do no good to the other. Far better to put his pride in his pocket and to come at once.

'Certainly,' he said. 'My duties leave me free at the moment.'

But this time, at least there was no need to dress up for the occasion. There was no call to put on his best silk stockings and his buckled shoes. The capture of the *Natividad* was a clearer proof of his bona fides than any gold-hilted sword.

It was only while giving final orders to Bush that Hornblower remembered that last night's success gave him adequate grounds for not flogging the erring Jenkins and Poole, and for not reprimanding Galbraith. That was an enormous relief, anyway. It helped to clear away the clouds of depression which always tended to settle on him after every success. It cheered him up as he mounted the minute horse which awaited him on shore, and rode past the mountain of stinking animal intestines, and along the avenue of dead men, up to el Supremo's house.

The appearance of el Supremo, sitting in his canopied chair on his dais, seemed for all the world to indicate that he had been sitting there, immobile, since the occasion four days ago (it seemed more like a month) when Hornblower had left him.

'So you have already done what I wished you to do, Captain?' were his opening words.

'I captured the *Natividad* last night,' said Hornblower.

'And the provisioning of your ship is, I understand, complete?'

'Yes.'

'Then,' said el Supremo, 'you have done what I wanted. That is what I said before.'

In the face of such sublime self-assurance there was no point in arguing.

'This afternoon,' said el Supremo, 'I shall proceed with my plan for the capture of the city of El Salvador and the man who calls himself Captain General of Nicaragua.'

'Yes?' said Hornblower.

'There are fewer difficulties before me now, Captain. You may not be aware that the roads between here and El Salvador are not as good as roads might be. At one place the path goes up one hundred and twenty seven steps cut in the lava between two precipices. It is difficult for a mule, to say nothing of a horse, to make the journey, and an evilly diposed person armed with a musket could cause much trouble.'

'I expect he could,' said Hornblower.

'However,' said el Supremo, 'El Salvador lies less than ten miles from the sea, and there is a good road from the city to its port of La Libertad. This afternoon I shall sail with five hundred men in the two ships to La Libertad. As this town is no more than a hundred miles away I shall reach there at dawn tomorrow. Tomorrow evening I shall dine in El Salvador.'

'Ho – h'm,' said Hornblower. He was wondering how best to present in argument the difficulties he could see ahead.

'You killed very few of the crew of the *Natividad*, Captain?' asked el Supremo, and thereby approaching directly some of the difficulties Hornblower had in mind.

'Eleven killed,' said Hornblower. 'And eighteen wounded, of whom four seem unlikely to recover.'

'So you left enough to work the ship?'

'Ample, señor, if—'

'That is what I wanted. And, Captain, human beings in addressing me do not use the expression 'señor'. That is insufficiently honorific. I am el Supremo.'

Hornblower could only bow in reply. El Supremo's marvellous manner was like a stone wall.

'The navigating officers are still alive?' went on el Supremo.

'Yes,' said Hornblower; and, because he could see trouble close ahead and was anxious to keep it to a minimum, he added, with a gulp, 'Supremo.'

'Then,' said el Supremo, 'I will take the *Natividad* into my service. I will kill the executive officers and replace them with men of my own. The others and the common sailors will serve me.'

There was nothing intrinsically impossible in what el Supremo suggested; Hornblower knew from experience that the Spanish navy, old fashioned as always, maintained a rigid distinction (such as was fast dying out in our own service) between the officers who worked the ship and the gentlemen who commanded it. And Hornblower had no doubt whatever as to what choice the seamen and sailing master would make if asked to choose between death by torture and serving el Supremo.

Nor could it be denied that el Supremo's suggestion was in many ways a good one; to transport five hundred men in the *Lydia* alone would be difficult, to say the least, while the *Lydia* by herself would find it impossible to blockade completely all the thousand miles of coast – two ships would cause far more than twice as much trouble to the enemy in that way. Yet to hand over the *Natividad* meant starting an endless and probably unsuccessful argument with the lords of the Admiralty on the question of prize money. And he could not in honour hand over the Spanish officers to the death el Supremo had in mind for them. He had to think quickly.

'The *Natividad* is the prize of my King,' he said. 'Perhaps he would not be pleased if I let her go.'

'He certainly would be displeased if he knew you had offended *me*,' said el Supremo. His eyebrows came closer together, and Hornblower heard Hernandez beside him take a quick breath. 'I have noticed before, Captain Hornblower, that you have verged upon disrespect towards me, and I have been mild enough to attribute it to your foreign breeding.'

Hornblower was still thinking hurriedly. A little more opposition would cause this madman to order him out for execution, and if her captain were killed the *Lydia* would certainly not fight for el Supremo. There would indeed be a complicated situation in the Pacific, and the *Lydia*, with friends neither among the rebels nor among the government, would probably never reach home again – especially with the unimaginative Bush in command. England would lose a fine frigate and a fine opportunity. He must sacrifice his prize money, the thousand pounds or so with which he had wanted to dazzle Maria's eyes. But at all costs he must keep his prisoners alive.

'I am sure it is my foreign breeding which is to blame, Supremo,' he said. 'It is difficult for me to express in a foreign tongue all the delicate shades of meaning which it is necessary to convey. How could it possibly be imagined that I could be lacking in respect to el Supremo?'

El Supremo nodded. It was satisfactory to see that a madman who attributed almightiness to himself was naturally inclined to accept the grossest flattery at its face value.

'The ship is yours, Supremo,' went on Hornblower, 'she has been yours since my men first set foot on her deck last night. And when in the future a vast Armada sails the Pacific under el Supremo's direction I only wish it to be remembered that the first ship of that fleet was taken from the Spaniards by Captain Hornblower at el Supremo's orders.'

El Supremo nodded again, and then turned to Hernandez.

'General,' he said, 'make arrangements for five hundred men to go on board the ships at noon. I will sail with them and so will you.'

Hernandez bowed and departed; it was easy to see that there was no chance of el Supremo doubting his own divinity as a result of disrespect or hesitation on the part of his subordinates. His lightest order, whether it dealt with a thousand pigs or five hundred men, was obeyed instantly. Hornblower made his next move at once.

'Is the *Lydia*,' he asked, 'to have the honour of carrying el Supremo to La Libertad? My crew would greatly appreciate the distinction.'

'I am sure they would,' said el Supremo.

'I hardly venture to ask it,' said Hornblower, 'but could my officers and I aspire to the honour of your dining with us before our departure?'

El Supremo considered for a moment.

'Yes,' he said, and Hornblower had to suppress the sigh of relief he was on the point of drawing. Once el Supremo was on board the *Lydia* it might be possible to deal with him with less difficulty.

El Supremo clapped his hands, and instantly, as though by clockwork, a knocking at the brass-studded door heralded the arrival of the swarthy major-domo. He received in a single sentence orders for the transfer of el Supremo's household to the *Lydia.*

'Perhaps,' said Hornblower, 'you will permit me to return to my ship now to make arrangements for your reception, Supremo.'

He received another nod in reply.

'At what time shall I be at the beach to receive you?'

'At eleven.'

Hornblower, as he came out into the patio, thought with sympathy of the oriental vizier who never came out of the royal presence without feeling to see if his head were still on his shoulders. And on the *Lydia's* deck, the moment the twittering of the pipes had died away, Hornblower was giving his orders.

'Have those men taken below at once,' he said to Bush, pointing to the Spanish prisoners. 'Put them in the cable tier under guard. Call the armourer and have them put in irons.'

Bush made no attempt to conceal his surprise, but Hornblower wasted no time on explanations to him.

'Señores,' he said, as the officers came by him. 'You are going to be harshly treated. But believe me, if you are as much as seen during the next few days you will be killed. I am saving your lives for you.'

Next Hornblower turned back to his first lieutenant.

'Call all hands, Mr Bush.'

The ship was filled with the sound of horny feet pattering over pine boards.

'Men!' said Hornblower. 'There is coming aboard today a prince of this country who is in alliance with our own gracious King. Whatever happens – mark my words, *whatever happens* – he is to be treated with respect. I will flog the man who laughs, or the man who does not behave towards Señor el Supremo as he would to me. And we shall be sailing tonight with this gentleman's troops on board. You will look after them as if they were Englishmen. And better than that. You would play tricks on English soldiers. The first man to play a trick on any of these men I shall flog within the hour. Forget their colour. Forget their clothes. Forget that they cannot speak English, and remember only what I say to you. You can pipe down now, Mr Bush.'

Down in the cabin Polwheal was waiting faithfully with the dressing gown and towel for his captain's bath, which ought according to time table have been taken two hours back.

'Put out my best uniform again,' snapped Hornblower. 'And I want the after cabin ready for a state dinner for eight at six bells. Go for'rard and bring my cook to me.'

There was plenty to do. Bush and Rayner the first and fourth lieutenants, and Simmonds the marine officer, and Crystal the master, had to be invited to the dinner and warned to be ready in full dress. Plans had to be made for the accommodation of five hundred men on board the two frigates.

Hornblower was just looking across to the *Natividad,* where she swung with her white ensign over the red and gold of Spain, wondering what steps he should take with regard to her, when a boat came running gaily out to him from the shore. The leader of the party which came on board was a youngish man of less than middle height, slight of figure and lithe as a monkey, with a mobile smile and an expression of indefeatable good humour. He looked more Spanish than American. Bush brought him up to where Hornblower impatiently trod his quarterdeck. Making a cordial bow, the newcomer introduced himself.

'I am Vice-Admiral Don Cristobal de Crespo,' he said.

Hornblower could not help but look him up and down. The Vice-Admiral wore gold earrings, and his gold embroidered coat did not conceal the raggedness of the grey shirt beneath. At least he wore boots, of soft brown leather, into which were tucked his patched white trousers.

'Of el Supremo's service?' asked Hornblower.

'Of course. May I introduce my officers. Ship-captain Andrade. Frigate-captain Castro. Corvette-captain Carrera. Lieutenants Barrios and Barillas and Cerno. Aspirants Diaz—'

The dozen officers introduced under these resounding titles were barefooted Indians, the red sashes round their waists stuck full of pistols and knives. They bowed awkwardly to Hornblower; one or two of them wore expressions of brutish cruelty.

'I have come,' said Crespo, amiably, 'to hoist my flag in my new ship *Natividad.* It is el Supremo's wish that you should salute it with the eleven guns due to a vice-admiral.'

Hornblower's jaw dropped a little at that. His years of service had grained into him despite himself a deep respect for the details of naval pageantry, and he was irked by the prospect of giving this ragged-shirted rascal as many guns as Nelson ever had. With an effort he swallowed his resentment. He knew he had to go through with the farce to the bitter end if he was to glean any success. With an empire at stake it would be foolish to strain at points of ceremony.

'Certainly, Admiral,' he said. 'It gives me great happiness to be one of the first to congratulate you upon your appointment.'

'Thank you, Captain. There will be one or two details to attend to first,' said the vice-admiral. 'May I ask if the executive officers of the *Natividad* are on board here or are still in the *Natividad*?'

'I greatly regret,' said Hornblower, 'that I dropped them overboard this morning after courtmartial.'

'That is indeed a pity,' said Crespo. 'I have el Supremo's orders to hang them at the *Natividad's* yardarms. You did not leave even one?'

'No one, Admiral. I am sorry that I received no orders from el Supremo on the subject.'

'There is no help for it, then. Doubtless there will be others. I will go on board my ship, then. Perhaps you will be good enough to accompany me so as to give orders to your prize crew?'

'Certainly, Admiral.'

Hornblower was curious to see how el Supremo's subordinates would deal with the problem of changing the allegiance of a whole ship's crew. He gave hurried orders to the gunner for the saluting of the flag when it should be hoisted in the *Natividad*, and went down into the boat with the new officers.

On board the *Natividad* Crespo swaggered on to the quarterdeck. The Spanish sailing master and his mates were grouped there, and under their startled eyes he walked up to the image of the Virgin and Child beside the taffrail and tossed it overboard. At a sign from him one of the aspirants hauled down the Spanish and British ensigns from the peak. Then he turned upon the navigating officers. It was a dramatic scene on that crowded quarterdeck in the brilliant sunshine. The British marines stood in rigid line in their red coats, with ordered arms. The British seamen stood by their carronades, matches smouldering, for no orders had yet relieved them of their duty. Gerard came over and stood beside Hornblower.

'Which is the sailing master?' demanded Crespo.

'I am,' quavered one of the Spaniards.

'Are you his mates?' rasped Crespo, and received frightened nods in reply.

All trace of humour had disappeared from Crespo's expression. He seemed to expand and dilate with cold anger.

'You,' he said, pointing at the youngest. 'You will now hold up your hand and declare your faith in our lord el Supremo. Hold up your hand.'

The boy obeyed as if in a trance.

'Now repeat after me. "I swear—" '

The boy's face was white. He tried to look round at his superior officer, but his gaze was held by Crespo's glaring eyes.

'"I swear,"' said Crespo, more menacingly. The boy's mouth opened and shut without a sound. Then convulsively he freed himself from the hypnotic stare. His hand wavered and came down, and he looked away from Crespo's pointing right forefinger. Instantly Crespo's left hand shot out; so quick was the motion that no one could see until afterwards that it held a pistol from his sash. The shot rang out, and the boy, with a pistol ball in his stomach, fell to the deck writhing in agony. Crespo disregarded his convulsions and turned to the next man.

'*You* will now swear,' he said.

He swore at once, repeating Crespo's words in quavering tones. The half dozen sentences were very much to the point; they declared the omnipotence of el Supremo, testified to the speaker's faith, and in a single sweeping blasphemy denied the existence of God and the virginity of the Mother of God. The others followed his example, repeating the words of the oath one after the other, while no one paid any attention to the dying boy at their feet. Crespo only condescended to notice him after the conclusion of the ceremony.

'Throw that overboard,' he said curtly. The officers only hesitated a moment under his gaze, and then one stooped and lifted the boy by his shoulders, another by his feet, and they flung the still living body over the rail.

Crespo waited for the splash, and then walked forward to the quarterdeck rail with its peeling gilt. The herded crew in the waist listened dumbly to his uplifted voice. Hornblower, gazing down at them, saw that there would be small resistance to Crespo's missionary efforts. To a man the crew were of non-European blood; presumably during the many years of the *Natividad's* commission in the Pacific the original European crew had quite died out. Only officers had been replaced from Spain; fresh hands had been recruited from the native races. There were Chinese among them, as Hornblower recognised, and negroes, and some whose physiognomy was unfamiliar to him – Philipinos.

In five minutes of brilliant speaking Crespo had won them all over. He made no more attempt to enunciate the divinity of el Supremo than was involved in the mention of his name. El Supremo, he said, was at the head of a movement which was sweeping the Spaniards from the dominion of America. Within the year the whole of the New World from Mexico to Peru would be at his feet. There would be an end of Spanish misrule, or brutal domination, of slavery in mine and field. There would be land for the asking for everybody, freedom and happiness under the benign supervision of el Supremo. Who would follow him?

They all would seemingly. Crespo had them all cheering wildly at the end of his speech. Crespo came back to Hornblower.

'Thank you, Captain,' he said. 'I think there is no more need for the presence of your prize crew. My officers and I will be able to attend to any insubordination which may arise later.'

'I think you will be quite able to,' said Hornblower, a little bitterly.

'Some of them *may* not easily be enlightened when the time comes for that,' said Crespo, grinning.

Pulling back to the *Lydia* Hornblower thought bitterly about the murder of the Spanish master's mate. It was a crime which he ought to have prevented – he had gone on board the *Natividad* expressly to prevent cruelty and he had failed. Yet he realised that that kind of cruelty would not have the bad effect on his own men that a cold-blooded hanging of the officers would have done. The crew of the *Natividad* was being forced to serve a new master against their will – but the pressgang had done the same for three-quarters of the crew of the *Lydia.* Flogging and death were the punishments meted out to Englishmen who refused to obey the orders of officers who had arbitrarily assumed command over them – English sailors were not likely to fret unduly over Dagoes in the same position, even though with English lower-class lack of logic they would have been moved to protest against a formal hanging of officers.

His train of thought was suddenly interrupted by the sound of a gun from the *Natividad,* instantly answered by another from the *Lydia.* He almost sprang to his feet in the sternsheets of the launch, but a glance over his shoulder reassured him. A new flag was now flying from the *Natividad's* peak. Blue with a yellow star in the middle, he saw. The sound of the saluting guns rolled slowly round the bay; the salute was still being fired as he went up the *Lydia's* side. Mr Marsh, the gunner, was pacing up and down the foredeck mumbling to himself – Hornblower guessed at the jargon.

'If I hadn't been a born bloody fool I shouldn't be here. Fire *seven.* I've left my wife; I've left my home and everything that's dear. Fire *eight.*'

Half an hour later Hornblower was at the beach to meet el Supremo, who came riding down, punctual to the minute, a ragged retinue of a dozen riding with him. El Supremo did not condescend to present his suite to the captain, but bowed and stepped straight into the launch; his suite introduced themselves, in a string of meaningless names, in turn as they came up to Hornblower. They were all nearly pure Indians; they were all Generals save for one or two Colonels, and they were all clearly most devotedly attached to their master. Their whole bearing, every little action of theirs, indicated not merely their fear of him but their admiration – their love, it might be said.

At the gangway sideboys and boatswain's mates and marines were ready to receive el Supremo with distinguished military formality, but el Supremo astonished Hornblower as he was about to go up the ladder, with the casual words—

'The correct salute for me, Captain, is twenty-three guns.'

That was two more guns than His Majesty King George himself would receive. Hornblower stared for a moment, thought wildly of how he could refuse, and finally salved his conscience with the notion that a salute of that number of guns would be entirely meaningless. He sent a message hurriedly to Mr Marsh ordering twenty-three guns – it was odd, the way in which the ship's boy almost reduplicated Hornblower's reactions, by staring, composing his features, and hurrying off comforted by the thought that it was the Captain's reponsibility and not his own. And Hornblower could hardly repress a grin as he thought of Marsh's certain astonishment, and the boiling exasperation in his voice when he reached – 'If I hadn't been a born bloody fool I shouldn't be here. Fire *twenty-three*.'

El Supremo stepped on to the quarterdeck with a keen glance round him, and then, while Hornblower looked at him, the interest faded from his face and he lapsed into the condition of abstracted indifference in which Hornblower had seen him before. He seemed to listen, but he looked over the heads of Bush and Gerard and the others as Hornblower presented them. He shook his head without a word when Hornblower suggested that he might care to inspect the ship. There was a little awkward pause, which was broken by Bush addressing his captain.

'*Natividad* hoisting another flag to the main yardarm, sir. No it's not, it's—'

It was the body of a man, black against the blue sky, rising slowly, jerking and twisting as it rose. A moment later another body rose at the other end of the yard. All eyes instinctively turned towards el Supremo. He was still gazing away into the distance, his eyes focused on nothing, yet everyone knew he had seen. The English officers cast a hasty glance at their captain for guidance, and followed his lead in lapsing into an uncomfortable pose of having noticed nothing. Disciplinary measures in a ship of another nation could be no affair of theirs.

'Dinner will be served shortly, Supremo,' said Hornblower with a gulp. 'Would you care to come below?'

Still without a word el Supremo walked over to the companion and led the way. Down below his lack of stature was made apparent by the fact that he could walk upright. As a matter of fact, his head just brushed the deck beams above him, but the nearness of the beams did nothing to make him stoop as he walked. Hornblower became conscious of a ridiculous feeling that el Supremo would never need to stoop, that the deck beams would raise themselves as he passed rather than commit the sacrilege of bumping his head – that was how el Supremo's quiet dignity of carriage affected him.

Polwheal and the stewards assisting him, in their best clothes, held aside the screens which still took the place of the discarded bulkheads, but at the entrance to the cabin el Supremo stopped for a moment and said the first words which had passed his lips since he came on board.

'I will dine alone here,' he said. 'Let the food be brought to me.'

None of his suite saw anything in the least odd about his request – Hornblower, watching their expressions, was quite sure that their unconcern was in no way assumed. El Supremo might have been merely blowing his noise for all the surprise they envinced.

It was all a horrible nuisance, of course. Hornblower and his other guests had to dine in makeshift fashion in the gunroom mess, and his one linen tablecloth and his one set of linen napkins, and the two last bottles of his old Madeira remained in the after cabin for el Supremo's use. Nor was the meal improved by the silence that prevailed most of the time; el Supremo's suite were not in the least talkative, and Hornblower was the only Englishman with conversational Spanish. Bush tried twice, valiantly, to make polite speeches to his neighbours, putting a terminal 'o' on the ends of his English words in the hope that so they might be transmuted into Spanish, but the blank stares of the men he addressed reduced him quickly to stammering inarticulation.

Dinner was hardly finished; everyone had hardly lighted the loose brown cigars which had been part of the stores handed over to the *Lydia* when a new messenger arrived from the shore and was brought in by the bewildered officer of the watch who could not understand his jabbering talk. The troops were ready to come on board. With relief Hornblower put away his napkin and went on deck, followed by the others.

The men whom the launch and the cutter, plying steadily between ship and shore, brought out, were typical Central American soldiers, barefooted and ragged, swarthy and lankhaired. Each man carried a bright new musket and a bulging cartridge pouch, but these were merely what Hornblower had brought for them; most of the men carried in their hands cotton bags presumably filled with provisions – some bore melons and bunches of bananas in addition. The crew herded them on to the maindeck; they looked about them curiously and chattered volubly, but they were amenable enough, squatting in gossiping groups between the guns where the grinning crew pushed them. They sat on the planking and most of them incontinently began to eat; Hornblower suspected them to be half starved and to be devouring the rations which were expected to last them for several days.

When the last man was on board Hornblower looked across to the *Natividad*; it appeared as if her share of the expeditionary force was already embarked. Suddenly the babble on the main deck died away completely, to be succeeded by a silence surprising in its intensity. Next moment el Supremo came on the quarterdeck – it must have been his appearance from the after cabin which had quelled the noise.

'We shall sail for La Libertad, Captain,' he said.

'Yes, Supremo,' replied Hornblower. He was glad that el Supremo had made his appearance when he did; a few seconds later and the ship's officers would have seen that their captain was awaiting his orders, and that would never have done.

'We will weigh anchor, Mr Bush,' said Hornblower.

VIII

The voyage up the coast was completed. La Libertad had fallen, and el Supremo and his men had vanished into the tangle of volcanoes surrounding the city of the Holy Saviour. Once again in the early morning Captain Hornblower was pacing the quarterdeck of His Britannic Majesty's 36-gun frigate *Lydia*, and Lieutenant Bush as officer of the watch was standing by the wheel rigidly taking no notice of him.

Hornblower was gazing round him, and filling his lungs deep with air at every respiration as he walked. He noticed that he was doing this, and grinned to himself at the realisation that what he was doing was to savour the sweet air of liberty. For a space he was free from the nightmare influence of el Supremo and his cut-throat methods, and the feeling of relief was inexpressible. He was his own master again, free to walk his quarterdeck undisturbed. The sky was blue, the sea was blue and silver – Hornblower caught himself making the old comparison with heraldic argent and azure, and knew that he was himself again; he smiled once more out of sheer high spirits, looking out to sea, nevertheless, so that his subordinates should not see that their captain was walking the deck grinning like a Cheshire cat.

There was just the gentlest wind abeam pushing the *Lydia* along at three or four knots; peeping over the horizon on the port side were the tops of the interminable volcanoes which formed the backbone of this benighted country. Perhaps after all el Supremo might accomplish his wild dream of conquering Central America; perhaps after all there might be some solid foundation in the hope that good communications might be opened across the Isthmus – by Panama if the Nicaraguan scheme proved impracticable. That would make a profound difference to the world. It would bring Van Diemen's Land and the Moluccas into closer relation to the civilised world. It would open the Pacific to England by evading the difficulties of the journey round the Horn or by the Cape of Good Hope and India, and in that case the Pacific might see squadrons of ships of the line cruising where hardly a frigate had penetrated up to that moment. The Spanish Empire of Mexico and California might acquire a new importance.

Hornblower told himself hastily that all this was only a wild dream at present. As a kind of punishment for dreaming he began to take himself to task regarding his present movements, and to subject himself to a severe examination regarding the motives which had brought him southwards towards Panama. He knew full well that the main one was to shake himself free from el Supremo, but he tried to justify his action in the face of his self-accusation.

If el Supremo's attempt upon San Salvador should fail, the *Natividad* would suffice to bring off what few might survive of his army. The presence of the *Lydia* could in no way influence the land operations. If el Supremo should succeed it might be as well that while he was conquering Nicaragua there should be a diversion in Panama to distract the Spaniards and to prevent them from concentrating their whole strength upon him. It was only right that the *Lydia's* crew should be given a chance of winning some prize money among the pearl fishers of the Gulf of Panama; that would compensate them for their probable loss of the prize money already gained – there would be no screwing money out of the Admiralty for the *Natividad*. The presence of the *Lydia* in the Gulf would hamper the transport of Spanish forces from Peru. Besides, the Admiralty would be glad of a survey of the Gulf and the Pearl Islands; Anson's charts were wanting in this respect. Yet for all these plausible arguments Hornblower knew quite well that why he had come this way was to get away from el Supremo.

A large flat ray, the size of a table top, suddenly leaped clear of the water close overside and fell flat upon the surface again with a loud smack, leaped clear again, and then vanished below, its pinky brown gleaming wet for a moment as the blue water closed over it. There were flying fish skimming the water in all directions, each leaving behind it a momentary dark furrow. Hornblower watched it all, carefree, delighted that he could allow his thoughts to wander and not feel constrained to keep them concentrated on a single subject. With a ship full of stores and a crew contented by their recent adventures he had no real care in the world. The Spanish prisoners whose lives he had saved from el Supremo were sunning themselves lazily on the forecastle.

'Sail ho!' came echoing down from the masthead.

The idlers thronged the bulwark, gazing over the hammock nettings; the seamen holystoning the deck surreptitiously worked more slowly in order to hear what was going on.

'Where away?' called Hornblower.

'On the port bow, sir. Lugger, sir, I think, an' standing straight for us, but she's right in the eye of the sun—'

'Yes, a lugger, sir,' squeaked midshipman Hooker from the fore top gallant masthead. 'Two masted. She's right to windward, running down to us, under all sail, sir.'

'Running down to us?' said Hornblower, mystified. He jumped up on the slide of the quarterdeck carronade nearest him, and stared into the sun and the wind under his hand, but at present there was still nothing to be seen from that low altitude.

'She's still holding her course, sir,' squeaked Hooker.

'Mr Bush,' said Hornblower. 'Back the mizzen tops'l.'

A pearling lugger from the Gulf of Panama, perhaps, and still ignorant of the presence of a British frigate in those waters; on the other hand she might be bearing a message from el Supremo – her course made that unlikely, but that might be explained. Then as the ship lifted, Hornblower saw a gleaming square of white rise for a second over the distant horizon and vanish again. As the minutes passed by the sails were more and more frequently to be seen, until at last from the deck the lugger was in plain view, nearly hull up, running goose-winged before the wind with her bow pointed straight at the *Lydia.*

'*She's* flying Spanish colours at the main, sir,' said Bush from behind his levelled telescope. Hornblower had suspected so for some time back, but had not been able to trust his eyesight.

'She's hauling 'em down, all the same,' he retorted, glad to be the first to notice it.

'So she is, sir,' said Bush, a little puzzled, and then – 'There they go again, sir. No! What do you make of that, sir?'

'White flag over Spanish colours now,' said Hornblower. 'That'll mean a parley. No, I don't trust 'em. Hoist the colours, Mr Bush, and send the hands to quarters. Run out the guns and send the prisoners below under guard again.'

He was not going to be caught unaware by any Spanish tricks. That lugger might be as full of men as an egg is of meat, and might spew up a host of boarders over the side of an unprepared ship. As the *Lydia's* gun ports opened and she showed her teeth the lugger rounded-to just out of gunshot, and lay wallowing, hove-to.

'She's sending a boat, sir,' said Bush.

'So I see,' snapped Hornblower.

Two oars rowed a dinghy jerkily across the dancing water, and a man came scrambling up the ladder to the gangway – so many strange figures had mounted that ladder lately. This new arrival, Hornblower saw, wore the full dress of the Spanish royal navy, his epaulette gleaming in the sun. He bowed and came forward.

'Captain Hornblower?' he asked.

'I am Captain Hornblower.'

'I have to welcome you as the new ally of Spain.'

Hornblower swallowed hard. This might be a ruse, but the moment he heard the words he felt instinctively that the man was speaking the truth. The whole happy world by which he had been encompassed up to that moment suddenly became dark with trouble. He could foresee endless worries piled upon him by some heedless action of the politicians.

'We have had the news for the last four days,' went on the Spanish officer. 'Last month Bonaparte stole our King Ferdinand from us and has named his brother Joseph King of Spain. The Junta of Government has signed a treaty of perpetual alliance and friendship with His Majesty of England. It is with great pleasure. Captain, that I have to inform you that all ports in the dominions of His Most Catholic Majesty are open to you after your most arduous voyage.'

Hornblower still stood dumb. It might all be lies, a ruse to lure the *Lydia* under the guns of Spanish shore batteries. Hornblower almost hoped it might be – better that than all the complications which would hem him in if it were the truth. The Spaniard interpreted his expression as implying disbelief.

'I have letters here,' he said, producing them from his breast. 'One from your admiral in the Leeward Islands, sent overland from Porto Bello, one from His Excellency the Viceroy of Peru, and one from the English lady in Panama.'

He tendered them with a further bow, and Hornblower, muttered an apology – his fluent Spanish had deserted him along with his wits – began to open them. Then he pulled himself up; on deck under the eye of the Spanish officer was no place to study these documents. With another muttered apology he fled below to the privacy of his cabin.

The stout canvas wrapper of the naval orders was genuine enough. He scrutinised the two seals carefully, and they showed no signs of having been tampered with; and the wrapper was correctly addressed in English script. He cut the wrapper open carefully and read the orders enclosed. They could leave him in no doubt. There was the signature – Thomas Troubridge, Rear Admiral, Bart. Hornblower had seen Troubridge's signature before, and recognised it. The orders were brief, as one would expect from Troubridge – an alliance having been concluded between His Majesty's Government and that of Spain Captain Hornblower was directed and required to refrain from hostilities towards the Spanish possessions, and, having drawn upon the Spanish authorities for necessary stores, to proceed with all dispatch to England for further orders. It was a genuine document without any doubts at all. It was marked 'Copy No. 2'; presumably other copies had been distributed to other parts of the Spanish possessions to ensure that he received one.

The next letter was flamboyantly sealed and addressed – it was a letter of welcome from the Viceroy of Peru assuring him that all Spanish America was at his disposal, and hoping that he would make full use of all facilities so that he would speedily be ready to help the Spanish nation in its sacred mission of sweeping the French usurper back to his kennel.

'Ha – h'm,' said Hornblower – the Spanish viceroy did not know yet about the fate of the *Natividad,* nor about the new enterprise of el Supremo. He might not be so cordial when he heard about the *Lydia's* part in these occurrences.

The third letter was sealed merely with a wafer and was addressed in a feminine hand. The Spanish officer had spoken about a letter from the English lady in Panama – what in the world was an English lady doing there? Hornblower slit open the letter and read it.

The Citadel,
Panama.

Lady Barbara Wellesley presents her compliments to the captain of the English frigate. She requests that he will be so good as to convey her and her maid to Europe, because Lady Barbara finds that owing to an outbreak of yellow fever on the Spanish Main she cannot return home the way she would desire.

Hornblower folded the letter and tapped it on his thumb nail in meditation. The woman was asking an impossibility, of course. A crowded frigate sailing round the Horn was no place for females. She seemed to have no doubt about it, all the same; on the contrary, she seemed to assume that her request would be instantly granted. That name Wellesley, of course, gave the clue to that. It had been much before the public of late. Presumably the lady was a sister or an aunt to the two well-known Wellesleys – the Most Hon. the Marquis Wellesley, K.P., late Governor General of India and now a member of the Cabinet, and General the Hon. Sir Arthur Wellesley, K.B., the victor of Assaye and now pointed at as England's greatest soldier after Sir John Moore. Hornblower had seen him once, and had noticed the high arched arrogant nose and the imperious eye. If the woman had that blood in her she would be the sort to take things for granted. So she might, too. An impecunious frigate captain with no influence at all would be glad to render a service to a member of that family. Maria would be pleased as well as suspicious when she heard that he had been in correspondence with the daughter of an Earl, the sister of a Marquis.

But this was no time to stop and think about women. Hornblower locked the letters in his desk and ran up on deck; forcing a smile as he approached the Spanish captain.

'Greeting to the new allies,' he said. 'Señor, I am proud to be serving with Spain against the Corsican tyrant.'

The Spaniard bowed.

'We were very much afraid, Captain,' he said, 'lest you should fall in with the *Natividad* before you heard the news, because she has not heard it either. In that case your fine frigate would have come to serious harm.'

'Ha – h'm,' said Hornblower. This was more embarrassing than ever; he turned and snapped out an order to the midshipman of the watch. 'Bring the prisoners up from the cable tier. Quickly!'

The boy ran, and Hornblower turned back again to the Spanish officer.

'I regret to have to tell you, señor, that by evil chance the *Lydia* met the *Natividad* a week ago.'

The Spanish captain looked his surprise. He stared round the ship, at the meticulous good order, the well set up rigging. Even a Spaniard frigate captain could see that the frigate had not been engaged in a desperate action lately.

'But you did not fight her, Captain?' he said. 'Perhaps—'

The words died away on his lips as he caught sight of a melancholy procession approaching them along the gangway. He recognised the captain and the lieutenants of the *Natividad*. Hornblower plunged feverishly into an explanation of their presence; but it was not easy to tell a Spanish captain that the *Lydia* had captured a Spanish ship of twice her force without receiving a shot or a casualty – it was harder still to go on and explain that the ship was now sailing under the flag of rebels who had determined to destroy the Spanish power in the new world. The Spaniard turned white with rage and injured pride. He turned upon the captain of the *Natividad* and received confirmation of Hornblower's story from that wretched man's lips; his shoulders were bowed with sorrow as he told the story which would lead inevitably to his courtmartial and his ruin.

Bit by bit the newcomer from the lugger heard the truth about recent events, about the capture of the *Natividad*, and the success of el Supremo's rebellion. He realised that the whole of the Spanish overlordship of the Americas was in jeopardy, and as he realised that, a fresh and harassing aspect of the situation broke in upon him.

'The Manila galleon is at sea!' he exclaimed. 'She is due to arrive at Acapulco next month. The *Natividad* will intercept her.'

One ship a year crossed the wide Pacific from the Philippines, never bearing less than a million sterling in treasure. Her loss would cripple the bankrupt Spanish government hopelessly. The three captains exchanged glances – Hornblower was telling himself that this was why el Supremo had agreed so readily to the *Lydia* sailing south westward; he had doubtless been pleased at the thought of the *Natividad* to the north eastward acquiring this wealth for him. It would take the Spaniards months to bring round the Horn a ship capable of dealing with the *Natividad*, and in the interval el Supremo would enjoy all those advantages of sea power which Hornblower had foreseen for the *Lydia*. The rebellion would be so firmly rooted that nothing would put it down, especially as, apparently, the Spaniards of Spain were engaged in a life-and-death struggle with Bonaparte and would have neither ships nor men to spare for America. Hornblower could see where lay his duty.

'Very well,' he announced abruptly. 'I will take my ship back to fight the *Natividad*.'

All the Spanish officers looked their relief at that.

'Thank you, Captain,' said the officer of the lugger. 'You will call in at Panama to consult the Viceroy first?'

'Yes,' snapped Hornblower.

In a world where news took months to travel, and where complete upheavals of international relationships were not merely possible but likely, he had learned now by bitter experience to keep in the closest contact with the shore; his misery was in no way allayed by the knowledge that the present difficulties were occasioned merely by his strict obedience to orders – and he knew, too, that the Lords of the Admiralty would not allow that point to influence them in their opinion of a captain who could cause such terrible trouble.

'Then,' said the captain of the lugger. 'I will bid you good-bye for the time. If I reach Panama first, I will be able to arrange a welcome for you. Perhaps you will allow my compatriots to accompany me?'

'No I won't,' rasped Hornblower. 'And you, sir, will keep under my lee until we drop anchor.'

The Spaniard shrugged and yielded. At sea one can hardly argue with a captain whose guns are run out and whose broadside could blow one's ship out of the water, especially as all Englishmen were as mad and as domineering as el Supremo. The Spaniard had not enough intuition to enable him to guess that Hornblower still had a lurking fear that the whole business might be a ruse to inveigle the *Lydia* helpless under the guns of Panama.

IX

It was not a ruse at all. In the morning when the *Lydia* came stealing before a three knot breeze into the roadstead of Panama the only guns fired were the salutes. Boatloads of rejoicing Spaniards came out to greet her, but the rejoicing was soon turned to wailing at the news that the *Natividad* now flew el Supremo's flag, that San Salvador had fallen, and that all Nicaragua was in a flame of rebellion. With cocked hat and gold-hilted sword ('a sword of the value of fifty guineas', the gift of the Patriotic Fund for Lieutenant Hornblower's part in the capture of the *Castilla* six years ago) Hornblower had made himself ready to go ashore and call upon the Governor and the Viceroy, when the arrival of yet one more boat was announced to him.

'There is a lady on board, sir,' said Gray, one of the master's mates, who brought the news.

'A lady?'

'Looks like an English lady, sir,' explained Gray. 'She seems to want to come aboard.'

Hornblower went on deck; close alongside a large rowing boat tossed and rolled; at the six oars sat swarthy Spanish Americans, bare armed and straw hatted, while another in the bows, boat hook in hand, stood waiting, face upturned for permission to hook on to the chains. In the stern sat a negress with a flaming red handkerchief over her shoulders, and beside her sat the English lady Gray had spoken about. Even as Hornblower looked, the bowman hooked on, and the boat closed in alongside, two men fending off. Somebody caught the rope ladder, and the next moment the lady, timing the movement perfectly, swung on to it and two seconds later came on deck.

Clearly she was an Englishwoman. She wore a wide shady hat trimmed with roses, in place of the eternal mantilla, and her grey-blue silk dress was far finer than any Spanish black. Her skin was fair despite its golden tan, and her eyes were grey-blue, of just the same evasive shade as her silk dress. Her face was too long for beauty and her nose too high arched, to say nothing of her sunburn. Hornblower saw her at that moment as one of the horsefaced mannish women whom he particularly disliked; he told himself that all his inclinations were towards clinging incompetence. Any woman who could transfer herself in that fashion from boat to ship in an open roadstead, and could ascend a rope ladder unassisted, must be too masculine for his taste. Besides, an Englishwoman must be unsexed to be in Panama without a male escort – the phrase 'globe trotting', with all its disparaging implications, had not yet been invented, but it expressed exactly Hornblower's feeling about her.

Hornblower held himself aloof as the visitor looked about her. He was going to do nothing to help her. A wild squawk from overside told that the negress had not been as handy with the ladder, and directly afterwards this was confirmed by her appearance on deck wet from the waist down, water streaming from her black gown on to the deck. The lady paid no attention to the mishap to her maid; Gray was nearest to her and she turned to him.

'Please be so good, sir,' she said, 'as to have my baggage brought up out of the boat.'

Gray hesitated, and looked round over his shoulder at Hornblower, stiff and unbending on the quarterdeck.

'The captain's here, ma'am,' he said.

'Yes,' said the lady. 'Please have my baggage brought up while I speak to him.'

Hornblower was conscious of an internal struggle. He disliked the aristocracy – it hurt him nowadays to remember that as the doctor's son he had had to touch his cap to the squire. He felt unhappy and awkward in the presence of the self-confident arrogance of blue blood and wealth. It irritated him to think that if he offended this woman he might forfeit his career. Not even his gold lace nor his presentation sword gave him confidence as she approached him. He took refuge in an icy formality.

'Are you the captain of this ship, sir?' she asked, as she came up. Her eyes looked boldly and frankly into his with no trace of downcast modesty.

'Captain Hornblower, at your service, ma'am,' he replied, with a stiff jerk of his neck which might charitably be thought a bow.

'Lady Barbara Wellesley,' was the reply, accompanied by a curtsy only just deep enough to keep the interview formal. 'I wrote you a note, Captain Hornblower, requesting a passage to England. I trust that you received it.'

'I did, ma'am. But I do not think it is wise for your ladyship to join this ship.'

The unhappy double mention of the word 'ship' in this sentence did nothing to make Hornblower feel less awkward.

'Please tell me why, sir.'

'Because, ma'am, we shall be clearing shortly to seek out an enemy and fight him. And after that, ma'am, we shall have to return to

England round Cape Horn. Your ladyship would be well advised to make your way across the Isthmus. From Porto Bello you can easily reach Jamaica and engage a berth in the West India packet which is accustomed to female passengers.'

Lady Barbara's eyebrows arched themselves higher.

'In my letter,' she said, 'I informed you that there was yellow fever in Porto Bello. A thousand persons died there of it last week. It was on the outbreak of the disease that I removed from Porto Bello to Panama. At any day it may appear here as well.'

'May I ask why your ladyship was in Porto Bello, then?'

'Because, sir, the West India packet in which I was a female passenger was captured by a Spanish privateer and brought there. I regret, sir, that I cannot tell you the name of my grandmother's cook, but I shall be glad to answer any further questions which a gentleman of breeding would ask.'

Hornblower winced and then to his annoyance found himself blushing furiously. His dislike for arrogant blue blood was if anything intensified. But there was no denying that the woman's explanations were satisfactory enough – a visit to the West Indies could be made by any woman without unsexing herself, and she had clearly come to Porto Bello and Panama against her will. He was far more inclined now to grant her request – in fact he was about to do so, having strangely quite forgotten the approaching duel with the *Natividad* and the voyage round the Horn. He recalled them just as he was about to speak, so that he changed at a moment's notice what he was going to say and stammered and stuttered in consequence.

'B-but we are going out in this ship to fight,' he said. '*Natividad*'s got twice our force. It will be d-dangerous.'

Lady Barbara laughed at that – Hornblower noted the pleasing colour contrast between her white teeth and her golden sunburn; his own teeth were stained and ugly.

'I would far rather,' she said, 'be on board your ship, whomsoever you have got to fight, than be in Panama with the *vomita negro*.'

'But Cape Horn, ma'am?'

'I have no knowledge of this Cape Horn of yours. But I have twice rounded the Cape of Good Hope during my brother's Governor-Generalship, and I assure you, captain, I have never yet been seasick.'

Still Hornblower stammered and hesitated. He resented the presence of a woman on board his ship. Lady Barbara exactly voiced his thoughts – and as she did so her arched eyebrows came close together in a fashion oddly reminiscent of el Supremo although her eyes still laughed straight into his.

'Soon, Captain,' she said 'I will come to think that I shall be unwelcome on board. I can hardly imagine that a gentleman holding the King's commission would be discourteous to a woman, especially to a woman with my name.'

That was just the difficulty. No captain of small influence could afford to offend a Wellesley. Hornblower knew that if he did he might never command a ship again, and that he and Maria would rot on the beach on half pay for the rest of their lives. At thirty-seven he still was not more than one-eighth the way up the captain's list – and the goodwill of the Wellesleys could easily keep him in employment until he attained flag rank. There was nothing for it but to swallow his resentment and to do all he could to earn that goodwill, diplomatically wringing advantage from his difficulties. He groped for a suitable speech.

'I was only doing my duty, ma'am,' he said, 'in pointing out the dangers to which you might be exposed. For myself there would be nothing that would give me greater pleasure than your presence on board my ship.'

Lady Barbara went down in a curtsy far deeper than her first, and at this moment Gray came up and touched his cap.

'Your baggage is all on board, ma'am,' he said.

They had hove the stuff up with a whip from the main yardarm, and now it littered the gangway – leather cases, ironbound wooden boxes, dome-topped trunks.

'Thank you, sir.' Lady Barbara brought out a flat leather purse from her pocket, and took from it a gold coin. 'Would you be so kind as to give this to the boat's crew?'

'Lord love you, ma'am, you don't need to give those Dago niggers gold. Silver's all they deserve.'

'Give them this, then, and thank you for your kindness.'

Gray hurried off, and Hornblower heard him bargaining in English with a boat's crew who knew no tongue but Spanish. The threat of having a cold shot hove down into the boat compelled it at length to shove off still spattering expostulation. A new little wave of irritation rose in Hornblower's mind. He disliked seeing his warrant officers running to do a woman's bidding, and his responsibilities were heavy, and he had been standing in a hot sun for half an hour.

'There will be no room in your cabin for a tenth of that baggage, ma'am,' he snapped.

Lady Barbara nodded gravely.

'I have dwelt in a cabin before this, sir. That sea chest there holds everything I shall need on board. The rest can be put where you will – until we reach England.'

Hornblower almost stamped on the deck with rage. He was unused to a woman who could display practical common-sense like this. It was infuriating that he could find no way of discomposing her – and then he saw her smiling, guessed that she was smiling at the evident struggle on his face, and blushed hotly again. He turned on his heel and led the way below without a word.

Lady Barbara looked round the captain's cabin with a whimsical smile, but she made no comment, not even when she surveyed the grim discomfort of the after-cabin.

'A frigate has few of the luxuries of an Indiaman you see, ma'am,' said Hornblower, bitterly. He was bitter because his poverty at the time when he commissioned the *Lydia* had allowed him to purchase none of the minor comforts which many frigate-captains could afford.

'I was just thinking when you spoke,' said Lady Barbara, gently, 'that it was scandalous that a King's officer should be treated worse than a fat John Company man. But I have only one thing to ask for which I do not see.'

'And that is, ma'am—?'

'A key for the lock on the cabin door.'

'I will have the armourer make you a key, ma'am. But there will be a sentry at this door night and day.'

The implications which Hornblower read into this request of Lady Barbara's angered him again. She was slandering both him and his ship.

'Quis custodiet ipsos custodes?' said Lady Barbara. 'It is not on my account, Captain, that I need a key. It is Hebe here whom I have to lock in unless she is directly under eye. She can no more keep from the men than a moth from a candle.'

The little negress grinned widely at this last speech, showing no resentment and a good deal of pride. She rolled her eyes at Polwheal, who was standing silently by.

'Where will she sleep, then?' asked Hornblower, disconcerted once more.

'On the floor of my cabin. And mark my words, Hebe, the first time I find you not there during the night I'll lace you so that you will have to sleep on your face.'

Hebe still grinned, although it was evident that she knew her mistress would carry out her threat. What mollified Hornblower was Lady Barbara's little slip in speaking of the 'floor' of her cabin instead of the deck. It showed that she was only a feeble woman after all.

'Very good,' he said. 'Polwheal, take my things into Mr Bush's cabin. Give Mr Bush my apologies and tell him he will have to berth in the wardroom. See that Lady Barbara has all that she wants, and ask Mr Gray with my compliments to attend to putting the baggage in my storeroom. You will forgive me, Lady Barbara, but I am already late in paying my call upon the Viceroy.'

X

The captain of the *Lydia* came on board again to the accompaniment of the usual twitterings of the pipes and the presenting of arms by the marine guard. He walked very carefully, for good news just arrived from Europe had made the Viceroy pressingly hospitable while the notification of the first case of yellow fever in Panama had made him apprehensive so that Hornblower had been compelled to drink one glass of wine too much. A naturally abstemious man, he hated the feeling of not being quite master of himself.

As always, he looked sharply round the deck as soon as his feet were on it. Lady Barbara was sitting in a hammock chair on the quarter-deck – someone must have had that chair made for her during the day; and someone had rigged for her a scrap of awning in the mizzen rigging so that she sat in the shade with Hebe crouching at her feet. She looked cool and comfortable, and smiled readily at him as he approached, but he looked away from her. He would not speak to her until his head was clearer.

'Call all hands to weigh anchor and make sail,' he said to Bush. 'We leave at once.'

He went below, checked himself with a gesture of annoyance at finding that habit had led him to the wrong cabin, and as he turned on his heel he hit his head a shattering crash on a deck beam. His new cabin, from which Bush had been evicted, was even smaller than the old one. Polwheal was waiting to help him change his clothes, and the sight of him reminded Hornblower of fresh troubles. He had been wearing his best gold laced coat and white breeches when Lady Barbara came on board, but he could not afford to continue to wear them lest they should grow too shabby for use on ceremonial occasions. He would have to appear before this woman in future in his old patched coats and cheap duck trousers. She would sneer at his shabbiness and poverty.

He cursed the woman as he stripped off his clothes, all wet with sweat. Then a new trouble came into his mind. He had to leave Polwheal to keep watch while he had his shower bath under the pump lest she should surprise him there naked. He would have to issue orders to the crew so as to make sure that her fastidious eyes would not be offended by the state of undress which they habitually affected in the tropics. He combed his hair and cursed its curliness as drawing additional attention to the way his hair was receding from his forehead.

Then he hurried on deck; he was glad that the need for looking after the ship saved him from meeting Lady Barbara's eyes and seeing her reaction to his shabby clothes. He felt her gaze upon him, all the same, as he stood with his back to her attending to the business of getting under weigh. Half of one watch were at the capstan with all their weight upon the bars, their bare feet seeking holds on the smooth deck while Harrison bellowed encouragement and threats, and stimulated the laggards with cuts from his cane. Sullivan the mad fiddler, the two Marine fifers and the two drummers were playing some lively tune – to Hornblower one tune was much the same as another – on the forecastle.

The cable came steadily in, the ship's boys with their nippers following it to the hatch-coamings and scuttling back immediately to take a fresh hold on cable and messenger. But the measured clank-clank of the capstan grew slower and slower and then came to a dead stop.

'Heave, you bastards! Heave!' bellowed Harrison. 'Here, you fo'c'sle men, bear a hand! Now, heave!'

There were twenty more men thrusting at the bars now. Their added strength brought one more solemn clank from the capstan.

'Heave! Christ damn you, heave!'

Harrison's cane was falling briskly first here and then there.

'Heave!'

A shudder ran through the ship, the capstan swung round so sharply that the hands at the bars fell in a tumbling heap to the deck.

'Messenger's parted, sir,' hailed Gerard from the forecastle. 'The anchor's foul, I think, sir.'

'Hell fire!' said Hornblower to himself. He was certain that the woman in the hammock chair behind him was laughing at his predicament, with a foul anchor and the eyes of all Spanish America on him. But he was not going to abandon an anchor and cable to the Spaniards.

'Pass the small bower cable for a messenger,' he shouted.

That meant unbearably hot and unpleasant work for a score of men down in the cable tier rousing out the small bower cable and manhandling it up to the capstan. The calls and curses of the boatswain's mates came echoing back to the quarterdeck – the warrant officers were as acutely conscious of the indignity of the ship's position as was their captain. Hornblower could not pace the deck as he wished to do, for fear of meeting Lady Barbara's eyes. He could only stand and fume, wiping the sweat with his handkerchief from his face and neck.

'Messenger's ready, sir!' hailed Gerard.

'Put every man to the bars that there's place for. Mr Harrison, see that they heave!'

'Aye aye, sir!'

Br-r-r-rm. Boom! Br-r-r-rm. Boom! The drum rolled.

'Heave, you sons of bitches,' said Harrison, his cane going crack-crack-crack on the straining backs.

Clank! went the capstan. Clank-clank-clank.

Hornblower felt the deck inclining a trifle under his feet. The strain was dragging down the ship's bows, not bringing home the anchor.

'God—,' began Hornblower to himself, and then left the sentence uncompleted. Of the fifty-five oaths he had ready to employ not one was adequate to the occasion.

'Avast heaving!' he roared, and the sweating seamen eased their aching backs.

Hornblower tugged at his chin as though he wanted to pull it off. He would have to sail the anchor out of the ground – a delicate manoeuvre involving peril to masts and rigging, and which might end in a ridiculous fiasco. Up to the moment only a few knowing people in Panama could have gussed the ship's predicament, but the moment sail was set telescopes would be trained upon her from the city walls and if the operation failed everyone would know and would be amused – and the *Lydia* might be delayed for hours repairing damage. But he was not going to abandon that anchor and cable.

He looked up at the vane at the masthead, and overside at the water; the wind was across the tide, which gave them a chance, at least. He issued his orders quietly, taking the utmost precaution to conceal his trepidation, and steadily keeping his back to Lady Barbara. The topmen raced aloft to set the fore topsail; with that and the driver he could get sternway upon the ship. Harrison stood by the capstan ready first to let the cable go with a run and then second to have it hove in like lightning when the ship came forward again. Bush had his men ready at the braces, and every idle hand was gathered round the capstan.

The cable roared out as the ship gathered sternway; Hornblower stood rooted to the quarterdeck feeling that he would give a week of his life for the chance to pace up and down without meeting Lady Barbara's eyes. With narrowed eyes he watched the progress of the ship, his mind juggling with a dozen factors at once – the drag of the cable on the bows, the pressure of the wind on the driver and the backed fore topsail, the set of the tide, the increasing sternway, the amount of cable still to run out. He picked his moment.

'Hard-a-starboard,' he rasped at the quartermaster at the wheel, and then to the hands forward 'Smartly with the braces now!'

With the rudder hard across the ship came round a trifle. The fore topsail came round. The jibs and fore staysails were set like lightning. There was a shuddering moment before the ship paid off. Her sternway checked, the ship hesitated, and then, joyfully, began slowly to move forward close hauled. Up aloft every sail that could draw was being set as Hornblower barked his orders. The capstan clanked ecstatically as Harrison's men raced round with the bars gathering the cable again.

Hornblower had a moment to think now, with the ship gathering forward way. The drag of the cable would throw her all aback if he gave her the least chance. He was conscious of the rapid beating of his heart as he watched the main topsail for the first signs of flapping. It took all his force of will to keep his voice from shaking as he gave his orders to the helmsman. The cable was coming in fast; the next crisis was at hand, which would see the anchor out of the ground or the *Lydia* dismasted. He nerved himself for it, judged his moment, and then shouted for all sail to be got in.

All the long and painful drill to which Bush had subjected the crew bore its fruit now. Courses, topsails and top gallants were got in during the few seconds which were left, and as the last shred of canvas disappeared a fresh order from Hornblower brought the ship round, pointing straight into the wind and towards the hidden anchor, the way she had gathered carrying her slowly forward. Hornblower strained his ears to listen to the capstan.

Clank-clank-clank-clank.

Harrison was driving his men round and round the capstan like madmen.

Clank-clank-clank.

The ship was moving perceptibly slower. He could not tell yet if all his effort was to end ignominiously in failure.

Clank-clank.

There came a wild yell from Harrison.

'Anchor's free, sir!'

'Set all sail, Mr Bush,' said Hornblower; Bush was making no attempt to conceal his admiration for a brilliant piece of seamanship, and Hornblower had to struggle hard to keep his voice at the hard mechanical pitch which would hide his elation and convince everyone that he had had no doubt from the very start of the success of his manoeuvre.

He set a compass course, and as the ship came round and steadied upon it he gave one final glance of inspection round the deck.

'Ha – h'm,' he rasped, and dived below, to where he could relax and recover, out of Bush's sight – and out of Lady Barbara's, too.

XI

Stretched flat on his back in his cabin, blowing thick greasy wreaths of smoke from one of General Hernandez' cigars towards the deck above him where sat Lady Barbara, Hornblower began slowly to recover from the strain of a very trying day. It had begun with the approach to Panama, with every nerve keyed up lest an ambush had been laid, and it had ended so far with this trying business of the fouled anchor. Between the two had come Lady Barbara's arrival and the interview with the Viceroy of New Granada.

The Viceroy had been a typical Spanish gentleman of the old school – Hornblower decided that he would rather have dealings with el Supremo any day of the week. El Supremo might have an unpleasant habit of barbarously putting men to death, but he found no difficulty in making up his mind and one could be confident that orders issued by him would be obeyed with equal promptitude. The Viceroy, on the other hand, while full of approval of Hornblower's suggestion that instant action against the rebels was necessary, had not been ready to act on it. He was obviously surprised at Hornblower's decision to sail from Panama on the same day as his arrival – he had expected the *Lydia* to stay for at least a week of fêtings and junketings and idleness. He had agreed that at least a thousand soldiers must be transported to the Nicaraguan coast – although a thousand soldiers constituted practically the whole of his command – but he had clearly intended to postpone until the morrow the issuing of the orders for that concentration.

Hornblower had had to use all his tact to persuade him to do it at once, to give his instructions from his very banqueting table, and to put his favourite aides de camp to the pain of riding with messages under a hot sun during the sacred hours of the siesta. The banquet had in itself been trying; Hornblower felt as if there was no skin left on his palate, so highly peppered had been every dish. Both because of the spiciness of the food and the pressing hospitality of the Viceroy it had been hard to avoid drinking too much; in an age of hard drinking Hornblower stood almost alone in his abstemiousness, from no conscientious motive but solely because he actively disliked the feeling of not having complete control of his judgment.

But he could not refuse that last glass of wine, seeing what news had just come in. He sat up on his cot with a jerk. That business with the anchor had driven the recollection out of his mind. Good manners compelled him to go and communicate the news to Lady Barbara, seeing how closely it concerned her. He ran up on deck, pitched his cigar overboard, and went towards her. Gerard, the officer of the watch, was in close conversation with her; Hornblower smiled grimly to himself when he saw Gerard hurriedly break off the conversation and move away.

She was still seated aft by the taffrail in her hammock chair, the negress at her feet. She seemed to be drinking in the cool wind against which the *Lydia* was standing out of the gulf close hauled. On the starboard beam the sun was ready at the horizon, a disc of orange fire in the clear blue of the sky, and she was exposing her face to its level beams with a total disregard for her complexion which accounted for her sunburn and, presumably, for the fact that she was now twenty-seven and still unmarried despite a trip to India. Yet there was a serenity in her expression which seemed to show that at the moment at least she was not worrying about being an old maid.

She acknowledged his bow with a smile.

'It is heavenly to be at sea again, Captain,' she said. 'You have given me no opportunity so far to tell you how grateful I am to you for taking me away from Panama. To be a prisoner was bad enough, but to be free and yet to be confined there by force of circumstances would have driven me out of my mind. Believe me, Captain, you have won my eternal gratitude.'

Hornblower bowed again.

'I trust the Dons treated your ladyship with all respect?'

She shrugged her shoulders.

'Well enough. But Spanish manners can grow trying. I was in charge of Her Excellency – an admirable woman. But insupportably dull. In Spanish America women are treated like Mohammedans. And Spanish-American food—'

The words recalled to Hornblower the banquet he had just endured, and the expression on his face made Lady Barbara break off her sentence to laugh so infectiously that Hornblower could not help but join in.

'Will you not sit down, Captain?'

Hornblower resented the suggestion. He had never once during this commission sat in a chair on his own deck, and he disliked innovations in his habits.

'Thank you, your ladyship, but I prefer to stand if I may. I came to give you good news.'

'Indeed? Then your company is doubly pleasant. I am all eagerness to hear.'

'Your brother, Sir Arthur, has won a great victory in Portugal over the French. Under the terms of a convention the French are evacuating the country and are handing over Lisbon to the English army.'

'That is very good news. I have always been proud of Arthur – this makes me prouder still.'

'It gives me great pleasure to be the first to congratulate his sister.'

Lady Barbara contrived miraculously to bow although seated in her hammock chair – Hornblower was conscious of the difficulty of the feat and grudgingly admitted to himself that it was well done.

'How did the news come?'

'It was announced to the Viceroy while I was at dinner with him. A ship had reached Porto Bello from Cadiz, and a messenger rode express by the waggon road. There was other news as well – how true is more than I can say.'

'To what effect, Captain?'

'The Spaniards claim a victory, too. They say a whole army of Bonaparte's has surrendered to them in Andalusia. They are already looking forward to an invasion of France in company with the English army.'

'And how true do you think it is?

'I distrust it. They may have cut off a detachment by good luck. But it will need more than a Spanish army to beat Bonaparte. I can foresee no speedy end to the war.'

Lady Barbara nodded a grave approval. She looked out to where the sun was sinking into the sea, and Hornblower looked with her. To him the disappearance of the sun each evening into those placid waters was a daily miracle of beauty. The line of the horizon cut the disc now. They watched silently as the sun sank farther and farther. Soon only a tiny edge was left; it vanished, reappeared for a second like a glint of gold as the *Lydia* heaved up over the swell, and then faded once more. The sky glowed red in the west, but overhead it grew perceptibly darker with the approach of night.

'Beautiful! Exquisite!' said Lady Barbara; her hands were tightly clasped together. She was silent for a moment before she spoke again, returning to the last subject of conversation. 'Yes. One gleam of success and the Spaniards will look on the war as good as over. And in England the herd will be expecting my brother to lead the army into Paris by Christmas. And if he does not they will forget his victories and clamour for his head.'

Hornblower resented the word 'herd' – by birth and by blood he was one of the herd himself – but he was aware of the profound truth of Lady Barbara's remarks. She had summed up for him his opinion both of the Spanish national temperament and of the British mob. Along with that went her appreciation of the sunset and her opinion of Spanish-American food. He actually felt well disposed towards her.

'I hope,' he said, ponderously, 'that your ladyship was provided to-day during my absence with everything necessary? A ship is poorly provided with comforts for women, but I hope that my officers did their best for your ladyship.'

'Thank you, Captain, they did indeed. There is only one more thing that I wish for, which I should like to ask as a favour.'

'Yes, your ladyship?'

'And that is that you do not call me "your ladyship." Call me Lady Barbara, if you will.'

'Certainly, your – Lady Barbara. Ha – h'm.'

Ghosts of dimples appeared in the thin cheeks, and the bright eyes sparkled.

'And if "Lady Barbara" does not come easily to you, Captain, and you wish to attract my attention, you can always say "ha – h'm." '

Hornblower stiffened with anger at this impertinence. He was about to turn on his heel, drawing a deep breath as he did so, and he was about to exhale that breath and clear this throat when he realised that he would never again, or at least until he had reached some port where he could get rid of this woman, be able to make use of that useful and noncommittal sound. But Lady Barbara checked him with outstretched hand; even at that moment he noticed her long slender fingers.

'I am sorry, Captain,' she said, all contrition, 'please accept my apologies, although I know now that it was quite unforgivable.'

She looked positively pretty as she pleaded. Hornblower stood hesitating, looking down at her. He realised that why he was angry was not because of the impertinence, but because this sharp-witted woman had already guessed at the use he made of this sound to hide his feelings, and with that realisation his anger changed into his usual contempt for himself.

'There is nothing to forgive, ma'am,' he said, heavily. 'And now, if you will forgive me in your turn, I will attend to my duties in the ship.'

He left her there in the fast falling night. A ship's boy had just come aft and lighted the binnacle lamps, and he stopped and read on the slate and traverse board the record of the afternoon's run. He wrote in his painstaking hand the instructions with regard to calling him – because some time that night they would round Cape Mala and have to change course to the northward – and then he went below again to his cabin.

He felt oddly disturbed and ill at ease and not merely because of the upsetting of all his habits. It was annoying that his own private water closet was barred to him now so that he had to use the ward-room one, but it was not just because of this. Not even was it merely because he was on his way to fight the *Natividad* again in the certain knowledge that with Vice-Admiral Cristobal de Crespo in command it would be a hard battle. That was part of what was troubling him – and then he realised with a shock that his disquiet was due to the added responsibility of Lady Barbara's presence on board.

He knew quite well what would be the fate of himself and his crew if the *Lydia* were beaten by the *Natividad*. They would be hanged or drowned or tortured to death – el Supremo would show no mercy to the Englishman who had turned against him. That possibility left him unmoved at present, because it was so entirely inevitable that he should fight the *Natividad*. But it was far different in Lady Barbara's case. He would have to see that she did not fall alive into Crespo's hands.

This brief wording of his difficulty brought him a sudden spasm of irritation. He cursed the yellow fever which had driven her on board; he cursed his own slavish obedience to orders which had resulted in the *Natividad's* fighting on the rebels' side. He found himself clenching his hands and gritting his teeth with rage. If he won his fight public opinion would censure him (with all public opinion's usual ignorance of circumstances) for risking the life of a lady – of a Wellesley. If he lost it – but he could not bear to think about that. He cursed his own weakness for allowing her to come on board; for a moment he even dallied with the notion of putting back to Panama and setting her on shore. But he put that notion aside. The *Natividad* might take the Manila galleon. His crew, already discomposed by all the recent changes of plan, would fret still more if he went back and then went to sea again. And Lady Barbara might refuse – and with yellow fever raging in Panama she would be justified in refusing. He could not exercise his authority so brutally as to force a woman to land in a fever-stricken town. He swore to himself again, senselessly, making use of all the filthy oaths and frantic blasphemies acquired during his sea experience.

From the deck came a shrilling of pipes and a shouting of orders and a clatter of feet; apparently the wind had backed round now with the fall of night. As the sound died away the feeling of oppression in the tiny cabin overcame him. It was hot and stuffy; the oil lamp swinging over his head stank horribly. He plunged up on deck again. Aft from the taffrail he heard a merry laugh from Lady Barbara, instantly followed by a chorus of guffaws. The dark mass there must be at least half a dozen officers, all grouped round Lady Barbara's chair. It was only to be expected that after seven months – eight, nearly, now – without seeing an English woman they would cluster round her like bees round a hive.

His first instinct was to drive them away, but he checked himself. He could not dictate to his officers how they spent their watch below, and they would attribute his action to his desire to monopolise her society to himself – and that was not in the least the case. He went down again, unobserved by the group, to a stuffy cabin and the stinking lamp. It was the beginning of a sleepless and restless night.

XII

Morning found the *Lydia* heaving and swooping lightly over a quartering sea. On the starboard beam, just jutting over the horizon, were the greyish-pink summits of the volcanoes of that tormented country; by ranging along just in sight of the coast the *Lydia* stood her best chance of discovering the *Natividad*. The captain was already afoot – indeed, his coxswain Brown had had apologetically to sand the captain's portion of the quarterdeck while he paced up and down it.

Far away on the port side the black shape of a whale broke the surface in a flurry of foam – dazzling white against the blue sea – and a thin plume of white smoke was visible as the whale emptied its lungs. Hornblower liked whales for some reason or other; the sight of this one, in fact, led him on his first step back towards good temper. With the imminent prospect of his cold shower bath before him the prickle of sweat under his shirt was gratifying now instead of irritating. Two hours ago he had been telling himself that he loathed this Pacific coast, its blue sea and its hideous volcanoes – even its freedom from navigational difficulties. He had felt himself homesick for the rocks and shoals and fogs and tides of the Channel, but now, bathed in sunshine, his opinion changed once more. There was something to be said in favour of the Pacific after all. Perhaps this new alliance between Spain and England would induce the Dons to relax some of their selfish laws prohibiting trade with America; they might even go so far as to try to exploit the possibility of that canal across Nicaragua which the British Admiralty had in mind, and in that case this blue Pacific could come into its own. El Supremo would have to be suppressed first, of course, but on this pleasant morning Hornblower foresaw less difficulty in that.

Gray the master's mate had come aft to heave the log. Hornblower checked in his walk to watch the operation. Gray tossed the little triangle of wood over the stern, and, log line in hand, he gazed fixedly with his boyish blue eyes at the dancing bit of wood.

'Turn!' he cried sharply to the hand with the sand glass, while the line ran out freely over the rail.

'Stop!' called the man with the glass.

Gray nipped the line with his fingers and checked it progress, and then read off the length run out. A sharp jerk at the thin cord which had run out with the line freed the peg so that the log now floated with its edge towards the ship, enabling Gray to pull the log in hand over hand.

'How much?' called Hornblower to Gray.

'Seven an' nigh on a half, sir.'

The *Lydia* was a good ship to reel off seven and a half knots in that breeze, even though her best point of sailing was with the wind on her quarter. It would not take long if the wind held to reach waters where the *Natividad* might be expected to be found. The *Natividad* was a slow sailer, as nearly all those two-decker fifty-gun ships were, and as Hornblower had noticed when he had sailed in her company ten days back – it might as well be ten years, so long did it seem – from the Gulf of Fonseca to La Libertad.

If he met her in the open sea he could trust to the handiness of his ship and the experience of his crew to out-manoeuvre her and discount her superior weight of metal. If the ships once closed and the rebels boarded their superior numbers would overwhelm his crew. He must keep clear, slip across her stern and rake her half a dozen times. Hornblower's busy mind, as he paced up and down the deck, began to visualise the battle, and to make plans for the possible eventualities – whether or not he might hold the weather gauge, whether or not there might be a high sea running, whether or not the battle began close inshore.

The little negress Hebe came picking her way across the deck, her red handkerchief brilliant in the sunshine, and before the scandalised crew could prevent her she had interrupted the captain in his sacred morning walk.

'Milady says would the captain breakfast with her,' she lisped.

'Eh – what's that?' asked Hornblower, taken by surprise and coming out of his day dream with a jerk, and then, as he realised the triviality for which he had been interrupted 'No no no! Tell her ladyship I will *not* breakfast with her. Tell her that I will *never* breakfast with her. Tell her that on *no* account am I to be sent messages during the morning. Tell her you are *not* allowed and neither is she on this deck before eight bells. *Get below!*'

Even then the little negress did not seem to realise how enormous had been her offence. She nodded and smiled as she backed away without a sign of contrition. Apparently she was used to white gentlemen who were irascible before breakfast and attributed little importance to the symptoms. The open skylight of the after cabin was close beside him as he walked, and through it he could hear, now that his reverie had been broken into, the clatter of crockery, and then first Hebe's and then Lady Barbara's voice.

The sound of the men scrubbing the decks, the harping of the rigging and the creaking of the timbers were noises to which he was used. From forward came the thunderous beat of a sledgehammer as the armourer and his mate worked upon the fluke of the anchor which had been bent in yesterday's misadventure. He could tolerate all the ship's noises, but this clack-clack-clack of women's tongues through the open skylight would drive him mad. He stamped off the deck in a rage again. He did not enjoy his bath after all, and he cursed Polwheal for clumsiness in handing him his dressing gown, and he tore the threadbare suit which Polwheal had put out for him and cursed again. It was intolerable that he should be driven in this fashion off his own deck. Even the excellent coffee, sweetened (as he liked it) to a syrup with sugar, did not relieve his fresh ill-temper. Nor, most assuredly, did the necessity of having to explain to Bush that the *Lydia* was now sailing to seek out and to capture the *Natividad*, having already been to enormous pains to capture her and hand her over to the rebels who were now their foes.

'Aye aye, sir,' said Bush gravely, having heard the new development. He was being so obviously tactful, and he so pointedly refrained from comment, that Hornblower swore at him.

'Aye aye, sir,' said Bush again, knowing perfectly well why he was being sworn at, and also knowing that he would be sworn at far worse if he said anything beyond 'aye aye, sir.' Really what he wanted to say was some expression of sympathy for Hornblower in his present situation, but he knew he dared not sympathise with his queer-tempered captain.

As the day wore on Hornblower came to repent of his ill-humour. The saw-edged volcanic coast was slipping past them steadily, and ahead of them somewhere lay the *Natividad*. There was a desperate battle awaiting them, and before they should fight it it would be tactful for him to entertain his officers to dinner. And he knew that any captain with an eye to his professional advancement would be careful not to treat a Wellesley in the cavalier fashion he had employed up to the present. And ordinary politeness dictated that he should at this, the earliest opportunity, arrange that his guest should meet his officers formally at dinner, even though he knew full well that she had already, in her emancipated manner, conversed with half of them in the darkness of the quarterdeck.

He sent Polwheal across to Lady Barbara with a politely worded request that Lady Barbara would be so kind as to allow Captain Hornblower and his officers to dine with her in the after cabin and Polwheal returned with a politely worded message to the effect that Lady Barbara would be delighted. Six was the maximum number that could sit round the after cabin table; and superstitiously Hornblower remembered that on the eve of his last encounter with the *Natividad* Galbraith, Clay, and Savage had been his guests. He would never have admitted to himself that it was for this reason that he invited them again in the hope of encountering similar good fortune, but it was the case nevertheless. He invited Bush as the sixth – the other possible choice was Gerard, and Gerard was so handsome and had acquired somehow such a knowledge of the world that Hornblower did not want to bring him into too frequent contact with Lady Barbara – solely, he hastened to assure himself, for the sake of peace and quiet in his ship. And when that was all settled he could go on deck again to take his noon sights and pace his quarterdeck in his consuming restlessness, feeling that he could (after this exchange of polite messages) meet Lady Barbara's eyes without the embarrassment that would previously have prevented him, unreasoningly.

The dinner at three o'clock was a success. Clay and Savage passed through the stages of behaviour that might have been expected of boys their age. At first they were brusque and shy in Lady Barbara's presence, and then, when the novelty had worn off and they had a glass of wine inside them they moved towards the other extreme of over-familiarity. Even the hard-bitten Bush, surprisingly, showed the same symptoms in the same order, while poor Galbraith was of course shy all the time.

But Hornblower was astonished at the ease with which Lady Barbara handled them. His own Maria would have been too gauche ever to have pulled that party together, and in a world where he knew few women Hornblower was prone to measure the ones he met by Maria's standard. Lady Barbara laughed away Clay's bumptiousness, listened appreciatively to Bush's account of Trafalgar (when he had been a junior lieutenant in the *Téméraire*) and then won Galbraith's heart completely by displaying a close knowledge of a remarkable poem called 'The Lay of the Last Minstrel' by an Edinburgh lawyer – every line of which Galbraith knew by heart, and which Galbraith thought was the greatest poem in the English language. His cheeks glowed with pleasure as they discussed it.

Hornblower kept his opinion of the work to himself. His model author was Gibbon, whose 'Decline and Fall of the Roman Empire' was to be found in the very locker on which he sat, and he was surprised that a woman who could quote Juvenal with ease should be so interested in a barbaric romantic poem with no polish about it whatever. He contented himself with sitting back and watching the faces round the table – Galbraith tense and pleased, Clay and Savage and Bush a little out of their depth but interested in spite of themselves, and Lady Barbara completely at ease, conversing with a fearless self-confidence which nevertheless (as Hornblower grudgingly admitted to himself) seemed to owe nothing to her great position.

She made no use of her sex, either, Hornblower realised, and yet she was, marvellously, neither cold nor masculine. She might have been Savage's aunt, or Galbraith's sister. She could talk to men as an equal, and yet could keep from her manner both invitation and hostility. She was very different from Maria. And when dinner was over and the officers rose to drink the health of the King, stooping under the deck beams (not until twenty-five more years had passed would a King who had been a sailor himself give permission to the Navy to drink his health sitting) she echoed 'God bless him!' and finished her single glass of wine with exactly the right touch of light-hearted solemnity which befitted the occasion. Hornblower suddenly realised that he was passionately anxious for the evening not to end.

'Do you play whist, Lady Barbara?' he asked.

'Why, yes,' she said, 'are there whist players on board this ship?'

'There are some who are not too enthusiastic,' replied Hornblower, grinning at his juniors.

But nobody had nearly as much objection to playing in a four with Lady Barbara, the more so as her presence might moderate the captain's dry strictness. The cut allotted Lady Barbara as the captain's partner against Clay and Galbraith. Clay dealt and turned up a heart as trump; it was Lady Barbara's lead. She led the king of hearts, and Hornblower writhed uneasily in his seat. This might well be the play of a mere tyro, and somehow it hurt him to think that Lady Barbara was a bad whist player. But the king of hearts was followed by the king of diamonds, which also took the trick, and that by the ace of hearts, followed by the seven. Hornblower took the trick with the queen – his last heart, making a total of eleven played, and returned a diamond. Down came Lady Barbara's queen. Next came the ace of diamonds, and then two small ones to follow. At his first discard Hornblower dropped the seven from his suit of four clubs headed by king and knave. His opponents each discarded small spades on that remorseless string of diamonds. From doubt Hornblower changed instantly to complete confidence in his partner, which was entirely justified. She led the ace of clubs followed by the three, Hornblower finessed his knave, played his king, on which his partner discarded her singleton spade and then claimed the last two tricks with her remaining trumps. They had made a slam even though their opponents held every trick in spades.

Lady Barbara had shown that she could play a good hand well; later she proved that she could fight out a losing hand with equal brilliance. She watched every discard, noted every signal, finessed boldly when there was a chance of profit, returned her partner's leads and yet resolutely ignored them if her hand justified the risk; she played low from a sequence and led high. Not since the *Lydia* left England had Hornblower had such a good partner. In his pleasure at this discovery Hornblower quite forgot to have any qualms at the fact that here was a woman who could do something well.

And the next evening she displayed another accomplishment, when she brought out a guitar on to the quarterdeck and accompanied herself in the songs which she sang in a sweet soprano – so sweet that the crew came creeping aft and crouched to listen under the gangways and coughed and fidgeted sentimentally at the close of each song. Galbraith was her slave, and she could play on his musical heartstrings as on her guitar. The midshipmen loved her. Even the barnacle-encrusted officers like Bush and Crystal softened towards her, and Gerard flashed his brilliant smile at her and made play with his good looks and told her stories of his privateering days and of his slaving adventures up the African rivers. Hornblower watched Gerard anxiously during that voyage up the Nicaraguan coast, and cursed his own tone deafness which made Lady Barbara's singing not merely indifferent to him but almost painful.

XIII

The long volcanic coast line slid past them day after day. Every day brought its eternal panorama of blue sea and blue sky, of slaty-pink volcanic peaks and a fringing coast line of vivid green. With decks cleared for action and every man at his post they ran once more into the Gulf of Fonseca and sailed round the island of Manguera in search of the *Natividad,* but they did not find her. They saw no sign of life on the shores of the bay, either. Someone fired a musket at the ship from the cliffs of Manguera – the spent bullet thudded into the mainchains – but they did not see the man who fired it. Bush steered the *Lydia* out of the gulf again and north eastward in his search for the *Natividad*.

The *Natividad* was not to be found in the roadstead of La Libertad, nor in any of the little ports farther along. There was much smoke to be seen at Champerico, and Hornblower, training his glass upon it, could see that for once it was not volcanic. Champerico was in flames, so that presumably el Supremo's men had come there spreading enlightenment, but there was no sign of the *Natividad*.

Storms awaited them in the Gulf of Tehuantepec, for that corner of the Pacific is always stormy, lashed by the wind which blows hither from the Gulf of Mexico through a gap in the sierras. Hornblower was made aware of the change by an increase in the motion of the ship. She was rising and swooping more violently than usual and a gusty wind was heeling her sharply over. It was just eight bells, and the watch was being called; he could hear the bellowings of the master's mates – 'Show a leg! Show a leg! Lash up and stow! Lash up and stow!' – as he ran up to the quarterdeck. The sky was still blue overhead and the sun was hot, but the sea was grey, now, and running high, and the *Lydia* was beginning to labour under her press of sail.

'I was just sending down to you, sir, for permission to shorten sail,' said Bush.

Hornblower glanced up at the canvas, and over towards the clouds towards the coast.

'Yes. Get the courses and t'gallants off her,' he said.

The *Lydia* plunged heavily as he spoke, and then rose again, labouring, the water creaming under her bows. The whole ship was alive with the creaking of timber and the harping of the rigging. Under shortened sail she rode more easily, but the wind of her beam was growing stronger, and she was bowing down to it as she crashed over the waves. Looking round, Hornblower saw Lady Barbara standing with one hand on the taffrail. The wind was whipping her skirts about her, and with her other hand she was trying to restrain the curls that streamed round her head. Her cheeks were pink under their tan, and her eyes sparkled.

'You ought to be below, Lady Barbara,' he said.

'Oh no, Captain. This is too delicious after the heat we have been enduring.'

A shower of spray came rattling over the bulwarks and wetted them both.

'It is your health, ma'am, about which I am anxious.'

'If salt water was harmful sailors would die young.'

Her cheeks were bright as if she had been using cosmetics. Hornblower could refuse her nothing, even though he bitterly remembered how last evening she had sat in the shadow of the mizzen rigging talking so animatedly to Gerard that no one else had been able to profit by her society.

'Then you can stay on deck, ma'am, since you wish it, unless this gale increases – and I fancy it will.'

'Thank you, Captain,' she replied. There was a look in her eye which seemed to indicate that the question as to what would happen if the gale increased was not nearly as decided as the captain appeared to think – but like her great brother she crossed no bridges until she came to them.

Hornblower turned away; he would clearly have liked to have stayed there talking, with the spray pattering about them, but his duty was with his ship. As he reached the wheel there came a hail from the masthead.

'Sail ho! Deck, there, a sail right ahead. Looks like *Natividad*, sir.'

Hornblower gazed up. The lookout was clinging to his perch, being swung round and round in dizzy circles as the ship pitched and swooped over the waves.

'Up you go, Knyvett,' he snapped to the midshipman beside him. 'Take a glass with you and tell me what you can see.' He knew that he himself would be of no use as a lookout in that wild weather – he was ashamed of it, but he had to admit it to himself. Soon Knyvett's boyish voice came calling down to him through the gale.

'She's the *Natividad,* sir. I can see the cut of her tops'ls.'

'How's she heading?'

'On the starboard tack, sir, same course as us. Her masts are in one line. Now she's altering course, sir. She's wearing round. She must have seen us, sir. Now she's on the port tack, sir, heading up to wind'ard of us, close hauled, sir.'

'Oh, is she,' said Hornblower to himself, grimly. It was an unusual experience to have a Spanish ship face about and challenge action – but he remembered that she was a Spanish ship no longer. He would not allow her to get the weather gauge of him, come what might.

'Man the braces, there!' he shouted, and then to the man at the wheel: 'Port your helm. And mark ye, fellow, keep her as near the wind as she'll lie. Mr Bush, beat to quarters, if you please, and clear for action.'

As the drum rolled and the hands came pouring up he remembered the woman aft by the taffrail, and his stolid fatalism changed to anxiety.

'Your place is below, Lady Barbara,' he said. 'Take your maid with you. You must stay in the cockpit until the action is over – no, not the cockpit. Go to the cable tier.'

'Captain—,' she began, but Hornblower was not in the mood for argument – if indeed she had argument in mind.

'Mr Clay!' he rasped. 'Conduct her ladyship and her maid to the cable tier. See that she is safe before you leave her. Those are my *orders,* Mr Clay. Ha – h'm.'

A cowardly way out, perhaps, to throw on Clay the responsibility of seeing his orders carried out. He knew it, but he was angry with the woman because of the sick feeling of worry which she was occasioning him. She left him, nevertheless, with a smile and a wave of the hand, Clay trotting before her.

For several minutes the ship was a turmoil of industry as the men went through the well-learned drill. The guns were run out, the decks sanded, the horses rigged to the pumps, the fires extinguished, the bulkheads torn down. The *Natividad* could be seen from the deck now, sailing on the opposite tack towards her, obviously clawing her hardest up to windward to get the weather gauge. Hornblower looked up at the sails to mark the least shiver.

'Steer small, blast you,' he growled at the quartermaster.

The *Lydia* lay over before the gale, the waves crashing and hissing overside, the rigging playing a wild symphony. Last night she had been stealing peacefully over a calm and moonlit sea, and now here she was twelve hours later thrashing through a storm with a battle awaiting her. The wind was undoubtedly increasing, a wilder puff almost took her aback, and she staggered and rolled until the helmsman allowed her to pay off.

'*Natividad* won't be able to open her lower deck ports!' gloated Bush beside him. Hornblower stared across the grey sea at the enemy. He saw a cloud of spray break over her bows.

'No,' he said heavily. He would not discuss the possibilities of the approaching action for fear lest he might be too talkative. 'I'll trouble you, Mr Bush, to have two reefs taken in those tops'ls.'

On opposite tacks the ships were nearing each other along the sides of an obtuse angle. Look as closely as he would, he could not decide which ship would be to windward when they met at the apex.

'Mr Gerard,' he called down to the lieutenant in charge of the port side maindeck battery. 'See that the matches in your tubs are alight.'

'Aye aye, sir.'

With all this spray breaking aboard the flint lock trigger mechanism could not be relied upon until the guns grew hot and the old-fashioned method of ignition might have to be used – in the tubs on deck were coils of slow-match to meet this emergency. He stared across again at the *Natividad*. She, too, had reefed her topsail now, and was staggering along, closehauled, under storm canvas. She was flying the blue flag with the yellow star; Hornblower glanced up overhead to where the dingy white ensign fluttered from the peak.

'She's opened fire, sir,' said Bush beside him.

Hornblower looked back at the *Natividad* just in time to see the last of a puff of smoke blown to shreds by the wind. The sound of the shot did not reach them, and where the ball went no one could say – the jet of water which it struck up somewhere was hidden in the tossing waves.

'Ha – h'm,' said Hornblower.

It was bad policy, even with a well-drilled crew, to open fire at long range. That first broadside, discharged from guns loaded carefully and at leisure, and aimed by crews with time to think, was too precious a thing to be dissipated lightly. It should be saved up for use at the moment when it would do maximum harm, however great might be the strain of waiting inactive.

'We'll be passing mighty close, sir,' said Bush.

'Ha – h'm,' said Hornblower.

Still there was no means of telling which ship would hold the weather gauge when they met. It appeared as if they would meet bow to bow in collision if both captains held rigidly to their present courses. Hornblower had to exert all his willpower to keep himself standing still and apparently unemotional as the tension increased.

Another puff of smoke from the *Natividad's* starboard bow, and this time they heard the sound of the shot as it passed overhead between the masts.

'Closer!' said Bush.

Another puff, and simultaneously a crash from the waist told where the shot had struck.

'Two men down at number four gun,' said Bush, stooping to look forward under the gangway, and then, eyeing the distance between the two ships: 'Christ! It's going to be a near thing.'

It was a situation which Hornblower had visualised several times in his solitary walks on the quarterdeck. He took a last glance up at the weathervane, and at the topsails on the point of shivering as the ship tossed on the heaving sea.

'Stand by, Mr Rayner. Fire as your guns bear,' he called. Rayner was in command of the starboard side maindeck battery. Then, from the corner of his mouth to the men at the wheel – 'Put your helm a-weather. Catch her! Hold her so!'

The *Lydia* spun round and shot down the lee side of the *Natividad* and her starboard side guns went off almost simultaneously in a rolling crash that shook the ship to her keel. The billow of smoke that enveloped her momentarily was blown away instantly by the gale. Every shot crashed into the *Natividad's* side; the wind brought to their ears the screams of the wounded. So unexpected had the manoeuvre been that only one single shot was fired from the *Natividad*, and that did no damage – her lower deck ports on this, her lee side, were closed because of the high sea.

'Grand! Oh, grand!' said Bush. He sniffed at the bitter powder smoke eddying round him as if it had been sweet incense.

'Stand by to go about,' rasped Hornblower.

A well-drilled crew, trained in months of storms under Bush's eagle eye, was ready at sheets and braces. The *Lydia* tacked about, turning like a machine, before *Natividad* could offer any counter to this unexpected attack, and Gerard fired his battery into her helpless stern. The ship's boys were cheering aimlessly in high piping trebles as they came running up from below with new charges for the guns. On the starboard side the guns were already loaded; on the port side the guns' crews were thrusting wet swabs down the bore to extinguish any residual fragments of smouldering cartridge, ramming in the charges and shot, and heaving the guns up into firing position again. Hornblower stared across the tossing water at the *Natividad*. He could see Crespo up on her poop; the fellow actually had the insolence to wave his hand to him, airily, while in the midst of bellowing orders at his unhandy crew.

The *Lydia* had wrung the utmost advantage out of her manoeuvre; she had fired her two broadsides at close range and had only received a single shot in reply, but now she had to pay for it. By her possession of the weather gauge the *Natividad* could force close action for a space if resolutely handled. Hornblower could just see her rudder from where he stood. He saw it kick over, and next moment the two-decker had swung round and was hurtling down upon them. Gerard stood in the midst of his battery gazing with narrowed eyes into the wind at the impressive bulk close overside. His swarthy beauty was accentuated by the tenseness of the moment and the fierce concentration of his expression, but for once he was quite unconscious of his good looks.

'Cock your locks!' he ordered. 'Take your aim! Fire!'

The roar of the broadside coincided exactly with that of the *Natividad's*. The ship was enveloped in smoke, through which could be heard the rattling of splinters, the sound of cut rigging tumbling to the deck, and through it all Gerard's voice continuing with his drill – 'Stop your vents!' The quicker the touch holes of the muzzle loaders were plugged after firing the less would be the wear caused by the rush of the acid gases through them.

The guns' crews strained at the tackles as the heave of the ship bade fair to send them surging back against the ship's sides. They sponged and they rammed.

'Fire as you will, boys!' shouted Gerard. He was up on the hammock-netting now, gazing through the smoke wreaths at the *Natividad* rising and swooping alongside. The next broadside crashed out raggedly, and the next more raggedly still, as the more expert gun crews got off their shots more quickly than the others; soon the sound of firing was continuous, and the *Lydia* was constantly a-tremble. At intervals through the roar of her cannon came the thunderous crash of the *Natividad's* broadside – Crespo evidently could not trust his crew to fire independently with efficiency, and was working them to the word of command. He was doing it well, too; at intervals as the sea permitted, her lower deck ports were opening like clockwork and the big twenty-four pounders were vomiting flame and smoke.

'Hot work, this, sir,' said Bush.

The iron hail was sweeping the *Lydia's* decks. There were dead men piled round the masts, whither they had been hastily dragged so as not to encumber the guns' crews. Wounded men were being dragged along the deck and down the hatchways to where the horrors of the cockpit awaited them. As Hornblower looked he saw a powder boy flung across the deck, dissolved into a red inhuman mass as a twenty-four pounder ball hit him.

'Ha – h'm,' said Hornblower, but the sound was drowned in the roar of the quarterdeck carronade beside him. It was hot work indeed, too hot. This five minutes of close firing was sufficient to convince him that the *Natividad's* guns were too well worked for the *Lydia* to have any chance against her overpowering strength broadside to broadside, despite the damage done in the first few minutes of the action. He would have to win by craft if he was to win at all.

'Hands to the braces!' he yelled, his voice, high-pitched, cutting through the din of the guns. He stared narrow-eyed at the *Natividad* with the smoke pouring from her sides, he estimated the force of the wind and the speeds of the ships. His mind was making calculations with delirious rapidity, keyed up by the excitement, as he began the new manoeuvre. Throwing the main topsail aback a trifle allowed the *Natividad* to shoot ahead without taking so much way off the *Lydia* to go about again, but even as the sheets were handed and the tacked his ship about so that the waiting starboard battery was able to fire into the *Natividad's* stern. The *Natividad* came up into the wind in the endeavour to follow her opponent round and keep broad-side to broadside with her, but the frigate was far quicker in stays than the clumsy, stumpy two-decker. Hornblower, watching his enemy with his keen gaze, tacked once more, instantly, and shot past the *Natividad's* stern on the opposite tack while Gerard, running from gun to gun, sent every shot crashing into the shattered timbers.

'Glorious! Damme! Damn my eyes! Damn my soul! Glorious!' spluttered Bush, thumping his right fist into his left hand and leaping up and down on the quarterdeck.

Hornblower had no attention to spare for Bush nor for Bush's good opinion, although later he was to remember hearing the words and find warm comfort in them. As the ships diverged he shouted for the *Lydia* to go about again, but even as the sheets were handed and the helm put over the *Natividad* wore round to pass her to leeward. So much the better. At the cost of a single exchange of broadsides he would be able to assail that vulnerable stern again, and if the *Natividad* attempted to circle, his was the handier ship and he could rely on getting in at least two effective shots to his opponent's one. He watched the *Natividad* come foaming up; her bulwarks were riddled with shot and there was a trickle of blood from her scuppers. He caught a glimpse of Crespo on the poop – he had hoped that he might have been killed in the last two broadsides, for that would mean, almost for certain, a slackening in the attack. But her guns were run out ready, and on this, her weather side, her lower deck ports were open.

'For what we are about to receive—,' said Bush, repeating the hackneyed old blasphemy quoted in every ship awaiting a broadside.

Seconds seemed as long as minutes as the two ships neared. They were passing within a dozen yards of each other. Bow overlapped bow, foremast passed foremast and then foremast passed mainmast. Rayner was looking aft, and as soon as he saw that the aftermost gun bore on the target he shouted the order to fire. The *Lydia* lifted to the recoil of the guns, ears were split with the sound of the discharge, and then, even before the gale had time to blow away the smoke, came the *Natividad's* crashing reply.

It seemed to Hornblower as if the heavens were falling round him. The wind of a shot made him reel; he found at his feet a palpitating red mass which represented half the starboard side carronade's crew, and then with a thunderous crackling the mizzen mast gave way beside him. The weather mizzen rigging entangled him and flung him down into the blood on the deck, and while he struggled to free himself he felt the *Lydia* swing round as she paid off despite the efforts of the men at the wheel.

He got to his feet, dizzy and shaken, to find ruin all round him. The mizzen mast was gone, snapped off nine feet from the deck, taking the main top gallant mast with it, and masts and yards and sails and rigging trailed alongside and astern by the unparted shrouds. With the loss of the balancing pressure of the mizzen topsail the *Lydia* had been unable to keep her course on the wind and was now drifting helplessly dead before the gale. And at that very moment he saw the *Natividad* going about to cross his stern and repay, with a crushing broadside, the several unanswered salvoes to which earlier she had been forced to submit. His whole world seemed to be shattered. He gulped convulsively, with a sudden sick fear of defeat at the pit of his stomach.

XIV

But he knew, and he told himself, at the moment of his getting to his feet, that he must not delay an instant in making the *Lydia* ready for action again.

'Afterguard!' he roared – his voice sounding unnatural to himself as he spoke – 'Mr Clay! Benskin! Axes here! Cut that wreckage away!'

Clay came pounding aft at the head of a rush of men with axes and cutlasses. As they were chopping at the mizzen shrouds he noticed Bush sitting up on the deck with his face in his hands – apparently a falling block had struck him down but there was no time to spare for Bush. The *Natividad* was coming down remorselessly on them; he could see exultant figures on her deck waving their hats in triumph. To his strained senses it seemed to him that even through the din on board the *Lydia* he could hear the creaking of *Natividad's* rigging and the rumble of her reloaded guns being run out. She was steering to pass as close as possible. Hornblower saw her bowsprit go by, felt her reefed fore topsail loom over him, and then her broadside crashed out as gun after gun bore on the *Lydia's* stern. The wind caught the smoke and whipped it round Hornblower, blinding him. He felt the deck leap as the shots struck home, heard a scream from Clay's party beside him, felt a splinter scream past his cheek, and then, just as annihilation seemed about to engulf him, the frightful succession of shots ended, the smoke was borne away, the *Natividad* had gone by, and he was still alive and could look round him. The slide of the aftermost carronade had been smashed, and one of Clay's men was lying screaming on the deck with the gun across his thighs and two or three of his mates striving futilely to prise it off them.

'Stop that!' screamed Hornblower – the necessity of having to give such an order sent his voice up to the same pitch as that of the miserable wretch in his agony – 'Cut that bloody wreckage away! Mr Clay, keep them at work!'

A cable's length away, over the grey topped waves the *Natividad* was slowly wearing round to return and deal a fresh blow at her helpless opponent. It was lucky that the *Natividad* was an unhandy ship, like all those stumpy fourth rates – it gave Hornblower more time between the broadsides to try and get the *Lydia* into a condition so that she could face her enemy again.

'Foretop, there! Mr Galbraith! get the headsails in.'

'Aye aye, sir.'

The absence of the fore-topmast-staysail and storm jib would balance to some extent the loss of the mizzen topsail and driver. He might, by juggling with the helm, get the *Lydia* to lie to the wind a trifle then, and hit back at his big opponent. But there was no hope of doing so while all this wreckage was trailing astern like a vast sea anchor. Until that was cut away she could only lie helpless, dead before the wind, suffering her enemy's blows in silence. A glance showed him that the *Natividad* had worn round now, and was heading to cross their stern again.

'Hurry up!' he screamed to the axe men. 'You, there, Holroyd, Tooms, get down into the mizzen chains.'

He suddenly realised how high-pitched and hysterical his voice had become. At all costs he must preserve before Clay and the men his reputation for imperturbability. He forced himself convulsively, to look casually at the *Natividad* as she came plunging down on them again, wicked with menace; he made himself grin, and shrug his shoulders, and speak in his normal voice.

'Don't mind about her, my lads. One thing at a time. Cut this wreckage away first, and we'll give the Dagoes their bellyful after.'

The men hacked with renewed force at the tough tangles of cordage. Something gave way, and a new extravagant plunge on the part of the *Lydia* as a huge wave lifted her stern caused the wreckage to run out a little farther before catching again, this time on the mizzen stay, which, sweeping the deck, tumbled three men off their feet. Hornblower seized one of the fallen axes, and fell desperately on the rope as it sawed back and forth with the roll of the ship. From the tail of his eye he saw the *Natividad* looming up, but he could spare no attention for her. For the moment she represented merely a tiresome interruption to his work, not a menace to his life.

Then once more he was engulfed in the smoke and din of the *Natividad's* broadside. He felt the wind of shot round him, and heard the scream of splinters. The cries of the man under the carronade ceased abruptly, and beneath his feet he could feel the crash as the shot struck home in the *Lydia's* vitals. But he was mesmerised by the necessity of completing his task. The mizzen stay parted under his axe; he saw another rope draw up taut, and cut that as well – the pattern of the seams of the deck planking at that point caught his notice – felt another severed and flick past him, and then knew that the *Lydia* was free from the wreckage. Almost at his feet lay young Clay, sprawled upon the deck, but Clay had no head. He noted that as an interesting phenomenon, like the pattern of the deck seams.

A sudden breaking wave drenched him with spray; he swept the water from his eyes and looked about him. Most of the men who had been on the quarterdeck with him were dead, marines, seamen, officers. Simmonds had what was left of the marines lined up against the taffrail, ready to reply with musketry to the *Natividad's* twenty-four pounders. Bush was in the main top, and Hornblower suddenly realised that to him was due the cutting of the mizzen top mast stay which had finally freed the ship. At the wheel stood the two quartermasters, rigid, unmoving, gazing straight ahead; they were not the same as the men who had stood there when the action began, but the iron discipline of the Navy and its unbending routine had kept the wheel manned through the vicissitudes of the battle.

Out on the starboard quarter the *Natividad* was wearing round again. Hornblower realised with a little thrill that this time he need not submit meekly to the punishment she was determined to adminster. It called for an effort to make himself work out the problem of how to work the ship round, but he forced his mind to concentrate on it, comparing the proportional leverages of the fore and main topsails, and visualising in his mind the relative positions of the centre of the ship and the mainmast – luckily this latter was stepped a little aft.

'Man the braces, there!' he called. 'Mr Bush, we'll try and bring her to the wind.'

'Aye aye, sir.'

He looked back at the *Natividad,* plunging and heaving towards them.

'Hard-a-starboard!' he snapped at the quartermaster. 'Stand to your guns, men.'

The crew of the *Natividad,* looking along their guns, suddenly saw the *Lydia's* battered stern slowly turn from them. For a fleeting half minute, while the English frigate held her way, the quartermasters straining at her wheel were able to bring the wind abeam of her as the *Natividad* swept by.

'Fire!' yelled Gerard – his voice, too, was cracking with excitement.

The *Lydia* heaved again with the recoil of the guns, and the smoke billowed over her deck, and through the smoke came the iron hail of the *Natividad's* broadside.

'Give it her again, lads!' screamed Gerard. 'There goes her fore-mast! Well done, lads.'

The guns' crews cheered madly, even though their two hundred voices sounded feeble against the gale. In that sudden flurry of action the enemy had been hard hit. Through the smoke Hornblower saw the *Natividad's* fore-mast shrouds suddenly slacken, tauten again, slacken once more, and then her whole foremast bowed forward; her main topmast whipped and then followed it, and the whole vanished over the side. The *Natividad* turned instantly up into the wind, while at the same time the *Lydia's* head fell off as she turned downwind despite the efforts of the men at the wheel. The gale screamed past Hornblower's ears as the strip of grey sea which divided the ships widened more and more. One last gun went off on the main deck, and then the two ships lay pitching upon the turbulent sea, each unable to harm the other.

Hornblower wiped the spray slowly from his eyes again. This battle was like some long drawn nightmare, where one situation of fantastic unreality merged into the next. He felt as if he were in a nightmare, too – he could think clearly, but only by compelling himself to do so, as though it was unnatural to him.

The gap between the ships had widened to a full half mile, and was widening further. Through his glass he could see the *Natividad's* forecastle black with men struggling with the wreck of the foremast. The ship which was first ready for action again would win. He snapped the glass shut and turned to face all the problems which he knew were awaiting his immediate solution.

XV

The captain of the *Lydia* stood on his quarterdeck while his ship, hove to under the main staysail and three-reefed main topsail, pitched and wallowed in the fantastic sea. It was raining now, with such violence that nothing could be seen a hundred yards away, and there were deluges of spray sweeping the deck, too, so that he and his clothes were as wet as if he had been swimming in the sea, but he was not aware of it. Everyone was appealing to him for orders – first lieutenant, gunner, boatswain, carpenter, surgeon, purser. The ship had to be made fit to fight again, even though there was every doubt as to whether she would even live through the storm which shrieked round her. It was the acting-surgeon who was appealing to him at the moment.

'But what am I to *do,* sir?' he said pathetically, white faced, wringing his hands. This was Laurie, the purser's steward, who had been appointed acting-surgeon when Hankey the surgeon died. He had fifty wounded down in the grim dark cockpit, maddened with pain, some with limbs torn off, and all of them begging for the assistance which he had no idea of how to give.

'What are you to *do,* sir?' mimicked Hornblower scornfully, beside himself with exasperation at this incompetence. 'After two months in which to study your duties you have to ask what to do!'

Laurie only blenched a little more at this, and Hornblower had to make himself be a little helpful and put some heart in this lily-livered incompetent.

'See here, Laurie,' he said, in more kindly fashion. 'Nobody expects miracles of you. Do what you can. Those who are going to die you must make easy. You have my orders to reckon every man who has lost a limb as one of those. Give them laudanum – twenty-five drops a man, or more if that won't ease them. Pretend to bandage 'em. Tell 'em they're certain to get better and draw a pension for the next fifty years. As for the others, surely your mother wit can guide you. Bandage 'em until the bleeding stops. You have rags enough to bandage the whole ship's crew. Put splints on the broken bones. Don't move any man more than is necessary. Keep every man quiet. A tot of rum to every wounded man, and promise 'em another at eight bells if they lie still. I never knew a Jack yet who wouldn't go through hell fire for a tot of rum. Get below, man, and see to it.'

'Aye aye, sir.'

Laurie could only think of his own responsibility and duty; he scuttled away below without a thought for the hell-turned-loose on the main deck. Here one of the twelve-pounders had come adrift, its breechings shot away by the *Natividad's* last broadside. With every roll of the ship it was rumbling back and forth across the deck, a ton and a half of insensate weight, threatening at any moment to burst through the ship's side. Galbraith, with twenty men trailing ropes, and fifty men carrying mats and hammocks, was trailing it cautiously from point to point in the hope of tying it or smothering it into helplessness. As Hornblower watched them, a fresh heave of the ship canted it round and sent it thundering in a mad charge straight at them. They parted wildly before it, and it charged through them, its trucks squealing like a forest of pigs, and brought up with a shattering crash against the mainmast.

'Now's your chance, lads! Jump to it!' yelled Hornblower.

Galbraith, running forward, risked limb and life to pass a rope's end through an eye tackle. Yet he had no sooner done it than a new movement of the ship swung the gun round and threatened to waste his effort.

'Hammocks, there!' shouted Hornblower. 'Pile them quick! Mr Galbraith, take a turn with that line round the mainmast. Whipple, put your rope through the breeching ring. Quick, man! Now take a turn!'

Hornblower had accomplished what Galbraith had failed to do – had correlated the efforts of the men in the nick of time so that now the gun was bound and helpless. There only remained the ticklish job of manoeuvring it back to its gun port and securing it with fresh breechings. Howell the carpenter was at his elbow now, waiting until he could spare a moment's attention from this business with the gun.

'Four feet an' more in the well, sir,' said Howell, knuckling his forehead. 'Nearer five, an' making fast as well as I could tell. Can I have some more men for the pumps, sir?'

'Not until that gun's in place,' said Hornblower, grimly. 'What damage have you found?'

'Seven shot holes, sir, below water line. There's no pluggin' of 'em not with this sea runnin', sir.'

'I know that,' snapped Hornblower. 'Where are they?'

'All of 'em for'rard, somehow, sir. One clean through the third frame timber, starboard side. Two more—'

'I'll have a sail forthered under the bottom as soon as there are enough men to spare. Your men at the pumps will have to continue pumping. Report to the first lieutenant's party with your mates now.'

The first lieutenant and the boatswain were busily engaged upon the duty of erecting a jury mizzen mast. Already the boatswain had come ruefully to the captain with the information that half the spare spars secured between the gangways had been damaged by shot, but there was a main topsail yard left which would serve. But to sway up its fifty-five foot length into a vertical position was going to be a tricky business – hard enough in a smooth sea, dangerous and prolonged out here with the Pacific running mad. In harbour an old ship – a sheer hulk – would be brought alongside, and would employ the two immense spars which constituted her sheers as a crane in which to lift the new mast vertically into the ship. Here there was nothing of the sort available, and the problem of raising the spar might seem insoluble, but Bush and Harrison between them were tackling it with all the resource and energy the navy could display.

Happily there was that stump of the old mizzen mast left – its nine feet of length relieved them of the tiresome complication of steeping the new mast, which they proposed instead merely to fish to the stump. The after part of the ship was alive with working parties each intent on its own contribution to the work in hand. With tackles and rollers the spar had been eased aft until its butt was solidly against the stump of the mizzen mast. Harrison was now supervising the task of noosing shrouds to the new masthead; after that he would have to prepare the masthead to receive the cap and the trussel trees which the carpenter and his mates would now have to make.

In the mizzen chains on either side Harrison's mates were supervising the efforts of two other parties engaged upon attaching the other ends of the shrouds to the channels, where with dead eyes and lanyards the shrouds could be kept taut as the mast rose. Bush was attending to the preparation of the jears and tackle at the mainmast which would help to accomplish a great part of the lift; the sailmaker and his mates were rousing out and adapting sails to fit the new mast, gaff, and yards. Another party of men under the gunner was engaged on the difficult task of remounting the dismounted quarterdeck carronade, while Gerard was aloft with the topmen attending to the repair of the damage done to the standing and running rigging of the remaining masts. All this was in the rain, with the wind shrieking round them; and yet the rain and the wind seemed warm to the touch, so oppressively hot was it. The half-naked seamen, slaving at their task, were running wet with sweat as well as with rainwater and spray. The ship was a nightmare of insane yet ordered activity.

A sudden flurry of rain heralded the arrival of a clear spell. Braced upon the heaving deck Hornblower set his glass to his eye; the *Natividad* was visible again, hull down now, across the tossing grey-flecked sea. She was hove-to as well, looking queerly lopsided in her partially dismasted condition. Hornblower's glass could discover no sign of any immediate replacement of the missing spars; he thought it extremely probable that there was nothing left in the ship to serve as jury masts. In that case as soon as the *Lydia* could carry enough sail aft to enable her to beat to windward he would have the *Natividad* at his mercy – as long as the sea was not running high enough to make gunnery impossible.

He glowered round the horizon; at present there was no sign of the storm abating, and it was long past noon. With the coming of night he might lose the *Natividad* altogether, and nightfall would give his enemy a further respite in which to achieve repairs.

'How much longer, Mr Harrison?' he rasped.

'Not long now, sir. Nearly ready, sir.'

'You've had long enough and to spare for a simple piece of work like that. Keep the men moving, there.'

'Aye aye, sir.'

Hornblower knew that the men were cursing him under their breath; he did not know they admired him as well, as men will admire a hard master despite themselves.

Now it was the cook come to report to him – the cook and his mates had been the only men in the ship who could be spared for the grisly work allotted to them.

'All ready, sir,' he said.

Without a word Hornblower strode forward down the starboard side gangway, taking his prayer book from his pocket. The fourteen dead were there, shrouded in their hammocks, two to a grating, a roundshot sewn into the foot of each hammock. Hornblower blew a long blast upon his silver whistle, and activity ceased on board while he read, compromising between haste and solemnity, the office for the burial of the dead at sea.

'We therefore commit their bodies to the deep—'

The cook and his mates tilted each grating in turn, and the bodies fell with sullen splashes overside while Hornblower read the concluding words of the service. As soon as the last words were said he blew his whistle again and all the bustle and activity recommenced. He grudged those few minutes taken from the work bitterly, but he knew that any unceremonious pitching overboard of the dead would be resented by his men, who set all the store by forms and ceremonies to be expected of the uneducated.

And now there was something else to plague him. Picking her way across the maindeck below him came Lady Barbara, the little negress clinging to her skirts.

'My orders were for you to stay below, ma'am,' he shouted to her. 'This deck is no place for you.'

Lady Barbara looked round the seething deck and then tilted her chin to answer him.

'I can see that without having it pointed out to me,' she said, and then, softening her manner: 'I have no intention of obstructing, Captain. I was going to shut myself in my cabin.'

'Your cabin?'

Hornblower laughed. Four broadsides from the *Natividad* had blasted their way through that cabin. The idea of Lady Barbara shutting herself up there struck him as being intensely funny. He laughed again, and then again, before checking himself in hurried mistrust as an abyss of hysteria opened itself before him. He controlled himself.

'There is no cabin left for you, ma'am. I regret that the only course open to you is to go back whence you have come. There is no other place in the ship that can accommodate you at present.'

Lady Barbara, looking up at him, thought of the cable tier she had just left. Pitch dark, with only room to sit hunched up on the slimy cable, rats squeaking and scampering over her legs; the ship pitching and rolling madly, and Hebe howling with fright beside her; the tremendous din of the guns, and the thunderous rumble of the gun trucks immediately over her head as the guns were run in and out; the tearing crash which had echoed through the ship when the mizzen mast fell; the ignorance of how the battle was progressing – at this very moment she was still unaware whether it had been lost or won or merely suspended: the stench of the bilge, the hunger and the thirst.

The thought of going back there appalled her. But she saw the captain's face, white with fatigue and strain under its tan, and she had noted that laugh with its hysterical pitch, abruptly cut off, and the grim effort that had been made to speak to her reasonably. The captain's coat was torn across the breast, and his white trousers were stained – with blood, she suddenly realised. She felt pity for him, then. She knew now that to speak to him of rats and stinks and baseless fears would be ridiculous.

'Very good, Captain,' she said quietly, and turned to retrace her steps.

The little negress set up a howl, and was promptly shaken into silence as Lady Barbara dragged her along.

XVI

'Ready now, sir,' said Bush.

The crew of the *Lydia* had worked marvellously. The guns were all secured now, and the main deck cleared of most of the traces of the fight. A sail stretched over the bottom of the ship had done much to check the inflow of water, so that now only twenty men were at work upon the pumps and the level in the well was measurably sinking. The sailmaster had his new sails ready, the boatswain his rigging, the carpenter his accessories. Already Harrison had his men at the windlass, and the mast lay ready for hoisting.

Hornblower looked round him. All the mad effort put into the work to get it done speedily was wasted, for the gale still showed no signs of abating and with this present wind blowing it would be hopeless to try to beat over to the *Natividad*. He had driven his men hard – overdriven them – to lose no time, and now it was obvious that they might have done it all at their leisure. But the work might as well be completed now. He ran his eye over the waiting groups of men; each knew their duty, and there was an officer at each strategic point to see that orders were carried out.

'Very good, Mr Bush,' he said.

'Hoist away, there!' yelled Bush to the windlass crew.

The windlass began to turn, the rope began to groan through the jears, and the mast rose, little by little, watched by every eye. The mad plunges of the ship threatened to ruin everything. There was danger of the masthead escaping from the ropes that held it; there was danger of the butt slipping away from the stump of the mizzen mast against which it rested. Everything had to be watched, every precaution taken, to see that neither of these possibilities developed. Bush watched the jears, while Gerard at the main masthead attended to the slings. Galbraith was in the mizzen chains on one side, Rayner on the other. Boatswain and carpenter stood with ropes and spars at the butt end of the mast, but it was the captain, leaning on the quarterdeck rail, whose duty it was to see that every part of the cumbrous machine did its work in its proper relation to the others. It was he whom the crew would blame for failure.

He knew it, too. He watched the dizzy heave and pitch of the ship, and the masthead wavering in the slings, and he heard the butt end grinding upon the deck as it moved uneasily between the two spars lashed as buttresses against the stump of the mizzen mast. It was an effort to think clearly, and he could only compel his mind to it by an exertion of all his will. He was sick and tired and nervous.

It was of vital importance that the hands at the shrouds and backstays only took up as much slack as was won for them by the jears, and refrained from tightening up when a roll of the ship swung the mast over on their side a trifle. Yet this was just what they persisted in doing, maddeningly, so obsessed were they with the necessity of keeping all taut to prevent the swaying mast from taking charge. Twice the grip of the slings on the masthead was imperilled in this way, and Hornblower had to key himself up to his highest pitch for several seconds, watching the roll of the ship, so as to time precisely the next heave which would obviate the danger. His voice was hoarse with shouting.

Slowly the mast left the horizontal and swayed up towards the perpendicular. Hornblower's calculating eye, measuring stresses and reactions, saw that the crisis was now come – the moment when the jears could raise the masthead no more and the final lifting must be accomplished by the pull of the backstays aft. The next few moments were tricky ones, because the masthead would not be deprived of the positive support of the slings. The jears had to be disconnected from the windlass and their work done by the backstays. Two lengths of cable had to be passed round the sloping jury mast and the vertical stump, with gangs of men ready to tighten them, tourniquet fashion, with capstan bars as each gain was made. Yet in these first seconds the backstays were at a mechanical disadvantage and would certainly not bear the strain which would be imposed on them if the windlass were employed in an endeavour to drag the mast upright by brute force.

The motion of the ship must be utilised to help. Hornblower had to watch the motion carefully, calling to the men to wait as the ship rolled and plunged, and then, as the bow slowly emerged from the creaming sea and climbed steadily skywards, he had to set windlass men and tourniquet men and lanyard men all in action at once, and then check them all instantly as the bow began to sink again and full strain came on to the rigging. Twice he managed it successfully, and then three times – although the third time an unexpected wave lifted the *Lydia's* stern at the wrong moment and nearly wrecked everything.

Then the fourth heave settled it all. The mast was now so nearly vertical that shrouds and backstays were at a mechanical advantage, and everything could be hove taut regardless of the ship's motion. Shrouds and backstays could be set up now in normal fashion, the jury mast adequately fished to the stump – in fact all the difficult part of the work was completed. Hornblower leaned against the rail, sick with weariness, wondering dully how these ironframed men of his could find the strength to cheer as they put the finishing touches to their work.

He found Bush beside him – Bush had a rag round his head, bloodstained because of the cut in his forehead inflicted by the falling block.

'A magnificent piece of work, if I may say so, sir,' he said.

Hornblower eyed him sharply, suspicious as ever of congratulation, knowing his own weakness so well. But Bush, surprisingly, seemed to mean in all sincerity what he said.

'Thank you,' said Hornblower, grudgingly.

'Shall I send up the topmast and yards, sir?'

Hornblower looked round the horizon once more. The gale was blowing as madly as ever, and only a grey smudge on the distant horizon marked where the *Natividad* was battling with it. Hornblower could see that there was no chance of showing any more canvas at present, no chance of renewing the fight while the *Natividad* was still unprepared. It was a bitter pill to swallow. He could imagine what would be said in service circles when he sent in his report to the Admiralty. His statement that the weather was too bad to renew the action, after having received such a severe handling, would be received with pitying smiles and knowing wags of the head. It was a hackneyed excuse, like the uncharted rock which explained faulty navigation. Cowardice, moral or even perhaps physical, would be the unspoken comment on every side – at ten thousand miles distance no one could judge of the strength of a storm. He could divest himself of some of his responsibility by asking Bush his opinion, and requesting him to go through the formality of putting it in writing; but he turned irritably from the thought of displaying weakness before his inferior.

'No,' he said, without expression. 'We shall stay hove-to until the weather moderates.'

There was a gleam of admiration in Bush's bloodshot eyes – Bush could well admire a captain who could make with such small debate a decision so nearly touching his professional reputation. Hornblower noticed it, but his cursed temperament forbade him to interpret it correctly.

'Aye aye, sir,' said Bush, warned by the scowl on his captain's forehead not to enlarge on the subject. But his affection for his captain compelled him to open a fresh one. 'If that's the case, sir, why not take a rest? You look mortally tired, sir, indeed you do. Let me send and have a berth screened off for you in the ward room.'

Bush found his hand twitching – he had been about to commit the enormity of patting his captain's shoulder, and restrained himself just in time.

'Fiddlesticks!' snapped Hornblower. As if a captain of a frigate could publicly admit that he was tired! And Hornblower could not trust himself to show any weakness at all – he always remembered how on his first commission his second-in-command had taken advantages of lapses on his part.

'It is rather you who need a rest,' said Hornblower. 'Dismiss the starboard watch, and go below and turn in. Have someone attend to that forehead of yours, first. With the enemy in sight I shall stay on deck.'

After that it was Polwheal who came to plague him – Hornblower wondered ineffectively whether he came of his own initiative or whether Bush sent him up.

'I've been to attend to the lady, sir,' said Polwheal; Hornblower's tired mind was just beginning to grapple with the problem of what to do with Lady Barbara in a damaged ship cleared for action. 'I've screened off a bit of the orlop for her, sir. The wounded's mostly quiet by now, sir. I slung a 'ammock for her – nipped into it like a bird, she did, sir. She's taken food, too, sir – what was left of that cold chicken an' a glass of wine. Not that she wanted to, sir, but I persuaded her, like.'

'Very good, Polwheal,' said Hornblower. It was an enormous relief to hear that one responsibility at least was lifted from his shoulders.

'An' now about you, sir,' went on Polwheal. 'I've got you up some dry clothes from your chest in your storeroom, sir – I'm afraid that last broadside spoilt everything in your cabin, sir. An' I've got your boat cloak, sir, all warm an' dry. Do you care to shift your clothes up here or down below, sir?'

Polwheal could take much for granted and could wheedle the rest. Hornblower had anticipated dragging his weary form in his water-logged clothes up and down the quarterdeck all through the night, his nervous irritation not permitting him to contemplate any other course. Polwheal unearthed Lady Barbara's hammock chair from somewhere and lashed it to the rail and persuaded Hornblower to sit in it and consume a supper of biscuit and rum. Polwheal draped the boat cloak about him and airily took it for granted that he would continue to sit there, since his determination was fixed not to turn in while the enemy was still close at hand.

And marvellously, as he sat there, with the spray wetting his face and the ship leaping and rolling under him, his head drooped upon his breast and he slept. It was only a broken and fitful sleep, but astonishingly restorative. He awoke every few minutes. Twice it was the sound of his own snores which roused him. At other times he woke with a start to see whether the weather was moderating; at other times still the thoughts which went running on through his mind despite his dozing called him out of his unconsciousness when they reached some fresh startling conclusion regarding what opinion England and his crew would hold of him after this battle.

Soon after midnight his sailor's instinct called him definitely into complete wakefulness. Something was happening to the weather. He scrambled stiffly to his feet. The ship was rolling more wildly than ever, but as he sniffed round him he knew that there was an improvement. He walked across to the binnacle, and Bush looked vastly out of the darkness beside him.

'Wind's shifting southerly an' moderating, sir,' said Bush.

The shift of the wind was breaking up the long Pacific waves into steeper seas, as the *Lydia's* antics displayed well enough.

'Black as the Earl of Hell's riding boots, all the same, sir,' grumbled Bush, peering into the darkness.

Somewhere, perhaps twenty miles from them, perhaps only two hundred yards, the *Natividad* was combating the same gale. If the moon were to break through the scurrying clouds they might be at grips with her at any moment, yet while they were talking it was so dark that they could hardly make out the loom of the main topsail from the quarterdeck.

'She was going away to leeward much faster than us when we saw her last,' said Bush meditatively.

'I happened to notice that myself,' snapped Hornblower.

In this present darkness, however much the gale might moderate, there was nothing they could do. Hornblower could foresee, awaiting them, another of those long intervals of time with nothing to do and everything ready which punctuate the life of a naval officer and which were so liable to irritate him if he allowed them to. He realised that here was another opportunity to show himself as an iron-nerved man whom no tension could disturb. He yawned elaborately.

'I think I shall got to sleep again,' he said, speaking with the utmost unconcern. 'See that the lookouts keep awake, if you please, Mr Bush. And have me called as soon as it grows lighter.'

'Aye aye, sir,' said Bush, and Hornblower went back to his boat cloak and his hammock chair.

He lay there for the rest of the night, unsleeping, and yet staying rigidly still so that the quarterdeck officers might think him asleep and admire the steadiness of his nerves. His mind was busy on the task of guessing what Crespo might be planning in the *Natividad*.

The latter was so badly crippled that probably he would be able to make no effective repairs while at sea. It would be much to his advantage to make for the Gulf of Fonseca again. There he could step a foremast and send up a new main topmast. If the *Lydia* tried to interfere with her there she could overwhelm her by her superior weight in those confined waters; and besides, she would have the assistance of shore boats and possibly even of shore batteries. Moreover he could land his wounded and refill the gaps in his crew caused by the recent action – even landsmen would be of use in a fight to a finish. Crespo was a man of sufficient flexibility of mind not to scorn a retreat if it were to his advantage. The doubtful point was whether Crespo would dare to face el Supremo after an unsuccessful action.

Hornblower lay considering the matter, balancing his estimate of Crespo's character against what he knew of el Supremo. He remembered Crespo's glibness of tongue; that man would be able to convince even el Supremo that his return to his base with the *Lydia* undefeated was all part of a cunning plan for the more certain destruction of the enemy. Certainly his best course would be to return, and probably that would be the course he would adopt, and that course implied an attempted evasion of the *Lydia*. In that case he would – Hornblower's mind began feverish calculations of the *Natividad's* present position and future course. In consequence of her bigger bulk, and her two decks, she would have made far more leeway during the night – she was far to leeward at nightfall, for that matter. With the wind shifting and moderating as it was doing at present she would soon be able to make what sail her crippled condition would permit. The wind would be nearly foul for a run to the Gulf of Fonseca. Making for the mainland would be dangerous in Crespo's opinion, for the *Lydia* could hem her in between sea and shore and compel her to fight. Most likely he would reach far out to sea, clawing southward at the same time as much as he could, and make for the Gulf of Fonseca by a long detour out of sight of land. In that case Hornblower must guess at what would be his position at dawn. He plunged into further tortuous mental calculations.

Eight bells sounded; the watch was called; he heard Gerard come to take over the deck from Bush. The wind was dropping fast, although the sea showed no sign of moderating as yet. The sky as he looked up at it was perceptibly lighter – here and there he could see stars between the clouds. Crespo would certainly be able to make sail now and attempt his escape. It was time for Hornblower to come to a decision. He climbed out of the hammock chair and walked across to the wheel.

'We will make sail, if you please, Mr Bush.'

'Aye aye, sir.'

Hornblower gave the course, and he knew as he gave it that it might be quite the wrong one. He might have completely miscalculated. Every yard that the *Lydia* was sailing now might be in a direction away from the *Natividad*. Crespo might at this very moment be heading past him to safety. He might never destroy the *Natividad* at all if she fortified herself in the Gulf of Fonseca. There would be some who would attribute his failure to incompetence, and there would be not a few who would call it cowardice.

XVII

From the *Lydia's* masthead, in the clear daylight of the Pacific, a ship might be seen at a distance of as much as twenty miles, perhaps. A circle of twenty miles' radius, therefore, covered the extent of sea over which she had observation. It kept Hornblower occupied, during the remaining hours of darkness, to calculate the size of the circle in which the *Natividad* would necessarily be found next morning. She might be close at hand; she might be as much as a hundred and fifty miles away. That meant that if pure chance dictated the positions of the ships at dawn, it was almost exactly fifty to one against the *Natividad* being in sight; fifty to one on the ruin of Hornblower's professional reputation and only his professional abilities to counterbalance those odds. Only if he had guessed his enemy's plans correctly would he stand justified, and his officers knew it as well as he. Hornblower was conscious that Gerard was looking at him with interest through the darkness, and the consciousness caused him to hold himself rigid and immobile on the deck, neither walking up and down nor fidgeting, even though he could feel his heart beating faster each time he realised that dawn was approaching.

The blackness turned to grey. Now the outlines of the ship could be ascertained. The main topsail could be seen clearly. So could the fore topsail. Astern of them now the faintest hint of pink began to show in the greyness of the sky. Now the bulk of the grey waves overside could be seen as well as their white edges. Overhead by now the stars were invisible. The accustomed eye could pierce the greyness for a mile about the ship. And then astern, to the eastward, as the *Lydia* lifted on a wave, a grain of gold showed over the horizon, vanished, returned, and grew. Soon it became a great slice of the sun, sucking up greedily the faint mist which hung over the sea. Then the whole disk lifted clear, and the miracle of the dawn was accomplished.

'Sail ho!' came pealing down from the masthead; Hornblower had calculated aright.

Dead ahead, and ten miles distant, she was wallowing along, her appearance oddly at contrast with the one she had presented yesterday morning. Something had been done to give her a jury rig. A stumpy topmast had been erected where her foremast had stood, raked far back in clumsy fashion; her main topmast had been replaced by a slight spar – a royal mast, presumably – and on this jury rig she carried a queer collection of jibs and foresails and spritsails all badly set – 'Like old Mother Brown's washing on the line,' said Bush – to enable her to keep away from the wind with main course and mizzen topsail and driver set.

At sight of the *Lydia* she put her helm over and came round until her masts were in line, heading away from the frigate.

'Making a stern chase of it,' said Gerard, his glass to his eye. 'He had enough yesterday, I fancy.'

Hornblower heard the remark. He could understand Crespo's psychology better than that. If it were profitable to him to postpone action, and it undoubtably was, he was quite right to continue doing so, even at the eleventh hour. At sea nothing was certain. Something might prevent the *Lydia's* coming into action; a squall of wind, the accidental carrying away of a spar, an opportune descent of mist – any one of the myriad things which might happen at sea. There was still a chance that the *Natividad* might get clear away, and Crespo was exploiting that chance to the last of his ability. That was logical though unheroic, exactly as one might expect of Crespo.

It was Hornblower's duty to see that the chance did not occur. He examined the *Natividad* closely, ran his eyes over the *Lydia's* sails to see that every one was drawing, and bethought himself of his crew.

'Send the hands to breakfast,' he said – every captain of a king's ship took his men into action with full bellies if possible.

He remained, pacing up and down the quarterdeck, unable to keep himself still any longer. The *Natividad* might be running away, but he knew well that she would fight hard enough when he caught her up. Those smashing twenty-four pounders which she carried on her lower deck were heavy metal against which to oppose the frail timbers of a frigate. They had wrought enough damage yesterday – he could hear the melancholy clanking of the pumps keeping down the water which leaked through the holes they had made; that clinking sound had continued without a break since yesterday. With a jury mizzen mast, and leaking like a sieve despite the sail under her bottom, with sixty-four of her attenuated crew *hors de combat,* the *Lydia* was in no condition to fight a severe battle. Defeat for her and death for him might be awaiting them across the strip of blue sea.

Polwheal suddenly appeared beside him on the quarterdeck, a tray in his hand.

'Your breakfast, sir,' he said, 'seeing as how we'll be in action when your usual time comes.'

As he proffered the tray Hornblower suddenly realised how much he wanted that steaming cup of coffee. He took it eagerly and drank thirstily before he remembered that he must not display human weakness of appetite before his servant.

'Thank you, Polwheal,' he said, sipping discreetly.

'An' 'er la'ships's compliments, sir, an' please may she stay where she is in the orlop when the action is renooed.'

'Ha – h'm,' said Hornblower, staring at him, thrown out of his stride by this unexpected question. All through the night he had been trying to forget the problem of Lady Barbara, as a man tries to forget an aching tooth. The orlop meant that Lady Barbara would be next to the wounded, separated from them only by a canvas screen – no place for a woman. But for that matter neither was the cable tier. The obvious truth was that there was no place for a woman in a frigate about to fight a battle.

'Put her wherever you like as long as she is not in reach of shot,' he said, irritably.

'Aye aye, sir. An' 'er la'ship told me to say that she wished you the best of good fortune today, sir, an' – an' – she was confident that you would meet with the success you – you deserve, sir.'

Polwheal stumbled over this long speech in a manner which revealed that he had not been quite as successful in learning it fluently as he wished.

'Thank you, Polwheal,' said Hornblower, gravely. He remembered Lady Barbara's face as she looked up at him from the main deck yesterday. It was clean cut and eager – like a sword, was the absurd simile which came up in his mind.

'Ha – h'm,' said Hornblower angrily. He was aware that his expression had softened, and he feared lest Polwheal should have noticed it, at a moment when he knew about whom he was thinking. 'Get below and see that her ladyship is comfortable.'

The hands were pouring up from breakfast now; the pumps were clanking with a faster rhythm now that a fresh crew was at work upon them. The guns' crews were gathered about their guns, and the few idlers were crowded on the forecastle eagerly watching the progress of the chase.

'Do you think the wind's going to hold, sir?' asked Bush, coming on to the quarterdeck like a bird of ill omen. 'Seems to me as if the sun's swallowing it.'

There was no doubting the fact that as the sun climbed higher in the sky the wind was diminishing in force. The sea was still short, steep, and rough, but the *Lydia's* motion over it was no longer light and graceful. She was pitching and jerking inelegantly deprived of the steady pressure of a good sailing wind. The sky overhead was fast becoming of a hard metallic blue.

'We're overhauling 'em fast,' said Hornblower, staring fixedly at the chase so as to ignore these portents of the elements.

'Three hours and we're up to 'em,' said Bush. 'If the wind only holds.'

It was fast growing hot. The heat which the sun was pouring down on them was intensified by its contrast with the comparative coolness of the night before. The crew had begun to seek the strips of shade under the gangways, and were lying there wearily. The steady clanking of the pumps seemed to sound louder now that the wind was losing its force. Hornblower suddenly realised that he would feel intensely weary if he permitted himself to think about it. He stood stubborn on the quarterdeck with the sun beating on his back, every few moments raising his telescope to stare at the *Natividad* while Bush fussed about the trimming of the sails as the breeze began to waver.

'Steer small, blast you,' he growled at the quartermaster at the wheel as the ship's head fell away in the trough of a wave.

'I can't, sir, begging your pardon,' was the reply. 'There aren't enough wind.'

It was true enough. The wind had died away so that the *Lydia* could not maintain the two knot speed which was sufficient to give her rudder power to act.

'We'll have to wet the sails. Mr Bush, see to it, if you please,' said Hornblower.

One division of one watch was roused up to this duty. A soaking wet sail will hold air which would escape if it were dry. Whips were rove through the blocks on the yards, and sea water hoisted up and poured over the canvas. So hot was the sun and so rapid the evaporation that the buckets had to be kept continually in action. To the clanging of the pumps was now added the shrilling of the sheaves in the blocks. The *Lydia* crept, still plunging madly, over the tossing sea and under the glaring sky.

'She's boxing the compass now,' said Bush with a jerk of his thumb at the distant *Natividad*. 'She can't compare with this beauty. She won't find the new rig of hers any help, neither.'

The *Natividad* was turning idly backwards and forwards on the waves, showing sometimes her broadside and sometimes her three masts in line, unable to steer any course in the light air prevailing. Bush looked complacently up at his new mizzen mast, a pyramid of canvas, and then across at the swaying *Natividad*, less than five miles away. The minutes crept by, their passage marked only by the monotonous noises of the ship. Hornblower stood in the scorching sunlight, fingering his telescope.

'Here comes the wind again, by God!' said Bush, suddenly. It was sufficient wind to make the ship heel a little, and to summon a faint harping from the rigging. ''Vast heaving with those buckets, there.'

The *Lydia* crept steadily forward, heaving and plunging to the music of the water under her bows, while the *Natividad* grew perceptibly nearer.

'It will reach him quickly enough. There! What did I say?'

The *Natividad's* sails filled as the breeze came down to her. She straightened upon her course.

' 'Twon't help him as much as it helps us. God, if it only holds,' commented Bush.

The breeze wavered and then renewed itself. The *Natividad* was hull-up now across the water when a wave lifted her. Another hour – less than an hour – and she would be in range.

'We'll be trying long shots at her soon,' said Bush.

'Mr Bush,' said Hornblower, spitefully, 'I can judge of the situation without the assistance of your comments, profound though they be.'

'I beg your pardon, sir,' said Bush, hurt. He flushed angrily for a moment until he noticed the anxiety in Hornblower's tired eyes, and then stumped away to the opposite rail to forget his rage.

As if by way of comment the big main-course flapped loudly, once, like a gun. The breeze was dying away as motivelessly as it had begun. And the *Natividad* still held it; she was holding her course steadily, drawing away once more, helped by the fluky wind. Here in the tropical Pacific one ship can have a fair wind while another two miles away lies becalmed, just as the heavy sea in which they were rolling indicated that last night's gale was still blowing, over the horizon, at the farther side of the Gulf of Tehuantepec. Hornblower stirred uneasily in the blazing sun. He feared lest he should see the *Natividad* sail clean away from him; the wind had died away so much that there was no point in wetting the sails, and the *Lydia* was rolling and sagging about aimlessly now to the send of the waves. Ten minutes passed before he was reassured by the sight of the *Natividad's* similar behaviour.

There was not a breath of wind now. The *Lydia* rolled wildly, to the accompaniment of a spasmodic creaking of woodwork, flapping of sails, and clattering of blocks. Only the clangour of the pumps sounded steadily through the hot air. The *Natividad* was four miles away now – a mile and a half beyond the farthest range of any of the *Lydia's* guns.

'Mr Bush,' said Hornblower. 'We will tow with the boats. Have the launch and the cutter hoisted out.'

Bush looked doubtful for a moment. He feared that two could play at that game. But he realised – as Hornblower had realised before him – that the *Lydia's* graceful hull would be more amenable to towing than the *Natividad's* ungainly bulk, even without counting the possibility that yesterday's action might have left her with no boat left that would swim. It was Hornblower's duty to try every course that might bring his ship into action with the enemy.

'Boats away!' roared Harrison. 'Cutter's crew, launch's crew.'

The pipes of his mates endorsed the orders. The hands tailed on to the tackles, and each boat in turn was swayed up into the air, and lowered outboard, the boats' crews fending off as the *Lydia* rolled in the swell.

There began for the boats' crews a period of the most exhausting and exasperating labour. They would tug and strain at the oars, moving the ponderous boats over the heaving waves, until the tow ropes tightened with a jerk as the strain came upon them. Then, tug as they would, they would seem to make no progress at all, the oar blades foaming impotently through the blue water, until the *Lydia* consented to crawl forward a little and the whole operation could be repeated. The heaving waves were a hindrance to them – sometimes every man on one side of a boat would catch a simultaneous crab so that the boat would spin round and become a nuisance to the other one – and the *Lydia,* so graceful and willing when under sail, was a perfect bitch when being towed.

She yawed and she sagged, falling away in the trough on occasions so much that the launch and the cutter were dragged, with much splashing from the oars, stern first after her wavering bows, and then changing her mind and heaving forward so fast after the two ropes that the men, flinging their weight upon the oar looms in expectation of a profitless pull, were precipitated backwards with the ease of progression while in imminent danger of being run down.

They sat naked on the thwarts while the sweat ran in streams down their faces and chests, unable – unlike their comrades at the pumps – to forget their fatigues in the numbness of monotonous work when every moment called for vigilance and attention, tugging painfully away, their agonies of thirst hardly relieved by the allowance of water doled out to them by the petty officers in the sternsheets, tugging away until even hands calloused by years of pulling and hauling cracked and blistered so that the oars were agony to touch.

Hornblower knew well enough the hardship they were undergoing. He went forward and looked down at the toiling seamen, knowing perfectly well that his own body would not be able to endure that labour for more than half an hour at most. He gave orders for an hourly relief at the oars, and he did his best to cheer the men on. He felt an uneasy sympathy for them – three-quarters of them had never been sailors until this commission, and had no desire to be sailors either, but had been swept up by the all-embracing press seven months ago. Hornblower was always able (rather against his will) to do what most of his officers failed to do – he saw his crew not as topmen or hands, but as what they had been before the press caught them, stevedores, wherry men, porters.

He had waggoners and potters – he had even two draper's assistants and a printer among his crew; men snatched without notice from their families and their employment and forced into this sort of labour, on wretched food, in hideous working conditions, haunted always by the fear of the cat or of Harrison's rattan, and with the chance of death by drowning or by hostile action to seal the bargain. So imaginative an individualist as Hornblower was bound to feel sympathy with them even when he felt he ought not, especially as he (in common with a few other liberals) found himself growing more and more liberal-minded with the progress of years. But to counterbalance this weakness of his there was his restless nervous anxiety to finish off well any task he had set himself to do. With the *Natividad* in sight he could not rest until he had engaged her, and when a captain of a ship cannot rest his crew certainly cannot – aching backs or bleeding hands notwithstanding.

By careful measurement with his sextant of the subtended angles he was able to say with certainty at the end of an hour that the efforts of the boats' crews had dragged the *Lydia* a little nearer to the *Natividad,* and Bush, who had taken the same measurements, was in agreement. The sun rose higher and the *Lydia* crept inch by inch towards the enemy.

'*Natividad's* hoisting out a boat, sir,' hailed Knyvett from the foretop.

'How many oars?'

'Twelve, sir, I think. They're taking the ship in tow.'

'And they're welcome,' scoffed Bush. 'Twelve oars won't move that old tub of a *Natividad* very far.'

Hornblower glared at him and Bush retired to his own side of the quarterdeck again; he had forgotten his captain was in this unconversational mood. Hornblower was fretting himself into a fever. He stood in the glaring sun while the heat was reflected up into his face from the deck under his feet. His shirt chaffed him where he sweated. He felt caged, like a captive beast, within the limitations of practical details. The endless clanking of the pumps, the rolling of the ship, the rattle of the rigging, the noise of the oars in the rowlocks, were driving him mad, as though he could scream (or weep) at the slightest additional provocation.

At noon he changed the men at the oars and pumps, and sent the crew to dinner – he remembered bitterly that he had already made them breakfast in anticipation of immediate action. At two bells he began to wonder whether the *Natividad* might be within extreme long range, but the mere fact of wondering told him that it was not the case – he knew his own sanguine temperament too well, and he fought down the temptation to waste powder and shot. And then, as he looked for the thousandth time through his telescope, he suddenly saw a disk of white appear on the high stern of the *Natividad*. The disk spread and expanded into a thin cloud, and six seconds after its first appearance the dull thud of the shot reached his ears. The *Natividad* was evidently willing to try the range.

'*Natividad* carries two long eighteens aft on the quarterdeck,' said Gerard to Bush in Hornblower's hearing. 'Heavy metal for stern chasers.'

Hornblower knew it already. He would have to run the gauntlet of those two guns for an hour, possibly, before he could bring the brass nine pounder on his forecastle into action. Another puff of smoke from the *Natividad,* and this time Hornblower saw a spout of water rise from the breast of a wave half a mile ahead. But at that long range and on that tossing sea it did not mean that the *Lydia* was still half a mile beyond the *Natividad's* reach. Hornblower heard the next shot arrive, and saw a brief fountain of water rise no more than fifty yards from the *Lydia's* starboard quarter.

'Mr Gerard,' said Hornblower. 'Send for Mr Marsh and see what he can do with the long nine forward.'

It would cheer the men up to have a gun banging away occasionally instead of being merely shot at without making any reply. Marsh came waddling up from the darkness of the magazine, and blinked in the blinding sunshine. He shook his head doubtfully as he eyed the distance between the ships, but he had the gun cleared away, and he loaded it with his own hands, lovingly. He measured out the powder charge on the fullest scale, and he spent several seconds selecting the roundest and truest shot from the locker. He trained the gun with care, and then stood aside, lanyard in hand, watching the heave of the ship and the send of the bows, while a dozen telescopes were trained on the *Natividad* and every eye watched for the fall of the shot. Suddenly he jerked the lanyard and the cannon roared out, its report sounding flat in the heated motionless air.

'Two cables' lengths astern of her!' yelled Knyvett from the foretop. Hornblower had missed the splash – another proof, to his mind, of his own incompetence, but he concealed the fact under a mask of imperturbability.

'Try again, Mr Marsh,' he said.

The *Natividad* was firing both stern chasers together now. As Hornblower spoke there came a crash forward as one of the eighteen-pounder balls struck home close above the water line. Hornblower could hear young Savage, down in the launch hurling shrill blasphemies at the men at the oars to urge them on – that shot must have passed just over his head. Marsh stroked his beard and addressed himself to the task of reloading the long nine pounder. While he was so engaged, Hornblower was deep in the calculation of the chances of battle.

That long nine, although of smaller calibre, was of longer range than his shorter main deck guns, while the carronades which comprised half of the *Lydia's* armament were useless at anything longer than close range. The *Lydia* would have to draw up close to her enemy before she could attack her with effect. There would be a long and damaging interval between the moment when the *Natividad* should be able to bring all her guns into action and the moment when the *Lydia* could hit back at her. There would be casualties, guns dismounted perhaps, serious losses. Hornblower balanced the arguments for and against continuing to try and close with the enemy while Mr Marsh was squinting along the sights of the nine pounder. Then Hornblower scowled to himself, and ceased tugging at his chin, his mind made up. He had started the action; he would go through with it to the end, cost what it might. His flexibility of mind could crystallise into sullen obstinacy.

The nine pounder went off as though to signal this decision.

'Just alongside her!' screamed Knyvett triumphantly from the foretop.

'Well done, Mr Marsh,' said Hornblower, and Marsh wagged his beard complacently.

The *Natividad* was firing faster now. Three times a splintering crash told of a shot which had been aimed true. Then suddenly a thrust as if from an invisible hand made Hornblower reel on the quarterdeck, and his ears were filled with a brief rending noise. A skimming shot had ploughed a channel along the planking of the quarterdeck. A marine was sitting near the taffrail stupidly contemplating his left leg, which no longer had a foot on the end of it; another marine dropped his musket with a clatter and clapped his hands to his face, which a splinter had torn open, with the blood spouting between his fingers.

'Are you hurt, sir?' cried Bush, leaping across to Hornblower.

'No.'

Hornblower turned back to stare through his glass at the *Natividad* while the wounded were being dragged away. He saw a dark dot appear alongside the *Natividad,* and lengthen and diverge. It was the boat with which they had been trying to row – perhaps they were giving up the attempt. But the boat was not being hoisted in. For a second Hornblower was puzzled. The *Natividad's* stumpy fore mast and main mast came into view. The boat was pulling the ship laboriously round so that her whole broadside would bear. Not two, but twenty-five guns would soon be opening their fire on the *Lydia.*

Hornblower felt his breath come a little quicker, unexpectedly, so that he had to swallow in order to regulate things again. His pulse was faster, too. He made himself keep the glass to his eye until he was certain of the enemy's manoeuvre, and then walked forward leisurely to the gangway. He was compelling himself to appear lighthearted and carefree; he knew that the fools of men whom he commanded would fight more diligently for a captain like that.

'They're waiting for us now, lads,' he said. 'We shall have some pebbles about our ears before long. Let's show 'em that Englishmen don't care.'

They cheered him for that, as he expected and hoped they would do. He looked through his glass again at the *Natividad*. She was still turning, very slowly – it was a lengthy process to turn a clumsy two-decker in a dead calm. But he could see a hint of the broad white stripes which ornamented her side.

'Ha – h'm,' he said.

Forward he could hear the oars grinding away as the men in the boats laboured to drag the *Lydia* to grips with her enemy. Across the deck a little group of officers – Bush and Crystal among them – were academically discussing what percentage of hits might be expected from a Spanish broadside at a range of a mile. They were coldblooded about it in a fashion he could never hope to imitate with sincerity. He did not fear death so much – nor nearly as much – as defeat and the pitying contempt of his colleagues. The chiefest dread at the back of his mind was the fear of mutilation. An ex-naval officer stumping about on two wooden legs might be an object of condolence, might receive lip service as one of Britain's heroic defenders, but he was a figure of fun, nevertheless. Hornblower dreaded the thought of being a figure of fun. He might lose his nose or his cheek and be so mutilated that people would not be able to bear to look at him. It was a horrible thought which set him shuddering while he looked through the telescope, so horrible that he did not stop to think of the associated details, of the agonies he would have to bear down there in the dark cockpit at the mercy of Laurie's incompetence.

The *Natividad* was suddenly engulfed in smoke, and some seconds later the air and the water around the *Lydia* and the ship herself, were torn by the hurtling broadside.

'Not more than two hits,' said Bush, gleefully.

'Just what I said,' said Crystal. 'That captain of theirs ought to go round and train every gun himself.'

'How do you know he did not?' argued Bush.

As punctuation the nine pounder forward banged out its defiance. Hornblower fancied that his straining eyes saw splinters fly amidships of the *Natividad*, unlikely though it was at that distance.

'Well aimed, Mr Marsh!' he called. 'You hit him squarely.'

Another broadside came from the *Natividad*, and another followed it, and another after that. Time after time the *Lydia's* decks were swept from end to end with shot. There were dead men laid out again on the deck, and the groaning wounded were dragged below.

'It is obvious to anyone of a mathematical turn of mind,' said Crystal, 'that those guns are all laid by different hands. The shots are too scattered for it to be otherwise.'

'Nonsense!' maintained Bush sturdily. 'See how long it is between broadsides. Time enough for one man to train each gun. What would they be doing in that time otherwise?'

'A Dago crew—,' began Crystal, but a sudden shriek of cannon balls over his head silenced him for a moment.

'Mr Galbraith!' shouted Bush. 'Have that main t'gallant stay spliced directly.' Then he turned triumphantly on Crystal. 'Did you notice,' he asked, 'how every shot from that broadside went high? How does the mathematical mind explain that?'

'They fired on the upward roll, Mr Bush. Really, Mr Bush, I think that after Trafalgar—'

Hornblower longed to order them to cease the argument which was lacerating his nerves, but he could not be such a tyrant as that.

In the still air the smoke from the *Natividad's* firing had banked up around about her so that she showed ghostly through the cloud, her solitary mizzen topmast protruding above it into the clear air.

'Mr Bush,' he asked, 'at what distance do you think she is now?'

Bush gauged the distance carefully.

'Three parts of a mile, I should say, sir.'

'Two-thirds, more likely, sir,' said Crystal.

'Your opinion was not asked, Mr Crystal,' snapped Hornblower.

At three-quarters of a mile, even at two-thirds, the Lydia's carronades would be ineffective. She must continue running the gauntlet. Bush was evidently of the same opinion, to judge by his next orders.

'Time for the men at the oars to be relieved,' he said, and went forward to attend it. Hornblower heard him bustling the new crews down into the boats, anxious that the pulling should be resumed before the *Lydia* had time to lose what little way she carried.

It was terribly hot under the blazing sun, even though it was now long past noon. The smell of the blood which had been spilt on the decks mingled with the smell of the hot deck seams and of the powder smoke from the nine pounder with which Marsh was still steadily bombarding the enemy. Hornblower felt sick – so sick that he began to fear lest he should disgrace himself eternally by vomiting in full view of his men. When fatigue and anxiety had weakened him thus he was far more conscious of the pitching and rolling of the ship under his feet. The men at the guns were silent now, he noticed – for long they had laughed and joked at their posts, but now they were beginning to sulk under the punishment. That was a bad sign.

'Pass the word for Sullivan and his fiddle,' he ordered.

The red-haired Irish madman came aft, and knuckled his forehead, his fiddle and bow under his arm.

'Give us a tune, Sullivan,' he ordered. 'Hey there, men, who is there among you who dances the best hornpipe?'

There was a difference of opinion about that, apparently.

'Benskin, sir,' said some voices.

'Hall, sir,' said others.

'No, MacEvoy, sir.'

'Then we'll have a tournament,' said Hornblower. 'Here, Benskin, Hall, MacEvoy. A hornpipe from each of you, and guinea for the man who does it best.'

In later years it was a tale told and retold, how the *Lydia* was towed into action with hornpipes being danced on her maindeck. It was quoted as an example of Hornblower's cool courage, and only Hornblower knew how little truth there was in the attribution. It kept the men happy, which was why he did it. No one guessed how nearly he came to vomiting when a shot came in through a forward gunport and spattered Hall with a seaman's brains without causing him to miss a step.

Then later in that dreadful afternoon there came a crash from forward, followed by a chorus of shouts and screams overside.

'Launch sunk, sir!' hailed Galbraith from the forecastle, but Hornblower was there as soon as he had uttered the words.

A round shot had dashed the launch practically into its component planks, and the men were scrambling in the water, leaping up for the bobstay or struggling to climb into the cutter, all of them who survived wild with fear of sharks.

'The Dagoes have saved us the trouble of hoisting her in,' he said, loudly. 'We're close enough now for them to feel our teeth.'

The men who heard him cheered.

'Mr Hooker!' he called to the midshipman in the cutter. 'When you have picked up those men, kindly starboard your helm. We are going to open fire.'

He came aft to the quarterdeck again.

'Hard a-starboard,' he growled at the quartermaster. 'Mr Gerard, you may open first when your guns bear.'

Very slowly the *Lydia* swung round. Another broadside from the *Natividad* came crashing into her before she had completed the turn, but Hornblower actually did not notice it. The period of inaction was now over. He had brought his ship within four hundred yards of the enemy, and all his duty now was to walk the deck as an example to his men. There were no more decisions to make.

'Cock your locks!' shouted Gerard in the waist.

'Easy, Mr Hooker. Way enough!' roared Hornblower.

The *Lydia* turned inch by inch, with Gerard squinting along one of the starboard guns to judge of the moment when it would first bear.

'Take your aim!' he yelled, and stood back, timing the roll of the ship in the heavy swell. 'Fire!'

The smoke billowed out amid the thunder of the discharge, and the *Lydia* heaved to the recoil of the guns.

'Give him another, lads!' shouted Hornblower through the din. Now that action was joined he found himself exalted and happy, the dreadful fears of mutilation forgotten. In thirty seconds the guns were reloaded, run out, and fired. Again and again and again, with Gerard watching the roll of the ship and giving the word. Counting back in his mind, Hornblower reckoned five broadsides from the Lydia, and he could only remember two from the *Natividad* in that time. At that rate of firing the *Natividad's* superiority in numbers of guns and weight of metal would be more than counterbalanced. At the sixth broadside a gun went off prematurely, a second before Gerard gave the word. Hornblower sprang forward to detect the guilty crew – it was easy enough from their furtive look and suspicious appearance of busyness. He shook his finger at them.

'Steady, there!' he shouted. 'I'll flog the next man who fires out of turn.'

It was very necessary to keep the men in hand while the range was as long as at present, because in the heat and excitement of the action the gun captains could not be trusted to judge the motion of the ship while preoccupied with loading and laying.

'Good old Horny!' piped up some unknown voice forward, and there was a burst of laughing and cheering, cut short by Gerard's next order to fire.

The smoke was banked thick about the ship already – as thick as a London fog so that from the quarterdeck it was impossible to see individuals on the forecastle, and in the unnatural darkness which it brought with it one could see the long orange flashes of the guns despite the vivid sunshine outside. Of the *Natividad* all that could be seen was her high smoke cloud and the single topmast jutting out from it. The thick smoke, trailing about the ship in greasy wreaths, made the eyes smart and irritated the lungs, and affected the skin like thundery weather until it pricked uncomfortably.

Hornblower found Bush beside him.

'*Natividad's* feeling our fire, sir,' he roared through the racket. 'She's firing very wild. Look at that, sir.'

Of the broadside fired only one or two shots struck home. Half a dozen plunged together into the sea astern of the *Lydia* so that the spray from the fountains which they struck up splashed round them on the quarterdeck. Hornblower nodded happily. This was his justification for closing to that range and for running the risks involved in the approach. To maintain a rapid fire, well aimed, amid the din and the smoke and the losses and the confusion of a naval battle called for discipline and practice of a sort that he knew the *Natividad's* crew could not boast.

He looked down through the smoke at the *Lydia's* main deck. The inexperienced eye, observing the hurry and bustle of the boys with the cartridge buckets, the mad efforts of the gun crews, the dead and the wounded, the darkness and the din, might well think it a scene of confusion, but Hornblower knew better. Everything that was being done there, every single action, was part of the scheme worked out by Hornblower seven months before when he commissioned the *Lydia,* and grained into the minds of all on board during the long and painful drills since. He could see Gerard standing by the mainmast, looking almost saintly in his ecstasy – gunnery was as much Gerard's ruling passion as women; he could see the midshipmen and other warrant officers each by his subdivision of guns, each looking to Gerard for his orders and keeping his guns working rhythmically, the loaders with their rammers, the cleaners with their sponges, the gun captains crouching over the breeches, right hands raised.

The port side battery was already depleted of most of its men; there were only two men to a gun there, standing idle yet ready to spring into action if a shift of the fight should bring their guns to bear. The remainder were on duty round the ship – replacing casualties on the starboard side, manning the pumps, whose doleful clanking continued steadily through the fearful din, resting on their oars in the cutter, hard at work aloft repairing damages. Hornblower found time to be thankful that he had been granted seven months in which to bring his crew into its present state of training and discipline.

Something – the concussion of the guns, a faint breath of air, or the send of the sea – was causing the *Lydia* to turn away a trifle from her enemy. Hornblower could see that the guns were having to be trained round farther and farther so that the rate of firing was being slowed down. He raced forward, running out along the bowsprit until he was over the cutter where Hooker and his men sat staring at the fight.

'Mr Hooker, bring her head round two points to starboard.'

'Aye aye, sir.'

The men bent to their oars and headed their boat towards the *Natividad*; the tow-rope tightened while another badly aimed broadside tore the water all round them into foam. Tugging and straining at the oars they would work the ship round in time. Hornblower left them and ran back to the quarterdeck. There was a white-faced ship's boy seeking him there.

'Mr Howell sent me, sir. Starboard side chain pump's knocked all to pieces.'

'Yes?' Hornblower knew that Howell the ship's carpenter would not merely send a message of despair.

'He's rigging another one, sir, but it will be an hour before it works, sir. He told me to tell you the water's gaining a little, sir.'

'Ha – h'm,' said Hornblower. The infant addressing him grew round-eyed and confidential now that the first strangeness of speaking to his captain had worn off.

'There was fourteen men all knocked into smash at the pump, sir. 'Orrible, sir.'

'Very good. Run back to Mr Howell and tell him the captain is sure he will do his best to get the new pump rigged.'

'Aye aye, sir.'

The boy dived down to the maindeck, and Hornblower watched him running forward, dodging the hurrying individuals in the crowded space there. He had to explain himself to the marine sentry at the fore hatchway – no one could go below without being able to show that it was his duty which was calling him there. Hornblower felt as if the message Howell had sent did not matter at all. It called for no decision on his part. All there was to do was to go on fighting, whether the ship was sinking under their feet or not. There was a comfort in being free of all responsibility in this way.

'One hour and a half already,' said Bush, coming up rubbing his hands. 'Glorious, sir. Glorious.'

It might have been no more than ten minutes for all Hornblower could tell, but Bush had in duty bound been watching the sand glass by the binnacle.

'I've never known Dagoes stick to their guns like this before,' commented Bush. 'Their aim's poor, but they're firing as fast as ever. And it's my belief we've hit them hard, sir.'

He tried to look through the eddying smoke, even fanning ridiculously with his hands in the attempt – a gesture which, by showing that he was not quite as calm as he appeared to be, gave Hornblower an absurd pleasure. Crystal came up as well as he spoke.

'The smoke's thinning a little, sir. It's my belief that there's a light air of wind blowing.'

He held up a wetted finger.

'There is indeed, sir. A trifle of breeze over the port quarter. Ah!'

There came a stronger puff as he spoke, which rolled away the smoke in a solid mass over the starboard bow and revealed the scene as if a theatre curtain had been raised. There was the *Natividad,* looking like a wreck. Her jury foremast had gone the way of its predecessor, and her mainmast has followed it. Only her mizzen mast stood now, and she was rolling wildly in the swell with a huge tangle of rigging trailing over her disengaged side. Abreast her foremast three ports had been battered into one; the gap looked like a missing tooth.

'She's low in the water,' said Bush, but on the instant a fresh broadside vomited smoke from her battered side, and this time by some chance every shot told in the *Lydia,* as the crash below well indicated. The smoke billowed round the *Natividad,* and as it cleared the watchers saw her swinging round head to the wind, helpless in the light air. The *Lydia* had felt the breeze. Hornblower could tell by the feel of her that she had steerage way again; the quartermaster at the wheel was twirling the spokes to hold her steady. He saw his chance on the instant.

'Starboard a point,' he ordered. 'Forward, there! Cast off the cutter.'

The *Lydia* steadied across her enemy's bows and raked her with thunder and flame.

'Back the main tops'l!' ordered Hornblower.

The men were cheering again on the maindeck through the roar of the guns. Astern the red sun was dipping to the water's edge in a glory of scarlet and gold. Soon it would be night.

'She must strike soon. Christ! Why don't she strike?' Bush was saying, as at close range the broadsides tore into the helpless enemy, raking her from bow to stern. Hornblower knew better. No ship under Crespo's command and flying el Supremo's flag would strike her colours. He could see the golden star on a blue ground fluttering through the smoke.

'Pound him, lads, pound him!' shouted Gerard.

With the shortening range he could rely on his gun captains to fire independently now. Every gun's crew was loading and firing as rapidly as possible. So hot were the guns that at each discharge they leaped high in their carriages, and the dripping sponges thrust down their bores sizzled and steamed at the touch of the scorching hot metal. It was growing darker, too. The flashes of the guns could be seen again now, leaping in long orange tongues from the gun muzzles. High above the fast fading sunset could be seen the first star, shining out brilliantly.

The *Natividad's* bowsprit was gone, splintered and broken and hanging under her forefoot, and then in the dwindling light the mizzen mast fell as well, cut through by shots which had ripped their way down the whole length of the ship.

'She must strike now, by God!' said Bush.

At Trafalgar Bush had been sent as prize master into a captured Spanish ship, and his mind was full of busy memories of what a beaten ship looked like – the dismounted guns, the dead and wounded heaped on the deck and rolling back and forth as the dismasted ship rolled on the swell, the misery, the pain, the helplessness. As if in reply to him there came a sudden flash and report from the *Natividad's* bows. Some devoted souls with tackles and hand-spikes had contrived to slew a gun round so that it would bear right forward, and were firing into the looming bulk of the *Lydia.*

'Pound him, lads, pound him!' screamed Gerard, half mad with fatigue and strain.

The *Lydia* by virtue of her top hamper was going down to leeward fast upon the rolling hulk. At every second the range was shortening. Through the darkness, when their eyes were not blinded with gun flashes, Hornblower and Bush could see figures moving about on the *Natividad's* deck. They were firing muskets now, as well. The flashes pricked the darkness and Hornblower heard a bullet thud into the rail beside him. He did not care. He was conscious now of his overmastering weariness.

The wind was fluky, coming in sudden puffs and veering unexpectedly. It was hard, especially in the darkness, to judge exactly how the two ships were nearing each other.

'The closer we are, the quicker we'll finish it,' said Bush.

'Yes, but we'll run on board of her soon,' said Hornblower.

He roused himself for a further effort.

'Call the hands to stand by to repel boarders,' he said, and he walked across to where the two starboard side quarterdeck carronades were thundering away. So intent were their crews on their work, so hypnotised by the monotony of loading and firing, that it took him several seconds to attract their notice. Then they stood still, sweating, while Hornblower gave his orders. The two carronades were loaded with canister brought from the reserve locker beside the taffrail. They waited, crouching beside the guns, while the two ships drifted closer and closer together, the *Lydia's* main deck guns still blazing away. There were shouts and yells of defiance from the *Natividad,* and the musket flashes from her bows showed a dark mass of men crowding there waiting for the ships to come together. Yet the actual contact was unexpected, as a sudden combination of wind and sea closed the gap with a rush. The *Natividad's* bow hit the *Lydia* amidships, just forward of the mizzenmast, with a jarring crash. There was a pandemonium of yells from the *Natividad* as they swarmed forward to board, and the captains of the carronades sprang to their lanyards.

'Wait!' shouted Hornblower.

His mind was like a calculating machine, judging wind and sea, time and distance, as the *Lydia* slowly swung round. With hand spikes and the brute strength of the men he trained one carronade round and the other followed his example, while the mob on the *Natividad's* forecastle surged along the bulwarks waiting for the moment to board. The two carronades came right up against them.

'Fire!'

A thousand musket balls were vomited from the carronades straight into the packed crowd. There was a moment of silence, and then the pandemonium of shouts and cheers was replaced by a thin chorus of screams and cries – the blast of musket balls had swept the *Natividad's* forecastle clear from side to side.

For a space the two ships clung together in this position; the *Lydia* still had a dozen guns that would bear, and these pounded away with their muzzles almost touching the *Natividad's* bow. Then wind and sea parted them again, the *Lydia* to leeward now, drifting away from the rolling hulk; in the English ship every gun was in action, while from the *Natividad* came not a gun, not even a musket shot.

Hornblower fought off his weariness again.

'Cease firing,' he shouted to Gerard on the main deck, and the guns fell silent.

Hornblower stared through the darkness at the vague mass of the *Natividad,* wallowing in the waves.

'Surrender!' he shouted.

'Never!' came the reply – Crespo's voice, he could have sworn to it, thin and high pitched. It added two or three words of obscene insult.

Hornblower could afford to smile at that, even through his weariness. He had fought his battle and won it.

'You have done all that brave men could do,' he shouted.

'Not all, yet, Captain,' wailed the voice in the darkness.

Then something caught Hornblower's eyes – a wavering glow of red about the *Natividad's* vague bows.

'Crespo, you fool!' he shouted. 'Your ship's on fire! Surrender, while you can.'

'Never!'

The *Lydia's* guns, hard against the *Natividad's* side, had flung their flaming wads in amongst the splintered timbers. The tinder-dry wood of the old ship had taken fire from them, and the fire was spreading fast. It was brighter already than when Hornblower had noticed it; the ship would be a mass of flames soon. Hornblower's first duty was to his own ship – when the fire should reach the powder charges on the *Natividad's* decks, or when it should attain the magazine, the ship would become a volcano of flaming fragments, imperilling the *Lydia*.

'We must haul off from her, Mr Bush,' said Hornblower, speaking formally to conceal the tremor in his voice. 'Man the braces, there.'

The *Lydia* swung away, close hauled, clawing her way up to windward of the flaming wreck. Bush and Hornblower gazed back at her. There were bright flames now to be seen, spouting from the shattered bows – the red glow was reflected in the heaving sea around her. And then, as they looked, they saw the flames vanish abruptly, like an extinguished candle. There was nothing to be seen at all, nothing save darkness and the faint glimmer of the wave crests. The sea had swallowed the *Natividad* before the flames could destroy her.

'Sunk, by God!' exclaimed Bush, leaning out over the rail.

Hornblower still seemed to hear that last wailing 'Never!' during the seconds of silence that followed. Yet he was perhaps the first of all his ship's company to recover from the shock. He put his ship about and ran down to the scene of the *Natividad's* sinking. He sent off Hooker and the cutter to search for survivors – the cutter was the only boat left, for gig and jolly boat had been shattered by the *Natividad's* fire, and the planks of the launch were floating five miles away. They picked up a few men – two were hauled out of the water by men in the *Lydia's* chains, and the cutter found half a dozen swimmers; that was all. The *Lydia's* crew tried to be kind to them, as they stood on her deck in the lantern light with the water streaming from their ragged clothes and their lank black hair, but they were sullen and silent; there was even one who struggled for a moment, as if to continue the battle which the *Natividad* had fought so desperately.

'Never mind, we'll make topmen of them yet,' said Hornblower, trying to speak lightly.

Fatigue had reached such a pitch now that he was speaking as if out of a dream, as if all these solid surroundings of his, the ship, her guns and masts and sails, Bush's burly figure, were unreal and ghostlike, and only his weariness and the ache inside his skull were existing things. He heard his voice as though he were speaking from a yard away.

'Aye aye, sir,' said the boatswain.

Anything was grist that came to the Royal Navy's mill – Harrison was prepared to make seamen out of the strangest human material; he had done so all his life, for that matter.

'What course shall I set, sir?' asked Bush, as Hornblower turned back to the quarterdeck.

'Course?' said Hornblower, vaguely. 'Course?'

It was terribly hard to realise that the battle was over, the *Natividad* sunk, that there was no enemy afloat within thousands of miles of sea. It was hard to realise that the *Lydia* was in acute danger, too; that the pumps, clanking away monotonously, were not quite able to keep the leaks under, that the *Lydia* still had a sail stretched under her bottom, and stood in the acutest need of a complete refit.

Hornblower came by degrees to realise that now he had to start a new chapter in the history of the *Lydia,* to make fresh plans. And there was a long line of people waiting for immediate orders, too – Bush, here, and the boatswain and the carpenter and the gunner and that fool Laurie. He had to force his tired brain to think again. He estimated the wind's force and direction, as though it were an academic exercise and not a mental process which for twenty years had been second nature to him. He went wearily down to his cabin and found the shattered chart cases amid the indescribable wreckage, and he pored over the torn chart.

He must report his success at Panama as soon as he could; that was obvious to him now. Perhaps he could refit there, although he saw small chance of it in that inhospitable roadstead, especially with yellow fever in the town. So he must carry the shattered *Lydia* to Panama. He laid off a course for Cape Mala, by a supreme effort compelled his mind to realise that he had a fair wind, and came up again with his orders to find that the mass of people who were clamouring for his attention had miraculously vanished. Bush had chased them all away, although he never discovered it. He gave the course to Bush, and then Polwheal materialised himself at his elbow, with boat cloak and hammock chair. Hornblower had no protest left in him. He allowed himself to be wrapped in the cloak, and he fell half fainting into the chair. It was twenty-one hours since he had last sat down. Polwheal had brought food, too, but he merely ignored that. He wanted no food! all he wanted was rest.

Then for a second he was wide awake again. He had remembered Lady Barbara, battened down below with the wounded in the dark and stifling bowels of the ship. But he relaxed at once. The blasted woman could look after herself – she was quite capable of doing so. Nothing mattered now. His head sank on his breast again. The next thing to disturb him was the sound of his own snores, and that did not disturb him long. He slept and he snored through all the din which the crew made in their endeavour to get the *Lydia* ship-shape again.

XVIII

What awoke Hornblower was the sun, which lifted itself over the horizon and shone straight into his eyes. He stirred and blinked, and for a space he tried, like a child, to shield his eyes with his hands and return to sleep. He did not know where he was, and for that time he did not care. Then he began to remember the events of yesterday, and he ceased trying to sleep and instead tried to wake up. Oddly, at first he remembered the details of the fighting and could not recall the sinking of the *Natividad*. When that recollection shot into his brain he was fully awake.

He rose from his chair, stretching himself painfully, for all his joints ached with the fatigues of yesterday. Bush was standing by the wheel, his face grey and lined and strangely old in the hard light. Hornblower nodded to him and received his salute in return; Bush was wearing his cocked hat over the dirty white bandage round his forehead. Hornblower would have spoken to him, but all his attention was caught up immediately in looking round the ship. There was a good breeze blowing which must have backed round during the night, for the *Lydia* could only just hold her course close hauled. She was under all plain sail; Hornblower's rapid inspection revealed to him innumerable splices both in standing and running rigging; the jury mizzenmast seemed to be standing up well to its work, but every sail that was spread seemed to have at least one shot hole in it – some of them a dozen or more. They gave the ship a little of the appearance of a tattered vagabond. The first part of today's work would be spreading a new suit of sails; new rigging could wait for a space.

It was only then, after weather and course and sail set had been noted, that Hornblower's sailor's eye came down to the decks. From forward came the monotonous clangour of the pumps; the clear white water which was gushing from them was the surest indication that the ship was making so much water that it could only just be kept in check. On the lee side gangway was a long, long row of corpses, each in its hammock. Hornblower flinched when he saw the length of the row, and it called for all his will to count them. There were twenty-four dead men along the gangway; and fourteen had been buried yesterday. Some of these dead might be – probably were – the mortally wounded of yesterday, but thirty-eight dead seemed certainly to indicate at least seventy wounded down below. Rather more than one-third of the *Lydia's* company were casualties, then. He wondered who they were, wondered whose distorted faces were concealed beneath those hammocks.

The dead on deck outnumbered the living. Bush seemed to have sent below every man save for a dozen men to hand and steer, which was sensible of him, seeing that every one must be worn out with yesterday's toil while one man out of every seven on board would have to be employed at the pumps until the shot holes could be got at and plugged. The rest of the crew, at first glance, were all asleep, sprawled on the main deck under the gangways. Hardly anyone had had the strength to sling a hammock (if their hammocks had survived the battle); all the rest lay as they had dropped, lying tangled here and there, heads pillowed on each other or on more unsympathetic objects like ring bolts and the hind axletrees of the guns.

There were still evident many signs of yesterday's battle, quite apart from the sheeted corpses and the dark stains, not thoroughly swabbed, which disfigured the white planking. The decks were furrowed and grooved in all directions, with jagged splinters still standing up here and there. There were shot holes in the ship's sides with canvas roughly stretched over them. The port sills were stained black with powder; on one of them an eighteen-pounder shot stood out, half buried in the tough oak. But on the other hand an immense amount of work had been done, from laying out the dead to securing the guns and frapping the breechings. Apart from the weariness of her crew, the *Lydia* was ready to fight another battle at two minutes' notice.

Hornblower felt a prick of shame that so much should have been done while he slept lazily in his hammock chair. He forced himself to feel no illwill on that account. Although to praise Bush's work was to admit his own deficiencies he felt that he must be generous.

'Very good indeed, Mr Bush,' he said, walking over to him; yet his natural shyness combined with his feeling of shame to make his speech stilted. 'I am both astonished and pleased at the work you have accomplished.'

'Today is Sunday, sir,' said Bush, simply.

So it was. Sunday was the day of the captain's inspection, when he went round every part of the ship examining everything, to see that the first lieutenant was doing his duty in keeping the ship efficient. On Sunday the ship had to be swept and garnished, all the falls of rope flemished down, the hands fallen in by divisions in their best clothes, divine service held, the Articles of War read – Sunday was the day when the professional ability of every first lieutenant in His Britannic Majesty's Navy was tried in the balance.

Hornblower could not fight down a smile at this ingenious explanation.

'Sunday or no Sunday,' he said, 'you have done magnificently, Mr Bush.'

'Thank you, sir.'

'And I shall remember to say so in my report to the Admiralty.'

'I know you'll do that, sir.'

Bush's weary face was illuminated by a gleam of pleasure. A successful single ship action was usually rewarded by promotion to Commander of the first lieutenant, and for a man like Bush, with no family and no connections, it was his only hope of making that vitally important step. But a captain who was anxious to enhance his own glory could word his report so that it appeared that he had won his victory despite of, instead of by the aid of, his first lieutenant – instances were known.

'They may make much of this in England, when eventually they hear about it,' said Hornblower.

'I'm certain of it, sir. It isn't every day of the week that a frigate sinks a ship of the line.'

It was stretching a point to call the *Natividad* that – sixty years ago when she was built she may have been considered just fit to lie in the line, but times had changed since then. But it was a very notable feat that the *Lydia* had accomplished, all the same. It was only now that Hornblower began to appreciate how notable it was, and his spirit rose in proportion. There was another criterion which the British public was prone to apply in estimating the merit of a naval action, and the Board of Admiralty itself not infrequently used the same standard.

'What's the butcher's bill?' demanded Hornblower, brutally, voicing the thoughts of both of them – brutally because otherwise he might be thought guilty of sentiment.

'Thirty-eight killed, sir,' said Bush, taking a dirty scrap of paper from his pocket. 'Seventy-five wounded. Four missing. The missing are Harper, Dawson, North, and Chump the negro, sir – they were lost when the launch was sunk. Clay was killed in the first day's action—'

Hornblower nodded; he remembered Clay's headless body sprawled on the quarterdeck.

'—and John Summers, master's mate, Henry Vincent and James Clifton, boatswain's mates, killed yesterday, and Donald Scott Galbraith, third lieutenant, Lieutenant Samuel Simmonds of the Marines, Midshipman Howard Savage and four other warrant officers wounded.'

'Galbraith?' said Hornblower. That piece of news prevented him from beginning to wonder what would be the reward of a casualty list of a hundred and seventeen, when frigate captains had been knighted before this for a total of eighty killed and wounded.

'Badly, sir. Both legs smashed below the knees.'

Galbraith had met the fate which Hornblower had dreaded for himself. The shock recalled Hornblower to his duty.

'I shall go down and visit the wounded at once,' he said, and checked himself and looked searchingly at his first lieutenant. 'What about you, Bush? You don't look fit for duty.'

'I am perfectly fit, sir,' protested Bush. 'I shall take an hour's rest when Gerard comes up to take over the deck from me.'

'As you will, then.'

Down below decks in the orlop it was like some canto in the Inferno. It was dark; the four oil lamps whose flickering, reddish yellow glimmer wavered from the deck beams above seemed to serve only to cast shadows. The atmosphere was stifling. To the normal stenches of bilge and a ship's stores were added the stinks of sick men crowded together, of the sooty lamps, of the bitter powder smell which had drifted in yesterday and had not yet succeeded in making its way out again. It was appallingly hot; the heat and the stink hit Hornblower in the face as he entered, and within five seconds of his entry his face was as wet as if it had been dipped in water, so hot was it and so laden was the atmosphere with moisture.

As complex as the air was the noise. There were the ordinary ship noises – the creaking and groaning of timber, the vibration of the rigging transmitted downward from the chains, the sound of the sea outside, the wash of the bilge below, and the monotonous clangour of the pumps forward intensified by the ship-timbers acting as sounding boards. But all the noises acted only as accompaniment to the din in the cockpit, where seventy-five wounded men, crammed together, were groaning and sobbing and screaming, blaspheming and vomiting. Lost souls in hell could hardly have had a more hideous environment, or be suffering more.

Hornblower found Laurie, standing aimlessly in the gloom.

'Thank God you've come, sir,' he said. His tone implied that he cast all responsibility, gladly, from that moment on the shoulders of his captain.

'Come round with me and make your report,' snapped Hornblower. He hated this business, and yet, although he was completely omnipotent on board, he could not turn and fly as his instincts told him to do. The work had to be done, and Hornblower knew that now Laurie had proved his incompetence he himself was the best man to deal with it. He approached the last man in the row, and drew back with a start of surprise. Lady Barbara was there; the wavering light caught her classic features as she knelt beside the wounded man. She was sponging his face and his throat as he writhed on the deck.

It was a shock to Hornblower to see her engaged thus. The day was yet to come when Florence Nightingale was to make nursing a profession in which women could engage. No man of taste could bear the thought of a woman occupied with the filthy work of a hospital. Sisters of Mercy might labour there for the good of their souls; boozy old women might attend to women in labour and occasionally take a hand at sick nursing, but to look after wounded men was entirely men's work – the work of men who deserved nothing better, either, and who were ordered to it on account of their incapacity or their bad record like men ordered to clean out latrines. Hornblower's stomach revolted at the sight of Lady Barbara here in contact with dirty bodies, with blood and pus and vomit.

'Don't do that!' he said, hoarsely. 'Go away from here. Go on deck.'

'I have begun this work now,' said Lady Barbara indifferently. 'I am not going to leave it unfinished.'

Her tone admitted no possibility of argument; she was apparently talking of the inevitable – much as she might say that she had caught cold and would have to bear with it until it had run its course.

'The gentleman in charge here,' she went on, 'knows nothing of his duties.'

Lady Barbara had no belief in the nobility of nursing, to her mind it was a more degrading occupation than cooking or mending clothes (work which had only occasionally, when the exigencies of travel demanded it, engaged her capable fingers) but she had found a job which was being inefficiently done when there was no one save herself to do it better, at a time when the King's service depended in part on its being done well. She had set herself to work with the same wholehearted attention to detail and neglect of personal comfort with which one of her brothers had governed India and another had fought the Mahrattas.

'This man,' went on Lady Barbara, 'has a splinter of wood under his skin here. It ought to be extracted at once.'

She displayed the man's bare chest, hairy and tattooed. Under the tattooing there was a horrible black bruise, stretching from the breast bone to the right armpit, and in the muscles of the armpit was a jagged projection under the skin; when Lady Barbara laid her fingers on it the man writhed and groaned with pain. In fighting between wooden ships splinter wounds constituted a high proportion of the casualties, and the hurtling pieces of wood could never be extracted by the route by which they entered, because their shape gave them natural barbs. In this case the splinter had been deflected by the ribs so as to pass round under the skin, bruising and lacerating, to its present place in the armpit.

'Are you ready to do it now?' asked Lady Barbara of the unhappy Laurie.

'Well, madam—'

'If you will not, then I will. Don't be a fool, man.'

'I will see that it is done, Lady Barbara,' interposed Hornblower. He would promise anything to get this finished and done with.

'Very well, then, Captain.'

Lady Barbara rose from her knees, but she showed no sign of any intention of retiring in a decent female fashion. Hornblower and Laurie looked at each other.

'Now, Laurie,' said Hornblower, harshly. 'Where are your instruments? Here, you, Wilcox, Hudson. Bring him a good stiff tot of rum. Now, Williams, we're going to get that splinter out of you. It is going to hurt you.'

Hornblower had to struggle hard to keep his face from writhing in disgust and fear of the task before him. He spoke harshly to stop his voice from trembling; he hated the whole business. And it was a painful and bloody business, too. Although Williams tried hard to show no weakness, he writhed as the incision was made, and Wilcox and Hudson had to catch his hands and force his shoulders back. He gave a horrible cry as the long dark strip of wood was dragged out, and then fell limp, fainting, so that he uttered no protest at the prick of the needle as the edges of the wound were clumsily sewn together.

Lady Barbara's lips were firmly compressed. She watched Laurie's muddled attempts at bandaging, and then she stooped without a word and took the rags from him. The men watched her fascinated as with one hand firmly behind Williams' spine she passed the roll dexterously round his body and bound the fast-reddening waste firmly to the wound.

'He will do now,' said Lady Barbara, rising.

Hornblower spent two stifling hours down there in the cockpit going the round with Laurie and Lady Barbara, but they were not nearly such agonising hours as they might have been. One of the main reasons for his feeling so unhappy regarding the care of the wounded had been his consciousness of his own incompetence. Insensibly he came to shift some of his responsibility on to Lady Barbara's shoulders; she was so obviously capable and so unintimidated that she was the person most fitted of all in the ship to be given the supervision of the wounded. When Hornblower had gone round every bed, when the five newly dead men had been dragged out, he faced her under the wavering light of the last lamp in the row.

'I don't know how I can thank you, ma'am,' he said. 'I am as grateful to you as any of these wounded men.'

'There is no gratitude needed,' said Lady Barbara, shrugging her slim shoulders, 'for work which had to be done.'

A good many years later her ducal brother was to say 'The King's government must be carried on,' in exactly the same tone. The man in the bed beside them waved a bandaged arm.

'Three cheers for her leddyship,' he croaked. 'Hip hip, hurrah!'

Some of the shattered invalids joined him in his cheers – a melancholy chorus, blended with the wheezing and groaning of the delirious men around them. Lady Barbara waved a deprecating hand and turned back to the captain.

'We must have air down here,' she said. 'Can that be arranged? I remember my brother telling me how the mortality in the hospital at Bombay declined as soon as they began to give the patients air. Perhaps those men who can be moved can be brought on deck?'

'I will arrange it, ma'am,' said Hornblower.

Lady Barbara's request was strongly accented by the contrast which Hornblower noticed when he went on deck – the fresh Pacific air, despite the scorching sunshine, was like champagne after the solid stink of the orlop. He gave orders for the immediate re-establishment of the canvas ventilating shafts which had been removed when the decks were cleared for action.

'And there are certain of the wounded, Mr Rayner,' he went on, 'who would do better if brought up on deck. You must find Lady Barbara Wellesley and ask her which men are to be moved.'

'Lady Barbara Wellesley, sir?' said Rayner, surprised and tactless, because he knew nothing of the last development.

'You heard what I said,' snapped Hornblower.

'Aye aye, sir,' said Rayner hurriedly, and dived away below in fear lest he should say anything further to annoy his captain.

So that on board H.M.S. *Lydia* that morning divisions were held and divine service conducted a little late, after the burial of the dead, with a row of wounded swaying in hammocks on each side of the maindeck, and with the faint echo of the horrible sounds below floating up through the air shafts.

XIX

Once more the *Lydia* held her course along the Pacific coast of Central America. The grey volcanic peaks, tinged with pink, slid past her to the eastward, with the lush green of the coastal strip sometimes just visible at their feet. The sea was blue and the sky was blue; the flying-fish skimmed the surface, leaving their fleeting furrows behind them. But every minute of the day and night twenty men toiled at the pumps to keep her from sinking, and the rest of the able bodied crew worked all their waking hours at the task of refitting.

The fortnight which elapsed before she rounded Cape Mala went far to reduce her list of wounded. Some of the men were by then already convalescent – the hard physical condition which they had enjoyed, thanks to months of heavy work at sea, enabled them to make light of wounds which would have been fatal to men of soft physique. Shock and exhaustion had relieved the ship of others, and now gangrene, the grim Nemesis which awaited so many men with open wounds in those pre-antiseptic days, was relieving her of still more. Every morning there was the same ceremony at the ship's side, when two or three or six hammock-wrapped bundles were slid over into the blue Pacific.

Galbraith went that way. He had borne the shock of his wound, he had even survived the torture to which Laurie submitted him when, goaded by Lady Barbara's urgent representations, he had set to work with knife and saw upon the smashed tangle of flesh and bone which had been his legs. He had bade fair to make a good recovery, lying blanched and feeble in his cot, so that Laurie had been heard to boast of his surgical skill and of the fine stumps he had made and of the neatness with which he had tied the arteries. Then, suddenly, the fatal symptoms had shown themselves, and Galbraith had died five days later after a fortunate delirium.

Hornblower and Lady Barbara drew nearer to each other during those days. Lady Barbara had fought a losing battle for Galbraith's life to the very end, had fought hard and without sparing herself, and yet seemingly without emotion as if she were merely applying herself to a job which had to be done. Hornblower would have thought this was the case if had not seen her face on the occasion when Galbraith was holding her hands and talking to her under the impression that she was his mother. The dying boy was babbling feverishly in the broad Scots into which he had lapsed as soon as delirium overcame him, clutching her hands and refusing to let her go, while she sat with him talking calmly and quietly in an effort to soothe him. So still was her voice, so calm and unmoved was her attitude, that Hornblower would have been deceived had he not seen the torment in her face.

And for Hornblower it was unexpectedly painful when Galbraith died. Hornblower always looked upon himself as a man content to make use of others, pleasingly devoid of human weaknesses. It was a surprise to him to find how hurt and sorry he was at Galbraith's death, and to find his voice trembling and tears in his eyes as he read the service, and to feel a shudder of distress at the thought of what the sharks were doing to Galbraith's body, down there below the blue surface of the Pacific. He told himself that he was being weak, and then hastened to assure himself that he was merely annoyed at the loss of a useful subordinate, but he could not convince himself. In a fury of reaction he flung himself into the business of driving his men harder in their task of refitting the *Lydia,* and yet now when his eyes met Lady Barbara's on deck or across the dinner table, it was not with the complete lack of sympathy which had previously prevailed. There was a hint of understanding between them now.

Hornblower saw little enough of Lady Barbara. They dined together on some occasions, always with at least one other officer present, but for the most part he was busy with his professional duties and she with her care of the sick. They neither of them had the time, and he at least had not the superfluous energy to spare for the flirtations that those mild tropic nights should have brought in their train. And Hornblower, as soon as they entered the Gulf of Panama, had sufficient additional worries for the moment to drive away all possibility of a flirtation.

The Pearl Islands were just in view over the port bow, and the *Lydia,* close hauled, was heading for Panama one day's sail ahead when the guarda-costa lugger which had encountered them before hove up over the horizon to windward. At sight of the *Lydia* she altered course and came running down wind towards her, while Hornblower kept steadily on his course. He was a little elated with the prospect of making even such a fever-ridden port as badly equipped as Panama, because the strain of keeping the *Lydia* afloat was beginning to tell on him.

The lugger hove-to a couple of cables' lengths away, and a few minutes later the same smart officer in the brilliant uniform came clambering on to the *Lydia's* deck as had boarded from her once before.

'Good morning, Captain,' he said, bowing profoundly. 'I trust Your Excellency is enjoying the best of health?'

'Thank you,' said Hornblower.

The Spanish officer was looking curiously about him; the *Lydia* still bore many marks of her recent battle – the row of wounded in hammocks told a good part of the story. Hornblower saw that the Spaniard seemed to be on his guard, as though determined to be noncommittal at present until something unknown had revealed itself.

'I see,' said the Spaniard, 'that your fine ship has been recently in action. I hope that Your Excellency had good fortune in the encounter?'

'We sank the *Natividad* if that is what you mean,' said Hornblower brutally.

'You sank her, Captain?'

'I did.'

'She is destroyed?'

'She is.'

The Spaniard's expression hardened – Hornblower was led for a moment to think that it was a bitter blow to him to hear that for a second time the Spanish ship had been beaten by an English ship of half her force.

'Then, sir,' said the Spaniard, 'I have a letter to give you.'

He felt in his breast pocket, but with a curious gesture of hesitation – Hornblower realised later that he must have had two letters, one in one pocket and one in another, of different import, one to be delivered if the *Natividad* were destroyed and the other if she were still able to do damage. The letter which he handed over when he was quite certain which was which was not very brief, but was worded with a terseness that implied (having regard to the ornateness of the Spanish official style) absolute rudeness, as Hornblower was quick to realise when he tore open the wrapper and read the contents.

It was a formal prohibition from the Viceroy of Peru for the *Lydia* to drop anchor in, or to enter into, any port of Spanish America, in the Viceroyalty of Peru, of the Vice-royalty of Mexico, or the Captain-Generalcy of New Granada.

Hornblower re-read the letter, and while he did so the dismal clangour of the pumps, drifting aft to his ears, made more acute the worries which instantly leaped upon him. He thought of his battered, leaking ship, his sick and wounded, his weary crew and attentuated stores, of the rounding of the Horn and the four thousand miles of Atlantic which lay between him and England. And more than that; he remembered the supplementary orders which had been given him when he left England, regarding the effort he was to make to open Spanish America to British trade and to establish an Isthmian canal.

'You are aware of the contents of this letter, sir?' he asked.

'Yes, sir.'

The Spaniard was haughty, even brazen about it.

'Can you explain this most unfriendly behaviour on the part of the Viceroy?'

'I would not presume to explain my master's actions, sir.'

'And yet they are in sore need of explanation. I cannot understand how any civilised man could abandon an ally who has fought his battles for him and is in need of help solely because of those battles.'

'You came unasked into these seas, sir. There would have been no battle for you to fight if you had stayed in those parts of the world where your King rules. The South Sea is the property of His Most Catholic Majesty, who will tolerate no intruder upon it.'

'I understand,' said Hornblower.

He guessed that new orders had come out to Spanish America now that the government of Spain had heard of the presence of an English frigate in the Pacific. The retention of the American monopoly was to the Spanish mind as dear as life itself. There was no length to which the Spanish government would not go to retain it, even though it meant offending an ally while in the midst of a life and death struggle with the most powerful despot in Europe. To the Spaniards in Madrid the *Lydia's* presence in the Pacific hinted at the coming of a flood of British traders, at the drying up of the constant stream of gold and silver on which the Spanish government depended, at – worse still – the introduction of heresy into a part of the world which had been kept faithful to the Pope through three centuries. It did not matter if Spanish America were poor, misgoverned, disease ridden, nor if the rest of the world felt the pinch of being shut out at a time when the Continental System had ruined European trade.

In a clear-sighted moment Hornblower foresaw that the world could not long tolerate selfishness carried to these lengths, and that soon, amid general approval, Spanish America would throw off the Spanish yoke. Later, if neither Spain nor New Granada would cut that canal, someone else would step in and do it for them. He was minded to say so, but his innate caution restrained him. However badly he had been treated, there was nothing to be gained by causing an open breach. There was a sweeter revenge in keeping his thoughts to himself.

'Very good, sir,' he said. 'My compliments to your master. I will call at no port on the Spanish Main. Please convey to His Excellency my lively sense of gratitude at the courtesy with which I have been treated, and my pleasure at this further proof of the good relations between the governments of which we have the good fortune to be subjects.'

The Spanish officer looked at him sharply, but Hornblower kept his face immobile while bending his spine with studied courtesy.

'And now, sir,' went on Hornblower drily, 'I must, much to my regret, wish you good day and a pleasant journey. I have much to attend to.'

It was irksome to the Spaniard to be dismissed in this cavalier fashion, but he could take no open exception to anything Hornblower had said. He could only return Hornblower's bow and walk back to the ship's side. No sooner was he back in his boat than Hornblower turned to Bush.

'Keep the ship hove-to, if you please, Mr Bush,' he said.

The *Lydia* rolled heavily, hove-to, on the swell, while her captain resumed his uninterrupted pacing of the quarterdeck, eyed furtively by those officers and men who had guessed at the bad news this latest despatch contained. Up and down, up and down, walked Hornblower, between the carronade slides on the one hand and the ring bolts on the other, while the clanking of the pumps, floating drearily on the heavy air, told him at every second how urgent it was that he should form some new decision.

First of all, however, before even the question of the condition of the ship arose, he must decide about stores and water – every ship's captain had to consider that problem first. Six weeks back he had filled his storerooms and his water barrels. But since that time he had lost a quarter of his crew. At a pinch, even allowing for a long time to refit, there was enough food to last them back to England, therefore; especially as the easterly rounding of the Horn was never as prolonged as the westerly one, and (now that all need of secrecy had disappeared) if necessary St Helena or Sierra Leone or Gibraltar would be open to him to replenish.

That was intensely satisfactory. He could devote his whole mind now to his ship. Refit he must. The *Lydia* could not hope to survive the storms of Cape Horn in her present condition, leaking like a sieve, jury rigged, and with a sail fothered under her bottom. The work could not be done at sea, and the harbours were barred to him. He must do as old buccaneers did – as Drake and Anson and Dampier had done in these very waters – find some secluded cove where he could careen his ship. It would not be easy on the mainland, for the Spaniards had settled round every navigable bay. It would have to be an island, therefore.

Those Pearl Islands on the horizon would not be suitable, for Hornblower knew them to be inhabited and to be frequently visited from Panama – besides, the lugger was still in sight and watching his movements. Hornblower went down below and got out his charts; there was the island of Coiba which the *Lydia* had passed yesterday. His charts told him nothing of it save its position, but it was clearly the place to investigate first. Hornblower laid off his course and then went on deck again.

'We will put the ship about, if you please, Mr Bush,' he said.

XX

Inch by inch His Britannic Majesty's frigate *Lydia* crept into the bay. The cutter was out ahead, with Rayner sounding industriously, while with a dying breath of air behind her and a shred of sail set the *Lydia* felt her way between the two headlands into the tortuous channel. Those capes, one each side of the entrance, were steep rocky cliffs, and the one overlapped the other a trifle so that only an eye sharpened by necessity, and which had made the most of its recent opportunities of learning the typical rock formations of that coast could have guessed at the possibility of an expanse of water behind them.

Hornblower took his eye from the ship's course as she crawled round the corner to study the bay before him. There were mountains all round it, but on the farther side the slope down to the water was not nearly as steep, and on the water's edge there, at the foot of the dazzling green which clothed the banks all round, there was a hint of golden sand which told of the sort of bottom which he sought. It would be shelving there, without a doubt, and free from rock.

'This seems very suitable,' said Hornblower to Bush.

'Aye aye, sir. Made for the job,' said Bush.

'Then you may drop anchor. We shall start work at once.'

It was terribly hot in that little bay in the island of Coiba. The lofty mountains all about cut off any wind that might be blowing, and at the same time reflected the heat to a focus in the bay. As the cable rasped out through the hawsehole Hornblower felt the heat descend upon him. He was wet with sweat even while he stood still on the quarterdeck; he longed for a bath and for a little leisure, to rest until the cool of the evening, but he could not allow himself any such luxury. Time was, as ever, of vital importance. He must make himself secure before the Spaniards could discover where he had hidden himself.

'Call back the cutter,' he said.

On land it was even hotter than on the water. Hornblower had himself rowed to the sandy beach, sounding as he went, and examining with care the sample of the bottom which the tallow on the bottom of the lead brought up for his inspection. It was sand without a doubt – he could beach the *Lydia* safely there. He landed in the breathless jungle; there was clearly no human life here, to judge by the pathlessness of the close-packed vegetation. Tall trees and scrub, creepers and parasites, were all tangled together in their silent struggle for life. Strange birds with strange cries flitted through the twilight of the branches; Hornblower's nostrils were assailed by the reek of the decaying matter beneath his feet. With a sweating escort, musket in hand, about him, he cut his way through the forest. He emerged where the rock was too steep for vegetation ever to have gained a foothold, into the blinding sunlight at the mouth of the bay. He climbed, sweating and exhausted, up the steep ledges. The *Lydia* floated idly on the dazzling blue of the little bay. The opposite headland frowned down upon him across the mouth, and he studied its soaring ledges through his glass. Then he went back to his ship, to goad his men into frantic activity.

Before she could be beached, before the carpenter and his men could set to work upon her bottom, the *Lydia* must be lightened. And also, before she could be laid defenceless on her side, this bay must be made secure from all aggressors. Tackles were rigged, and the two-ton eighteen pounders were swayed up from the maindeck. With careful management and exact balancing the cutter could just carry one of these monsters. One at a time they were ferried to the headlands, where Rayner and Gerard were ready at work with parties preparing emplacements. Toiling gangs were set to work preparing rough paths up the faces of the cliffs, and no sooner were these complete than the men were turned on with tackles and ropes to drag the guns up the paths. Powder and shot for the guns followed them, and then food and water for the garrisons. At the end of thirty-six hours of exacting labour the *Lydia* was a hundred tons lighter, and the entrance to the bay was so defended that any vessel attempting it would have to brave the plunging fire of twenty guns.

In the meanwhile another party had been working like furies on shore above the sandy beach. Here they cleared away a section of forest, and dragged the fallen trees into a rough breast work, and into the rude fort so delimited, among the tree stumps, another party brought up beef barrels, and flour bags, and spars, and guns, and shot, and powder barrels, until the *Lydia* was a mere empty shell rolling in the tiny waves of the bay. The men stretched canvas shelters for themselves as protection against the frequent tropical showers which deluged on them, and for their officers they built rude timber huts – and one for the women as well.

In giving that order Hornblower made his sole acknowledgment of the women's existence. During this flurry of work, and under the strain of the responsibility which he bore, he had neither the time nor the surplus energy to spare for conversation with Lady Barbara. He was tired, and the steamy heat drained his energies, but his natural reaction to these conditions, having in mind the need for haste, was to flog himself into working harder and harder, obstinately and unreasonably, so that the days passed in a nightmare of fatigue, during which the minutes he passed with Lady Barbara were like the glimpses a man has of a beautiful woman during delirium.

He drove his men hard from earliest dawn as long as daylight lasted, keeping them slaving away in the crushing heat until they shook their heads over him in rueful admiration. They did not grudge him the efforts he called for; that would have been impossible for British sailors led by a man who was so little prepared to spare himself. And besides, the men displayed the constant characteristics of British crews of working the more cheerfully the more unusual the conditions. Sleeping on beds of sand instead of in their far more comfortable hammocks, working on solid earth instead of on board ship, hemmed in by dense forest instead of engirdled by a distant horizon – all this was stimulating and cheering.

The fireflies in the forest, the strange fruits which were found for them by their impressed prisoners from the *Natividad,* the very mosquitoes which plagued them, helped at the same time to keep them happy. Down the cliff face beside one of the entrance batteries there tumbled a constant stream of clear water, so that for once in their lives the men were allowed as much fresh water as they could use, and to men who for months at a time had to submit to having a sentry standing guard over their drinking water this was an inexpressible luxury.

Soon, on the sandy shore, and as far as possible from the stored powder barrels, canvas covered and sentry guarded, there were fires lit over which was melted the pitch brought from the boatswain's store. There had not been enough defaulters during those days to pick all the oakum required – some of the ship's company had to work at oakum picking while the *Lydia* was hove over and the carpenter applied himself to the task of settling her bottom to rights. The shot holes were plugged, and strained seams caulked and pitched, the missing sheets of copper were replaced by the last few sheets which the *Lydia* carried in reserve. For four days the tiny bay was filled with the sound of the caulking hammers at work, and the reek of melting pitch drifted over the still water as the smoking cauldrons were carried across to the working parties.

At the end of that time the carpenter expressed himself as satisfied, and Hornblower, anxiously going over every foot of the ship's bottom, grudgingly agreed with him. The *Lydia* was hove off, and still empty, was kedged and towed across the bay until she lay at the foot of the high cliff where one of the batteries was established – the shore was steep enough at this point to allow her to lie close in here when empty of guns and stores. At this point Lieutenant Bush had been busy setting up a projecting gallows, a hundred feet above, and vertically over, the ship's deck. Painfully, and after many trials, the *Lydia* was manoeuvred until she could be moored so that the stump of her mizzen mast stood against the plumb line which Bush dropped from the tackles high above. Then the wedges were knocked out, the tackles set to work, and the stump was drawn out of her like a decayed tooth.

That part of the work was easy compared with the next step. The seventy-five foot main yard had to be swayed up to the gallows, and then hung vertically down from them; if it had slipped it would have shot down like some monstrous arrow and would have sunk her for certain. When the yard was exactly vertical and exactly above the mizzen mast step it was lowered down, inch by inch, until its solid butt could be coaxed by anxious gangs through the maindeck and through the orlop until it came at last solidly to rest in its step upon the kelson. It only remained then to wedge it firmly in, to set up new shrouds, and the *Lydia* had once more a mizzen mast which could face the gales of the Horn.

Back at her anchorage, the *Lydia* could be ballasted once more, with her beef barrels and water barrels, her guns and her shot, save what was left in the entrance batteries. Ballasted and steady upon her keel, she could be re-rigged and her topmasts set up again. Every rope was re-rove, her standing rigging newly set up, replacements affected until she was as efficient a ship as when she had left Portsmouth newly commissioned.

It was then that Hornblower could allow himself time to draw breath and relax. The captain of a ship that is no ship, but only a mere hulk helpless in a landlocked inlet, cannot feel a moment's peace. A heretic in an Inquisitor's dungeon is happy compared with him. There is the menacing land all about him, the torment of helplessness as a perpetual goad, the fear of an ignominious siege to wake him in the night. Hornblower was like a man released from a sentence of death when he trod the *Lydia's* deck once more and allowed his eye to rove contentedly upward and ever upward through the aspiring rigging, with the clangour of the pumps which had echoed in his ears during the last fortnight's cruise completely stilled, happy in the consciousness of a staunch ship under his feet, comfortable in the knowledge that there would be no more campaigns to plan until he reached England.

At this very moment they were dismantling one of the entrance batteries, and the guns were being ferried out to the *Lydia* one by one. Already he had a broadside battery which could fire, a ship which could manoeuvre, and he could snap his fingers at every Spaniard in the Pacific. It was a glorious sensation. He turned and found Lady Barbara on the quarterdeck beside him, and he smiled at her dazzlingly.

'Good morning, ma'am,' he said. 'I trust you found your cabin comfortable again?'

Lady Barbara smiled back at him – in fact she almost laughed, so comical was the contrast between this greeting and the scowls she had encountered from him during the last eleven days.

'Thank you, Captain,' she said. 'It is marvellously comfortable. Your crew has worked wonders to have done so much in so little time.'

Quite unconsciously he had reached out and taken both her hands in his, and was standing there holding them, smiling all over his face in the sunshine. Lady Barbara felt that it would only need a word from her to set him dancing.

'We shall be at sea before nightfall,' he said, ecstatically.

She could not be dignified with him, any more than she could have been dignified with a baby; she knew enough of men and affairs not to resent his previous preoccupation. Truth to tell, she was a trifle fond of him because of it.

'You are a very fine sailor, sir,' she said to him suddenly. 'I doubt if there is another officer in the King's service who could have done all you have done on this voyage.'

'I am glad you think so, ma'am,' he said, but the spell was broken. He had been reminded of himself, and his cursed self-consciousness closed in upon him again. He dropped her hands, awkwardly, and there was a hint of a blush in his tanned cheeks.

'I have only done my duty,' he mumbled, looking away.

'Many men can do that,' said Lady Barbara, 'but few can do it well. The country is your debtor – my sincerest hope is that England will acknowledge the debt.'

The words started a sudden train of thought in Hornblower's mind; it was a train he had followed up often before. England would only remember that his battle with the *Natividad* had been unnecessary; that a more fortunate captain would have heard of the new alliance between Spain and England before he had handed the *Natividad* over to the rebels, and would have saved all the trouble and friction and loss which had resulted. A frigate action with a hundred casualties might be glorious, but an unnecessary action with a hundred casualties was quite inglorious. No one would stop to think that it was his careful obedience to orders and skill in carrying them out which had been the reason of it. He would be blamed for his own merits, and life was suddenly full of bitterness again.

'Your pardon, ma'am,' he said, and he turned away from her and walked forward to bawl orders at the men engaged in swaying an eighteen pounder up from the launch.

Lady Barbara shook her head at his back.

'Bless the man!' she said to herself, softly. 'He was almost human for a while.'

Lady Barbara was fast acquiring, in her forced loneliness, the habit of talking to herself like the sole inhabitant of a desert island. She checked herself as soon as she found herself doing so, and went below and rated Hebe soundly for some minor sin of omission in the unpacking of her wardrobe.

XXI

The rumour had gone round the crew that the *Lydia* was at last homeward bound. The men had fought and worked, first on the one side and then on the other, without understanding the trend of high politics which had decided whom they should fight and for whom they should work. That Spaniards should be first enemies, and then friends, and then almost hostile neutrals, had hardly caused one of them a single thought. They had been content to obey orders unthinkingly; but now, it seemed certain, so solidly based was the rumour, that the *Lydia* was on her way home. To the scatter-brained crew it seemed as if England was just over the horizon. They gave no thought to the five thousand stormy miles of sea that lay before them. Their heads were full of England. The pressed men thought of their wives; the volunteers thought of the women of the ports and of the joys of paying off. The sun of their rapture was not even overcast by any cloud of doubt as to the chances of their being turned over to another ship and sent off half round the world again before ever they could set foot on English soil.

They had flung themselves with a will into the labour of warping out of the bay, and not one of them looked back with regret to the refuge which alone had made their homeward voyage possible. They had chattered and played antics like a crew of monkeys when they dashed aloft to set sail, and the watch below had danced and set to partners through the warm evening while the *Lydia* bowled along with a favourable breeze over the blue Pacific. Then during the night the wind died away with its usual tropical freakishness, from a good breeze to a faint air, and from a faint air to a slow succession of fluky puffs which set the sails slatting and the rigging creaking and kept the watch continually at work at the braces trimming the sails.

Hornblower awoke in his cot in the cool hour before dawn. It was still too dark to see the tell-tale compass in the deck over his head, but he could guess from the long roll of the ship and the intermittent noises overhead that calm weather had overtaken them. It was almost time for him to start his morning walk on the quarterdeck, and he rested, blissfully free of all feeling of responsibility, until Polwheal came in to get out his clothes. He was putting on his trousers when a hail from the masthead lookout came echoing down through the scuttle.

'Sail ho! Broad on the larboard beam. It's that there lugger again, sir.'

That feeling of freedom from worry vanished on the instant. Twice had that ill-omened lugger been seen in this very Gulf of Panama, and twice she had been the bearer of bad news. Hornblower wondered, with a twinge of superstition, what this third encounter would bring forth. He snatched his coat from Polwheal's hands and put it on as he dashed up the companionway.

The lugger was there, sure enough, lying becalmed some two miles away; there were half a dozen glasses trained on her – apparently Hornblower's officers shared his superstition.

'There's something about that craft's rig which gives me the horrors,' grumbled Gerard.

'She's just a plain Spanish guarda-costa,' said Crystal. 'I've seen 'em in dozens. I remember off Havana—'

'Who hasn't seen 'em?' snapped Gerard. 'I was saying – hullo! Theres a boat putting off.'

He glanced round and saw his captain appearing on the deck.

'Lugger's sending a boat, sir.'

Hornblower did his best to make his expression one of sturdy indifference. He told himself that commanding, as he did, the fastest and most powerful ship on the Pacific coast, he need fear nothing. He was equipped and ready to sail half round the world, to fight any ship up to fifty guns. The sight of the lugger ought to cause him no uneasiness, but it did.

For long minutes they watched the boat come bobbing towards them over the swell. At first it was only a black speck showing occasionally on the crests Then the flash of the oar blades could be seen, as they reflected the rays of the nearly level sun, and then the oars themselves, as the boat grew like some great black water beetle creeping over the surface, and at last she was within hail, and a few minutes after for the third time the young Spanish officer in his brilliant uniform mounted to the *Lydia's* deck and received Hornblower's bow.

He made no attempt to conceal his curiosity, nor the admiration which blended with it. He saw that the jury mizzen mast had disappeared and had been replaced by a new spar as trim and as efficient as any set up in a navy yard; he saw that the shot holes had been expertly patched; he noticed that the pumps were no longer at work – that in fact during the sixteen days since he last saw her the ship had been entirely refitted, and, to his certain knowledge, without any aid from the shore and in no harbour save perhaps for some deserted inlet.

'It surprises me to see you here again, sir,' he said.

'To me,' said Hornblower, with perfect courtesy, 'it is a pleasure as well as a surprise.'

'To me also it is a pleasure,' said the Spaniard quickly, 'but I had thought you were far on your way home by now.'

'I am on my way home,' said Hornblower, determined to give no cause for offence if possible, 'but as you see, sir, I have not progressed far as yet. However, I have effected, as perhaps you may notice, the repairs that were necessary, and now nothing will delay me from proceeding to England with the utmost despatch – unless, sir, there is some new development which makes it advisable, for the sake of the common cause of our two countries, for me to remain longer in these waters.'

Hornblower said these last words anxiously, and he was already devising in his mind excuses to free himself from the consequences of this offer if it were accepted. But the Spaniard's reply reassured him.

'Thank you, sir,' he said, 'but there is no need for me to take advantage of your kindness. His Most Catholic Majesty's dominions are well able to guard themselves. I am sure that His Britannic Majesty will be glad to see such a fine frigate returning to forward his cause.'

The two captains bowed to each other profoundly at this exchange of compliments before the Spaniard resumed his speech.

'I was thinking, sir,' he went on, 'that perhaps if you would do me the great honour of visiting my ship for a moment, taking advantage of this prevailing calm, I should be able to show Your Excellency something which would be of interest and which would demonstrate our ability to continue without your kind assistance.'

'What is it?' asked Hornblower, suspiciously.

The Spaniard smiled.

'It would give me pleasure if I could show it to you as a surprise. Please, sir, would you not oblige me?'

Hornblower looked automatically round the horizon. He studied the Spaniard's face. The Spaniard was no fool; and only a fool could meditate treachery when almost within range of a frigate which could sink his ship in a single broadside. And mad though most Spaniards were, they were not mad enough to offer violence to a British captain. Besides, he was pleased with the thought of how his officers would receive his announcement that he was going on board the lugger.

'Thank you, sir,' he said. 'It will give me great pleasure to accompany you.'

The Spaniard bowed again, and Hornblower turned to his first lieutenant.

'I am going to visit the lugger, Mr Bush,' he said. 'I shall only be gone a short time. Call away the cutter and send her after me to bring me back.'

Hornblower was delighted to see how Bush struggled to conceal his consternation at the news.

'Aye aye, sir,' he said. He opened his mouth and shut it again; he wanted to expostulate and yet did not dare, and finally repeated feebly 'Aye aye, sir.'

In the small boat rowing back to the lugger the Spaniard was the mirror of courtesy. He chatted politely about weather conditions. He mentioned the latest news of the war in Spain – it was quite undoubted that a French army had surrendered to the Spaniards in Andalusia, and that Spanish and British armies were assembling for a march into France. He described the ravages of yellow fever on the mainland. He contrived, all the same, to allow no single hint to drop as to the nature of the surprise which he was going to show Hornblower in the lugger.

The two captains were received with Spanish ceremony as they swung themselves up into the lugger's waist. There was a great deal of bustle and parade, and two bugles and two drums sounded a resounding march horribly out of tune.

'All in this ship is yours, sir,' said the Spaniard with Castilian courtesy, and seeing no incongruity in his next sentence. 'Your Excellency will take some refreshment? A cup of chocolate?'

'Thank you,' said Hornblower. He was not going to imperil his dignity by asking what was the nature of the surprise in store for him. He could wait – especially as he could see the launch already half-way towards the lugger.

The Spaniard was in no hurry to make the revelation. He was evidently savouring in anticipation the Englishman's certain astonishment. He pointed out certain peculiarities in the lugger's rig; he called up his officers to present to Hornblower; he discussed the merits of his crew – nearly all native Indians as on board the *Natividad*. In the end Hornblower won; the Spaniard could wait no longer to be asked.

'Would you please to come this way, sir?' he said. He led the way on to the foredeck, and there, chained by the waist to a ring bolt, with irons on his wrist and ankles, was el Supremo.

He was in rags – half naked in fact, and his beard and hair were matted and tangled, and his own filth lay on the deck about him.

'I think,' said the Spanish captain, 'that you have already had the pleasure, sir, of meeting His Excellency Don Julian Maria de Jesus de Alvarado y Moctezuma, who calls himself the Almighty?'

El Supremo showed no signs of being disconcerted by the gibe.

'Captain Hornblower has indeed been presented to me already,' he said loftily. 'He has worked for me long and devotedly. I trust you are enjoying the best of health, Captain?'

'Thank you, sir,' said Hornblower.

Despite his rags, and his filth, and his chains, el Supremo bore himself with the same elaborate dignity as Hornblower remembered so well those many weeks ago.

'I too,' he said, 'am as well as the world could desire. It is a source of continual satisfaction to me to see my affairs progressing so well.'

A negro servant appeared on the deck at that moment with a tray of chocolate; another followed him with a couple of chairs. Hornblower, at the invitation of his host, sat down. He was glad to do so, as his knees seemed suddenly weak under him, but he had no desire at all for his chocolate. The Spanish captain drank noisily, and el Supremo eyed him as he did so. There came a gleam of appetite in his face. His lips moistened and smacked softly together, his eyes brightened, his hand came out, and then next moment he was calm and indifferent again.

'I trust that the chocolate is to your liking, sirs,' he said. 'I ordered it specially for you. My own appetite for chocolate has long since disappeared.'

'That is just as well,' said the Spanish captain. He laughed loudly and drank again, smacking his lips.

El Supremo ignored him, and turned to Hornblower.

'You see I wear these chains,' he said. 'It is a strange whim on the part of myself and my servants that I should do so. I hope you agree with me that they set off my figure quite admirably?'

'Y-yes, sir,' stammered Hornblower.

'We are on our way to Panama, where I shall mount the throne of the world. They talk of hanging; these fellows here say that there is a gallows awaiting us on the bastion of the Citadel. That will be the framework of my golden throne. Golden, it will be, with diamond stars and a great turquoise moon. It will be from there that I shall issue my next decrees to the world.'

The Spanish captain guffawed again, but el Supremo still stood in quiet dignity, hugging his chains, with the sun blazing down on his tangled head.

'He will not last long in this mood,' said the Spanish captain to Hornblower behind his hand. 'I can see signs of the change coming. It gives me great felicity that you have had the opportunity of seeing him in both his moods.'

'The sun grows in his splendour every day,' said el Supremo. 'He is magnificent and terrible, as I am. He can kill – kill – kill, as he killed the men I exposed to him – when was it? And Moctezuma is dead, and all his line save me, in the hundreds of years ago. I alone remain. And Hernandez is dead, but it was not the sun that killed him. They hanged Hernandez even while the blood dripped from his wounds. They hanged him in my city of San Salvador, and as they hanged him he still called upon the name of el Supremo. They hanged the men and they hanged the women, in long rows at San Salvador.

Only el Supremo is left, to govern from his golden throne. His throne! His throne!'

El Supremo was staring about him now. There was a hint of bewildered realisation in his face as he jangled his chains. He peered at them stupidly.

'Chains! These are chains!'

He was bawling and shouting. He laughed madly, and then he wept and he cursed, flinging himself about on the deck, biting at his chains. His words were no longer articulate as he slobbered and writhed.

'It is interesting, is it not?' said the Spanish captain. 'He will struggle and shout sometimes for twenty-four hours without a stop.'

'Bah!' said Hornblower, and his chair fell with a clatter to the deck as he got to his feet. He was on the verge of vomiting. The Spaniard saw his white face and trembling lips, and was faintly amused, and made no attempt to conceal it.

But Hornblower could give no vent to the flood of protest which was welling up within him. His cautious mind told him that a madman in a ship as small as the lugger must of necessity be chained to the deck, and his conscience reminded him uneasily of the torments he had seen el Supremo inflict without expostulation. This Spanish way of making a show out of insanity and greatness was repulsive enough, but could be paralleled often enough in English history. One of the greatest writers of the English language, and a dignitary of the Church to boot, had once been shown in his dotage for a fee. There was only one line of argument which he could adopt.

'You are going to hang him, mad as he is?' he asked. 'With no chance of making his peace with God?'

The Spaniard shrugged.

'Mad or sane, rebels must hang. Your Excellency must know that as well as I do.'

Hornblower did know it. He was left without any argument at all, and was reduced to stammering inarticulation, even while he boiled with contempt for himself on that account. All that was left for him to do, having lost all his dignity in his own eyes, was to try and retain some few shreds of it in the eyes of his audience. He braced himself up, conscious of the hollowness of the fraud.

'I must thank you very much, sir,' he said, 'for having given me the opportunity of witnessing a most interesting spectacle. And now, repeating my thanks, I fear that I must regretfully take my departure. There seems to be a breath of wind blowing.'

He went down the side of the lugger as stiffly as he might, and took his seat in the sternsheets of the launch. He had to brace himself again to give the word to cast off, and then he sat silent and gloomy as he was rowed back to the *Lydia.* Bush and Gerard and Lady Barbara watched him as he came on deck. It was as if there was death in his face. He looked round him, unseeing and unhearing, and then hurried below to hide his misery. He even sobbed, with his face in his cot, for a second, before he was able to take hold of himself and curse himself for a weak fool. But it was days before he lost that deathly look, and during that time he kept himself solitary in his cabin, unable to bring himself to join the merry parties on the quarterdeck whose gay chatter drifted down to him through the skylight. To him it was a further proof of his weakness and folly that he should allow himself to be so upset by the sight of a criminal madman going to meet the fate he richly deserved.

XXII

Lady Barbara and Lieutenant Bush were sitting talking in the warm moonlight night beside the taffrail. It was the first time that Bush had happened to share a *tête-à-tête* with her, and he had only drifted into it by chance – presumably if he had foreseen it he would have avoided it, but now that he had drifted into conversation with her he was enjoying himself to the exclusion of any disquietude. He was sitting on a pile of the oakum-filled cushions which Harrison had had made for Lady Barbara, and he nursed his knees while Lady Barbara leaned back in her hammock chair. The *Lydia* was rising and falling softly to the gentle music of the waves and the harping of the rigging in the breeze. The white sails glimmered in the brilliant moon; overhead the stars shone with strange brightness. But Bush was not talking of himself, as any sensible man would do under a tropic moon with a young woman beside him.

'Aye, ma'am,' he was saying. 'He's like Nelson. He's nervous, just as Nelson was, and for the same reason. He's thinking all the time – you'd be surprised, ma'am, to know how much he thinks about.'

'I don't think it would surprise me,' said Lady Barbara.

'That's because you think, too, ma'am. It's us stupid ones who'd be surprised, I meant to say. He has more brains than all the rest of us in the ship put together, excepting you, ma'am. He's mighty clever, I do assure you.'

'I can well believe it.'

'And he's the best seaman of us all, and as for navigation – well, Crystal's a fool compared with him, ma'am.'

'Yes?'

'Of course, he's short with me sometimes, the same as he is with everyone else, but bless you, ma'am, that's only to be expected. I know how much he has to worry him, and he's not strong, the same as Nelson wasn't strong. I am concerned about him sometimes, ma'am.'

'You are fond of him.'

'Fond, ma'am?' Bush's sturdy English mind grappled with the word and its sentimental implications, and he laughed a trifle self-consciously. 'If you say so I suppose I must be. I hadn't ever thought of being fond of him before. I like him, ma'am, indeed I do.'

'That is what I meant.'

'The men worship him, ma'am. They would do anything for him. Look how much he has done this commission, and the lash not in use once in a week, ma'am. That is why he is like Nelson. They love him not for anything he does or says, but for what he is.'

'He's handsome, in a way,' said Barbara – she was woman enough to give that matter consideration.

'I suppose he is, ma'am, now you come to mention it. But it wouldn't matter if he were as ugly as sin as far as we was concerned.'

'Of course not.'

'But he's shy, ma'am. He never can guess how clever he is. It's that which always surprises me about him. You'd hardly believe it, ma'am, but he has no more faith in himself than – than I have in myself, ma'am, to put it that way. Less, ma'am, if anything.'

'How strange!' said Lady Barbara. She was accustomed to the sturdy self-reliance of her brothers, unloved and unlovable leaders of men, but her insight made her comment only one of politeness – it was not really strange to her.

'Look, ma'am,' said Bush, suddenly, dropping his voice.

Hornblower had come up on deck. They could see his face, white in the moonlight, as he looked round to assure himself that all was well with his ship, and they could read in it the torment which was obsessing him. He looked like a lost soul during the few seconds he was on deck.

'I wish to God I knew,' said Bush as Hornblower retreated again to the solitude of his cabin, 'what those devils did to him or said to him when he went on board the lugger. Hooker who was in the cutter said he heard someone on board howling like a madman. The torturing devils! It was some of their beastliness, I suppose. You could see how it has upset him, ma'am.'

'Yes,' said Lady Barbara softly.

'I should be grateful if you could try to take him out of himself a little, ma'am, begging your pardon. He is in need of distraction, I suspicion. Perhaps you could – if you'll forgive me, ma'am.'

'I'll try,' said Lady Barbara, 'but I don't think I shall succeed where you have failed. Captain Hornblower has never taken a great deal of notice of me, Mr Bush.'

Yet fortunately the formal invitation to dine with Lady Barbara, which Hebe conveyed to Polwheal and he to his captain, arrived at a moment when Hornblower was just trying to emerge from the black fit which had engulfed him. He read the words as carefully as Lady Barbara had written them – and she had devoted much care to the composition of the note. Hornblower read Lady Barbara's pretty little apology for breaking in upon him at a time when he was obviously engrossed in his work, and he went on to read how Lady Barbara had been informed by Mr Bush that the *Lydia* was about to cross the Equator, and that she thought such an occasion merited some mild celebration. If Captain Hornblower, therefore, would give Lady Barbara the pleasure of his company at dinner and would indicate to her which of his officers he considered should be invited at the same time, Lady Barbara would be delighted. Hornblower wrote back to say that Captain Hornblower had much pleasure in accepting Lady Barbara's kind invitation to dinner, and hoped that Lady Barbara would invite whomever she pleased in addition.

Yet even in the pleasure of returning to society there was some alloy. Hornblower had always been a poor man, and at the time when he commissioned the *Lydia* he had been at his wits' end about where to turn for money in the need for leaving Maria comfortably provided for. In consequence he had not outfitted himself satisfactorily, and now, all these months later, his clothes were in the last stages of decay. The coats were all patched and darned; the epaulettes betrayed in their brassy sheen the fact that they had begun life merely coated with bullion; the cocked hats were all wrecks; he had neither breeches nor stockings fit to be seen; his once white scarves were all coarsened now, and could never be mistaken again for silk. Only the sword 'of fifty guineas' value' retained its good appearance, and he could not wear that at a dinner party.

He was conscious that his white duck trousers, made on board the *Lydia*, had none of the fashionable appearance to which Lady Barbara was accustomed. He looked shabby and he felt shabby, and as he peered at himself in his little mirror he was certain that Lady Barbara would sneer at him. There were grey hairs in his brown curls, too, and then, to his horror, as he straightened his parting, he caught a glimpse of pink scalp – his baldness had increased beyond all measure of late. He eyed himself with complete disgust, and yet he felt that he would gladly give a limb or his remaining hair in exchange for a ribbon and star with which to dazzle Lady Barbara; yet even that would be of no avail, for Lady Barbara had lived all her life in an atmosphere of Garters and Thistles, orders which he could never hope to wear.

He was on the verge of sending a message to Lady Barbara to say that he had changed his mind and would not dine with her that evening, until he thought that if he did so, after all these preparations, Polwheal would guess that it was the result of his realisation of his shabbiness and would laugh at him (and his shabbiness) in consequence. He went into dinner and had his revenge upon the world by sitting silent and preoccupied at the head of the table, blighting with his gloomy presence all attempts at conversation, so that the function began as a frigid failure. It was a poor sort of revenge, but there was a slight gratification to be found in observing Lady Barbara looking down the table at him in concern. In the end he was deprived even of that, for Lady Barbara suddenly smiled and began talking lightly and captivatingly, and led Bush into describing his experiences at Trafalgar – a tale she had heard, to Hornblower's certain knowledge, twice at least already.

The conversation became general, and then animated, for Gerard could not bear to leave all the talking to Bush, and he had to break in with the story of his encounter with an Algerine corsair off Cape Spartel in his old slaving days. It was more than Hornblower's flesh and blood could stand, to stay silent with everyone talking in this fashion. Against his will he found himself entering into the conversation, and an artless question from Lady Barbara about Sir Edward Pellew inveigled him still further in, for Hornblower had been both midshipman and lieutenant in Pellew's ship, and was proud of it. Not until the end of dinner was he able to steady himself, and decline, after the drinking of the King's health, Lady Barbara's invitation to a rubber of whist. That at least, he thought, would make an impression on her – it certainly did upon his officers, for he saw Bush and Gerard exchange startled glances on hearing their captain refuse to play whist. Back in his cabin again he listened through the bulkhead to the uproarious game of *vingt-et-un* which Lady Barbara had suggested instead. He almost wished he was playing, too, even though in his opinion *vingt-et-un* was a game for the feeble-minded.

The dinner had served its purpose, however, in making it possible to meet Lady Barbara's eye again on deck. He could converse with her, too, discussing with her the condition of the few wounded who remained upon the sick list, and after a few morning encounters it was easy to fall into conversation with her during the breathless afternoons and the magic tropical nights as the *Lydia* held her course over the calm Pacific. He had grown hardened again to his shabby coats and his shapeless trousers; he was forgetting the resentful plans he had once turned over in his mind to confine Lady Barbara to her cabin; and mercifully, his memory was no longer being so acutely troubled by the pictures of el Supremo chained to the deck, of Galbraith dying, and of poor little Clay's body sprawled headless on the bloody planks – and when those memories lapsed he could no longer accuse himself of being a coward for being worried by them.

Those were happy days indeed. The routine of the *Lydia* progressed like clockwork. Almost every hour of every day there was enough wind to give her steerage way, and sometimes it blew just hard enough to relieve the monotony. There were no storms during that endless succession of golden days, and the mind could contemplate its endlessness with tranquillity, for 50 degrees South Latitude seemed impossibly far away; they could enjoy the blissfulness of eternity, disregarding the constant warning conveyed to them as every noontide showed the sun lower in the sky and every midnight showed the South Cross higher.

They could be friends during those heavenly nights when the ship's wake showed as a long trail or fire on the faintly luminous water. They learned to talk together, endlessly. She could chatter about the frivolities of the Vice-Regal court at Dublin, and of the intrigues which could enmesh a Governor-General of India; of penniless French émigrés putting purse-proud northern iron-masters in their places; of Lord Byron's extravagancies and of the Royal Dukes' stupidities; and Hornblower learned to listen without a twinge of envy.

He could tell, in return, of months spent on blockade, combating storms off the ironbound Biscay coast, of how Pellew took his frigates into the very surf to sing the *Droits-de-l'homme* with two thousand men on board, of hardship and cruelty and privation – a monotonous toilsome life as fantastic to her as hers appeared to him. He could even tell her, as his self-consciousness dwindled, of the ambitions which he knew would seem to her as trivial as those of a child yearning for a hobby horse; of the two thousand pounds in prize money which he had decided would be all that he would require to eke out his half-pay, the few acres and the cottage and the shelves and shelves of books.

And yet she heard without a smile, with even a trace of envy in her calm face as the moon shone down on them; for her own ambitions were far more vague and far less likely to be realised. She hardly knew what it was that she wanted, and she knew that whatever it was, she could only hope to attain it by ensnaring a husband. That an earl's daughter could envy a penniless frigate captain moved Hornblower inexpressibly, as he watched her face in the moonlight; he was glad even while he was unhappy that Lady Barbara should have to envy anything of anyone.

They could talk of books and of poetry, and Hornblower championed the cause of the classical school who looked back to the days of Queen Anne against the barbarous leaders of the revolt who seemed to delight in setting every established rule at defiance. She heard him with patience, even with approval, as he talked of Gibbon (the object of his sincerest admiration) and Johnson and Swift, when he quoted from Pope and Gray, but she could approve of the barbarians as well. There was a madman called Wordsworth of whose revolutionary opinions in literature Hornblower had heard with vague horror; Lady Barbara thought there was something to be said for him. She turned the tables neatly on Hornblower by claiming Gray as a precursor of the same school; she quoted Campbell and that Gothic innovator, Scott, and she won Hornblower's grudging approval of an ungainly poem called 'The Rime of the Ancient Mariner,' although he maintained sturdily, in the last ditch, that its only merit lay in its content, and that it would have been infinitely better had Pope dealt with the theme in heroic couplets – especially if Pope had been assisted by someone who knew more about navigation and seamanship than did this Coleridge fellow.

Lady Barbara wondered vaguely, sometimes, whether it was not strange that a naval officer should be so earnest a student of literature, but she was learning rapidly. Sea captains were not all of a class, as the uninitiated might carelessly decide. From Bush and Gerard and Crystal as well as from Hornblower she had heard of captains who write Greek elegiacs, of captains who cluttered up their cabins with marbles looted from the Greek islands, captains who classified sea-urchins and corresponded with Cuvier – these on the one hand, just as there were captains who delighted in seeing human back lacerated with the cat-o'-nine-tails, captains who drank themselves insensible every night and who raised hell in their ships during bouts of delirium tremens, captains who starved their crews and captains who turned up all hands at every bell, night and day. She found that she was sure, all the same, that Hornblower was an outstanding member of a class which people on shore tended not to credit with nearly as much ability as they actually possessed.

She had, from the time of her first arrival on board, found pleasure in Hornblower's society. Now they had formed a habit of each other, as though they were insidious drugs, and were vaguely uneasy when out of sight of each other. The voyage had been monotonous enough, as the *Lydia* held steadily southwards, for habits to be easily formed; it had become a habit to exchange a smile when they met on the quarterdeck in the morning – a smile illumined by secret memories of the intimacy of the conversation of the night before. It was a habit now for Hornblower to discuss the ship's progress with Lady Barbara after he had taken the noon sights, a habit now for him to drink coffee with her in the afternoons, and especially was it a habit for them to meet at sunset by the taffrail, although no appointment had been made and no hint of their meeting had ever been suggested, and to lounge in the warm darkness while conversation grew up, seemingly from no roots at all, and blossomed and flowered exotically, under the magic brilliance of the stars until with a reluctance of which they were hardly conscious they drifted off to bed, hours after midnight.

They could even sit silent together now, watching, wordlessly, the mastheads circling amid the stars with the rolling of the ship, listening to the faint orchestra of the ship's fabric, and their thoughts paralleling each other's so that when eventually one of them spoke it was to harmonise completely with what was in the other's mind. At those times Lady Barbara's hand, like a healthy young woman's, was at her side where it could be touched without too great effort. When she had not wanted them to do so men had taken her hand often before, at London balls and Governor-Generals' receptions, but now, conscious though she was of how reckless and imprudent it would be to encourage the slightest physical intimacy on this voyage with months more to last, she still was reckless and imprudent enough to risk it without attempting to analyse her motives. But Hornblower seemed unconscious of that hand. She would see her face lifted to the stars, peaceful and immobile, and she found pleasure in giving herself credit for the change in it from that evening when she had talked with Bush and seen Hornblower's torment.

For happy weeks that phase of the voyage lasted, while the *Lydia* ran steadily south and still more south, until the evenings grew chill and the mornings misty, until the blue sky changed to grey and the first rain they had known for three weeks wetted the *Lydia's* decks, and the west wind blew more blustering and searching, so that Lady Barbara had to wrap herself in a boat cloak to be able to sit on deck at all. Those evenings by the taffrail came to an imperceptible end, and the *Lydia* thrashed along through half a gale, and it grew steadily colder, even though this was the Antipodean summer. For the first time in her life Lady Barbara saw Hornblower dressed in tarpaulins and sou'wester, and she thought oddly, how well those hideous garments suited him. There were times when he would come sauntering into the cabin, his eyes bright and his cheeks flushed with wind, and she felt her pulses leap in sympathy with his.

She knew she was being foolish. She told herself that this weakness of hers only arose because Hornblower was the one man with any culture or any trace of eligibility on board the *Lydia,* and because life in close contact with him for four continuous months was bound to make her either love him or hate him – and as there was no room for hatred in her system the other thing was inevitable. She told herself, too, that as soon as she returned to civilisation, as soon as she could see Hornblower against that usual background of hers which had faded with the passage of the months almost out of her memory, he would lose his interest and his charm.

On board ship one saw things in a false perspective, she informed herself. Salt beef and salt pork, weevilly bread and dried peas, with a glass of lemon juice twice a week; that meant monotony. Trifles assumed an exaggerated importance when leading a life like that. Just as toothache tended to disappear when something occurred to distract the mind, so would this heartache of hers disappear when she had other things to think about. It was all very true; but strangely it made not the least difference to her present feelings.

They had reached the region of westerly trade winds now. Every day they roared harder and harder, and every day the sea rose higher and higher. The *Lydia* was thrashing along magnificently now; there were two or three days when she logged over two hundred and forty nautical miles as her day's run from noon to noon. It was cold, and it rained in torrents, and the main deck was often knee deep in water. There were days when all Lady Barbara could do was to brace herself in her cot while the ship tossed and rolled as though at any moment she would turn completely over, while Hebe (who never succeeded quite in overcoming her seasickness) moaned in her blankets on the deck and her teeth chattered with the cold. No fire could be kept alight; nothing could be cooked, while the groaning of the ship's timbers swelled into a volume of sound comparable with that of an organ in a church.

At the very climax of the voyage, at their farthest south, the freakishness of Cape Horn weather displayed itself, when Lady Barbara awoke one morning to find the ship rising and swooping once more in orderly fashion, and Polwheal knocked at the cabin door with a message from the captain to the effect that this morning Lady Barbara might, if she wished, take advantage of the break in the weather to take the air on deck. She found the sky blue and the air clear though keen enough to make the duffle coat which Gerard had lent her grateful. The wind had died away to a mere fresh breeze, before which the *Lydia* was careering gaily along under all sail to the royals, and there was a bright sun shining all around them. It was a joy to walk the deck once more. It was if anything an even greater joy to drink hot coffee, steaming hot, again, served by a grinning Polwheal to Lady Barbara and the officers on the quarterdeck. There was an excruciating pleasure in filling her lungs with pure air after days of breathing the mephitic vapours of below decks. She caught Hornblower's eyes and they exchanged smiles of delight. In all the rigging the sailors' clothes, spread hastily to dry, were gesticulating as though with joy waving a thousand glad arms and legs in the sparkling air.

Cape Horn allowed them just that one pleasurable morning; before noon a thin cloud had spread itself over the sun, and the wind was increasing in force again, and to windward there were solid banks of black clouds coming up and overhauling them rapidly.

'Get the royals in, Mr Bush,' growled Hornblower, glowering aft. 'Lady Barbara, I am afraid that you will have to retire to your cabin again.'

The gale fell on them with a shriek when Lady Barbara had hardly reached her cabin; they ran before it all the afternoon, and at evening Lady Barbara could tell by the motion of the ship (so experienced a sailor had she become) that Hornblower had been compelled to heave her to. For thirty-six hours the *Lydia* remained hove to, while the heavens tore themselves to pieces around her, but there was comfort in the knowledge that on her easterly course all her drift to leeward helped her on her way. Lady Barbara found it hard to believe that men had ever succeeded in sailing a ship westward round the Horn. It helped her to agree with Hornblower that before very long, at the latest as soon as a general peace was concluded, the whole world would arise and write in the demand for the cutting of a canal through the Isthmus of Panama. Meanwhile there was nothing to do except to wait for the happy day when they would reach St Helena, and could enjoy fresh meat again, and vegetables, even – impossibly Utopian though it might seem – milk and fruit.

XXIII

On that voyage the change in conditions after rounding the Horn was most dramatic. It seemed to Lady Barbara almost as if one day they were labouring along over grey seas before the south-westerly gales, cold and uncomfortable, with waves running as high as the yard arms, and the next they were enjoying blue skies and gentle breezes from the south-east. They had in fact been fortunate, for the last thundering gale from the south-west had carried them well into the region of the southerly trades. They were leaving the Antipodean autumn behind them, and the northern spring was coming down in the track of the sun to meet them. The sea was blue again, as blue as any blue well could be, in its usual marvellous contrast with the white foam. There were flying-fish furrowing the enamelled surface. In a flash the privations and discomforts of the Horn were forgotten.

It seemed the most natural thing in the world that as night fell Lady Barbara should find herself seated as ever by the taffrail, and just as natural that Hornblower should loom up in the half light beside her and should accept her unvaryingly polite invitation to a seat beside her. It was perfectly natural that the officers should accept this state of affairs as one which had long existed, and that the officer of the watch should confine his walk to the forward part of the quarter-deck. At eight bells when Gerard came up to relieve Rayner the latter with a jerk of his thumb and a cock of his head called the former's attention to the little dark group by the taffrail. Gerard grinned, his white teeth in his swarthy face gleaming in the starlight.

He had made his trial of the lady's virtue in the long ago, before the captain had noticed her existence. He did not think that Hornblower would succeed where he had failed, and in any case Gerard prided himself on having sufficient sense not to try to compete with his own captain. Gerard had conquests enough to think about during the silent night watches, and he was philosopher enough to wish his captain good luck while keeping his back turned squarely to them as they talked quietly, only just out of earshot of him.

Yet to Hornblower – and to Lady Barbara – things were not the same here in the Atlantic as they had been in the Pacific. Hornblower seemed to feel a tension he had not felt before. Perhaps the rounding of the Horn had forced it home upon him that even sailing ship voyages must end some time, that even the five thousand odd miles that lay between them and Portsmouth would not last for ever. In the Pacific, appropriately enough, he had found peace in Lady Barbara's company. Here in the Atlantic he was conscious of uneasiness, as he might if the barometer were falling rapidly in a glassy calm in West Indian waters.

For some reason – perhaps merely because he had been thinking of England – the image of Maria had been much before his eyes of late; Maria, short and tubby, with a tendency to spots in her complexion, with the black silk parasol which she affected; or Maria in her flannel nightshift and curl papers with a loving note sounding hoarsely in her voice; Maria arguing with a lodging-house keeper, and Maria on board the ship at Portsmouth, her poor opinion of common sailors evident in her expression. It was disloyal to think of Maria like that; rather should he think of her as she was that feverish night in the Southsea lodgings, her eyes red with weeping, struggling bravely to keep her lips from trembling while little Horatio died of the smallpox in her arms and little Maria lay dead in the next room.

'Ha – h'm,' said Hornblower, harshly, and he stirred uneasily in his seat.

Lady Barbara looked at his face in the starlight. It bore that bleak, lonely expression which she had come to dread.

'Can you tell me what is the matter, Captain?' she asked gently.

Hornblower sat silent for some seconds before he shook his head. No, he could not tell her. For that matter he did not know himself; introspective though he was, he had not dared to admit to himself that he had been making comparisons between someone short and stout and someone tall and slender, between someone with apple cheeks and someone with a classic profile.

Hornblower slept badly that night, and his morning walk which followed was not devoted to the purpose for which it had originally been destined. He could not keep his mind at work upon the problems of stores and water, of how to keep the crew busy and out of mischief, of winds and courses, which he was accustomed to solve at this time so as to appear a man of decision the rest of the day. Part of the time he was too unhappy to think connectedly, and for the rest his mind was busy wrestling with suppositions so monstrous that they appalled him. He was tempted to make advances to Lady Barbara; that, at least, he could admit to himself. He wanted to do so badly. There was an ache in his breast, a most painful yearning as he thought of it.

What was monstrous about his thoughts was the suspicion that possibly Lady Barbara would not repulse him. It seemed inconceivable and yet possible, like something in a nightmare. He might even put his hot hand on her cool bosom – a thought which made him writhe in strange anguish. His longing to taste her sweetness was excruciating. He had been nearly a year cooped up in the *Lydia* now, and a year of unnatural living breeds strange fancies. Somewhere just over the gloomy horizon of Hornblower's mind there lurked fancies stranger yet; dark phantoms of rape and murder.

Yet even while Hornblower thus toyed with madness his cursed analytical powers were at work upon other pros and cons. Whether he offended Lady Barbara, or whether he seduced her, he was playing with fire. The Wellesley family could blast him at their whim. They could snatch him from his command and leave him to rot for ever on half pay; even worse, they could find, somewhere in his actions of the past year, if their animosity were sufficient, grounds for a court martial, and a court martial under Wellesley pressure could strip him of his commission and leave him a pauper dependent on parish relief. That was the worst that could happen – save perhaps for a duel with a result fatal to himself – and the very best was not much better. Supposing, as was just conceivable, the Wellesleys could tolerate the seduction of their sister – supposing that, confronted with a *fait accompli,* they resolved to try to make the best of things. No, that was not conceivable at all. He would have to produce a divorce from Maria, and that would involve an act of parliament and the expenditure of five thousand pounds.

To meddle with Lady Barbara would mean risking utter ruin – professional, social, and financial. And he knew he could not trust himself where risks were concerned. When he had had the *Lydia* towed into range of the *Natividad* and had fought it out with her gun to gun he had run such appalling risks that to this day he felt a little chill down his spine on recalling them. Risk and danger lured him even while he knew he was a fool to expose himself to them, and he knew that no risk would deter him once he had embarked on a course of action. Even at this moment, thinking about it in cold blood, there was something dangerously fascinating in the thought of wiping the eye of the whole Wellesley family and then daring them to do their worst.

And then all these cold-blooded considerations were swept away to nothing again in a white hot wave of passion as he thought of her, slim and lovely, understanding and sweet. He was trembling with passion, the hot blood running under his skin, and muddled images streamed through his mind in a fantastic panorama. He stood by the rail staring unseeing over the blue sea with its patches of golden weed, conscious of nothing save the riot in his own body and mind. When his heart had at last slowed down to normal, and he turned to look round over the ship, everything was oddly sharp and clear. He could see the smallest details of the complicated splicing which one of the hands was engaged upon on the forecastle a hundred and twenty feet away. Immediately afterwards he was heartily glad that he had regained his self control, for Lady Barbara came on deck, smiling as she always did when the sun shone on her face on emerging from the deck cabin, and soon he was in conversation with her.

'I spent last night dreaming dreams,' said Lady Barbara.

'Indeed?' said Hornblower, awkwardly. He, too, had been dreaming.

'Yes,' said Lady Barbara. 'I was dreaming mostly of eggs. Fried eggs, and buttered eggs. And slices of white bread spread thick with butter. And café au lait with plenty of cream. And cabbage – plain boiled cabbage. My dreams were not extravagant enough to run to a purée of spinach, but I almost attained to a dish of young carrots. And behold, this morning Hebe brings me my black coffee and my weevilly maize bread, and Polwheal sends in to ask me if I will be pleased to take beef or pork for my dinner. Today I think I start on the seventh brother of the pig whose chops I first tasted at Panama. I know his breed by now.'

Lady Barbara could still laugh and show her white teeth in her brown face, as she made this speech, and her laugh whisked away Hornblower's passion for a space. He was in sympathy with her – months of ship's fare set everyone literally dreaming of fresh food – but her fine naturalness acted upon Hornblower's state of mind like an open window on a stuffy room. It was that talk about food which staved off the crisis for a few more days – golden days, during which the *Lydia* kept the south-east trades on her beam and reached steadily across the south Atlantic for St Helena.

The wind did not fail her until the very evening when the lookout at the masthead, the setting of the sun in a golden glory having enabled him to gaze ahead once more, caught sight of the tip of the mountain top just as the light was fading from the sky, and his cry of 'Land ho!' told Hornblower that once more he had made a perfect landfall. All day long the wind had been dying away, and with the setting of the sun it dwindled to nothing, tantalisingly, just when a few more hours of it would have carried the *Lydia* to the island. From the deck there was still no sign of land, and as Gerard pointed out to Lady Barbara, she would have to take its proximity on trust until the wind condescended to blow again. Her disappointment at this postponement of her promised buttered eggs was so appealing that Crystal hastened forward and stuck his open clasp-knife in the mainmast. That was a sure way of raising a wind, he said – and if by any mishap it should fail on this occasion he would set all the ship's boys whistling in unison and chance the tempest such imprudence might summon from the deep.

It may have been the mere fact of this respite working on Hornblower's subconscious mind which precipitated the crisis; for undoubtedly Hornblower had a lurking fear that the call at St Helena might well bring about some undesired alteration in affairs on board the *Lydia*. On the other hand, the thing was bound to happen, and perhaps coincidence merely allotted that evening for it. It was coincidence that Hornblower should come into the main cabin in the half light at a moment when he thought Lady Barbara was on deck, and it was coincidence that his hand should brush against her bare arm as they stood cramped between the table and the locker and he apologised for his intrusion. She was in his arms then, and they kissed, and kissed again. She put one hand behind his shoulder and touched the back of his neck, and they were giddy with passion. Then a roll of the ship forced him to let her go, and she sank down upon the locker, and she smiled at him as she sat so that he came down on his knees beside her, his head on her breast, and she stroked his curls, and they kissed again as if they would never tire. She spoke to him with the endearments which her nurse had used to her when she was a child – she had never learned yet to use endearments.

'My dear,' she whispered. 'My sweet. My poppet.'

It was hard to find words that would tell him of her love for him.

'Your hands are beautiful,' she said, spreading one of them on her own palm, and playing with the long slender fingers. 'I have loved them ever since Panama.'

Hornblower had always thought his hands bony and ugly, and the left one bore the ingrained powder stain he had acquired at the boarding of the *Castilla*. He looked at her to see if she were teasing him, and when he saw that she was not he could only kiss her again – her lips were so ready for his kisses. It was like a miracle that she should want to be kissed. Passion carried them away once more.

Hebe's entrance made them part; at least it made Hornblower spring up, to sit bolt upright and self-conscious, while Hebe grinned at them with sly eyes. To Hornblower it was a dreadful thing for a captain to be caught toying with a woman on board his ship actually in commission. It was contrary to the Articles of War – worse, it was undignified, subversive of discipline, dangerous. Lady Barbara remained quite unruffled.

'Go away, Hebe,' she said, calmly. 'I shall not need you yet.'

And she turned back to Hornblower, but the spell was broken. He had seen himself in a new light, grovelling furtively on a couch with a passenger. He was blushing hotly, angry with himself, and already wondering how much the officer of the watch and the man at the wheel had heard of their murmurings through the open skylight.

'What are we to do?' he asked feebly.

'Do?' she replied. 'We are lovers, and the world is ours. We do as we will.'

'But—,' he said, and again 'but—'

He wanted to explain to her in half a dozen words the complications he could see hedging him in. There was a cold fit on him; he wanted to tell her of how he dreaded the ill-concealed amusement of Gerard, the utterly tactless tactfulness of Bush, and how the captain of a ship was not nearly as much his own master as she apparently thought, but it was hopeless. He could only stammer, and his hands flapped feebly, and his face was averted. He had forgotten all these practical details in those mad dreams of his. She put her hand on his chin and made him turn to her.

'Dear,' she asked. 'What is troubling you? Tell me, dear.'

'I am a married man,' he said, taking the coward's way out.

'I know that. Are you going to allow that to interfere with – us?'

'Besides—,' he said, and his hands flapped again in the hopeless effort to express all the doubts which consumed him.

She condescended to sink her pride a little further.

'Hebe is safe,' she said, softly. 'She worships me. Nor would she dare to be indiscreet.'

She saw the look in his face, and rose abruptly. Her blood and lineage were outraged at this. However veiled her offer had been, it had been refused. She was in a cold rage now.

'Please have the kindness, Captain,' she said, 'to open that door for me.'

She swept out of the cabin with all the dignity of an earl's daughter, and if she wept when in the privacy of her own cabin, Hornblower knew nothing of it. He was pacing the deck above, up and down, up and down, endlessly. This was the end of his fine dreams. This was how he showed himself a man to whom danger and risk only made a plan more attractive. He was a fine lady-killer, a devil of a buck. He cursed himself in his shame, he jeered at himself as a man who could face the wrath of the Wellesleys in imagination and who flinched from the amusement of Gerard in practice.

It all might have come right in the end. If the calm had persisted for two or three days, so that Lady Barbara could have forgotten her wrath and Hornblower his doubts, more might have happened. There might have been an echoing scandal in high life. But as it was, at midnight a little wind began to blow – perhaps it was Crystal's clasp-knife which had summoned it – and Gerard came to him for orders. Again he could not flout public opinion. He could not face the thought of the suspicions which would arise and the secret questions which would be asked if he gave orders for the ship to be put about and to head away from St Helena at a time when the wind held fair.

XXIV

'There's the devil of a lot of shipping there,' said Bush, his glass to his eye, as they opened up the roadstead in the dawn. 'The devil of a lot. Men o' war, sir. No, Indiamen. Men o' war *and* Indiamen, sir. There's a three decker! It's the old *Téméraire,* sir, or I'm a Dutchman, with a rear-admiral's flag. Must be the rendezvous for the homeward bound convoy, sir.'

'Pass the word for Mr Marsh,' said Hornblower.

There would be salutes to be fired, calls to be paid – he was caught up in the irresistible current of naval routine, and he would be too busy now for hours to have a word with Lady Barbara even if she condescended to allow him one. He did not know whether to be glad or sorry.

The *Lydia* made her number, and the sound of the salutes began to roll slowly round the bay. Hornblower was in his shabby full dress – the faded blue coat with the brassy epaulettes, the worn white breeches, the silk stockings with the innumerable ladders which Polwheal had cobbled roughly together. The port officer came up the side to receive his certificate of the absence of infectious disease on board. A moment later the anchor roared out overside, then Hornblower called for the cutter to take him over to the Admiral. He was actually going over the side when Lady Barbara came on deck – he saw her, just for a second, gazing with pleasure up the green mountain slopes, and looking with surprise at the massed shipping inshore. He longed to stop and speak to her, but once more the dignity expected of a captain checked him. Nor could he take her with him – no captain starting on an official round of calls could go round in his boat with a woman in the sternsheets beside him, not even when subsequent explanation would reveal her to be a Wellesley.

The cutter pulled steadily over to the *Téméraire*.

'*Lydia*,' shouted the coxswain in reply to the hail from her deck, and he held up four fingers which indicated the presence in the boat of a captain as a warning for them to prepare the correct ceremonial.

Sir James Saumarez received Hornblower in the quarter gallery of his flagship. He was tall and spare, of youthful appearance until he took off his hat and revealed his snow-white hair. He listened courteously to Hornblower's brief explanation of his presence; after forty years at sea and sixteen years of continuous warfare he could guess at the wild adventures which remained undescribed in Hornblower's verbal report. There was a gleam of approval in his fierce blue eyes when he heard that the *Lydia* had sunk a fifty-gun twodecker in a ship to ship duel.

'You can accompany me and the convoy,' he said, at the end. 'I have no more than two ships of the line and not a single frigate to escort the whole East Indian convoy. One would have thought that the Government would have learnt the need of frigates since the war started in 'ninety-three, don't you think? I will send you written orders this morning. And now, sir, perhaps you will give me the pleasure of your company at the breakfast party at which I am about to be host?'

Hornblower pointed out that it was his duty to call upon the governor.

'His Excellency is breakfasting with me,' said the Admiral.

Hornblower knew that it was ill to continue to raise a series of objections to a suggestion by an Admiral, but he had to raise a fresh one.

'There is a lady on board the *Lydia,* sir,' he said, and when the Admiral's eyebrows went up he hurriedly began to explain Lady Barbara's presence to him.

The Admiral whistled.

'A Wellesley!' he said. 'And you brought her round the Horn? Here, we must tell Lady Manningtree of this.'

He led the way unceremoniously into the lofty Admiral's cabin. There was a long table with a snowy cloth, glittering with crystal and silver, and by the table there stood chatting a little group of men and women, beautifully dressed. The Admiral made hurried introductions – His Excellency the Governor, and Her Excellency; the Earl and Countess of Manningtree, Sir Charles and Lady Wheeler.

Lady Manningtree was a short and dumpy woman with good humour in every line of her face. She showed no sign of the dignity and reserve which might be expected of the wife of an ex-governor-general returning from his term of office.

'Captain Hornblower has brought Lady Barbara Wellesley with him from Darien,' said Sir James, and plunged into rapid explanation. Lady Manningtree listened in perfect horror.

'And you have left her there? On that little ship?' she said. 'The poor lamb! She must not stay there another moment! I shall go and bring her away this very instant! Sir James, you must excuse me. I will not have a moment's peace until she is comfortably in the cabin next to mine on board the *Hanbury Castle.* Sir James, would you be so good as to order a boat for me?'

She left in a whirl of apologies and explanations, a fluttering of petticoats and a perfect torrent of objurgations, mainly directed at Hornblower.

'When women take charge,' said Sir James philosophically, after she had departed, 'it is best for the men to stand from under. Will you sit here, Captain?'

Curiously, Hornblower could eat almost nothing of that delicious breakfast. There were heavenly mutton cutlets. There was coffee with fresh milk. There was new wheaten bread. There was butter, there were fruits, there were vegetables, all the things Hornblower had dreamed about when his thoughts had not been occupied with Lady Barbara, and now he could only eat a mouthful here and there. Fortunately his lack of appetite went unnoticed because he was kept so busy answering the questions which were rained on him, about Lady Barbara, about his adventures in the Pacific, about his passage round the Horn, and then back to Lady Barbara again.

'Her brother is doing great things in Spain,' said Sir James. 'Not the eldest one, the Marquis, but Arthur – the one who won the battle of Assaye. He came well out of that court of inquiry after Vimiero. Now he has bundled Soult out of Portugal, and when I left Lisbon he was in full march on Madrid. Since Moore was killed he is the most promising soldier in the army.'

'Humph,' said Lady Wheeler. The name of Wellesley was still anathema to a certain section of Anglo-Indians. 'This Lady Barbara is a good deal younger than he is, I fancy? I remember her as quite a child in Madras.'

Eyes were turned towards Hornblower, but Lord Manningtree in the kindness of his heart spared him the embarrassment of having to explain Lady Barbara's age.

'She's no child,' he said, bluffly. 'She's a very talented young woman. Declined a dozen good offers in India, too, and God knows how many since then.'

'Humph,' said Lady Wheeler again.

The breakfast began to seem interminable to Hornblower, and he was glad when the party showed signs of breaking up. The Governor seized the opportunity to discuss with him the matter of the stores for which the *Lydia* would have to indent – naval routine still claimed him for her own. There was urgent need for him to return to his ship; he made his excuses to Sir James and said good-bye to the rest of the company.

The Admiral's barge was still hooked on to the *Lydia's* chains when he returned to her; her crew were dressed in crimson coats with gold-laced hats. Hornblower had known frigate captains who dressed their gig's crews in fancy costumes in this fashion, too, but they were wealthy men who had been fortunate in the matter of prize money, not penniless fellows like himself. He went on board; Lady Barbara's baggage was piled on the gangway waiting to be swung down into the barge. Down in the main cabin could be heard a continuous chatter of female voices. Lady Manningtree and Lady Barbara were sitting there deep in conversation; obviously there had been so much to say that they could not wait until they had reach the *Hanbury Castle*. One topic had led to another so enthralling that they had forgotten the barge, forgotten the waiting baggage, forgotten even about breakfast.

Apparently Lady Barbara had taken the opportunity, when her baggage had been brought up from the storeroom, to unpack some new clothes. She was wearing a new gown which Hornblower had not seen before, and a new turban and veil. She was very obviously the great lady now. To Hornblower's startled mind she seemed as she stood up to be six inches taller than when he saw her last. And clearly Hornblower's arrival, breaking the thread of their conversation, constituted for them a signal for their departure.

'Lady Barbara has been telling me all about your voyage,' said Lady Manningtree, buttoning her gloves. 'I think you deserve a world of thanks for the care you have taken of her.'

The kind-hearted old lady was one of those people who can never think evil. She looked round the tiny ugly cabin.

'Nevertheless,' she went on, 'I think that it is high time that she enjoyed a little more comfort than you can offer her here.'

Hornblower managed to gulp out a few words regarding the superior arrangements for passengers on board a luxurious Indiaman.

'I don't mean to imply that it is your fault, Captain,' protested Lady Manningtree, hastily. 'I'm sure your ship is a very beautiful ship. A frigate, isn't it? But frigates were never made to carry females, and that's all one can say. And now we must say good-bye, Captain. I hope we may have the pleasure of receiving you on the *Hanbury Castle* later. There will be sure to be opportunities during this very tedious voyage home. Good-bye, Captain.'

Hornblower bowed and allowed her to pass before him. Lady Barbara followed.

'Good-bye,' she said. Hornblower bowed again as she went down in a curtsy. He was looking straight at her, but somehow he could see no detail of her face – only a white blur.

'Thank you for all your kindness,' said Lady Barbara.

The barge left the ship's side, and rowed steadily away. She was all blurred, too, a vague patch of red and gold. Hornblower found Bush beside him.

'The victualling officer's signalling, sir,' he said.

Hornblower's duties were clamouring for his attention. As he turned away from the ship's side to plunge into them he found himself, idiotically, remembering that in two months' time or so he would be seeing Maria again. He felt vaguely glad about that before it passed out of his mind again. He felt he would be happy with Maria. Overhead the sun was shining brightly, and before him rose the steep green slopes of St Helena.

A Ship of the Line

I

Captain Horatio Hornblower was reading a smudgy proof which the printers had just sent round to his lodgings.

'To all Young Men of *Spirit*,' he said. 'Seamen, Landsmen, and Boys, who wish to strike a Blow for Freedom and to cause the Corsican Tyrant to wish that he had never dared the Wrath of these British Isles. His Majesty's Ship *Sutherland* of two decks and seventy-four guns is at present commissioning at Plymouth, and a few *Vacancies* still exist to complete her Crew. Captain *Horatio Hornblower* in command has lately returned from a Cruise in the *South Sea* during which in command of the Frigate *Lydia* of thirty-six guns, he engaged and *sank* the Spanish vessel *Natividad* of two decks and more than *twice the force*. The Officers, Petty Officers, and men of the *Lydia* have all joined him in the *Sutherland*. What Heart of Oak can resist this Appeal to Join this Band of Heroes and Share with them the new Glories which await them? Who will teach Monsieur *Jean Crapaud* that the Seas are *Britannia's* where no Frog-eating *Frenchman* can show his Face? Who wishes for a Hatful of Golden Louis d'or for *Prize Money?* There will be *Fiddlers* and *Dancing* every evening, and Provisions at *sixteen* ounces to the Pound, the Best of Beef, and Best of Bread, and *Grog* at midday every Day of the Week and *Sundays*, all in addition to the *Pay* under the *Warrant* of His Most Gracious Majesty King *George!* In the *Place* where this notice is read can be found an Officer of His Majesty's Ship *Sutherland* who will enlist any *Willing Hearts* who Thirst for Glory.'

Captain Hornblower struggled against hopelessness as he read the proof. Appeals of this sort were to be read in dozens in every market town. It hardly seemed likely that he could attract recruits to a humdrum ship of the line when dashing frigate captains of twice his reputation were scouring the country and able to produce figures of prize money actually won in previous voyages. To send four lieutenants, each with half a dozen men, round the southern counties to gather recruits in accordance with this poster was going to cost him practically all the pay he had accumulated last commission, and he feared lest it should be money thrown away.

Yet something had to done. The *Lydia* had supplied him with two hundred able bodied seamen (his placard said nothing of the fact that they had been compulsorily transferred without a chance of setting foot on English soil after a commission of two years' duration) but to complete his crew he needed another fifty seamen and two hundred landsmen and boys. The guardship had found him none at all. Failure to complete his crew might mean the loss of his command, and from that would result unemployment and half pay – eight shillings a day – for the rest of his life. He could form no estimate at all of with how much favour he was regarded at the Admiralty, and in the absence of data it was natural to him to believe that his employment hung precariously in the balance.

Anxiety and strain brought oaths to his lips as he tapped on the proof with his pencil – silly blasphemies of whose senselessness he was quite well aware even as he mouthed them. But he was careful to speak softly; Maria was resting in the bedroom through the double doors behind him, and he did not want to rouse her. Maria (although it was too early to be certain) believed herself to be pregnant, and Hornblower was sated with her cloy tenderness. His irritation increased at the thought of it; he hated the land, the necessity of recruiting, the stuffy sitting-room, the loss of the independence he had enjoyed during the months of his last commission. Irritably he took his hat and stole quietly out. The printer's messenger was waiting, hat in hand, in the hall. To him Hornblower abruptly handed back the proof with a curt order for one gross of placards to be struck off, and then he made his way into the noisy streets.

The tollkeeper at the Halfpenny Gate Bridge at sight of his uniform let him through without payment; a dozen watermen at the ferry knew him as the captain of the *Sutherland* and competed to catch his eye – they could expect an ample fee for rowing a Captain to his ship up the long length of the Hamoaze. Hornblower took his seat in a pair-oared wherry; it gave him some satisfaction to say no word at all as they shoved off and began the long pull through the tangle of shipping. Stroke oar shifted his quid and was about to utter some commonplace or other to his passenger, but at sight of his black brow and ill-tempered frown he thought better of it and changed his opening word to a self-conscious cough – Hornblower, acutely aware of the bye-play although he had spared the man no open glance, lost some of his ill-temper as a result. He noticed the play of muscles in the brown forearms as the man strained at his oar; there was tattooing on the wrist, and a thin gold ring gleamed in the man's left ear. He must have been a seaman before he became a waterman – Hornblower longed inexpressibly to have him haled on board when they should reach the *Sutherland*; if he could only lay his hands on a few dozen prime seamen his anxiety would be at an end. But the fellow of course would have a certificate of exemption, else he would never be able to ply his trade here in a part where a quarter of the British Navy came seeking for men.

The victualling yard and the dock yard as they rowed past were swarming with men, too, all of them able bodied, and half of them seamen – shipwrights and riggers – at whom Hornblower stared at longingly and as helplessly as a cat at goldfish in a bowl. The rope walk and the mast house, the sheer hulk and the smoking chimneys of the biscuit bakery went slowly by. There was the *Sutherland*, riding to her moorings off Bull Point; Hornblower, as he gazed at her across the choppy water, was conscious of a queer admixture of conservative dislike in the natural pride which he felt in his new command. Her round bow looked odd at a time when every British built ship of the line had the beakhead to which his eye had long grown accustomed; her lines were ungainly and told their tale (as Hornblower noticed every time he looked at her) of more desirable qualities sacrificed for shallow draught. Everything about her – save for the lower masts which were of English origin – proved that she was Dutch built, planned to negotiate the mudbanks and shallow estuaries of the Dutch coast. The *Sutherland*, in fact, had once been the Dutch 74 *Eendracht*, captured off the Texel and, now rearmed, the ugliest and least desirable two-decker in the Navy List.

God help him, thought Hornblower, eyeing her with a distaste accentuated by his lack of men to man her, if ever he should find himself trying to claw off a lee shore in her. She would drift off to leeward like a cocked-hat paper boat. And at the subsequent court-martial nobody would believe a word of the evidence regarding her unweatherly qualities.

'Easy!' he snapped at the wherrymen, and the oars ceased to grind in the rowlocks as the men rested; the sound of the waves slapping the side of the boat became suddenly more apparent.

As they drifted over the dancing water Hornblower continued his discontented examination. She was newly painted, but in as niggardly a fashion as the dockyard authorities could manage – the dull yellow and black was unrelieved by any white or red. A wealthy captain and first lieutenant would have supplied the deficiency out of their own pockets, and would have shown a lick of gold leaf here and there, but Hornblower had no money to spare for gold leaf, and he knew that Bush, who kept four sisters and a mother on his pay, had none either – not even though his professional future depended in some part on the appearance of the *Sutherland*. Some captains would by hook or by crook have cozened more paint – gold leaf, too, for that matter – out of the dockyard, as Hornblower ruefully told himself. But he was not good at cozening; not the prospect of all the gold leaf in the world could lead him to slap a dockyard clerk on the back and win his favour with flattery and false bonhomie; not that his conscience would stop him, but his self-consciousness would.

Someone on deck spied him now. He could hear the pipes twittering as preparations were made to receive him. Let 'em wait a bit longer; he was not going to be hurried today. The *Sutherland,* riding high without her stores in her, was showing a wide streak of her copper. That copper was new, thank God. Before the wind the ugly old ship might show a pretty turn of speed. As the wind swung her across the tide she revealed her run to him. Looking over her lines, Hornblower occupied his mind with estimates of how to get the best performance out of her. Twenty-two years of sea going experience helped him. Before his mind's eye he called up a composite diagram of all the forces that would be at work on her at sea – the pressure of the wind on her sails, the rudder balancing the headsails, the lateral resistance of the keel, the friction of the skin, the impact of waves against her bows. Hornblower sketched out a preliminary trial arrangement, deciding just how (until practical tests gave him more data) he would have the masts raked and the ship trimmed. But next moment he remembered bitterly that at present he had no crew to man her, and that unless he could find one all these plans would be useless.

'Give way,' he growled to the wherry men, and they threw their weight on the oars again.

'Easy, Jake,' said bow oar to stroke, looking over his shoulder.

The wherry swung round under the *Sutherland's* stern – trust those men to know how a boat should be laid alongside a ship of war – giving Hornblower a sight of the stern gallery which constituted to Hornblower one of the most attractive points about the ship. He was glad that the dockyard had not done away with it, as they had done in so many ships of the line. Up in that gallery he would be able to enjoy wind and sea and sun, in a privacy unattainable on deck. He would have a hammock chair made for use there. He could even take his exercise there, with no man's eye upon him – the gallery was eighteen feet long, and he would only have to stoop a little under the overhanging cove. Hornblower yearned inexpressibly for the time when he would be out at sea, away from all the harassing troubles of the land, walking his stern gallery in the solitude in which alone he could relax nowadays. Yet without a crew all this blissful prospect was withheld from him indefinitely. He must find men somewhere.

He felt in his pockets for silver to pay the boatmen, and although silver was woefully short his self-consciousness drove him into overpaying the men in the fashion he attributed to his fellow captains of ships of the line.

'Thank 'ee, sir. Thank 'ee,' said the stroke oar, knuckling his forehead.

Hornblower went up the ladder and came in through the entry port with its drab paint where in the Dutchmen's time gilding had blazed bravely. The pipes of the boatswain's mates twittered wildly, the marine guard presented arms, the sideboys stood rigidly at attention. Gray, master mate – lieutenants kept no watch in harbour – was officer of the watch and saluted as Hornblower touched his hat to the quarterdeck. Hornblower did not condescend to speak to him, although Gray was a favourite of his; the rigid guard he kept on himself for fear of unnecessary loquacity forbade. Instead he looked round him silently.

The decks were tangled with gear as the work of rigging the ship proceeded, but the tangle, as Hornblower was careful to note, carried under its surface the framework of orderliness. The coils of rope, the groups at work on the deck, the sailmaker's party sewing at a topsail on the forecastle, gave an impression of confusion, but it was disciplined confusion. The severe orders which he had issued to his officers had borne fruit. The crew of the *Lydia* when they had heard that they were to be transferred bodily to the *Sutherland* without even a day on shore, had nearly mutinied. They were in hand again now.

'Master-at-arms wishes to report, sir,' said Gray.

'Send for him, then,' answered Hornblower.

The master-at-arms was the warrant officer responsible for enforcing discipline, and was a man new to Hornblower, named Price. Hornblower concluded that he had allegations of indiscipline to lodge, and he sighed even while he set his face in an expression of merciless rigidity. Probably it would be a matter of flogging, and he hated the thought of the blood and the agony. But, at the beginning of a commission like this, with a restive crew under his orders, he must not hesitate to flog if necessary – to have the skin and flesh stripped from the offenders' backbones.

Price was coming along the gangway now at the head of the strangest procession. Two by two behind him came a column of thirty men, each one handcuffed to his neighbour, save for the last two who clanked drearily along with leg irons at their ankles. Nearly all of them were in rags, and the rags had no sort of nautical flavour about them at all. The rags of a great many of them were sacking, some had corduroy, and Hornblower, peering closer, saw that one wore the wrecks of a pair of moleskin breeches. Yet another wore the remains of what had once been a respectable black broadcloth suit – white skin showed through a rent in the shoulder. All of them had stubbly beards, black, brown, golden, and grey, and those who were not bald had great mops of tangled hair. The two ship's corporals brought up the rear.

' 'Alt,' ordered Price. 'Orf 'ats.'

The procession shuffled to a halt, and the men stood sullenly on the quarterdeck. Some of them kept their eyes on the deck, while the others gaped sheepishly round them.

'What the devil's all this?' demanded Hornblower sharply.

'New 'ands, sir,' said Price. 'I signed a receipt to the sodgers what brought 'em, sir.'

'Where did they bring them from?' rasped Hornblower.

'Exeter Assizes, sir,' said Price, producing a list. 'Poachers, four of 'em. Waites, that's 'im in the moleskin breeches, sir, 'e was found guilty of sheepstealing. That 'un in black, 'is crime's bigamy, sir – 'e was a brewer's manager before this 'appened to 'im. The others is larceny mostly, sir, 'cept for them two in front what's in for rick burning and t'other two in irons. Robbery with violence is what they done.'

'Ha – h'm,' said Hornblower, wordless for the moment. The new hands blinked at him, some with hope in their eyes, some with hatred, some with indifference. They had chosen service at sea rather than the gallows, or transportation, or the gaol. Months in prison awaiting trial accounted for their dilapidated appearance. Here was a fine addition to the ship's company, thought Hornblower, bitterly – budding mutineers, sullen skulkers, half-witted yokels. But hands they were and he must make the most of them. They were frightened, sullen, resentful. It would be worth trying to win their affection. His naturally humanitarian instincts dictated the course he decided to pursue after a moment's quick thinking.

'Why are they still handcuffed?' he demanded, loud enough for them all to hear. 'Release them at once.'

'Begging you pardon, sir,' apologised Price. 'I didn't want to without orders, sir, seeing what they are and 'ow they come 'ere.'

'That's nothing to do with it,' snapped Hornblower. 'They're enlisted in the King's service now. And I'll have no man in irons in *my* ship unless he's given *me* cause to order it.'

Hornblower kept his gaze from wavering towards the new hands, and steadily addressed his declamation to Price – it was more effective delivered that way, he knew, even while he despised himself for using rhetorical tricks.

'I never want to see new hands in charge of the master-at-arms again,' he continued, hotly. 'They are recruits in an honourable service, with an honourable future before them. I'll thank you to see to it another time. Now find one of the purser's mates and see that each of these men is properly dressed in accordance with my orders.'

Normally it might be harmful to discipline to rate a subordinate officer in front of the men, but in the case of the master-at-arms Hornblower knew that little damage was being done. The men would come to hate the master-at-arms any way sooner or later – his privileges of rank and pay were given him so that he might be a whipping boy for the crew's discontent. Hornblower could drop the rasp in his voice and address the hands directly, now.

'A man who does his duty as best he can,' he said, kindly, 'has nothing to fear in this ship, and everything to hope for. Now I want to see how smart you can look in your new clothes, and with the dirt of the place you have come from washed off you. Dismiss.'

He had won over some of the poor fools, at least, he told himself. Some of the faces which had been sullen with despair were shining with hope now, after this experience of being treated as men and not as brutes – for the first time for months, if not the first time in their lives. He watched them off the gangway. Poor devils; in Hornblower's opinion they had made a bad bargain in exchanging the gaol for the navy. But at least they represented thirty out of the two hundred and fifty additional human bodies which he needed to drag at ropes and to heave at capstan bars so as to take this old *Sutherland* out to sea.

Lieutenant Bush came hastening on to the quarterdeck, and touched his hat to his captain. The stern swarthy face with its incongruous blue eyes broke into a smile just as incongruous. It gave Hornblower a queer twinge, almost of conscience, to see the evident pleasure which Bush experienced at sight of him. It was odd to know that he was admired – it might even be said that he was loved – by this very capable sailor, this splendid disciplinarian and fearless fighter who boasted so many of the good qualities in which Hornblower felt himself to be lacking.

'Good morning, Bush,' he said. 'Have you seen the new draft?'

'No, sir. I was rowing guard for the middle watch and I've only just turned out. Where do they hail from, sir?'

Hornblower told him, and Bush rubbed his hands with pleasure.

'Thirty!' he said. 'That's rare. I never hoped for more than a dozen from Exeter Assizes. And Bodmin Assizes open today. Please God we get another thirty there.'

'We won't get topmen from Bodmin Assizes,' said Hornblower, comforted beyond measure at the equanimity with which Bush regarded the introduction of gaolbirds into the *Sutherland's* crew.

'No, sir. But the West India convoy's due this week. The guards ought to nab two hundred there. We'll get twenty if we get our rights.'

'M'm,' said Hornblower, and turned away uneasily. He was not the sort of captain – neither the distinguished kind nor the wheedling kind – who could be sure of favours from the Port Admiral. 'I must look round below.'

That changed the subject effectively enough.

'The women are restless,' said Bush. 'I'd better come, too, sir, if you don't object.'

The lower gun deck offered a strange spectacle, lit vaguely by the light which came through half a dozen open gun ports. There were fifty women there. Three or four were still in their hammocks, lying on their sides looking out on the others. Some were sitting in groups on the deck, chattering loud-voiced. One or two were chaffering for food through the gun ports with the occupants of shore boats floating just outside; the netting which impeded desertion had a broad enough mesh to allow a hand to pass through. Two more, each backed by a supporting group, were quarrelling violently. They were in odd contrast – one was tall and dark, so tall as to have to crouch round-shouldered under the five foot deck beams, while the other, short, broad, and fair, was standing up boldly before her menacing advance.

'That's what I said,' she maintained stoutly. 'And I'll say it again. I ain't afeared o' *you,* Mrs Dawson, as you call yourself.'

'A-ah,' screamed the dark one at this crowning insult. She swooped forward, and with greedy hands she seized the other by the hair, shaking her head from side to side as if she would soon shake it off. In return her face was scratched and her shins were kicked by her stout-hearted opponent. They whirled round in a flurry of petticoats, when one of the women in the hammocks screamed a warning to them.

'Stop it, you mad bitches! 'Ere's the cap'n.'

They fell apart, panting and tousled. Every eye was turned towards Hornblower as he walked forward in the patchy light, his head bowed under the deck above.

'The next woman fighting will be put ashore instantly,' growled Hornblower.

The dark woman swept her hair from her eyes and sniffed with disdain.

'You needn't put *me* ashore, Cap'n,' she said. 'I'm goin'. There ain't a farden to be had out o' this starvation ship.'

She was apparently expressing a sentiment which was shared by a good many of the women, for the speech was followed by a little buzz of approval.

'Ain't the men *never* goin' to get their pay notes?' piped up the woman in the hammock.

'Enough o' that,' roared Bush, suddenly. He pushed forward anxious to save his captain from the insults to which he was exposed, thanks to a government which left its men still unpaid after a month in port. 'You there, what are you doing in your hammock after eight bells?'

But this attempt to assume a counter offensive met with disaster.

'I'll come out if you like, Mr Lieutenant,' she said, flicking off her blanket and sliding to the deck. 'I parted with my gown to buy my Tom a sausage, and my petticoat's bought him a soop o' West Country ale. Would you have me on deck in my shift, Mr Lieutenant?'

A titter went round the deck.

'Get back and be decent,' spluttered Bush, on fire with embarrassment.

Hornblower was laughing, too – perhaps it was because he was married that the sight of a half-naked woman alarmed him not nearly as much as it did his first lieutenant.

'Never will I be decent now,' said the woman, swinging her legs up into the hammock and composedly draping the blanket over her, 'until my Tom gets his pay warrant.'

'An' when he gets it,' sneered the fair woman. 'What can he do with it without shore leave? Sell it to a bumboat shark for a quarter!'

'Fi' pound for twenty-three months' pay!' added another. 'An me a month gone a'ready.'

'Avast there,' said Bush.

Hornblower beat a retreat, abandoning – forgetting, rather – the object of his visit of inspection below. He could not face those women when the question of pay came up again. The men had been scandalously badly treated, imprisoned in the ship within sight of land, and their wives (some of them certainly were wives, although by Admiralty regulations a simple verbal declaration of the existence of a marriage was sufficient to allow them on board) had just cause of complaint. No one, not even Bush, knew that the few guineas which had been doled out among the crew represented a large part of Hornblower's accumulated pay – all he could spare, in fact, except for the necessary money to pay his officers' expenses when they should start on their recruiting journeys.

His vivid imagination and absurd sensitiveness between them perhaps exaggerated part of the men's hardships. The thought of the promiscuity of life below decks, where a man was allotted eighteen inches' width in which to swing his hammock, while his wife was allowed eighteen inches next to him, all in a long row, husbands, wives, and single men, appalled him. So did the thought of women having to live on the revolting lower deck food. Possibly he made insufficient allowance for the hardening effect of long habit.

He emerged through the fore hatchway on to the maindeck a little unexpectedly. Thompson, one of the captains of the forecastle, was dealing with the new hands.

'P'raps we'll make sailors of you,' he was saying, 'and p'raps we won't. Overside with a shot at your feet, more likely, before we sight Ushant. And a waste o' good shot, too. Come on wi' that pump, there. Let's see the colour o' your hides, gaol-birds. When the cat gets at you we'll see the colour o' your backbones, too, you—'

'Enough of that, Thompson,' roared Hornblower, furious.

In accordance with his standing orders the new hands were being treated to rid them of vermin. Naked and shivering, they were grouped about the deck. Two of them were having their heads shorn down to the bare skin; a dozen of them, who had already submitted to this treatment (and looking strangely sickly and out of place with the prison pallor still on them) were being herded by Thompson towards the wash-deck pump which a couple of grinning hands were working. Fright was making them shiver as much as cold – not one of them, probably, had ever had a bath before, and what with the prospect, and Thompson's bloodcurdling remarks and the strange surroundings, they were pitiful to see.

It enraged Hornblower, who somehow or other had never forgotten the misery of his early days at sea. Bullying was abhorrent to him like any other sort of wanton cruelty, and he had no sympathy whatever with the aim of so many of his brother officers, to break the spirit of the men under him. One of these days his professional reputation and his future might depend on these very men risking their lives cheerfully and willingly – sacrificing them, if need be – and he could not imagine cowed and broken-spirited men doing that. The shearing and the bath were necessary, if the ship was to be kept clear of the fleas and bugs and lice which could make life a misery on board, but he was not going to have his precious men cowed more than was unavoidable. It was curious that Hornblower, who never could believe himself to be a leader of men, would always lead rather than drive.

'Under the pump with you, men,' he said kindly, and when they still hesitated – 'When we get to sea you'll see *me* under that pump, every morning at seven bells. Isn't that so, there?'

'Aye aye, sir,' chorused the hands at the pump – their captain's strange habit of having cold seawater pumped over him every morning had been a source of much discussion on board the *Lydia*.

'So under with you, and perhaps you'll all be captains one of these days. You, there, Waites, show these others you're not afraid.'

It was blessed good fortune that Hornblower was able not only to remember the name, but to recognise in his new guise Waites, the sheepstealer with the moleskin breeches. They blinked at this resplendent captain in his gold lace, whose tone was cheerful and whose dignity still admitted taking a daily bath. Waites steeled himself to dive under the spouting hose, and, gasping, rotated heroically under the cold water. Someone threw him a lump of holystone with which to scrub himself, while the others jostled for their turn – the poor fools were like sheep; it was only necessary to set one moving to make all the rest eager to follow.

Hornblower caught sight of a red angry welt across one white shoulder. He beckoned Thompson out of earshot.

'You've been free with that starter of yours, Thompson,' he said.

Thompson grinned uneasily, fingering the two-foot length of rope knotted at the end, with which petty officers were universally accustomed to stimulate the activity of the men under them.

'I won't have a petty officer in my ship,' said Hornblower, 'who doesn't know when to use a starter and when not to. These men haven't got their wits about 'em yet, and hitting 'em won't remedy it. Make another mistake like that, Thompson, and I'll disrate you. And then you'll clean out the heads of this ship every day of this commission. That'll do.'

Thompson shrank away, abashed by the genuine anger which Hornblower displayed.

'Keep your eye on him, Mr Bush, if you please,' added Hornblower. 'Sometimes a reprimand makes a petty officer take it out of the men more than ever to pay himself back. And I won't have it.'

'Aye aye, sir,' said Bush, philosophically.

Hornblower was the only captain he had ever heard of who bothered his head about the use of starters. Starters were as much part of Navy life as bad food and eighteen inches per hammock and peril at sea. Bush could never understand Hornblower's disciplinary methods. He had been positively horrified when he had heard his captain's public admission that he, too, had baths under the washdeck pump – it seemed madness for a captain to allow his men to guess that they were of the same flesh as his. But two years under Hornblower's command had taught him that Hornblower's strange ways sometimes attained surprising results. He was ready to obey him, loyally though blindly, resigned and yet admiring.

II

'The boy from the Angel has brought a note, sir,' said the landlady, when Hornblower called her in in reply to her knock at the sitting-room door. 'He waits an answer.'

Hornblower felt a shock as he read the address – the clear feminine handwriting which he recognised although it was months since he saw it last meant so much to him. He tried to disguise his feelings as he spoke to his wife.

'It is addressed to both of us, my dear,' he said. 'Shall I open it?'

'As you please,' said Maria.

Hornblower broke the wafer and unfolded the note.

The Angel Inn,
Plymouth.
Fourth May, 1810.

Rear Admiral Sir Percy and Lady Barbara Leighton would esteem it an Honour if Captain and Mrs Horatio Hornblower would dine with them at this address Tomorrow, the Fifth, at four o'clock.

'The Admiral is at the Angel. He wants us to dine with him tomorrow,' said Hornblower, as casually as his beating heart would allow. 'Lady Barbara is with him. I think we must accept, my dear.'

He passed the note over to his wife.

'I have only my blue sack gown,' said Maria, looking up from reading it.

The first thing a woman ever thought about on receiving an invitation was what she should wear. Hornblower tried to bend his mind to the consideration of the blue sack gown, when all the time his heart was singing songs at the knowledge that Lady Barbara was only two hundred yards away.

'It looks perfect on you, my dear,' he said. 'You know how much I have always liked it.'

It would call for a far better gown to look well on Maria's dumpy figure. But Hornblower knew that they must – they *must* – accept the invitation, and it would be a kindness to reassure Maria. It did not matter what clothes Maria wore as long as she thought she looked well in them. Maria smiled happily at the compliment, giving Hornblower a prick of conscience. He felt like Judas. Maria would look coarse and badly dressed and stupid beside Lady Barbara, and yet he knew that as long as he pretended to be in love with her she would be happy and unconscious.

He wrote a careful acceptance, and rang the bell for it to be given to the messenger. Then he buttoned his uniform coat.

'I must go down to the ship,' he said.

Maria's reproachful look hurt him. He knew that she had been looking forward to spending the afternoon with him, and indeed he had not intended to visit the ship that day. It was only an excuse to gain privacy for himself. He could not bear the thought of being mewed up in that sitting-room with Maria and her platitudes. He wanted to be alone to hug to himself the thought that Lady Barbara was in the same town, that he was going to see her tomorrow. He could not sit still with those thoughts bubbling within him. He could have sung for joy as he walked briskly down to the ferry, thrusting aside all remembrance of Maria's dutiful acquiescence in his departure – well she knew how great were the demands made upon a captain by the commissioning of a ship of the line.

In his yearning for solitude he urged the rowers of his boat until they sweated. On deck he gave the briefest of salutes to the quarter-deck and to the officer of the watch, before plunging below to the security and peace for which he had been yearning. There were a hundred matters to which he could have devoted his attention but he would not stay for one of them. He strode across his cabin – littered with the preparations made for when he should come on board – and out through the stern window into the great stern gallery. There, sheltered from all interruption, he could lean against the rail, and stare across the water.

The ebb was running, and with the wind light from the north-east the *Sutherland's* stern gallery looked southward down the length of the Hamoaze. To his left lay the dockyard, as busy as a beehive. Before him the glittering water was studded with shipping, with shore boats rowing hither and thither. In the distance beyond the roofs of the victualling yard he could see Mount Edgcumbe – Plymouth was out of his sight, round the corner from the Devil's Point; he would not have the satisfaction of gazing upon the roof that sheltered Lady Barbara.

Still, she was there, and he would see her tomorrow. He gripped the rail in his ecstasy until his fingers hurt him. He turned away and began to walk up and down the gallery, his hands behind his back to counterbalance the stoop necessitated by the cove above. The pain he had felt at first, three weeks back, when he had heard of Lady Barbara's marriage to Admiral Leighton was gone by now. There was only the joy in the thought that she still remembered him. Hornblower dallied with the idea that she might have travelled down to Plymouth with her husband in the expectation of seeing him. It was possible – Hornblower would not stop to think that she might have been influenced by the desire to spend a few more days with her new husband. She must have cajoled Sir Percy into sending this invitation on the moment of his arrival; Hornblower would not make allowance for the fact that any admiral must be anxious for an early opportunity to study an unknown captain placed under his command. She must have made Sir Percy ask at the Admiralty for his services – that would explain why they had found for him a new ship and a new command without a single month's interval of half pay. It was to Lady Barbara that he owed the very comforting addition of ten shillings a day to his pay which went with the command of a ship of the line.

He was a quarter of the way up the captains' list now. In less than twenty years' time – long before he was sixty – if he continued to obtain commands in this fashion he would hoist his flag as an Admiral. Then they might yellow him if they wanted to; he would be satisfied with Admiral's rank. On Admiral's half pay he could live in London, find a patron who would nominate him to a seat in Parliament. He would know power, and dignity, and security. All this was possible – and Lady Barbara still remembered him, cherished a kindly thought of him, was anxious to see him again despite the ludicrous way in which he had behaved towards her. High spirits bubbled within him again.

A seagull, wheeling motionless up wind, suddenly flapped its wings until it hovered stationary, and screamed raucously in his face. It flapped and screamed aimlessly along the gallery, and then, equally aimlessly, wheeled away again. Hornblower followed it with his eyes, and when he resumed his walk the thread of his thoughts was broken. Instantly there loomed up again into his consciousness the knowledge of the frightful need of men under which he laboured. Tomorrow he would have to confess miserably to his Admiral that the *Sutherland* was still a hundred and fifty men short of complement; he would be found wanting in the very first of a captain's duties. An officer might be the finest possible seaman, the most fearless fighter (and Hornblower did not think himself either) and yet his talents were useless if he could not man his ship.

Probably Leighton had never asked for his services at all, and he had been allotted to Leighton's squadron by some trick of fate. Leighton would suspect him of having been his wife's lover, would be consumed with jealousy, and would watch for every opportunity to achieve his ruin. He would make his life a misery to him, would plague him to madness, and would finally have him broken and dismissed the service – any admiral could break any captain if he set his mind to it. Perhaps Lady Barbara had planned to put him thus in Leighton's power, and was working his ruin in revenge for his treatment of her. That seemed much more likely than his earlier wild imaginings, thought Hornblower, the cold fit working on him.

She must have guessed just what Maria was like, and must have sent the invitation so as to have the pleasure of gloating over her weaknesses. The dinner tomorrow would be one long humiliation for him. He could not venture to draw on his next quarter's pay for another ten days at least; otherwise he would have taken Maria out to buy her the finest gown in Plymouth – although what would a Plymouth gown avail in the sight of an Earl's daughter who would undoubtedly buy all her clothes from Paris? He had not twenty pounds in the whole world now, having sent Bush and Gerard and Rayner and Hooker, his four lieutenants, out to drum up recruits. They had taken thirty men with them, the only trustworthy men in the whole ship, too. Probably there would be trouble on the lower deck in consequence – probably reaching a head tomorrow while he was dining with his admiral.

Gloomy anticipation could go no further than that. He jerked his head up with irritation, and hit it hard against one of the beams of the cove above. Then he clenched his fists and cursed the service, as he had cursed it a thousand times before. That made him laugh at himself – if Hornblower had never been able to laugh at himself he would have been, long ago, another of the mad captains in the Navy List. He took a firmer grip on his emotions and set himself to thinking seriously about the future.

The orders which had attached him to Admiral Leighton's squadron had stated briefly that he was destined for service in the Western Mediterranean, and it was an uncovenanted mercy on the part of the lords of the Admiralty to give him that much warning. He had known of captains who had laid in personal stores in the expectation of service in the West Indies only to find that they had been allotted to the Baltic convoy. The Western Mediterranean meant the Toulon blockade, the protection of Sicily, harassing the Genoese coasters, and, presumably, taking a hand in the war in Spain. It meant a more variegated life than the blockade of Brest, at least, although now that Spain was England's ally there would be far less chance of prize money.

His ability to speak Spanish seemed to make it certain that the *Sutherland* would be employed on the coast of Catalonia in concert with the Spanish army. Lord Cochrane had distinguished himself there, but Cochrane was under a cloud now. The courts martial which had followed the action in the Basque Roads were still echoing through the service, and Cochrane would be lucky if he ever got another ship – he was the standing example of the folly of an officer on the active list taking part in politics. Perhaps, thought Hornblower, trying to combat both optimism and pessimism simultaneously, he was intended by the Admiralty to supply Cochrane's place. If that were the case, it meant that his professional reputation was far higher than he dared believe. Hornblower had to battle sternly with his feelings at that thought; he found himself grinning when he warned himself that excess of emotion only resulted in his hitting his head on the beams above.

That quieted him, and he began to tell himself philosophically that all this anticipation was merely waste of effort; he would know sooner or later anyway, and all the worrying in the world would not alter his destiny a ha'porth. There were a hundred and twenty British ships of the line at sea, and nearly two hundred frigates, and in every one of these three hundred and twenty ships there was a post captain, each one a god to his crew, and presumably each one a puppet to the Admiralty. He must act like a sensible man, empty his mind of all these imaginings, and go home and spend a quiet evening with his wife untroubled by thoughts of the future.

Yet even as he left the stern gallery to pass the word for his gig to take him back a new wave of delirious anticipation surged through him at the thought of seeing Lady Barbara tomorrow.

III

'Do I look well?' asked Maria, her toilet completed.

Hornblower was buttoning his full-dress coat as he stood and looked at her; he made himself smile admiringly at her.

'Admirable, my dear,' he said. 'The gown sets off your figure better than any you have ever worn.'

His tact was rewarded by a smile. It was no use speaking the truth to Maria, telling her that that particular shade of blue revolted against the heavy red of her cheeks. With her thick figure and coarse black hair and bad complexion Maria could never appear well dressed. At best she looked like a shopkeeper's wife; at worst like some scrub woman dressed in finery cast off by her mistress. Those stubby red hands of hers, thought Hornblower, looking at them, were very like a scrub woman's.

'I have my Paris gloves,' said Maria, noting the direction of his glance. It was the very devil, the way in which she was eager to anticipate every wish of his. It was in his power to hurt her horribly, and the knowledge made him uncomfortable.

'Better and better,' he said gallantly. He stood before the mirror and twitched his coat into position.

'Full dress suits you well,' said Maria, admiringly.

Hornblower's first act when he had returned to England in the *Lydia* had been to buy himself new uniforms – there had been humiliating incidents last commission as a result of the poverty of his wardrobe. He eyed himself tolerantly in the glass. This coat was of the finest blue broadcloth. The heavy epaulettes that hung at the shoulders were of real bullion, and so was the broad gold lace round the edges and the buttonholes. Buttons and cuffs flashed as he moved; it was pleasant to see the heavy gold stripes on his cuffs that marked him as a Captain with more than three years' seniority. His cravat was of thick China silk. He approved the cut of his white kerseymere breeches. The thick white silk stockings were the best that he could find – he remembered with a twinge of conscience as he gloated over them that Maria wore concealed under her skirt only cheap cotton stockings at four shillings a pair. From the crown of his head to his ankles he was dressed as a gentleman should be dressed; only about his shoes was he doubtful. Their buckles were merely pinchbeck, and he feared lest their brassiness should be accentuated by contrast with the genuine gold everywhere else – funds had begun to run low when he bought them, and he had not dared spend twenty guineas on gold buckles. He must take care this evening to do nothing to call attention to his feet. It was a pity that the sword of one hundred guineas' value voted him by the Patriotic Fund for his fight with the *Natividad* had not yet reached him. He still had to wear the fifty guinea sword which had been awarded him eight years ago after the capture of the *Castilla* as a mere lieutenant.

He took up his cocked hat – the button and lace on it were real gold, too – and his gloves.

'Are you ready, my dear?' he asked.

'Quite ready, Horatio,' said Maria. She had early learned how he hated unpunctuality, and dutifully took care never to offend in this respect.

The afternoon sunlight in the street sparkled on his gold; a militia subaltern whom they passed saluted him respectfully. Hornblower noted that the lady who hung on the subaltern's arm looked more keenly at Maria than at him, and he thought he read in her glance the pitying amusement he expected. Maria was undoubtedly not the sort of wife one would expect to see on the arm of a distinguished officer. But she was his wife all the same, the friend of his childhood, and the self-indulgent soft-heartedness which had moved him to marry her had to be paid for now. Little Horatio and little Maria had died of the smallpox in a Southsea lodging – he owed her his devotion on account of that if for nothing else. And she thought she was carrying another child of his now. That had been madness, of course, but madness excusable in a man whose heart was torn with jealousy at the news that Lady Barbara was married. Still, it had to be paid for in more devotion to Maria; all his decent instincts as well as his soft-heartedness and irresolution compelled him to remain faithful to her, to give her pleasure, to act as if he were her truly devoted husband.

Nor was that all. His pride would never permit him to make public acknowledgment that he had made a mistake, a silly blunder worthy of any foolish boy. On that account alone, even if he could steel himself to break Maria's heart, he would never come to an open breach with her. Hornblower could remember the lewd comments of the navy over Nelson's matrimonial affairs, and there were Bowen's and Samson's after that. As long as he held loyally to his wife that kind of thing would never be said about him. People were tolerant of eccentricity while they laughed at weakness. They might marvel at his devotion, but that was all. While he carried himself as if Maria was the only woman in the world for him people would be forced to assume that there was more in her constitution than was apparent to an onlooker.

'It is the Angel to which we are bidden, is it not, my dear?' asked Maria, breaking in on his thoughts.

'Why, yes.'

'We have walked straight past it. You did not hear me when I spoke before.'

They retraced their steps, and a jolly Devon servant maid led them through into the cool dark depths at the back of the inn. There were several persons in the oak-panelled room into which they were ushered, but for Hornblower there was only one. Lady Barbara was there in a blue silk dress, blue-grey, the exact colour of her eyes. From a gold chain round her neck hung a sapphire pendant, but the sapphires seemed lifeless compared with her glance. Hornblower made his bow, and mumbled as he presented Maria. The fringes of the room seemed to be deep in mist; only Lady Barbara could be clearly seen. The golden sunburn which Hornblower had last seen in her cheeks had disappeared now; her complexion was as creamy white as any great lady's should be.

Hornblower became aware that someone else was speaking to him – had been speaking for some time.

'A most pleasurable occasion, Captain Hornblower,' he was saying. 'May I present you? Captain Hornblower, Mrs Elliott. Captain Hornblower, Mrs Bolton. My Flag-captain, Captain Elliott, of the *Pinto*. And Captain Bolton of the *Caligula*, who tells me he was shipmates with you in the old *Indefatigable*.'

The mists were clearing from Hornblower's eyes a little. He was able to stammer a few words, but fortunately the entrance of the innkeeper with the announcement of dinner gave him a little longer in which to collect himself. It was a circular table at which they were seated. Opposite him sat Bolton, with his ruddy cheeks and open, honest face. Hornblower still felt Bolton's grip lingering on his palm and remembered the horniness of his hand. There was nothing of the elegant world about Bolton, then. Nor was there about Mrs Bolton, who sat on Hornblower's right, between him and the Admiral. She was as plain and as dowdy as Maria herself – to Hornblower's infinite relief.

'I must congratulate you, Captain, on your appointment to the *Sutherland*,' said Lady Barbara on his left. A breath of perfume was wafted from her as she spoke, and Hornblower's head swam. To smell the scent of her, and to hear her voice again, was still some romantic drug to him. He did not know what he said in reply.

'The innkeeper here,' announced the Admiral to the table at large, dipping a ladle into the silver tureen before him, 'swore to me that he knew the art of turtle soup, and I entrusted a turtle to his care. God send he spoke the truth. The sherry wine – George, the sherry – I trust you will find tolerable.'

Hornblower incautiously took a mouthful of soup far too hot, and the pain he experienced while swallowing it down helped to bring him back to reality. He turned his head to study the Admiral to whom he would owe obedience for the next two or three years, who had won Lady Barbara's hand in marriage after a courtship that could not have endured more than three weeks. He was tall and heavily built and darkly handsome. The star of the Bath and the red ribbon set off his glittering uniform. In age he could hardly be much over forty – only a year or two older than Hornblower – so that he must have attained to post rank at the earliest age family influence could contrive it. But the perceptible fullness about his jowl indicated to Hornblower's mind either self-indulgence or stupidity; both, perhaps.

So much Hornblower saw in a few seconds' inspection. Then he forced himself to think of his manners, although between Lady Barbara and the Admiral it was hard to think clearly.

'I trust you are enjoying the best of health, Lady Barbara?' he said. A quaint quarterdeck rasp of formality crept into his voice as he tried to hit the exact tone he thought the complicated situation demanded. He saw Maria on the other side of Captain Elliott beyond Lady Barbara, raise her eyebrows a little – Maria was always sensitive to his reactions.

'Indeed, yes,' said Lady Barbara, lightly. 'And you, Captain?'

'I have never known Horatio better,' said Maria interposing.

'That is good news,' said Lady Barbara, turning towards her. 'Poor Captain Elliott here is still shaken sometimes with the ague he acquired at Flushing.'

It was deftly done; Maria and Lady Barbara and Elliott were at once engaged in a conversation which left no room for Hornblower. He listened for a moment, and then forced himself to turn to Mrs Bolton. She had no fund of small talk. 'Yes' and 'No' were all she could say, seemingly, and the Admiral on her other side was deep in talk with Mrs Elliott. Hornblower lapsed into gloomy silence. Maria and Lady Barbara continued a conversation from which Elliott soon dropped out, and which was continued across his unresisting body with a constancy which not even the arrival of the next course could interrupt.

'Can I carve you some of this beef, Mrs Elliot?' asked the Admiral. 'Hornblower, perhaps you will be good enough to attend to those ducks before you. Those are neats' tongues, Bolton, a local delicacy – as you know, of course. Will you try them, unless this beef claims your allegiance? Elliott, tempt the ladies with that ragout. They may be partial to foreign kickshaws – made dishes are not to my taste. On the sideboard there is a cold beefsteak pie which the landlord assures me is exactly like those on which his reputation is founded, and a mutton ham such as one only finds in Devonshire. Mrs Hornblower? Barbara, my dear?'

Hornblower, carving the ducks, felt a real pain in his breast at this casual use of the Christian name which was sacred to him. For a moment it impeded his neat dissection of long strips from the ducks' breasts. With an effort he completed his task, and, as no one else at the table seemed to want roast duck, he took for himself the plateful he had carved. It saved him from having to meet anyone's eyes. Lady Barbara and Maria were still talking together. It seemed to his heated imagination as if there was something specially pointed about the way Lady Barbara turned her shoulder to him. Perhaps Lady Barbara had decided that it was a poor compliment to her that he should have loved her, now that she had discovered the crudity of his taste from his choice of a wife. He hoped Maria was not being too stupid and gauche – he could overhear very little of their conversation. He could eat little of the food with which the table was covered – his appetite, always finicking, had quite disappeared. He drank thirstily of the wine which was poured for him until he realised what he was doing, and he checked himself; he disliked being drunk even more than over-eating. Then he sat and fiddled with his food on his plate, making a pretence at eating; fortunately Mrs Bolton beside him had a good appetite and was content to be silent while indulging it, as otherwise they would have made a dull pair.

Then the table was swept clear to make room for cheese and dessert.

'Pineapples not as good as we enjoyed at Panama, Captain Hornblower,' said Lady Barbara, turning back to him unexpectedly. 'But perhaps you will make a trial of them?'

He was almost too flustered to cut the thing with the silver knife, so much was he taken off his guard. He helped her eventually, awkwardly. Now that he had her attention again he longed to talk to her, but the words would not come – or rather, seeing that what he found he wanted to ask her was whether she liked married life, and, while he just had enough sense not to blurt out that question, he did not have enough to substitute another for it.

'Captain Elliott and Captain Bolton,' she said, 'have been plying me incessantly with questions about the battle between the *Lydia* and the *Natividad*. Most of them were of too technical a nature for me to answer, especially, as I told them, since you kept me immured in the orlop where I could see nothing of the fight. But everyone seems to envy me even that experience.'

'Her ladyship's right,' roared Bolton, across the table – his voice was even louder than when Hornblower had known him as a young lieutenant. 'Tell us about it, Hornblower.'

Hornblower flushed and fingered his neckcloth, conscious of every eye upon him.

'Spit it out, man,' persisted Bolton; no lady's man, and oppressed by the company, he had said hardly a word so far, but the prospect of having the battle described found his tongue for him.

'The Dons put up a better fight than usual? 'asked Elliott.

'Well—' began Hornblower, lured into explaining the conditions in which he had fought. Everybody listened; apt questions from one or other of the men drew him on, bit by bit. Gradually the story unfolded itself, and the loquaciousness against which Hornblower was usually on his guard led him into eloquence. He told of the long duel in the lonely Pacific, the labour and slaughter and agony, up to the moment when, leaning weakly against the quarterdeck rail, he had known triumph at the sight of his beaten enemy sinking in the darkness.

He stopped self-consciously there, hot with the realisation that he had been guilty of the unforgivable sin of boasting of his own achievements. He looked round the table from face to face, expecting to read in them awkwardness or downright disapproval, pity or contempt. It was with amazement that instead he saw expressions which he could only consider admiring. Bolton, over there, who was at least five years his senior as a captain and ten in age, was eyeing him with something like hero-worship. Elliott, who had commanded a ship of the line under Nelson, was nodding his massive head with intense appreciation. The admiral, when Hornblower could bring himself to steal a glance at him, was still sitting transfixed. There might possibly be a shade of regret in his dark handsome face that his lifetime in the navy had brought him no similar opportunity for glory. But the simple heroism of Hornblower's tale had fascinated him, too; he stirred himself and met Hornblower's gaze admiringly.

'Here's a toast for us,' he said, lifting his glass. 'May the captain of the *Sutherland* rival the exploits of the captain of the *Lydia*.'

The toast was drunk with a murmur of approval while Hornblower blushed and stammered. The admiration of men whose approval he valued was overwhelming; more especially as now he was beginning to realise that he had won it under false pretences. Only now was the memory returning to him of the sick fear with which he had waited the *Natividad's* broadsides, the horror of mutilation which had haunted him during the battle. He was one of the contemptible few, not like Leighton and Elliott and Bolton, who had never known fear in their lives. If he had told the whole truth, told of his emotions as well as of the mere manoeuvres and incidents of the fight, they would be sorry for him, as for a cripple, and the glory of the *Lydia's* victory would evaporate. His embarrassment was relieved by Lady Barbara arising from the table and the other women following her example.

'Do not sit too long over your wine,' said Lady Barbara, as the men stood for them. 'Captain Hornblower is a whist player of renown, and there are cards waiting for us.'

IV

When they walked away from the Angel through the pitch dark street Maria clung eagerly to Hornblower's arm.

'A delightful evening, my dear,' she said. 'Lady Barbara seems to be a very genteel person.'

'I'm glad you have enjoyed yourself,' said Hornblower. He knew only too well that Maria after any party to which he accompanied her delighted in discussing the others who had been present. He shrank from the inevitable dissection of Lady Barbara which was bound to come.

'She had breeding,' said Maria, inexorably, 'far beyond what I was led to expect by what you told me about her.'

Searching back in his memory Hornblower realised that he had only laid stress on her fine courage and her ability to mix with men without embarrassment. At that time it had pleased Maria to think of an Earl's daughter as a masculine hoyden; now she was just as pleased to revert to the traditional attitude, admiring her for her breeding, and being gratified at her condescension.

'She is a very charming woman,' he said, cautiously falling in with Maria's mood.

'She asked me if I were going to accompany you on your approaching voyage, and I explained that with the hopes of the future which we were beginning to cherish it was inadvisable.'

'You told her *that?*' asked Hornblower sharply. At the last moment he was able to keep the anguish out of his voice.

'She wished me joy,' said Maria, 'and asked me to give you her fe-felicitations.'

It irked Hornblower inexpressibly to think of Maria's discussing her pregnancy with Lady Barbara. He would not allow himself to think why. But the thought of Lady Barbara's knowledge was one more complexity in the whirl of thoughts in his mind, and there was no chance of straightening anything out in the course of the short walk to their lodgings.

'Oh,' said Maria when they were in their bedroom. 'How tight those shoes were!'

She chaffed her feet in the white cotton stockings as she sat in the low chair; from the candle on the dressing table her shadow danced on the opposite wall. The shadow of the bed tester lay in a grim black rectangle on the ceiling.

'Hang up that best coat of yours carefully,' said Maria, beginning to take the pins out of her hair.

'I'm not ready for sleep,' said Hornblower, despairingly.

He felt that no price would be too great to pay at the moment to be able to slip away to the solitude of his ship. But he certainly could not do that; the hour would make such a thing odd and the full dress uniform he wore would make it preposterous.

'Not ready for sleep!' It was so like Maria to repeat his words. 'How strange, after this tiring evening! Did you eat too much roast duck?'

'No,' said Hornblower. It was hopeless to try to explain a too rapidly working mind to Maria, hopeless to try to escape. Any attempt to do so would only hurt her feelings, and he knew by experience he could never make himself do that. With a sigh he began to unbuckle his sword.

'You have only to compose yourself in bed and you will sleep,' said Maria, from her own constant experience. 'We have few enough nights together left to us now, darling.'

That was so; Admiral Leighton had told them that the *Pluto, Caligula* and *Sutherland* were ordered to escort as far as the Tagus an East India convoy which was even then assembling. And that raised once more the cursed question of the shortage of men – how the devil was he to complete his crew in time? Bodmin Assizes might send him a few more criminals. His lieutenants, due to return any day now, might bring in a few volunteers. But he needed fifty more topmen, and topmen could not be picked up in gaols, nor in the market squares.

'It is a hard service,' said Maria, thinking of the approaching separation.

'Better than counters at eightpence a week,' replied Hornblower, forcing himself to speak lightly.

Before their marriage Maria had taught in a school with graduated fees – readers paid fourpence, writers sixpence, and counters eightpence.

'Indeed yes,' said Maria. 'I owe much to you, Horatio. Here's your nightshirt, ready for you. The torment I went through when Miss Wentworth found I had taught Alice Stone the multiplication table although her parents only paid fourpence! And then the ungrateful minx egged that little Hopper boy to let those mice loose in the schoolroom. But I'd suffer it all again, darling, if – if that would keep you near me.'

'Not while duty calls, my dear,' said Hornblower, diving into his nightshirt. 'But I'll be back with a bagful of guineas for prize money before two years are up. Mark my words.'

'Two years!' said Maria pitifully.

Hornblower yawned elaborately, and Maria rose to the bait thus deftly cast, just as Hornblower had been sure she would.

'And you said you were not ready for sleep!' she said.

'It has come upon me now,' said Hornblower. 'Perhaps the admiral's port is beginning to take effect. I can hardly keep my eyes open. I shall say "good night" now, my love.'

He kissed her as she sat before the dressing table, and, turning hastily away, he climbed up into the big bed. There, lying on the farthest edge, keeping rigidly still, he lay until Maria had blown out the candle and climbed up beside him, until her breathing grew quiet and regular. Only then could he relax and change position and give rein to the galloping thoughts coursing through his mind.

He remembered what Bolton had said to him with a wink and a nod when they found themselves together at one time during the evening in a corner where they could not be overheard.

'He means six votes to the Government,' said Bolton, jerking his head towards the Admiral.

Bolton was as stupid as a good seaman could be, but he had been in London recently and attended a levee and had heard the gossip. The poor old King was going mad again, a Regency was imminent, and with the Regency the Tories might go out and the Whigs might come in – the six votes of the Leighton interests were valuable. With the Marquis Wellesley as Foreign Secretary, and Henry Wellesley as Ambassador in Spain, and Sir Arthur Wellesley – what was his new title? Lord Wellington of course – as Commander in Chief in the Peninsula it was not surprising to find Lady Barbara Wellesley married to Sir Percy Leighton, and still less to find the latter given a command in the Mediterranean. The virulence of the Opposition was growing day by day, and the history of the world hung in the balance.

Hornblower shifted restlessly in bed at the thought, but a slight movement by Maria in reply fixed him rigid again. It was only a small party of men – the Wellesleys chief among them – who still had the resolution to continue the struggle against the Corsican's dominion. The smallest check, on land, at sea, or in Parliament, might pull them from their high positions, bring their heads perilously near the block, and tumble all Europe into ruin.

Some time during the evening Lady Barbara had been pouring tea, and Hornblower had found himself standing alone beside her, waiting for his refilled cup.

'It gave me pleasure,' she had murmured, 'when my husband told me you had been given the *Sutherland*. England needs all her best captains at present.'

She must have meant more than she said then. Probably she was hinting at the necessity for maintaining Leighton in his command. It had been no indication, all the same, that she had exerted herself to obtain the appointment for Hornblower. But it was satisfactory to be able to think that she had married Sir Percy for some other reason than love. Hornblower hated the thought of Lady Barbara being in love with anyone. He began to remember every word she had said to her husband, every look she had given him. Certainly she did not seem in the least like an adoring bride. But the fact remained that she was Leighton's wife – that she was in bed with him at this very minute. Hornblower writhed in fresh anguish at the thought.

Then he checked himself. He told himself very sensibly that only misery and madness lay before him if he allowed himself to think about that, and, grasping resolutely at the tail of the first train of thought which recurred to him, he began to analyse the whist he had been playing. If he had not taken that unsuccessful finesse against that lead of Elliott's he would have saved the rubber. His play had been correct – the chances were three to two – but a gambler would not have stopped to consider that. He would have gone baldheaded for results and in this case would have achieved them. But only a gambler could risk a king being unguarded. He prided himself on the precision and science of his play. Nevertheless, he was two guineas the poorer as the result of this evening, and the loss of two guineas was a devilish serious matter at present.

He wanted to buy a litter of pigs, and two dozen fowls – a couple of sheep as well, for that matter – before weighing anchor in the *Sutherland*. There was the wine he needed, too. Some he could buy later and more advantageously in the Mediterranean, but it would be well to have five or six dozen on board at the start. The effect on the officers and men might be bad for discipline if he were not provided with every luxury as a captain should be; and if the voyage out were long and lazy he would have to entertain his brother captains – the Admiral, too, most likely – and they would look at him askance if he offered them the ship's fare on which he was content to live. The list of things he needed stretched longer and longer in his imagination. Port, sherry, and madeira. Apples and cigars. Raisins and cheeses. A dozen at least of shirts. Four more pairs of silk stockings if there was to be much shore-going formality, as seemed likely. A chest of tea. Pepper and cloves and allspice. Prunes and figs. Wax candles. All these things were necessary to his dignity as captain – and to his own pride, for he hated the idea of people thinking him poor.

He could spend all the next quarter's pay on these things and still not have bought too much. Maria would feel the pinch during the next three months, but Maria, fortunately, was used to poverty and to staving off creditors. It was hard on Maria, but if ever he became an admiral he would repay her loyalty with luxury. There were books which he wanted to buy as well; not for entertainment – he had a chest of books, including Gibbon's *Decline and Fall of the Roman Empire* for bedside reading, all old friends – but to fit him for the coming campaign. In the *Morning Chronicle* yesterday there had been a notice of 'An Account of the Present War in Spain' which he would like to have, and there were half a dozen others. The more he knew about the peninsula on whose coast he was going to fight, and of the leaders of the nation he was to help, the better. But books cost money, and he did not know where to turn for money.

He rolled over again and thought of the ill-fortune which had always dogged him in the matter of prize money. The Admiralty had refused to pay out a penny on account of the sunk *Natividad*.

Since the capture of the *Castilla* when he was a young lieutenant he had never had a windfall, while frigate captains whom he knew had made thousands of pounds. It was maddening – especially as in his present poverty-stricken condition he was hampered in his exertions to complete the *Sutherland's* crew. That shortage of men was the most harassing of all his worries – that and the thought of Lady Barbara in Leighton's arms. Hornblower's thoughts had gone a full circle now, and were starting all over again. There was plenty to keep him restless and wakeful all through the weary night, until the dawn began to creep through the curtains; fantastic theories about Lady Barbara's state of mind, and hard-headed plans for making the *Sutherland* efficient for sea.

V

Captain Hornblower was walking up and down his quarterdeck amid all the last minute bustle of getting ready for sea. He was raging to himself at the length of time necessary for these final preparations although he knew quite well that every factor causing delay was susceptible to a reasonable explanation. Two-thirds of the men scurrying about the decks, urged on by the cane of Harrison the boatswain and the rope's ends of the petty officers, were landsmen most of whom until lately had never seen the sea, let alone been in a ship. The simplest order left them merely bewildered, and they had to be led to their tasks and the ropes actually put into their hands; even then they were far more inefficient than trained seamen, because they had not learned the knack of throwing all their weight simultaneously on the rope and walking away with it. And having once set them heaving, it was hard for a petty officer to remember that a shout of 'Avast' or 'Belay' meant nothing to them. More than once the few trained seamen among them, obeying promptly, were thrown off their feet and trampled upon by the rush of landsmen still heaving away. On one occasion of this sort a water butt while being hove up by a whip to the main yardarm had simply gone away with a run again, and only the mercy of providence had saved it from going clean through the bottom of the longboat overside.

It was owing to Hornblower's own orders that the water was so late in being brought aboard. Water left months in cask became so foul and so alive with living things that he had put off bringing it aboard until the last possible moment. Even a gain of a day or two was desirable. That twelve tons of biscuit had also been delayed was the result of the usual incompetence of the victualling yard, whose officials seemed incapable of reading or writing or figuring. The complication due to the fact that a shore boat with captain's stores was having to be unloaded at the same time, and its precious cargo passed carefully down the after hatchway, was due to the Patriotic Fund's delay in sending down to him the sword value one hundred guineas which he had been awarded for his fight with the *Natividad*. No shopkeeper or ship chandler would give credit to a captain about to sail on a new commission. The sword had only arrived yesterday, barely in time for him to pledge it with Duddingstone the chandler, and Duddingstone had only grudgingly given him credit on it, forcing him to promise faithfully to redeem it at the earliest opportunity.

'A sight too much writing on this for me,' said Duddingstone, pointing with a stubby forefinger at the wordy legend which the Patriotic Fund had had engraved, at vast expense, upon the blue steel of the blade.

Only the gold on the hilt and scabbard, and the seed pearls on the pommel, had any intrinsic value. Duddingstone, to give him his due, had been quite right in saying that it was hardly worth forty guineas' credit at his shop, even allowing for his profit and the chance of its being redeemed. But he had kept his word and had sent off the stores at dawn next morning – one more complication in the business of preparing for sea.

Along the gangway Wood the purser was dancing with rage and anxiety.

'God damn and blast all you hamfisted yokels!' he was saying. 'And you, sir, down there. Take that grin off your face and be more careful, or I'll have you clapped under hatches to sail with us today. Easy, there, easy! Christ, rum at seven guineas an anker isn't meant to be dropped like pig iron!'

Wood was supervising the loading of the rum. The old hands were doing their best to make sure that the clumsiness of the new ones would result in the staving of a keg or two, so as to swill from the leaks, and the grinning lightermen overside were abetting them. Hornblower could see by the red faces and uncontrollable hilarity that some of the men had succeeded in getting at the spirits, despite Wood's eagle eye and the marine sentries on guard; but he had no intention of interfering. It would merely compromise his dignity to try and keep sailors from stealing rum if they had the barest opportunity – no one had ever yet succeeded in that task.

From this position of vantage beside the quarterdeck rail he looked down upon a curious bit of bye-play on the main deck. A bewildered young giant – a tin miner, Hornblower guessed, from his biceps – had rounded upon Harrison, apparently driven frantic by the volley of orders and blasphemy hurled at him. But Harrison at forty-five had fought his way up to the boatswain's rank through hundreds of such encounters, and in his prime might have contested the highest honours of the prize ring. He slipped the Cornishman's clumsy punch and felled him with a crashing blow on the jaw. Then without ceremony he seized him by the scruff of the neck and kicked him across the deck to the tackle which was waiting. Dazed, the Cornishman took hold with the others and heaved with them, while Hornblower nodded approvingly.

The Cornishman had made himself liable to 'death, or such less penalty' – as the Articles of War said, by raising his hand to his superior officer. But it was not the moment to invoke the Articles of War, even though they had been read over to the Cornishman last night on his compulsory enlistment. Gerard had sailed round with the longboat and had raided Redruth and Camborne and St Ives, taking each place by surprise and returning with fifty stout Cornishmen who could hardly be expected yet to appreciate the administrative machinery of the service which they had joined. In a month's time, perhaps, when everyone on board would have learnt the heinousness of such an offence, a court martial might be needed, and a flogging – death, perhaps – but at the present time it was best to do what Harrison had just done, and crack the man on the jaw and set him to work again. Hornblower found time to thank God he was a captain and out of the hurly burly, for any attempt on his part at cracking men on the jaw would be a lamentable failure, he knew.

He shifted his weight from one leg to the other, and was reminded of the fact that he was horribly tired. Night after night now he had not slept, and his days had been spent in all the numerous activities necessitated by commissioning a ship of the line. The nervous tension induced by his worrying about Lady Barbara and Maria, by money troubles and manning troubles, had prevented him from leaving the details to Bush and Gerard, even though he knew they were perfectly capable of dealing with everything. Worry and anxiety would not allow him to rest, and had goaded him into activity. He felt sick and stupid and weary. Day after day he had longed for the moment when he should get to sea, and could settle down into the comfortable solitude which surrounds a ship's captain, leaving all shore worries behind him, even leaving Lady Barbara behind him.

He had the sense to realise that this new meeting with her had thoroughly upset him. He had given up as insoluble the problem of whether or not she had secured his nomination to the *Sutherland;* he had tried his hardest to combat his consuming jealousy of her husband. He had persuaded himself in the end that what he had wanted more than anything else was to escape from her, just as he wanted to escape from Maria's cloying sweetness and lovable stupidity, from all the complex misery of life on land. He had yearned for the sea as a castaway yearns for a drink of water. Two days ago the prospect of thus standing on the deck in the final bustle of departure seemed marvellously desirable to him. Now, he realised with a gulp, he was not quite so sure. It was like having a limb torn out by the roots to be leaving Lady Barbara like this. And, oddly enough, he was distressed at leaving Maria, too. There would be a child born before he could be home again, a child well over a year old, running about, perhaps even saying its first few words. Maria would have to go through her pregnancy and confinement without his moral support; and he knew, despite the brave way in which she had dismissed the subject, and despite her stout-hearted good-bye, how much she would miss him. It was that which made it so painful to leave her.

With all her courage her lips had trembled and her eyes had been wet when she lifted her face to him, in the sitting-room of their lodgings; they had agreed long ago that it was foolish to prolong the pangs of parting by her accompanying him on board. Even then the urge to be off had still been strong enough to take him from her arms without a pang, but it was different now. Hornblower mentally spurned himself as a sentimental fool, and glanced impatiently up at the masthead vane. Without a doubt the wind was backing northerly. If it should come round to north or nor'east the admiral would be anxious to start. The convoy, and the *Pluto* and *Caligula*, were assembled now, or pretty nearly, in Cawsand Bay; if the admiral decided not to wait for the stragglers he would be irritated at the *Sutherland's* delay, be it never so unavoidable.

'Keep the men to it, Mr Bush,' shouted Hornblower.

'Aye aye, sir,' answered Bush, patiently.

That patience in his voice irritated Hornblower further. It implied a slight rebuke, a rebuke only apparent to Bush and Hornblower. Hornblower knew that Bush was working as hard as he could, and that he was working the men as hard as he could, too. Hornblower's order had been a mere manifestation of impatience, and Bush knew it. Hornblower was annoyed with himself for having so unguardedly broken his rule of never saying an unnecessary word to his officers, and by way of advancing a reason for having spoken he went down below to his cabin, as he had not intended to do.

The sentry stood aside for him as he entered the door of his sleeping cabin on the half deck. There was plenty of room here; even the present of a twelve pounder left ample space for his cot and his desk and his chest. Polwheal had set everything to rights here already; Hornblower passed through into the main cabin. Here there was ample room, too; the Dutchmen who designed the *Sutherland* had lofty ideas regarding the comfort of the captain. The cabin extended across the whole width of the stern, and the great stern windows gave plenty of light. The stone-coloured paint made the cabin sunny and cheerful, and the black bulks of a twelve pounder on each side made an effective colour scheme. A couple of hands were standing by Polwheal in here while he lay on his stomach packing away cases of wine into the lockers. Hornblower glared at them, realising that he could not yet retire to the solitude of the stern gallery while he should be under their observation through the stern windows.

He went back to the sleeping cabin and threw himself with a sigh on his cot, but his restlessness brought him to his feet again and across to his desk. He took out a crackling document and sat down to look through it again.

Orders to the Inshore Squadron, Western Mediterranean, by Sir Percy Gilbert Leighton, K.B., Rear Admiral of the Red, Commanding.

There was nothing unusual about them at all – night signals, private signals, British, Spanish, and Portuguese; rendezvous in case of separation; a line or two regarding the tactics to be adopted in the event of encountering while with the convoy a hostile squadron of any force. The flagship would accompany the Lisbon convoy of transports into the Tagus – calling for orders, presumably; the *Caligula* was to take the storeships *Harriet* and *Nancy* to Port Mahon; the *Sutherland* was to escort the East Indiamen as far as Latitude 35° before heading for the Straits, to the final rendezvous off Palamos Point. Captains of His Britannic Majesty's Ships were informed that the coast of Andalusia, with the exception of Cadiz and Tarifa, was in the hands of the French, and so also was the coast of Catalonia from the frontier of Tarragona. At the same time captains entering any Spanish port whatever must take the most careful precautions lest the French should be in occupation there. The attached schedule of instructions to masters of ships in the convoy was mostly repetition of all this.

But to Hornblower, musing over these orders, they told a very full and complicated story. They told how, although Trafalgar had been fought five years back, and although England was maintaining at sea the greatest fleet the world had ever seen, she was still having to strain every nerve in the struggle. The Corsican was still building fleets in nearly every port in Europe, Hamburg, Antwerp, Brest, Toulon, Venice, Trieste, and a score of places in between, so that outside every port storm-beaten squadrons of English battleships had to maintain an unceasing watch – a hundred and twenty ships of the line could be found employment, if they could have been spared, on the blockade alone, without regard to the other duties. And at the same time every creek and fishing harbour along half the coasts of Europe maintained privateers, even if hardly better than big rowboats full of men, always ready to dash out and capture the helpless British merchant ships to be found in every sea. To guard against these depredations British frigates had to maintain unceasing patrol, and no King's ship could be despatched on any mission whatever without taking advantage of the opportunity given to convoy merchant shipping on part of their journey at least. In this war against the world only the most careful and scientific distribution of force could prevail, and now, mustering all her strength, England was taking the offensive. Her armies were on the march in Spain, and three ships of the line, scraped together from other duties from which they might just be spared, were being sent to attack the vulnerable flank which Bonaparte had incautiously exposed by his advance into the Peninsula. The *Sutherland* was destined to be the point of the spear-head which was making the thrust against the tyranny which dominated all Europe.

All very well, said Hornblower to himself. Automatically he was pacing up and down again, his head bent under the deck beams, and his walk limited to four strides between the twelve pounder and the door. It was an honourable and responsible position, and yet he had not the men to man his ship. To make or set sail in the way it should be done in a King's ship – or rather, with the rapidity and facility which might make the difference between defeat and victory – called for two hundred and fifty trained seamen. And if all the trained men were aloft at once there would be none at the guns. To serve the guns, if both broadsides were in action at once, called for four hundred and fifty men – two hundred of them, he admitted, might be untrained – and nearly a hundred more carrying powder and engaged upon necessary duties about the ship.

He had a hundred and ninety trained men from the *Lydia* and a hundred and ninety raw landsmen. During the commissioning of the *Sutherland* only twenty old *Lydias* had deserted, abandoning two years' pay and risking the penalty of a thousand lashes, and he knew he was lucky at that. Some captains would have lost two-thirds of their crews during as long a stay as this in a home port. But those twenty missing men would have been desperately useful now. He was a hundred and seventy men – a hundred and seventy *trained* men – short of complement. In six weeks he might drill his landsmen, all except that proportion of hopeless ones, diseased, crippled, or idiotic whom he could expect to find among them, into passable seamen and gunners. But in less than six weeks, possibly in less than three, he would be in action on the coast of Spain. By tomorrow night, even, he might be at grips with the enemy – the wind was backing towards the east and might bring out a French squadron of ships of the line from Brest, evading the blockading squadron, and crammed with men, to fall upon such a tempting prize as the East India convoy. What chance would the *Sutherland* stand, yardarm to yardarm with a French first rate, with only two-thirds of her proper crew, and half of them seasick?

Hornblower clenched his fists again, boiling with exasperation at the thought. It was he who would be held responsible for any disaster, who would have to sustain the contempt or the pity – either alternative horrible to contemplate – of his brother captains. He yearned and hungered for men, more passionately than ever a miser desired gold, or a lover his mistress. And now he had no more chance of finding any. Gerard's raid upon St Ives and Redruth had been his last effort; he knew that he had been fortunate to get as many as fifty men from there. There would be no chance of obtaining any from the convoy. Government transports to Lisbon, government storeships to Port Mahon, East India Company's ships – he could not take a man from any of those. He felt like a man in a cage.

He went across to his desk again and took out his private duplicate of the ship's watch bill, which he and Bush had sat up through most of the night to draw up. It was largely upon that watch bill that the efficiency of the ship would depend in her short-handed condition; the trained men had to be distributed evenly over every strategic point, with just the right proportion of landsmen to facilitate training, and yet not to impede the working of the ship. Foretop, maintop, and mizzen top; forecastle and afterguard; every man had to be assigned a duty, so that whatever evolution out of the thousand possible was being carried out, in fair weather or foul, in daylight or darkness, he would go to his position without confusion or waste of time knowing exactly what he had to do. He had to have his place at the guns allotted him under the command of the officer of his division.

Hornblower looked through the watch bill again. It was satisfactory as far as it went. It had a kind of cardcastle stability – adequate enough at first sight, but incapable of standing any strain or alteration. Casualties or disease would bring the whole thing down in ruins. He flung the watch bill down as he remembered that, if the cruise were a healthy one, he might expect one death every ten days from accident or natural causes without regard to hostile action.

Fortunately it was the unseasoned men who were the more likely to die.

Hornblower cocked his ear at the din on the main deck. The hoarse orders, the pipes of the boatswain's mates, and the stamp-and-go of many feet told him that they were heaving up the longboat from overside. A strange squeaking, unlike that of the sheaves in the blocks, which had reached him for some time and which he had been unable to identify so far, he suddenly realised was the noise of the various families of pigs – captain's stores and wardroom stores – at last come on board. He heard a sheep bleating and then a cock crowing to the accompaniment of a roar of laughter. He had brought no cock along with his hens; it must belong to someone in the wardroom or the midshipmen's berth.

Someone thumped on the cabin door, and Hornblower snatched up his papers and dropped into his chair. Not for worlds would he be seen standing up and obviously awaiting the hour of departure with discomposure.

'Come in!' he roared.

A scared young midshipman put his head round the door – it was Longley, Gerard's nephew, newly come to sea.

'Mr Bush says the last of the stores are just coming on board, sir,' he piped.

Hornblower eyed him with a stony indifference which was the only alternative to grinning at the frightened little imp.

'Very good,' he growled, and busied himself with his papers.

'Yes, sir,' said the boy, after a moment's hesitation, withdrawing.

'Mr Longley!' roared Hornblower.

The child's face, more terrified than ever, reappeared round the door.

'Come inside, boy,' said Hornblower, testily. 'Come in and stand still. What was it you said last?'

'Er – sir – I said – Mr Bush—'

'No, nothing of the sort. What was it you said *last*?'

The child's face wrinkled into the extreme of puzzlement, and then cleared as he realised the point of the question.

'I said "Yes, sir" ' he piped.

'And what ought you to have said?'

'Aye aye, sir.'

'Right. Very good.'

'Aye aye, sir.'

That boy had a certain amount of quickness of wit, and did not allow fright to bereave him entirely of his senses. If he learned quickly how to handle the men he would make a useful warrant officer. Hornblower put away his papers and locked his desk; he took a few more turns up and down his cabin, and then, a sufficient interval having elapsed to conserve his dignity, he went up to the quarterdeck.

'Make sail when you're ready, Mr Bush,' he said.

'Aye aye, sir. Easy with those falls there, you— you—'

Even Bush had reached the condition when there was no more savour in oaths. The ship was in a horrible state of muddle, the decks were filthy, the crew exhausted. Hornblower stood with his hands behind him in a careful attitude of Olympian detachment as the order was given for all hands to make sail, and the petty officers drove the crew, stupid with weariness, to their stations. Savage, the senior midshipman, whom Hornblower had seen grow from boyhood to manhood under his eye, came shouting for the afterguard to man the main topsail halliards. Savage was wan and his eyes were bloodshot; a night of debauchery in some foul haunt in Plymouth had not left him in the best of conditions. As he shouted he put his hand to his temple, where clearly the din he was making was causing him agony. Hornblower smiled to himself at the sight – the next few days would sweat him clean again.

'Captain of the afterguard!' yelled Savage, his voice cracking. 'I don't see the afterguard coming aft! Quicker than that, you men! Clap on to the main topsail halliards, there! I say, you master-at-arms. Send the idlers aft. D'ye hear, there!'

A boatswain's mate headed a rush to the mizzen rigging at Hornblower's elbow. Hornblower saw young Longley standing hesitating for a second, looking up at the men preceding him, and then, with a grimace of determination, the boy leaped for the ratlines and scrambled up after them. Hornblower appreciated the influences at work upon him – his fear of the towering height above him, and then his stoical decision that he could follow wherever the other men could venture. Something might be made of that boy.

Bush was looking at his watch and fuming to the master.

'Nine minutes already! God, look at them! The marines are more like sailors!'

The marines were farther aft, at the mizzen topsail halliards. Their booted feet went clump-clump-clump on the deck. They did their work like soldiers, with soldierly rigidity, as if at drill. Sailors always laughed at that, but there was no denying that at the present moment it was the marines who were the more efficient.

The hands scurried from halliards to braces. A roar from Harrison forward told that the mooring was slipped, and Hornblower, casting a final glance up at the windvane, saw that the wind had backed so far easterly that rounding Devil's Point was not going to be simple. With the yards braced round the *Sutherland* turned on her keel and slowly gathered way. Women's screeches and a fluttering of handkerchiefs from the shore boats told how some of the wives whom Hornblower had turned out twenty-four hours ago had put off to say good-bye. Close overside he saw a woman in the sternsheets of a boat blubbering unashamed, her mouth wide open and the tears running like rivers. It was no more than an even chance that she would never see her man again.

'Keep your eyes inboard, there!' yelled Harrison, who had detected some member of the crew waving farewell. Every man's attention must be kept strictly to the business in hand now.

Hornblower felt the ship heel as Bush directed her course as near to the wind as she would lie; with Devil's Point ahead, and an unfamiliar ship to handle, it was clearly as well to get as far to windward as possible. That heeling of the ship awakened a storm of memories. It was not until one was in a ship under sail, with the deck unstable under one's feet, and the familiar rattle of the blocks and piping of the rigging in one's ear, that the thousand and one details of life at sea became vivid and recognisable again. Hornblower found himself swallowing hard with excitement.

They were shaving the Dockyard Point as closely as possible. Most of the dockyard hands left their work to stare at them, stolidly, but not a soul among them raised a cheer. In seventeen years of warfare they had seen too many King's ships putting out to sea to be excited about this one. Hornblower knew that he ought to have a band on board, to strike up 'Britons, Strike Home' or 'Come cheer up, my lads, 'tis to glory we steer,' but he had no band; he had not the money for one, and he was not going to call on the marine fifer or the ship's fiddler to make a tinny little noise at this moment. Stonehouse Pool was opening up before them now, and beyond it lay the roofs of Plymouth. Maria was there somewhere; perhaps she could see the white topsails, closehauled to the wind. Perhaps Lady Barbara was there, looking out at the *Sutherland*. Hornblower gulped again.

A little flaw of wind, blowing down Stonehouse Pool, took the ship nearly aback. She staggered until the helmsman allowed her to pay off. Hornblower looked round to starboard. They were coming dangerously close in to Cremyll – he had been correct in his surmise that the *Sutherland* would make plenty of leeway. He watched the wind, and the set of the tide off the point. He looked ahead at Devil's Point on the starboard bow. It might be necessary at any moment to put the ship about and beat up to the northward again before breasting the tide once more. At the very moment when he saw that they would weather the point he saw Bush raise his head to bark the orders to go about.

'Keep her steady as she goes, Mr Bush,' he said; the quiet order was an announcement that he had taken charge, and Bush closed the mouth which had opened to give the order.

They cleared the buoy a bare fifty yards from any danger, with the water creaming under the lee now as she lay over to the fresh breeze. Hornblower had not interfered to demonstrate the superiority of his seamanship and judgment, but merely because he could not stand by and watch something being done a little less artistically than was possible. In the cold-blooded calculation of chances he was superior to his lieutenant, as his ability at whist proved. Hornblower stood sublimely unconscious of his motives; in fact he hardly realised what he had done – he never gave a thought to his good seamanship.

They were heading straight for the Devil's Point now; Hornblower kept his eye on it as they opened up the Sound.

'You can put the helm aport now,' he said. 'And set the t'gallant sails, Mr Bush.'

With the wind abeam they headed into the Sound, the rugged Staddon Heights to port and Mount Edgcumbe to starboard. At every yard they advanced towards the open sea the wind blew fresher, calling a keener note from the rigging. The *Sutherland* was feeling the sea a little now, heaving perceptibly to the waves under her bows. With the motion, the creaking of the wooden hull became audible – noticeable on deck, loud below until the ear grew indifferent to the noise.

'God blast these bloody farmers!' groaned Bush, watching the way in which the top gallant sails were being set.

Drake's Island passed away to windward; the *Sutherland* turned her stern to it as with the wind on her port quarter she headed down the Sound. Before the top gallant sails were set they were abreast of Picklecomb Point and opening up Cawsand Bay. There was the convoy – six East Indiamen with their painted ports like men of war, all flying the gridiron flag of the Honourable Company and one sporting a broad pendant for all the world like a king's commodore; the two naval storeships and the four transports destined for Lisbon. The three-decker *Pluto* and the *Caligula* were rolling to their anchors to seaward of them.

'Flagship's signalling, sir,' said Bush, his glass to his eye. 'You ought to have reported it a minute ago, Mr Vincent.'

The *Pluto* had not been in sight more than thirty seconds, but there was need for promptness in acknowledging this, the first signal made by the admiral.

'*Sutherland*'s pendant, sir,' said the unfortunate signal midshipman, staring through his glass. 'Negative. No. 7. Number Seven is "Anchor," sir.'

'Acknowledge,' snapped Hornblower. 'Get those t'gallants in again and back the main topsail, Mr Bush.'

With his telescope Hornblower could see men racing up the rigging of the ships. In five minutes both the *Pluto* and the *Caligula* had a cloud of canvas set.

'They commissioned at the Nore, blast 'em,' growled Bush.

At the Nore, the gateway of the busiest port in the world, ships of the Royal Navy had the best opportunity of completing their crews with prime seamen taken from incoming merchant vessels, in which it was not necessary to leave more than half a dozen hands to navigate their ships up to London river. In addition, the *Pluto* and *Caligula* had enjoyed the advantage of having been able to drill their crews during the voyage down channel. Already they were standing out of the bay. Signals were soaring up the flagship's halliards.

'To the convoy, sir,' said Vincent. 'Make haste. Up anchor. Make all sail con-conformable with the weather, sir. Jesus, there's a gun.'

An angry report and a puff of smoke indicated that the admiral was calling pointed attention to his signals. The Indiamen, with their heavy crews and man o' war routine, were already under weigh. The shoreships and transports were slower, as was only to be expected. The other ships were backing and filling outside for what seemed an interminable time before the last of them came creeping out.

''Nother signal from the flagship, sir,' said Vincent, reading the flags and then hurriedly referring to the signal book. 'Take up stations as previously ordered.'

That would be to windward of the convoy, and, with the wind abaft as it was, in the rear. Then the ships of war could always dash down to the rescue if a Frenchman tried to cut off one of the convoy under their noses. Hornblower felt the freshening breeze on his cheek. The flagship's top gallants were set, and as he looked, he saw her royals being spread as well. He would have to conform, but with the wind increasing as it was he fancied that it would not be long before they would have to come in again. Before nightfall they would be reefing topsails. He gave the order to Bush, and watched while the crew gathered at Harrison's bellow of 'All hands make sail.' He could see the landsmen flinch, not unnaturally – the *Sutherland's* main royal yard was a hundred and ninety feet above the deck and swaying in a dizzy circle now that the ship was beginning to pitch to the Channel rollers.

Hornblower turned his attention to the flagship and the convoy; he could not bear the sight of frightened men being hounded up the rigging by petty officers with ropes' ends. It was necessary, he knew.

The Navy did not – of necessity could not – admit the existence of the sentences 'I cannot' and 'I am afraid.' No exceptions could be made, and this was the right moment to grain it into the men, who had never known compulsion before, that every order must be obeyed. If his officers were to start with leniency, leniency would always be expected, and leniency, in a service which might at any moment demand of a man the willing sacrifice of his life, could only be employed in a disciplined crew which had had time to acquire understanding. But Hornblower knew, and sympathised with, the sick terror of a man driven up to the masthead of a ship of the line when previously he had never been higher than the top of a haystack. It was a pitiless, cruel service.

'Peace'll be signed' grumbled Bush to Crystal, the master, 'before we make sailors out of these clodhoppers.'

A good many of the clodhoppers in question had three days before been living peacefully in their cottages with never a thought of going to sea. And here they were under a grey sky, pitching over a grey sea, with a keener breeze than ever they had known blowing round them, overhead the terrifying heights of the rigging, and underfoot the groaning timbers of a reeling ship.

They were well out to sea now, with the Eddystone in sight from the deck, and under the pressure of the increased sail the *Sutherland* was growing lively. She met her first big roller, and heaved as it reached her bow, rolled corkscrew fashion, as it passed under her, and then pitched dizzily as it went away astern. There was a wail of despair from the waist.

'Off the decks, there, blast you!' raved Harrison. 'Keep it off the decks!'

Men were being seasick already, with the freedom of men taken completely by surprise. Hornblower saw a dozen pale forms staggering and lurching towards the lee rails. One or two men had sat down abruptly on the deck, their hands to their temples. The ship heaved and corkscrewed again, soaring up and then sinking down again as if she would never stop, and the shuddering wail from the waist was repeated. With fixed and fascinated eyes Hornblower watched a wretched yokel vomiting into the scuppers. His stomach heaved in sympathy, and he found himself swallowing hard. There was sweat on his face although he suddenly felt bitterly cold.

He was going to be sick, too, and that very soon. He wanted to be alone, to vomit in discreet privacy, away from the amused glances of the crowd on the quarterdeck. He braced himself to speak with his usual stern indifference, but his ear told him that he was only achieving an unsuccessful perkiness.

'Carry on, Mr Bush,' he said. 'Call me if necessary.'

He had lost his sea legs, too, during this stay in harbour – he reeled as he crossed the deck, and he had to cling with both hands to the rail of the companion. He reached the halfdeck safely and lurched to the after cabin door, stumbling over the coaming. Polwheal was laying dinner at the table.

'Get out!' snarled Hornblower, breathlessly. 'Get out!'

Polwheal vanished, and Hornblower reeled out into the stern gallery, fetching up against the rail, leaning his head over towards the foaming wake. He hated the indignity of seasickness as much as he hated the misery of it. It was of no avail to tell himself, as he did, despairingly, while he clutched the rail, that Nelson was always seasick, too, at the beginning of a voyage. Nor was it any help to point out to himself the unfortunate coincidence that voyages always began when he was so tired with excitement and mental and physical exertion that he was ready to be sick anyway. It was true, but he found no comfort in it as he leaned groaning against the rail with the wind whipping round him.

He was shivering with cold now as the nor'easter blew; his heavy jacket was in his sleeping cabin, but he felt he could neither face the effort of going to fetch it, nor could he call Polwheal to bring it. And this, he told himself with bitter irony, was the calm solitude for which he had been yearning while entangled in the complications of the shore. Beneath him the pintles of the rudder were groaning in the gudgeons, and the sea was seething yeastily in white foam under the counter. The glass had been falling since yesterday, he remembered, and the weather was obviously working up into a nor'easterly gale. Hounded before it, across the Bay of Biscay he could see no respite before him for days, at this moment when he felt he could give everything he had in the world for the calm of the Hamoaze again.

His officers were never sick, he thought resentfully, or if they were they were just sick and did not experience this agonising misery. And forward two hundred seasick landsmen were being driven pitilessly to their tasks by overbearing petty officers. It did a man good to be driven to work despite his seasickness, always provided that discipline was not imperilled thereby as it would be in his case. And he was quite, quite sure that not a soul on board felt as miserable as he did, or even half as miserable. He leaned against the rail again, moaning and blaspheming. Experience told him that in three days he would be over all this and feeling as well as ever in his life, but at the moment the prospect of three days of this was just the same as the prospect of an eternity of it. And the timbers creaked and the rudder groaned and the wind whistled and the sea hissed, everything blending into an inferno of noise as he clung shuddering to the rail.

VI

When the first paroxysm was over Hornblower was able to note that the breeze was undoubtedly freshening. It was gusty, too, sudden squalls bringing flurries of rain which beat into the stern gallery where he was standing. He was suddenly consumed with anxiety as to what would happen aloft if the *Sutherland* were caught in a wilder squall than usual with a crew unhandy at getting in sail. The thought of the disgrace involved in losing spars or canvas in sight of the whole convoy drove all thought of seasickness out of his head. Quite automatically he went forward to his cabin, put on his pilot coat, and ran up on deck. Gerard had taken over from Bush.

'Flagship's shortening sail, sir,' he said, touching his hat.

'Very good. Get the royals in,' said Hornblower, turning to look round the horizon through his glass.

The convoy was behaving exactly as convoys always did, scattering before the wind as if they really wanted to be snapped up by a privateer. The Indiamen were in a fairly regular group a mile ahead to leeward, but the six other ships were hull down and spread out far beyond them.

'Flagship's been signalling to the convoy, sir,' said Gerard.

Hornblower nearly replied 'I expect she has,' but refrained himself in time and limited himself to the single word 'Yes'. As he spoke a fresh series of flaghoists soared up the *Pluto's* halliards.

'*Caligula's* pendant,' read off the signal midshipman. 'Make more sail. Take station ahead of convoy.'

So Bolton was being sent ahead to enforce the orders which the transports had disregarded. Hornblower watched the *Caligula* re-set her royals and go plunging forward over the grey sea in pursuit of the transports. She would have to run down within hailing distance and possibly have to fire a gun or two before she could achieve anything; masters of merchant ships invariably paid no attention at all to flag signals even if they could read them. The Indiamen were getting in their top gallants as well – they had the comfortable habit of shortening sail at nightfall. Happy in the possession of a monopoly of the Eastern trade, and with passengers on board who demanded every luxury, they had no need to worry about slow passages and could take care that their passengers ran no risk of being disturbed in their sleep by the stamping and bustle of taking off sail if the weather changed. But from all appearances it might have been deliberately planned to spread the convoy out still farther. Hornblower wondered how the admiral would respond, and he turned his glass upon the *Pluto*.

Sure enough, she burst into hoist after hoist of signals, hurling frantic instructions at the Indiamen.

'I'll lay he wishes he could court martial 'em,' chuckled one midshipman to the other.

'Five thousand pounds, those India captains make out of a round voyage,' was the reply. 'What do they care about admirals? God, who'd be in the Navy?'

With night approaching and the wind freshening there was every chance of the convoy being scattered right at the very start of its voyage. Hornblower began to feel that his admiral was not showing to the best advantage. The convoy should have been kept together; in a service which accepted no excuses Sir Percy Leighton stood already condemned. He wondered what he would have done in the admiral's place, and left the question unanswered, vaguely telling himself the profound truth that discipline did not depend on the power to send before a court martial; he did not think that he could have done better.

'*Sutherland's* pendant,' said the signal midshipman, breaking in on his reverie. 'Take – night – station.'

'Acknowledge,' said Hornblower.

That was an order easy to obey. His night station was a quarter of a mile to windward of the convoy. Here he was drawing up fast upon the Indiamen to his correct position. He watched the *Pluto* go down past the Indiamen in the wake of the *Caligula*; apparently the admiral had decided to make use of his flagship as a connecting link between the halves of the convoy. Night was coming down fast and the wind was still freshening.

He tried to walk up and down the reeling deck so as to get some warmth back into his shivering body; his stomach was causing him terrible misgivings again now with this period of waiting. He fetched up against the rail, hanging on while he fought down his weakness. Of all his officers, Gerard, handsome, sarcastic, and able, was the one before whom he was least desirous of vomiting. His head was spinning with sickness and fatigue, and he thought that if he could only lie down he might perhaps sleep, and in sleep he could forget the heaving misery of his interior. The prospect of being warm and snug in his cot grew more and more urgent and appealing. Hornblower held on grimly until his eye told him, in the fast fading light, that he was in his correct station. Then he turned to Gerard.

'Get the t'gallants in, Mr Gerard.'

He took the signal slate, and wrote on it, painfully, while warring with his insurgent stomach, the strictest orders his mind could devise to the officer of the watch with regard to keeping in sight, and to windward, of the convoy.

'There are your orders, Mr Gerard,' he said. He quavered on the last word, and he did not hear Gerard's 'Aye aye, sir', as he fled below.

This time it was agony to vomit, for his stomach was completely empty. Polwheal showed up in the cabin as he came staggering back, and Hornblower cursed him savagely and sent him away again. In his sleeping cabin he fell across his cot, and lay there for twenty minutes before he could rouse himself to sit up. Then he dragged off his two coats, and, still wearing his shirt and waistcoat and breeches, he got under the blankets with a groan. The ship was pitching remorselessly as she ran before the wind, and all the timbers complained in spasmodic chorus. Hornblower set his teeth at every heave, while the cot in which he lay soared upward twenty feet or more and then sank hideously downward under the influence of each successive wave. Nevertheless, with no possibility of consecutive thinking, it was easy for exhaustion to step in. He was so tired that with his mind empty he fell asleep in a few minutes, motion and noise and seasickness notwithstanding.

So deeply did he sleep that when he awoke he had to think for a moment before he realised where he was. The heaving and tossing, of which he first became conscious, was familiar and yet unexpected. The door into the after cabin, hooked open, admitted a tiny amount of grey light, in which he blinked round him. Then, simultaneously with the return of recollections, his stomach heaved again. He got precariously to his feet, staggered across the after cabin, to the rail of the stern gallery, and then peered miserably across the grey sea in the first faint light of dawn, with the wind whipping round him. There was no sail in sight from there, and the consequent apprehension helped him to recover himself. Putting on coat and greatcoat again, he walked up to the quarterdeck.

Gerard was in charge of the deck, so that the middle watch was not yet ended. Hornblower gave a surly nod in reply to Gerard's salute, and stood looking forward over the grey sea, flecked with white. The breeze was shrilling in the rigging, just strong enough for it to be unnecessary to reef topsails, and right aft, blowing round Hornblower's ears as he stood with his hands on the carved rail. Ahead lay four of the Indiamen, in a straggling line ahead, and then he saw the fifth and sixth not more than a mile beyond them. Of the flagship, of the transports, of the store ships, of the *Caligula,* there was nothing to be seen at all. Hornblower picked up the speaking trumpet.

'Masthead, there! What do you see of the flagship!'

'Northin', sir. Northin' in sight nowhere, sir, 'cepting for the Indiamen, sir.'

And that was that, thought Hornblower, replacing the speaking trumpet. A rare beginning to a voyage. The traverse board showed that the *Sutherland* had held steadily on her course through the night, and the deck log on the slate showed speeds of eight and nine knots. Before long Ushant should be in sight in this clear weather; he had done all his duty in keeping the Indiamen under his eye, on their course, and under canvas conformable with the weather. He only wished that the queasiness of his stomach would permit him to be quite confident about it, for the gloomy depression of seasickness filled him with foreboding. If a victim had to be found, it would be he, he felt sure. He gauged the strength of the wind and decided that it would be inadvisable to set more sail in the hope of overtaking the rest of the convoy. And with that, having reached the satisfactory conclusion that he could do nothing to avert blame if blame were coming to him, he felt more cheerful. Life at sea had taught him to accept the inevitable philosophically.

Eight bells sounded, and he heard the call for the watch below. Bush arrived on the quarterdeck to relieve Gerard. Hornblower felt Bush's keen glance directed at him, and ignored it in surly silence. He had made it a rule never to speak unnecessarily, and he had found so much satisfaction in it that he was never going to break it. There was satisfaction to be found now, in paying no attention to Bush, who kept stealing anxious glances at him, ready to respond the moment he was spoken to, like a dog with his master. Then it occurred to Hornblower that he must be cutting a very undignified figure; unshaved and tousled, and probably pale green with seasickness. He went off below in a pet again.

In the cabin where he sat with his head in his hands all the hanging fitments were swaying in the slow time set by the creaking of timbers. But as long as he did not look at them he was not uncontrollably sick. When Ushant had been sighted he would lie down and close his eyes. Then Polwheal came in, balancing a tray like a conjuror.

'Breakfast, sir,' said Polwheal in a flood of garrulity. 'I didn't know you was up, sir, not till the port watch told me when they came below. Coffee, sir. Soft bread, sir. Galley fire's bright an' I could have it toasted for you in two twos, sir, if 'uld like it that way.'

Hornblower looked at Polwheal in a sudden flood of suspicion. Polwheal was making no attempt to offer him any of the fresh food, except for bread, which he had sent on board; not a chop or a steak nor rashers of bacon, nor any other of the other delicacies he had bought so recklessly. Yet Polwheal knew he had eaten no dinner yesterday, and Polwheal was usually insistent that he should eat and overeat. He wondered why, therefore, Polwheal should be offering him a Frenchman's breakfast like this. Polwheal's stony composure wavered a little under Hornblower's stare, confirming Hornblower's suspicions. Polwheal had guessed the secret of his captain's seasickness.

'Put it down,' he rasped, quite unable to say more at the moment. Polwheal put the tray on the table and still lingered.

'I'll pass the word when I want you,' said Hornblower sternly.

With his head between his hands he reviewed all of what he could remember of yesterday. Not merely Polwheal, he realised now, but Bush and Gerard – the whole ship's company, for that matter – knew that he suffered from seasickness. Subtle hints in their bearing proved it, now that he came to think about it. At first the thought merely depressed him, so that he groaned again. Then it irritated him. And finally his sense of humour asserted itself and he smiled. While he smiled, the pleasant aroma of the coffee reached his nostrils, and he sniffed at it wondering, reacting to the scent in two opposite ways at once, conscious both of the urge of hunger and thirst and of the revulsion of his stomach. Hunger and thirst won in the end. He poured coffee for himself and sipped it, keeping his eyes rigidly from the swaying of the cabin fitments. With the blessed warmth of the strong sweet coffee inside him he instinctively began to eat the bread, and it was only when he had cleared the tray that he began to feel qualms of doubt as to the wisdom of what he had done. Even then his luck held, for before the waves of seasickness could overcome him a knock on the cabin door heralded the news that land was in sight, and he could forget them in the activity the news demanded of him.

Ushant was not in sight from the deck, but only from the masthead, and Hornblower made no attempt to climb the rigging to see it. But as he stood with the wind whipping round him and the rigging harping over his head he looked over the grey sea eastward to where France lay beyond the horizon. Of all landfalls perhaps this one loomed largest in English naval history. Drake and Blake, Shovell and Rooke, Hawke and Boscawen, Rodney and Jervis and Nelson had all of them stood as he was standing, looking eastward as he was doing. Three-quarters of the British mercantile marine rounded Ushant, outward and homeward. As a lieutenant under Pellew in the *Indefatigable* he had beaten about in sight of Ushant for many weary days during the blockade of Brest. It was in these very waters that the *Indefatigable* and the *Amazon* had driven the *Droits de l'Homme* into the breakers, and a thousand men to their deaths. The details of that wild fight thirteen years ago were as distinct in his memory as those of the battle with the *Natividad* only nine months back; that was a symptom of approaching old age.

Hornblower shook off the meditative gloom which was descending on him, and applied himself to the business of laying a fresh course for Finisterre and directing the Indiamen upon it – the first was a far easier task than the second. It called for an hour of signalling and gunfire before every one of his flock had satisfactorily repeated his signals; it appeared to Hornblower as if the masters of the convoy took pleasure in misunderstanding him, in ignoring him, in repeating incorrectly. The *Lord Mornington* flew the signal for ten minutes at the dip, as if to indicate that it was not understood; it was only when the *Sutherland* had borne down almost within hail of her, with Hornblower boiling with fury, that she was able to clear the jammed signal halliards and hoist the signal properly.

Bush chuckled sardonically at the sight, and began some remark to his captain to the effect that even Indiamen were as inefficient as men of war at the beginning of a commission, but Hornblower stamped away angrily out of earshot, leaving Bush staring after him. The ridiculous incident had annoyed Hornblower on account of his fear lest he himself should appear ridiculous; but it had its effect in prolonging his forgetfulness of his seasickness. It was only after a spell of standing solitary on the starboard side while Bush gave the orders that brought the *Sutherland* up to windward of the convoy again that he calmed down and began to experience internal misgivings once more. He was on the point of retiring below when a sudden cry from Bush recalled him to the quarterdeck.

'*Walmer Castle's* hauled her wind, sir.'

Hornblower put his glass to his eye. The *Walmer Castle* was the leading ship of the convoy, and the farthest to port. She was about three miles away, and there was no mistaking the fact that she had spun round on her heel and was now clawing frantically up to windward towards them.

'She's signalling, sir,' said Vincent, 'but I can't read it. It might be No. 29, but that's "Discontinue the action" and she can't mean that.'

'Masthead!' bellowed Bush. 'What can you see on the port bow?'

'Northin', sir.'

'She's hauled it down now, sir,' went on Vincent. 'There goes another one! No. 11, sir. Enemy in sight.'

'Here, Savage,' said Bush. 'Take your glass and up with you.'

The next ship in the straggling line had come up into the wind, too; Savage was halfway up the rigging, when the masthead lookout hailed.

'I can see 'em now, sir. Two luggers, sir, on the port bow.'

Luggers off Ushant could only mean French privateers.

Swift, handy, and full of men, with a length of experience at sea only equalled by that of the British navy, they would court any danger to make a prize of a fat East Indiaman. Such a capture would make their captains wealthy men. Bush, Vincent, everyone on the quarterdeck looked at Hornblower. If he were to lose such a ship entrusted to his charge he would forfeit every bit of credit at the Admiralty that he possessed.

'Turn up the hands, Mr Bush,' said Hornblower. In the excitement of instant action he had no thought for the dramatic aspect of affairs, forgot the need to pose, and made no attempt to impress his subordinates with his calm; and the calculations which came flooding up into his mind had so rapidly engrossed him that he betrayed no excitement whatever, as they saw.

The Indiamen all carried guns – the *Lord Mornington* actually had eighteen ports a side – and could beat off any long range attack by a small privateer. The luggers' tactics would be to swoop alongside and board; no boarding nettings manned by an Indiaman's crew would keep out a hundred Frenchmen mad for gold. They would manoeuvre so as to cut off a ship to windward of him – while he was beating up against the wind they could rush her in three minutes and carry her off under his very eyes. He must not allow such a situation to arise, and yet the Indiamen were slow, his crew was undrilled, and French luggers were as quick as lightning in stays – there were two of them, as well, and he would have to parry two thrusts at once.

They were in sight now from the deck, their dark sails lifting above the horizon, two-masted and closehauled. The dark squares of their sails were urgent with menace, and Hornblower's eye could read more than the mere dreams of the silhouettes against the clear horizon. They were small, with not more than twenty guns apiece, and no more than nine pounders at that – the *Sutherland* could sink them with a couple of broadsides if they were ever foolish enough to come within close range. But they were fast; already they were hull-up, and Hornblower could see the white water under their bows. And they were lying at least a point nearer the wind than ever he could induce the *Sutherland* to lie. Each would have at least a hundred and fifty men on board, because French privateers had little thought for the comfort of their crews, nor needed to when they only intended to dash out of port, snap up a prize, and dash back again.

'Shall I clear for action, sir,' asked Bush, greatly daring.

'No,' snapped Hornblower. 'Send the men to quarters and put out the fires.'

There was no need to knock down bulwarks and risk spoiling his property and imperil the live-stock on board, because there was no chance of a stand-up fight. But a stray nine-pounder ball into the galley fire might set the whole ship ablaze. The men went to their stations, were pushed there, or led there – some of the men were still confused between port and starboard sides – to the accompaniment of the low-voiced threats and curses of the petty officers.

'I'll have the guns loaded and run out, too, if you please, Mr Bush.'

More than half the men had never seen a cannon fired in their lives. This was the first time they had even heard the strange mad music of the gun trucks rumbling over the planking. Hornblower heard it with a catch in his breath – it called up many memories. The privateers gave no sign of flinching when the *Sutherland* showed her teeth, as Hornblower, watching them closely, saw. They held steadily on their course, heading closehauled to meet the convoy. But their appearance, Hornblower was glad to see, had done more to herd the merchantmen together than his orders had done. They were huddled together in a mass, each ship closer aboard its neighbour than any merchant captain could be induced to steer save under the impulse of fear. He could see boarding nettings being run up on board them, and they were running out their guns. The defence they could offer would only be feeble, but the fact that they could defend themselves at all was important in the present state of affairs.

A puff of smoke and a dull report from the leading privateer showed that she had opened fire; where the shot went Hornblower could not see, but the tricolour flag soared up each of the luggers' main masts, and at a word from Hornblower the red ensign rose to the *Sutherland's* peak in reply to this jaunty challenge. Next moment the luggers neared the *Walmer Castle,* the leading ship to port, with the evident intention of running alongside.

'Set the t'gallants, Mr Bush,' said Hornblower. 'Helm a-starboard. Meet her. Steady.'

The *Walmer Castle* had sheered off in fright, almost running on board her starboard side neighbour, who had been forced to put her helm over as well. Then, in the nick of time, the *Sutherland* came dashing down. The luggers put up their helms and moved away to avoid the menace of her broadside, and their first clumsy rush had been beaten off.

'Main tops'l aback!' roared Hornblower.

It was of supreme importance to preserve his position of advantage to windward of the convoy, whence he could dash forward to the threatened point of danger. The convoy drew slowly ahead, with the luggers leading them. Hornblower watched them steadily, the practice of years enabling him to keep them in the focus of his telescope as he stood on the heaving deck. They spun round suddenly on the starboard tack again, moving like clockwork, leaping to meet the *Lord Mornington* on the starboard wing like hounds at the throat of a stag. The *Lord Mornington* sheered out of her course, the *Sutherland* came tearing down upon her, and the luggers went about, instantly, heading for the *Walmer Castle* again.

'Hard a-starboard,' rasped Hornblower. The *Walmer Castle,* to his vast relief, managed to throw her topsails aback, and the *Sutherland* reached her just in time. She swept across her stern; Hornblower could see her whiskered captain in his formal blue frockcoat beside her wheel, and half a dozen Lascar sailors leaping hysterically over her deck. The luggers wore away, just out of gunshot of the *Sutherland.* There was smoke eddying round one of the other Indiamen; apparently she had loosed off her broadside straight into the blue.

'They're wasting powder there, sir,' volunteered Bush, but Hornblower made no reply, being too busy with his mental calculations.

'As long as they have the sense not to scatter—' said Crystal.

That was an important consideration; if the convoy once divided he could not hope to defend every portion of it. There was neither honour nor glory to be won in this contest between a ship of the line and two small privateers – if he beat them off the world would think nothing of it, while if any one of the convoy was lost he could imagine only too well the ensuing public outcry. He had thought of signalling to his charges that they should keep together, but he had rejected the idea. Signalling would only confuse them, and half of them would probably misread the signal. It was better to rely on their natural instinct of self-preservation.

The privateers had come up into the wind again, and were working to windward directly astern of the *Sutherland*. From the very look of them, of their sharp black hulls and far-raked masts, Hornblower could guess that they had concerted some new move. He faced aft, watching them closely. Next moment the plan revealed itself. He saw the bows of the leader swing to starboard, those of the second one to port. They were diverging, and each with the wind on her quarter came racing down, white water foaming at their bows, lying over to the stiff breeze, each of them a picture of malignant efficiency. As soon as they were clear of the *Sutherland* they would converge again attacking opposite wings of the convoy. He would hardly have time to beat off the first one and then return to chase the other away.

He thought wildly for a moment of trying to bring the whole convoy to the wind together, and rejected the plan at once. They would probably spread out in the attempt, if they did not fall foul of each other, and in either case, scattered or crippled, they would fall easy victims to their enemies. All he could do was to attempt to tackle both ships in succession. It might seem hopeless, but there was nothing to be gained in abandoning the only plan possible. He would play it out to the last second.

He dropped his telescope on the deck, and sprang up on to the rail, hanging on by the mizzen rigging. He stared at his enemies, turning his head from side to side, calculating their speeds and, observing their courses, his face set rigid in an intensity of concentration. The lugger to starboard was slightly nearer, and consequently would arrive at the convoy first. He would have a minute or so more in hand to get back to deal with the second if he turned on this one. Another glance confirmed his decision, and he risked his reputation upon it – without a thought now, in the excitement of action, for that reputation of his.

'Starboard two points,' he called.

'Starboard two points,' echoed the quartermaster.

The *Sutherland* swung round, out of the wake of the convoy and headed to cross the bows of the starboard side lugger. In turn, to avoid the ponderous broadside which was menacing her, the latter edged away, farther and farther as the *Sutherland* moved down upon her. By virtue of her vastly superior speed she was forereaching both upon the convoy and the escort; and the *Sutherland* in her effort to keep between the privateer and the merchantmen was being lured farther and farther away from her proper position to interfere with the designs of the other lugger. Hornblower was aware of that, but it was a risk he was compelled to take, and he knew, despairingly, that if the Frenchmen played the right game he would be beaten. He could never drive the first lugger so far away and to leeward as to render her innocuous and still have time enough to get back and deal with the other. Already he was dangerously astray, but he held on his course, almost abreast now both of the convoy and of the lugger to starboard. Then he saw the other lugger turn to make its dash in upon the convoy.

'Hands to the braces, Mr Bush!' he called. 'Hard a-starboard!'

The *Sutherland* came round, heeling over with the wind abeam and a trifle more canvas than was safe. She seemed to tear through the water as she raced for the convoy, which was wheeling in confusion away from the attack. As if through a forest of masts and sails Hornblower could see the dark sails of the lugger swooping down upon the helpless *Walmer Castle,* which must have responded slowly to her helm, or been badly commanded, and was being left astern by the others. A dozen simultaneous calculations raced through Hornblower's mind. He was thinking like a highly complex machine, forecasting the course of the lugger, and of the six Indiamen, and making allowances for the possible variations resulting from their captains' personal traits. He had to bear in mind the speed of the *Sutherland,* and the rate at which she was drifting to leeway under her press of canvas. To circumnavigate the scattering convoy would take too much time and would deprive him of any opportunity of surprise. He called his orders quietly down to the helmsman, steering for the narrowing gap between two ships. The *Lord Mornington* saw the two-decker rushing down upon her, and swerved as Hornblower had anticipated.

'Stand to your guns, there!' he bellowed. 'Mr Gerard! Give the lugger a broadside as we pass her!'

The *Lord Mornington* was past and gone in a flash; beyond her was the *Europe* – she had worn round a little and seemed to be heading straight for a collision.

'God blast her!' roared Bush. 'God—' The *Sutherland* had shaved across her bows her jib boom almost brushing the *Sutherland's* mizzen rigging. Next moment the *Sutherland* had dashed through the narrowing gap between two more ships. Beyond was the *Walmer Castle,* and alongside her the lugger taken completely by surprise at this unexpected appearance. In the stillness which prevailed on board the *Sutherland* they could hear the pop-popping of small arms – the Frenchmen were scrambling up to the lofty deck of the Indiaman. But as the big two-decker came hurtling down upon him the French captain tried for safety. Hornblower could see the French boarders leaping down again to the lugger and her vast mainsail rose ponderously under the united effort of two hundred frantic arms. She had boomed off from the Indiamen and came round like a top, but she was five seconds too late.

'Back the mizzen tops'l,' snapped Hornblower to Bush. 'Mr Gerard!'

The *Sutherland* steadied herself for a crashing blow.

'Take your aim!' screamed Gerard, mad with excitement. He was by the forward section of guns on the main deck, which would bear first. 'Wait till your guns bear! Fire!'

The rolling broadside which followed, as the ship slowly swung round, seemed to Hornblower's tense mind to last for at least five minutes. The intervals between the shots was ragged, and some of the guns were clearly fired before they bore. Elevation was faulty, too, as the splashes both this side of, and far beyond, the lugger bore witness. Nevertheless, some of the shot told. He saw splinters flying in the lugger, a couple of shrouds part. Two sudden swirls in the crowd on her deck showed where cannon balls had ploughed through it.

The brisk breeze blew the smoke of the straggling broadside clear instantly, so that his view of the lugger a hundred yards away was uninterrupted. She had still a chance of getting away. Her sails were filled, and she was slipping fast through the water. He gave the orders to the helmsman which would cause the *Sutherland* to yaw again and bring her broadside to bear. As he did so nine puffs of smoke from the lugger's side gave warning that she was firing her nine-pounder popguns.

The Frenchmen were game enough. A musical tone like a brief expiring note on an organ sang in his ear as a shot passed close overhead, and a double crash below told him that the *Sutherland* was hit. Her thick timbers ought to keep out nine-pounder shot at that range.

He heard the rumble of the trucks as the *Sutherland's* guns were run out again, and he leaned over the rail to shout to the men on the maindeck.

'Take your aim well!' he shouted. 'Wait till your sights bear!'

The guns went off in ones or twos down the *Sutherland's* side as she yawed. There was only one old hand at each of the *Sutherland's* seventy-four guns, and although the officers in charge of the port side battery had sent over some of their men to help on the starboard side they would naturally keep the trained layers in case the port side guns had to be worked suddenly. And there were not seventy-four good gun layers left over from the *Lydia's* old crew – he remembered the difficulty he had experienced in drawing up the watch bill.

'Stop your vents!' shouted Gerard, and then his voice went up into a scream of excitement. 'There it goes! Well done, men!'

The big main mast of the lugger, with the mainsail and topmast and shrouds and all, was leaning over to one side. It seemed to hang there naturally, for a whole breathing space, before it fell with a sudden swoop. Even then a single shot fired from her aftermost gun proclaimed the Frenchman's defiance. Hornblower turned back to the helmsman to give the orders that would take the *Sutherland* within pistol shot and complete the little ship's destruction. He was aflame with excitement. Just in time he remembered his duty; he was granting the other lugger time to get in among the convoy, and every second was of value. He noted his excitement as a curious and interesting phenomenon, while his orders brought the *Sutherland* round on the other tack. As she squared away a long shout of defiance rose from the lugger, lying rolling madly in the heavy sea, her black hull resembling some crippled water-beetle. Someone was waving a tricolour flag from the deck.

'Good-bye, Mongseer Crapaud,' said Bush. 'You've a long day's work ahead of you before you see Brest again.'

The *Sutherland* threshed away on her new course; the convoy had all turned and were beating up towards her, the lugger on their heels like a dog after a flock of sheep. At the sight of the *Sutherland* rushing down upon her she sheered off again. Obstinately, she worked round to make a dash at the *Walmer Castle* – steering wide as usual – but Hornblower swung the *Sutherland* round and the *Walmer Castle* scuttled towards her for protection. It was easy enough, even in a clumsy ship like the *Sutherland,* to fend off the attacks of a single enemy. The Frenchman realised this after a few minutes more, and bore away to the help of her crippled consort.

Hornblower watched the big lugsail come round and fill, and the lugger lying over as she thrashed her way to windward; already the dismasted Frenchman was out of sight from the *Sutherland's* quarterdeck. It was a relief to see the Frenchman go – if he had been in command of her he would have left the other to look after herself and hung on to the convoy until nightfall; it would have been strange if he had not been able to snap up a straggler in the darkness.

'You can secure the guns, Mr Bush,' he said, at length.

Someone on the main deck started to cheer, and the cheering was taken up by the rest of the crew. They were waving their hands or their hats as if a Trafalgar had just been won.

'Stop that noise,' shouted Hornblower, hot with rage. 'Mr Bush, send the hands aft here to me.'

They came, all of them, grinning with excitement, pushing and playing like schoolboys; even the rawest of them had forgotten his seasickness in the excitement of the battle. Hornblower's blood boiled as he looked down at them, the silly fools.

'No more of that!' he rasped. 'What have you done? Frightened off a couple of luggers not much bigger than our long boat! Two broadsides from a seventy-four, and you're pleased with yourselves for knocking away a single spar! God, you ought to have blown the Frenchie out of the water! Two broadsides, you pitiful baby school! You must lay your guns better than that when it comes to real fighting, and I'll see you learn how – me and the cat between us. And how d'you make sail? I've seen it done better by Portuguese niggers!'

There was no denying the fact that words spoken from a full heart carry more weight than all the artifices of rhetoric. Hornblower's genuine rage and sincerity had made a deep impression, so stirred up had he been at the sight of botched and bungling work. The men were hanging their heads now, and shifting uneasily from one foot to the other, as they realised that what they had done had not been so marvellous after all. And to do them justice, half their exhilaration arose from the mad excitement of the *Sutherland's* rush through the convoy, with ships close on either hand. In later years, when they were spinning yarns of past commissions, the story would be embroidered until they began to affirm that Hornblower had steered a two-decker in a howling storm through a fleet of two hundred sail all on opposing courses.

'You can pipe down now, Mr Bush,' said Hornblower. 'And when the hands have had their breakfasts you can exercise them aloft.'

In the reaction following his excitement he was yearning to get away to the solitude of the stern gallery again. But here came Walsh the surgeon, trotting up the quarterdeck and touching his hat.

'Surgeon's report, sir,' he said. 'One warrant officer killed. No officers and no seamen wounded.'

'Killed?' said Hornblower, his jaw dropping. 'Who's killed?'

'John Hart, midshipman,' answered Walsh.

Hart had been a promising seaman in the *Lydia*, and it was Hornblower himself who had promoted him to the quarterdeck and obtained his warrant for him.

'Killed?' said Hornblower again.

'I can mark his "mortally wounded", sir, if you prefer it,' said Walsh. 'He lost a leg when a nine-pounder ball came in through No. 11 gun port on the lower deck. He was alive when they got him down to the cockpit, but he died the next minute. Popliteal artery.'

Walsh was a new appointment, who had not served under Hornblower before. Otherwise he might have known better than to indulge in details of this sort with so much professional relish.

'Get out of my road, blast you,' snarled Hornblower.

His prospect of solitude was spoiled now. There would have to be a burial later in the day, with flag half mast and yards a-cockbill. That in itself was irksome. And it was Hart who was dead – a big gangling young man with a wide, pleasant smile. The thought of it robbed him of all pleasure in his achievements this morning. Bush was there on the quarterdeck, smiling happily both at the thought of what had been done today and at the thought of four solid hours' exercise aloft for the hands. He would have liked to talk, and Gerard was there, eager to discuss the working of his beloved guns. Hornblower glared at them, daring them to address one single word to him; but they had served with him for years, and knew better.

He turned and went below; the ships of the convoy were sending up flags – the sort of silly signals of congratulation one might expect of Indiamen, probably half of them mis-spelled. He could rely on Bush to hoist 'Not understood' until the silly fools got it right, and then to make a mere acknowledgment. He wanted nothing to do with them, or with anybody else. The one shred of comfort in a world which he hated was that, with a following wind and the convoy to leeward, he would be private in his stern gallery, concealed even from inquisitive telescopes in the other ships.

VII

Hornblower took a last pull at his cigar when he heard the drum beating to divisions. He exhaled a lungful of smoke, his head thrown back, looking out from under the cover of the stern gallery up at the blissful blue sky, and then down at the blue water beneath, with the dazzling white foam surging from under the *Sutherland's* counter into her wake. Overhead he heard the measured tramp of the marines as they formed up across the poop deck, and then a brief shuffle of heavy boots as they dressed their line in obedience to the captain's order. The patter of hundreds of pairs of feet acted as a subdued accompaniment as the crew formed up round the decks. When everything had fallen still again Hornblower pitched his cigar overboard, hitched his full dress coat into position, settled his cocked hat on his head, and walked with dignity, his left hand on his swordhilt, forward to the halfdeck and up the companion ladder to the quarterdeck. Bush was there, and Crystal, and the midshipman of the watch. They saluted him, and from farther aft came the snick-snack-snick of the marines presenting arms.

Hornblower stood and looked round him in leisurely fashion; on this Sunday morning it was his duty to inspect the ship, and he could take advantage of the fact to drink in all the beauty and the artistry of the scene. Overhead the pyramids of white canvas described slow cones against the blue sky with the gentle roll of the ship. The decks were snowy white – Bush had succeeded in that in ten days' labour – and the intense orderliness of a ship of war was still more intense on this morning of Sunday inspection. Hornblower shot a searching glance from under lowered eyelids at the crew ranged in long single lines along the gangways and on the maindeck. They were standing still, smart enough in their duck frocks and trousers. It was their bearing that he wished to study, and that could be done more effectively in a sweeping glance from the quarterdeck than at the close range of the inspection. There could be a certain hint of insolence in the way a restive crew stood to attention, and one could perceive lassitude in a dispirited crew. He could see neither now, for which he was thankful.

Ten days of hard work, of constant drill, of unsleeping supervision, of justice tempered by good humour, had done much to settle the hands to their duty. He had had to order five floggings three days ago, forcing himself to stand apparently unmoved while the whistle and crack of the cat o' nine tails sickened his stomach. One of those floggings might do a little good to the recipient – an old hand who had apparently forgotten what he had learned and needed a sharp reminder of it. The other four would do none to the men whose backs had been lacerated; they would never make good sailors and were mere brutes whom brutal treatment could at least make no worse. He had sacrificed them to show the wilder spirits what might happen as a result of inattention to orders – it was only by an actual demonstration that one could work on the minds of uneducated men. The dose had to be prescribed with the utmost accuracy, neither too great nor too small. He seemed, so his sweeping glance told him, to have hit it off exactly.

Once more he looked round to enjoy the beauty of it all – the orderly ship, the white sails, the blue sky; the scarlet and pipeclay of the marines, the blue and gold of the officers; and there was consummate artistry in the subtle indications that despite the inspection the real pulsating life of the ship was going on beneath it. Where four hundred and more men stood at attention awaiting his lightest word the quartermaster at the wheel kept his mind on the binnacle and the leach of the main course, the lookouts at the masthead and the officer of the watch with his telescope were living demonstrations of the fact that the ship must still be sailed and the King's service carried on.

Hornblower turned aside to begin his inspection. He walked up and down the quadruple ranks of the marines, but although he ran his eye mechanically over the men he took notice of nothing. Captain Morris and his sergeants could be relied upon to attend to details like the pipeclaying of belts and the polishing of buttons. Marines could be drilled and disciplined into machines in a way sailors could not be; he could take the marines for granted and he was not interested in them. Even now, after ten days, he hardly knew the faces and names of six out of the ninety marines on board.

He passed on to the lines of seamen, the officers of each division standing rigidly in front. This was more interesting. The men were trim and smart in their whites – Hornblower wondered how many of them ever realised that the cost of their clothing was deducted from the meagre pay they received when they were paid off. Some of the new hands were horribly sunburned, as a result of unwise exposure to the sudden blazing sun of yesterday. A blond burly figure here had lost the skin from his forearms as well as from his neck and forehead. Hornblower recognised him as Waites, condemned for sheepstealing at Exeter assizes – that explained the sunburn, for Waites had been blanched by months of imprisonment awaiting trial. The raw areas looked abominably painful.

'See that this man Waites,' said Hornblower to the petty officer of the division, 'attends the surgeon this afternoon. He is to have goose grease for those burns, and whatever lotions the surgeon prescribes.'

'Aye aye, sir,' said the petty officer.

Hornblower passed on down the line, scanning each man closely. Faces well remembered, faces it was still an effort to put a name to. Faces that he had studied two years back in the far Pacific on board the *Lydia,* faces he had first seen when Gerard brought back his boat load of bewildered captures from St Ives. Swarthy faces and pale, boys and elderly men, blue eyes, brown eyes, grey eyes. A host of tiny impressions were collecting in Hornblower's mind; they would be digested together later during his solitary walks in the stern gallery, to form the raw material for the plans he would make to further the efficiency of his crew.

'That man Simms ought to be rated captain of the mizzen-top. He's old enough now. What's this man's name? Dawson? No, Dawkins. He's looking sulky. One of Goddard's gang – it looks as if he's still resenting Goddard's flogging. I must remember that.'

The sun blazed down upon them, while the ship lifted and swooped over the gentle sea. From the crew he turned his attention to the ship – the breechings of the guns, the way the falls were flemished down, the cleanliness of the decks, the galley and the forecastle. At all this he need only pretend to look – the skies would fall before Bush neglected his duty. But he had to go through with it, with a show of solemnity. Men were oddly influenced – the poor fools would work better for Bush if they thought Hornblower was keeping an eye on him, and they would work better for Hornblower if they thought he inspected the ship thoroughly. This wretched business of capturing men's devotion set Hornblower smiling cynically when he was unobserved.

'A good inspection, Mr Bush,' said Hornblower, returning to the quarterdeck. 'The ship is in better order than I hoped for. I shall expect the improvement to continue. You may rig the church now.'

It was a Godfearing Admiralty who ordered church service every Sunday morning, otherwise Hornblower would have dispensed with it, as befitted a profound student of Gibbon. As it was, he had managed to evade having a chaplain on board – Hornblower hated parsons. He watched the men dragging up mess stools for themselves, and chairs for the officers. They were working diligently and cheerfully, although not with quite that disciplined purposefulness which characterised a fully trained crew. His coxswain Brown covered the compass box on the quarterdeck with a cloth, and laid on it, with due solemnity, Hornblower's Bible and prayer book. Hornblower disliked these services; there was always the chance that some devout member of his compulsory congregation might raise objections to having to attend – Catholic or Nonconformist. Religion was the only power which could ever pit itself against the bonds of discipline; Hornblower remembered a theologically minded master's mate who had once protested against his reading the Benediction, as though he, the King's representative at sea – God's representative, when all was said and done – could not read a Benediction if he chose!

He glowered at the men as they settled down, and began to read. As the thing had to be done, it might as well be done well, and, as ever, while he read he was struck once more by the beauty of Cranmer's prose and the deftness of his adaptation. Cranmer had been burned alive two hundred and fifty years before – did it benefit him at all to have his prayer book read now?

Bush read the lessons in a tuneless bellow as if he were hailing the foretop. Then Hornblower read the opening lines of the hymn, and Sullivan the fiddler played the first bars of the tune. Bush gave the signal for the singing to start – Hornblower could never bring himself to do that; he told himself he was neither a mountebank nor an Italian opera conductor – and the crew opened their throats and roared it out.

But even hymn singing had its advantages. A captain could often discover a good deal about the spirits of his crew by the way they sang their hymns. This morning either the hymn chosen was specially popular or the crew were happy in the new sunshine, for they were singing lustily, with Sullivan sawing away at an ecstatic obbligato on his fiddle. The Cornishmen among the crew apparently knew the hymn well, and fell upon it with a will, singing in parts to add a leavening of harmony to the tuneless bellowings of the others. It all meant nothing to Hornblower – one tune was the same as another to his tone-deaf ear, and the most beautiful music was to him no more than comparable with the noise of a cart along a gravel road. As he listened to the unmeaning din, and gazed at the hundreds of gaping mouths, he found himself wondering as usual whether or not there was any basis of fact in this legend of music – whether other people actually heard something more than mere noise, or whether he was the only person on board not guilty of wilful self-deception.

Then he saw a ship's boy in the front row. The hymn meant something to him, at least. He was weeping broken-heartedly, even while he tried to keep his back straight and to conceal his emotions, with the big tears running down his cheeks and his nose all beslobbered. The poor little devil had been touched in one way or another – some chord of memory had been struck. Perhaps the last time he had heard that hymn was in the little church at home, beside his mother and brothers. He was homesick and heartbroken now.

Hornblower was glad for his sake as well as for his own when the hymn came to an end; the next ceremony would steady the boy again.

He took up the Articles of War and began to read them as the Lords Commissioners of the Admiralty had ordained should be done each Sunday in every one of His Britannic Majesty's Ships. He knew the solemn sentences by heart at this, his five hundredth reading, every cadence, every turn of phrase, and he read them well. This was better than any vague religious service or Thirty Nine Articles. Here was a code in black and white, a stern, unemotional call to duty pure and simple. Some Admiralty clerk or pettifogging lawyer had had a gift of phrasing just as felicitous as Cranmer's. There was no trumpet-call about it, no clap-trap appeal to sentiment; there was merely the cold logic of the code which kept the British Navy at sea, and which had guarded England during seventeen years of a struggle for life. He could tell by the death-like stillness of his audience as he read that their attention had been caught and held, and when he folded the paper away and looked up he could see solemn, set faces. The ship's boy in the front row had forgotten his tears. There was a far away look in his eyes; obviously he was making good resolutions to attend more strictly to his duty in future. Or perhaps he was dreaming wild dreams of the time to come when he would be a captain in a gold-laced coat commanding a seventy-four, or of brave deeds which he would do.

In a sudden revulsion of feeling Hornblower wondered if lofty sentiment would armour the boy against cannon shot – he remembered another ship's boy who had been smashed into a red jam before his eyes by a shot from the *Natividad*.

VIII

In the afternoon Hornblower was walking his quarterdeck; the problem before him was so difficult that he had quitted his stern gallery – he could not walk fast enough there, owing to his having to bend his head, to set his thoughts going. The people on the quarterdeck saw his mood, and kept warily over to the lee side, leaving the whole weather side, nearly thirty yards of quarterdeck and gangway, to him. Up and down, he walked, up and down, trying to nerve himself to make the decision he hankered after. The *Sutherland* was slipping slowly through the water with a westerly breeze abeam; the convoy was clustered together only a few cables' lengths to leeward.

Gerard shut his telescope with a snap.

'Boat pulling toward us from *Lord Mornington,* sir,' he said. He wanted to warn his captain of the approach of visitors, so that if he thought fit he could make himself unapproachable in his cabin; but he knew, as well as Hornblower did, that it might be unwise for a captain to act in too cavalier a fashion towards the notabilities on board the East India convoy.

Hornblower looked across at the boat creeping beetle-like towards him. Ten days of a strong north-easterly wind had not merely hurried the convoy to the latitude of North Africa where he was to leave them to their own devices, but had prevented all intercourse and visiting between ships, until yesterday. Yesterday there had been a good deal of coming and going between the ships of the convoy; it was only natural that today he should receive formal calls, which he could not well refuse. In another two hours they would be parting company – it could not be a prolonged ordeal.

The boat ran alongside, and Hornblower walked forward to receive his own guests – Captain Osborn of the *Lord Mornington,* in his formal frock coat, and someone else, tall and bony, resplendent in civilian full dress with ribbon and star.

'Good afternoon, Captain,' said Osborn. 'I wish to present you to Lord Eastlake, Governor-designate of Bombay.'

Hornblower bowed; so did Lord Eastlake.

'I have come,' said Lord Eastlake, clearing his throat, 'to beg of you, Captain Hornblower, to receive on behalf of your ship's company this purse of four hundred guineas. It has been subscribed by the passengers of the East India convoy in recognition of the skill and courage displayed by the *Sutherland* in the action with the two French privateers off Ushant.'

'In the name of my ship's company I thank your Lordship,' said Hornblower.

It was a very handsome gesture, and as he took the purse he felt like Judas, knowing what designs he was cherishing against the East India convoy.

'And I,' said Osborn, 'am the bearer of a most cordial invitation to you and to your first lieutenant to join us at dinner in the *Lord Mornington.*'

At that Hornblower shook his head with apparent regret.

'We part company in two hours,' he said. 'I was about to hang out a signal to that effect. I am deeply hurt by the necessity of having to refuse.'

'We shall all be sorry on board the *Lord Mornington,*' said Lord

Eastlake. 'Ten days of bad weather have deprived us of the pleasure of the company of any of the officers of the navy. Cannot you be persuaded to alter your decision?'

'This has been the quickest passage I have made to these latitudes,' said Osborn. 'I begin to regret it now that it appears to have prevented our seeing anything of you.'

'I am on the King's service, my Lord, and under the most explicit orders from the Admiral.'

That was an excuse against which the Governor-designate of Bombay could not argue.

'I understand,' said Lord Eastlake. 'At least can I have the pleasure of making the acquaintance of your officers?'

Once more that was a handsome gesture; Hornblower called them up and presented them one by one; horny-handed Bush, and Gerard handsome and elegant, Captain Morris of the marines and his two gawky subalterns, the other lieutenants and the master, down to the junior midshipman, all of them delighted and embarrassed at this encounter with a lord.

At last Lord Eastlake turned to go.

'Good-bye, Captain,' he said, proffering his hand. 'A prosperous voyage in the Mediterranean to you.'

'Thank you, my lord. And a good passage to Bombay to you. And a successful and historic term of office.'

Hornblower stood weighing the purse – an embroidered canvas bag at which someone had laboured hard recently – in his hand. He felt the weight of the gold, and under his fingers he felt the crackle of the banknotes. He would have liked to treat it as prize money, and take his share under prize money rules, but he knew he could not accept that sort of reward from civilians. Still, his crew must show full appreciation.

'Mr Bush,' he said, as the boat shoved off. 'Man the yards. Have the men give three cheers.'

Lord Eastlake and Captain Osborn acknowledged the compliment as they pulled away; Hornblower watched the boat creep back to the *Lord Mornington*. Four hundred guineas. It was a lot of money, but he was not going to be bought off with four hundred guineas. In that very moment he came to his decision after twenty-four hours of vacillation. He would display to the East India convoy the independence of Captain Hornblower.

'Mr Rayner,' he said. 'Clear away the launch and the long-boat. Have the helm put up and run down to leeward of the convoy. I want those boats in the water by the time we reach them. Mr Bush. Mr Gerard. Your attention please.'

Amid the bustle and hurry of wearing the ship, and tailing on at the stay tackles, Hornblower gave his orders briefly. For once in his life Bush ventured to demur when he realised what Hornblower had in mind.

'They're John Company's ships, sir,' he said.

'I had myself fancied that such was the case,' said Hornblower with elaborate irony. He knew perfectly well the risk he was running in taking men from ships of the East India Company – he would be both offending the most powerful corporation in England and contravening Admiralty orders. But he needed the men, needed them desperately, and the ships from whom he was taking them would sight no land until they reached St Helena. It would be three or four months before any protest could reach England, and six months before any censure could reach him in the Mediterranean. A crime six months old might not be prosecuted with extreme severity, and perhaps in six months' time he would be dead.

'Give the boats' crews pistols and cutlasses,' he said, 'just to show that I'll stand no nonsense. I want twenty men from each of those ships.'

'Twenty!' said Bush, gaping with admiration. This was flouting the law on the grand scale.

'Twenty from each. And mark you, I'll have only white men. No Lascars. And able seamen every one of them, men who can hand, reef, and steer. And find out who their quarter gunners are and bring them. You can use some trained gunners, Gerard?'

'By God I can, sir.'

'Very good.'

Hornblower turned away. He had reached his decision unaided, and he did not want to discuss it further. The *Sutherland* had run down to the convoy. First the launch and then the cutter dropped into the water and pulled over to the clustered ships while the *Sutherland* dropped farther down to leeward to wait their return, hove to with main topsail to the mast. Through his glass Hornblower saw the flash of steel as Gerard with his boarding party ran up on to the deck of the *Lord Mornington* – he was displaying his armed force early so as to overawe any thought of resistance. Hornblower was in a fever of anxiety which he had to struggle hard to conceal. He shut his glass with a snap and began to pace the deck.

'Boat pulling towards us from *Lord Mornington*, sir,' said Rayner, who was as excited as his captain, and far more obviously.

'Very good,' said Hornblower with careful unconcern.

That was a comfort. If Osborn had given Gerard a point blank refusal, had called his men to arms and defied him, it might give rise to a nasty situation. A court of law might call it murder if someone got killed in a scuffle while illegal demands were being enforced. But he had counted on Osborn being taken completely by surprise when the boarding party ran on to his deck. He would be able to offer no real resistance. Now Hornblower's calculations were proving correct; Osborn was sending a protest, and he was prepared to deal with any number of protests – especially as the rest of the convoy would wait on their Commodore's example and could be relieved of their men while the protesting was going on.

It was Osborn himself who came in through the entry port, scarlet with rage and offended dignity.

'Captain Hornblower!' he said, as he set foot on the deck. 'This is an outrage! I must protest against it, sir. At this very moment your lieutenant is parading my crew with a view to impressment.'

'He is acting by my orders, sir,' said Hornblower.

'I could hardly believe it when he told me so. Are you aware, sir, that what you propose to do is contrary to the law? It is a flagrant violation of Admiralty regulations. A perfect outrage, sir. The ships of the Honourable East India Company are exempt from impressment, and I, as Commodore, must protest to the last breath of my body against any contravention of the law.'

'I shall be glad to receive your protest when you make it, sir.'

'But—but—' spluttered Osborn. 'I have delivered it. I have *made* my protest, sir.'

'Oh, I understand,' said Hornblower. 'I thought these were only remarks preliminary to a protest.'

'Nothing of the sort,' raved Osborn, his portly form almost dancing on the deck. 'I have protested, sir, and I shall continue to protest. I shall call the attention of the highest in the land to this outrage. I shall come from the ends of the earth, gladly, sir, to bear witness at your court martial. I shall not rest – I shall leave no stone unturned – I shall exert all my influence to have this crime punished as it deserves. I'll have you cast in damages, sir, as well as broke.'

'But, Captain Osborn—' began Hornblower, changing his tune just in time to delay the dramatic departure which Osborn was about to make. From the tail of his eye Hornblower had seen the *Sutherland's* boats pulling towards two more victims, having presumably stripped the first two of all possible recruits. As Hornblower began to hint at a possible change of mind on his part, Osborn rapidly lost his ill temper.

'If you restore the men, sir, I will gladly retract all I have said,' said Osborn. 'Nothing more will be heard of the incident, I assure you.'

'But will you not allow me to ask for volunteers from among your crews, Captain?' pleaded Hornblower. 'There may be a few men who would like to join the King's service.'

'Well – yes, I will even agree to that. As you say, sir, you may find a few restless spirits.'

That was the height of magnanimity on Osborn's part, although he was safe in assuming that there would be few men in his fleet foolish enough to exchange the comparative comfort of the East India Company's service for the rigours of life in the Royal Navy.

'Your seamanship in that affair with the privateers, sir, was so admirable that I find it hard to refuse you anything,' said Osborn, pacifically. The *Sutherland's* boats were alongside the last of the convoy now.

'That is very good of you, sir,' said Hornblower, bowing. 'Allow me, then, to escort you into your gig. I will recall my boats. Since they will have taken volunteers first, we can rely upon it that they will have all the willing ones on board, and I shall return the unwilling ones. Thank you, Captain Osborn. Thank you.'

He saw Captain Osborn over the side and walked back to the quarterdeck. Rayner was eyeing him with amazement on account of his sudden volte-face, which gave him pleasure, for Rayner would be still more amazed soon. The cutter and launch, both of them as full of men as they could be, were running down now to rejoin, passing Osborn's gig as it was making its slow course to windward. Through his glass Hornblower could see Osborn wave his arm as he sat in his gig; presumably he was shouting something to the boats as they went by. Bush and Gerard very properly paid him no attention. In two minutes they were alongside, and the men came pouring on deck, a hundred and twenty men laden with their small possessions, escorted by thirty of the *Sutherland's* hands. They were made welcome by the rest of the crew all with broad grins. It was a peculiarity of the British pressed sailor that he was always glad to see other men pressed – in the same way, thought Hornblower, as the fox who lost his brush wanted all the other foxes to lose theirs.

Bush and Gerard had certainly secured a fine body of men; Hornblower looked them over as they stood in apathy, or bewilderment, or sullen rage, upon the *Sutherland's* main deck. At no warning they had been snatched from the comfort of an Indiaman, with regular pay, ample food, and easy discipline, into the hardships of the King's service, where the pay was problematic, the food bad, and where their backs were liable to be flogged to the bones at a simple order from their new captain. Even a sailor before the mast could look forward with pleasure to his visit to India, with all its possibilities; but these men were destined instead now to two years of monotony only varied by danger, where disease and the cannon balls of the enemy lay in wait for them.

'I'll have those boats hoisted in, Mr Rayner,' said Hornblower.

Rayner's eyelids flickered for a second – he had heard Hornblower's promise to Captain Osborn, and he knew that more than a hundred of the new arrivals would refuse to volunteer. The boats would only have to be hoisted out again to take them back. But if Hornblower's wooden expression indicated anything at all, it was that he meant what he said.

'Aye aye, sir,' said Rayner.

Bush was approaching now, paper in hand, having agreed his figures regarding the recruits with Gerard.

'A hundred and twenty, total, sir, as you ordered,' said Bush. 'One cooper's mate – he was a volunteer, one hundred and nine able seamen – two of 'em volunteered; six quarter gunners; four landsmen, all volunteers.'

'Excellent, Mr Bush, Read 'em in. Mr Rayner, square away as soon as those boats are inboard. Mr Vincent! Signal to the convoy. "All-men-have-volunteered. Thank you. Good-bye." You'll have to spell out "volunteered" but it's worth it.'

Hornblower's high spirits had lured him into saying an unecessary sentence. But when he took himself to task for it he could readily excuse himself. He had a hundred and twenty new hands, nearly all of them able seamen – the *Sutherland* had nearly her full complement now. More than that, he had guarded himself against the wrath to come. When the inevitable chiding letter arrived from the Admiralty he would be able to write back and say that he had taken the men with the East India Company's Commodore's permission; with any good fortune he could keep the ball rolling for another six months. That would give him a year altogether in which to convince the new hands that they had volunteered – by that time some of them at least might be sufficiently enamoured of their new life to swear to that; enough of them to befog the issue, and to afford to an Admiralty, prepared of necessity to look with indulgence on breaches of the pressing regulations, a loophole of excuse not to prosecute him too hard.

'*Lord Mornington* replying, sir,' said Vincent. ' "Do not understand the signal. Await boat" !'

'Signal "Good-bye" again,' said Hornblower.

Down on the maindeck Bush had hardly finished reading through the Articles of War to the new hands – the necessary formality to make them servants of the King, submissive to the hangman and the cat.

IX

The *Sutherland* had reached her rendezvous off Palamos Point, apparently the first of the squadron, for there was no sign as yet of the flagship or of the *Caligula*. As she beat slowly up under easy sail against the gentle south-easterly wind Gerard was taking advantage of this period of idleness to exercise the crew at the guns. Bush had too long had his way in drilling the crew aloft; it was time for practice with the big guns, as Hornblower had agreed. Under the scorching sun of a Mediterranean midsummer the men, naked to the waist, had sweated rivers running the guns out and in again, training round with handspikes, each man of the crew learning the knack of the flexible rammer – all the mechanical drill which every man at the guns had to learn until he could be trusted to run up, fire, clean, and reload, and to go on doing so for hour after hour, in thick powder smoke and with death all round him. Drill first, marksmanship a long way second, but all the same it was policy to allow the men to fire off the guns a few times – they found compensation in that for the arduous toil at the guns.

A thousand yards to port the quarter boat was bobbing over the glittering sea. There was a splash, and then they could see the black dot of the cask she had thrown overboard before pulling hastily out of the line of fire.

'No. 1 gun!' bellowed Gerard. 'Take your aim! Cock your locks! Fire – stop your vents!'

The foremost eighteen-pounder roared out briefly while a dozen glasses looked for the splash.

'Over and to the right!' announced Gerard. 'No. 2 gun!'

The maindeck eighteen-pounders, the lower deck twenty-four-pounders, spoke each in turn. Even with experienced gun layers it would have been too much to expect to hit a cask at such a long range in thirty-seven shots; the cask still bobbed unharmed. Every gun of the port battery tried again, and still the cask survived.

'We'll shorten the range. Mr Bush, have the helm put up and run the ship past the cask at a cable's length away. Now, Mr Gerard.'

Two hundred yards was a short enough range even for carronades; the forecastle and quarterdeck carronades' crews stood to their weapons as the *Sutherland* ran down to the cask. The guns went off nearly simultaneously as they bore, the ship trembling to the concussions, while the thick smoke eddied upwards round the naked men. The water boiled all round the cask, as half a ton of iron tore it up in fountains, and in the midst of the splashes the cask suddenly leaped clear of the water, dissolving into its constituent staves as it did so. All the guns' crews cheered while Hornblower's silver whistle split the din as a signal to cease fire, and the men clapped each other on the shoulder exultantly. They were heartily pleased with themselves. As Hornblower knew, the fun of knocking a cask to pieces was full compensation for two hours' hard work at gun drill.

The quarter boat dropped another cask; the starboard side battery prepared to bombard it, while Hornblower stood blinking gratefully in the sunshine on the quarterdeck, feeling glad to be alive. He had as full a crew as any captain could hope for, and more trained topmen than he could ever have dared to expect. So far everyone was healthy; his landsmen were fast becoming seamen, and he would train them into gunners even quicker than that. This blessed midsummer sunshine, hot and dry, suited his health admirably. He had left off fretting over Lady Barbara, thanks to the intense pleasure which it gave him to see his crew settling down into a single efficient unit. He was glad to be alive, with high spirits bubbling up within him.

'Good shot, there!' said Hornblower. An extraordinary lucky shot from one of the lower deck guns had smashed the second cask to fragments. 'Mr Bush, see that every man of that gun's crew gets a tot of rum tonight.'

'Aye aye, sir.'

'Sail ho!' came from the masthead. 'Deck, there. Sail right to wind'ard, an' coming down fast.'

'Mr Bush, have the quarter boat recalled. Heave the ship to on the starboard tack, if you please.'

'Aye aye, sir.'

Even here, no more than fifty miles from France, and not more than twenty from a corner of Spain under French domination, there was very small chance of any sail being French, especially on the course this one was steering – any French vessel crept along the coast without venturing a mile to sea.

'Masthead! What do you make of the sail?'

'She's a ship, sir, wi' all sail set. I can see her royals an' t'garn stuns'ls.'

'Belay!' roared the boatswain's mate to the hands hoisting in the quarter boat.

The fact that the approaching vessel was a full-rigged ship made it more unlikely still that she was French – French commerce was confined to small craft, luggers and brigs and tartanes, now. Probably she was one of the ships the *Sutherland* had come to meet. A moment later the suspicion was confirmed from the masthead.

'Deck, there! Sail looks like *Caligula* to me, sir. I can see her torps'ls now, sir.'

So she was; Captain Bolton must have completed his task of escorting the storeships into Port Mahon. Within an hour the *Caligula* was within gunshot.

'*Caligula* signalling, sir,' said Vincent. 'Captain to Captain. Delighted to see you. Will you dine with me now?'

'Hoist the assent,' replied Hornblower.

The pipes of the boatswain's mates twittered into one last weird wail as Hornblower went up the side of the *Caligula;* the sideboys stood at attention; the marines presented arms; and Captain Bolton came forward, his hand held out and his craggy face wreathed in smiles.

'First at the rendezvous!' said Bolton. 'Come this way, sir. It does my heart good to see you again. I've twelve dozen sherry here I'll be glad to hear your opinion of. Where are those glasses, steward? Your very good health, sir!'

Captain Bolton's after cabin was furnished with a luxury which contrasted oddly with Hornblower's. There were satin cushions on the lockers; the swinging lamps were of silver, and so were the table appointments on the white linen cloth on the table. Bolton had been lucky in the matter of prize money when in command of a frigate – a single cruise had won him five thousand pounds – and Bolton had started life before the mast. The momentary jealousy which Hornblower experienced evaporated as he noted the poor taste of the cabin fittings, and remembered how dowdy Mrs Bolton had looked when he saw her last. More than anything else, Bolton's obvious pleasure at seeing him, and the genuine respect he evinced in his attitude towards him, combined to give Hornblower a better opinion of himself.

'From the rapidity with which you reached the rendezvous, it appears that your passage was even quicker than ours,' said Bolton, and the conversation lapsed into technicalities, which endured even after dinner was served.

And clearly Bolton had little idea of what kind of dinner to offer in this scorching heat. There was pea soup, excellent, but heavy. Red mullet – a last minute purchase in Port Mahon at the moment of sailing. A saddle of mutton. Boiled cabbage. A Stilton cheese, now a little past its best. A syrupy port which was not to Hornblower's taste. No salad, no fruit, not one of the more desirable products of the Minorca Bolton had just left.

'Minorquin mutton, I fear,' said Bolton, carvers in hand. 'My last English sheep died mysteriously at Gibraltar and provided dinner for the gunroom. But you will take a little more, sir?'

'Thank you, no,' said Hornblower. He had eaten manfully through a vast helping, and, gorged with mutton fat, was sitting sweating now in the sweltering cabin. Bolton pushed the wine back to him, and

Hornblower poured a few drops into his half empty glass. A lifetime of practice had made him adept at appearing to drink level with his host while actually drinking one glass to three. Bolton emptied his own glass and refilled it.

'And now,' said Bolton, 'we must await in idleness the arrival of Sir Mucho Pomposo, Rear Admiral of the Red.'

Hornblower looked at Bolton quite startled. He himself would never have risked speaking of his superior officer as Mucho Pomposo to anyone. Moreover, it had not occurred to him to think of Sir Percy Leighton in that fashion. Criticism of a superior who had yet to demonstrate to him his capacity one way or the other was not Hornblower's habit; and possibly he was specially slow to criticise a superior who was Lady Barbara's husband.

'Mucho Pomposo, I said,' repeated Bolton. He had drunk one glass more of port than was quite wise, and was pouring himself out another one. 'We can sit and polish our backsides while he works that old tub of a *Pluto* round from Lisbon. Wind's sou'easterly. So it was yesterday, too. If he didn't pass the Straits two days back it'll be a week or more before he appears. And if he doesn't leave all the navigation to Elliott he'll never arrive at all.'

Hornblower looked up anxiously at the skylight. If any report of his conversation were to reach higher quarters it would do Bolton no good. The latter interpreted the gesture correctly.

'Oh, never fear,' he said. 'I can trust my officers. They don't respect an admiral who's no seaman any more than I do. Well, what have you to say?'

Hornblower proffered the suggestion that one of the two ships might push to the northward and begin the task of harassing the French and Spanish coast while the other stayed on the rendezvous awaiting the admiral.

'That's a worthy suggestion,' said Bolton.

Hornblower shook off the lassitude occasioned by the heat and the vast meal inside him. He wanted the *Sutherland* to be despatched on this duty. The prospect of immediate action was stimulating. He could feel his pulse quickening at the thought, and the more he considered it the more anxious he was that the choice should fall on him. Days of dreary beating about on and off the rendezvous made no appeal to him at all. He could bear it if necessary – twenty years in the navy would harden anyone to waiting – but he did not want to have to. He did not want to.

'Who shall it be?' said Bolton. 'You or me?'

Hornblower took a grip of his eagerness.

'You are the senior officer on the station, sir,' he said. 'It is for you to say.'

'Yes,' said Bolton, meditatively. 'Yes.'

He looked at Hornblower with a considering eye.

'You'd give three fingers to go,' he said suddenly, 'and you know it. You're the same restless devil that you were in the *Indefatigable*. I remember beating you for it, in '93, or was it '94?'

Hornblower flushed hotly at the reminder. The bitter humiliation of being bent over a gun and beaten by the lieutenant of the midshipman's berth rankled to this day when it was recalled to him. But he swallowed his resentment; he had no wish to quarrel with Bolton, especially at this juncture, and he knew he was exceptional in regarding a beating as an outrage.

' '93, sir,' he said. 'I'd just joined.'

'And now you're a post captain, and most noteworthy one in the bottom half of the list,' said Bolton. 'God, how time flies. I'd let you go, Hornblower, for old times' sake, if I didn't want to go myself.'

'Oh,' said Hornblower. His evident disappointment made his expression ludicrous. Bolton laughed.

'Fair's fair,' he said. 'I'll spin a coin for it. Agreed?'

'Yes, sir,' said Hornblower, eagerly. Better an even chance than no chance at all.

'You'll bear me no malice if I win?'

'No, sir. None.'

With maddening slowness Bolton reached into his fob and brought out his purse. He took out a guinea and laid it on the table, and then, with the same deliberation, while Hornblower wrestled with his eagerness, he replaced the purse. Then he took up the guinea, and poised it on his gnarled thumb and forefinger.

'King or spade?' he asked, looking across at Hornblower.

'Spade,' said Hornblower, swallowing hard.

The coin rang as Bolton spun it in the air; he caught it, and crashed it on to the table.

'Spade it is,' he said, lifting his hand.

Bolton went through all the motions once more of taking out his purse, putting the guinea back, and thrusting the purse into his fob, while Hornblower forced himself to sit still and watch him. He was cool again now, with the immediate prospect of action.

'Damn it, Hornblower,' he said. 'I'm glad you won. You can speak the Dago lingo, which is more than I can. You've had experience with 'em in the South Sea. It's the sort of duty just made for you. Don't be gone more than three days. I ought to put that in writing, in case his High Mightiness comes back. But I won't trouble. Good luck to you, Hornblower, and fill your glass.'

Hornblower filled it two-thirds full – if he left a little in the bottom he would only have drunk half a glass more than he wanted then. He sipped, and leaned back in his chair, restraining his eagerness as long as possible. But it overcame him at last, and he rose.

'God damn it, man, you're not going?' said Bolton. Hornblower's attitude was unmistakable, but he could not believe the evidence of his eyes.

'If you would permit me, sir,' said Hornblower. 'There's a fair wind—'

Hornblower was actually stammering as he tried to make all his explanations at once. The wind might change; if it was worth while separating it was better to go now than later; if the *Sutherland* were to stand in towards the coast during the dark hours there was a chance that she might snap up a prize at dawn – every sort of explanation except the true one that he could not bear to sit still any longer with immediate action awaiting him just over the horizon.

'Have it your own way, then,' grumbled Bolton. 'If you must, you must. You're leaving me with a half empty bottle. Does that mean you don't like my port?'

'No, sir,' said Hornblower, hastily.

'Another glass, then, while your boat's crew is making ready. Pass the word for Captain Hornblower's gig.'

The last sentence was bellowed towards the closed door of the cabin, and was immediately repeated by the sentry outside.

Boatswain's pipes twittered as Hornblower went down the *Caligula's* side, officers stood to attention, side boys held the lines. The gig rowed rapidly over the silver water in the fading evening; Coxswain Brown looked sidelong, anxiously, at his captain, trying to guess what this hurried and early departure meant. In the *Sutherland* there was similar anxiety; Bush and Gerard and Crystal and Rayner were all on the quarterdeck awaiting him – Bush had obviously turned out of bed at the news that the captain was returning.

Hornblower paid no attention to their expectant glances. He had made it a rule to offer no explanation – and there was a pleasurable selfish thrill in keeping his subordinates in ignorance of their future. Even as the gig came leaping up to the tackles he gave the orders which squared the ship away before the wind, heading back to the Spanish coast where adventure awaited them.

'*Caligula's* signalling, sir,' said Vincent. 'Good luck.'

'Acknowledge,' said Hornblower.

The officers on the quarterdeck looked at each other, wondering what the future held in store for them for the commodore to wish them good luck. Hornblower noted the interchange of glances without appearing to see them.

'Ha-h'm,' he said, and walked with dignity below, to pore over his charts and plan his campaign. The timbers creaked faintly as the gentle wind urged the ship over the almost placid sea.

X

'Two bells, sir,' said Polwheal, waking Hornblower from an ecstatic dream. 'Wind East by South, course Nor' by East, an' all sail set to the royal, sir. An' Mr Gerard says to say land in sight on the larboard beam.'

This last sentence jerked Hornblower from his cot without a moment's more meditation. He slipped off his nightshirt and put on the clothes Polwheal held ready for him. Unshaved and uncombed he hurried up to the quarterdeck. It was full daylight now, with the sun half clear of the horizon and looking over the starboard quarter, and just abaft the port beam a grey mountain shape reflecting its light. That was Cape Creux, where a spur of the Pyrenees came jutting down to the Mediterranean, carrying the Spanish coast line out of its farthest easterly point.

'Sail ho!' yelled the lookout at the masthead. 'Nearly right ahead. A brig, sir, standing out from the land on the starboard tack.'

It was what Hornblower had been hoping for; it was for this reason that he had laid his course so as to be on this spot at this moment. All the seaboard of Catalonia, as far south as Barcelona and beyond, was in the hands of the French, and a tumultuous French army – the 'Account of the Present War in Spain' estimated it at nearly eighty thousand men – was endeavouring to extend its conquests southwards and inland.

But they had Spanish roads to contend against as well as Spanish armies. To supply an army eight thousand strong, and a large civilian population as well, was impossible by land over the Pyrenean passes, even though Gerona had surrendered last December after a heroic defence. Food and siege materials and ammunition had to be sent by sea, in small craft which crept along the coast, from shore battery to shore battery, through the lagoons and the shallows of the coast of the Gulf of Lions, past the rocky capes of Spain, as far as Barcelona.

Since Cochrane's recall, this traffic had met with hardly any interference from the British in the Mediterranean. When Hornblower first reached his rendezvous off Palamos Point he had been careful to disappear again over the horizon immediately, so as to give no warning of the approach of a British squadron. He had hoped that the French might grow careless. With the wind nearly in the east, and Cape Creux running out almost directly eastwards, there was a chance that some supply ship or other, compelled to stand far out from the land to weather the point, might be caught at dawn out of range of the shore batteries, having neglected to make this dangerous passage at night. And so it had proved.

'Hoist the colours, Mr Gerard,' said Hornblower. 'And call all hands.'

'The brig has wore, sir,' hailed the lookout. 'She's running before the wind.'

'Head so as to cut her off, Mr Gerard. Set stu'ns'ls both sides.'

Before the wind, and with only the lightest of breezes blowing, was the *Sutherland's* best point of sailing, as might be expected of her shallow build and clumsy beam. In these ideal conditions she might easily have the heels of a deep-laden coasting brig.

'Deck, there!' hailed the lookout. 'The brig's come to the wind again, sir. She's on her old course.'

That was something very strange. If the chase had been a ship of the line, she might have been challenging battle. But a mere brig, even a brig of war, would be expected to fly to the shelter of the shore batteries. Possibly she might be an English brig.

'Here, Savage. Take your glass and tell me what you can see.'

Savage dashed up the main rigging at the word.

'Quite right, sir. She's closehauled again on the starboard tack. We'll pass her to leeward on this course. She's wearing French national colours, sir. And she's signalling now, sir. Can't read the flags yet, sir, and she's nearly dead to leeward, now.'

What the devil was the brig up to? She had settled her own fate by standing to windward again; if she had dashed for the land the moment she had sighted the *Sutherland* she might possibly have escaped. Now she was a certain capture – but why was the French brig signalling to a British ship of the line? Hornblower sprang up on to the rail; from there he could see the brig's topsails over the horizon, as she held her windward course.

'I can read the signal now, sir. MV.'

'What the devil does MV mean?' snapped Hornblower to Vincent, and then regretted that he had said it. A look would have done as well.

'I don't know, sir,' said Vincent, turning the pages of the signal book. 'It's not in the code.'

'We'll know soon enough,' said Bush. 'We're coming up to her fast. Hullo! She's wearing round again. She's come before the wind.

But it's no use now, Mongseer. You're ours. A handsome bit of prize money there for us, my lads.'

The excited chatter of the quarterdeck reached Hornblower's ears to be unheard. This last attempt at flight on the Frenchman's part had explained his previous movements. Bush, Gerard, Vincent, Crystal, were all too careless to have thought about it, too excited at the prospect of prize money. Hornblower could guess now what had happened. At first sight of the *Sutherland,* the brig had turned to fly. Then she had seen the red ensign which the *Sutherland* had hoisted, and misread it as the French colours – both sides had made the same mistake before this, the red fly both of tricolour and of red ensign led easily to confusion.

It was fortunate this time that Leighton had been Rear-Admiral of the Red, so that the *Sutherland* had worn his colours. What was more, the *Sutherland* had the round bow given her by her Dutch builders, the same as nearly every French ship of the line, and unlike every English ship save three or four. So the brig had taken the *Sutherland* to be French, and as soon as she was sure of this had held to the wind again, anxious to make her offing so as to weather Cape Creux. Then the MV signal which she had flown had been the private French recognition signal – that was something well worth knowing. It was only when the *Sutherland* did not make the expected conventional reply that the French captain had realised his mistake, and made one last dash for liberty.

A quite unavailing dash, for the *Sutherland* had cut her off from all chance of escape to leeward. The ships were only two miles apart now, and converging. Once more the brig came round, this time with the very faint hope of clawing away out of range to windward. But the *Sutherland* was hurtling close upon her.

'Fire a shot near him,' snapped Hornblower.

At that threat the French captain yielded. The brig hove to, and the tricolour came down from her peak. A cheer went up from the *Sutherland's* main deck.

'Silence, there!' roared Hornblower. 'Mr Bush, take a boat and board her. Mr Clarke, you're prize-master. Take six hands with you and navigate her to Port Mahon.'

Bush was all smiles on his return.

'Brig *Amelie,* sir. Six days out from Marseilles for Barcelona. General cargo of military stores. Twenty-five tons powder. One hundred and twenty-five tons of biscuit. Beef and pork in casks. Brandy. Admiralty agent at Port Mahon'll buy her, sure as a gun, ship, stores, and all.' Bush rubbed his hands. 'And we the only ship in sight!'

If any other British ship had been in sight she would have shared the prize money. As it was the only shares to be given away were those of the Admiral commanding in the Mediterranean and of Admiral Leighton commanding the squadron. Between them they would have one-third of the value, so that Hornblower's share would be about two-ninths – several hundred pounds at least.

'Bring the ship before the wind,' said Hornblower. Not for worlds would he give any sign of his delight at being several hundred pounds richer. 'We've no time to lose.'

He went below to shave, and as he scraped the lather from his cheeks and contemplated the melancholy face in the glass he meditated once more on the superiority of sea over land. The *Amelie* was a small vessel, almost inconsiderable in size. But she carried between two and three hundred tons of stores; and if the French had tried to send that amount overland to Barcelona it would have called for a first-class military convoy – a hundred or more waggons, hundreds of horses, taking up a mile or more of road and needing a guard of thousands of troops to protect it from the attacks of the Spanish partisans. Troops and horses would have needed food, too, and that would call for more waggons still, all crawling along at fifteen miles a day at most over the Spanish roads. Small wonder, then, that the French preferred to run the risk of sending their stores by sea. And what a blow it would be for the harassed French army to find a British squadron on their flank, and their best route of communication broken.

Walking forward to take his bath with Polwheal in attendance, a new idea struck him.

'Pass the word for the sailmaker,' he said.

Potter the sailmaker came aft and stood at attention while Hornblower rotated himself under the jet of the washdeck pump.

'I want a French ensign, Potter,' said Hornblower. 'There's not one on board?'

'French ensign, sir? No, sir.'

'Then make one. I'll give you twenty minutes, Potter.'

Hornblower continued to rotate under the jet of the pump, rejoicing in its refreshing impact on this hot morning. The chances were that no Frenchman had observed the capture of the *Amelie* from Cape Creux, and that was the only land in sight at the time. Even if someone had done so, it would take many hours to warn all the coast line of the presence of a British ship of the line. Having taken the French by surprise, the right game to play was to go on exploiting that surprise to the utmost, making use of every device that would make the blow effective. He went back to his cabin and put on refreshing clean linen, still turning over in his mind the details of his plans which were now losing their nebulousness of the night before and growing more and more clear cut.

'Breakfast, sir?' asked Polwheal, tentatively.

'Bring me some coffee on the quarterdeck,' said Hornblower. He could not bear the thought of food – perhaps because of his present excitement, perhaps because of his vast dinner of the night before.

From the quarterdeck could be seen shadowy blue masses on the horizon right ahead – the peaks of the Pyrenees; between them and the sea crawled the road from France to Spain. The sailmaker's mate came running aft with his arms full of a vast bundle.

'Mr Vincent,' said Hornblower. 'I'll have this flag hoisted instead of our own.'

The officers of the quarterdeck eyed the strange tricolour as it rose to the peak, and they looked from the flag to their captain, whispering among themselves. Grouped on the lee side, not one of them dared to try to open a conversation with Hornblower on the weather side. Hornblower exulted both in their excitement and their silence.

'Send the hands to quarters as soon as they have breakfasted, Mr Bush,' said Hornblower. 'Clear for action, but keep the ports shut, I want the long boat and launch ready to be hoisted out at a moment's notice.'

The hands came tumbling up from breakfast in a perfect babble of sound – the order to clear for action, the tricolour at the peak, the mountains of Spain ahead, the morning's capture, all combining to work them up into wild excitement.

'Keep those men silent on the maindeck, there!' bellowed Hornblower. 'It sounds like Bedlam turned loose.'

The noise dwindled abruptly, the men creeping about like children in a house with an irascible father. The bulkheads came down, the galley fire was tipped overside. The boys were running up with powder for the guns; the shot garlands between the guns were filled with the black iron spheres ready for instant use.

'Cleared for action, sir,' said Bush.

'H-h'm,' said Hornblower. 'Captain Morris, if I send away the long boat and launch, I want twenty marines in each. Have your men told off ready.'

Hornblower took his glass and studied once more the rapidly nearing coast line. There were cliffs there, and the coast road wound at the foot of them, at the water's edge, and the shore was steep-to, according to his charts. But it would be a sensible precaution to start the lead going soon. He was taking a risk in approaching a lee shore guarded by heavy batteries – the *Sutherland* might be badly knocked about before she could beat to windward out of range again. Hornblower was counting not merely on the disguise he had adopted, but on the very fact that the French would not believe that an English ship could take that risk.

To the French in the batteries the presence of a French ship of the line off that coast was susceptible of explanation – she might have ventured forth from Toulon, or have come in from the Atlantic, or she might be a refugee from some Ionian island attacked by the British, seeking refuge after long wanderings. He could not believe that they would open fire without allowing time for explanation.

At a word from Hornblower the *Sutherland* turned on a course parallel with the shore, heading northward with the wind abeam. She was creeping along now, in the light breeze, only just out of gunshot of the shore. The sun was blazing down upon them, the crew standing silently at their stations, the officers grouped on the quarterdeck, Hornblower with the sweat running down his face, sweeping the coast with his glass in search of an objective. The little wind was calling forth only the faintest piping from the rigging; the rattle of the blocks to the gentle roll of the ship sounded unnaturally loud in the silence as did the monotonous calling of the man at the lead. Suddenly Savage hailed from the foretop.

'There's a lot of small craft, sir, at anchor round the point, there. I can just see 'em from here, sir.'

A dark speck danced in the object glass of Hornblower's telescope. He lowered the instrument to rest his aching eye, and then he raised it again. The speck was still there; it was a tricolour flag waving lazily in the wind from a flagstaff on the point. That was what Hornblower had been seeking. A French battery perched on the top of the cliff. Forty-two pounders, probably, sited with a good command, probably with furnaces for heating the shot – no ship that floated could fight them. Clustered underneath, a little coasting fleet, huddling there for shelter at the sight of a strange sail.

'Tell your men to lie down,' said Hornblower to Morris. He did not want the red coats of the marines drawn up on the quarterdeck to reveal his ship prematurely for what she was.

The *Sutherland* crept along, the grey cliffs growing more clearly defined as at Hornblower's order she was edged closer in shore. Beyond the cliffs mountain peaks were revealing themselves with startling suddenness whenever Hornblower's rigid concentration on the battery relaxed. He could see the parapets now in his glass, and he almost thought he could see the big guns peeping over them. At any moment now the battery might burst into thunder and flame and smoke, and in that case he would have to turn and fly, baffled. They were well within gunshot now. Perhaps the French had guessed the *Sutherland's* identity, and were merely waiting to have her well within range. Every minute that the *Sutherland* approached meant another minute under fire when she tried to escape. The loss of a mast might mean in the end the loss of the ship.

'Mr Vincent,' said Hornblower, without shifting his gaze from the battery. 'Hoist MV.'

The words sent a stir through the group of officers. They could be certain now of what plan Hornblower had in mind. The trick increased the risk of detection at the same time as, if it were successful, it gave them more opportunity of approaching the battery. If MV were the French recognition signal, and was being correctly employed, well and good. If not – the battery would soon tell them so. Hornblower, his heart thumping in his breast, judged that at any rate it might confuse the issue for the officer in the battery and induce him to delay a little longer. The signal rose up the halliards, and the battery still stayed silent. Now a signal hoist soared up the battery's flagstaff.

'I can't read that, sir,' said Vincent. 'One of 'em's a swallowtail we don't use.'

But the mere fact of the battery's signalling in reply meant that they were at least doubtful of the *Sutherland's* identity – unless it were part of the plan to lure her closer in. Yet if the battery delayed much longer it would be too late.

'Mr Bush, do you see the battery?'

'Yes, sir.'

'You will take the long boat. Mr Rayner will take the launch, and you will land and storm the battery.'

'Aye aye, sir.'

'I will give you the word when to hoist out.'

'Aye aye, sir.'

'Quarter less eight,' droned the leadsman – Hornblower had listened to each cast subconsciously; now that the water was shoaling he was compelled to give half his attention up to the leadsman's cries while still scrutinising the battery. A bare quarter of a mile from it now; it was time to strike.

'Vrey good, Mr Bush. You can go now.'

'Aye aye, sir.'

'Back the main tops'l, Mr Gerard.'

At Bush's orders the dormant ship sprang to life. The shrilling of the pipes brought the boats' crews to the falls at the run. This was the time when the painful drill would reveal its worth; the more quickly those boats were swung out, manned, and away, the less would be the danger and the greater the chance of success. Long boat and launch dropped to the water, the hands swarming down the falls.

'Throw the guns down the cliff, Mr Bush. Wreck the battery if you can. But don't stay a moment longer than necessary.'

'Aye aye, sir.'

They were off, the men tugging like maniacs at the oars.

'Helm a-lee! Mr Gerard, put the ship about. And down with that flag, and send up our own. Ah!'

The air was torn with the passage of cannon shot overhead. The whole ship shook as something struck her a tremendous blow forward. Hornblower saw the smoke billow up round the battery – it had opened fire at last. And thank God it was firing at the ship; if one of those shots hit a boat he would be in a pretty scrape. So pleased was he at the thought that it never occurred to him to wonder about his own personal safety.

'Mr Gerard, see if the guns can reach the battery. See that every shot is properly aimed. It is no use unless the embrasures can be swept.'

Another salvo from the battery, and too high again, the shot howling overhead. Little Longley, strutting the quarterdeck with his dirk at his hip, checked in his stride to duck, instinctively, and then, with a side glance at his captain, walked on with his neck as stiff as a ramrod. Hornblower grinned.

'Mr Longley, have that main top gallant halliard spliced at once.'

It was a kindness to keep the boy busy so that he would have no time to be afraid. Now the *Sutherland's* starboard broadside began to open fire, irregularly, as the gun captains fancied their weapons bore. Flying jets of dust from the face of the cliff showed that most of the shot were hitting thirty feet too low. But if even one or two shots got in through the embrasures and killed someone working the guns it would be a valuable help in unsettling the artillery men. Another salvo. This time they had fired at the boats. The launch almost vanished under the jets of water flung up by the plunging fire, and Hornblower gulped with anxiety. But the next moment the launch reappeared, limping along crabwise – a shot must have smashed some of the oars on one side. But the boats were safe now; close up to the cliffs as they were the guns up above could surely not be depressed sufficiently to hit them. The long boat was in the very surf now, with the launch at her heels. Now the men were tumbling out and splashing up to the beach.

For a moment Hornblower wished that, contrary to etiquette he had taken command of the landing party, fearing lest a disorderly and piecemeal attack should waste all the advantages gained. No, Bush was safe enough. He could see him through his glass, leaping up on to the road and then turning to face the landing party. Hornblower could see Bush's arms wave as he gave his orders. Someone led off a party of seamen to the right – that was Rayner, for Hornblower's straining eyes could perceive his bald head and unmistakable round shouldered gait. Morris was taking the marines – a solid block of scarlet – off to the left. Bush was forming up the remainder in the centre – Bush was clearheaded enough. There were three gullies in the face of the cliff, marked with straggling greenery, and indicating the easiest points of ascent. As the flanking parties reached the bottom of their paths, Hornblower saw Bush's sword flash as he called his men on. They were breasting the cliffs now, all three parties simultaneously. A tiny faint cheer crept out over the water to the ship.

One or two of the main deck guns were making better practice now. Twice Hornblower thought he saw earth flying from the embrasures as shots struck them; so much the better, but the firing must stop now that the men were mounting the cliff. He pealed on his whistle and bellowed the order. In dead silence the ship slid on through the water while every eye watched the landing party. They were pouring over the top now. Sudden gusts of smoke showed that the guns were firing again – canister or grape, probably. Any of those parties caught in a whirlpool of canister from a forty-two pounder might well be wiped out. Weapons were sparkling on the parapet; little pinpricks of smoke indicated small arm fire. Now out on the left the red coats of the marines were on the very top of the parapet, a white clad sailor was waving from the centre. They were pouring over, although red dots and white dots littered the face of the parapet to mark where men had fallen. One anxious minute with nothing to see seemed to last for hours. And then the tricolour flag came slowly down its staff, and the hands on the main deck burst into a storm of cheering. Hornblower shut his glass with a snap.

'Mr Gerard, put the ship about. Send in the quarter boats to take possession of the craft in the bay.'

There were four tantanes, a felucca, and two cutter-rigged boats clustered at anchor in the tiny bay below the battery – a fine haul especially if they were fully laden. Hornblower saw the dinghies pulling madly from them for the shore on the side away from the battery, as the crews fled to escape captivity. Hornblower was glad to see them go; he did not want to be burdened with prisoners, and he had been a prisoner himself for two weary years in Ferrol. Something fell in an avalanche down the cliff, crashing on to the road at its foot in a cloud of dust and debris. It was a forty-two pounder heaved up by brute force over the parapet; Bush had got to work quickly enough at dismantling the battery – if Bush were still alive. Another gun followed at an interval, and another after that.

The small craft, two of them towing the quarter boats, were beating out towards the *Sutherland* where she lay hove-to awaiting them, and the landing party was coming down the cliff face again and forming up on the beach. Lingering groups indicated that the wounded were being brought down. All these necessary delays seemed to stretch the anticlimax into an eternity. A bellowing roar from the battery and a fountain of earth and smoke – momentarily like those volcanoes at whose foot the *Lydia* had anchored last commission – told that the magazine had been fired. Now at last the launch and the long boat were pulling back to the ship, and Hornblower's telescope, trained on the sternsheets of the long boat, revealed Bush sitting there, alive and apparently well. Even then, it was a relief to see him come rolling aft, his big craggy face wreathed in smiles, to make his report.

'The Frogs bolted out of the back door as we came in at the front,' he said. 'They hardly lost a man. We lost—'

Hornblower had to nerve himself to listen to a pitiful list. Now that the excitement was over he felt weak and ill, and it was only by an effort that he was able to keep his hands from trembling. And it was only by an effort that he could make himself smile and mouth out words of commendation first to the men whom Bush singled out for special mention and then to the whole crew drawn up on the maindeck. For hours he had been walking the quarterdeck pretending to be imperturbable, and now he was in the throes of the reaction. He left it to Bush to deal with the prizes, to allot them skeleton crews and send them off to Port Mahon, while without a word of excuse he escaped below to his cabin. He had even forgotten that the ship had been cleared for action, so that in his search for privacy he had to sit in his hammock chair at the end of the stern gallery, just out of sight from the stern windows, while the men were replacing the bulkheads and securing the guns. He lay back, his arms hanging and his eyes closed, with the water bubbling under the counter below him and the rudder pintles groaning at his side. Each time the ship went about as Bush worked her out to make an offing his head sagged over to the opposite shoulder.

What affected him most was the memory of the risks he had run; at the thought of them little cold waves ran down his back and legs. He had been horribly reckless in his handling of the ship – only by the greatest good fortune was she not now a dismasted wreck, with half her crew killed and wounded, drifting on to a lee shore, with an exultant enemy awaiting her. It was Hornblower's nature to discount his achievements to himself, to make no allowance for the careful precautions he had taken to ensure success, for his ingenuity in making the best of circumstances. He cursed himself for a reckless fool, and for his habit of plunging into danger and only counting the risk afterwards.

A rattle of cutlery and crockery in the cabin recalled him to himself, and he sat up and resumed his unmoved countenance just in time as Polwheal came out into the stern gallery.

'I've got you a mouthful to eat, sir,' he said. 'You've had nought since yesterday.'

Hornblower suddenly knew that he was horribly hungry, and at the same time he realised that he had forgotten the coffee Polwheal had brought him, hours ago, to the quarterdeck. Presumably that had stayed there to grow cold until Polwheal fetched it away. With real pleasure he got up and walked into the cabin; so tempting was the prospect of food and drink that he felt hardly a twinge of irritation at having Polwheal thus fussing over him and trying to mother him and probably getting ready to make overmuch advantage of his position. The cold tongue was delicious, and Polwheal with uncanny intuition had put out a half bottle of claret – not one day a month did Hornblower drink anything stronger than water when by himself, yet today he drank three glasses of claret, knowing that he wanted them, and enjoying every drop.

And as the food and the wine strengthened him, and his fatigue dropped away, his mind began to busy itself with new plans, devising, without his conscious volition, fresh methods of harassing the enemy. As he drank his coffee the ideas began to stir within him, and yet he was not conscious of them. All he knew was the cabin was suddenly stuffy and cramped, and that he was yearning again for the fresh air and fierce sunshine outside. Polwheal, returning to clear the table, saw his captain through the stern windows pacing the gallery, and years of service under Hornblower had taught him to make the correct deductions from Hornblower's bent, thoughtful head, and the hands which, although clasped behind him, yet twisted and turned one within the other as he worked out each prospective development.

In consequence of what Polwheal had to tell, the lower deck all knew that another move was imminent, fully two hours before Hornblower appeared on the quarterdeck and gave the orders which precipitated it.

XI

'They're shooting well, sir,' said Bush, as a fountain of water leaped suddenly and mysteriously into brief life a hundred yards from the port beam.

'Who couldn't shoot well with their advantages?' answered Gerard.

'Forty-two pounders, on permanent mounts fifty feet above the water, and soldiers to serve 'em ten years in the ranks?'

'I've seen 'em shoot worse, all the same,' said Crystal.

'It's a mile an' a half if it's a yard,' said Bush.

'More than that,' said Crystal.

'A scant mile,' said Gerard.

'Nonsense,' said Bush.

Hornblower broke into their wrangling.

'Your attention, please, gentlemen. And I shall want Rayner and Hooker – pass the word, there, for Mr Rayner and Mr Hooker. Now, study the place with care.'

A dozen telescopes trained on Port Vendres, with the sunset reddening behind. In the background Mount Canigou stood out with a startling illusion of towering height; to the left the spurs of the Pyrenees ran clean down into the sea at Cape Cerbera, marking where Spain had ended and France began. In the centre the white houses of Port Vendres showed pink under the sunset, clustering round the head of the little bay. In front of them a vessel swung at anchor, under the protection of the batteries on either side of the bay which were marked by occasional puffs of smoke as the guns there tried repeatedly, at extremely long range, to hit the insolent ship which was flaunting British colours within sight of the Empire's coasts.

'Mark that battery to the left, Mr Gerard,' said Hornblower. 'Mr Rayner, you see the battery to the right – there goes a gun. Mark it well. I want no mistake made. Mr Hooker, you see how the bay curves? You must be able to take a boat straight up to the ship there tonight.'

'Aye aye, sir,' said Hooker, while the other officers exchanged glances.

'Put the ship upon the port tack, Mr Bush. We must stand out to sea, now. These are your orders, gentlemen.'

Turning from one officer to another, Hornblower ran briefly through their instructions. The ship sheltering in Port Vendres was to be cut and taken that night as a climax to the twenty-four hours which had begun with the capture of the *Amelie* and continued with the storming of the battery at Llanza.

'The moon rises at one o'clock. I shall take care to be back in our present position here at midnight,' said Hornblower.

With good fortune, the garrison of Port Vendres might be lured into tranquillity by the sight of the *Sutherland* sailing away now, and she could return unobserved after nightfall. An hour of darkness would suffice to effect a surprise, and the rising moon would give sufficient light for the captured ship to be brought out if successful, and for the attackers to rally and escape if unsuccessful.

'Mr Bush will remain in command of the ship,' said Hornblower.

'Sir!' protested Bush. 'Please sir—'

'You've won sufficient distinction today, Bush,' said Hornblower.

Hornblower was going in with the attack. He knew that he would not be able to bear the anxiety of waiting outside with the firing and the fighting going on inside – he was in a fever already, now that he was allowing his mind to dwell on the prospective action, although he was taking care not to show it.

'Every man in the boarding party must be a seaman,' said Hornblower. 'Mr Gerard and Mr Rayner can divide the marines between them.'

His listeners nodded, understanding. To set sail in a strange ship and get her under way in darkness would call for seamanship.

'You all understand what is expected of you?' asked Hornblower, and they nodded again. 'Mr Hooker, repeat your orders.'

Hooker repeated them accurately. He was a good officer as Hornblower had known when he had recommended him for promotion to lieutenant on the *Lydia's* return.

'Good,' said Hornblower. 'Then, gentlemen, you will please set your watches with mine. There will be enough light from the stars to read them. What, no watch, Mr Hooker? Perhaps Mr Bush will be good enough to lend you his.'

Hornblower could see, from his officers' expressions, that this synchronisation of the watches had impressed upon them the necessity for accurately conforming to the timetable which he had laid down, in a fashion nothing else could have done. Otherwise they would have paid only casual attention to the intervals of 'five minutes' and 'ten minutes' which he had given, and he could appreciate in a manner they could not, the necessity for exact adherence to schedule in a complex operation carried out in the darkness.

'You are all agreed now? Then perhaps all you gentlemen with the exception of the officer of the watch will give me the pleasure of your company at dinner.'

Again the officers interchanged glances; those dinners in Hornblower's cabin on the eve of action were famous. Savage could remember one on board the *Lydia* before the duel with the *Natividad*. The other two present then had been Galbraith the lieutenant of his division, and Clay, his best friend. And Galbraith had died of gangrene in the far Pacific, and Clay's head had been smashed by a cannon ball.

'There'll be no whist tonight, Savage,' smiled Hornblower, reading his thoughts. 'There will be too much to do before midnight.'

Often before Hornblower had insisted on whist before action, and had concealed his own nervousness by criticism of the play of his preoccupied fellow players. Now he was forcing himself to be smiling, genial, and hospitable as he led the way into the cabin. His nervous tension inclined to make him talkative, and this evening, when his guests were more tongue-tied even than usual, he could for once give rein to his inclinations, and chat freely in an attempt to keep conversation going. The others eyed him, wondering as he smiled and gossiped. They never saw him in this mood except on the eve of action, and they had forgotten how human and fascinating he could be when he employed all his wiles to captivate them. For him it was a convenient way to keep his mind off the approaching action, thus to exercise himself in fascination while still drawing the rigid line which divided the captain from his subordinates.

'I am afraid,' said Hornblower in the end, crumpling his napkin and tossing it on to the table, 'it is time for us to go on deck again, gentlemen. What a mortal pity to break up this gathering!'

They left the lamplit brilliance of the cabin for the darkness of the deck. The stars were glowing in the dark sky, and the *Sutherland* was stealing ghostlike over the sea which reflected them; her pyramids of canvas soared up to invisibility, and the only sounds to be heard were the rattle of the rigging and the periodic music of the water under her forefoot as she rode over the tiny invisible waves. The crew was resting on the gangways and the maindeck, conversing in whispers, and when the subdued voices of their officers called them to duty they mustered silently, each division assembling for its particular duty. Hornblower checked the position of the ship with Bush, and strained his eye through his nightglass towards the invisible shore.

'Longboat crew here!' called Gerard softly.

'Launch crew here!' echoed Rayner, and their allotted parties formed up quietly abreast the main mast.

The cutters' crews were assembling on the quarterdeck; Hornblower was taking two hundred and fifty men altogether – if the expedition were a complete disaster Bush would hardly have sufficient men to navigate the *Sutherland* back to the rendezvous.

'You can heave-to, Mr Bush,' he said.

One by one the boats were hoisted out, and lay on their oars a few yards off. Last of all, Hornblower went down the side and seated himself beside Brown and Longley in the stern of the barge; the men at the oars pushed off at a growl from Brown, and the flotilla, with muffled oars, began to pull steadily away from the ship. The darkness was intense, and, by the usual optical illusion, seemed still more intense close to the surface of the sea than up on the deck of the *Sutherland*. Slowly the barge drew ahead, and as the longboat and launch diverged out on each quarter they were rapidly lost to sight. The oars seemed to touch the velvety blackness of the sea without a sound.

Hornblower made himself sit still, his hand resting on the hilt of his fifty-guinea sword. He wanted to crane his neck round and look at the other boats; with every minute's inaction he grew more nervous. Some fool of a marine might fiddle with the lock of his musket, or someone's pistol, carelessly left at full cock, might go off as its owner tugged at his oar. The slightest warning given on shore would ruin the whole attack; might mean the loss of hundreds of lives, and call down upon his head – if he survived – a withering rebuke from his admiral. Grimly he made himself sit still for five more minutes before taking up his nightglass.

Then at last he caught the faintest possible glimpse of grey cliff. With his hand on the tiller he altered course until they were almost in the mouth of the inlet.

'Easy!' he breathed, and the boat glided silently forward under the stars. Close astern two tiny nuclei of greater darkness indicated where the two cutters rested on their oars. Holding his watch under his nose he could just see the time – he must wait three full minutes.

A distant sound reached his ear; there were oars pulling in the harbour. He heard them splashing two hundred yards ahead; he fancied he could see the splashes. The French were, as he expected, rowing a guard round their precious ship. Yet her captain had not realised that a guard boat rowing with muffled oars, creeping very slowly along, would be a far more dangerous obstacle to a cutting-out expedition than any boat merely busily rowing up and down across the entrance. He looked at his watch again.

'Oars,' he whispered, and the men braced themselves ready to pull. 'There's the guard boat ahead. Remember, men, cold steel. If any man fires before I do I'll shoot him with my own hand. Give way!'

The barge crept forward again, stealing into the harbour. In a few more seconds she would be at the point where the batteries' fire crossed, the point which sentries would have under constant observation, upon which the guns would be laid at nightfall so that a salvo would blow any approaching boat out of the water. For a horrible second Hornblower wondered whether launch and longboat had gone astray. Then he heard it. A loud challenge on his right, heard clearly across the water, followed by another on his left, and both instantly drowned in a wild rattle of musketry fire. Rayner and Gerard were leading their parties against the batteries, and both of them as their orders had dictated, were making an infernal noise about it so as to distract the gunners at the vital moment.

His eye caught the splashes of the guard boat's oars, more noticeable than ever with the crew pulling wildly as they paid attention to the din on shore instead of to their own business. The barge shot silently and unnoticeable towards it. She was only fifty yards from the guard boat when someone at last caught sight of her.

'Qui va là!' cried someone, sharply, but before any answer could be expected the barge came crashing up against the guard boat's side, as Hornblower dragged the tiller round.

His quick order had got the oars in a second before the collision, while the impact of the barge swept the oars of the guard boat away, tumbling half her crew in a tangle into the bottom of the boat. Hornblower's sword was out, and at the instant of contact he leaped madly from the barge to the guard boat, choking with excitement and nervousness as he did so. He landed with both feet on someone in the stern, trod him down, and miraculously kept his own footing. There was a white face visible down by his knee, and he kicked at it, wildly, felt a jar up his leg as the kick went home, and at the same moment he cut with all his strength at another head before him. He felt the sword bite into bone; the boat rolled frightfully under him as more of the barge's crew came tumbling into the guard boat. Someone was heaving himself upright before him – someone with a black gash of a moustache across his face in the starlight, and therefore no Englishman. Hornblower lunged fiercely as he reeled in the rocking boat, and he and his opponent came down together upon the men under their feet. When he scrambled up the struggle was over, without a shot being fired. The guard boat's crew was dead, or overboard, or knocked unconscious. Hornblower felt his neck and his wrist wet and sticky – with blood, presumably, but he did not have time to think about that.

'Into the barge, men,' he said. 'Give way.'

The whole fight had hardly taken more than a few seconds. At the batteries the racket of the attack was still continuing, and even as the barge pushed away from the derelict guard boat there came a sudden splutter of musketry fire from higher up the bay. The two cutters had reached the anchored ship without impediment, rowing, as Hornblower's orders had dictated, past the two locked boats straight for her. With his hand on the tiller he set a course for the musket flashes. Apparently the cutters' crews had not succeeded in carrying the ship at the first rush, for the sparkle of the firing stayed steady along the ship's bulwark – she must have had her boarding nettings rigged and her crew fairly wide awake.

The child Longley at his side was leaping about in his seat with excitement.

'Sit still, boy,' growled Hornblower.

He put the tiller over and the barge swept under the ship's stern towards the disengaged side of the ship.

'Oars!' hissed Hornblower. 'Take hold, there, bowman. Now, all together, men, and give a cheer.'

It was a hard scramble up the side of the ship, and her boarding nettings were rigged, sure enough. Hornblower found foothold on the bulwark through the netting, swaying perilously, leaning far out over the water, for the nettings were rigged from the yardarms and sloped sharply outwards. He struggled in them like a fly in a web. Beside him he saw Longley, writhing similarly. The boy had his dirk between his teeth in the fashion he had heard about in sailors' yarns. He looked so foolish hanging in the netting with that great clumsy weapon in his mouth that Hornblower giggled insanely on his insecure foothold. He snatched his sword from its sheath, clutching with the other hand, and slashed at the tarry cordage. The whole net was heaving and tossing as the barge's crew wrenched at it; he was almost jerked from his hold.

But everyone around him was cheering madly. This surprise attack on the unguarded side must be shaking the nerve of the defenders trying to beat off the cutters' crews. The fifty-guinea sword was of the finest steel and had a razor edge; it was cutting through strand after strand of the netting. Suddenly something parted with a rush. For one horrible second Hornblower lost his footing and nearly fell outwards, but with a convulsive effort he recovered and swung himself forward, falling through the net on his hands and knees, the sword clattering on the deck before him. A Frenchman was rushing at him; his eye caught a glimpse of the steel head of a levelled pike. He snatched hold of the shaft, twisting on to his back, guiding the weapon clear. The Frenchman's knee crashed into the back of his head, and his neck was badly wrenched as the Frenchman tumbled over on top of him. He kicked himself clear, found his sword, miraculously, and stood to face the other dark shapes rushing at him.

A pistol banged off at his ear, half deafening him, and it seemed as if the whole mass of those attacking him melted away into nothing at the finish. Those others crossing the deck now were English; they were cheering.

'Mr Crystal!'

'Sir!'

'Cut the cable. Is Mr Hooker there?'

'Aye aye, sir.'

'Get aloft with your boat's crew and set sail.'

There was no time for self congratulation yet. Boats might come dashing out from the shore with reinforcements for the ship's crew; and Rayner and Gerard might be repulsed by the garrisons of the batteries so that he would have to run the gauntlet of the guns.

'Brown!'

'Sir!'

'Send up that rocket.'

'Aye aye, sir.'

The rocket which Brown had brought with him at Hornblower's orders was to be the signal to the landing parties that the ship was taken. And there was a decided breath of air coming off the land which would carry the ship out of the bay; Hornblower had counted on that – after the scorching heat of the day a land breeze was only to be expected.

'Cable's parted, sir!' hailed Crystal from forward.

Hooker had loosed the main topsail, and the ship was already gathering sternway.

'Hands to the braces, there, barge's crew, first cutter's crew. Benskin! Ledly! Take the wheel. Hard a-starboard.'

Brown's flint and steel were clicking and flashing as he crouched on the deck. The rocket rose in an upward torrent of sparks and burst high above into stars. As the fore stay sail was set the ship's head came round, and as she steadied on her course down the bay with the wind abaft the moon cleared the horizon right ahead – a gibbous, waning moon, giving just enough light for Hornblower to be able to con the ship easily out of the bay between the batteries. Hornblower could hear whistles blowing, piercing the sound of the musketry which was still popping round the batteries. Rayner and Gerard were calling off their men now.

Two splashes overside indicated that a couple of the ship's crew were swimming for the shore rather than face captivity. It had been a well-timed and successful operation.

XII

This Gulf of the Lion was not likely to be a very profitable cruising ground so Hornblower decided as he scanned the French coast through his telescope. It was so deeply embayed that any wind from north to west through south would find his ship with land under her lee; it was shallow, treacherous, and liable to be whipped by storms into a tremendous sea. Navigational risks were worth taking if a suitable prize offered, but, thought Hornblower looking at the coast, there was small chance of any prize. From Port Vendres as far round as Marseille – the limit of the Inshore Squadron's sector – the flat shore was bordered by vast dreary lagoons which were separated from the sea by long spits of sand and even by peninsulas of cultivated land. There were batteries here and there upon the sand spits, and regular forts to support them, and the little towns, Cette, Aigues-Mortes, and so on were encompassed by mediaeval fortifications which could defy any effort he could make against them.

But the main factor was that chain of lagoons, linked together since Roman times by a series of canals. Vessels up to two hundred tons could creep along inside the coast line – he could actually see through his glass, at this very moment, brown sails apparently sailing over the green vineyards. The entrances to the chain were all defended by solid works, and if he were to try to surprise one of these it would involve running all the risk of taking his ship in through the tortuous channels between the sandbanks, under gunfire. Even if he should succeed he could still hardly attack the shipping in the lagoons.

The blue Mediterranean under the glaring blue sky shaded to green and even to yellow as it shoaled here and there in patches, a constant reminder to Hornblower as he walked his deck of the treacherous water he was navigating. Forward the ship was a hive of industry. Bush, watch in hand, had fifty men whom he was drilling aloft – they had set and furled the fore top gallant sail a dozen times in the last hour and a half, which must be puzzling the numerous telescopes trained on the ship from the shore. Harrison the boatswain down on the maindeck was squatting on a stool with two of his mates and twenty landsmen crosslegged in a ring round him – he was teaching the advanced class some of the refinements of knotting and splicing. From the lower gun deck the squeal and rumble of gun trucks told how Gerard was exercising embryo gun layers at the six forward twenty-four pounders – Gerard's ambition was to have six trained gun captains at every gun, and he was a long way yet from achieving it. On the poop Crystal with his sextant was patiently trying to instruct the midshipmen in the elements of navigation – the young devils were fidgety and restless as Crystal droned on. Hornblower was sorry for them. He had delighted in mathematics since his boyhood; logarithms had been playthings to him at little Longley's age, and a problem in spherical trigonometry was to him but a source of pleasure, analogous, he realised, to the pleasure some of those lads found in the music which was so incomprehensible to him.

A monotonous hammering below indicated that the carpenter and his mates were putting the finishing touches to their repair of the big hole which had been made yesterday morning – incredible that it was hardly more than twenty-four hours ago – by the forty-two pounder at Llanza, while the clanking of the pumps showed that the petty criminals of the ship were pumping her out. The *Sutherland*, thanks to her recent docking, leaked extraordinarily little, less than an inch a day in calm weather, and Hornblower was able to deal with this small amount by an hour's pumping every morning, allotting to it the miscreants who had found themselves in Bush's or Harrison's black books by being last up the hatchway, or lashing up their hammocks by fore and aft turns, or by committing any of the numerous crimes of omission or commission which annoy boatswains and first lieutenants. A turn at pumping – the most monotonous and uninviting work in the ship – was a far more economical punishment than the cat, and Hornblower believed it to be more deterrent, rather to Bush's amusement.

Smoke was pouring from the galley chimney, and even on the quarterdeck Hornblower could smell the cooking that was going on. The men were going to have a good dinner today, with duff; yesterday they had eaten and drunk nothing save biscuit and cold water, thanks to the ship having been engaged three times in twenty-four hours. They did not mind that as long as they were successful – it was amazing how beneficial a little success was to discipline. Today, with eleven dead and sixteen wounded, with thirty-four men away in prizes – less two prisoners who had elected to serve the King of England rather than face one of his prisons – the *Sutherland* was more effective as a fighting unit than the day before yesterday with practically a full complement. Hornblower could see, from the quarterdeck, the cheerfulness and high spirits of everyone in sight.

He was cheerful and in high spirits himself. For once his self-depreciation was in abeyance. He had forgotten his fears of yesterday, and three successful actions in a day had re-established his self-confidence. He was at least a thousand pounds the richer by his captures, and that was good to think about. He had never before in his life had a thousand pounds. He remembered how Lady Barbara had tactfully looked away after a single glance at the pinchbeck buckles on his shoes. Next time he dined with Lady Barbara he would be wearing solid gold buckles, with diamonds set in them if he chose, and by some inconspicuous gesture he would call her attention to them. Maria would have bracelets and rings to flaunt his success before the eyes of the world.

Hornblower remembered with pride that he had not known a moment's fear last night in Port Vendres, not when he leaped on board the guard boat, not even when he had found himself in the nightmare embrace of the boarding netting. Just as he now had the wealth for which he had longed, so he had proved to himself to his own surprise that he possessed the brute physical courage which he had envied in his subordinates. Even though, characteristically, he attached no importance to the moral courage and organising ability and ingenuity he had displayed he was on the crest of a wave of optimism and self-confidence. With high spirits bubbling inside him he turned once more to scan the flat repulsive coast on his left hand, applying himself to the problem of how to stir up confusion there. Down below there were the captured French charts with which the Admiralty had supplied him – as they had the *Pluto* and *Caligula* as well, presumably. Hornblower spent the earliest hours of daylight in poring over them. He called up their details before his mind's eye as he looked across the shallows at the green bar of coast, and the brown sails beyond. He was as close in as he dared, and yet that sail was half a mile beyond cannon shot.

Over to the left was Cette, perched up on the top of a little hill prominent above the surrounding flat land. Hornblower was reminded of Rye overlooking Romney Marsh, but Cette was a gloomy little town of a prevailing black colour, unlike Rye's cheerful grey and reds. And Cette, he knew, was a walled town, with a garrison, against which he could attempt nothing. Behind Cette was the big lagoon called the Etang de Thau, which constituted a major link in the chain of inland waterways which offered shelter and protection to French shipping all the way from Marseille and the Rhone Valley to the foot of the Pyrenees. Cette was invulnerable as far as he was concerned, and vessels on the Etang de Thau were safe from him.

Of all the whole inland route he was opposite the most vulnerable part, this short section where the navigable channel from Aigues Mortes to the Etang de Thau was only divided from the sea by a narrow spit of land. If a blow were to be struck, it was here that he must strike it; moreover, at this very moment he could see something at which to strike – that brown sail no more than two miles away. That must be one of the French coasters, plying between Port Vendres and Marseille with wine and oil. It would be madness to attempt anything against her, and yet – and yet – he felt mad today.

'Pass the word for the captain's coxswain,' he said to the midshipman of the watch. He heard the cry echo down the main deck, and in two minutes Brown was scurrying towards him along the gangway, halting breathless for orders.

'Can you swim, Brown?'

'Swim, sir? Yes, sir.'

Hornblower looked at Brown's burly shoulders and thick neck.

There was a mat of black hair visible through the opening of his shirt.

'How many of the barge's crew can swim!'

Brown looked first one way and then the other before he made the confession which he knew would excite contempt. Yet he dared not lie, not to Hornblower.

'I dunno, sir.'

Hornblower refraining from the obvious rejoinder was more scathing than Hornblower saying 'You ought to know.'

'I want a crew for the barge,' said Hornblower. 'Everyone a good swimmer, and everyone a volunteer. It's for a dangerous service, and, mark you, Brown, they must be true volunteers – none of your pressgang ways.'

'Aye aye, sir,' said Brown, and after a moment's hesitation. 'Everyone'll volunteer, sir. It'll be hard to pick 'em. Are you going, sir?'

'Yes. A cutlass for every man. And a packet of combustibles for every man.'

'Com-combustibles, sir?'

'Yes. Flint and steel. A couple of port-fires, oily rags, and a bit of slowmatch, in a watertight packet for each man. Go to the sail-maker and get oilskin for them. And a lanyard each to carry it if we swim.'

'Aye aye, sir.'

'And give Mr Bush my compliments. Ask him to step this way, and then get your crew ready.'

Bush came rolling aft, his face alight with excitement; and before he had reached the quarterdeck the ship was abuzz with rumours – the wildest tales about what the captain had decided to do next were circulating among the crew, who had spent the morning with one eye on their duties and the other on the coast of France.

'Mr Bush,' said Hornblower. 'I am going ashore to burn that coaster over there.'

'Aye aye, sir. Are you going in person, sir?'

'Yes,' snapped Hornblower. He could not explain to Bush that he was constitutionally unable to send men away on a task for which volunteers were necessary and not go himself. He eyed Bush defiantly, and Bush eyed him back, opened his mouth to protest, thought better of it, and changed what he was going to say.

'Longboat and launch, sir?'

'No. They'd take the ground half a mile from the shore.'

That was obvious; four successive lines of foam showed where the feeble waves were breaking, far out from the water's edge.

'I'm taking my barge and a volunteer crew.'

Still Hornblower, by his expression, dared Bush to make any protest at all, but this time Bush actually ventured to make one.

'Yes, sir. Can't I go, sir?'

'No.'

There was no chance of further dispute in the face of that blank negative. Bush had the queer feeling – he had known it before – as he looked at Hornblower's haughty expression that he was a father dealing with a high-spirited son; he loved his captain as he would have loved a son if ever he had had one.

'And mark this, too, Bush. No rescue parties. If we're lost, we're lost. You understand? Shall I give you that in writing?'

'No need, sir. I understand.'

Bush said the words sadly. When it came to the supreme test of practice, Hornblower, however much he respected Bush's qualities and abilities, had no opinion whatever of his first lieutenant's capacity to make original plans. The thought of Bush blundering about on the mainland of France throwing away valuable lives in a hopeless attempt to rescue his captain frightened him.

'Right. Heave the ship to, Mr Bush. We'll be back in half an hour if all goes well. Stand off and wait for us.'

The barge pulled eight oars; as Hornblower gave the word he had high hopes that her launching had passed unobserved from the shore. Bush's morning sail drill must have accustomed the French to seemingly purposeless manoeuvres by the *Sutherland;* her brief backing of her topsails might be unnoticed. He sat at Brown's side while the men went to their oars. The boat danced quickly and lightly over the sea; he set a course so as to reach the shore a little ahead of the brown sail which was showing just over the green strip of coast. Then he looked back at the *Sutherland,* stately under her pyramids of sails, and dwindling with extraordinary rapidity as the barge shot away from her. Even at that moment Hornblower's busy mind set to work scanning her lines and the rake of her masts, debating how he could improve her sailing qualities.

They had passed the first line of breakers without taking ground – breakers they could hardly be called, so sluggish was the sea – and darted in towards the golden beach. A moment later the boat baulked as she slid over the sand, moved on a few yards, and grounded once more.

'Over with you, men,' said Hornblower.

He threw his legs over the side and dropped thigh deep into the water. The crew were as quick as he, and seizing the gunwales, they ran the lightened boat up until the water was no higher than their ankles. Hornblower's first instinct was to allow excitement to carry him away and head a wild rush inland, but he checked himself.

'Cutlasses?' he asked, sternly. 'Fire packets?'

Running his eye over his nine men he saw that every one was armed and equipped, and then he started his little expedition steadily up the beach. The distance was too great to expect them to run all the way and swim afterwards. The sandy beach was topped by a low shingle bank where samphire grew. They leaped over this and found themselves among green vines; not twenty yards away an old, bent man and two old women were hoeing along the rows. They looked up in blank surprise at this sudden apparition, standing and staring voiceless at the chattering group of seamen. A quarter of a mile away, across the level vineyard, was the brown spritsail. A small mizzen was visible now behind it. Hornblower picked out a narrow path leading roughly in that direction.

'Come along, men,' he said, and broke into a dog trot. The old man shouted something as the seamen tramped the vines; they laughed like children at hearing French spoken for the first time in their lives. To most of them this was their first sight of a vineyard, too – Hornblower could hear them chattering behind him in amazement at the orderly rows of seemingly worthless stumps, and the tiny bunches of immature grapes.

They crossed the vineyard; a sharp drop on the further side brought them on to a rough towpath along the canal. Here the lagoon was no more than two hundred yards wide, and the navigable channel was evidently close up to the towpath, for a sparse line of beacons a hundred yards out presumably marked the shallows. Two hundred yards away the coaster was creeping slowly towards them, still unconscious of her danger. The men uttered a wild cheer and began tearing off their jackets.

'Quiet, you fools,' growled Hornblower. He unbuckled his sword belt and stripped off his coat.

At the sound of the men's shouting the crew of the coaster came tumbling forward. There were three men, and a moment later they were joined by two sturdy women, looking at them from under their hands. It was one of the women, quicker witted, who guessed what the group of men stripping on the bank implied. Hornblower, tearing off his breeches, heard one of them give a shriek and saw her running aft again. The coaster still crept over the water towards them, but when it was nearly opposite the big spritsail came down with a run and she swung away from the towpath as her helm was put over. It was too late to save her, though. She passed through the line of beacons and grounded with a jerk in the shallows beyond. Hornblower saw the man at the wheel quit his charge and turn and stare at them, with the other men and the women grouped round him. He buckled his sword about his naked body. Brown was naked, too, and was fastening his belt round his waist, and against his bare skin lay a naked cutlass.

'Come along, then,' said Hornblower; the quicker the better. He put his hands together and dropped into the lagoon in an ungainly dive; the men followed him, shouting and splashing. The water was as warm as milk, but Hornblower swam as slowly and steadily as he could. He was a poor swimmer, and the coaster a hundred and fifty yards away seemed very distant. The sword dangling from his waist already seemed heavy. Brown came surging past him, swimming a lusty overarm stroke, with the lanyard of his packet of combustibles between his white teeth, and his thick black hair sleek with water. The other men followed; by the time they neared the coaster Hornblower was a long way last. They all scrambled up before him into the low waist of the vessel, but then discipline reasserted itself and they turned and stooped to haul him on board. He pressed aft, with sword drawn. Women and men were there in a sullen group, and for a moment he was puzzled to know what to do with them. French and English faced each other in the dazzling sunlight, the water streaming from the naked men, but in the tenseness of that meeting no one thought of their nakedness. Hornblower remembered with relief the dinghy towing behind; he pointed to it and tried to remember his French.

'Au bateau,' he said. 'Dans le bateau.'

The French hesitated. There were four middle-aged men and one old one; one old woman and one middle-aged. The English seamen closed up behind their captain, drawing their cutlasses from their belts.

'Entrez dans le bateau,' said Hornblower. 'Hobson, pull that dinghy up alongside.'

The middle-aged woman broke into a storm of invective, screeching, high pitched, her hands gesticulating wildly and her wooden shoes clattering on the deck.

'I'll do it, sir,' interposed Brown. ''Ere, you, 'op in there.'

He took one of the men by the collar, flourished his cutlass and dragged him across the deck to the side. The man yielded, and lowered himself over the side, and once the example was set, the others followed it. Brown cast off the painter and the crowded dinghy drifted away, the woman still shrieking curses in her Catalan French.

'Set the ship on fire,' said Hornblower. 'Brown, take three men below and see what you can do there.'

The late crew had got out a couple of oars and were paddling cautiously over to the towpath, the dinghy laden down to within an inch of the water's edge. Hornblower watched them as they crawled across, and climbed the bank to the path.

His picked crew did their work quickly and neatly. A mighty crashing from below showed that Brown's party was bursting into the cargo to make a nest for a fire. Smoke emerged almost at once from the cabin skylight; one of the men had piled the furniture there together, soused it in oil from the lamps, and got the whole thing into a blaze at once.

'Cargo is oil in barr'ls and grain in sacks, sir,' reported Brown. 'We stove in some barr'ls an' ripped some sacks open, sir. That'll burn. Look, sir.'

From the main hatchway a thin ghost of black smoke was already rising, and the heat pouring up from the hatch made all the forward part of the ship appear to dance and shimmer in the sunshine. There was a fire in the dry timberwork of the deck just forward of the hatch, too. It was crackling and banging explosively, although this fire was hardly visible thanks to the strong sunlight and the absence of smoke, and there was fire in the forecastle – smoke was billowing out of the bulkhead door and rolling towards them in a sullen wave.

'Get some of the deck planks up,' said Hornblower hoarsely.

The splintering crash of the work was followed by a contrasting silence – and yet no silence, for Hornblower's ear caught a muffled, continuous roaring. It was the noise of the flames devouring the cargo, as the increased draught caused by the piercing of the decks set the flames racing through the inflammable stuff.

'God! There's a sight!' exclaimed Brown.

The whole waist of the ship seemed to open as the fire poured up through the deck. The heat was suddenly unbearable.

'We can go back now,' said Hornblower. 'Come along, men.'

He set the example by diving once more into the lagoon, and the little naked band began to swim softly back to the towpath. Slowly, this time; the high spirits of the attack had evaporated. The awful sight of the red fire glowing under the deck had sobered every man. They swam slowly, clustered round their captain, while he set a pace limited by his fatigue and unscientific breaststroke. He was glad when he was able at last to stretch out a hand and grasp the weeds growing on the towpath bank. The others scrambled out before him; Brown offered him a wet hand and helped him up to the top.

'Holy Mary!' said one of the men. 'Will ye look at th' old bitch?'

They were thirty yards from where they had left their clothes, and at that spot the coaster's crew had landed. At the moment when the Irishman called their attention to them the old woman who had reviled them cast one last garment into the lagoon. There was nothing left lying on the bank. One or two derelict shirts still floated in the lagoon, buoyed up by the air they contained, but practically all their clothes were at the bottom.

'What did you do that for, damn you?' raved Brown – all the seamen had rushed up to the coaster's crew and were dancing and gesticulating naked round them. The old woman pointed across at the coaster. It was ablaze from end to end, with heavy black smoke pouring from her sides. They saw the rigging of the mainmast whisk away in smouldering fragments, and the mast suddenly sag to one side, barely-visible flames licking along it.

'I'll get your shirt back for you, sir,' said one of the men to Hornblower, tearing himself free from the fascination of the sight.

'No. Come along,' snapped Hornblower.

'Would you like the old man's trousers, sir?' asked Brown. 'I'll take 'em off him and be damned to him, sir. 'Tisn't fit—'

'No!' said Hornblower again.

Naked, they climbed up to the vineyard. One last glance down showed that the two women were weeping, heartbroken, now. Hornblower saw one of the men patting one of the women on the shoulder; the others watched with despairing apathy the burning of their ship – their all. Hornblower led the way over the vines. A horseman was galloping towards them; his blue uniform and cocked hat showed that he was one of Bonaparte's gendarmes. He reined up in front of them, reaching for his sabre, but at the same time, not too sure of himself, he looked to right and to left for the help which was not in sight.

'Ah, would you!' said Brown, dashing to the front waving his cutlass.

The other seamen closed up beside him, their weapons ready, and the gendarme hastily wheeled his horse out of harm's way; a gleam of white teeth showed under his black moustache. They hurried past him; he had dismounted when Hornblower looked back, and was trying, as well as his restless horse would allow, to take his carbine out of the boot beside his saddle. At the top of the beach stood the old man and the two women who had been hoeing; the old man brandished his hoe and threatened them, but the two women stood smiling shamefaced, looking up under lowered eyelids at their nakedness. There lay the barge, just in the water, and far out there was the *Sutherland* – the men cheered at the sight of her.

Lustily they ran the boat out over the sand, paused while Hornblower climbed in, pushed her out farther, and then came tumbling in over the side and took the oars. One man yelped with pain as a splinter in a thwart pricked his bare posterior; Hornblower grinned automatically, but the man was instantly reduced to silence by a shocked Brown.

' 'Ere 'e comes, sir,' said stroke oar, pointing aft over Hornblower's shoulder.

The gendarme was leaping clumsily down the beach in his long boots, his carbine in his hand. Hornblower, craning round, saw him kneel and take aim; for a second Hornblower wondered, sickly, whether his career was going to be ended by the bullet of a French gendarme, but the puff of smoke from the carbine brought not even the sound of the bullet – a man who had ridden far, and run fast in heavy boots, could hardly be expected to hit a ship's boat at two hundred yards with a single shot.

Over the spit of land between sea and lagoon they could see a vast cloud of smoke. The coaster was destroyed beyond any chance of repair. It had been a wicked waste to destroy a fine ship like that, but war and waste were synonymous terms. It meant misery and poverty for the owners; but at the same time it would mean that the length of England's arm had been demonstrated now to the people of this enemy land whom the war had not affected during these eighteen years save through Bonaparte's conscription. More than that; it meant that the authorities responsible for coast defence would be alarmed about this section of the route from Marseille to Spain, the very section which they had thought safest. That would mean detaching troops and guns to defend it against future raids, stretching the available forces thinner still along the two hundred miles of coast. A thin screen of that sort could easily be pierced at a selected spot by a heavy blow struck without warning – the sort of blow a squadron of ships of the line, appearing and disappearing at will over the horizon, could easily strike. If the game were played properly, the whole coast from Barcelona to Marseille could be kept in a constant state of alarm. That was the way to wear down the strength of the Corsican colossus; and a ship favoured by the weather could travel ten, fifteen times as fast as troops could march, as fast even as a well-mounted messenger could carry a warning. He had struck at the French centre, he had struck at the French left wing. Now he must hasten and strike at the French right wing on his way back to the rendezvous. He uncrossed and recrossed his knees as he sat in the sternsheets of the barge, his desire for instant action filling him with restlessness while the boat drew closer to the *Sutherland*.

He heard Gerard's voice saying 'What the devil—?' come clearly over the water to him; apparently Gerard had just detected the nakedness of everyone in the approaching boat. The pipes twittered to call the watch's attention to the arrival of the ship's captain. He would have to come in naked through the entry port, receiving the salutes of the officers and marines, but keyed up as he was he gave no thought to his dignity. He ran up to the deck with his sword hanging from his naked waist – it was an ordeal which could not be avoided, and he had learned in twenty years in the Navy to accept the inevitable without lamentation. The faces of the side boys and of the marines were wooden in their effort not to smile, but Hornblower did not care. The black pall of smoke over the land marked an achievement any man might be proud of. He stayed naked on the deck until he had given Bush the order to put the ship about which would take the *Sutherland* southward again in search of fresh adventure. The wind would just serve for a south-westerly course, and he was not going to waste a minute of a favourable wind.

XIII

The *Sutherland* had seen nothing of the *Caligula* during her long sweep south-westward. Hornblower had not wanted to, and, more, had been anxious not to. For it was just possible that the *Pluto* had reached the rendezvous, and in that case the admiral's orders would override Captain Bolton's, and he would be deprived of this further opportunity before his time limit had elapsed. It was during the hours of darkness that the *Sutherland* had crossed the latitude of Cape Bugar – the Palamos Point of the rendezvous – and morning found the *Sutherland* far to the south-westward, with the mountains of Catalonia a blue streak on the horizon over the starboard bow.

Hornblower had been on deck since dawn, a full hour before the land was sighted; at his orders the ship wore round and stood close-hauled to the north-eastward again, edging in to the shore as she did so until the details of the hilly country were plainly visible. Bush was on deck, standing with a group of other officers; Hornblower, pacing up and down, was conscious of the glances they were darting at him, but he did his best not to notice them, as he kept his telescope steadily directed at the land. He knew that Bush and all the others thought he had come hither with a set purpose in mind, and that they were awaiting the orders which would plunge the ship again into the same kind of adventures which had punctuated the last two days. They credited him with diabolical foresight and ingenuity; he was not going to admit to them how great a part good fortune had played, nor was he going to admit that he had brought the *Sutherland* down here, close in to Barcelona, merely on general principles and in the hope that something might turn up.

It was stifling hot already; the blue sky glared with a brassy tint to the eastward, and the easterly breeze seemed not to have been cooled at all by its passage across four hundred miles of the Mediterranean from Italy. It was like breathing the air of a brick kiln; Hornblower found himself running with sweat within a quarter of an hour of cooling himself off under the washdeck pump. The land slipping by along their larboard beam seemed to be devoid of all life. There were lofty grey-green hills, many of them capped with a flat table-top of stone with precipitous rocky slopes; there were grey cliffs and brown cliffs, and occasional dazzling beaches of golden sand. Between the sea and those hills ran the most important high road in Catalonia, that connecting Barcelona with France. Surely, thought Hornblower, something ought to show up somewhere along here. He knew there was a bad mountain road running parallel ten miles inland, but the French would hardly use it of their own free will. One of the reasons why he had come here was to force them to abandon the high road in favour of the bye road where the Spanish partisans would have a better chance of cutting up their convoys; he might achieve that merely by flaunting the British flag here within gunshot of the beach, but he would rather bring it about by administering a sharp lesson. He did not want this blow of his against the French right flank to be merely a blow in the air.

The hands were skylarking and laughing as they washed the decks; it was comforting to see their high spirits, and peculiarly comforting to allow oneself to think that those high spirits were due to the recent successes. Hornblower felt a glow of achievement as he looked forward, and then, as was typical of him, began to feel doubts as to whether he could continue to keep his men in such good order. A long, dreary cruise on blockade service might soon wear down their spirits. Then he spurned away his doubts with determined optimism. Everything had gone so well at present; it would continue to go well. This very day, even though the chances were a hundred to one against, something was certain to happen. He told himself defiantly that the vein of good fortune was not yet exhausted. A hundred to one against or a thousand to one, something was going to happen again today, some further chance of distinction.

On the shore over there was a little cluster of white cottages above a golden beach. And drawn up on the beach were a few boats – Spanish fishing boats, presumably. There would be no sense in risking a landing party, for there was always the chance that the village would have a French garrison. Those fishing boats would be used to supply fish to the French army, too, but he could do nothing against them, despite that. The poor devils of fishermen had to live; if he were to capture or burn those boats he would set the people against the alliance with England – and it was only in the Peninsula, out of the whole world, that England had any allies.

There were black dots running on the beach now. One of the fishing boats was being run out into the sea. Perhaps this was the beginning of today's adventure; he felt hope, even certainty, springing up with him. He put his glass under his arm and turned away, walking the deck apparently deep in thought, his head bent and his hands clasped behind him.

'Boat putting off from the shore, sir,' said Bush, touching his hat.

'Yes,' said Hornblower carelessly.

He was endeavouring to show no excitement at all. He hoped that his officers believed that he had not yet seen the boat and was so strong-minded as not to step out of his way to look at her.

'She's pulling for us, sir,' added Bush.

'Yes,' said Hornblower, still apparently unconcerned. It would be at least ten minutes before the boat could near the ship – and the boat must be intending to approach the *Sutherland*, or else why should she put off so hurriedly as soon as the *Sutherland* came in sight? The other officers could train their glasses on the boat, could chatter in loud speculation as to why she was approaching. Captain Hornblower could walk his deck in lofty indifference, awaiting the inevitable hail. No one save himself knew that his heart was beating faster. Now the hail came, high pitched, across the glittering water.

'Heave to, Mr Bush,' said Hornblower, and stepped with elaborate calm to the other side to hail back.

It was Catalan which was being shouted to him; his wide and exact knowledge of Spanish – during his two years as a prisoner on parole when a young man he had learned the language thoroughly to keep himself from fretting into insanity – and his rough and ready French enabled him to understand what was being spoken, but he could not speak Catalan. He hailed back in Spanish.

'Yes,' he said. 'This is a British ship.'

At the sound of his voice someone else stood up in the boat. The men at the oars were Catalans in ragged civilian dress; this man wore a brilliant yellow uniform and a lofty hat with a plume.

'May I be permitted to come on board?' he shouted in Spanish. 'I have important news.'

'You will be very welcome,' said Hornblower, and then, turning to Bush. 'A Spanish officer is coming on board, Mr Bush. See that he is received with honours.'

The man who stepped on to the deck and looked curiously about him, as the marines saluted and the pipes twittered, was obviously a hussar. He wore a yellow tunic elaborately frogged in black, and yellow breeches with broad stripes of gold braid. Up to his knees he wore shiny riding boots with dangling gold tassels in front and jingling spurs on the heels; a silver grey coat trimmed with black astrakhan, its sleeves empty, was slung across his shoulders. On his head was a hussar busby, of black astrakhan with a silver grey bag hanging out of the top behind an ostrich plume, and gold cords from the back of it round his neck, and he trailed a broad curved sabre along the deck as he advanced to where Hornblower awaited him.

'Good day, sir,' he said, smiling. 'I am Colonel José Gonzales de Villena y Danvila, of His Most Catholic Majesty's Olivenza Hussars.'

'I am delighted to meet you,' said Hornblower. 'And I am Captain Horatio Hornblower, of His Britannic Majesty's ship *Sutherland*.'

'How fluently your Excellency speaks Spanish!'

'Your Excellency is too kind. I am fortunate in my ability to speak Spanish, since it enables me to make you welcome on board my ship.'

'Thank you. It was only with difficulty that I was able to reach you. I had to exert all my authority to make those fishermen row me out. They were afraid lest the French should discover that they had been communicating with an English ship. Look! They are rowing home already for dear life.'

'There is no French garrison in that village at present, then?'

'No, sir, none.'

A peculiar expression played over Villena's face as he said this. He was a youngish man of fair complexion, though much sunburned, with a Hapsburg lip (which seemed to indicate that he might owe his high position in the Spanish army to some indiscretion on the part of his female ancestors) and hazel eyes with drooping lids. Those eyes met Hornblower's with a hint of shiftiness. They merely seemed to be pleading with him not to continue his questioning, but Hornblower ignored the appeal – he was far too anxious for data.

'There are Spanish troops there?' he asked.

'No, sir.'

'But your regiment, Colonel?'

'It is not there, Captain,' said Villena, and continued hastily. 'The news I have to give you is that a French army – Italian, I should say – is marching along the coast road there, three leagues to the north of us.'

'Ha!' said Hornblower. That was the news he wanted.

'They were at Malgret last night, on their way to Barcelona. Ten thousand of them – Pino's and Lecchi's divisions of the Italian army.'

'How do you know this?'

'It is my duty to know it, as an officer of light cavalry,' said Villena with dignity.

Hornblower looked at Villena and pondered. For three years now, he knew, Bonaparte's armies had been marching up and down the length and breadth of Catalonia. They had beaten the Spaniards in innumerable battles, had captured their fortresses after desperate sieges, and yet were no nearer subjecting the country than when they had first treacherously invaded the province. The Catalans had not been able to overcome in the field even the motley hordes Bonaparte had used on this side of Spain – Italians, Germans, Swiss, Poles, all the sweepings of his army – but at the same time they had fought on nobly, raising fresh forces in every unoccupied scrap of territory, and wearing out their opponents by the incessant marches and counter-marches they imposed on them. Yet that did not explain how a Spanish colonel of hussars found himself quite alone near the heart of the Barcelona district where the French were supposed to be in full control.

'How did you come to be there?' he demanded, sharply.

'In accordance with my duty, sir,' said Villena, with lofty dignity.

'I regret very much that I still do not understand, Don José. Where is your regiment?'

'Captain—'

'Where is it?'

'I do not know, sir.'

All the jauntiness was gone from the young hussar now. He looked at Hornblower with big pleading eyes as he was made to confess his shame.

'Where did you see it last?'

'At Tordera. We – we fought Pino there.'

'And you were beaten?'

'Yes. Yesterday. They were on the march back from Gerona and we came down from the mountains to cut them off. Their cuirassiers broke us, and we were scattered. My – my horse died at Arens de Mar there.'

The pitiful words enabled Hornblower to understand the whole story in a wave of intuition. Hornblower could visualise it all – the undisciplined hordes drawn up on some hillside, the mad charges which dashed them into fragments, and the helter-skelter flight. In every village for miles round there would be lurking fugitives today. Everyone had fled in panic. Villena had ridden his horse until it dropped, and being the best mounted, had come farther than anyone else – if his horse had not died he might have been riding now. The concentration of the French forces to put ten thousand men in the field had led to their evacuation of the smaller villages, so that Villena had been able to avoid capture, even though he was between the French field army and its base at Barcelona.

Now that he knew what had happened there was no advantage to be gained from dwelling on Villena's misfortunes; indeed it was better to hearten him up, as he would be more useful that way.

'Defeat,' said Hornblower, 'is a misfortune which every fighting man encounters sooner or later. Let us hope we shall gain our revenge for yesterday today.'

'There is more than yesterday to be revenged,' said Villena.

He put his hand in the breast of his tunic and brought out a folded wad of paper; unfolded it was a printed poster, which he handed over to Hornblower who glanced at it and took in as much of the sense as a brief perusal of the Catalan in which it was printed permitted. It began, 'We, Luciano Gaetano Pino, Knight of the Legion of Honour, Knight of the Order of the Iron Crown of Lombardy, General of Division, commanding the forces of His Imperial and Royal Majesty Napoleon, Emperor of the French and King of Italy in the district of Gerona hereby decree—' There were numbered paragraphs after that, dealing with all the offences anyone could imagine against His Imperial and Royal Majesty. And each paragraph ended – Hornblower ran his eye down them – 'will be shot'; 'penalty of death'; 'will be hanged'; 'will be burned' – it was a momentary relief to discover that this last referred to villages sheltering rebels.

'They have burned every village in the uplands,' said Villena. 'The road from Figueras to Gerona – ten leagues long, sir – is lined with gallows, and upon every gallows is a corpse.'

'Horrible!' said Hornblower, but he did not encourage the conversation. He fancied that if any Spaniard began to talk about the woes of Spain he would never stop. 'And this Pino is marching back along the coast road, you say?'

'Yes.'

'Is there deep water close into the shore at any spot?'

The Spaniard raised his eyebrows in protest at that question, and Hornblower realised that it was hardly fair to ask a colonel of hussars about soundings.

'Are there batteries protecting the road from the sea?' he asked, instead.

'Oh yes,' said Villena. 'Yes, I have heard so.'

'Where?'

'I do not know exactly, sir.'

Hornblower realised that Villena was probably incapable of giving exact topographical information about anywhere, which was what he would expect of a Spanish colonel of light cavalry.

'Well, we shall go and see,' he said.

XIV

Hornblower had shaken himself free from the company of Colonel Villena, who showed, now that he had told of his defeat, a hysterical loquacity and a pathetic unwillingness to allow him out of his sight. He had established him in a chair by the taffrail out of the way, and escaped below to the security of his cabin, to pore once more over the charts. There were batteries marked there – most of them apparently dated from the time, not so long ago, when Spain had been at war with England, and they had been erected to protect coasting vessels which crept along the shore from battery to battery. In consequence they were established at points where there was not merely deep water close in, but also a bit of shelter given by projecting points of land in which the fugitives could anchor. There had never been any thought in men's minds then that marching columns might in the future be attacked from the sea, and exposed sections of the coast – like this twenty miles between Malgret and Arens de Mar – which offered no anchorage might surely be neglected. Since Cochrane was here a year ago in the *Impérieuse* no British ship had been spared to harass the French in this quarter.

The French since then had had too many troubles on their hands to have time to think of mere possibilities. The chances were that they had neglected to take precautions – and in any case they could not have enough heavy guns and trained gunners to guard the whole coast. The *Sutherland* was seeking a spot a mile and a half at least from any battery, where the water was deep enough close in for her to sweep the road with her guns. She had already hauled out of range of one battery, and that was marked on his chart and, moreover, was the only one marked along the stretch. It was most unlikely that the French had constructed others since the chart was last brought up to date. If Pino's column had left Malgret at dawn the *Sutherland* must be nearly level with it now. Hornblower marked the spot which his instinct told him would be the most suitable, and ran up on deck to give the orders which would head the *Sutherland* in towards it.

Villena climbed hastily out of his chair at sight of him, and clinked loudly across the deck towards him, but Hornblower contrived to ignore him politely by acting as if his whole attention was taken up by giving instructions to Bush.

'I'll have the guns loaded and run out, too, if you please, Mr Bush,' he concluded.

'Aye aye, sir,' said Bush.

Bush looked at him pleadingly. This last order, with its hint of immediate action, set the pinnacle on his curiosity. All he knew was that a Dago colonel had come on board. What they were here for, what Hornblower had in mind, he had no means of guessing. Hornblower always kept his projected plans to himself, because then if he should fail his subordinates would not be able to guess the extent of the failure. But Bush felt sometimes that his life was being shortened by his captain's reticence. He was pleasantly surprised this time when Hornblower condescended to make explanations, and he was never to know that Hornblower's unusual loquaciousness was the result of a desire to be saved from having to make polite conversation with Villena.

'There's a French column expected along the road over there,' he said. 'I want to see if we can get in a few shots at them.'

'Aye aye, sir.'

'Put a good man in the chains with the lead.'

'Aye aye, sir.'

Now that Hornblower actually wanted to be conversational he found it impossible – for nearly three years he had checked every impulse to say an unnecessary word to his second in command; and Bush's stolid 'Aye aye, sirs', were not much help. Hornblower took refuge from Villena by gluing his eye to his telescope and scanning the nearing shore with the utmost diligence. Here there were bold grey-green hills running almost to the water's edge, and looping along the foot of them, now ten feet up, and now a hundred feet, ran the road.

As Hornblower looked at it his glass revealed a dark tiny speck on the road far ahead. He looked away, rested his eye, and looked again. It was a horseman, riding towards them. A moment later he saw a moving smudge behind, which fixed his attention by an occasional sparkle and flash from the midst of it. That was a body of horsemen; presumably the advanced guard of Pino's army. It would not be long before the *Sutherland* was up opposite to them. Hornblower gauged the distance of the ship from the road. Half a mile, or a little more – easy cannon shot, though not as easy as he would like.

'By the deep nine!' chanted the man at the lead. He could edge in a good deal closer at this point if, when he turned the ship about and followed Pino along the shore, they came as far as here. It was worth remembering. As the *Sutherland* proceeded to meet the advancing army, Hornblower's brain was busy noting landmarks on the shore and the corresponding soundings opposite them. The leading squadron of cavalry could be seen distinctly now – men riding cautiously, their sabres drawn, looking searchingly on all sides as they rode; in a war where every rock and hedge might conceal a musketeer determined on killing one enemy at least their caution was understandable.

Some distance behind the leading squadron Hornblower could make out a longer column of cavalry, and beyond that again a long, long line of white dots, which puzzled him for a moment with its odd resemblance to the legs of a caterpillar all moving together. Then he smiled. They were the white breeches of a column of infantry marching in unison; by some trick of optics their blue coats as yet showed up not at all against their grey background.

'And a half ten!' called the leadsman.

He could take the *Sutherland* much closer in here when he wanted to. But at present it was better to stay out at half gunshot. His ship would not appear nearly as menacing to the enemy at that distance. Hornblower's mind was hard at work analysing the reactions of the enemy to the appearance of the *Sutherland* – friendly hat-waving by the cavalry of the advanced guard, now opposite him, gave him valuable additional data. Pino and his men had never yet been cannonaded from the sea, and had had no experience so far of the destructive effect of a ship's heavy broadside against a suitable target. The graceful two-decker, with her pyramids of white sails, would be something outside their experience. Put an army in the field against them, and they could estimate its potentialities, but they had never encountered ships before. His reading told him that Bonaparte's generals tended to be careless of the lives of their men; and any steps taken to avoid the *Sutherland's* fire would involve grave inconvenience – marching back to Malgret to take the inland road, or crossing the pathless hills to it direct. Hornblower guessed that Pino, somewhere back in that long column and studying the *Sutherland* through his glass, would make up his mind to chance the *Sutherland's* fire and would march on hoping to get through without serious loss. Pino would be disappointed, thought Hornblower.

The cavalry at the head of the main column were opposite them. The second regiment twinkled and sparkled in the flaming sunlight like a river of fire.

'Those are the cuirassiers!' said Villena, gesticulating wildly at Hornblower's elbow. 'Why do you not fire, Captain?'

Hornblower realised that Villena had probably been gabbling Spanish to him for the last quarter of an hour, and he had not heard a word he had said. He was not going to waste his surprise attack on cavalry who could gallop away out of range. This opening broadside must be reserved for slow-moving infantry.

'Send the men to the guns, Mr Bush,' he said, forgetting all about Villena again in a flash, and to the man at the wheel 'Starboard a point.'

'And a half nine,' called the leadsman.

The *Sutherland* headed closer into shore.

'Mr Gerard!' hailed Hornblower. 'Train the guns on the road, and only fire when I give you the signal.'

A horse artillery battery had followed the cavalry – popgun six-pounders whose jolting and lurching showed well how bad was the surface of the road, one of the great highways of Spain. Then men perched on the limbers waved their hands in friendly fashion to the beautiful ship close in upon them.

'By the mark six!' from the leadsman.

He dared not stand closer in.

'Port a point. Steady!'

The ship crept on through the water; not a sound from the crew, standing tense at their guns – only the faint sweet music of the breeze in the rigging, and the lapping of the water overside. Now they were level with the infantry column, a long dense mass of blue-coated and white-breeched soldiers, stepping out manfully, a little unreal in the haze of dust. Above the blue coats could be seen the white lines of their faces – every face was turned towards the pretty white-sailed ship creeping over the blue-enamel water. It was a welcome diversion in a weary march, during a war when every day demanded its march. Gerard was giving no orders for change of elevation at the moment – here the road ran level for half a mile, fifty feet above the sea. Hornblower put his silver whistle to his lips. Gerard had seen the gesture. Before Hornblower could blow, the centre maindeck gun had exploded, and a moment later the whole broadside followed with a hideous crash. The *Sutherland* heeled to the recoil, and the white, bitter-tasting smoke came billowing up.

'God, look at that!' exclaimed Bush.

The forty-one balls from the *Sutherland's* broadside and carronades had swept the road from side to side. Fifty yards of the column had been cut to fragments. Whole files had been swept away; the survivors stood dazed and stupid. The guntrucks roared as the guns were run out again, and the *Sutherland* lurched once more at the second broadside. There was another gap in the column now, just behind the first.

'Give it 'em again, boys!' yelled Gerard.

The whole column was standing stock still and silly to receive the third broadside; the smoke from the firing had drifted to the shore now, and was scattering over the rocks in thin wreaths.

'Quarter less nine!' called the leadsman.

In the deepening water Hornblower could close nearer in. The next section of the column, seeing the terrible ship moving down upon them implacably, about to blast them into death, was seized with panic and bolted wildly down the road.

'Grape, Mr Gerard!' shouted Hornblower. 'Starboard a point!'

Farther down the road the column had not fled. Those who stood firm and those who ran jammed the road with a struggling mass of men, and the *Sutherland*, under the orders of her captain, closed in upon them pitilessly, like a machine, steadied again, brought her guns to bear upon the crowd, and then swept the road clear with her tempest of grapeshot as though with a broom.

'God blast me!' raved Bush. 'That'll show 'em.'

Villena was snapping his fingers and dancing about the deck like a clown, dolman flying, plume nodding, spurs jangling.

'By the deep seven!' chanted the leadsman. But Hornblower's eye had caught sight of the little point jutting out from the shore close ahead, and its hint of jagged rock at its foot.

'Stand by to go about!' he rasped.

His mind was working at a feverish pace – there was water enough here, but that point indicated a reef – a ridge of harder rock which had not been ground away like the rest of the shore, and remained as a trap below the surface on which the *Sutherland* might run without warning between two casts of the lead. The *Sutherland* came up to the wind, and stood out from the shore. Looking aft, they could see the stretch of road which she had swept with her fire. There were dead and wounded in heaps along it. One or two men stood among the wreck; a few were bending over the wounded, but most of the survivors were on the hillside above the road, scattered on the steep slopes, their white breeches silhouetted against the grey background.

Hornblower scanned the shore. Beyond the little point there would be deep water close in again, as there had been on the other side of it.

'We will wear ship again, Mr Bush,' he said.

At the sight of the *Sutherland* heading for them the infantry on the road scattered wildly upon the hillside, but the battery of artillery beyond had no such means of escape open to it. Hornblower saw drivers and gunners sitting helplessly for an instant; then saw the officer in command, his plume tossing, gallop along the line, calling the men to action with urgent gesticulations. The drivers wheeled their horses on the road, swinging their guns across it, the gunners leaning down from the limbers, unhooking the gun trails, and bending over their guns as they worked frantically to bring them into action. Could a battery of nine-pounder field pieces effect anything against the *Sutherland*'s broadside?

'Reserve your fire for the battery, Mr Gerard,' shouted Hornblower.

Gerard waved his hat in acknowledgment. The *Sutherland* swung slowly and ponderously round. One gun went off prematurely –

Hornblower was glad to see Gerard noting the fact so as to punish the gun's crew later – and then the whole broadside was delivered with a crash, at the moment when the Italian artillerymen were still at work with the rammers loading the guns. The rush of smoke obscured the view from the quarterdeck; it did not clear until already one or two well-served guns were rumbling up into firing position again. By that time the wind had rolled it away in a solid bank, and they could see the hard hit battery. One gun had had a wheel smashed, and was leaning drunkenly over to one side; another, apparently hit full on the muzzle, had been flung back from its carriage and was pointing up to the sky. There were dead men lying around the guns, and the living were standing dazed by the torrent of shot which had delayed them. The mounted officer had just flung himself from his saddle and let his horse go free while he ran to the nearest gun. Hornblower could see him calling the men about him, determined on firing one shot at least in defiance of the thundering tormentor.

'Give 'em another, men!' shouted Gerard, and the *Sutherland* heeled once more to the broadside.

By the time the smoke cleared away the *Sutherland* had passed on, leaving the battery behind. Hornblower could see it wrecked and ruined, another of its guns dismounted, and not a soul visible on his feet near the guns. Now the *Sutherland* was opposite more infantry – the second division of the column, presumably – which shredded away in a panic up the hillside section by section as the *Sutherland* neared them. Hornblower saw them scattering. He knew that it was as damaging to an army to be scattered and broken up like this as for it to be decimated by fire; he would as soon not kill the poor devils, except that his own men would be more delighted at casualties among the enemy than at a mere demoralisation whose importance they could not appreciate.

There was a group of horsemen on the hillside above the road. Through his telescope he could see that they were all splendidly mounted, and dressed in a variety of uniforms flashing with gold and diversified with plumes. Hornblower guessed them to be the staff of the army; they would serve well as a target in the absence of larger bodies of formed troops. He attracted Gerard's notice and pointed. Gerard waved back. His two midshipmen-messengers went running below to point out the new target to the officers on the lower gun deck; Gerard himself bent over the nearest gun and squinted along it, while the gun captains set the tangent sights in accordance with the orders he bellowed through his speaking trumpet. Gerard stood aside and jerked the lanyard, and the whole broadside followed the shot he fired.

The blast of shot reached the group of horsemen. Men and horses went down together; there was hardly a rider left in his saddle. So universal was the destruction that Hornblower guessed that close under the surface soil must be rock, flying chips of which had scattered like grapeshot. He wondered if Pino were among those hit, and found himself to his surprise hoping that Pino had had both legs shot off. He told himself that until that morning he had not even heard Pino's name, and he felt a momentary scorn for himself, for feeling a blind animosity towards a man merely because he was his opponent.

Some officer a little farther down the road had kept his men together, drawn up stubbornly in a mass along the road, refusing to allow them to scatter. It was small advantage that this stern discipline brought his men. Hornblower brought his ship steadily round until the guns bore, and then tore the steady regiment to fragments with a fresh broadside. As the smoke eddied around him a sharp rap on the rail at his side made him look down. There was a musket ball stuck there – someone had fired at long range, two hundred yards or more, and succeeded in hitting the ship. The ball must have been nearly spent when it arrived, for it was embedded to half its depth and had retained its shape. It was just too hot to touch; he picked it out with his handkerchief over his fingers, and juggled with it idly, as he had done, he told himself, with hot chestnuts when he was a boy.

The clearing smoke revealed the new destruction he had wrought, the slaughtered files and heaped up dead; he fancied that he could hear even the screaming of the wounded. He was glad that the troops were scattering up the hillside and presented no target, for he was sick of slaughter although Bush was still blaspheming with excitement and Villena still capering at his side. Surely he must reach the rear of the column soon – from advanced guard to rearguard the army could not occupy more than eight or nine miles of road. As the thought came into his head he saw the road here was full of stationary waggons – the baggage train of the army. Those squat vehicles with four horses apiece must be ammunition caissons; beyond was a string of country carts, each with its half-dozen patient oxen, duncoloured, with sheepskins hanging over their foreheads. Filling the rest of the road beside the carts were packmules, hundreds of them, looking grotesquely malformed with their ungainly burdens on their backs. There was no sign of a human being – the drivers were mere dots, climbing the hillside having abandoned their charges.

The 'Account of the Present War in the Peninsula' which Hornblower had so attentively studied had laid great stress on the difficulties of transport in Spain. A mule or horse was as valuable –

several times as valuable, for that matter – as any soldier. Hornblower set his expression hard.

'Mr Gerard!' he shouted. 'Load with grape. I want those baggage animals killed.'

A little wail went up from the men at the guns who heard the words. It was just like those sentimental fools to cheer when they killed men and yet to object to killing animals. Half of them would deliberately miss if they had the chance.

'Target practice. Single guns only,' bellowed Hornblower to Gerard.

The patient brutes would stand to be shot at, unlike their masters, and the gun layers would have no opportunity to waste ammunition. As the *Sutherland* drifted slowly along the shore her guns spoke out one by one, each one in turn hurling a hatful of grape, at extreme grapeshot range, on to the road. Hornblower watched horses and mules go down, kicking and plunging. One or two of the packmules, maddened with fear, managed to leap the bank out of the road and scrambled up the hill, scattering their burdens as they did so. Six oxen attached to a cart all went down together, dead simultaneously. Held together by their yokes they stayed, two by two, on their knees and bellies, their heads stretched forward, as if in prayer. The main deck murmured again in pity as the men saw the result of the good shot.

'Silence there!' roared Gerard, who could guess at the importance of the work in hand.

Bush plucked at his captain's sleeve, daring greatly in thus breaking in on his preoccupation with a suggestion.

'If you please, sir. If I took a boat's crew ashore I could burn all those waggons, destroy everything there.'

Hornblower shook his head. It was like Bush not see the objections to such a plan. The enemy might fly before guns to which they had no chance of replying, but if a landing party were put within their reach they would fall upon it fiercely enough – more fiercely than ever as a result of their recent losses. It was one thing to land a small party to attack fifty artillery men in a battery taken completely by surprise, but it was quite another to land in the face of a disciplined army ten thousand strong. The words with which Hornblower tried to soften his refusal were blown into inaudibility by the explosion of the quarterdeck carronade beside them, and when Hornblower again opened his mouth to speak there was a fresh distraction on the shore to interrupt him.

Someone was standing up in the next cart destined to receive fire, waving a white handkerchief frantically. Hornblower looked through his glass; the man appeared to be an officer of some sort, in his blue uniform with red epaulettes. But if he were trying to surrender he must know that his surrender could not be accepted in that it could not be put into effect. He must take his chance of the next shot. The officer suddenly seemed to realise it. He stooped down in the cart and rose again still waving his handkerchief and supporting someone who had been lying at his feet. Hornblower could see that the man hung limp in his arms; there was a white bandage round his head and another round his arm, and Hornblower suddenly realised that these carts were the ambulance vehicles of the army, full of the sick and of the wounded from yesterday's skirmish. The officer with the handkerchief must be a surgeon.

'Cease fire!' bellowed Hornblower, shrilling on his whistle. He was too late to prevent the next shot being fired, but luckily it was badly sighted and merely raised a cloud of dust from the cliff face below the road. It was illogical to spare draught animals which might be invaluable to the French for fear of hitting wounded men who might recover and again be active enemies, but it was the convention of war, deriving its absurdity from war itself.

Beyond the waggon train was the rearguard, but that was scattered over the hillside sparsely enough not to be worth powder and shot. It was time to go back and harass the main body once more.

'Put the ship about, Mr Bush,' said Hornblower. 'I want to retrace our course.'

It was not so easy on a course diametrically opposite to the previous one. The wind had been on the *Sutherland's* quarter before; now it was on her bow and she could only keep parallel to the shore by lying as close-hauled as she would sail. To make any offing at all when they reached the little capes which ran out from the shore the ship would have to go about, and the leeway she made might drift her into danger unless the situation were carefully watched. But the utmost must be done to harass the Italians and to demonstrate to them that they could never use the coast road again; Bush was delighted – as Hornblower could see from the fierce light in his eyes – that his captain was going to stick to his task and not sail tamely off after defiling once along the column, and the men at the starboard side guns rubbed their hands with pleasure at the prospect of action as they bent over the weapons that had stood unused so far.

It took time for the *Sutherland* to go about and work into position again for her guns to command the road; Hornblower was pleased to see the regiments which had re-formed break up again as their tormentor neared them and take to the hillside once more. But close-hauled the *Sutherland* could hardly make three knots past the land, allowing for the vagaries of the coast line and the wind; troops stepping out as hard as they could go along the road could keep their distance from her if necessary, and perhaps the Italian officers might realise this soon enough. He must do what damage he could now.

'Mr Gerard!' he called, and Gerard came running to his beckoning, standing with face uplifted to hear his orders from the quarter-deck. 'You may fire single shots at any group large enough to be worth it. See that every shot is well aimed.'

'Aye aye, sir.'

There was a body of a hundred men or so massed on the hillside opposite them now. Gerard himself laid the gun and estimated the range, squatting on his heels to look along the dispart sights with the gun at full elevation. The ball struck the rock in front of them and ricocheted into the group; Hornblower saw a sudden swirl in the crowd, which scattered abruptly leaving two or three white-breeched figures stretched on the ground behind them. The crew cheered at the sight of it. Marsh the gunner had been hurriedly sent for by Gerard to take part in this accurate shooting; the gun he was training killed more men in another group, over which flashed something on a pole which Hornblower, straining his eye through his telescope, decided must be one of the imperial eagles which Bonaparte's bulletins so often mentioned, and at which British cartoonists so often jeered.

Shot after shot crashed out from the *Sutherland's* starboard battery as she made her slow way along the coast. Sometimes the crew cheered when some of the scrambling midgets on the hillside were knocked over; sometimes the shot was received in chill silence when no effect could be noted. It was a valuable demonstration to the gunners on the importance of being able to lay their guns truly, to estimate range and deflection, even though it was traditional in a ship of the line that all the gunners had to do was to serve their guns as fast as possible with no necessity for taking aim with their ship laid close alongside the enemy.

Now that the ear was not deafened by the thunder of a full broadside, it could detect after each shot the flattened echo thrown back by the hills, returning from the land with its quality oddly altered in the heated air. For it was frightfully hot. Hornblower, watching the men drinking eagerly at the scuttle butt as their petty officers released them in turns for the purpose, wondered if those poor devils scrambling over the rocky hillsides in the glaring sun were suffering from thirst. He feared they were. He had no inclination to drink himself – he was too preoccupied listening to the chant of the man at the lead, with watching the effect of the firing and with seeing that the *Sutherland* was running into no danger.

Whoever was in command of the shattered field artillery battery farther along the road was a man who knew his duty. Midshipman Savage in the foretop attracted Hornblower's attention to it with a hail. The three serviceable guns had been slewed round to point diagonally across the road straight at the ship, and they fired the moment Hornblower trained his glass on them. Wirra-wirra-wirra; one of the balls passed high over Hornblower's head, and a hole appeared in the *Sutherland's* main topsail. At the same time a crash forward told where another shot had struck home. It would be ten minutes before the *Sutherland's* broadside could bear on the battery.

'Mr Marsh,' said Hornblower. 'Turn the starboard bowchasers on that battery.'

'Aye aye, sir.'

'Carry on with your target practice, Mr Gerard.'

'Aye aye, sir.'

As part of the programme for training his men into fighting machines it would be invaluable to give them firing practice while actually under fire from the enemy – no one knew better than Hornblower the difference between being fired at and not being fired at. He found himself in the act of thinking that one or two unimportant casualties might be worth receiving in these circumstances as part of the crew's necessary experience, and then he drew back in horror from the thought that he was casually condemning some of his own men to mutilation or death – and he might himself be one of those casualties. It was intolerably easy to separate mentally the academic theories of war from the human side of it, even when one was engaged in it oneself. To his men down below the little uniformed figures scrambling over the hillside were not human beings suffering agonies from heat and thirst and fatigue; and the still figures which littered the road here were not disembowelled corpses, lately fathers or lovers. They might as well be tin soldiers for all his men thought about them. It was mad that at that moment, irrelevantly in the heat, and the din of firing, he should start thinking about Lady Barbara and her pendant of sapphires, and Maria, who must now be growing ungainly with her child within her. He shook himself free from such thoughts – while they had filled his mind the battery had fired another salvo whose effect he actually had not noticed.

The bow-chasers were banging away at the battery; their fire might unsteady the men at the field guns. Meanwhile the broadside guns were finding few targets offered them, for the Italian division opposite them had scattered widely all over the hillside in groups of no more than half a dozen at the most – some of them were right up on the skyline. Their officers would have a difficult time reassembling them, and any who wished to desert – the 'Account of the Present War in the Peninsula' had laid stress on the tendency of the Italians to desert – would have ample opportunity today.

A crash and a cry below told that a shot from the battery had caused one at least of the casualties Hornblower had been thinking about – from the high-pitched scream of agony it must have been one of the ship's boys who had been hit; he set his lips firm as he measured the distance the ship still had to sail before bringing her broadside to bear. He would have to receive two more salvoes; it was the tiniest bit difficult to wait for them. Here came one – it passed close overhead with a sound like an infinity of bees on an urgent mission; apparently the gunners had made inadequate allowance for the rapidly decreasing range. The main top gallant backstay parted with a crack, and a gesture from Bush sent a party to splice it. The *Sutherland* would have to swing out now in readiness to weather the point and reef ahead.

'Mr Gerard! I am going to put the ship about. Be ready to open fire on the battery when the guns bear.'

'Aye aye, sir.'

Bush sent the hands to the braces. Hooker was forward in charge of the headsail sheets. The *Sutherland* came beautifully up into the wind as her helm was put down, and Hornblower watched the field guns, now less than a quarter of a mile away, through his glass. The gunners saw the *Sutherland* swinging round – they had seen that before, and knew the tempest of shot that would follow. Hornblower saw one man run from the guns, and saw others follow him, clawing their way desperately up the bank on to the hillside. Others flung themselves flat on their faces – only one man was left standing, raving and gesticulating beside the guns. Then the *Sutherland* heaved to the recoil of her guns once more, the acrid smoke came billowing up, and the battery was blotted out of sight. Even when the smoke cleared the battery could not be seen. There were only fragments – shattered wheels, an axle tree pointing upwards, the guns themselves lying tumbled on the ground. That had been a well-aimed broadside; the men must have behaved as steadily as veterans.

Hornblower took his ship out round the reef and stood in again for the shore. On the road just ahead was the rear of an infantry column; the leading division must have been formed up again on the road while the *Sutherland* was dealing with the second one. Now it was marching off down the road at a great pace, embanked in a low, heavy cloud of dust.

'Mr Bush! We must try and catch their column.'

'Aye aye, sir.'

But the *Sutherland* was a poor sailor close-hauled, and time and again when she was on the point of overtaking the rear of the column she had to go about and head out from the shore in order to weather a projecting point of land. Sometimes she was so close to the hurrying infantry that Hornblower could see through his glass the white faces above the blue tunics of the men looking back over their shoulders. And here and there along the road in the track of the division he saw men who had fallen out – men sitting by the roadside with their heads in their hands, men leaning exhausted on their muskets staring at the ship gliding by, sometimes men lying motionless and unconscious on their faces where they had fallen, overwhelmed by fatigue and heat.

Bush was fretting and fuming as he hastened about the ship trying to coax a little more speed out of her, setting every spare man to work carrying hammocks laden with shot from the lee side to the weather side, trimming the sails to the nicest possible degree of accuracy, blaspheming wildly whenever the gap between the ship and men showed signs of lengthening.

But Hornblower was well content. An infantry division which had been knocked about as badly as this one, and then sent flying helter skelter in panic for miles, dropping stragglers by the score, and pursued by a relentless enemy, would have such a blow to its self-respect as to be vastly weakened as a fighting force for weeks. Before he came into range of the big coastal battery on the farther side of Arens de Mar he gave over the pursuit – he did not want the flying enemy to recover any of its lost spirit by seeing the *Sutherland* driven off by the fire of the heavy guns there, and to circle round out of range would consume so much time that night would be upon them before they could be back on the coast again.

'Very good, Mr Bush. You can put the ship on the starboard tack and secure the guns.'

The *Sutherland* steadied to an even keel, and then heeled over again as she paid off on the other tack.

'Three cheers for the cap'n,' yelled someone on the maindeck – Hornblower could not be sure who it was, or he would have punished him. The storm of cheering that instantly followed drowned his voice and prevented him from checking the men, who shouted until they were tired, all grinning with enthusiasm for the captain who had led them to victory five times in three days. Bush was grinning, too, and Gerard, beside him on the quarterdeck. Little Longley was dancing and yelling with an utter disregard for an officer's dignity, while Hornblower stood sullenly glowering down at the men below. Later he might be delighted at the recollection of this spontaneous proof of the men's affection and devotion, but at present it merely irritated and embarrassed him.

As the cheering died away the voice of the leadsman made itself heard again.

'No bottom! No bottom with this line!'

He was still doing the duty to which he had been assigned, and would continue to do it until he received orders to rest – a most vivid example of the discipline of the navy.

'Have that man taken out of the chains at once, Mr Bush!' snapped Hornblower, annoyed at the omission to relieve the man.

'Aye aye, sir,' said Bush, chagrined at having been for once remiss in his work.

The sun was dipping in purple and red into the mountains of Spain, in a wild debauch of colour that made Hornblower catch his breath as he looked at the extravagant beauty of it. He was mazed and stupid now, in reaction from his exalted quickness of thought of the preceding hours; too stupid as yet even to be conscious of any fatigue. Yet he must still wait to receive the surgeon's report. Someone had been killed or wounded today – he remembered vividly the crash and the cry when the shot from the field guns hit the ship.

The gunroom steward had come up on the quarterdeck and touched his forehead to Gerard.

'Begging your pardon, sir,' he said. 'But Tom Cribb's been killed.'

'What?'

'Yes indeed, sir. Knocked 'is 'ead clean off. Dretful, 'e looks, laying there, sir.'

'What's this you say?' interrupted Hornblower. He could remember no man on board of the name of Tom Cribb – which was the name of the heavyweight champion of England – nor any reason why the gunroom steward should report a casualty to a lieutenant.

'Tom Cribb's been killed, sir,' explained the steward. 'And Mrs Siddons, she's got a splinter in 'er – in 'er backside, begging your pardon, sir. You could 'ave 'eard 'er squeak from 'ere, sir.'

'I did,' said Hornblower.

Tom Cribb and Mrs Siddons must be a pig and a sow belonging to the gunroom mess. It was a comfort to realise that.

'She's all right now, sir. The butcher clapped a 'andful o' tar on the place.'

Here came Walsh the surgeon with his report that there had been no casualties in the action.

'Excepting among the pigs in the manger, sir,' added Walsh, with the deprecating deference of one who proffers a joke with his superior officer.

'I've just heard about them,' said Hornblower.

Gerard was addressing the gunroom steward.

'Right!' he was saying. 'We'll have his chitterlings fried. And you can roast the loin. See that you get the crackling crisp. If it's leathery like the last time we killed a pig, I'll have your grog stopped. There's onions and there's sage – yes, and there's a few apples left. Sage and onions and apple sauce – and mark you this, Loughton, don't put any cloves in that sauce. No matter what the other officers say. I won't have 'em. In an apple pie, yes, but not with roast pork. Get started on that at once. You can take a leg to the bos'n's mess with my compliments, and roast the other one – it'll serve cold for breakfast.'

Gerard was striking the fingers of one hand into the palm of the other to accentuate his points; the light of appetite was in his face – Hornblower fancied that when there were no women available Gerard gave all the thought he could spare from his guns to his belly. A man whose eyes could go moist with appetite at the thought of fried chitterlings and roast pork for dinner on a scorching July afternoon in the Mediterranean, and who could look forward with pleasure to cold leg of pork for breakfast next day should by right have been fat like a pig himself. But Gerard was lean and handsome and elegant. Hornblower thought of the developing paunch within his own waistband with momentary jealousy.

But Colonel Villena was wandering about the quarterdeck like a lost soul. Clearly he was simply living for the moment when he would be able to start talking again – and Hornblower was the only soul on board with enough Spanish to maintain a conversation. Moreover, as a colonel he ranked with a post captain, and could expect to share the hospitality of the captain's cabin. Hornblower decided that he would rather be overfed with hot roast pork than have to endure Villena's conversation.

'You seemed to have planned a feast for tonight, Mr Gerard,' he said.

'Yes, sir.'

'Would my presence be unwelcome in the gunroom to share it?'

'Oh no, sir. Of course not, sir. We would be delighted if you would honour us, sir.'

Gerard's face lit with genuine pleasure at the prospect of acting as host to his captain. It was such a sincere tribute that Hornblower's heart was warmed, even while his conscience pricked him at the memory of why he had invited himself.

'Thank you, Mr Gerard. Then Colonel Villena and myself will be guests of the gunroom tonight.'

With any luck, Villena would be seated far enough from him to save him from the necessity for Spanish conversation.

The marine sergeant drummer had brought out all that the ship could boast of a band – the four marine fifers and the four drummers. They were marching up and down the gangway to the thunder and the rumble of the drums while the fifes squealed away bravely at the illimitable horizon.

'Hearts of oak are our ships
Jolly tars are our men—'

The bald words and the trite sentiments seemed to please the crew, although every man-jack of it would have been infuriated if he had been called a 'jolly tar'.

Up and down went the smart red coats, and the jaunty beat of the drums thrilled so that the crushing heat was forgotten. In the west the marvellous sky still flamed in glory, even while in the east the night was creeping up over the purple sea.

XV

'Eight bells, sir,' said Polwheal.

Hornblower woke with a start. It seemed to him as if he could not have been asleep more than five minutes, while actually it had been well over an hour. He lay on his cot in his nightshirt, for he had thrown off his coverings during the sweltering heat of the night; his head ached and his mouth had a foul taste. He had retired to bed at midnight, but – thanks to roast pork for supper – he had tossed and turned in the frightful heat for two or three hours before going to sleep, and now here he was awakened at four o'clock in the morning, simply because he had to prepare his report to Captain Bolton or to the admiral (if the latter had arrived) for delivery that morning at the rendezvous. He groaned miserably with fatigue, and his joints ached as he put his feet to the deck and sat up. His eyes were gummy and hard to open, and they felt sore when he rubbed them.

He would have groaned again except for the need to appear in Polwheal's eyes superior to human weaknesses – at the thought of that he stood up abruptly and posed as somebody feeling perfectly wide awake. A bath under the washdeck pump, and a shave made the pose almost a reality, and then, with dawn creeping up over the misty horizon, he sat down at his desk and cut himself a new pen, licked its point meditatively before dipping it into ink, and began to write.

'I have the honour to report that in accordance with the orders of Captain Bolton, on the 20th inst., I proceeded—'

Polwheal came in with his breakfast, and Hornblower turned to the steaming hot coffee for a spur to his already flagging energies. He flipped the pages of the ship's log to refresh his memory – so much had happened latterly that he was actually vague already about the details of the capture of the *Amelie*. The report had to be written badly, avoiding Gibbonesque antitheses or high-flying sentiment, yet at the same time Hornblower disliked the use of the kind of phrasing which was customary in captains' reports. When listing the prizes taken from beside the battery at Llanza he was careful to write 'as named in the margin' instead of the irritating phrase 'as per margin' which had become stereotyped in the Navy since its classic use by an unlettered captain nearly a hundred years before in the War of Jenkins' Ear. He was compelled to use the word 'proceed' even though he hated it – in official reports the Navy never set sail, nor went, nor put to sea, nor journeyed, but always proceeded, just as in the same way captains never suggested or advised or recommended, but always respectfully submitted. Hornblower had respectfully to submit that until the French battery was re-established at Llanza the coastal route from France to Spain was now most vulnerable between Port Vendres and Rosas Bay.

While he struggled with the wording of his description of the raid on the Etang de Thau near Cette he was interrupted by a knock on his door. Longley entered in response to his call.

'Mr Gerard sent me, sir. The squadron's in sight on the starboard bow.'

'The flagship's there, is she?'

'Yes, sir.'

'Right. My compliments to Mr Gerard, and will he please alter course to close her.'

'Aye aye, sir.'

His report would have to be addressed to the admiral, then, and not to Captain Bolton, and it would have to be finished within the next half hour. He dashed his pen into the ink and began to scribble feverishly, describing the harassing of the divisions of Pino and Lecchi on the coast road between Malgret and Arens de Mar. It came as a shock to him when he computed the casualties inflicted on the Italians – they must have numbered five or six hundred, exclusive of stragglers. He had to word that carefully, otherwise he would probably be suspected of gross exaggeration, a serious crime in the eyes of authority. Yesterday five or six hundred men were killed or mutilated who today would have been alive and well if he had not been an active and enterprising officer. The mental eyes with which Hornblower viewed his exploit saw a double image – on the one hand he saw corpses, widows and orphans, misery and pain, while on the other he saw white breeched figurines motionless on a hillside, tin soldiers knocked over, arithmetical digits recorded on paper. He cursed his analytical mind at the same time as he cursed the heat and the need for writing the report. He was even vaguely conscious of his own cross-grainedness, which always plunged him into depression after a success.

He dashed off his signature to the document, and shouted for Polwheal to bring a candle to melt the sealing wax while he peppered sand over the wet ink. Thanks to the heat his hands stuck clammily to the limp paper. When he came to address the report – 'Rear Admiral Sir P. G. Leighton, K.B.' – the ink spread and ran on the smeared surface as though on blotting paper. But at any rate the thing was done; he went on deck, where already the sunshine was oppressive. The brassiness of the sky, noticeable yesterday, was far more marked today, and Hornblower had noticed that the barometer in his cabin indicated a steady fall which had begun three days ago. There was a storm coming, without a doubt, and moreover a storm which had so long been foretold would be all the more violent when it did come. He turned to Gerard with orders to keep a sharp eye on the weather and to be ready to shorten sail at the first hint of trouble.

'Aye aye, sir,' said Gerard.

Over there rolled the two other ships of the squadron, the *Pluto* with her three tiers of ports, and the red ensign at the mizzen masthead indicating the presence on board of a rear-admiral of the red, and the *Caligula* astern of her.

'Pass the word to Mr Marsh to salute the Admiral's flag,' said Hornblower.

While the salute was being returned a hoist of flags ran up the *Pluto's* rigging.

'*Sutherland's* pendant,' read off Vincent. 'Take station astern.'

'Acknowledge.'

The hoist was succeeded by another.

'*Sutherland's* pendant,' said Vincent again. 'Flag to captain. Come on board and report.'

'Acknowledge. Mr Gerard, clear away my barge. Where's Colonel Villena?'

'Not seen him yet this morning, sir.'

'Here, Mr Savage, Mr Longley. Run down and get Colonel Villena out of bed. I want him ready as soon as my barge is cleared away.'

'Aye aye, sir.'

It took two and a half minutes before the captain's barge was in the water with Hornblower seated in the stern, and at the very last second Villena made his appearance at the ship's side. He looked as disagreeable as might be expected, at having been routed out of bed by two brusque midshipmen who could speak no word of his language and dressed with their clumsy and hurried aid. His busby was awry and his coat incorrectly hooked, and his sabre and pelisse still hung over his arm. He was hauled down into the boat by the impatient boat's crew, who did not want to imperil their ship's reputation for smartness by waiting for him after the admiral had signalled for them.

Villena lurched miserably to his thwart beside Hornblower. He was unshaven and bedraggled, and his eyes were as gummy as Hornblower's had been on his awakening. He sat down, muttering and grumbling, still half asleep, trying in dazed fashion to complete his dressing, while the men bent to their oars and sent the barge skimming over the water. It was only as they neared the flagship that Villena was able to open his eyes fully and begin to talk, and for the short remaining period Hornblower felt no need for elaborate politeness. He was full of hope that the admiral would invite Villena to be his guest for the sake of any information he could give regarding conditions ashore.

Captain Elliott was at the ship's side to greet him as they came on board.

'Glad to see you, Hornblower,' he said, and then in response to Hornblower's introduction he mumbled incoherently to Villena eyeing the latter's gaudy uniform and unshaven chin in blank astonishment. He was obviously relieved when the formality was over and he could address himself to Hornblower again. 'The admiral's in his cabin. This way, gentlemen please.'

The flag lieutenant in the admiral's cabin along with the admiral was young Sylvester, whom Hornblower had heard of as a capable young officer even though he was – as might have been expected – a sprig of the nobility. Leighton himself was ponderous and slow of speech this morning; in the stifling heat the sweat was visible in little rivers running down the sides of his heavy chin. He and Sylvester made a brave attempt to welcome Villena. They both of them spoke French fairly well and Italian badly, and by amalgamating what they knew of those two languages with what remained of their schoolboy Latin they were able to make themselves understood, but it was heavy going. Obviously with relief Leighton turned to Hornblower.

'I want to hear your report, Hornblower,' he said.

'I have it here in writing, sir.'

'Thank you. But let us hear a little about your doings verbally. Captain Bolton tells me he spoke a prize you had taken. Where did you go?'

Hornblower began his account – he was glad that events had moved so fast that he was able to omit all reference to the circumstances in which he had parted company from the East India convoy. He told of his capture of the *Amelie* and of the little fleet of small vessels at Llanza. The admiral's heavy face showed a gleam of extra animation when he heard that he was a thousand pounds the richer as a result of Hornblower's activity, and he nodded sympathetically when Hornblower explained the necessity of burning the last prize he had taken – the coaster near Cette. Cautiously Hornblower put forward the suggestion that the squadron might be most profitably employed in watching between Port Vendres and Rosas, on which stretch, thanks to the destruction of the battery at Llanza, there was now no refuge for French shipping. A hint of a groove appeared between the admiral's eyebrows at that, and Hornblower swerved away from the subject. Clearly Leighton was not the sort of admiral to welcome suggestions from his inferiors.

Hornblower hurriedly began to deal with the next day's action to the south-westward.

'One moment, Captain,' said Leighton. 'You mean you went southward the night before last?'

'Yes, sir.'

'You must have passed close to this rendezvous during the darkness?'

'Yes, sir.'

'You made no attempt to ascertain whether the flagship had arrived?'

'I gave orders for a specially good lookout to be kept, sir.'

The groove between Leighton's eyebrows was very noticeable now. Admirals were always plagued by the tendency of their captains, when on blockade service, to make excuses to get away and act independently – if only because it increased their share of prize-money – and obviously Leighton was not merely determined to deal drastically with any such tendency but also he guessed that Hornblower had been careful to arrange his cruise so as to pass the rendezvous at night.

'I am extremely annoyed, Captain Hornblower, that you should have acted in such a fashion. I have already admonished Captain Bolton for allowing you to go, and now that I find you were within ten miles of here two nights ago I find it difficult to express my displeasure. I reached the rendezvous that very morning, as it happened, and as a result of your behaviour two of His Majesty's ships of the line have been kept idle here for nearly forty-eight hours until you should see fit to rejoin. Please understand, Captain Hornblower, that I am very annoyed indeed, and I shall have to report my annoyance to the admiral commanding in the Mediterranean, for him to take any action he thinks necessary.'

'Yes, sir,' said Hornblower. He tried to look as contrite as he could, but his judgment told him that it was not a court martial matter – he was covered by Bolton's orders – and it was doubtful if Leighton would really carry out his threat of reporting to higher authority.

'Please continue,' said Leighton.

Hornblower began to describe the action against the Italian divisions. He could see by Leighton's expression that he attached little importance to the moral effect achieved, and that his imagination was not powerful enough to allow him to gauge the effect on the Italians of an ignominious retreat before an invulnerable enemy. At Hornblower's suggestion that they had lost five hundred men at least Leighton moved restlessly and exchanged glances with Sylvester – he clearly did not believe him. Hornblower decided discreetly not to put forward his estimate that the Italians had lost at least another five hundred men through straggling and desertion.

'Very interesting,' said Leighton, a trifle insincerely.

A knock at the cabin door and the entrance of Elliott eased the situation.

'The weather's looking very nasty, sir,' he said. 'I was thinking that if Captain Hornblower wishes to rejoin his ship—'

'Yes, of course,' said Leighton, rising.

From the deck they could see black clouds to leeward, rising rapidly against the wind.

'You'll only just have time,' said Elliott, looking at the sky as Hornblower prepared to go down into his barge.

'Yes indeed,' said Hornblower. His main anxiety was to get away from the *Pluto* before anyone noticed that he was leaving Villena behind – the latter, with no understanding of the English conversation, was hanging back on the quarterdeck, and Hornblower was able to scramble down into the boat without anyone thinking of him.

'Give way,' said Hornblower, before he was fairly seated, and the barge shot away from the *Pluto's* side.

With an admiral and his staff on board the accommodation, three-decker though she was, must already be strained. The presence of a Spanish colonel would mean that some unfortunate lieutenant would be rendered extremely uncomfortable. But Hornblower could harden his heart to the troubles of the unknown lieutenant.

XVI

The thunder was already rolling on the horizon when Hornblower set foot on the *Sutherland's* deck again, although the heat showed no signs of diminishing at present and the wind had dropped away almost to nothing. The black clouds had stretched over the sky nearly overhead, and what blue was left was of a hard metallic tint.

'It'll be coming soon, sir,' said Bush. He looked complacently upwards; the *Sutherland's* sail had already been reduced by his orders to topsails only, and now the crew were busy taking a reef in them. 'But where it'll come from, God only knows.'

He mopped his sweating forehead; the heat was frightful, and the ship, with no wind to steady her, was heaving painfully on the uneasy sea. The blocks were chattering loudly as she rolled.

'Oh, come *on,* blast you,' grumbled Bush.

A breath of air, hot as though from a brick kiln, stole upon them, and the *Sutherland* steadied for a moment. Then came another, hotter and stronger.

'There it comes!' said Bush pointing.

The black sky was suddenly split by dazzling lightning, followed almost instantaneously by a tremendous crash of thunder, and the squall came racing down upon them; they could see its hard, metallic line on the surface of the grey sea. Almost taken aback, the *Sutherland* shuddered and plunged. Hornblower bellowed orders to the helmsman, and she paid off before it, steadying again. The shrieking wind brought hail with it – hailstones as big as cherries, which bit and blinded and stung, rattling with an infernal din on the decks, and whipping the sea into a yeasty foam whose hiss was audible even through the other noises. Bush held the big collar of his tarpaulin coat up round his face, and tried to shield his eyes with the brim of his sou'wester, but Hornblower found the keen wind so delicious that he was unconscious of the pain the hailstones caused him. Polwheal, who came running up on deck with his tarpaulin and sou'wester, had positively to jog his elbow to attract his attention and get him to put them on.

The *Pluto,* hove to, came drifting down two cables' lengths clear of the *Sutherland's* starboard bow; the big three-decker was even more unhandy and made more leeway than the *Sutherland* herself. Hornblower watched her and wondered how Villena was feeling now, battened down below with the timbers groaning round him. He was commending himself to the saints, presumably. The *Caligula* was still up to windward under reefer topsails, her man o' war pendant blown out stiff and as straight as a pole. She was the most weatherly of the three ships, for her British designers had had in mind as principal object the building of a ship to contend with storms – not, as in the case of the *Pluto,* of cramming the utmost artillery into a given length and beam, nor, as the Dutch designers had been compelled to do in the case of the *Sutherland,* to give the minimum of draught compatible with a minimum of sea-worthiness.

Almost without warning the wind whipped round four whole

points, and the *Sutherland* lurched and plunged, her storm canvas slatting like a discharge of guns, before she paid off again. The hail had given place to torrential rain now, driven along almost horizontally by the howling wind, and the sudden change in the wind called up a short, lumpy sea over which the *Sutherland* bucked and plunged in ungainly fashion. He looked over to the *Pluto* – she had been caught nearly aback, but Elliott was handling her well and she had paid off in time. Hornblower felt that he would rather command the flat-bottomed old *Sutherland* than a clumsy three-decker ninety-eight guns and thirty-two pounders and first-rate's pay notwithstanding.

The wind shrieked at him again, nearly tearing his tarpaulin from his back. The *Sutherland* trying to lie over on her side in a gale like this was like a cow trying to waltz. Bush was yelling something at him. Hornblower caught the words 'relieving tackles' and nodded, and Bush vanished below. Four men at the wheel, aided by the powerful leverage of the barrel of the wheel, might possibly manage to control it despite the *Sutherland's* frantic behaviour, but the strain thrown on the tiller ropes would be enormous, and as precautionary measure it would be better to place six or eight men at relieving tackles in the gunroom, to share the strain both on the men at the wheel and on the tipper ropes. A petty officer would have to be posted at the grating nearest the wheel to shout down instructions to the men at the relieving tackles – all highly skilled work, the thought of which made Hornblower bless his own resolution in stripping the East India convoy of seamen.

To windward the horizon was concealed in a pearly mistiness of rare beauty, but to leeward it was clearer, and reaching up to the sky in that direction there was a bar of blue – the mountains of Spain. In that direction there was Rosas Bay, poor shelter with the present south-easterly gale blowing, and closed to British ships in any case because of the French guns mounted there; Rosas was a fortress whose siege and capture by the French had provided Cochrane with opportunities for distinguishing himself a year ago. The northern extremity of Rosas Bay was Cape Creux – the *Sutherland* had captured the *Amelie* while the latter was endeavouring to weather this point. Beyond Cape Creux the coast trended away again north-westerly, giving them ample sea room in which to ride out the gale, for these summer storms in the Mediterranean never lasted long, violent though they were.

'Flagship's signalling, sir,' yelled the midshipman of the watch. 'No. 35, make all sail conformable with the weather.'

The *Pluto* was showing storm-staysails as well as her close reefed topsails; apparently the admiral had decided that Cape Creux was dangerously near, and wished to claw out a little farther to windward in case of emergencies. It was a sensible precaution; Hornblower gave the necessary orders to set the *Sutherland* on the same course, although it was all that the men at the wheel and relieving tackles could do to keep her from coming up into the wind. The guns' crews were busy double-breeching the guns lest the heavings of the ship should cause any to break loose, and there was already a party of men at work on the two chain pumps. The working of the ship was not causing her to take in much water as yet, but Hornblower believed in keeping the well as clear as possible in case the time should come when pumping would be urgently necessary. The *Caligula* was far to windward already – Bolton was making the fullest use of the weatherly qualities of his ship and was keeping, very properly, as far as possible out of harm's way. But the *Sutherland* and the *Pluto* were safe enough, always excepting accidents. The loss of a spar, a gun breaking loose, a sudden leak developing, and the situation might be dramatically changed, but at present they were safe enough.

Overhead the thunder was rolling so unceasingly that Hornblower noticed it no longer. The play of the lightning among the black clouds was dazzling and beautiful. At this rate the storm could not last much longer; equilibrium was restoring itself fast. But there would be some flurries yet, and the wind had already kicked up a heavy sea, here in this shallow corner of the Mediterranean; there was plenty of water washing over the maindeck as the *Sutherland* rolled. The air, even the deluges of rain and spray, were exhilarating after the stifling heat of the past few days, and the wind screaming in the rigging made a music which even Hornblower's tone-deaf ear could appreciate. He was surprised that so much time had passed when Polwheal came to tell him his dinner was ready – what dinner there was, with the galley fire extinguished.

When he came on deck again the wind had sensibly diminished, and over to the windward there were patches of clear sky to be seen, of a steely green-blue, and the rain had ceased, although the sea was wilder than ever.

'It's blown itself out quick enough, sir,' said Bush.

'Yes,' answered Hornblower, but with mental reservation. That steely sky was not the blue of returning calm, and he never yet had known one of these Mediterranean storms die away without at least one expiring effort. And he was still very conscious of Cape Creux on the horizon to leeward. He looked keenly round him, at the *Pluto* to leeward, veiled in spray, and the *Caligula* far to windward and her canvas only rarely visible across the tossing grey water.

Then it happened – a sudden howling squall, which laid the *Sutherland* over and then veered round with astonishing quickness.

Hornblower clung to the mizzen weather rigging, bellowing orders. It was wild while it lasted; for a moment it felt as if the *Sutherland* would never rise again, and then as if she might be driven under stern-foremost as the wind took her aback. It howled and shrieked round them with a violence which it had not yet displayed. Only after a long struggle was the ship brought to the wind again and hove to; the shift in the wind had made the sea lumpier and more erratic than ever, so that she was bucking and plunging in a senseless fashion which made it hard even for those who had spent a lifetime at sea to keep their footing. But not a spar had carried away, and not a rope had parted – clear proof of the efficient work of Plymouth Dockyard and of the seamanship of Bush and Harrison.

Bush was shouting something now, and pointing away over the quarter, and Hornblower followed the gesture with his eyes. The *Pluto* had vanished, and for a moment Hornblower thought she must have sunk with all hands. Then a breaking wave revealed her, right over on her beam ends, the grey waves breaking clean over her exposed bottom, her yards pointing to the sky, sails and rigging showing momentarily black through the white foam in the lee of her.

'Jesus Christ!' yelled Bush. 'The poor devils have gone!'

'Set the main topmast stays'l again!' yelled Hornblower back.

She had not sunk yet; there might possibly be some survivors, who might live long enough in the wild sea to grab a rope's end from the *Sutherland's* deck and who might be hauled on board without being beaten to death; it had to be tried even though it was a hundred to one against one of the thousand men on board being saved. Hornblower worked the *Sutherland* slowly over towards the *Pluto*. Still the latter lived, with the waves breaking over her as if she were a half tide rock. Hornblower's imagination pictured what was happening on board – the decks nearly vertical, with everything carrying away and smashing which could. On the weather side the guns would be hanging by their breechings; the least unsoundness there and they would fall straight down the decks, to smash holes on the opposite side which would sink her in a flash. Men would be crawling about in the darkness below decks; on the main deck the men who had not been washed away would be clinging on like flies on a windowpane, soused under as the waves broke.

Through his levelled glass he caught sight of a speck on the exposed upper side of the *Pluto*, a speck that moved, a speck which survived the breach of a wave over it. There were other specks, too, and there was a gleam of something in swift regular movement. Some gallant soul had got a party together to hack at the weather shrouds of the mainmast, and as the *Sutherland* closed he saw the shrouds part, and the foremast shrouds as well. With a shuddering roll the *Pluto* heaved herself out of the water like a whale, water cascading from her scuppers, and as she rolled towards the *Sutherland* her mizzen-mast went as well, on the opposite side. Freed from the overpowering leverage of her top hamper she had managed to recover – naval discipline and courage had won her a further chance of life during the few seconds which had been granted her while she lay on her beam ends. Hornblower could see men still hard at work, hacking madly at the uncut shrouds to free the ship from the wreckage thrashing alongside.

But she was in poor case. Her mast had gone, a few feet from the deck; even her bowsprit had disappeared. And with the loss of their steadying weight the bare hull was rolling insanely, heaving right over until her bottom copper was exposed on one side, and then rolling equally far back again taking only a few seconds to accomplish a roll which extended through far more than a right angle. The wonder was that she did not roll over and over, as a wooden ninepin might do, floating on one side. Inside the ship it must be like an inferno, like a madman's nightmare; and yet she lived, she floated, with some at least of her crew alive on her decks. Overhead the thunder pealed a final roll. Even westward, to leeward, there was a gap visible through the clouds, and the Spanish sun was trying to break through. The wind was no more now than a strong gale. It was the last hurricane effort of the storm which had done the damage.

And yet that last effort must have endured longer than Hornblower could have guessed. He was suddenly conscious of Cape Creux large upon the horizon, and the wind was driving nearly straight from the ship towards it. It would only be a matter of an hour or two before the dismantled hulk was in the shallows at the foot of the cape where certain destruction awaited her – and to make it doubly certain there were French guns on Cape Creux ready to pound a helpless target.

'Mr Vincent,' said Hornblower. 'Make this signal. "*Sutherland* to flagship. Am about to give assistance." '

That made Bush jump. In that boiling sea, on a lee shore, the *Sutherland* would find it difficult to give assistance to a mastless hulk twice her size. Hornblower turned upon him.

'Mr Bush, I want the bower cable got out through a stern port. As quickly as you can, if you please. I am going to tow the flagship off.'

Bush could only look his expostulations – he knew his captain too well to demur openly. But anyone could see that for the *Sutherland* to attempt the task was to take her into danger probably uselessly. The scheme would be practically impossible from the start, owing to the difficulty of getting the cable to the *Pluto* as she rolled and lunged, wildly and aimlessly, in the trough. Nevertheless, Bush was gone before Hornblower could do more than read his expression. With that wind steadily thrusting them towards the land every second was of value.

With her flat bottom and with all her top hamper exposed to the wind the *Sutherland* was going off to leeward a good deal faster than the *Pluto*. Hornblower had to work his ship with the utmost care, fighting his way to windward close-hauled before heaving-to and allowing her to drop back again; there was only the smallest margin to spare. The gale was still blowing strongly, and the least clumsiness in handling, the slightest accident to sail, or spar, meant danger. Despite the chill of the wind and the steady rain the *Sutherland's* topmen were sweating freely soon, thanks to the constant active exertion demanded of them by their captain, as he backed and filled, worked up to windward and went about, keeping his ship hovering round the dismasted *Pluto* like a seagull round a bit of wreckage. And Cape Creux was growing nearer and nearer. From below came a steady tramp and thumps and dragging noises as Bush's party slaved away to haul the ponderous twenty-inch cable aft along the lower gun deck.

Now Hornblower was measuring distances with his eye, and gauging the direction of the wind with the utmost care. He could not hope to haul the *Pluto* bodily out to sea – it was as much as the *Sutherland* could do to work herself to windward – and all he intended was to tow her aside a trifle to gain advantage of the respite, the additional sea room which would be afforded by avoiding the cape. Postponement of disaster was always a gain. The wind might drop – probably would – or change, and given time the *Pluto's* crew would be able to set up jury masts and get their ship under some sort of control. Cape Creux was nearly due west, and the wind was a little north of east, the tiniest trifle north. It would be best from that point of view to drag the *Pluto* away southerly; in that case they stood a better chance of weathering the cape. But southwards from Cape Creux stretched Rosas Bay, limited southward by Cape Bagur, and such a course might drift them under the guns of Rosas, expose them to the annoyance of the gunboats which were probably stationed there, and end in worse disaster than before. Northwards there would be no such danger, the guns at Llanza could not be remounted yet, and there were twenty miles of clear water from the tip of the cape to Llanza anyway. Northwards was safer – if only he could be sure of weathering the cape. Hornblower's imagination was hard at work trying to calculate, on quite insufficient data, the rate of drift he could expect and the possible distance the *Sutherland* would be able to tow the dismasted three-decker in the time granted. With the data insufficient, imagination was all he had to go upon.

He had decided on a northward course when a young seaman came running breathless up to the quarterdeck.

'Mr Bush says the cable'll be ready in five minutes, sir,' he said.

'Right,' answered Hornblower. 'Mr Vincent, signal to the flagship "Stand by to receive a line." Mr Morkell, pass the word for my coxswain.'

A line! The quarterdeck officers stared at each other. The *Pluto* was plunging and lunging quite irrationally in the trough of the sea. She was still heeling over so as to show her copper before rolling back to bury the white streaks between her gunports, but in addition, in the irregular sea, she was lunging now forward, now aft, as incalculable whim took her. She was as dangerous to approach as a gun loose on a rolling deck. Any sort of collision between the ships might well, in that sea, send them both incontinently to the bottom.

Hornblower ran his eyes over Brown's bulging muscles as he stood before him.

'Brown,' he said, 'I've selected you to heave a line to the flagship as we go down past her. D'you know anyone in the ship who could do it better? Frankly, now.'

'No, sir. I can't say as I do, sir.'

Brown's cheerful self confidence was like a tonic.

'What are you going to use, then?'

'One o' them belayin' pins, sir, an' a lead line, if I can have one, sir.'

Brown was a man of instant decision – Hornblower's heart warmed to him, not for the first time.

'Make ready, then. I shall lay our stern as close to the flagship's bows as is safe.'

At the moment the *Sutherland* was forging slowly ahead under storm jib and close reefed topsails, two hundred yards to windward of the *Pluto*. Hornblower's mind became a calculating machine again, estimating the *Sutherland's* relative drift down upon the *Pluto*, the latter's drunken reelings and plungings, the *Sutherland's* present headway, the send of the waves and the chances of a cross-wave intervening. He had to wait for two long minutes before the moment for which he was waiting should arrive, his eyes glued upon the *Pluto* until their relative positions should be exactly what he wanted.

'Mr Gerard,' said Hornblower – his mind was too busy for him to be afraid. 'Back the main tops'l.'

The *Sutherland's* way was checked. At once the gap between the two ships began to narrow, as the *Sutherland* drifted down upon the *Pluto* – a gap of grey angry water with bearded waves. Fortunately the *Pluto* was lying fairly constantly in the trough without yawing, only surging forward or back as some unexpected sea struck her.

Brown was standing statuesquely on the taffrail, balancing superbly. The lead line was coiled on the deck at his side, attached to the belaying pin which he swung pendulum fashion, idly, from his fist. He made a magnificent picture there against the sky, with no hint of nervousness as he watched the distance dwindle. Even at that moment Hornblower felt a hint of envy of Brown's physique and robust self-confidence. The *Sutherland* was coming down fast upon the *Pluto* – upon the latter's wave-swept forecastle Hornblower could see a group of men waiting anxiously to catch the line. He looked to make sure that Brown's assistants were ready with the stouter line to bend on the lead line.

'We'll do it, by God!' said Gerard to Crystal.

Gerard was wrong – at the present relative rate of drift the ships would pass at least ten yards farther apart than Brown could be expected to throw the belaying pin and its hampering trailer of line.

'Mr Gerard,' said Hornblower coldly. 'Back the mizzen tops'l.'

The hands were ready at the braces; the order was hardly given before it was executed. The *Sutherland* was making a tiny trifle of sternway now, and the gap was closing farther still. The *Pluto's* towering bow, lifting to a wave, seemed right upon them. Gerard and Crystal were swearing softly in unison, without the slightest idea of what they were saying, as they watched, fascinated. Hornblower felt the wind blowing cold about his shoulders. He wanted to call to Brown to throw, and with difficulty checked himself. Brown was the better judge of what he could do. Then he threw, with the *Sutherland's* stern lifting to a wave. The belaying pin flew with the line wavering behind it in the wind. It just reached the *Pluto's* beak-head bows and caught round a remnant of the standing rigging of the bowsprit, where a ragged sailor astride the spar seized it with a wave of his arm. Next moment a wave broke clean over him, but he held on, and they saw him pass the end of the line up to the waiting group on the forecastle.

'Done it!' shrieked Gerard. 'Done it, done it, done it!'

'Mr Gerard,' said Hornblower. 'Brace the mizzen tops'l sharp up.'

The line was uncoiling fast from the deck as the *Pluto* hauled it in; soon the heavier line was on its way out to the dismasted ship. But they had not long to spare; with their different rates of drift it was impossible for Hornblower in that gale to keep the two ships that same distance apart – impossible and dangerous. The *Sutherland* hove-to went to leeward faster than the *Pluto;* closehauled she forged ahead, and it was Hornblower's task to combine these two factors so that the increasing distance between the ships was kept down to a minimum – a nice algebraic problem in convergent series which

Hornblower had to convert into mental arithmetic and solve in his head.

When suddenly the *Pluto* decided irrationally to rush forward upon the *Sutherland* he found himself recasting his estimates at the very moment when everyone else was holding their breath and waiting for the collision. Gerard had a couple of parties standing by with spars to try to bear the *Pluto* off – not that they could have achieved much against her three thousand tons deadweight – and the bight of an old sail filled with hammocks as a fend-off, and there was wild activity on the forecastle of the *Pluto* as well, but at the very last moment, with blasphemy crackling all round, the dismasted ship suddenly sheered off and everyone breathed again more freely, except Hornblower. If the *Pluto* could surge in that fashion towards the *Sutherland,* she could surge away from her also, and if she were to do so while the line was hauling in the twenty-three inch cable she would part the line for certain and leave the whole business to be done again – and Cape Creux was looming very near now.

'*Caligula* signalling, sir,' said Vincent. 'How can I help?'

'Reply "Wait", said Hornblower over his shoulder to him; he had actually forgotten the *Caligula's* existence. Bolton would be a fool if he came down unnecessarily to leeward, towards a hostile lee shore.

A mighty splash over the stern indicated that Bush down below was paying out some of the hawser through the after-port so as to provide some slack if the *Pluto* surged away, but the process might be overdone – it was a hemp cable, which sank in water, and to have out too much would imperil the line which was drawing it in. Hornblower leaned over the heaving stern.

'Mr Bush!' he bellowed.

'Sir!' said Bush's voice from below through the open port.

'Avast there, now!'

'Aye aye, sir.'

The line was taking the strain now, and the cable was creeping slowly out towards the *Pluto* like some sea worm. Hornblower watched as it straightened – this was a business demanding calculation as close as any so far. He had to shout his orders for Bush to pay out more cable, or to wait, his eyes on the ships, on the sea, on the wind. The cable was two hundred yards long, but fifty of these lay in the *Sutherland* herself – the job had to be completed before the ships were a hundred and fifty yards apart. Hornblower only began to feel relieved when he saw the end of the cable curve up out of the sea on to the *Pluto's* bows, and the waving of flags told him that the end had been taken inboard and made fast.

Hornblower looked at the nearing land, felt the wind on his cheek. His earlier calculations were proving correct, and if they held on this tack they would be drifted into Rosas Bay even if they cleared the land.

'Mr Vincent,' he said. 'Signal to the Flagship "I am preparing to go about on the other tack".'

Gerard looked his amazement. It appeared to him that Hornblower was going to unnecessary trouble and imperilling both ships by this manoeuvre – he could see no farther than Cape Creux, only the friendly sea and the dangerous land. With a seamen's instinct he wanted to get both ships comfortably under control with sea room under their lee, and he did not stop to consider beyond that. He could see the land and feel the wind, and his reaction to those circumstances was instinctive.

'Mr Gerard,' said Hornblower. 'Go to the wheel. When the strain comes on the hawser—'

Gerard did not need to be told about that. With three thousand tons trailing on her stern the *Sutherland* would behave unlike any ship the quartermasters had ever steered, and extraordinary and unexpected measures would have to be taken to keep her from flying up into the wind. The hawser was tightening already. The bight of it rose slowly out of the sea, straightening like a bar, the water spouting out of it in fountains, while a thunderous creaking below told how the bitts were feeling the strain. Then the cable slackened a trifle, the creaking diminished, and the *Sutherland* had got the *Pluto* under way. With every yard they went, and every bit of way the *Pluto* received, the latter sagged less and less to leeward. As soon as she could answer the helm the strain on the *Sutherland's* quartermasters would be eased.

Bush came up on the quarterdeck again, his task below completed.

'I want you to work the ship, Mr Bush, when we go about.'

'Aye aye, sir,' said Bush. He looked at the land, and felt the wind, and his thoughts followed an exact parallel to Gerard's, but Bush by now never dreamed of doubting his captain's judgment in a matter of seamanship. His mental state was now that if Hornblower thought it right, it must be so, and there was no need to wonder about it.

'Send the hands to the braces. It must be like lightning when I give the word.'

'Aye aye, sir.'

The *Pluto* was gathering way, and every yard after this that they made in a southerly direction would be a dead loss when they turned northerly.

'Back the mizzen tops'l,' said Hornblower.

The *Sutherland* lost way, and the *Pluto* came steadily forging down upon her. Hornblower could actually see Captain Elliott come running forward to see for himself what was happening. He could not guess what Hornblower was intending.

'Have the signal "Tack" bent and ready to send up, Mr Vincent.'

The *Pluto* was very near now.

'Brace the mizzen tops'l up, Mr Bush.'

The *Sutherland* gathered speed again – she had just the distance allowed by the slackening of the hawser in which to gather way and go about before the two began to interfere. Hornblower watched the cable and estimated the speed of the ship through the water.

'Now, Mr Bush! That signal, Mr Vincent!'

The helm was put down, the yards braced up, with Rayner forward attending to the fore topmast staysail. She was coming round, her canvas volleying as she came into the wind; on board the *Pluto* as they read the signal they had the sense to put their own helm down too, and with steerage way upon her she began to come round a little and allow Hornblower a little more room for his manoeuvres. Now the *Sutherland* was over on the opposite tack, and gathering way, but the *Pluto* was only half way round. There would be a terrific jerk in a moment. Hornblower watched the tightening cable rising from the sea.

'Stand by, Mr Gerard!'

The jerk came, and the *Sutherland* shuddered. The drag of the cable across her stern was doing the most fantastic things to her – Hornblower could hear Gerard volleying orders to the quartermasters at the wheel and down the grating to the men at the relieving tackles below. For one palpitating second it seemed as if she must be dragged back and thrown in irons, but Gerard at the wheel and Bush at the braces and Rayner forward fought her tooth and nail. Shuddering, she paid off again, and the *Pluto* followed her round. They were over on the other tack at least heading northwards towards the comparative safety of the Gulf of the Lion.

Hornblower looked at the green-topped Cape Creux, close in now, and a little forward of the port beam. It was going to be a very near-run thing, for besides her own natural leeway the *Sutherland* was being dragged to leeward by the dead weight of the *Pluto,* and her speed through the water towards safety was diminished by the same dead weight. It was going to be a very near thing indeed. Hornblower stood with the wind howling round him, his busy mind plunged into calculations of drift and distance again. He looked back at the *Pluto,* not rolling so badly now that she had way on her. The towrope was at an angle to the length of the *Sutherland,* and the *Pluto* was at a further angle to the towrope. He could rely on Elliott to make the most economical use of his helm, but the drag on the *Sutherland* must be tremendous. He ought to try to get a little more speed out of the *Sutherland,* but with a full gale blowing it was dangerous to spread any more canvas. If a sail were to split or a spar carry away they would be on the shore in no time.

He looked towards the land again, to measure the diminishing distance, and as he looked a warning rose out of the sea a cable's length away like a ghost. It was a pillar of water six feet high, which rose from the breast of a wave and vanished as quickly and as mysteriously as it had risen. Hornblower could hardly believe he had seen it, but a glance at Crystal's and Bush's faces, intentionally immobile, assured him that he had. A cannon ball had plunged into the water there, calling up that splash, although in the high wind he had neither heard the shot nor seen the smoke from the land. The battery on Cape Creux was firing at him, and he was nearly in range. Soon there would be forty-two-pounder balls coming about his ears.

'Flagship's signalling, sir,' said Vincent.

On board the *Pluto* they had managed to attach a block to the top of the stump of the foremast and sent up a signal; the fluttering flags could be seen clearly from the *Sutherland's* quarterdeck.

'"Flag to *Sutherland*,"' read Vincent. '"Cast off – two – if necessary".'

'Reply "Submit not necessary".

They must make more speed through the water, there was no doubt about that. It was an interesting problem in chances, but more of the sort to appeal to a player of hazard than a whist player. To set more sail increased the danger to both ships at the same time as it gave them a greater chance of reaching safety. Yet if he set more sail and lost a spar he still might possibly struggle with the *Sutherland* out of danger, and the *Pluto* would be no more lost than she would be if he cast her off ignominiously now.

'Mr Bush, I'll have the reefs shaken out of the fore tops'l.'

'Aye aye, sir,' said Bush. He had anticipated the necessity for it, and he had guessed that his captain would choose the bolder course – he was learning fast, even at his age, was Bush.

The topmen went running up the rigging and out along the fore topsail yard; standing on the swaying foot ropes with the gale howling round them, holding on by their elbows over the yard, they struggled with the reef points. The sail shook itself out with a loud flap, and the *Sutherland* heeled sharply over under the increased pressure. Hornblower noticed the flat catenary curve of the heavy cable astern flatten itself a trifle more, but the rope gave no sign of breaking under the strain. Despite the increased heel of the ship the men at the wheel were actually finding their task a little easier, for the leverage of the big fore topsail forward tended to balance the ternal drag of the tow aft.

He glanced at the land just in time to see a puff of smoke from the summit of Cape Creux, blown instantly into invisibility by the gale. Where the shots fell he could not tell at all, for he neither saw nor heard them; the sea was too rough for the splashes to be easily seen. But the fact that the battery was firing showed that they must at least be almost in range – they were circling on the very edge of ruin. Nevertheless, the *Sutherland* was making better speed through the water, and looking aft he could see preparations advancing on the *Pluto's* deck for setting up a jury main mast. Any fragment of sail which the *Pluto* could carry would ease the *Sutherland's* task enormously, and in an hour they might have the work completed. Yet in an hour darkness would have come to shield them from the fire of the battery; in an hour their fate would be decided one way or another. Everything depended on the occurrences of the next hour.

The sun had broken through the westerly clouds now, changing the hills and mountains of Spain from grey to gold. Hornblower nerved himself to endure the waiting during the next hour, and the *Sutherland* and the *Pluto* came through that hour successfully. At the end of that time they had weathered Cape Creux, and had drawn so far to the northward that the land under their lee had dropped away abruptly from a mile and a half distant to fifteen miles. Night found them safe, and Hornblower very weary.

XVII

'Captain Hornblower will command the landing party,' said Admiral Leighton, finally.

Elliott and Bolton both nodded in entire agreement as they sat round the council table in the *Pluto's* cabin. A landing party six hundred strong, contributed by three ships of the line, was certainly a captain's command, and Hornblower was equally certainly the best captain to command it. They had been expecting some such move as this ever since the *Pluto* had returned refitted from Port Mahon, and Leighton had shifted his flag back into her from the *Caligula*. The coming and going of Colonel Villena from the shore had heralded it, too. For three weeks the *Caligula* and the *Sutherland* had ranged along the coast of Catalonia, and the *Pluto* returning had brought back welcome fresh provisions, the *Sutherland's* prize crews, and even a dozen new hands for each ship. With the crews at full strength they might well strike a heavy blow, and the capture of Rosas, if it could be effected, would undoubtedly throw the whole of the French arrangements for the subjection of Catalonia into confusion.

'Now, are there any comments?' asked the admiral. 'Captain Hornblower?'

Hornblower looked round the big cabin, the cushioned lockers, the silver on the table, Elliott and Bolton gorged with the vast dinner they had consumed, Sylvester with paper and ink before him, Villena in his gaudy yellow uniform staring idly about him while the English conversation which he did not understand went on round him. On the bulkhead opposite him hung a portrait of Lady Barbara, a likeness so good as to be startling – Hornblower felt as if he might hear her voice at any moment. He caught himself wondering what they did with it when they cleared for action, tore his thoughts away from Lady Barbara with an effort, and tried as tactfully as he could to show his distaste for the whole scheme.

'I think,' he said at length, 'that it might be unwise to trust so entirely to the co-operation of the Spanish army.'

'There are seven thousand men ready to march,' said Leighton. 'From Olot to Rosas is no more than thirty miles.'

'But Gerona lies between.'

'Colonel Villena assures me that there are bye roads round the town passable to an army without cannon. He himself, as you know, has made the journey four times.'

'Yes,' said Hornblower. Sending a single horseman was a different proposition entirely from marching seven thousand men by mountain paths. 'But can we be certain of seven thousand men? And can we be sure that they will come?'

'Four thousand men would suffice for the siege,' said Leighton. 'And I have General Rovira's definite promise to march.'

'Still they might not come,' said Hornblower. He realised it was hopeless to try and argue with a man who had not had personal experience of Spanish promises, and who had not imagination enough to visualise the difficulties of arranging combined action between forces separated by thirty miles of mountainous country. The tell-tale groove had appeared between Leighton's eyebrows.

'What alternative do you suggest then, Captain Hornblower?' he asked, impatience evident at having thus to reopen the whole question.

'I should suggest that the squadron confines itself to actions within its own strength, without having to depend on Spanish help. The coast battery at Llanza has been re-established. Why not try that? Six hundred men ought to be able to storm it.'

'My instructions,' said Leighton ponderously, 'are to the effect that I must act in the closest co-operation with the Spanish forces. Rosas has a garrison of no more than two thousand men, and Rovira has seven thousand only thirty miles away. The main body of the French Seventh Corps is to the southward of Barcelona – we have a week at least in which to effect something against Rosas. From the squadron we can supply heavy guns, men to work them, and more men to head a storming column when we have effected a breach. It appears to me to be an eminently suitable opportunity for combined action, and I quite fail to understand your objections, Captain Hornblower. But perhaps they are not so cogent, now?'

'I did no more than to state them at your request, sir.'

'I did not ask for objections, but for comments, or helpful suggestions. I looked for more loyalty from you, Captain Hornblower.'

That made the whole argument pointless. If Leighton only wanted servile agreement there was no sense in continuing. He had clearly made up his mind, and on the face of it he had a very strong case. Hornblower knew that his objections were more instinctive than reasoned, and a captain could not very well put forward a plea of greater experience to an admiral.

'I can assure you of my loyalty, sir.'

'Very well. Captain Bolton? Captain Elliott? No comments? Then we can start work at once. Mr Sylvester will let you have your orders in writing. I trust that we are on the eve of the most resounding success the east coast of Spain has seen since this Spanish war began.'

The fall of Rosas would indeed be a resounding success if it could be achieved. As a town with practicable communication with the sea it could hardly be retaken by the French now that there was a strong English squadron on the spot to sustain it. It would be a constant threat to the French communications, a base where Spanish armies from anywhere in the Peninsula could be thrown on shore, of such importance that the Seventh Corps would be bound to cease their attempts at the conquest of Catalonia and concentrate all their strength on the task of retaking it or observing it. But it was Spanish information that there was no French field army within reach. It was a Spanish promise to bring Rovira down from Olot to effect a siege, and a Spanish promise to have transport animals ready to drag the siege train from the landing point.

But with Leighton set upon it, there was nothing for it but to go through with the affair wholeheartedly. If everything went right, they would win a great success, and although Hornblower had never yet heard of a combined operation of war in which everything went right, he could still hope for one, and draft his arrangements for the landing of the siege train from the fleet in accordance with that hope.

Two nights later the squadron came gliding in the early darkness, with the hills and cliffs of the Cape Creux peninsula looming faintly in the distance, to drop anchor together off the sand cove beside Selva de Mar which had been agreed upon as the best place for landing. Four miles to the westward was the battery at Llanza; five miles to the east was the battery on the end of Cape Creux, and six miles due southward, across the root of the long peninsula of which Cape Creux forms the tip, lay the town of Rosas.

'Good luck, sir,' said Bush, looming up in the darkness of the quarterdeck as Hornblower made ready to go down into his barge.

'Thank you, Bush,' answered Hornblower. The punctilious 'Mr' could be dropped occasionally in unofficial speeches of this sort. But the fact that he found his hand sought and gripped by Bush's large horny one was an indication that Bush took the most serious view of the impending operation.

The barge took him quickly over the placid water which reflected the numberless stars overhead; soon the noise of the gentle waves breaking on the sandy beach was louder than the subdued rumbling of the landing force in process of embarkation. A sharp challenge came from the beach to the approaching boat; it was pleasant to hear that it was worded in Spanish, which made it appear much less likely that it was a French force posted there to oppose a landing, and probable that it was the party of guerilleros who had been promised. Hornblower stepped ashore, and a group of cloaked figures, just visible in the starlight, came down the beach towards them.

'The English captain?' asked one of them in Spanish.

'Captain Horatio Hornblower, at your service.'

'I am Colonel Juan Claros, of the third tercio of Catalan migueletes. I bid you welcome in the name of Colonel Rovira.'

'Thank you. How many men have you here?'

'My tercio. That is to say a thousand men.'

'How many animals?'

'Fifty horses and a hundred mules.'

Villena had promised that all northern Catalonia would be swept for draught animals for the siege train. There were four miles of hill paths and a mile of flat plain to be covered between here and Rosas – it would take fifty horses to drag one of the two and a half ton twenty-four pounders over rough country. Had there been fewer animals than this Hornblower would have refused to move, but the Spaniards had provided the barest minimum necessary.

'Take the barge back,' said Hornblower to Longley. 'The landing can proceed.'

Then he turned again to Claros.

'Where is Colonel Rovira?'

'He is over beyond Castellon, closing in on Rosas.'

'What is his force?'

'He has every Spaniard able to carry arms in northern Catalonia, Captain, except for my tercio. Seven thousand men at least.'

'H'm.'

That was exactly according to plan. The army was to be under the walls at dawn, and to be joined as quickly as possible by the siege train, so that the battering could start without delay immediately upon the alarm being given. There was only the barest minimum of time available to reduce Rosas before the main French army could come up from Barcelona. Hornblower felt that he must make every effort to carry out his part of the programme, since the Spaniards were adhering so closely to theirs.

'Have you any patrol watching Rosas?' asked Hornblower.

'A squadron of regular cavalry. They will give the alarm if any sortie comes from the fortress.'

'Excellent.'

He would not be able to get the guns far from the beach before dawn, and by that time Rovira would have hemmed Rosas in, while any hitch would be reported by the cavalry. It was a good piece of organisation. Hornblower felt he had misjudged the Spaniards, or perhaps these Catalan irregulars were better soldiers than the ordinary Spanish army – which was not unlikely.

The steady splash of oars heralded the approach of the boats of the squadron; the leading ones were up to the beach and the men in them came tumbling out, stirring up a faint phosphorescence in the water. The white crossbelts of the marines showed up in startling contrast with their red coats, which appeared black in the faint light.

'Major Laird!'

'Sir!'

'Take a party to the top of the cliff. Post your pickets where you think best, but remember your orders. Allow nobody out of earshot.'

Hornblower wanted to have a solid disciplined force out as a screen in front of him, not trusting Spanish precautions against surprise, but in darkness, and with three languages – Spanish, Catalan, and English – in use, he did not want to risk any muddle or misunderstanding. It was the sort of minor technical difficulty which could not be appreciated by an admiral without experience. The long boats with the guns were grounding far out in the shallows. Men were already hauling into position the rough landing pontoon of spars lashed into rafts, the outer sections buoyed up by casks, which Hornblower had had prepared. Cavendish, the first lieutenant of the *Pluto,* was doing this part of the work thoroughly well and without troubling Hornblower for orders.

'Where are the horses and mules, Colonel?'

'Up above.'

'I shall want them down here shortly.'

It was only a matter of minutes for most of the material to be brought ashore, even though a thousand rounds of shot for the twenty-four pounders – a hundred rounds per gun, one day's consumption – weighed over ten tons. Three hundred seamen and three hundred marines, working under naval discipline, could land ten tons of shot, and the necessary powder barrels, and the beef and bread for one day's rations, in no time worth mentioning. It was the guns which presented the greatest difficulty. The first of the ten twenty-four pounders was only now being coaxed on to the pontoon, for it was a desperate business to run it up the brief ramp from the platform built on the thwarts, where it had been precariously perched during its passage from the ship, over the boat's gunwale. The pontoon sank under its ponderous weight until its surface was awash. Two hundred men, thigh deep in water, toiled on the dragropes which were attached to the gun, and floundering and splashing, their feet seeking foothold in the soft sand below and finding none, they gradually hauled the thing towards the beach.

Like all guns Hornblower had ever seen, it behaved with a pig-headed obstinacy that might have been instigated by infernal powers with a perverted sense of humour. Although it had been fitted, by Hornblower's orders, with specially large trucks to make it more easy to surmount inequalities of surface, it caught and stuck, over and over again, in its passage over the spars. Handspikes and crow-bars were handled diligently in the dark by Cavendish and his men to coax it over the inequalities. And then it would slew round, with Cavendish bellowing to the men to avast, for fear lest the maddening thing should run clean off the platform in the water alongside; only when it had been pushed and heaved straight again could the men tail on to the dragropes once more. There were ten of these guns; Hornblower reflected, and four miles of paths, uphill and down, over which they had to be dragged.

He had had the base of the pier prolonged over the sand by further rafts of timber laid out there, right up to where the sand gave place to the rock bottom of the steep combe which seamed the cliff here and led to the summit. The horses and mules, each with a man at its head whose rags were obvious in the darkness, were waiting here in a great herd, but of course the Spaniards, although they knew they had come to drag guns, had provided no sort of harness for the operation.

'Here, you men,' said Hornblower, turning to a waiting group of sailors. 'There's plenty of line over there. Harness up these horses to the gun. You can find some spare canvas if you look for it.'

'Aye aye, sir.'

It was quite fantastic to see what seamen could turn their hands to. They fell to work with a will, knotting and tying. The English words they used may have sounded strange to the Spanish horses' ears as they wheeled the animals into position, but they seemed to be effective enough. Even the horse-holders, gabbling Catalan, pushed and shoved until they were more help than hindrance. Whinnying and clattering in the darkness – barely relieved by the light of a dozen lanterns – the puzzled brutes were got into line. Rope collars padded with canvas were slipped over their heads, rope traces were passed back to the eyebolts in the gun carriage.

'Avast!' roared one of the sailors just as the strain was beginning to come on. 'This beggar's got his starboard leg over the line.'

By the time the second gun had reached the water's edge they were ready to start hauling up the first. Whips cracked and sailors shouted. The horses plunged as they sought foothold in the sand, but the gun began to move, with a vast creaking and cracking of timber under the trucks. The movement was spasmodic and jerky, and when they began to breast the steep slope of the combe it died away altogether. Twenty Spanish horses, underfed and undersized, could not haul that gun up the slope.

'Mr Moore,' said Hornblower, irritably. 'See that that gun is hauled up.'

'Aye aye, sir.'

A hundred men on dragropes as well as twenty horses managed it, aided by a party behind with crowbars to help over the worst inequalities and to sprag the wheels with rocks at moments when neither men nor horses could pull for another second. Hornblower felt he had really accomplished a great deal when he stood on the summit, with dawn creeping out of the sea, and looked at the line of ten guns, and the mountain of stores, which had been all dragged up in the course of the night.

The gradual coming of the light enabled him to look about him. Down below was the golden beach, dotted with details of the landing party, and beyond that the blue sea, with the ships of the squadron rolling to their anchors. On his own level the summit of the peninsula stretched in a rocky, uneven expanse before him. Over to his right the rock broke completely through in a vast table-topped hill, but southward, in the direction of Rosas which he would have to follow, a narrow goat path wound through the low scrub of arbutus bushes. Claros beside him was revealed as a lean man, sunburnt to the colour of tobacco, with a long black moustache above an excellent set of white teeth, which he displayed in a smile.

'I have a horse for you, Captain.'

'Thank you, Colonel. That is very kind of you.'

There were a few brown figures creeping dispiritedly about the rocks; in the dips between the low crests there were brown masses which were just beginning to disintegrate in the sunlight from huddles of sleeping men into sleepy groups, who, still clutching their blankets about them, moved aimlessly here and there. Hornblower regarded his allies with a disfavour which was not diminished by the fact that it was exactly what he had anticipated, and which was intensified by his sleepless night.

'Would you be so kind,' he said, 'as to send a message to Colonel Rovira, telling him that we are about to march on Rosas, and that I hope to reach there with at least some of the guns at noon?'

'Certainly, Captain.'

'And I must ask you for the help of your men in the transport of my guns and stores.'

Claros looked more dubious at that, and more dubious still when he was told that of his men four hundred would be needed to help with the guns while another four hundred would have to carry a twenty-four pound cannon ball each all the way to Rosas. Hornblower overrode his objections a little crossly.

'And after that, Colonel,' he said, 'they will have to return here for more. I was promised a sufficiency of pack animals; if you do not supply me with four-legged ones, I must use those with two. Now, if you please, I want to get the column started.'

Ten horses or mules to every gun, with a hundred men at the drag-ropes. A hundred men ahead to labour on the task of improving the path, rolling rocks out of the way and filling up holes. Four hundred men carrying cannonballs, some of them leading the packmules with gunpowder kegs slung over their backs. Claros looked still more askance when it became apparent that every man of his tercio would be at work, while Hornblower proposed to leave two hundred of his marines free of any labouring duty.

'That is how I wish it arranged, Colonel. If you do not like it, you can try to find a Spanish battering train.'

Hornblower was determined upon keeping a substantial portion of his disciplined force closed up and ready for an emergency, and his determination was obvious enough to silence Claros' protests.

There was already an outcry behind them where the mules were being loaded up. Hornblower strode over with Claros at his heels, to find a Spanish officer threatening Gray with a drawn sword, his ragged guerilleros behind him handling their muskets.

'What's all this? What is happening here?' demanded Hornblower, first in English and then in Spanish. Everybody turned to him all speaking at once, like schoolboys in a playground dispute. The officer's explosive Catalan was almost incomprehensible to him, and he turned to listen to Gray.

'It's like this, sir,' said the master's mate, displaying a lighted cigar in his hand. 'This Dago lieutenant here, sir, he was a-smoking this while we was loading up the mules. I says to him, very respectful, sir, "No smoking in the magazine, sir," but he didn't take no notice, not understanding, maybe. So I says to him, I says, "No smokingo, magazino, señor," an' he just blew out a puff of smoke and turned his back on me. So I took away his cigar, an' he drew his sword, sir.' – Claros had at the same time heard his officer's explanation, and Claros and Hornblower faced each other.

'Your sailor has insulted my officer,' said Claros.

'Your officer has been very foolish,' said Hornblower.

It seemed like an impasse.

'Look, sir,' said Gray, suddenly. He pointed to one of the barrels swinging against the ribs of the patient mule who bore it. It was slightly stove, and a thin black trickle of powder had run from it. There was powder on the mule's flank, powder on the ground. The danger of fire was obvious, must be obvious even to a Catalan. Claros could not suppress a half smile as he looked.

'My sailor acted hastily,' said Hornblower, 'but I think you will admit, Colonel, that he was in part justified. He will tender a profound apology, and then, perhaps, you will issue strict orders against smoking near the powder.'

'Very well,' said Claros.

Hornblower turned to Gray.

'Say to the officer "God save our gracious king, señor." Say it humbly.'

Gray looked startled.

'Go on, man,' said Hornblower testily. 'Do what I say.'

'God save our gracious king, señor,' said Gray, in a tone that was at least unnatural, if not humble.

'The man wishes to express to you his profound regret for his rudeness,' explained Hornblower to the officer, and Claros nodded approvingly, spat out a couple of brief orders, and turned away. The crisis was over, and no feelings hurt on either side. The sailors were grinning and cheerful, while the Catalans looked proudly down upon the lighthearted barbarians.

XVIII

Captain Hornblower checked his horse on the top of the last of the hitherto interminable rocky undulations. The August sun was blazing overhead, and innumerable flies plagued him and his horse and his companions. At his side rode Claros, behind them Longley and Brown sat uneasily their rawboned Rosinantes along with the three Spanish staff officers. Far back along the path was a solid block of scarlet. Major Laird had his marines formed up as an advance guard, while here and there on the grey-green hills scarlet dots showed where he had posted pickets as a precaution against surprise. Farther back still could be seen a caterpillar of men, naked to the waist, labouring at their task of improving the path for the guns, and beyond that a sort of multiple caterpillar with a black dot at the end showed where the first gun had reached. In five hours it had travelled little more than three miles. Hornblower, looking up at the sun, saw that he had an hour and a half left in which to keep his appointment – in which to haul his guns over a mile of rock and over a mile of the plain which lay below him. He felt a twinge of conscience at the thought that he would probably be a little late with the first of the guns, and he certainly would not be able to open fire against the walls before five or six o'clock in the evening.

There below him, a mile away but seemingly much nearer in the clear air, lay the town of Rosas. Hornblower could recognise all the features of the place which his map indicated. To the right was the citadel – from his elevated position Hornblower could see the pentagonal outline of its grey ramparts, with the blue sea behind. In the centre was the town itself, a single long street lying close to the shore, with a line of earthworks guarding it on the landward side. To the left was the high tower of Fort Trinidad on the other flank. The weakest point was undoubtedly the centre, but it would be of little use assailing that, as the citadel and the Trinidad could hold out independently. The best course would be to take the bull by the horns and breach and storm the citadel by an attack delivered from close by the water's edge. The town could not be held if the citadel fell, although the Trinidad might cause further trouble.

Hornblower had allowed his thoughts to run away with him. He had been so busy planning the reduction of Rosas that he had not even noticed the general peacefulness of the scene. The tricoloured flags flapped idly from the flagstaffs in the citadel and the Trinidad, and they were the most warlike things in sight. There was no sign on the bare plain of any besieging army. Meanwhile it could only be a question of hours before the garrison discovered how near to them lay a valuable convoy, and how weak was the force guarding it.

'Where is the army of Catalonia?' Hornblower demanded angrily, of Claros. He received a deprecatory shrug of the shoulders.

'I do not know, Captain.'

To Hornblower it meant that his precious convoy, and his far more precious landing party, were strung out over three miles of country within easy reach of any column which the governor of Rosas might send out.

'You told me Colonel Rovira was marching on Rosas last night!'

'He seems to have been delayed.'

'The messenger – the one you said you would send at dawn – has he returned?'

Claros, by a raising of his eyebrows and a jerk of the head, passed this question on to the chief of staff.

'He did not go,' said this officer.

'*What?*' said Hornblower in English. He had to fight down his bewilderment and struggle with his dazed senses in order to speak Spanish again. 'Why not?'

'It would have put the officer to unnecessary trouble,' said the chief of staff. 'If Colonel Rovira comes, he comes. If he cannot, no message of ours will bring him.'

Hornblower pointed over to the right. In a fold of the hills a line of some fifty picketed horses and a few groups of seated men indicated the position of the squadron of cavalry which had been watching the town since yesterday.

'Why did they not report that Colonel Rovira had not arrived?' he demanded.

'The officer commanding had my orders to report when he *did* arrive,' answered Claros.

He was showing no signs of indignation at the barely concealed contempt in Hornblower's expression, but Hornblower kept his rage in hand for a little longer in his endeavour to keep the enterprise alive.

'We are in a very considerable danger here,' he said.

Claros shrugged his shoulders again at the Englishman's timidity.

'My men are used to the mountains. If the garrison comes out to attack us we can get away by goat paths over there,' he answered, pointing away to the precipitous sides of the mesa in the distance. 'They will never dare to follow us there, and if they did they would never catch us.'

'But my guns? My men?'

'In war there is always danger,' said Claros loftily.

Hornblower's answer was to turn to Longley.

'Ride back at once,' he said to the boy. 'Halt the guns. Halt the convoy. Halt every man on the path. Nothing is to move a yard farther without orders from me.'

'Aye aye, sir.'

Longley wheeled his horse round and clattered off; the boy had somewhere learned to ride well before coming to sea. Claros and his staff, Hornblower and Brown, all watched him go, and then turned back to face each other. The Spaniards could guess what were the orders that had been given him.

'Not a gun or a man of mine will stir,' said Hornblower, 'until I see Colonel Rovira's army on the plain there. Will you be good enough to send a message to him now?'

Claros tugged at his long moustache and then gave the order to his staff; his junior officers argued sulkily with each other before one of them took the note written by the chief of staff and set off with it. Clearly no one relished the prospect of a ride of perhaps twenty miles under a hot sun in search of Rovira's column.

'It is nearly the hour for dinner,' said Claros. 'Will you have my men's food served out to them, Captain?'

Hornblower's jaw dropped at that. He had thought nothing more could surprise him, and he was proved wrong. Claros' tobacco-brown face gave no indication that he thought there was anything other than what was strictly ordinary in his assumption that his thousand men were to feed on the stores laboriously landed from the squadron. It was on the tip of Hornblower's tongue to refuse pointblank, but he stopped to consider. He guessed that if they were not fed, Claros' men would simply melt away in search of food, and there was still a faint chance that Rovira might arrive and the siege be taken in hand. For the sake of that chance, it was as well to make this concession and make the most of the few hours granted them before their presence should be discovered.

'I will give orders for it,' he said, and the dignified colonel's expression showed no change at either demanding or receiving favours from the Englishman with whom he had just been on the verge of quarrelling.

Soon sailors and Catalans were all of them eating heartily. Even the squadron of cavalry smelt food from afar, like vultures, and rode hastily back to join in the feast, leaving only an unhappy half dozen to continue the watch over Rosas. Claros and his staff seated themselves in a group ministered to by orderlies. And as was to be expected, comida was followed by siesta – after a vast meal every Spaniard stretched himself in the shade which the shrub afforded, and snored, flat on his back, with a Peninsula disregard for the flies which buzzed over his open mouth.

Hornblower neither ate nor slept. He dismounted and gave his horse over into Brown's charge, and then hobbled up and down on his hill top looking down at Rosas, with his heart full of bitterness. He had written carefully to the admiral to explain the reason of his halt – carefully, because he did not want to belong to the type of officer who sees difficulties at every turn – and the answer had simply enraged him. Was it not possible, Leighton had asked in his reply, to attempt something against the fortress with the fifteen hundred men he had in hand? Where was Colonel Rovira? The tone of that question indicated that Hornblower was somehow at fault regarding Rovira's non-arrival. Captain Hornblower must remember the need to work in the closest and most cordial co-operation with England's allies. The squadron could not possibly continue to supply Rovira's force with food for long; Hornblower must tactfully call Colonel Rovira's attention to the need of drawing upon his own sources of supplies. It was highly important that the arrival of the British squadron should be signalised by a great success, but on no account was any operation to be undertaken which might imperil the safety of the landing party. Leighton's letter was a completely futile piece of writing, having regard for the present facts, but a Court of Inquiry who knew nothing of them would consider it eminently sane and sensible.

'Begging your pardon, sir,' said Brown, suddenly. 'The Froggies down there is on the move.'

Startled, Hornblower looked down at Rosas. There were three serpents issuing out of the fortress – three long narrow columns of troops creeping out on to the plain, one each from the citadel, the village, and the Trinidad. A hoarse shout from the Spanish cavalry picket proclaimed that they had seen the same phenomenon; the little party left their post and rode headlong back to the scattered Spanish army. Hornblower went on staring for two more minutes; the columns showed no sign of ending, but wound on interminably out of the fortifications. Two were heading towards him, while the one from the citadel was taking a different route, off to his right, with the clear intention of cutting off the Spanish retreat to the mainland. Hornblower's eye caught the flash of musket barrels in the sunlight; still the columns were winding out – there must be a thousand men at least in each. The Spanish information which had estimated the garrison's strength at two thousand as a maximum must be as faulty as all the rest.

Claros came clattering up with his staff to gaze out over the plain. He paused only for an instant to take in the significance of what he saw – every man with him pointed simultaneously to the outflanking column – and then he wheeled about and spurred back again. As he wheeled his eyes met Hornblower's; they were expressionless as ever, but Hornblower knew what he intended. If he abandoned the convoy and marched his men with all haste for the mesa, he could just get away in time, and he was set upon it. Hornblower knew in that instant that there was not the least use appealing to him to cover the retreat of the convoy, even if the Catalans were steady enough to fight a rearguard action against greatly superior numbers.

The safety of the landing party was dependent solely on its own exertions, and there was not a moment to be lost. Hornblower scrambled on to his horse – the heads of the French columns were well out on to the plain now, and some would be soon ascending the steep escarpment of the plateau – and dashed back after Claros. Then, as he neared the place where Major Laird had his marines already drawn up into line, he checked the pace of his weary horse to a sober trot. It would never do to display too much haste or anxiety. That would only unsteady the men.

And he had a difficult problem to decide, too. The obvious best course was to abandon everything, guns, stores, and all, and march his men back to the ship headlong. The lives of trained seamen were too valuable to be lightly thrown away, and if he did as common sense directed he would have every man safely on board before the French column caught them up; in any matter-of-fact scale of relative values even a few seamen were worth more than ten twenty-four pounders, and their ammunition and whatever food stuffs had been landed. Yet in war the matter-of-fact frequently held only second place. A headlong flight to the ships, and abandonment of guns and stores, would depress the spirits of the men inordinately; a fighting retreat with next to no loss would raise them. He made up his mind as he halted his horse beside Major Laird.

'We'll have three thousand French on us in an hour, Laird,' he said quietly. 'You'll have to hold them back while we get the stores on board again.'

Laird nodded. He was a tall red-faced Scot, red-haired and inclined to stoutness; his cocked hat was tilted back off his forehead and he mopped his face with a lilac-coloured silk handkerchief which clashed dreadfully in the sunlight with his red coat and sash.

'Aye,' he said. 'We'll do that.'

Hornblower spared a second to glance down the double line of marines, the homely brown faces under the shakos, and the white cross belts in Euclidean line. The disciplined composure the marines displayed was comforting and reassuring. He kicked his heels into the shaggy sides of his horse and trotted down the path. Here came Longley, tearing back on his pony.

'Ride to the beach, Longley. Tell the admiral it is necessary to re-embark the men and stores, and ask that all the boats of the squadron should be ready to take us off.'

A column of Spaniards was already hurrying off in disorderly fashion up a cross path towards the mainland. A Spanish petty officer was collecting the remainder of his men; a British petty officer was looking on in puzzled fashion as they unhitched a team of horses from one of the guns and began to lead them away.

'Stop!' shouted Hornblower, riding up in the nick of time and delving hurriedly into his mind for adequate Spanish. 'We shall keep those horses. Here, Sheldon, Drake, bring those horses back. Brown, ride on. Tell every officer that the Spaniards can go, but they're not to take a mule or horse with them.'

There were sullen looks among the Spaniards. In a country in whose every corner war had raged bitterly for two years draught and pack animals were of the utmost imaginable value. The meanest Spanish peasant in the ranks knew it, knew that the loss of those animals would mean an empty belly for him in some new campaign a month off. But the British sailors were equally determined. They handled their pistols and cutlasses with every intention of using them if necessary, and the Spaniards remembered the French column which was marching to cut off their retreat. All down the path they abandoned the animals and drew off, sulkily, while Hornblower kicked his weary horse into renewed activity, as he rode along, turning back towards the beach all the guns and material which had been dragged so far with such exertion. He reached the head of the steep gully and rode down it to the beach. On that tranquil afternoon the sea was blue and smooth like enamel; far out the squadron rode peacefully at anchor, and below him lay the golden sand of the beach, while over the enamelled surface plied the boats of the squadron like huge beetles. All round him grasshoppers were singing deafeningly. The beach party was already hard at work re-embarking the beef barrels and bread bags piled there. He could safely leave this part of the work to Cavendish, and he turned back again and rode up the gully. At the top a party of seamen arrived with the first of the mule train. He left orders for the animals to be brought back to the guns as soon as their loads were taken off, and rode on.

The nearest gun was within half a mile of the gully, men and horses labouring to drag it up the path – for this half mile the land sloped away fairly steeply inland from the top of the cliffs. The men gave him a cheer, and he waved his hand and tried to sit his horse as if he were an accomplished rider; it was comforting to think that Brown behind him was an even worse horseman, so that the contrast might help. Then a distant pop-pop-popping, its tone unnatural in the heated air, told him that Laird's rearguard was in action.

He rode hastily along the path, Brown and Longley at his heels, past the other gun teams labouring on the steep hillsides, towards the firing. At one point along the path there was a long line of cannon-balls, lying where the Spanish carrying party had dropped them when the alarm came. Those would have to be lost – there was no chance at all of getting them back to the ship. He arrived unexpectedly at the scene of the firing. Here the country was a succession of short steep ups and downs, the rocky soil covered with a dense undergrowth, amid which grasshoppers were still singing loudly through the musketry. Laird had his men strung out along the summit of one of the major ridges; Hornblower came upon him standing on a lump of rock overlooking the path, the lilac handkerchief still in one hand and his sword in the other, and muskets banging away all along the ridge on either side of him. He had the air of a man completely enjoying himself, and he looked down at Hornblower with the irritation of a man disturbed while composing a work of art.

'All well?' said Hornblower.

'Aye,' said Laird, and then, grudgingly, 'come up and see for yourself.'

Hornblower got off his horse and scrambled up the rock, balancing precariously on its slippery summit beside the major.

'Ye'll observe,' said Laird, academically, and rolling his r's, 'the formed troops must keep to the paths in this terrain. Moreover, detached skirmishers lose their sense of direction rapidly, and this thorny vegetation is admirably adapted to hinder free movement.'

From the rock Hornblower looked down upon a sea of green – the nearly impenetrable maquis which clothes the stony hillsides of Mediterranean Spain – through which the red coats of the marines, shoulder deep in the scrub, were hardly visible. Here and there puffs of white smoke, drifting over the surface, marked where recently there had been firing. On the opposite hillside there were other puffs of smoke and faint stirrings among the undergrowth. Hornblower saw white faces, and blue coats, and sometimes even white breeches over there where the French struggled through the thorny scrub. Much farther back he could see part of a column of troops waiting on a section of the path. Two or three musket bullets came whizzing through the air close over his head.

'We are quite safe here,' said Laird, 'until the enemy turns our flank. If ye look over there to the right, ye'll observe a French regiment advancing along a path roughly parallel to this one. As soon as it reaches that thorn tree there, we shall have to retreat and take up a fresh position and leave them all their work to do again. Fortunately that path is only a sheep track of uncertain direction. It may never reach that thorn tree.'

Hornblower could see a long line of French shakos bobbing along above the maquis as he followed Laird's pointing finger; its loops and winds showed that the path must be, as Laird had suggested, a mere chance sheep track. Another bullet buzzed past them.

'The French standard of musketry,' said Laird, 'is lower now even than it was at Maida, where I had the honour of being engaged as an officer on Sir John Stuart's staff. Those fellows have been firing at me for half an hour now without hitting me, nor even the remotest chance of hitting me. But with two of us up here the possibility is doubled. I would recommend you sir, to descend and devote your attention to accelerating the march of the convoy.'

They looked at each other keenly. Hornblower knew quite well that the command of the rearguard was Laird's duty, in which he should not interfere as long as it was properly performed. It was the fear of being thought afraid which made him hesitate to descend. As he stood, he felt his cocked hat struck a violent blow which twisted it on his head so that it toppled off; with an instinctive grab he caught it as it fell.

'That outflanking column,' said Laird, steadily, 'is about to reach that thorn tree. I must ask you officially, sir' – he dragged out the long word into 'offeeecially' – 'to go back before I call on my men to retreat. Our retirement will necessarily be hurried.'

'Very well, major,' said Hornblower, grinning despite himself, and slipping down from the rock with all the dignity he could muster. He got on his horse and trotted down the path again; he examined his hat with a little thrill of pride to see that the bullet had hit the gold loop at the front, passing within two inches of his head, and he had felt no fear. Where the path crossed the summit of the next ridge he drew rein again; the musketry in the rear had suddenly become more intense. He waited, and then a detachment of marines came running along the path with Captain Morris at their head. They had no attention to spare for him as they turned aside and plunged into the undergrowth on either side of the path seeking points of vantage from which their fire would cover the retreat of their comrades. The musketry fire spluttered out abruptly, and then up the path they came, Laird at their head, half a dozen men under a young lieutenant bringing up the rear and turning to keep back the nearest enemy with warning shots.

Confident that the rearguard was under efficient direction, Hornblower was able to ride on to where the rearmost gun was standing stubbornly at the foot of a slope. The weary horses were plunging and slipping on the rocky surface as they strove to drag the thing up under the urgings of the sailors, but now there were only half a dozen seamen in place of the fifty Spaniards who had helped to drag it from the beach. They were reduced to heaving the gun up the slope foot by foot with crowbars; their naked ribs – most of them had thrown off their shirts – were glistening with sweat. Hornblower racked his brains for the appropriate thing to say.

'Heave away, my lads. Boney hasn't any guns as good as these. Don't let the Dagoes give him a birthday present.'

The column of Spaniards could now be seen like a long worm ascending the precipitous sides of the mesa. They had made their escape. Hornblower, looking after them felt a sudden feeling of hatred for them and the race they represented. They were a proud nation, yet never so proud as to disdain favours from others, hating foreigners only a little more than they hated each other, ignorant, misgoverned, misusing the wealth with which nature had endowed their country; Spain was a natural prey to any stronger nation. France had made this attempt at conquest, and it was only England's jealousy which was defeating it. Some time in the future the country would be torn to pieces in the strife between Liberals and Conservatives, and at some period in that struggle the European powers would find sufficient accord to seize upon the fragments. Civil war and foreign aggression, centuries of them, perhaps constituted the future of Spain unless the Spaniards set their house in order.

He brought back his mind with an effort from profitless speculation on the future to deal with the petty problems in hand – detailing the returning mule teams to assist in dragging the guns, portioning out the failing strength of his men so as to make the best speed with the mass of material yet remaining; the spluttering musketry to the rear told how men were suffering wounds and death for the sake of preserving it from the enemy. He sternly cast out the doubt which assailed him as to whether the gesture were worth the price, and kicked his exhausted horse into a last effort as he clattered along the path.

Half the guns were on the beach at last – for the final run down the steep gully to the sand little exertion was needed – and the remainder were fast nearing the head of the gully. The beach was cleared of all the stores that had been landed, and the first gun was even now being dragged along the landing pier for transfer to the ships. Cavendish, in command at the beach, came up to Hornblower.

'What about the horses and mules, sir?'

Shipping a hundred and fifty animals would be as difficult a task as shipping the guns, and they would be an intolerable nuisance on board. Certainly they must not be allowed to fall into the hands of the French; in Spain at the present time they were the most valuable form of booty. The sensible thing to do would be to cut the brutes' throats on the beach. Yet they were enormously valuable. If only they could be got away, and kept alive on board for a few days, they might be landed again and handed back to the Spaniards. To slaughter the wretched beasts would have as bad a moral effect on the men as losing the guns. Crushed biscuit would feed them on board – from the look of them it would be better fare than they had experienced for some time – and the fresh water problem was hardly insurmountable. In the rear Laird was still fighting his successful rearguard action, and the sun was fast setting over the mesa.

'Send them on board with the other stores,' said Hornblower, at last.

'Aye aye, sir,' said Cavendish, allowing no shade of expression in his face to hint at his conviction that mules were far more trouble than guns to coax into small boats and to heave up into ships.

The work went on. One of the guns, with the malicious ingenuity of all its tribe, fell over and dismounted itself during its passage down the gully, but the men did not allow the accident to delay them long. With crowbars they heaved the huge mass of iron down the slope and over the sand, rolling it, like a barrel, along the pier and into the long boat awaiting it. The ships had tackle which would make light of its weight and would remount it in no time. Hornblower gave up his horse to be led to the water's edge and to be coaxed into a boat, while he walked away along the summit of the cliff to take his stand on a high point from which he could overlook both the beach and the head of the gully where Laird would make his final stand.

'Run to Major Laird,' he said to Brown. 'Tell him everything is on the beach now.'

Ten minutes later events suddenly moved with a rush. Brown must have met the marines in their final movement of retreat, for the scarlet uniforms came pouring back up the path, to take up their position along the summit of the cliff, their line reaching nearly to where Hornblower was standing. The French were hard on their heels; Hornblower could see their uniforms moving through the scrub, and the musketry popped furiously along the line.

'Look out, sir!' called Longley, suddenly. He pushed his captain violently in the ribs, jostled him off the flat rock on which he was standing. Hornblower heard two or three bullets pass over his head as he struggled to keep his footing, and at the same moment a group of French infantry, fifty or more, came bursting out of the bush, running hard for them. They were between Hornblower and the nearest marines; the only way of escape was down the steep face of the cliff, and he had no more than a second in which to make up his mind to take it.

'This way, sir!' squeaked Longley. 'Down here!'

Longley dropped like a monkey to a narrow ledge below, beckoning him down with waving arms. Two blue-coated infantry men were close upon him, their bayonets levelled; one of them was shouting something which Hornblower could not understand. He turned and jumped after Longley, his feet just reaching the ledge a dozen feet below; and he swayed there with a vertical drop of over a hundred feet below him. Longley caught his arm, and, leaning outwards, scanned the descent keenly and yet with a nightmare coolness.

'That is the best way, sir. You see that bush? If we can reach that, we ought to get over there. There's a bit of a gully there joining the big one. Shall I go first, sir?'

'Yes,' said Hornblower.

A musket banged over his head and he felt the wind of the bullet – the French were leaning over the top of the cliff firing down at them. Longley braced himself, and then leaped wildly along the face of the cliff, slid down it in a cloud of dust and fragments, and caught the stout bush he had pointed out to Hornblower. Then, moving cautiously away from it, he found an inequality on which to rest, and from there beckoned again to his captain. Hornblower tried to nerve himself for the leap, and then drew back. Another bullet – it actually struck the ledge close to his feet. Hornblower plunged heavily from the end of the ledge, turning his face to the cliff. He felt the rock tearing at his clothes as he slid. Then he crashed into the bush and grasped it madly, his feet seeking foothold.

'Now, over here, sir. Catch hold of that lump with your hands. Put your foot into that crack, sir. No! Not that foot! T'other one!'

Longley's voice went up into a squeak like a bat's in the excitement as he edged himself along the cliff and at the same time instructed his captain where to put his hands and feet. Hornblower clung to the cliff face like a fly on a window pane. His hands and arms were aching already – the activities of two days and a night had already drained his strength. A bullet whacked into the rock between him and the midshipman, a chip which it displaced struck his knee a sharp tap. He looked down, and his head swam at the sight of the drop below him. In his exhausted state he felt he would gladly loose his hold and drop down to the quick death awaiting him.

'Come on, sir!' said Longley. 'Not much more now, sir. Don't look down!'

He recalled himself to sanity. Changing foothold and handhold inch by inch, he shuffled along in accordance with Longley's instructions.

'Just a minute,' said Longley. 'Are you all right, sir? Wait here while I go and have a look.'

Hornblower clung on with aching arms and legs. He kept his face against the cliff, stupid with fatigue and fear. Then he heard Longley beside him again.

'It's all right, sir. There's only one nasty bit. Get your feet down on to that knob, there. Where that bit of grass is.'

They had to get past a projecting boss in the face of the cliff; there was one awful second when Hornblower had no foothold, and with his legs dangling had to stretch to a new handhold.

'They can't see us here, sir. You can rest a bit, if you'd like to,' said Longley solicitously.

Hornblower lay on his face in the shallow depression which grooved the cliff, conscious for a space of nothing save the cessation of strain. Then with a rush he remembered everything – his dignity, the work on the beach, the fighting on the summit. He sat up and looked down; with a solid lump of the cliff under him his head would stand that. The beach was clear of guns now, in the darkening evening, and only a few animals stood waiting their turn to be coaxed into the boats. Up above the firing seemed to have died down for a space; either the French had begun to despair of achieving anything further or they were gathering for a last effort.

'Come on,' said Hornblower, abruptly.

The rest of the descent was easy; they could slide and scramble all the way until he felt the welcome sand under his feet. A worried-looking Brown materialised here, his face clearing as he caught sight of his captain. Cavendish was standing supervising the despatch of the last cutter.

'Very good, Mr Cavendish. The seamen can go next. Are the armed boats ready?'

'Yes, sir.'

It was nearly dark now, and the sky gave only a faint light when the marines began to pour down the gully and over the sand. The last shots in the long retreat were fired by the four-pounders mounted in the bows of the two longboats which lay nosing the sand while the final section of marines splashed out into the water to them. The long red tongues of flame lit up the dark masses of Frenchmen swarming down on to the beach, and the blast of grape which they had hurled was followed by a gratifying chorus of screams and cries from the stricken masses.

'A very handsome operation indeed,' said Major Laird from his seat in the stern of the longboat beside Hornblower.

Hornblower drooping in weariness was inclined to agree with him, although he was shivering with the chill of his soaked breeches, and his hands smarted from cuts and abrasions, and other parts of him pained him with saddlesoreness as if they were being held before a fierce fire. They rowed out over the silent sea to a ship strange with the whinnying of horses and smelling stable-like already.

Hornblower staggered on board; he saw the boatswain's mate who held the lantern for him glance curiously at his ragged clothes and white face. He walked blindly past the dark line of horses and mules, picketed head and heel to the deck ringbolts, to the security of his cabin. He ought to make his report to the admiral – surely he could leave that until daylight. The deck seemed to be heaving under him rhythmically. Polwheal was there, and food was laid on the candle-lighted table, but Hornblower later could never remember eating any. Faintly he could remember Polwheal helping him into bed, and a vivid, clearcut memory always abode with him of hearing Polwheal, through the closed cabin door, arguing with the sentry outside.

'Twarn't Horny's fault,' said Polwheal, didactically.

Then sleep swooped down upon Hornblower, sleep which held him fast, even though he was conscious through it of the aches and pains which assailed him, of the perils he had encountered that day, of the fear which had tortured him on the cliff.

XIX

The *Sutherland* was wallowing through the stormy waters of the Gulf of the Lion, under a grey sky, with flecked wave tops all round her, while her captain stood on his heaving quarterdeck enjoying the cold blast of the mistral round his ears. The nightmare adventure on the Spanish mainland was three weeks past now, for over a fortnight the ship had been clear of horses and mules, and the stable-smell had nearly disappeared, and the decks were white once again. Much more important, the *Sutherland* had been sent away on detached duty with orders to examine the French coast line all the way along to Toulon; he was free from the clogging authority of the admiral again, and he breathed the keen air with the delight of someone released from slavery. Barbara's husband was not a man whom it was a pleasure to serve.

The whole ship seemed to be infected with this feeling of freedom – unless it was the pleasure in the contrast between the present weather and the tranquil skies and calm seas which had prevailed so long. Here came Bush, rubbing his hands and grinning like a gargoyle.

'Blowing a little, sir,' said Bush, 'and it'll blow harder than this before it's over.'

'Very likely,' said Hornblower.

He grinned back, light heartedly, with a bubbling of high spirits within him. It was quite fantastic how stimulating it was to be thrashing to windward again against a stiff breeze, especially with the nearest admiral a hundred miles away. In Southern France that same wind would be causing grumbling and complaints, and the French would be going about hugging their cloaks to them, but here at sea it was perfectly delightful.

'You can put the hands to any work you please, Mr Bush,' said Hornblower magnanimously, as discretion returned to him and he evaded the tempting snares of falling into idle conversation.

'Aye aye, sir.'

Young Longley came aft with the sand glass to attend to the hourly heaving of the log, and Hornblower watched him from the corner of his eye. The boy was carrying himself with assurance now, and gave his orders easily. He was the only one of all the midshipmen whose calculations of the day's work made any pretence at accuracy, and the incident on the cliff had shown him to be a lad of quick decision. Towards the end of this commission, and at a suitable opportunity, Hornblower decided, he would appoint him acting lieutenant; he watched him bending over the traverse board marking up the hour's run with a queer wonder as to whether he was observing a future Nelson, an admiral who would some day rule forty ships of the line.

He was an ugly little fellow, with this stubby hair and monkey face, yet it was hard not to feel a surge of affection for him. If little Horatio, the child whom smallpox had killed on the third day in those Southsea lodgings, had grown up in this fashion Hornblower would have been proud of him. Perhaps he might have done – but it was not a good thing to think himself into gloom on a fresh morning like this about the little boy he had loved. There would be another child by the time he reached home. Hornblower hoped it might be a boy; and he was nearly sure that Maria hoped the same. Not that any little boy could quite take the place of Horatio – Hornblower felt a new flood of depression when he remembered how Horatio had said 'Papa! Want papa!' and had rested his face against his shoulder that evening when the first malaise of the illness was creeping over him. He shook his depression off; if his return to England was at the earliest moment he could hope for the child would be crawling about the floor with all a baby's misdirected zeal. He might even be talking a little, and would hang his head in shyness when his strange papa arrived, so that Hornblower would have the task of winning his confidence and affection. It would be a pleasant task.

Maria was going to ask Lady Barbara to be godmother to the child – it would be delightful if Lady Barbara agreed. Any child with the influence of the Wellesley family behind it could contemplate a secure future. Without a doubt it was the Wellesley influence which had put Leighton in command of the squadron he was mismanaging. And by this time Hornblower was sure that it was the Wellesley influence which had put him in command of one of the ships of that squadron and retained him in employment without a single day of half pay. He was still in doubt about what had been Lady Barbara's motive, but on a stimulating morning like this he could almost venture to believe that it was because she loved him; he would far rather it were that than it should merely be because she admired his professional ability. Or it might be just an amused and tolerant kindliness towards an inferior whom she knew to love her.

That thought called up a surge of revolt. She had been his for the asking, once. He had kissed her, clasped her. No matter that he had been afraid to take her – he slurred that memory over in his present indignation – she had offered, and he had declined. As a suppliant once, she had no right to pose to herself now as his patroness. He stamped his feet with mortification as he paced the deck.

But his clairvoyance was instantly blurred by his idealism. His memory of a cool and self collected Lady Barbara, the perfect hostess, the dignified wife of an admiral, was overlaid by mental pictures of a tender Lady Barbara, a loving Lady Barbara, with a beauty which would take a man's breath away. His heart was torn with longing for her; he felt sick and sad and lonely in his rush of desire for her, for the angel of goodness and sweetness and kindliness he thought her to be. His pulse beat faster as he remembered her white bosom with the sapphire pendant resting on it, and animal desire came to reinforce the boyish affection he bore her.

'Sail ho!' bellowed the masthead lookout, and Hornblower's dreaminess was stripped from him in a flash, like the straw wrapping from a bottle.

'Where away?'

'Right in the wind's eye, sir, an' comin' up fast.'

A brisk nor'easterly wind like the present meant ideal weather conditions for French ships which wished to escape from the blockade of Marseille and Toulon. It was a fair wind for the escaping ship, enabling her to get out of harbour and cover a long distance during the first night, while at the same time it pushed the blockading squadron away to leeward. This might well be a ship engaged in breaking the blockade, and if such were the case she would have small chance of escape with the *Sutherland* right to leeward of her. It would be consistent with the good fortune he had enjoyed on detached service during the present commission if this were to be another prize for him.

'Keep her steady as she goes,' said Hornblower, in reply to Bush's look of inquiry. 'And turn the hands up, if you please, Mr Bush.'

'Deck, there!' hailed the lookout. 'She's a frigate, and British by the look of her.'

That was a disappointment. There were fifty possible explanations of a British frigate's presence here and on her present course which offered no chance of action as opposed to one which might involve the proximity of an enemy. Her topsails were in sight already, white against the grey sky.

'Begging your pardon, sir,' said the gunlayer of one of the port side quarterdeck carronades. 'Stebbings here thinks he knows who she is.'

Stebbings was one of the hands taken from the East India convoy, a middle-aged man with grey hairs in his beard.

'*Cassandra,* sir, thirty-two, seems to me. She convoyed us last v'yage.'

'Captain Frederick Cooke, sir,' added Vincent, flipping hastily over the pages of the printed list.

'Ask her number and make sure,' ordered Hornblower.

Cooke had been posted six months later than he had; in the event of any combined operations he would be the senior officer.

'Yes, she's the *Cassandra,* sir,' said Vincent, his eye to his telescope, as a hoist of flags went up to the frigate's foretopsail yardarm.

'She's letting fly her sheets,' said Bush, with a hint of excitement in his voice. 'Queer, that is, sir.'

From time immemorial, dating back long before a practical flag signalling system had been devised, letting fly the sheets had been a conventional warning all the world over of the approach of a fleet.

'She's signalling again, sir,' said Vincent. 'It's hard to read with the flags blowing straight towards us.'

'Damn it, sir,' blazed Bush. 'Use your eyes, or I'll know the reason why not.'

'Numeral. Four. Literal. Seventeen – astern – to windward – source – sou'west,' translated Longley with the signal book.

'Beat to quarters, if you please, Mr Bush. And wear the ship directly.'

It was not the *Sutherland's* task to fight odds of four to one. If there were any British ships in pursuit he could throw himself in the enemy's path and reply on crippling at least two Frenchmen so as to ensure their capture, but until he knew more about the situation he must keep as clear as was possible.

'Ask "Are any British ships at hand?"' he said to Vincent while the *Sutherland* first lay over on her side and then rose to an even keel as Bush brought her before the wind.

'Reply negative, sir,' said Vincent, a minute later, through the din of clearing for action.

It was as he expected, then. The four French ships of the line had broken out of Toulon during the darkness, and while the blockading squadron had been blown away to leeward. Only the *Cassandra,* the inshore lookout, had caught sight of them, and had run before them so as to keep them under observation.

'Ask "Where is the enemy?"' said Hornblower. It was an interesting exercise, calling for familiarity with the signal book, to frame a message so as to use the fewest number of flags.

'Six – miles – astern – bearing – nor'east,' translated Longley from the code book as Vincent read out the numbers.

So the French were lying right before the wind. That might merely be because they wanted to put as great a distance as possible between them and the blockading squadron off Toulon, but it was not likely that the officer in command would run wastefully direct to leeward unless that was the course most suited to his plan. It ruled out completely any thought of Sicily or the Adriatic or the Eastern Mediterranean as objective, and it pointed directly to the Spanish coast near Barcelona and beyond that to the Straits of Gibraltar.

Hornblower on his quarterdeck set himself to try and think the thoughts of Bonaparte at the Tuileries. Beyond the Straits lay the Atlantic and the whole world. Yet it was hard to imagine any useful objective for four French ships of the line out there; the French West Indies had been nearly all reduced by English expeditions, the Cape of Good Hope was in English hands, Mauritius was about to fall. The French squadron might be intended for a mere commerce destroying raid, but in that case an equal number of frigates would be both cheaper and more effective. That was not like Bonaparte. And on the other hand exactly enough time had elapsed for the appearance of Leighton's squadron on the Catalan coast and the resultant dearth of supplies to have been reported to the Tuileries, and for orders to have been transmitted thence to Toulon. Those orders would bear the Bonaparte stamp. Three British ships on the Catalan coast? Then send four French ones against them. Man with crews picked from all the ships rotting in Toulon harbour. Load them with all the stores for which the Barcelona garrison is clamouring. Let them slip out one dark night, hack their way through to Barcelona, crush the British squadron if they can, and return if they are lucky. In a week they might be safe and sound, and if not – every omelette demands the breaking of eggs.

That must be the French plan, and he would gladly bet all he had that he was right. It only remained to decide how to defeat the French aims, and the opening moves were obvious. First, he must keep between the French and their objective, and second, it would be desirable to keep out of sight of the French, over their horizon, as long as possible – it would be a surprise to them to find a ship of considerable force, and not a mere frigate, in their path; and surprise was half a battle. In that case his first instinctive move had been correct, and the *Sutherland* was on the right course to achieve both these ends – Hornblower wondered uneasily whether his unthinking mind had jumped at once to the conclusions which his thinking mind had only just reached. All that remained to be done was to call down the *Pluto* and the *Caligula.* Three British ships of the line and a frigate could fight four French ships, picked crews or not, and Bonaparte's opinion notwithstanding.

'Cleared for action, sir,' said Bush, touching his hat. His eyes were bright with the anticipation of action. Hornblower saw in him a fighting man of the type to which he regretted he did not belong – a man who relished the prospect of a battle for its own sake, who loved physical danger, who would never stop to count the odds against him.

'Dismiss the watch below, if you please,' said Hornblower. There was no object in keeping every man at his station when action was far distant, and Hornblower saw Bush's expression alter when he heard the words. They meant that the *Sutherland* was not going to plunge immediately into action against odds of four to one.

'Aye aye, sir,' he said, reluctantly.

There was something to be said for Bush's point of view, for the *Sutherland* well handled might knock away so many French spars as to leave two or three at least of the French so crippled as to fall a certain prey into British hands sooner or later. It would be at the cost of her own destruction, however, and he could think about it again later. A fair wind today might still mean a foul wind tomorrow; there might still be time for the *Pluto* and the *Caligula* to come up if only they could be informed of the proximity of their prey.

'Give me that signal book,' said Hornblower to Longley.

He turned its pages, refreshed his memory regarding the wording of some of the arbitrary signals. In sending a long message there was always danger of misunderstanding. And he pulled his chin while he composed his message. Like every British officer retreating, he was running the risk of having his motives misunderstood, even though as he told himself petulantly, not even the mad British public, gorged with past victories, could condemn him for refusing action against odds of four to one. But if everything went wrong the Wellesley faction might seek a scapegoat; and the order he was about to transmit might mean the difference between success and failure, between a court of inquiry and the thanks of Parliament.

'Send this message,' he said abruptly to Vincent.

Hoist after hoist the flags crept up the mast. The *Cassandra* was to set all sail she could carry, and to make use of her frigate's turn of speed to turn westward, seek out the *Pluto* and *Caligula* – Hornblower could not be exact in his description of their position – and bring them down to Barcelona. Phrase by phrase the *Cassandra* acknowledged the signal. Then there was a pause after its completion, before Vincent, glass to eye, reported.

'*Cassandra* signalling, sir. "Submit—".'

It was the first time Hornblower had ever had that word addressed to him. He had used it so often in signals to admirals and senior captains, had included it so often in reports, and now another officer was beginning a signal to him with the word 'Submit.' It was a clear, definite proof of his growing seniority, and gave him a thrill keener even than he had known when a ship had first piped the side for him on his being posted. Yet naturally the word 'submit' ushered in a protest. Cooke of the *Cassandra* was not in the least anxious to be thus summarily dismissed from the scene of a promising action. He submitted that it would be better for the *Cassandra* to stay in sight of the French.

'Signal "Carry out orders acknowledged",' said Hornblower, tersely.

Cooke was wrong and he was right – Cooke's protest helped his decision to crystallise. A frigate's whole function, what she was built for, was to enable the ships of the line to come into action. The *Cassandra* could not face a single broadside from one of the ships rolling along after her; if she could bring the *Pluto* and the *Caligula* into action she would have multiplied her own value an infinity of times. It was heart-warming to Hornblower to be not only convinced that he was right, but to be able to enforce the course of action he had decided upon. That six months' difference in seniority made Cooke obedient to him, and would make him obedient all their lives – if ever Cooke and he flew their flags together as admirals, he would still be the senior and Cooke the junior. He watched the *Cassandra* shake out the reefs from her topsails and bear away westwards, with all her five knots' superiority of speed being put to its best use now.

'Shorten sail, Mr Bush,' said Hornblower.

The French would see the *Cassandra* vanish over their horizon; there was a chance that the *Sutherland* might keep them under observation without being seen. He stuck his telescope into his pocket and set himself to climb the mizzen rigging, sedately – even a little laboriously; it was imperilling his dignity to do so, when every hand in the ship could climb the mast quicker than he, but he had to see with his own eyes the enemy astern of him. The ship was plunging heavily in the following sea, and the wind blew keenly about his ears. It called for resolution to continue his ascent without undignified pauses, so as to appear merely as leisurely as a captain had a right to be, and yet neither timid nor awkward.

At last he found a secure perch on the mizzen topmast cross trees, and could train his glass on the heaving horizon. With her main topsail taken in the *Sutherland's* speed was considerably reduced, and it could not be long before the French appeared. He saw them soon enough – a tiny rectangle of white just lifting over the horizon, then another beside it, and another, and another.

'Mr Bush!' he roared. 'Set the main tops'l again, if you please. And send Mr Savage up here.'

The four French ships were rolling along in lubberly French fashion in a wide line abreast, half a mile apart – presumably their captains were afraid of collision if they drew closer – and it was a hundred to one that their lookouts would never notice the tiny dot which would be all they could see of the *Sutherland*. Savage came tumbling up beside him, hardly out of breath after his lightning scramble up the ratlines.

'Take this glass,' said Hornblower. 'You see the French squadron? I want to hear instantly if they alter course, or if they headreach upon us, or we on them.'

'Aye aye, sir,' said Savage.

He had done all he could do now, when he reached the deck again. It only remained to wait, patiently, until tomorrow. Tomorrow would see some sort of battle, hopeless or even – or if there were no battle it would mean that the French had disappeared and he would go before a court martial. He was careful to keep his expression quite composed, and to try and appear as if he did not feel the tension of waiting in the least. It would be in the old tradition if he invited his officers to dinner and whist tonight.

XX

The situation was one likely to disturb any captain's sleep, with four hostile ships of the line to windward needing to be kept under observation, and with calculations continually bobbing up from the subconscious to the conscious regarding the chances of the *Cassandra* bringing down Admiral Leighton in time to cut off the enemy. The weather conditions were unsettling, too – the wind, having worked up nearly to a gale force towards evening, diminished until midnight, increased again, and then, with the inconsequence of Mediterranean winds, began to die away steadily.

Certainly Hornblower never expected sleep. He was too excited, and his mind was too active. He lay down on his cot when the watch was changed in the evening to have a rest, and, being quite convinced that he had no chance of sleeping he naturally fell into a heavy dreamless sleep so heavy that Polwheal had to shake him by the shoulder at midnight to awaken him. He came on deck to find Bush standing by the binnacle.

'Too dark for anything to be seen, sir,' said Bush, and then, excitement and exasperation getting the better of his formality, he growled, 'Black as Newgate Knocker.'

'Have you seen anything of the enemy?'

'I thought I did, sir, half an hour back, but nothing to be sure of. Wind's dropped a lot, too.'

'Yes,' said Hornblower.

As so often was the case at sea, there was nothing to do but wait. Two screened lanterns swayed down on the maindeck, where the watch lay at their stations by the guns; the keen wind harped in the rigging, and the ship rose and plunged in the following sea with a lightness and grace no one would expect of her who had only seen her with the wind abeam. Nothing to do but to wait; if he stayed on deck he would only fidget and display his nervousness, so that he might as well go and conceal his nervousness in his screened-off cot.

'Send for me at once if you catch sight of the enemy,' he said, with elaborate carelessness, and went back again below.

He lay on his cot with his mind busy, for he knew that having slept once there was no chance whatever of sleeping again. So perfect was this conviction that sleep ambushed him once more, leaped upon him unawares, as he lay thinking about the *Cassandra,* so that it only seemed two minutes later that he heard Polwheal speaking to him as if from another world.

'Mr Gerard's compliments, sir, an' it's beginnin' to get lighter, sir.'

It called for quite an effort to rouse himself and get up from his cot; only when he was drowsily on his feet did he begin to feel pleased at having been genuinely asleep each time that Polwheal came to call him. He could picture Polwheal telling his cronies about the iron nerves of the captain, who could sleep like a child on a night when the ship was aboil with the prospect of action.

'Anything to report, Mr Gerard?' he said, as he reached the quarterdeck.

'No, sir. I had to reef down for an hour at two bells, it blew so hard. But it's dropping fast now, sir, and backing sou'easterly.'

'H'm,' said Hornblower.

The faintest hint of light was beginning to tinge the gloomy sky, but nothing could be seen yet more than a cable's length away. A south-easterly wind would be nearly foul for the French on their course to Barcelona; it would be dead foul for the *Pluto* and *Caligula*.

'Thought I felt the loom o' the land, sir, before the light came,' said Gerard.

'Yes,' said Hornblower. Their course during the night would bring them close into Cape Creux of hated memory; he picked up the slate beside the binnacle, and, calculating from the hourly readings of the log, he made their position to be some fifteen miles off the cape. If the French had held the same course during the night they would soon have Rosas Bay and comparative security under their lee – of course, if they had not, if they had evaded him in the darkness, the consequence to him did not bear thinking about.

The light was broadening fast. Eastwards the watery clouds seemed to be thinning; just above the horizon. Undoubtedly they were thinning; for a second they parted, and a speck of gold could be seen through them, just where the white-flecked sea met the sky, and a long beam of sunlight shone level over the sea.

'Land-ho!' yelled the masthead lookout, and westward they could see a bluish smudge on the horizon where the mountains of Spain loomed faintly over the curve of the world.

And Gerard glanced anxiously at his captain, took a turn or two up and down the deck, gnawed at his knuckles, and then could restrain his impatience no longer.

'Masthead, there! What do you see of the enemy?'

The pause that followed seemed ages long before the reply came.

'Northin', sir. Northin' in sight barrin' the land to looard.'

Gerard renewed his anxious glance at his captain, but Hornblower, during that pause, had set his face sternly so that his expression was unmoved. Bush was coming on to the quarterdeck now; anyone could see that he was wild with anxiety. If four French ships of the line had evaded action it would mean half pay for Hornblower for life, if nothing worse. Hornblower retained his stony expression; he was proud of being able to do so.

'Put the ship about, Mr Gerard, if you please, and lay her on the starboard tack.'

The French might perhaps have altered course in the darkness, and might now be lost in the centre of the Western Mediterranean, but Hornblower still did not think it likely. His officers had made insufficient allowance for the lubberliness of the unpractised French. If Gerard had had to reef topsails in the night they might well have had to heave to; and both Bush and Gerard were over-eager – during the night the *Sutherland* might have gained twenty miles on the

French. By retracting his course he was confident that he would sight them again.

Confident as far as the whist-playing part of his mind was concerned, that is to say. He could not control the sick despair in his breast, nor the acceleration of his heart beats; he could only conceal them, keeping his face a mask and forcing himself to stand still instead of pacing about in his anxiety. Then he thought of an activity which would help to occupy his mind and yet not betray his nervousness.

'Pass the word for my steward,' he said.

His hands were just steady enough to permit him to shave, and a chill bath under the washdeck pump gave him new vigour. He put on clean clothes and parted his lessening hair with elaborate exactitude, for under the washdeck pump he had told himself that they would sight the French again before he had completed his toilet. It was with a sense of acute disappointment that he laid down the comb when he had no more smallest excuse to continue its use, and turned to put on his coat, with no news of the French. And then, with his foot on the companion, there came a wild yell from Midshipman Parker at the masthead.

'Sail in sight! Two – three of 'em, sir. Four! It's the enemy!'

Hornblower continued his progress up the companion without faltering in his step, and he hoped people noticed it. Bush was half way up the rigging with his glass, and Gerard was pacing – almost prancing – about the quarterdeck in his delight. Observing them, Hornblower was glad he had had no childish doubts about the correctness of his actions.

'Wear the ship, if you please, Mr Bush. Lay her on the port tack.'

A talkative captain might supplement the order with a brief explanation of the necessity for keeping the ship between the French and Spain, but Hornblower bit off the explanation as it rose to his lips. No unnecessary words would escape him.

'The wind's still working round southerly, sir,' said Gerard.

'Yes,' said Hornblower.

And it would drop a good deal, too, as the day progressed, he decided. The sun was fast breaking through the clouds, with every prospect of a warm day – a Mediterranean autumn day, with a rising barometer and only the faintest of breezes. The hammocks had been piled in the netting, and the watch not at their stations were clattering on to the deck with buckets and holystones. The routine of the navy had to be maintained, even though there was every chance that the decks they were swabbing would be running with blood before the day was over. The men were skylarking and joking – Hornblower felt a little thrill of pride as he looked at them and remembered the sullen despondent crowd with which he had sailed. Consciousness of real achievement was some compensation for the thankless service which employed him; and it helped him to forget, too, the uneasy feeling that today or tomorrow – soon, anyway – he would know again, as the whirl of battle eddied round him, the physical fear of which he was so intolerably ashamed.

As the sun climbed up the sky the wind dropped steadily, moving round even more southerly, and the mountains of Spain came nearer and nearer and grew more and more defined as their course brought them closer to the land. Hornblower held on as long as he could, bracing up his yards as the wind veered, and then finally heaving to while the French squadron crept up over the horizon. The shift in the wind had deprived them of the windward position; if they moved down to attack him he could escape northwards so that if they pursued him they would be running towards the *Pluto* and *Caligula*, but he had no hope that they would. French ships of the line who had evaded the blockading squadron would race to accomplish their mission first, and would only fight afterwards, however tempting the bait dangled before them. If the wind shifted no farther round they could just hold their course for Barcelona, and he had not the least doubt that they would do so if not prevented. He would hang on to them and try to attack some isolated ship during the night if no help arrived.

'They're signalling a lot, sir,' said Bush, his glass to his eye. They had been signalling all day, for that matter – the first flurry of bunting, Hornblower shrewdly surmised, had been occasioned by their catching sight of the *Sutherland*, unaware that she had been keeping company with them for fifteen hours. Frenchmen retained their talkative habits at sea, and no French captain was happy without messages passing back and forth along the squadron.

The *Sutherland* was clear of the Cape Creux peninsula now, and Rosas Bay was opening out on her beam. It was in these very waters, but in very different weather conditions, that the *Pluto* had lost her masts and had been towed to safety by the *Sutherland*; over there, on those green-grey slopes, had occurred the fiasco of the attack on Rosas; through his glass Hornblower thought he could discern the precipitous face of the mesa up which Colonel Claros had led his fugitive Catalans. If the wind came farther round now, the French had a refuge open to them under the guns of Rosas, where they would be safe until the British could bring up fireships and explosion vessels to drive them out again; actually it would be a more secure refuge for them than the anchorage at Barcelona.

He looked up at the pendant flapping at the masthead – the wind was certainly more southerly. It was growing doubtful whether the French would weather Palamos Point on their present tack, while he would certainly have to go about soon and stand out into the Frenchmen's wake, with all his advantages of position lost by the inconstancy of the weather. And the wind was beginning to come in irregular puffs now – a sure sign of its diminishing force. He turned his glass on the French squadron again to see how they were behaving. There was a fresh series of signals fluttering at their yardarms.

'Deck, there!' yelled Savage from the masthead.

Then there was a pause. Savage was not too sure of what he could see.

'What is it, Mr Savage?'

'I think – I'm not quite sure, sir – there's another sail, right on the horizon, sir, abaft the enemy's beam.'

Another sail! It might be a stray merchant ship. Otherwise it could only be Leighton's ships or the *Cassandra.*

'Keep your eye on her, Mr Savage.'

It was impossible to wait for news. Hornblower swung himself up into the shrouds and climbed upwards. At Savage's side he trained his glass in the direction indicated. For a second the French squadron danced in the object glass, disregarded, as he searched.

'A bit farther round, sir. About there, I think, sir.'

It was the tiniest flash of white, too permanent for a wave crest, of a different shade from the few clouds against the blue. Hornblower nearly spoke, but succeeded in limiting himself to 'Ha – h'm.'

'It's nearer now, sir,' said Savage, telescope to eye. 'I should say, sir, it's a ship's fore-royal.'

There could be no doubt about it. Some ship under full sail was out there beyond the Frenchmen, and standing in to cross their wake.

'Ha – h'm,' said Hornblower. He said no more, but snapped his telescope shut and addressed himself to the descent.

Bush dropped to the deck to meet him from the shrouds he had ascended; Gerard, Crystal, they were all on the quarterdeck eyeing him anxiously.

'The *Cassandra,*' said Hornblower, 'standing in towards us.'

By saying that, he was risking his dignity to demonstrate his good sight. No one could guess the new arrival to be the *Cassandra* from just that glimpse of her royals. But it could only be the *Cassandra* who would be on that course, unless his judgment were sadly at fault. Should she be revealed not to be, he would appear ridiculous – but the temptation to appear to recognise her when Savage was not even sure whether she was a ship or a cloud was too strong.

All the implications of the *Cassandra's* appearance were evident to the officers' minds at once.

'Where's the flagship and *Caligula*?' demanded Bush, of no one in particular.

'May be coming up, too,' said Gerard.

'The Frogs are cut off if they are,' said Crystal.

With the *Pluto* and *Caligula* to seaward of them, and the *Sutherland* to landward, Palamos Point to windward, and a fluky wind veering foul, it would be only by good fortune they could escape a battle. Every eye turned towards the French squadron; they were nearly hull-up now, heading south-by-west closehauled, a three-decker in the van followed by three two-deckers, admiral's flags flying at the foremasts of the first and third ships. The broad white stripes which decorated their sides stood out sharp and clear in the pure air. If the *Pluto* and *Caligula* were far astern of the *Cassandra* the Frenchmen would still be as much in ignorance of their proximity as was the *Sutherland*, which would explain why they were still holding their course.

'Deck there!' hailed Savage. 'The strange sail's *Cassandra*. I can see her tops'l now, sir.'

Bush and Gerard and Crystal looked at Hornblower with a strange respect for his penetrating vision; it had been well worth risking his dignity for that.

The sails suddenly flapped loudly; a puff of wind had followed a comparative lull, and from a more southerly point than before. Bush turned to shout orders for the trimming of the sails, and the others turned instantly to watch the French reaction.

'They're going about!' said Gerard, loudly.

Undoubtedly they were doing so; on the new tack they would weather Palamos Point but would be standing out to sea nearer to the British squadron – if the British were there.

'Mr Bush,' said Hornblower. 'Put the ship about, if you please.'

'*Cassandra's* signalling, sir,' yelled Savage.

'Up with you!' snapped Hornblower to Vincent and Longley. Telescope and signal book in hand, they raced for the masthead; everyone on the quarterdeck watched their progress anxiously.

'*Cassandra's* signalling to the flagship, sir!' yelled Vincent.

So Leighton was out there over the horizon – over the Frenchmen's horizon, too, judging from their actions. Bonaparte might send out four French ships to fight three English ones, but no French admiral safely at sea and knowing the capacity of his crews far better than his emperor, would obey those orders if he could help it.

'What's she saying, boy?' hailed Hornblower.

'She's too far off to be sure, sir, but I think she's reporting the enemy's new course.'

Let the Frenchmen hold that course for an hour, and they were lost, cut off from Rosas and certain to be overhauled before they reached Barcelona.

'They're going about again, by God!' said Gerard, suddenly.

Wordless, they watched the four French ships come up into the wind, and come over on to the other tack. Then they came round, farther and farther still, until in all four ships their three masts were in line; every one of them was heading straight for the *Sutherland*.

'Ha – h'm,' said Hornblower, watching his fate bearing down upon him: and again, 'Ha – h'm.'

The French lookouts must have glimpsed Leighton's mastheads. With Rosas Bay six miles under his lee and Barcelona a hundred miles almost to the windward the French admiral could have taken little time to reach a decision in face of those strange sails on the horizon. He was dashing instantly for shelter; the single ship of the line which lay directly in his path must be destroyed if she could not be evaded.

The sick wave of excitement and apprehension which Hornblower experienced did not prevent calculations pouring into his mind. The French had six miles to go with a fair wind. He still did not know whereabouts on the circumference of the possible circle whose centre was the French flagship Leighton was on at the moment. But he would have twenty miles, perhaps a little more, to sail for certain, and with the wind – such wind as there was – abeam, if he were in the most advantageous position, and on his port bow if he were far astern. And shifting as it was, it would be dead foul for him in two hours. Twenty to one, Hornblower estimated the odds against the admiral being able to catch the French before they reached the protection of the guns of Rosas. Only unheard-of flukes of wind would do it, and only then if the *Sutherland* were able to knock away a good many spars before she was beaten into helplessness. So keenly had Hornblower been calculating that it was only then that he remembered, with a gulp of excitement, that the *Sutherland* was his ship, and the responsibility his, as well.

Longley came sliding down the backstay, the whole height from topmast head to the deck, his face white with excitement.

'Vincent sent me, sir. *Cassandra's* signalling, and he thinks it's "Flag to *Sutherland,* no. 21". Twenty-one's "Engage the enemy", sir. But it's hard to read the flags.'

'Very good. Acknowledge.'

So Leighton at least had the moral courage to assume the responsibility for sending one ship against four. In that respect he was worthy of being Barbara's husband.

'Mr Bush,' he said. 'We've a quarter of an hour. See that the men get a bite to eat in that time.'

'Aye aye, sir.'

He looked again at the four ships all steering slowly down upon him. He could not hope to turn them back, but he could only hope to accompany them in their race to Rosas Bay. Any ship that he could totally dismast would fall a prey to Leighton; the others he must damage so sorely that they could not repair themselves in Rosas, which had the smallest dockyard facilities. Then they would stay there until fireships, or a large scale cutting out expedition, or a properly organised attack by land on the fortress, should result in their destruction. He thought he ought to succeed in that, but he could not bring himself to visualise what would happen to the *Sutherland* meanwhile. He swallowed hard, and set himself to plan the manoeuvres of the first encounter. The leading French ship mounted eighty guns – they were run out and grinning at him through her open ports, while each of the Frenchmen had, as though in bravado, at least four tricolour flags floating in the rigging. He looked up at the battered red ensign hanging from the peak against the blue of the sky, and then he plunged into realities.

'Hands to the braces, Mr Bush. I want the ship handled like lightning when the time comes. Mr Gerard! I'll have every gun captain flogged tomorrow who fires before his gun bears.'

The men at the guns grinned; they would give of their best for him without any threat of flogging, and they knew he knew it.

Bow to bow the *Sutherland* was approaching the eighty-gun ship, unwavering; if both captains held their courses steadily there would be a collision which might sink both ships. Hornblower kept his eye on the Frenchman to detect the first signs of irresolution; the *Sutherland* was lying as near to the wind as she could, with her sails on the point of flapping. If the French captain had the sense to bring his ship to the wind the *Sutherland* could do nothing decisive against her, but the chances were he would leave his decision to the last moment and then instinctively put his ship before the wind as the easiest course with an unhandy crew. At half a mile smoke suddenly eddied round the Frenchman's bows, and a shot came humming overhead. She was firing her bow chasers, but there was no need to warn Gerard not to reply – he knew the value of that first unhurried broadside too well. With the distance halved two holes appeared in the *Sutherland's* main topsail; Hornblower did not hear the passing of the shot, so intent was he on noting the Frenchman's actions.

'Which way will he go?' said Bush, beating one hand with the other. 'Which way? He's holding on farther than I thought.'

The farther the better; the more hurried the Frenchman's manoeuvre the more helpless he would be. The bowsprits were only a hundred yards apart now, and Hornblower set his teeth so as not to give the instinctive order to up helm. Then he saw a flurry on the Frenchman's decks, and her bow swung away from him – to leeward.

'Hold your fire!' Hornblower shouted to Gerard, fearful lest a premature broadside should waste the opportunity. Gerard waved his hat in reply, with a flash of white teeth in his brown face. The two ships were overlapping now, not thirty yards apart, and the Frenchman's guns were beginning to bear. In the bright sunlight Hornblower could see the flash of the epaulettes of the officers on the quarterdeck, the men at the forecastle cannonades stooping to look along the sights. This was the moment.

'Helm a-weather, slow,' he said to the helmsman. A glance at Bush was enough – he was anticipating this order. The *Sutherland* began to wear round slowly, beginning her turn to cross the Frenchman's stern before the two ships were alongside. Bush began to bellow the orders to the men at the braces and the headsail sheets, and as he did so the Frenchman's broadside burst into thunder and flame and smoke. The *Sutherland* shook and jarred with the impact of the shot; one of the mizzen shrouds above Hornblower's head parted with a twang at the same moment as a hole appeared in the quarterdeck bulwark near him amid a shower of splinters. But the *Sutherland's* bow was already almost touching the Frenchman's stern. Hornblower could see an eddy of panic on her quarterdeck.

'Keep her at that!' he shouted to the helmsman.

Then with a series of heavy crashes, one following another as the *Sutherland* crossed her enemy's stern and each section of guns bore in turn, she fired her broadside into her, heeling slightly at each discharge, with every shot tearing its destructive course from end to end of the ship. Gerard came leaping on to the quarterdeck, having run down the whole length of the maindeck, keeping pace with the firing. He bent eagerly over the nearest carronade, altered its elevation with a quick twist of the screw, and jerked the lanyard, with a wave of the hand to the other gun captains to do the same. The carronades roared out, sweeping the Frenchman's quarterdeck with grape on top of the roundshot. Hornblower saw the officers there dashed to the deck like lead soldiers, saw rigging parting, and the big stern windows of the French ship disappear like a curtain jerked from its pole.

'That's given him a bellyful,' said Bush.

That was the sort of broadside which won battles. That single discharge had probably knocked half the fight out of the Frenchmen, killing and wounding a hundred men or more, dismounting half a dozen guns. In a single-ship duel she would strike her flag in less than half an hour. But now she had drawn ahead while the *Sutherland* was completing her turn, and the second Frenchman, the one with the rear-admiral's flag, was loose on the weather quarter. She had all plain sail set, and was overhauling them fast; in a moment she would be able to rake the *Sutherland* as the *Sutherland* had raked her consort.

'Starboard!' said Hornblower to the helmsman. 'Stand to your guns on the port side!' His voice rang uncannily loud in the stillness following the firing.

The Frenchman came on undeviating, not disdaining a broadside to broadside duel, but not attempting to manoeuvre, especially against an enemy who had proved himself alert, at a time when manoeuvring meant delay in gaining the shelter of Rosas. The ships inclined together, growing nearer and nearer as the Frenchman headreached upon the *Sutherland* and the *Sutherland's* course approached hers. From the *Sutherland's* deck they could hear the excited orders which the French officers were shouting to their men, trying to restrain their eagerness until the decisive moment.

They were not entirely successful all the same, as first one gun and then another went off as excitable gunners let fly – where the shots went Heaven alone knew. A word from Hornblower swung the *Sutherland* round till she lay parallel to her opponent, and as she steadied on her new course Hornblower waved his hand to Gerard as a signal to open fire. There was not more than half a second between the two broadsides; the *Sutherland*, heaving up her side to the recoil of her guns, heaved over farther still to the impact of the shot. As the smoke came billowing up round her the air was filled with the splintering crash of the shot striking her sides; there were screams and cries from below in proof of the damage received.

'Keep at it now, lads! Fire as you will!' shouted Gerard.

Those hours of drill bore fruit now. The sponges were thrust into the reeking gun muzzles, and the moment they were withdrawn the powder and the rammer and the shot were ready for insertion. Almost simultaneously the gun trucks rumbled as the crews flung themselves on the tackles and ran the guns up; almost simultaneously the guns roared out. This time there was a perceptible and measurable interval before the Frenchman replied in a straggling and irregular salvo. The gentle wind blowing on the engaged quarter kept the ship engulfed in the smoke; the gunners labouring on the main-deck were as vague as in a dense fog to Hornblower, but the masts and sails of the Frenchman still stood out clear against the blue sky. The *Sutherland's* third broadside followed close on the heels of the Frenchman's second.

'Three to her two, as usual,' said Bush, coolly. A shot struck the mizzen mast bitts and sprayed the deck with splinters. 'She's still drawing ahead, sir.'

It was hard to think clearly in this frightful din, with death all round. Captain Morris had his marines all along the port side gangway firing away at everyone visible on the other ship's decks; the two ships were within easy musket shot. The *Sutherland's* broadsides were growing irregular now, as the most efficient crews worked their guns faster than the others, while the Frenchman was delivering a running fire in which there were occasional louder explosions to be heard when several guns went off together. It was like the clattering of the hoofs of four coach horses on a hard road, sometimes in unison for a space, and then spreading out again.

'I fancy his fire's slackening, sir,' said Bush. 'It doesn't surprise me.'

The *Sutherland* had not suffered mortally yet, judging by the number of dead on the maindeck. She could still fight for a long time yet.

'See his main mast, sir!' yelled Bush.

His main topmast was bowing forward, slow and dignified, with the topgallant mast bowing further forward still. Through the smoke they could see the main mast inclining aft. Then all dignity left the soaring mass of spars and canvas. It hung S-shaped in the air for a breathless second, and then tumbled down with a rush, fore and mizzen topmasts falling with it. Hornblower felt a grim satisfaction at the sight – there were no spare main masts to be had in Rosas. The *Sutherland's* crew cheered piercingly, and hastened to fire in a few last shots as their ship drew ahead of her crippled opponent. A minute later the din of the firing ceased, the tiny breeze blew away the smoke, and the sun came shining through upon the littered deck again.

Aft lay their late antagonist, a great mass of wreckage trailing alongside, the second lower deck gun from the bow pointing out of its port at an impossible angle of elevation to show she had one gun at least knocked useless. A quarter of a mile ahead was the first ship they had fired into; she had paid no attention to the duel behind her but had continued under all sail for the safety of Rosas Bay, just like a Frenchman. And beyond her, sweeping round the horizon, were the cruel mountains of Spain, and the white roofs of Rosas were clearly visible above the golden shore. The *Sutherland* was close to the wide mouth of the bay; half way between her and Rosas lay two gigantic beetles on the flat blue surface – gunboats coming out of Rosas under sweeps.

And close astern of the crippled ship came the other two ships of the French squadron, the three-decker with the vice-admiral's flag and a two-decker in her wake. It was the moment for decision.

'Masthead there!' hailed Hornblower. 'Can you see anything of the flagship?'

'No, sir. Nothing but *Cassandra*.'

Hornblower could see the *Cassandra's* royals himself, from the deck, pearly white on the horizon; the *Pluto* and *Caligula* must still be nearly twenty miles away – possibly becalmed. The tiny breeze which was urging the *Sutherland* into the bay was probably a sea breeze; the day was hot enough for that. Leighton would hardly arrive in time to take part in this battle. Hornblower could put his ship about now, and tack into safety, beating off the two enemies if they interfered with him, or he could throw himself into their path; and with every second carrying him a yard nearer Rosas he must decide quickly. If he fought, there was the faintest possible chance that Leighton might be brought up in time to pick up the cripples, but so faint a chance as to be negligible.

The *Sutherland* would be destroyed, but her enemies would be so knocked about as to be detained in Rosas for days or even weeks. And that was desirable, because it would be several days before preparations could be made to attack them in their anchorage, and during those days there would always be the chance of their escaping – three of them, at least – from Rosas as they had escaped from Toulon.

Hornblower balanced in his mind the loss of a seventy-four to England against the certain loss of four ships of the line to France. And then he knew, suddenly, that his cogitation had been wasted. If he withdrew, he would all the rest of his life suspect himself of having done so out of cowardice, and he foresaw with clarity the years of mental uneasiness it would bring. He would fight whether it was the right thing or not, and as he reached that decision he realised with relief that it was the correct course as well. One more second he wasted, looking up at the blue sky which he loved, and then he gulped down his muddled emotions.

'Lay the ship on the port tack, if you please, Mr Bush,' he said.

The crew cheered again, the poor fools, when they saw that they were about to face the rest of the French, even though it meant the certain death of half of them at least. Hornblower felt pity – or was it contempt? – for them and their fighting madness or thirst for glory. Bush was as bad as any of them, judging by the way his face had lit up at the order. He wanted the Frenchman's blood just because they were Frenchmen, and thought nothing of the chance of being a legless cripple if he were granted the chance of smashing a few French legs first.

The crippled two-decker with the rear-admiral's flag came drifting down on them – this sea breeze would push all wrecks into Rosas Bay under the guns of the fortress – and the men working lackadaisically at clearing the wreckage ran from their work when they looked up and saw the *Sutherland's* guns swinging around towards them.

The *Sutherland* fired three broadsides into her with hardly a gun in reply before she drifted clear – another fifty or so dead Frenchmen for Bush, thought Hornblower, viciously, as the rumble of the gun trucks died away and the men stood waiting once more, silent now, beside their guns. Here came the three-decker, now, beautiful with her towering canvas, hideous with her grinning guns. Even at that moment Hornblower marked, with professional interest, the decided tumble-home of her sides, much greater than English shipwrights allowed.

'Let her pay off slowly, Mr Bush,' he said. He was going to set his teeth into the three-decker like a bulldog.

Round came the *Sutherland,* slowly, slowly. Hornblower saw that his last manoeuvre with the *Sutherland* was going to be as well timed as ever he could wish. She was on the same course as the three-decker at exactly the moment the latter drew up opposite to her; the guns of both ships bore simultaneously, a hundred yards apart, and burst simultaneously into thunder and smoke.

In the earlier encounters time had seemed to pass slowly. Now it seemed to be passing fast, the infernal din of the broadsides seeming almost unintermitting, the figures hurrying about in the smoke seeming to be moving twice as fast as normally.

'Edge in closer on her,' said Hornblower to the helmsman, and then, his last order given, he could abandon himself to the mad inconsequence of it all. Shots seemed to be tearing up the deck all around him, smashing great gashes in the planking. With the clear unreality of a nightmare he saw Bush fall, with blood running from the stump of one leg where a foot was missing. Two men of the surgeon's crew bent over him to carry him below.

'Leave me on deck,' said Bush. 'Let go of me, you dogs.'

'Take him away,' said Hornblower. The harshness of his voice was a piece with the madness of everything else, for he was glad to be able to order Bush into a place of safety where he might yet live.

The mizzen topmast fell, and spars and blocks and tackle came raining all round him – death falling from the heavens as well as hurtling in from overside, but still he lived. Now the foretopsail yard was shot through in the slings; dimly through the smoke he could see Hooker leading a party aloft to repair it. Out of the tail of his eye he saw something new and strange looming through the smoke – it was the fourth French ship, coming up on the *Sutherland's* disengaged side. He found himself waving his hat and shrieking some nonsense or other to his men, who cheered him back as they brought the starboard side guns into action. The smoke was thicker, and the din more tremendous, and the whole ship throbbing with every gun in action.

Little Longley was at his side now, white faced, miraculously alive after the fall of the mizzen topmast.

'I'm *not* frightened. I'm *not* frightened,' the boy said; his jacket was torn clean across the breast and he was trying to hold it together as he denied the evidence of the tears in his eyes.

'No, sonny, of course you're not,' said Hornblower.

Then Longley was dead, hands and breast smashed into pulp. There was a maindeck gun not run out, he saw as he looked away from Longley's body. He was about to call attention to the abandoned gun, when he noticed its slaughtered crew lying in fragments round it, and he saw that there were no longer any men to spare to get it into action again. Soon there would be more guns than one out of action. The very carronade beside him had but three men to man it – so had the next one, and the next. Down on the maindeck there were marines carrying powder and shot; Gerard must have set them to that work, and the powder boys must be mostly dead. If only this din would stop, and allow him to think!

It seemed to him as if at that the din redoubled. Foremast and mainmast came down together with a splintering crash audible high above the gunfire, the mass of wreckage tumbling over the starboard side. He ran forward, to find Hooker there already hard at work with a group of men drawn from the blinded guns hacking away at the rigging to cut it clear. The three-feet-thick end of the broken mainmast had smashed a gun carriage and killed the crew during its fall. Shots from the two-decker on that side were smashing through the men at work, and already smoke was pouring up from the canvas hanging over the side where the flame of the guns had set it on fire. Hornblower took an axe from the hand of a dead man and fell to work hacking and cutting along with the others. When the last rope was cut, and the flaring mass had dropped overside, and hasty inspection showed that the timber of the ship had not caught fire, he swept the sweat from his forehead and looked around the ship from his new point of view.

The whole deck was heaped and littered with dead men and fragments of dead men. The wheel was gone, the masts, the bulwarks were beaten flat, the very hatch coamings indicated by a mere fringe of splinters. But the guns which could still be worked were still firing, each manned by its attenuated crew. On either side the enemy loomed through the smoke, but the three-decker had lost two topmasts and the two-decker her mizzen mast, and their sails were in shreds and their rigging hanging in festoons, seen dimly in the smoke. The firing was as fierce as ever. He wondered dully by what miracle he survived to walk through the tempest of shot back to his post on the quarterdeck.

Some puff of wind was altering the relative position of the ships. The three-decker was swinging round, coming closer; Hornblower was already running forward down the port side, with seeming feet of lead, when the three-decker's starboard bow came with a grinding bump against the *Sutherland's* port bow. Frenchmen were gathering to leap down on to the *Sutherland's* deck, and Hornblower drew his sword as he ran.

'Boarders!' he yelled. 'All hands repel boarders! Boom them off, there, Hooker, Crystal.'

High above his head towered the three-decker. Musketry was spattering along her bulwarks, and Hornblower heard bullets rapping into the deck around him. Men with swords and pikes in their hands were scrambling down the three-decker's sides, and more were spewing out of the middle-deck gunport on to the *Sutherland's* gangway. Hornblower found himself caught up in a wave of British sailors with cutlasses and pikes, rammers and handspikes, men naked to the waist and grey with powder smoke. Everyone was jostling and slipping and struggling. He was flung up against a dapper little French lieutenant with his hat rakishly awry. For the moment his arms were pinned to his sides by the press, and the Frenchman was struggling to pull a pistol from his waistband.

'Rends-toi,' he spluttered, as the weapon came free, but Hornblower brought up his knee and the Frenchman's head went back in agony and he dropped the pistol.

And the three-decker was swinging away clear again, urged by the puff of wind and the thrust of the spar Crystal and Hooker and their party were pushing against her side. Some of the Frenchmen leaped back to the ship. Some leaped into the sea. A dozen who were left dropped their weapons – one of them too late to check the pike which was thrust into his stomach. The puff of wind was still blowing, drifting the French ships away from the dismasted *Sutherland* and rolling away the smoke. The sun came out and shone upon them and the hideous decks as though from behind a cloud, and the din of the firing ended magically as the guns ceased to bear.

Sword in hand, Hornblower stood while the men about him secured the prisoners. The cessation of the noise had not brought him the relief he had hoped for – on the contrary, he was amazed and stupid, and in his weariness he found it a desperate effort to think clearly. The wind had drifted the *Sutherland* well inside the bay, and there was no sign at all of the *Pluto* and *Caligula* – only the *Cassandra,* hull down over the horizon, a helpless spectator of the fight. The two battered French ships, almost as helpless as the *Sutherland,* thanks to the damage they had received aloft, were floating a short distance off; down the side of the three-decker, dribbling from the scuppers,

Hornblower noticed a dark streak – human blood.

The two-decker was still swinging round; her shattered side was out of sight, now she was presenting her stern, and now her other side to the *Sutherland's* bow. Hornblower watched her stupidly. And then – a bellowing roar, and her broadside came tearing into the *Sutherland*. A cloud of splinters flew from the shattered stump of the foremast, and the gun beside Hornblower rang like a bell to a glancing shot.

'Oh, stop!' muttered Hornblower. 'For God's sake!'

The men on the *Sutherland's* deck were dragging themselves to the guns again. Gerard was nowhere to be seen, but Hooker – a good boy, that – was walking along the main deck apportioning the men to the guns so that some at least might be worked. But the men were faint with fatigue, and at present no gun would bear, while the dismasted *Sutherland* could do nothing to save herself. Another broadside, ripping and tearing through the ship. Hornblower became conscious of a faint undercurrent of noise – the feeble chorus of the wounded men huddled in every corner of the ship. The gunboats were working round cautiously with their sweeps to take up a position under the *Sutherland's* stern; soon they would be firing their forty-two pounders into her on the water line. Sun and blue sea and blue sky; the grey-green mountains of Spain, the golden beach and white houses of Rosas – Hornblower looked round him at them all, despairingly, and it was agony to look.

Another broadside; Hornblower saw two men knocked into a bloody mess a. Hooker's side.

'Strike,' he said to himself. 'We must strike.'

But the *Sutherland* had no colours flying that she could strike, and Hornblower's dazed mind wrestled with this problem as he walked aft. The forty-two pounder in one of the gun boats boomed out loudly, and Hornblower felt the jar as the shot smashed into the ship's side below him. Hooker was on the quarterdeck now, and Crystal, and Howell the carpenter.

'There's four feet of water in the well, sir,' said this last, 'an' no pump left.'

'Yes,' said Hornblower, dully. 'I shall surrender.'

He read agreement in the grey faces of his officers, but they said nothing. If only the *Sutherland* would sink under them the problem would solve itself but that would be too much to hope for. She would only grow more and more waterlogged, sinking as each deck in turn was submerged, while the pitiless cannonade would continue. It might be as much as twenty-four hours before she sank completely and in that time the little wind would have drifted her aground under the guns of Rosas. All he could do was to surrender. He thought of the other British captains who had found themselves in similar positions. Thompson of the *Leander* and the captain of the *Swiftsure* and the unfortunate man under Saumarez' command in Algeciras Bay; they, too, had hauled down their flags after a long fight against heavy odds.

Somebody was hailing from the two-decker; he could not understand what was said, but it must be a demand to surrender.

'Oui,' he shouted back. 'Oui.'

For answer there came another broadside, smashing home with a splintering of timber and to the accompaniment of a shriek from below.

'Oh God!' said Hooker.

Hornblower realised that he must have misunderstood the question, and with the realisation came a solution of the difficulty. He ran as fast as his stiff legs would carry him down to the indescribable chaos which represented what was left of his cabin. Hurriedly he turned over the litter there, while the men at the guns watched him expressionless as animals. He found what he sought at last, and came up on the quarterdeck with his arms full of it.

'Here,' he said, giving it to Crystal and Howell. 'Hang that over the side.'

It was the tricolour flag he had had made to deceive the batteries at Llanza. At sight of it the men in the gunboats bent to their oars to propel their craft alongside, while Hornblower stood with the sun shining on his bare head waiting for them. They would take his sword of honour away from him. And the other sword of honour was still in pawn to Duddingstone the ship chandler, and he would never be able to redeem it now, with his career wrecked. And the shattered hull of the *Sutherland* would be towed in triumph under the guns of Rosas – how long would it be before the Mediterranean fleet came down to avenge her, to retake her from the captors, or burn her in one vast pyre along with her shattered conquerors? And Maria was going to bear him a child, whom he would never see during all the years of his captivity. And Lady Barbara would read of his capture in the newspapers – what would she think of his surrendering? But the sun was hot on his head, and he was very weary.